Praise for Nancy McKenzie's first book, THE CHILD QUEEN

By Nancy McKenzie
Published by Ballantine Books:

THE CHILD QUEEN
THE HIGH QUEEN

THE HIGH QUEEN

The Tale of Guinevere and King Arthur Continues

NANCY MCKENZIE

A Del Rey® Book

BALLANTINE BOOKS • NEW YORK

For
Elizabeth, Katie, and
Caroline

A Del Rey® Book
Published by Ballantine Books

Library of Congress Catalog Card Number: 94-94647

ISBN 0-345-38245-5

Printed in Canada

First Edition: March 1995

10 9 8 7 6 5 4 3 2 1

✸ CONTENTS

The Princes	1	*The Dragon Sail*	3
	2	*All Hallow's Eve*	13
	3	*The Dark Prince*	23
	4	*The Witch's Sons*	31
	5	*The Meeting*	44
	6	*The Boar Hunt*	57
The Queens	7	*The Return*	75
	8	*The Slander*	88
	9	*The Honor of Lancelot*	101
	10	*The Witch of Orkney*	118
	11	*The Accusation*	134
	12	*The Prophecy*	147
	13	*The Witch of Rheged*	159
The Druids	14	*The Homecoming*	179
	15	*The Messengers*	197
	16	*The Isle of Mona*	207
	17	*The Prisoner*	224
	18	*The Judgment*	238
The Men of Orkney	19	*Seeds of Discord*	261
	20	*The Murder*	273
	21	*The Beating*	283
	22	*The Heir*	303
	23	*The Slaughter*	319
The High King	24	*The Threat*	339
	25	*The Queen's Dilemma*	354
	26	*The Rescue*	370
	27	*The King*	385
	28	*The Wicked Day of Destiny*	403
		Epilogue	424

I. The Descent of Pendragon

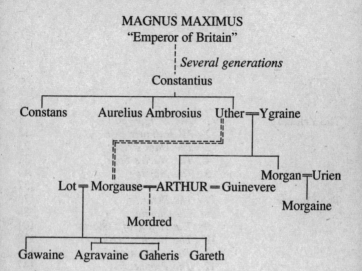

MAGNUS MAXIMUS
"Emperor of Britain"

Several generations

Constantius

Constans   Aurelius Ambrosius   Uther = Ygraine

Lot = Morgause — ARTHUR = Guinevere   Morgan = Urien

Mordred

Morgaine

Gawaine   Agravaine   Gaheris   Gareth

II. The House of Gwynedd

THE PRINCES

The Dragon Sail
All Hallow's Eve
The Dark Prince
The Witch's Sons
The Meeting
The Boar Hunt

1 ✹ The Dragon Sail

"Come on, Bedwyr! I wager you a gold coin I can beat you to the top of Nob's Hill!"

"You're on!" he cried, and dug in his heels. I crouched low over my gelding's withers and buried my fist in his whipping mane. "Faster, Pallas, faster, my brave boy!" The horse responded, pounding up the hill, his haunches bunching powerfully, his forelegs striking out for the rising ground. Halfway up, we caught Bedwyr and his stallion; around the last turn we nosed ahead.

We pulled up together, gasping for breath and laughing. "Good boy!" I cried, patting Pallas' sweated neck as he lowered his head and blew. "You beat him! That's twice this week—you're losing your touch, Bedwyr."

"And my purse." He grinned, tossing me the coin. "Arthur should never have given you that horse."

"No doubt he'd have picked another, if he'd known how poor it would make you!" I tucked the coin in my pouch. Behind us, the rest of the escort thundered up the hill.

Bedwyr sidled closer. "Ah, Gwen, it's good to see you laugh again. It's been awhile."

I turned away, the smile gone, as the escort cantered into view. Bless Bedwyr, he kept them at a distance and left the two of us alone on the hilltop.

We walked the horses slowly around the summit clearing. I loosed my hair from Ailsa's careful braiding and let it all blow free in the rising wind. I would catch it from my dear nurse later, but just now I did not care. The sun pulled free of streaming clouds and a shaft of light, golden with the lateness of the day, stabbed down at the bare emptiness of autumn. From the brown marshes below us most of the fowl were already gone. It is a mel-

3

ancholy time of year, when the sun sets early and darkness comes in the afternoon, when the west wind sweeps everything before it and summer's memories lie like summer's fruit, dead and forgotten underfoot.

"Give yourself time," Bedwyr said gently. "All wounds heal with time."

I shrugged. "You sound like Merlin, may he rest in peace."

In the last six months my world had changed forever. It seemed like only yesterday I outrode my escort on a foggy April morning, lost my way, and fell into the trap Elaine had set for me. I shuddered at the memory of it—King Melwas rising out of the mists to grab me, the long row to his hidden island while the thick fog shrouded us in silence and all I could hear was the creak of oarlocks and the eager panting of his breath. The miserable cabin where he kept me prisoner, the bars on the windows, the rich hangings around the bed—they haunted my dreams and set me weeping in the night. And this, all this, Elaine had planned herself, down to the last detail. She had betrayed me to him; she had as good as given me into the villain's hands.

This was not a thing I could put behind me. I still saw Melwas standing half dressed before the fire, gloating, taunting me with his smug certainty Arthur was about to put me away and the whole world knew it. What need had Britain's King for a childless Queen? I still felt his hands and lips upon my flesh and heard his coarse whispers in my ear! Oh, the blackguard! He was sure that if he took me, Arthur would want me no longer. And Elaine, my cousin Elaine, had thought so, too.

Sometimes I thought I would never get past it, even though Arthur assured me that in time, the terror of it would fade. Bless Arthur, he had sworn to keep me; more than that, he had publicly proclaimed it. Yet still the nightmares cursed my sleep, terror burning deep into my soul. If Lancelot had not come to rescue me—ah, God! If he had been less than he was—I turned sharply, and Pallas threw up his head in alarm.

"Look at the Tor," Bedwyr said lightly. "It looks close enough to touch, and yet it's a good hour's ride away."

I pulled my cloak tighter around me and looked westward toward the Tor. Ynys Witrin, the Isle of Glass, the Holy Hill, dominated the view. Alone and forbidding, it rose from the Lake of Avalon like a giant sentry guarding Arthur's western flank. The signal fires at its summit could be seen for a hundred leagues. The last time they had lit—was it already five years ago?—they had warned the King of Badon.

Below the summit sat the little Christian monastery, a small place, but growing. It was best known for its peace and solitude, since few cared to go there. The brothers lived in mean huts, worshipped in a crude and tiny chapel, and went to bed unwashed, or so the bishop said. But then, he was one of those men who must make little of others to make more of himself, so it might well be untrue.

Further down the Tor stood Melwas' fortress, just visible through the naked trees. As King of the Summer Country, he guarded the estuary that fed the Lake and oversaw the safety of the King's ships and of all the trading vessels along his coasts when the seas were open. Until last spring he had proved a true friend to Arthur, but now he was lucky to be alive. To abduct the Queen, survive two attacks by Lancelot, and face the High King in single combat—I shut my eyes tightly. Oh, how I wished Arthur had killed him! God knows he had the right! But Arthur had thought it wise to show him mercy; in the long run it was more politic to let him live. Melwas had acknowledged defeat and sworn solemn oaths of fealty. Only time would tell how much he meant them.

At the foot of the Tor lay the Lady's shrine of Avalon, the whitewashed walls of the pavilions nestled among the apple orchards, a peaceful place, famous for its gift of healing. Niniane was Lady of the Lake, and under her the shrine had grown in power, for she was Arthur's chief advisor. Merlin himself, may God rest his pagan soul, had trained her. Last summer, when the old enchanter died, she alone had inherited his magics and his Sight. Behind her back, I heard it whispered that she stole them from him, that she wove a spell and robbed him of his gifts. But no one who ever knew Merlin gave the whispers credence. He was no fool, even in his dotage. He had chosen Niniane as his successor, and she had proved worthy of the gift. I owed her much. It was to Avalon Lancelot had brought me, half crazed with fear, from Melwas' cabin. There, Niniane and her women had healed Lancelot of his grievous wounds—dear God!—which he got for my sake, crossing Melwas' bridge of swords. My throat ached. My rescuer! He had braved death to save me from a cruel fate, and what was his reward? My false friend, the companion of my girlhood, and my own kin: Elaine.

Unable to bear it any longer, I bowed my head and turned away from Bedwyr, shoving my fist against my lips to keep from sobbing. Sweet Lancelot! My protector and my friend! Where was he now? Gone from me, gone perhaps forever! Gone across the sea with Elaine, my cousin, who hated him worse than death and had married him to spite me! How on God's earth could such things happen?

"My lady Guinevere." At my elbow, Bedwyr spoke softly. "He is not gone forever. He will winter at home in Lanascol and be back come spring."

I shook my head. "Elaine will keep him there. Forever. She told me so."

"You should know, Gwen, she does not have that power. His heart is here in Britain. He will return."

I shrugged. "She hates him, Bedwyr, and will make him as miserable as she can. What will his life be like?"

"Forgive me, my lady," Bedwyr said slowly, "but this he knew before he wed her."

He was right. And Lancelot had married her anyway, because it was the only thing he could in honor do. Bedwyr was watching me worriedly. I wiped away my tears with the back of my hand. "Forgive me, Bedwyr. A moment ago you had me laughing. I am sorry to be so changeable."

"Nonsense. I understand it. And Arthur warned me that the state of your temper might be uncertain."

"Did he?" I managed a bitter smile and stared out over the gray lake waters, ruffled by the wind into frothy waves.

"He misses Lancelot as much as you do."

I bit off a cry of protest. I knew what he meant—the two friends had not been parted since they met, ten years ago. Even so, to compare Arthur's grief to mine!

"Time will heal you both, Gwen. Let time pass."

How could I expect Bedwyr to understand? Unless he were a woman denied a woman's gift—unless he were a barren Queen, whose barrenness shamed her lord; unless he were betrayed by his own cousin and childhood companion, who seduced and then married the one he loved; unless he sat helplessly by while the wicked girl grew heavy with Lancelot's child—I shut my eyes as the tears slid out—unless he were me, he could not know the horror of his comfortless words. "Time," I whispered, thinking of Elaine's bulging belly, "will only make it worse."

He waited patiently until I had myself in hand. "My dear Guinevere, whatever comes, you have the strength to bear it. Think of what you have already borne. Why, Melwas—"

"I pray you, do not speak to me of Melwas!"

"Whatever is ahead cannot be worse. How can you doubt your courage? Think back five years. You were barely fifteen when

Kay, Lancelot, and I rode into Wales to fetch you, take you from your home and kin, and bring you to a strange country to marry a man you had never even seen. If that does not take courage, what does?"

I looked up. "Indeed, but I am surprised you saw it so. Lancelot did not understand it. Yet had it not been for Lancelot, perhaps I could not have borne it." I remembered the very clearing in the oak wood where I had seen him first, a tall knight of twenty with an odd, endearing face, handsome but for a nose broken in childhood and grown awry, with soft black hair shading great gray eyes that spoke right to my soul. A whole month he had spent in Gwynedd, talking to me about Arthur while the wedding party prepared for the journey south, but all I had heard in a month of words was the sweet timbre of his voice and the promise that lay hidden in his whispers.

I shook myself. "Gwynedd was not my real home. King Pellinore and Queen Alyse were kind enough to take me in when my father died, as company for Elaine. And I owe them much. Have you ever seen my real home, Bedwyr? Northgallis is a tiny kingdom. You might have ridden through it and not even known."

"Indeed, my lady, I have been there twice. Your brother Gwarthgydd received me most kindly at Cameliard."

"Did he? I'm pleased to hear it. He's a good man, and supports Arthur. Did you meet Gwillim, Gwarth's youngest son? He was my playmate in those years, being near my age. They are pagan still, in Northgallis. Old ways die hard. It wasn't until I reached Gwynedd I even saw a Christian. I have not been back since the day I left. At seven." I sighed. "Let be. I do not regret my childhood. But you are right about the time you came to Wales. At fifteen, I was not prepared for marriage." I glanced at him quickly and smiled. "Do you have any idea how terrified I was of Arthur?"

He laughed. "Do I not! Aside from what Lancelot let drop, I saw your face when he was mentioned and your awe at coming to Caer Camel. He must have been more legend than flesh and blood to you."

"How not, when I knew him only by his reputation? The High King of all Britain, the Saxon-Slayer himself, who turned the tide of the Saxon invasions and made them stay behind the borders that he set them. Crowned at fourteen and never once defeated. Outshining Uther and Ambrosius who came before him, outshining even Maximus the Great. All the kings of Britain bent a knee to him, from Lothian and Strathclyde in the north, to Elmet in the east, to Wales and Cornwall in the west and south—everyone revered him, everyone wanted to fight under his Dragon banner. Everything he did was sung by bards all over Britain. Come out of obscurity at the moment of Britain's greatest need, guided by the most powerful enchanter the world has ever known, wielding a Sword of light and a wearing a mantle of glory—my dear Bedwyr, he was a man of a thousand legends before he was twenty. Do you wonder at my terror? To you, it was a matter of fetching him his bride. To me, it was being sacrificed to a god." I stopped and laughed. "How Arthur would hate to hear me say that!"

Bedwyr shook his head. "I remember, when Lancelot told us you were frightened of him, we found it hard to believe. Now I understand it. But now you know the man."

"Ahhh. I do indeed. I thank God every day for Arthur. There is no one like him."

"Before you met him, did you ever wish he had chosen someone else?"

"A thousand times!" I cried, smiling at his surprise. "Elaine and I used to lie in bed and pray nightly for my death, or his change of mind, or a great flood or a cataclysm—for some sort of deliverance!"

"Well," he replied, grinning, "it's your own fault he chose you. Your kinsman Gwillim proposed you, though you had been gone seven years from his home, and King Fion of Ireland sang your praises with such persuasive charm, Arthur was convinced you could have no peer."

I laughed. "If you could have seen Fion the night he washed up on the beach outside Pellinore's castle! A wounded pirate, he was then, no more. It was weeks before we found out he was actually a prince. What fun we had, Elaine and I, flirting with him behind her mother's back!"

"It seemed to us he remembered you with more than fondness."

"Oh, come, Bedwyr. It was a girlish romance, nothing more."

"Did Elaine love him, as well? Is that why she refused all her suitors here in Camelot?"

I looked back toward the Tor. "No. From childhood Elaine loved only one man. She had no wish to be Queen of Ireland. She wanted only to be Britain's Queen." I paused as he started. "She loved Arthur. You knew that, surely?" But from the shock on his face, I saw he had not known it. "Oh, yes," I continued softly. "All her life, for as long as I have known her, she has wanted to be Arthur's wife."

"Then—then why did you bring her with you to Camelot?"

"Why, indeed? Now I curse the day I did. But think back, Bedwyr, to what I said about my terror. Leaving my home for a strange man and a strange country, knowing nothing about marriage, close to panic at the thought of the marriage bed—I was beside myself with relief and joy when Alyse permitted her to come and stay with me. One friend I had, that's all. One friend in the world. And we two together made a pact that she would deny her love for the King and strive to conquer her affection, and I would do the same for—well, let it go unsaid."

Bedwyr smiled sadly. "You were very young."

"Indeed. And neither of us succeeded. I know it was hard for her, to be so near him and go so unnoticed, but I never dreamed she would betray me. But then, Elaine could never put anyone's welfare above her own, even the Kingdom's."

"Betrayal is a hard word. Say she married Lancelot for revenge."

"She married him for spite. But that's not all."

"What else?"

"I may not tell you. Lancelot himself does not know it and I pray he never will. I will say only this: She wanted Arthur to put me away, so she could take my place."

"Gwen, what are you saying?"

"It is true, Bedwyr. Only Arthur knows it. If you love Lancelot, you will not tell him. Her plan failed, but she confessed it when I faced her with it. I was to marry Lancelot, and she Arthur—that was her goal."

"By the Bull of Mithra!" he cried. "The wicked girl!"

"Oh, yes. That is my dear cousin Elaine. When she failed, she married Lancelot to spite me. To take him from me. She seduced him for the purpose." I shut my eyes and drew a deep breath. "Dear God, may she show some kindness to him! But I fear she has nothing in her soul but hate. He took her to Lanascol to bear his child, and he will never bring her back, even if he manages to come himself. Arthur says it will work out all right eventually, but I don't see how it can. She will hate him as long as he lives, and he will be miserable as long as she does—how will it end?"

Bedwyr shrugged. "Perhaps there is some middle road, for both of them."

"Arthur tells me to take the longer view—how like a man! Britain is whole, and likely to stay so, barring some unforeseen threat. With Fion now king in Ireland we have friendships in the west. Since Badon, treaties have bound the Saxons in the east.

Lothian and Strathclyde are our buffer against the Picts. Arthur's cousin Hoel of Brittany has been a staunch ally, like his father before him, and with Lancelot as king in Lanascol, all of Less Britain is stronger. Arthur says we are stronger with him there than with him here, but I know he says it only to bring me comfort. You are right, Bedwyr, he misses Lancelot as much as I do."

"No," Bedwyr said gently, "I was wrong. No one will miss him as much as you." He lifted his head suddenly and pointed. "Look yonder! Toward the fringes of the Lake! Isn't that a sail?" Bedwyr narrowed his eyes. "By Mithra, it is! Whoever can it be? It's late in the year for ships."

"Ships!" I gasped. "Bedwyr, do you see a ship?"

He eyed me cautiously. "Er, my dear Gwen, he cannot be back so soon."

I forced a smile. "Rest easy, my lord. My wits still serve me. I'm not looking for Lancelot, I am looking for the King's ship. With the Dragon sail. Is this the one?"

"I can't make it out quite yet. I didn't know we were expecting visitors so late in the season."

The question was casually dropped. He was not asking me for news, he was simply curious. But I, who had been so consumed with Elaine's treachery and Lancelot's leaving, had forgotten all about the High King's ship! This, of course, was the reason Arthur had been like a cat on hot bricks these last few weeks. Once Lancelot had sailed for Less Britain, there was nothing else to occupy his mind. He had been edgy and quick-tempered, which was unlike him, but in my selfish suffering I had never paused to wonder why.

"Yes," I said slowly, wondering how much Bedwyr knew, "the King awaits a ship from Orkney."

His head whipped round. "Orkney! At this time of year?"

"Yes." I watched his face carefully for any sign that he guessed the truth, but he looked genuinely astonished.

"Queen Morgause? The Witch of Orkney is coming to Camelot? *This* will be a tale to tell my children!"

"No, not Queen Morgause. Arthur has sent only for the princes."

Bedwyr let out a low whistle. "And left the queen in exile? I know he has no love for her, but I wonder if that's wise. That insult may bear rotten fruit in years to come." He paused. "His half sister, isn't she? Uther's daughter, born before he married Queen Ygraine?"

"That's right. Half sister. Wife to Lot of Lothian, may he rest in peace."

Bedwyr grinned. "You'd not say that if you'd known him! *There* was a living devil of a man! A fierce fighter and an ambitious lord, who tried to grab the Kingship at Uther's death. But for Merlin, he might have done it, too. Yes, I remember Lot well. I fought in the battle of the Caledonian Forest, where he was slain. Wherever he is now, I wager he's not at peace."

I peered anxiously across the Lake but as yet, could not make out the device upon the sail. It might only be a trader bound for Melwas' castle.

"So he's sent for his nephews?" Bedwyr mused. "They must be nearly old enough to serve him. If they *will* serve him."

"What have you heard about the princes?" I asked quickly, too quickly. His eyes narrowed. What a fool I was to give myself away! Now he was watching me with interest.

"That they are hotheads who care nothing beyond the interests of their clan. Oh, yes, the Orkney boys are known throughout the north. Wild boys, all four of them, like Lot."

"Five," I said, and watched his face. "Five princes."

He frowned. "Beg pardon, my lady. I have heard of only four. Gawaine, the firstborn, the twins Agravaine and Gaheris, and the little one, Gareth."

I looked away from him, out toward the Tor. "There is another, older than Gawaine. His name is Mordred."

"Trueborn?"

"No. A bastard."

Bedwyr's frown deepened. "But surely he isn't coming! What would Arthur want with his sister's bastard?"

Pallas began to fret; I found I had a death grip on the reins and dropped them on his withers. Gratefully he lowered his head and began to crop the dry grass. I stared with concentration at the Lake. There was an answer to his question, but Bedwyr would never hear it from me. It was the King's own secret, to keep or to reveal.

No one knew that Mordred was Arthur's son, begotten on his own half sister, the witch Morgause. Rumors went round from time to time—I had heard them as a child in Gwynedd—but as Morgause stayed in Orkney, and Arthur in Camelot, the rumors always died for lack of fuel.

He had been a boy then, a nameless bastard in Sir Ector's keeping, and she had been a woman in the full bloom of her beauty, betrothed to Lot of Lothian and ripe for bedding. She seduced him. He did not know, when he lay with her, who his father was. But she did.

Since Mordred's birth, Morgause had kept the boy hidden, and Arthur, ashamed of his great sin, had been content to keep it so. And even though he had sinned in innocence, the horror of what he had done ate at him like a canker from within. I had learned the truth only four months ago, on the night of the summer solstice, the fifth anniversary of our marriage, and he told me only because I asked him, straight out.

And I asked him to send for his son. I had begged him to do it, that we might have a boy to raise together. After five years of waiting in vain for Arthur's seed to grow within my body, driving myself half mad with tears every time I bled, listening to rumors about the Kingdom's discontent at the High Queen's failure, and fearing the constant talk that the King was bound to put me away, I had at last faced the hard truth God had sent me. I was barren and would never bear the King a son. My only hope was Mordred. And when I had asked him to send for the boy, Arthur's joy had told me what his lips had been so careful not to say—he had loved the child more dearly with every passing year, and longed to have him near. Now we looked forward together to his coming, but in secret. Arthur had sent for them all, princes and bastard, but until he found the courage to reveal himself to his son, no whisper of the boy's true parentage could be allowed. Even the boy himself did not know it.

"I wonder—" Bedwyr began.

"Look yonder! That's the Dragon on the sail! It *is* the High King's ship!"

Bedwyr leaned forward eagerly and squinted. "You are right, my lady! I see it now."

I gathered the reins quickly in my hand. "Hurry, Bedwyr, alert the soldiers. We must get back as fast as we can and warn the King."

He stared at me. "*Warn* the King?"

Silently I cursed my unthinking words. What had happened to me since Lancelot's departure? I seemed to have lost every vestige of finesse I had ever possessed. "I mean give him notice. There are preparations to be made."

He looked at me a long moment. "You are hiding something from me, Guinevere. It is unlike you."

I sidled my mare closer and touched his arm. "Forgive me, Bedwyr. It is not by choice."

"Then I may assume that the King knows it—that there is nothing in the Orkney ship that can bring him harm?"

"I wish I could be certain, but in truth, I do not know. Pray hard, Bedwyr."

2 ⬤ all hallow's eve

Arthur and I sat silently in the hall after coming from mass. It was All Hallow's Eve. We had had frosts lately, and the night air carried a tang of sea salt. Down in the town and all over Britain, Samhain fires were burning, honoring the end of the old year after taking in the harvest, welcoming the new with prayers and incantations. On this night, Christian and pagan alike felt kinship with spirits, both blessed and fey.

I looked around the hall. Torches danced in the cool breeze; everyone was robed. Half the benches stood empty, so many were gone from us. The latest band of knights errant had left three days before: Lamorak, Bellangere, Dryaunt, Gillymer, Gauter, Gryfflet, and Agglavall, all good men and sorely missed. Thank goodness the King could not part with Bedwyr; with Lancelot gone, our fellowship was thinned beyond bearing.

The King picked at his food. Even silver-tongued Bedwyr ran out of patter and finally sat silent. We shared a heaviness of spirit that oppressed us like a fever in midwinter, with no escape but through suffering. Beside me, Arthur fidgeted. Normally he sat as still as stone. The knowledge that his son stood on ground that he commanded, so nearby but not yet within his gates, nearly drove him wild. And Arthur was the most patient man I knew.

We had no bard with us. The King called early for the wine to go around, and would, I knew, when the torture of dinner was over, stride off to his workroom to pace endlessly, hour upon hour, until the signal came. I prayed that the commander of the escort would have the sense to ride to Camelot tonight, and not wait on Ynys Witrin until daylight. For secrecy's sake, the King had sent no orders, and so must wait upon the commander's judgment.

"Gwen," he said suddenly, "I nearly forgot to tell you—we had a courier today while you were out with Bedwyr. From Lancelot."

I caught my breath. "So soon? He is well?"

Arthur smiled and covered my hand with his own. "Very well. The crossing was a calm one, and they reached Benoic without trouble. His brother Galyn was there to greet him. They held a great feast in his honor."

"And to welcome his queen." I looked up into his warm brown eyes and somehow smiled. "Don't try to spare me, Arthur. I know full well the nature of the celebration. Lancelot is returned at last to take up the kingship of Lanascol, and he has brought home a bride already heavy with his heir. No doubt they are celebrating all over Less Britain. And so they should, to have such a king in their midst." The ache in my throat stopped my words.

Arthur lifted my fingers to his lips. "I cannot spare you when you face the truth so bravely. But that is behind you, Guinevere. Now look ahead."

I tried to smile. "As to that, now that the boy is almost here, I am scared to death to meet him!"

Arthur flashed a grin that lit his face. "And so am I!"

Suddenly we heard a commotion in the forecourt, raised voices and the clatter of hooves. I glanced quickly at Arthur; he had gone perfectly still. Minutes later, Kay entered the room, coughed politely, and went down on one knee beside the High King's chair.

"My lord," he announced, "the Orkney party are without. Sir Lukan, the commander, wishes to know if you will receive them tonight or wait until the morning. They are"—he paused, and his stony face revealed a shade of consternation—"not quite presentable, my lord, and he knows the hour is late."

The hall went quiet. Slowly Arthur surveyed all the faces and then stood. Everyone rose. "Where are they, Kay?"

"In the courtyard, my lord. Dismounting. The wagons are just coming in King's Gate."

Arthur drew breath and squared his shoulders. "Take the boys to the barracks. Gereint will assign them sleeping places. He shall have their keeping, and Bedwyr their training. I will give them time to wash and rest. But I will see them all tonight. All five, Kay. Send Lukan to me in the library. Now."

"Yes, my lord."

Arthur turned and nodded to his Companions. "Bedwyr, Bors,

Lamorak, Berys, Sagramor, you may attend me. Guinevere—" He looked down at me and held out a hand. "Will you come?"

"Of course, my lord. I wouldn't for the world miss meeting your nephews."

He laughed, half in pleasure, half in sheer excitement. "I don't expect much; they're clearly not up to Kay's standards. But I can't sleep until I know what they are made of. Let's hope, when the night is over, we have cause for celebration."

It was our custom to spend our evenings with the King in his pleasant workroom, where all the scrolls were kept. It gave onto the big garden, where we would stroll on summer evenings to take the air. In winter, we would sit around the log fire, discussing the day's events, or making plans for the spring, or honoring a guest. Sometimes I sang to them, sometimes we read aloud from the precious scrolls Arthur had got from overseas. Tonight, the King sat nervously behind his great marble table in the corner, fiddling with his winecup and talking to Bedwyr. The others stood by the fire, or sat on the cushioned benches, making small talk, wondering in lowered voices why a visit from his own nephews, boys not yet near manhood, should make the King so obviously uneasy.

The door swung open. Sir Lukan entered, face and hands wet from a hasty washing. Arthur rose.

"Welcome, Lukan. I'm glad to see you safely back."

Sir Lukan knelt at his feet and kissed the great Pendragon ruby on his finger. "My lord, I am glad to be back. It was not an easy journey, but we made it without losing a single man. As to your nephews, my lord, they were raised upon the sea and thrive in stormy weather!"

Arthur smiled and raised him. When he had thanked Lukan, served him wine, and sat him near the fire, he paused, his face solemn and intent.

"Tell me," he said simply.

"Well, my lord, we had good weather going and made Orkney at midsummer. The queen gave us a gracious welcome, and at first I thought it would be plain sailing with her as well. But—" He paused. Nothing moved in Arthur's face, but his eyes darkened. "She seemed to find a thousand excuses to prevent our leaving. First it was the preparations. Her boys had nothing fine enough to wear to greet the King."

Arthur snorted. I shot him a startled look, and Bedwyr hid a smile.

"Then it was a pox among the sailors, then the mast was damaged the night before our sailing, and we had to stay to build another." A thin, hard note of anger crept into his voice. "There is not a tree on Orkney, my lord King, that will make a decent mast. Our sailors had to row the queen's vessels clear to the mainland and float the lumber back. In midchannel a storm arose and nearly drowned us." He stopped and took a deep breath. "They do not call her a witch for nothing, begging your pardon, my lord. But we made it back alive."

"Do not beg my pardon, Lukan," Arthur replied coldly. "What she is, she has made herself. It is nothing to me."

I moved closer to his side and laid my hand upon his shoulder. He relaxed a little and beckoned Lukan to taste his wine, which the commander did with some relief. "She's a beauty, my lord," he said in a warmer voice. "I can't deny it, and there's not a man in Orkney who doesn't do her bidding. For all that, I believe she's false at heart."

Arthur smiled bitterly. "If you have just now learned it, Lukan, you come late to the lesson. How did she take my summons? Well or ill?"

Lukan put down his winecup with care. "Well enough, my lord, at first. She acted pleased her sons were called to Camelot to serve the King."

"Lukan." Arthur sat down opposite him and leaned forward, hands on knees. "Lukan, she is my half sister because my father's lusts got the better of his sense. Understand that she is nothing to me. I neither like her nor trust her; if you call her a venomous viper to my face, I will feel no insult. Now, man, tell me the truth. How did the witch take my summons?"

Lukan sat up straighter. "She was furious, my lord. Mad as a hellcat. Not that the boys were called to court, but that she was not. There was the devil to pay among her women. Half of them carried black eyes for weeks." Arthur grimaced. "For six weeks," Lukan continued, "she fought me. First, she threatened to disobey and bring her sons to you herself. She was certain I must have misunderstood the orders, but there it was, on parchment, for her scribe to read aloud. Then she refused to let them go. Beyond her protection, she said, they would fare ill at her tyrant brother's hands. Or—or—"

"Go on."

"Suffer poison, or castration, by his barren Queen."

Arthur's nostrils flared. "Did she say this in their hearing?"

"Indeed, my lord, these tirades were for their sake more than mine. But I think they knew it."

Arthur's expression hardened. "All right, Lukan. Go on."

"Then she tried fits of weeping, that we might pity her misfortune in losing all her sons at a single stroke, but she is not convincing in the pose of helplessness. Last she tried her witch's curses. She has cursed my line down to the sixteenth generation, my lord. They are all to be halfwit savages, every one."

Arthur managed a stiff smile. "I'd say you got off lightly. She has wished much worse on me. Good man, Lukan, to withstand her. She's known to be chancey to cross, but you have done it for me, and I thank you from my heart."

Lukan looked relieved. "At the end, my lord, she gave in with such grace and willingness, it quite surprised me. I was even on the lookout for some trick, but in the end, she let us go in peace, if you don't count the storms that assailed us as soon as we were through the straits."

"Well, she is nothing if not changeable."

Or perhaps, I thought, she had some new plan afoot; but I did not say it. They drank together in fellowship and talked about the weather. I watched Arthur's hands around the winecup, lean, strong hands, with nimble fingers, playing nervously with the beaten silver, turning and turning, as if he could not stop.

"And the princes?" he asked suddenly. "Fared they well upon the journey? No seasickness?"

Lukan laughed. "Those boys? Not a bit of it. Why, they were bred upon the sea and know her moods and tempers. They eat like young wolves and are never sated. You've no worry with your nephews my lord. A healthier, rowdier lot I've seen only in the kennels."

Arthur smiled and listened as Lukan recounted their shipboard antics, but I knew his mind was in the barracks. At last he rose, and Lukan stood. "I thank you for your service, Lukan. You've done splendidly, and I'll reward you. Go now to your well earned rest. Tomorrow we'll speak again."

"Thank you, my lord. It is ever my pleasure to serve you."

When the door had closed behind him, Arthur whirled. "Bedwyr, send to Gereint. Say I wish to see my sister's sons as soon as they are ready."

But Bedwyr had not got halfway to the door before it flew open in his face. Tall and graceful, dark haired and pale complexioned, the Lady of the Lake herself strode in unannounced and stood before the King.

"Arthur!" she cried. "He is transformed! He is free! He is among us!"

Everyone stared. She was not wearing the white robe of the Goddess' servant, but her riding clothes—leggings, tunic, and mantle—and her hair had come loose from its braiding, falling in wild, ragged wisps about her face. Without a doubt, she had ridden straight from Avalon to see the King.

"Niniane!" He took her elbow and led her to the bench. "Be still a moment. My lords, I would speak with her alone." The men bowed and began to file out. I made Arthur a quick reverence and turned to follow,.but he looked up swiftly. "No, Gwen, stay. And you, too, Bedwyr. Gwen, what have we to offer her to drink? She's had a vision of some sort—look at her eyes—and she's ridden instead of resting."

I passed him a winecup, and he lifted it to her lips. She drank without knowing it, her dark eyes wide and unfocused, her whole body trembling with some strong emotion.

"Arthur!"

"I am here, Niniane. Take a moment."

"I must speak to you alone!"

"Go ahead."

"Arthur, I have seen him! He is living!"

"Who, Niniane?"

"Merlin."

I gasped. The King went white. Slowly he slid to one knee and took both her hands. "Niniane. Calm yourself."

"Arthur, I have seen him! In the flesh!"

"How can that be? I buried him myself, there in the hill, and filled the cave mouth with stones not a company of my strongest men could move. He is dead, my dear, and beyond our call. You have said so yourself."

She met his eyes, and her breathing slowed a little. "Yes," she whispered, "I know it. When he lay dying, with his head in my arms, he told me to trust the Sight we shared. He—he must go to his grave, he said, and I must bear his mantle in the world of men. But—" She paused and looked at Arthur pleadingly. "I can't be sure. I thought I felt his death come. But as much as I took from him—I did as he bade me, Arthur, when I entered his mind. You must believe that! I did not steal his thoughts; he offered them to me—I did not take all. There was something else I could not reach; the god we serve forbade it. I don't know what it was."

Arthur held her hands firmly between his own and spoke kindly. "I know he wanted you to take his power. Don't torture yourself with the rest. But as you love him, Niniane, let him rest in peace."

"But Arthur! I saw him tonight. *Tonight!* He is alive!"

Bedwyr moved closer to me; the candles flickered in the draft. Arthur's voice came cool and calm and steady. "Tell me what you saw."

"In the workroom at Avalon, I sat before the peat fire, mixing herbs. Suddenly he was there with me. Not in the fire, Arthur. *In the room!* He spoke, and it wasn't a vision voice; it was his own. He bade me bring you to Caerleon and said he would see you there."

"Niniane—"

She fumbled with her pouch and drew forth an old copper ring. "He gave me this, as a token of the truth. He said you would have trouble believing me, else."

Arthur gasped and shot to his feet. "This was on his body, that we buried!"

"I know."

"But it cannot be!"

"It is."

In that moment his whole being changed. He lit from within. "Niniane, tell me only this—is it possible?"

"Not with ordinary men," she whispered, "but if he is, or was, or has become—a shapeshifter—then—"

Arthur tossed the ring in the air and let out a whoop of joy. "Bless you, Niniane! A thousand thanks! Bedwyr, stay here as Queen's Protector. Guinevere, I leave the boys to you." He strode for the door. "Geoff! My horse! My sword! Five minutes!" He turned. "I shall be back in ten days, or a fortnight, or whenever I can. Think of it! Merlin is alive!"

He was gone; the room still rang with his echoes. I stared at Bedwyr, who shook from head to foot. I crossed myself and for the second time that day I wondered how such things could be.

Bedwyr whirled and whistled sharply. Men came running. "Sagramor! Tell Gereint to send an escort after the King! Quickly, man! Or he'll ride all the way to Caerleon alone!"

"Sir Bedwyr." Niniane spoke quietly. "Would you arrange an escort for me, as well?"

"Do you wish to accompany the King? If so, we must hurry—"

"No. Let them have their private meeting. As soon as you are able is soon enough for me."

"It will be done, my lady. I will see to it directly."

"Thank you."

Bedwyr turned to me and hastily bowed. "My lady, I will attend you in a moment; I want a word with Gereint before the escort leaves."

"Of course, Bedwyr. Go on."

The quiet castle came suddenly alive, with sentries running through the halls, pages fetching swords and cloaks, the calls of soldiers and the clatter of shod hooves on the courtyard stone. Niniane rose, looking more herself again, and thanked me formally for the wine and the escort.

"Anything we can do to please you, Niniane, is our pleasure to perform. You have brought the King great news."

She shrugged lightly. "Great news, indeed. But it is not without danger."

"What do you mean? Danger to whom?"

"A gift from the god is a double-edged sword. There is always another side. There is always a price to pay."

"Do you mean Merlin?"

She nodded slowly, her eyes, normal now, looked far away. "So long as Arthur walks on middle earth, the serpent shadows him that will one day strike at his heel. If my lord Merlin hopes to save him from it—if this is why he has returned—he risks disaster. He may not interfere. It is forbidden. He knows it well, but"— she sighed—"he loves the King."

I went up to her and took her arm. "Niniane, I understand your words but not their meaning. What is it you are telling me?"

She shrugged again and smiled. "Only that on occasion, love gets the better of sense. But this you know already, my lady Queen. . .I should be going."

"Will you tell me what a—a shapeshifter is?"

She laughed lightly. "What have you heard from bards' tales? An ancient spirit, neither god nor man nor beast, and yet all three. Never mind it; I don't even know if it is true. Perhaps, after all, he did not die. With Merlin, all things are possible."

With that, she left me, but I paced about in agitation. I never understood enchanters' talk, so garbled and so dire. Where lay the threat to Arthur? Who was the snake? How everything had changed in the space of a lightning flash the instant she appeared! Here I was, alone in the library, when so short a time ago, Arthur and his Companions had sat here and interviewed Sir Lukan about the High King's nephews! Who would have believed that he would ride from Camelot without so much as speaking to them? To have his own son here at last, to be on the verge of meeting him face to face—and to leave everything, without a look back, just on the chance Merlin might still live! How he loved the man! How he trusted Niniane!

I sat in the King's favorite chair, near the fire. The King's hound Cabal raised himself from the hearth and shoved his wet nose under my hand.

"Well, Cabal," I said, scratching his ears, "here we are, we two, sitting in the corner, waiting upon events. How often, my old friend, has it been so? Men ride in, and men ride out, and we two are ever faithful, waiting. Always before when the King left, I had Lancelot for company. But I suppose I must count myself lucky, to be married five years to a traveling soldier and not find myself lonely until now."

Bedwyr returned within the hour. The escorts were gone, he reported, and the princes housed in the barracks, though not abed. They were far too excited for sleep.

"Well, I'm glad someone remembered them. But tell me, Bedwyr, what did Niniane mean? What is a shapeshifter? It is possible Merlin could endure death and return?"

He shuddered and covered it with a scowl. "Old wives' tales, if you ask me, my lady. I hope Arthur's not gone off on a goose chase. Haven't you ever heard the term before?"

"When I was a child my nurse told me tales at bedtime, about elves and witches and fairy people and such, who lived when the world was young. I think I remember a tale about a wolfboy who was a shapeshifter. But I thought these things were fantasy only and not something a grown man, or woman either, could seriously believe."

"Well, I suppose no one really knows. When our ancestors were children, when gods lived in every tree and rock and stream, people believed in spirits who had strange powers and who lived between the worlds of gods and men. They were real to touch and sight, and yet were creatures of the nether world, who came and went at their own bidding. In the songs I've heard, they were more evil than good. Nuisances, mostly. But really, Guinevere, it's been ages since anyone believed in them, much less saw one. I can't image what possessed Niniane to say that—perhaps it's true she stole Merlin's powers from him and is now pursued by guilt?"

I nearly laughed. "Not Niniane. I don't believe she betrayed him, but if she did, she'd never suffer a backward glance. No, I think she truly believes what she told Arthur. And how quickly Arthur accepted it!"

Bedwyr shrugged. "Well, he knows Merlin best. Perhaps it's

possible. I've heard him say often enough, anything is possible with Merlin."

"Well. I suppose we will have to wait the arrival of a courier to know the truth. Now he has flown off without greeting his nephews, and it is left for me to do it. You must tell me what you know about them, Bedwyr. What are they like?"

With relief, he plunged into a subject much more to his liking. "They are a wild lot, which is not surprising, since they've grown up far from civilization and worship outland gods."

"What do you mean, 'outland gods'? You are a pagan yourself."

He grinned. "Mithra is a soldier and a gentleman. But in Orkney, their gods are animals, as well. I have seen the Mother represented as a pregnant fish!"

"Not so strange," I murmured. "In Wales, I have seen her likened to a pregnant boar. But I mean, what do the princes look like? How did they fare on the journey? Did you speak with them?"

"Oh, yes. I felt it was my duty to get them settled, since Gereint and Kay had so much else to do. They are strong boys all, and none of them the worse for the journey. But then, as Lukan said, they have all but grown up on the sea. Fight like dogs they do, the redheads. Gawaine is first among them, although he is not firstborn. You were right, the eldest is a bastard. Half prince, they tease him. They are all five safely stowed away."

I was nervous and pressed my hands together to keep them still. "What did they look like?"

Bedwyr's eyes narrowed. "Short and thickly built, my lady, red-headed with high color and short tempers. Except for the youngest, Gareth, who is a pleasant, cheerful child, and the bastard, who is of a different breed."

"Oh?" I failed in my attempt to sound casual. "And what is he like, this strange one?"

Bedwyr's gaze sharpened. "Altogether different. Tall and dark. Restrained. Thoughtful. A boy who keeps to himself. A comely lad, too, by the look of him, but not of warrior stock."

"Indeed! You forget yourself!" I cried indignantly, and then flushed, biting my tongue too late. Bedwyr's eyes were alive with excitement. I rose and turned away from him, fighting to calm myself. Bedwyr waited, silent, until I came back and sat beside him.

"Another cup of wine, my lord?"

Gently he laid a hand upon my arm. "Guinevere, if I am to protect the Orkney princes, don't you think you had better tell me what you know about them?"

"I know nothing about them."

Bedwyr smiled. "Who is this dark lad you're so sure is made of warrior stock?"

I bit my lip and lowered my eyes. "Please, Bedwyr, do not ask me. I cannot tell you. I have sworn it."

"To whom?"

I shook my head.

"It is true, then," he said softly, unable to hide his elation. "So, it is true! I have often wondered. There was talk about them at Caer Eden, I remember. Ector's fosterling and Uther's daughter. But he was so young, and she already a woman. Few believed it. Anyway, it was long ago and nothing came of it, I thought, so I forgot it."

I raised my eyes to him. "It is better so," I said softly.

"He does not know who his father is," he said, smiling. "They tease him about it." I said nothing. "I will not press you for the truth, for clearly you have promised not to tell. But I have seen the boy. And I think I know why Arthur sent for him."

"Bedwyr." I looked into his eyes. "Whatever conclusions you come to, will you keep them to yourself?"

"Of course I will." His voice was gentle. "I swear by the Light of Mithra, all of the King's secrets are safe with me."

3 ⚙ The Dark Prince

I rose early the next morning and went to the stables. I was far too excited to sit and do nothing; I did not want to ride out and perhaps miss a glimpse of the boys. So I went to Lyonel, Lancelot's apprentice and now Master of the Horse in his absence, and bade him make ready the young bay stallion Rajid.

Lancelot had three years hence begun to train the war stallions

along the lines set down in an old book the King had procured for
him. It was a short scroll written by a Greek, one Xenophon. This
man knew horses, and gave instructions for gentling them and
training them for war. Lancelot had begun to follow his methods,
and Arthur was well pleased with the result. Now he had developed a system of training that began when they were colts in the
field, just weaned from the mares, and continued until their full
maturity at the age of five. Lancelot and two others, Lyonel and
a lowborn stable boy named Griff, were the only riders good
enough to do this training. But Lancelot had desperately needed
another pair of hands and, over time, had persuaded the High
King to let me try. For two years now, I had helped them, and indeed, although it was ring work, I loved it nearly as much as a
fast gallop over the downs.

What the soldiers thought of a woman riding a war stallion, I
did not know. But ever since I had lifted the High King's Sword
and lived, they had been more accepting of the strange things I
did. They saw I was not like other women: I rode astride without
a saddle, and hawked, and raced, and bore no children. They
shrugged, and muttered to one another that it was Arthur's problem, thank God, and not theirs.

The young horse was put through a series of simple exercises
to supple and strengthen him, and increase his willingness to obey.
There were bending exercises, changes of gait, and turns and
sprints and calm halts. Like dancing, it required control and was
hard for young stallions whose instincts were for running, fighting, and breeding mares. It always took all my concentration, and
it was for this reason that I went to the stable that morning. I
could not bear the thought of Arthur's son so near—I, unable to
go to him, and he, not knowing who he was.

By the time the rest of the palace was up and about, Rajid and
I were hard at work in the big paddock. He moved like a dream,
easy and fluid, and when he outgrew his fits of temper, would
make one of the best fighting stallions in the High King's stable.
We were doing changes of pace at the canter, and he sweated
freely, lathering the oiled reins and chewing the bit as he worked.
Suddenly a group of rowdy grooms burst from the stable door,
shouting and pushing; the horse took fright, reared, spun, landed
and bucked twice, and tried to bolt. By the time I had him in hand
again and made him stand, trembling and blowing with fear, the
shouting match had progressed to a fistfight. I turned, furious, to
give the grooms a tongue-lashing—anyone who worked around
horses should know better than that!

But I saw instantly, in a single glance, who it was. Three red-headed boys in outlandish clothes wrestled in the dust of the stableyard, cursing each other in barely intelligible speech, scratching and kicking, fighting by no rules at all that I could see. At the fence, staring open-mouthed, stood a slim, dark-haired boy holding the hand of a small, red-headed imp, who looked up at me with wide green eyes and grinned delightedly.

"Dred," he said, tugging at the other's hand. "Dred, it's a girl."

I stared back at Mordred, Arthur's son. His father's face was so clearly stamped upon him, I did not see how anyone could doubt his birth who had ever seen the King. The wide brow, the straight planes of the face, the strong chin, generous mouth—these were Arthur's. Even his hands, well shaped and strong, were not his own. But his eyes were black; his hair, cut roughly by someone unskilled, was blue-black; his body slender without the promise of breadth—these belonged to him alone. He looked so like Arthur that I expected to feel the familiar warmth flow from him, of greeting, of recognition, or just of joy of living. But the eyes were fathomless and gave nothing back. He had run up with the child when the stallion was misbehaving, but now he just stood and watched me, whether in admiration or disapproval it was impossible to tell.

I saluted him gravely. "My lord," I said slowly, in case he had trouble understanding cultured speech, "can you not exert some control over yonder unruly brood? This is a stableyard, not a battlefield. They are frightening the horse."

His eyes widened. I could see he was pleased to be taken for the eldest, the man in charge.

"My lady," he began bravely, and then faltered. His voice was just changing; it had that tentative quality, as if he never could be certain when he opened his mouth which voice would emerge, the man's or the boy's. Suddenly he squared his shoulders in a gesture so like Arthur's, it brought a blush to my cheek. "My lady, please forgive them. They—we—are from a foreign land, where customs differ. Besides"—and suddenly the boy was back—"they cannot keep from fighting five minutes out of six."

I could not keep from smiling.

"Hey, Gawaine!" cried the little imp, leaving Mordred's side to run toward the tussling boys. "Gawaine! Look at the lady on the horse! She rides just like a man! And better than you!"

At this the fight stopped, and the three boys all turned toward me. Two were identical: red-headed, green-eyed, and freckled, with the type of short, blunt nose that begs for a blow. Gawaine, a little taller and stronger featured, but no less unkempt, had at least some shred of dignity about him. As I was to learn, he always knew what was due him and saw that he got it.

He gaped at me and approached the fence.

"What's this?" he cried. "Since when do maidens ride the High King's horses? And without a saddle, no less! This is a bit high-handed—whose woman are you? Who's your lord? Why don't you answer? Do you think you can insult my uncle, the High King, without redress?"

"Shut up, Gawaine! Can't you see she's—" Mordred whispered, and was cuffed for his pains. I nearly cried out in indignation, but stopped myself in time. Mordred was used to such treatment, it seemed, and took it with even temper.

But Gawaine saw my anger and smiled. "There's more where that came from. Now give me an answer or get off the horse."

In a flash I understood why they did not know me. I had bound up my hair and covered it with a scarf, to keep it secure during the workout. And it was by the freakish color of my hair that strangers knew me. Only children had hair of such pale gold it was nearly white, but at twenty, I had yet to outgrow this color.

I had opened my mouth to tell them, when I thought of a better way to teach Gawaine a lesson. Sir Ferron, one of the King's commanders, had come into the yard behind them. He had obviously been looking for the boys and was out of patience. When he saw me he saluted; the greeting was upon his lips, when I shook my head, and he went silent.

"Sir?" I said to Gawaine. "Who is it who speaks to me so rudely? Before I answer your accusations, give me your name and family."

Gawaine threw his chest out and shouldered Mordred aside. His speech was British, but with a thick, guttural accent and hard to follow.

"I am Gawaine, Prince of Orkney. Firstborn of Lot and his queen Morgause. The High King is my uncle. And what business is it of yours, I should like to know?"

Ferron gasped, but saw my signal and was still. Beneath me the stallion, grown bored, began to paw the ground. I corrected him gently and he stood quiet.

"Is this the way you are taught to greet strangers, my lord? Here in Camelot, we are polite to those we do not know."

Mordred nudged him ever so slightly. "It's a stallion, Gawaine. Use your head."

But the hint was lost on Gawaine.

"I respect my betters, wench, and when you are one, you shall have it."

"That's enough!" Ferron cried, unable to bear silence any longer. He grabbed Gawaine by the collar and shook him, lifting the boy completely from the ground. "You'll be whipped for this, my lad! King's nephew or no! No one speaks to the—"

"Ferron!" I cut him off in time. "Spare him this once. For me. I should have told him. But I wanted to see his nature first."

"Well, my lady, you have seen it," he said angrily. Gawaine stared at me in bewilderment, and then at Mordred, who had already bent his knee to the ground. I beckoned to the twins; they came forward, surly and uncertain.

"Are you princes of Orkney, as well?"

One of them nodded, glancing quickly at Ferron. "Agravaine, my lady, and this is Gaheris."

"Have you no manners?" Ferron growled. "Has no one taught you how to bow?"

I slid off Rajid's back and beckoned to a groom to come and take the reins. Gawaine's eyes widened as I approached him. He came no higher than my shoulder. I knelt down to look the youngest in the face.

"And who are you, my wise little man?" He went suddenly shy and reached for Mordred's hand.

"His name is Gareth, my lady," Mordred answered quietly.

I stood. The top of Mordred's head came to eye level. I looked gently into the face of Arthur's son. "And you, sir? You are the eldest, surely?"

It was as good as asking him his parentage, but he did not blush or hesitate. "My name is Mordred, lady," he replied. "I am half brother to the princes, a bastard of the queen Morguase." He paused. I was not going to press him further, but he gave me the rest without my asking, baring his shame without a tremor. "I do not know my father's name."

I could not read his expression; he was so self-contained. I could see nothing there but bright intelligence, the flash of a mind working.

"Your father's name is none of my concern." I looked at them all. "You are nephews to the High King Arthur. On his behalf, I welcome you to Camelot."

I made them a reverence, and Ferron made them kneel. I walked past them and unfastened the scarf, letting my hair fall down my back. Gawaine and his brothers made the sign against bewitchment.

"Tell them, Ferron, after I am gone."

I left through the archway that led back to the palace. But before I had slipped into its shadows, I heard Ferron's angry hiss: "Now you've done it, you pagan scoundrels! Cooked your goose your first day here! Can't you tell breeding when you see it? That was the Queen!"

I had no sleep that night. My restless pacing awakened Ailsa, and she came into my chamber with a sleeping draught. But I refused it. "Thank you for the thought, dear Ailsa. I'm sorry that I woke you. Return to your rest, and I will walk in the garden."

"At this time of year, my lady? You'll catch your death of cold! I will not hear of it! Come to me, child, and tell me what disturbs you so." She sat me on the bed and held me, as she had done ever since I could remember. "Now, what is it, Gwen? Share it, make it easier to bear."

"It is Mordred," I whispered.

"Prince Mordred?" She looked puzzled. "He is the eldest of that wild bunch from Orkney, is he not? Why ever do you bother your pretty head about him?"

My hands twisted together in my lap, and I looked away. "He is more than that, Ailsa. He is Arthur's son."

She gasped and clutched her amulets, mumbling her ancient protections.

"I bind you to secrecy, Ailsa. You must not tell a soul. No one may know, until the King makes himself known to the boy."

She nodded, her eyes wide. "I swear by the ancient oak of Bilis, and by the black stone of Eroth, and by Shaitan, the beheader."

I smiled faintly. "It's not as dark a secret as all that. Be easy."

She glanced swiftly toward the King's empty chamber. "I am surprised, my lady, that he would bring him here without your consent," she said nervously. "Is all not well between you?"

I took her hand, amused, for it was she who had come to comfort me. "All is very well between us. Arthur would never have done that. I asked him to send for the boy. Only—now I am beginning to have second thoughts."

"You *knew* he had a child?" She gasped. "Who told you?"

I shook my head. "I have known for years," I said slowly. "I heard it from a soldier."

"Eavesdropping!" Ailsa cried. "Listening at doors with Elaine! I knew it would land you in hot water one day!"

I nearly laughed and was surprised to feel tears spring to my eyes. "I hope I am not in hot water now," I cried, rising. "It's just that—he is so like his father!" I took a turn around the room, brushing the tears away.

"You have seen him, then," she said firmly, "and he upset you."

"No," I whispered, clasping my hands tight together, "he was perfectly behaved. He—it is the *fact* of him that upsets me. That he exists."

Ailsa knew me and said nothing, waiting.

"Knowing that he existed was one thing—and hard to bear—when he was in Orkney. But now that he is here—Oh, Ailsa! How I wish he had never been born! No, no, I don't mean that—I want nothing more than for Arthur to have an heir of his body—but I cannot look at Mordred and not resent it! It is unfair to him, and to Arthur, I know, but—but there he stands, flesh of Arthur's flesh, with the face to prove it, and I cannot—it fills me with jealousy and—and loathing for my rage—but I cannot stand the thought of it!"

Even to my own ears, my words sounded like ravings. I took a deep breath.

"Is is not jealousy of Arthur, exactly," I said slowly. "The King has a right to share his bed with anyone he chooses. Although," I added with some spirit, "I do not like it, and I think it is unfair that I am not allowed the same—and I have told him so."

"Gwen!" Ailsa cried, scandalized. "You never did!"

"I did. What's more, he agrees with me." I managed a small smile. "So you see, Ailsa, not even Arthur is perfect."

"May the saints preserve you! You always were a headstrong child! To say such a thing to the King!"

I sighed and drew aside the long curtain that covered the terrace doors. But the night was black with clouds; not even the stars were out. "He was not angry," I said, half to myself, "or even annoyed. He saw the justice of my complaint. But he said men were creatures less perfect than women; they were given greater strength, but less control."

"What a tongue he has in his head!" Ailsa laughed, relieved.

"Yes. That is what I said, too." I pulled the curtain shut and closed my eyes. "Oh, how I wish he was here! I need his strength now."

"Have you talked to the King about the boy, my lady?"

"Of course," I replied. "How not? And he is always careful of his speech, not wanting to hurt me." I turned to her then, as the tears splashed down. "But, Ailsa, how it *does* hurt! To see the boy here, to know he is Arthur's and not mine—it is a knife in my heart, truly it is!"

I fell at her feet, buried my face in her skirts, and wept. She stroked my hair and crooned in her gravelly voice, but the wound was deep and I had not yet shared it all.

"I am jealous of his mother," I went on, between sobs, "not of who she is, or of her night with the King, but—but simply that she bore him to Arthur. That is all. Only that. She bore him a son, and I did not!" I wept bitterly. Ailsa said nothing. When I looked up at last, I saw tear tracks on her face, and her sturdy body shook. It was easier for me then, and I kissed her rough hands in gratitude.

"Tell me, Gwen," she said at last, "why did you ask the King to send for the boy? What made you do it?"

I shrugged. "I don't know, really. It came suddenly, one night. I thought it came straight from God. But I did not know, then, how hard it would be." I relaxed against her and closed my eyes as she stroked my hair. "It was the night of the solstice—you remember, don't you? There was something special in the very air. Arthur was so loving, and he—we both—" I sighed, and started over. "He gave me great pleasure that night, and I wished to please him in return."

"Ahhhh," Ailsa said softly. "I remember. I remember his face when he saw you in that gown. Stirred his soul, you did."

"I remember you compared him to King Uther, your girlhood hero."

"Aye. And with reason. They say King Uther had the gift of giving women pleasure. Wherever he went, young girls would flock to his tent. He was known for it. Why, there was a maid in Northgallis, when I was your age, spent a night with him as he passed through Wales. And when she married, her husband prized her for the joy she took in the marriage bed. Like you."

"Ailsa! How you talk!"

"Would you care to hear the story?"

"Certainly not!"

Ailsa chuckled. "Very well, my lady, But Uther was as skilled in love as in war, they used to say."

I grinned at her. "Like father, like son."

"Well, then, Gwen," she breathed, "you are a lucky woman indeed."

I patted her hand. "How you have diverted my thoughts! Now you have made me lonely. I shall make you stay with me the night and keep me company."

"That I will do with pleasure, my lady. And I will tell you a
true tale, by your leave, of something that happened in my village
when I was a girl."

"Does King Uther come into it?"

"Not once," she said, smiling. "Not King Uther, but the Saxons. They burned our village when I was small, and we all took
to the hills. One woman lost her husband and all her children. Another family was murdered as they sat eating round the fire, all
but the baby in the cradle. The woman was wild with grief, I can
tell you. She tore her hair and blackened her face with soot until
you would have taken her for a hill witch. The orphaned babe was
taken in by a family with seven children, and wailed all day, never
getting the attention he deserved. One day a Druid priest came by.
Everyone in the village came out to do him reverence, for it is as
much as your life is worth to pass a Druid by. He took this
woman by the hand, gave the babe into her arms, and bade her
raise and tend it. He sang an incantation and blessed her, and her
grief was healed. It is a fact that she raised that boy to manhood,
and all his life he honored her and called her 'Mother' and cared
for her in her old age, and buried her with tears when she died."

I took her hand and kissed it. "I don't believe a single word—
Saxons in Northgallis! But I take your point."

"Take him under your wing," she whispered. "No one else will
have time for him. Make him your own, Gwen. It will bring you
joy."

4 ❋ The Witch's Sons

The King did not return within the fortnight, but sent a courier
to say he would stay at Caerleon with Merlin and we should join
him there for Christmas. It really was Merlin the Enchanter, the
courier said, returned in solid flesh, with nothing much worse to
show for suffering entombment than a haunted look about his

eyes. This news caused great rejoicing throughout the city. The people were proud of their Enchanter and revered his powers; over the bishop's objections we gave public thanks for his escape from death.

As for the Orkney boys, they were chagrined to miss the King, but the soldier's life at Camelot was exactly what they had always wanted. Indeed, their response to kind, even-handed treatment led me to believe they had not seen much of it before. They were given good horses to ride, only to discover that they could not ride them. They must have had only ponies on their island home, for handling a horse was beyond them. Lyonel himself took them in charge, but it was slow work, except for Mordred. The others had got into the habit of hauling their mounts around by the mouth; but the King's horses had never been handled so, and when the boys tried it they usually ended on their backsides in the dust. Only Mordred watched quietly and learned new ways. He even practiced his speaking and so slowly lost his accent. He was determined, he let fall to Ferron in a rare confidence, never to go back. All his life he had dreamed of the mainland and now he was here, he meant to stay.

They came to me in the King's library every day for lessons. The King had sent instructions only for Gareth, on account of his age. But I had them all brought, the first day, and questioned them on what they knew. None of them could write or read or figure; yet Gawaine hoped to be King of Lothian one day, and the others were not without ambition. Bedwyr was there, and a Roman scholar named Valerius who had gone adventuring in his middle years, ended up in Britain, and had recognized in Arthur the sort of man he said had vanished now from Rome. He shook his head in distress at such lack of refinement and learning in kings' sons.

Of them all, only Mordred noticed he was lacking something others around him possessed. He asked if he might have lessons with Gareth and learn to read and write and sum. This pleased Valerius, and it pleased me. Bedwyr, when he could take his eyes from the boy's face, noted my pleasure and marked it. The other boys sniggered at Mordred. They called him "baby-tender" and "nursemaid," and I guessed that he and Gareth stuck together, either from liking or for the child's protection.

"Prince Gawaine," I said firmly, and saw his chin go up. "Let us say you are a grown man of twenty, and King of Lothian." His eyes glowed, and he smiled contentedly. "You are out hunting with a troop of thirty men. You have made your kill and set up camp. Suddenly you find you are surrounded by your enemy, one hundred twenty strong. By how much are you outnumbered?"

Gawaine's mouth dropped open. Mordred grinned. It lit his face, and he looked so exactly like his father that I drew in my breath sharply. Bedwyr glanced sideways at me, smiling.

"However many they were, I should attack!" Gawaine exclaimed, embarrassed and therefore angry. "I would beat them back!"

"Hmmm." I did not laugh at him, but answered gravely. "When you learn the art of war from Lancelot, or from my lord Bedwyr, King of Brydwell, you will learn what are the odds on winning such an attack, if it is two to one, or three to one, or four to one. You will learn what strategies are best employed. But how can you know what to do, if you cannot tell by how many you are outnumbered?"

I turned next to his brother. "Prince Agravaine, tell me, if your ship is charged fifteen silver pieces in harbor dues, and you pay the customs collector three gold coins, how much should you receive in return?"

He colored deeply, resenting it. "I don't know . . . my lady." This last after a sharp look from Bedwyr.

"Then you cannot know if you are cheated or dealt with fairly. For your sake, I hope the King employs honest men as tax collectors."

I looked at Gaheris, who was already blushing, and decided enough was enough.

"It is not my wish to advise you," I said calmly, watching them bridle at the very thought, "and your uncle the High King has left no orders regarding your instruction, although I am sure he assumed these were things you knew already . . . Be that as it may, you are free to attend lessons with Valerius. Prince Gareth and Prince Mordred and I will be here every afternoon after the midday meal. You are welcome to join us."

Valerius bowed low, and the boys shifted from foot to foot.

"When does war training begin?" Gawaine wanted to know.

"In the spring," Bedwyr said. "And with any luck, Sir Lancelot will be here to teach you. There is no one better."

"Where is he when he's wanted, and why did he go away?" Gawaine was petulant. Bedwyr sprang forward and cuffed him on the side of the head. The boy whirled and his hand flew to his dagger, but recognizing Bedwyr as his superior in rank as well as age and strength, he gave way.

"You will address the Queen as 'my lady' in every sentence

you utter," muttered Bedwyr in a flat voice, "or I myself will send you back to Orkney and answer to the King for it. See you behave yourself."

To save Gawaine embarrassment, I answered quickly. "He is gone to take charge of his lands across the Narrow Sea. He is newly married and is settling his wife there. When the seas open, we hope he will return to us, and then your training will begin in earnest. Meanwhile, learn to ride and not abuse his horses, for he loves them dearly, and if he sees you haul at their mouths he will mount you on something that can take such abuse."

When they were gone, I turned to Bedwyr. "Well, Bedwyr, your conclusions must be drawn. The evidence is clear enough, I think."

He smiled. "Wonderfully clear, my lady."

"Have you ever seen such a likeness? It is disconcerting. On the surface, he is so like."

"But underneath, different, I think." His voice was thoughtful.

"What is it? What do you see?"

"Don't misunderstand me. I like the boy. He's quick, and respectful. I don't think he carries hate in him. He's just not . . . open."

"Would you be, I wonder, in his boots?"

"Probably not," he said, musing. "But Arthur would. In that they are different."

"Well, it is a beginning."

Until the court moved to Caerleon for Christmas, all five boys came every day. Between the three of us we taught them their letters, their numbers, and some elementary history of Britain. It was amazing how ignorant they were. They seemed to have learned nothing on Orkney but fighting, court gossip, curses, and the ways of the sea. They knew who Maximus was only because their mother descended from him. They were amazed to learn I descended from him, as well. After that, Gawaine forgot to say "my lady" less often. I thought Valerius would faint when he found they did not know where Rome was. To them, the civilized world ended at Britain's border.

But it was Bedwyr who truly astounded them. One day, he brought out his lap harp, tuned it, and gave them the Lay of Arthur in his clear tenor voice. They had never heard the whole of Arthur's story, which was known to every British child, and yes, Saxon, too, in those days, but that was not the only source of their astonishment. They simply could not believe that a grown man, a king, no less, would take up a harp and sing of his own will. This was bard's work and not the proper pastime for a soldier. But Bedwyr only smiled and sang with pride.

They sat with their mouths open when it was over, and then Bedwyr informed them he would give it to them again and expected them to have it by heart by week's end, certainly before they left to see the King. They stared aghast. Only Mordred listened with shining eyes and a stillness that went to his very soul.

On most days, I enjoyed these sessions and enjoyed watching Mordred, who learned quickly and took great pleasure in it. But oftentimes, in the evening, I would find myself in unexpected tears and weep against my will. I argued with myself and told myself I was behaving like a foolish, weak-willed woman, but this great grief, like love, seemed beyond my control. Sometimes the light would catch his cheek just so, and I would see Arthur, as he sat upon his horse in a sunlit clearing. Or suddenly, by the movement of a hand, I would see Arthur as he sat at table, toasting his Companions. It was a torture to me, to see the King reflected in this child; and yet it gave me joy, as well. Only when I looked into his eyes, black and secret, did I see the boy himself, and not the King. Thus I took to sitting near him, where I could see those eyes, and gradually, as time passed, was better able to bear his presence. He was not a shy child, but very reserved, and seldom spoke to me on his own. But he seemed to like it when I sat near, and slowly we grew easier with one another.

One day, I was in the library alone when the princes arrived. Bedwyr was at council in the Round Hall, and Valerius lay abed with a cold. I knelt in a recess by the window, looking in the chest for a scroll, and they did not see me. After the first words, I was afraid to show myself.

Gawaine went over to the fire and pushed Cabal out of his way, not gently. "Well, it looks like the bitch has forgotten us. The cat's away, let's have some fun."

"Hold your tongue, Gawaine! Are you mad?" It was Mordred, quickly.

Gawaine laughed. "Why should it offend you, bastard brother? You're no kin of hers. Come on, let's see who's strongest. Give me your hand, Gaheris."

"I know why," Agravaine crowed. "He's fallen in love, has Mordred. Can't you see it when he looks at her? Always fawning and bending his knee. Not content with a kitchen maid, he must have the High King's wife!"

The hackles rose on the back of my neck, as if some phantom breathed upon it. I would not have moved for the world.

"Ha-ha!" Gaheris taunted. "Lord Mordred, is that what you're after? King Mordred perhaps?"

There came a strangled cry from Mordred. "Shut up, all of you! I don't care what you say of me! But leave the Queen alone! Call me what you like. Call me landless bastard, that's your favorite. It's true enough. Well, I pity you heartily. Here you are at last on the mainland, in a civilized country, in the very heart of Arthur's Kingdom, where you have wanted to be since you first drew breath, and all you can do is moan about how hard it is to be a good knight, and make fun of his Queen because she cares about you. And I don't for the life of me understand why she bothers! Our upbringing is no concern of hers. As you so rightly pointed out, we are not her kin. Yet here she is, every afternoon, trying to make us fit to meet the King. Why can't you see that you are being done honor?"

There was a general grumbling. None of them had Mordred's power of fluid speaking. But Gawaine finally voiced his predictable objection. "I'm the boss here, Mordred. Just because Bedwyr treats you specially. That's because you like his music. He's just the Queen's fancy boy, anyone can see it."

"Gawaine." Mordred's voice was exasperated and tightly controlled. "She is grooming us. Patiently. Carefully. Think of what that means. In two weeks we go to Caerleon. Why is such care being taken over us? Can't you understand? Can't you tell how different we are? Everyone else you have met since you came to Camelot speaks politely, wears plain clothes and keeps them clean, eats a meal without spraying it over his neighbor, washes his hands and face daily and cleans his fingers after eating, goes about his work without complaint, and is never rude to a woman. Is it any wonder we stand out? If the Queen works hard at refining our behavior, have you wondered why? Could it possibly be"—he paused, having their attention—"could it possibly be because the King will not receive us else?"

There was a stunned silence as the boys watched their futures go up in smoke.

"He's our uncle!" Agravaine cried. "He may not receive *you*, Mordred, you fatherless bastard. Why, you could be the son of a wandering harper, for all we know. But we're the sons of a king. He brought us here. He'll receive us."

"Are you so certain? Where is our mother, then? His own sister?" Silence followed. "If he so valued bonds of kinship, he'd have sent for her, as well. Yet you heard the orders. She stays in exile. And we don't even know why."

"She's a witch!" Gaheris stated proudly. "He fears her power!"

"Are you jesting? Why should King Arthur fear a witch, when he's been a friend of Merlin the Enchanter all his life? She's no threat to him."

"She is, though," Agravaine asserted. "She hates him. Doesn't she, Gawaine? We've all heard her say so, often enough."

"Bah!" Gawaine said gruffly. "She'll say anything in a temper. She's jealous of his power, is all. Even she is afraid of it."

"She is not!" Gaheris screamed on a rising note.

"Then why isn't she here, of her own will?" Mordred's quiet voice cut through the panic. "She feared even the King's commander, who led our escort. And what she fears, she hates."

"Let her come," Gawaine declared, "if she dares. I, for one, would welcome her, but as a King's man, not as a witch's son."

"She *will* come!" bleated Gaheris. "You wait and see! She *will*!"

"She'd better not," Mordred warned.

"Arthur will not harm her if she does," Agravaine replied with defiance. "After all, she is his blood kin, the daughter of his father. And he would not dare, with us here—"

"Would not dare?" Mordred cried, aghast. "Would not dare *what*? Do you imagine Arthur fears you? Listen to yourselves! What are you, Agravaine, and you, Gaheris, against even one of the High King's knights? They are trained men, with real swords, and fine horses. My lord Bedwyr, whom you dare to call a fancy boy, has killed more men in battle than you have even *seen*! Don't make me laugh. What possible threat could you pose? You have not even reached manhood."

There was much shouting and some fisticuffs, but they recognized the truth of Mordred's argument and changed the subject. But I, huddled in my corner, I wished Arthur had heard it; if there was ever a boy ready and eager and worthy of the challenge before him, it was Mordred.

They talked about Morgause awhile, and what she was doing all alone on Orkney, and whether they could ever persuade their uncle to ask her south.

"At least she acts like a queen," Gaheris said finally. "Not like this Queen of Arthur's, who looks like a woman but acts like a man."

"Just because she can ride as well as you can walk!" Mordred returned hotly.

"See! I told you he is soft on her!" crowed Agravaine.

"I like her," Gareth piped up. "She smells good. Not like Mother."

Here they all laughed, and I hoped they would let it rest. The Queen of Orkney was known for her use of perfumes and aging creams.

"Don't forget what Mother warned us about her—"

"Do you mean about poison and—"

"Perhaps she *is* evil, in spite of the way she looks—"

"Evil!" Mordred cried, beside himself. "How can you think it? There is not a wicked hair on her head! What has she done to you but paid you honor? And this is how you speak of her behind her back?"

"He has a point," Gawaine granted. "Mother might have been jealous and told us that to make us keep our distance. I don't think the High Queen means us ill. But even so, Gaheris is right, she is too—straightforward."

"Too bold," Gaheris said.

"Too forthcoming," Agravaine said.

"By the Light!" swore Mordred, and I smiled, hearing by the way he said it that the oath was new to him, something recently picked up from the soldiers' barracks. "Is it not refreshing to deal straight with a woman, and not always be wondering what she really meant, where things are as they are, and have no double meaning? Speak for yourselves, of course, but it's a relief to me."

"But she orders Bedwyr around," Gawaine complained, coming to the rub. "He's the Queen's Protector. He's in command here. But she leads in everything and he follows."

"She doesn't lead the soldiers," Mordred said patiently.

"But I heard that she drew the High King's Sword Excalibur!" Agravaine hissed. "And the High King nearly slew her for it!"

"I heard he kissed her for it!" laughed Gareth. I put my hand over my mouth to cover a giggle.

"And guess what else I heard?" Gaheris whispered. "You know this Lancelot they keep telling us all about? They say he is her lover." He paused, having their attention. "And King Melwas, too, who took her and kept her on his island!"

"Well, and what of that?" countered Agravaine. "Mother's had plenty of lovers, and some of them kings."

"Shut up!" Gaheris cried, weeping. "She has not!"

"She has so! How do you think Mordred got here?"

"You fools!" Gawaine spoke with contempt. "A queen without a husband has a right to take a man to her bed. But if Queen

Guinevere takes a man to her bed, it is betrayal to the High King. He would kill her."

At last Mordred spoke. "I think you had better not repeat palace gossip until you know more about it. Do you think the High King would have spared Melwas' life if he'd lain with the Queen? These are rumors. How do we know there is truth in them? Men will say anything that sounds interesting in their cups. Wait until you have seen the King and Queen together, and until you have met Sir Lancelot, before repeating such gossip. You might regret it."

"Very wise words," came a cold voice from the doorway. It was Bedwyr, come at last from council. I turned my head a little. The boys all faced him, their backs to me.

"My lord Bedwyr," Gawaine said boldly, "is this Sir Lancelot everyone talks about the High Queen's lover? Has she betrayed our uncle behind his back?"

Then I rose, and then Bedwyr saw me. He never blinked an eye.

"Why don't you ask her yourself, if you dare?" And he bowed low in my direction.

They turned and gasped, all except little Gareth, who ran to me and hugged my skirts.

I looked at them, huddling together in fear, Mordred alone blushing for the shame of his brothers. He went down on one knee, bowing his head, and after a moment, the others followed.

"I am ashamed of you," I whispered.

The slither of metal lifted their heads. Bedwyr had drawn his sword and held it level with their throats.

"King's nephews or not," he said evenly, "I will slay the first man that so much as whispers aught against the Queen. I am the Queen's Protector. Never did I think to have to protect her honor from the likes of you! Uncouth outlanders all! Be gone! Out of my sight before I lose my temper!"

They went white and edged toward the door. Gaheris grabbed Gareth's hand and dragged him away.

"Prince Mordred," I said quickly, "stay a moment. I want a word with you."

Relieved, the others gladly left Mordred to his fate.

Mordred fell to his knees. "Please forgive us, my lady! Although I know it was unforgivable to say such things in the King's house. It is barracks talk only. We—we are not ready yet to live among you here. I—"

"Prince Mordred." I extended a hand and raised him. He stood facing me, shaking. "I wish to thank you. Not only for your defense of me, but more, for your defense of the High King and the way he has ordered life here. I know it must seem strange to you and your brothers, and it is hard to learn new ways, but your efforts will be rewarded. The King shall receive you. You will have a place here."

His eyes were shining with hope and excitement. "If that could only be possible, my lady—it is what I have wished for! Will we really get to see the King?"

"Yes. At Christmas. In Caerleon."

"And is he really—what they say of him?"

I smiled, looking into the image of Arthur's face, eager and bright and quick. "He is all that. And more. You will see."

He touched my hand very lightly to his lips. "Thank you, my lady."

They all gave me a good apology the next day, with downcast eyes and bent knees and humble demeanors, even little Gareth, who did not know what it was all about. After that, we were easier with one another, but it was never a pleasure to me to be with Gawaine, Agravaine, and Gaheris. The words they had said could not be unspoken. I knew, of course, as Arthur did, that rumors about Lancelot were as plentiful as daisies in summer, but no one had ever voiced them in my hearing.

And what was worse, I knew the three middle boys believed them, for I would catch them staring at me furtively from time to time, whenever Lancelot's name was mentioned, as if hoping to catch me out in a blush or a fever, like some village maiden with a crush upon her lord. It angered me, but there was naught that I could do. They had no sense bred in them. They were hot for one idea at a time, and that idea changed as quickly as the wind. Only Mordred was steady and cool.

As time for our departure neared I found myself growing anxious, and I did not know why. Bedwyr asked me thrice what ailed me, and I could not tell him. I would have shared it with him if I had known myself. I needed Mordred's company; I would seek him out and then when I was with him, I wished myself away. I did not know what drove me. As always, I sought solace riding and spent more and more of my days galloping over the downs at breakneck speeds. One day, I was out so long I made my escort late for the soldiers' mess; my apology made little difference; they would have to get what they could from the kitchens. Myself, I was not hungry, but stayed in the stable to tend my horse and be alone with my tormented thoughts.

Bedwyr found me in Pallas' stall, weeping mindlessly. "Gwen!" he called softly, but I could not answer. He put a hand on my arm. "Better my shoulder, sweet, than the horse's mane." He held me in silence until at last the storm abated, and I could draw breath without sobbing.

"Forgive me, Bedwyr."

"My dear Guinevere, what is there to forgive? Tell me only why you weep, that I may know how I can help."

I shook my head.

"It is Mordred, is it not?" I made no answer, and he laid a hand against my cheek. "I know it's Mordred. I've seen the way you look at him. Tell me, Gwen, what it is that hurts you so."

"Don't mistake me, I—I love the boy, Bedwyr."

"Yes," he said. "I know."

"If only—if only he did not look so like Arthur!"

"He is very like. Even Kay is beginning to wonder."

"I don't want Arthur to see me like this."

"He would understand it."

"But he would take it upon himself. And it is not his doing, it is mine."

"Yours?" He sounded surprised. "How so?"

I drew a long breath and steadied my shaking voice. "In a moment of . . . tenderness, I asked him to send for the boy. I wanted—I wanted to give him a son. It was the only way I could."

"Ahhhhh." His face warmed, and he lifted my hand to his lips. "What a gift, Gwen! I did not know it."

I shrugged. "So you see, I brought it upon myself. But now I find—and it is too late. We cannot send him back!"

"Is that what you would like to do, if you could?"

"No," I whispered, "no. He will bring Arthur such joy. And— and I do not wish to part with him myself, now that I have got to know him. But I weep at nights. It comes upon me of a sudden, like a fainting fit. I don't know why."

"I know why." Gently Bedwyr took my arm and drew me out of the stall. We walked in silence to the small room where the saddles were kept, and there he sat me on a bench. I had not realized, until I sat, how weak my knees were. Bedwyr closed the door behind us and lit the lamp. He sat beside me and took my hands in his. "My wife's sister cannot bear, so I know the signs of that grief. She grieves because she thinks she cannot be a woman without children," he said softly. I gasped; the blow hit me squarely and took my breath. "She is not a fool," he went on, "but she is wrong."

"She is right!" I cried, trembling. "All the world thinks so! If you do not believe it, you have not seen their faces or heard their whispers! Ask Kay! Ask anyone!"

"Ask Lancelot," he responded. "Ask Arthur. Ask me."

"No, you are kind and wish to ease my pain. But truly, Bedwyr. Why did the High King marry a second time? He did not wish to. He married to get himself an heir. Do not deny it."

"I do not deny it. It is true."

"That is a woman's duty. We do not fight battles, or rule kingdoms. Do not say I am his companion, for he does not take me with him, and he is gone more than he is here. What purpose do I serve? Out of kindness—all right, love—he keeps me. But there is not another like him in the world. I am not whole, Bedwyr— can you not see it? I am but half a woman, and to hear others talk, half a man. I ride, I hawk, I jest with his Companions, I dared to lift the Sword—what am I fit for? Truly, I do wonder: Why am I here?"

Bedwyr had bowed his head, but now he lifted his face to me, and I caught my breath at the glow of love and compassion I saw there. He rose and looked down upon me.

"Guinevere," he said, "I can hardly believe my ears." He took a turn around the room and returning, knelt before me. "Listen to me a moment. I am going to talk to you about Arthur."

Surprised, for I had expected him to try and appease me with the usual compliments, I nodded.

"I have known him a long time, and I know him well. We were boys together. He was always a leader; I know that is not hard to imagine. He was always the best at games, the swiftest runner, the most daring rider, had the truest aim and the quickest arm. He led and I followed. His bravery astonished me. His compassion won my love. But even at ten I knew he was not whole." He paused. "There is that in Arthur which drives him to—reach out, to share, to draw in others to him. He has always been seeking something. Back then, though we thought him the bastard of one of Ector's petty nobles, in my eyes he was a king. He was so able, so confident, so sure."

"Yes," I said quickly. "I know what you mean."

"But in his soul, Gwen, he was lonely. He had no one to match him. For a time, Merlin filled that space. Those early years, just after his crowning, they were good ones. Good fellowship with soldiers, planning battles, knowing Merlin was behind him—he was almost at peace. Then, as he grew, Lancelot and I were dearer to him, almost dear enough. But his is a great heart, and a great need. Together, we could not fill it. When he married the Cornish princess, we had hopes—she was bright and gay and made him laugh. But, for whatever reason, he did not love her, and until her dreadful death, she touched him not."

"Bedwyr, you are very kind, but—"

"Hear me out. This is important. I cannot begin to tell you what you mean to him. But I can tell you that what he always sought, he has found in you. Now he is the man it was always in him to be. Now he is whole. Now he lacks for nothing. Shall I tell you what he was like when you lay on Ynys Witrin, a prisoner of Melwas? Do you think you have seen anger? Or agony? Or cold fury? You have not, if you did not see the King. Do you want to know what he was like when he learned of your abduction? I am a strong man, yet I wept for him. Ask Bishop Landrum if any other of his congregation has knelt two days before the altar, praying, taking no food or rest."

I stared. "Arthur did that?"

"And more. It is not so much a passion of the heart, Gwen, as a need in his very soul. I cannot explain it. But it is real. From the first moment he saw you he has needed you. I pray you will consider this carefully. I am talking about much more than carnal love. You are his rest when he is weary; his joy when he is low; his quiet song when his ears are filled with human pleas and blandishments. What purpose do you serve? You give the King life. Without you, he would not be who he is."

"What a gift you have for words, dear Bedwyr! I see you feel the truth of what you say, and I thank you from my heart. No praise has ever touched me so. But—"

He gripped my wrist suddenly. "Gwen! Why can't you see that he would not love you if you were like other women? If you were coy or flirtatious or secretive or light-headed, if you filled your talk with gossip or your days with household chores and cares about children—you know the man! *Then* would you be like other wives, and *then* would your barrenness be a curse to him. But you are a woman a man can speak to! Why, even I—" He blushed suddenly and grinned. "Even I cannot speak to my dear wife as I speak to you. This is a gift, Gwen. Do not mistake it for manliness. That you, of all people, could ever think yourself unwomanly!"

I pressed a finger against his lips to stop him. "Oh, Bedwyr, I do thank you. I take your meaning. You are telling me that the things I do not value in myself are the very things the King values in me. If it is true—"

"Yes!" he cried.

"Then I do Arthur a disservice to have such doubts. Then I have done the right thing, after all, in bringing his son to Camelot."

"Yes!"

"Then I can serve him just by—just by being?"

"Yes, Gwen. Just by being yourself."

"Well, then," I whispered, looking past the window to the young stars, "perhaps the future will be possible to bear. I know his need of me—I have felt it often, although I have never understood it. It if truly means what you tell me, then—why then, I am able to give to Arthur the gift he gives to me."

Bedwyr smiled and uttered a quiet prayer to Mithra. "Blessed are the givers, for they are the bearers of Light."

5 ⚘ ThE MEETING

We rode into Caerleon on the twelfth day of December. It had snowed hard all day, and the going was slow. To prevent our freezing, Bedwyr rode ahead with those of us on horseback and half a troop of mounted soldiers, leaving Kay and the wagons, litters, and rest of the force behind. I rode beside Bedwyr near the front, and the boys rode behind us. They had a hard time of it. I enjoyed talking with Mordred and often beckoned him to come up between us; but I had to be sure and pay Gawaine his due and spend as much time with him, even though he bounced so much in the saddle he could barely talk. Little Gareth had refused to ride in a litter with the women when we separated from those who moved more slowly, and he clung happily to Ferron's saddlehorn, held by a strong arm, never complaining. The Orkney boys were more used to snow than we were and had several names for it in their own language, names for all its textures and forms. Of course they argued among themselves which name best applied. It kept them occupied.

We reached the garrison before dusk. Bedwyr halted at the King's house and lifted me down from my horse, an unnecessary display of gallantry, done to instruct the boys. He brushed the snow from my hood and cloak and offered me his arm. The sentries saluted as we walked to the door.

"Ailsa and the litters will be hours yet, I fear," Bedwyr said. "I will send another troop out to escort them, and see the boys safely housed in the barracks. You will be all right?"

"The King is here?"

"I understand he is expected. He might be here."

"No matter. I will be attended. Join us later, if you can, Bedwyr. He will have lots of questions."

"Does he know I know?"

I smiled. "No, but it will only need a look at your face. Go now. They are waiting. And thank you for all your kindnesses."

The house was warm, the tiled floors heated from below by the old Roman hypocaust system of heating water to boiling point in the cellar pit and sending steam through pipes laid under the floors. It was the one advantage the King's house at Caerleon had over the castle at Camelot, and it was why we always spent the cold months there. The women's quarters were deserted, for I was the first one there, all but young Hanna and Mary having chosen the litters. I had a hot bath, and Hanna washed my hair. She was shy and said little, but I was tired from the journey and the cold and enjoyed the peace.

I sat before the grate in my sitting room, while Hanna brushed out and braided my hair, and Mary brewed a hot posset over the fire. I must have dozed off, for I woke to their voices, whispering in the corner.

"Did you see him?"

"I saw him well. He rode beside me part of the way."

"So? What did he say?"

"Practically nothing. He is very shy."

"He has eyes only for the Queen."

"Not in that way, surely. She is old enough to be his—"

"Hush, she will hear you. She is not. Only eight or nine years between them. Less than between Queen Morgan and King Urien."

"Well, and what are you suggesting? That he is six weeks at court and plans to usurp the King?"

"Oh, hush, that is treason! I meant no such thing! Only that he admires the Queen and that he is old enough to."

"Perhaps. I say, Mary, do you know who he resembles? I saw it suddenly, when we rode along, and he turned to me. It came to me out of the blue—he looks like the—"

I coughed gently and sat up. At once they came to attend me, but they saw from my face I had overheard them. They were young, Hanna fifteen and Mary a year younger; even so, I had thought them old for Mordred. I made them sit before me, and I took both their hands.

"Listen to me, for this is serious. Young maids will talk and may be overheard sometimes and perhaps misunderstood. You would not willingly do the High King a disservice by your careless prattle, would you?"

"Oh, no, my lady," they said together, eyes wide.

"Well, then, keep a guard upon your tongues, especially where it concerns the princes of Orkney. They are his kin, and it would not do to start rumors you cannot put fact to."

"We spoke only of Mordred the bastard, madam."

"Treat Mordred no differently. He, too, is the High King's nephew."

Hanna nodded, but Mary was braver. "We have heard rumors, madam, about a different parentage for Mordred."

I looked her full in the face, and she lowered her eyes. "I have heard those rumors, too. Do you find me sharing them with others? Do you know if the rumors are true? Well, then, repeat them not. They are told by people as ignorant of the facts as yourselves. Let be, child, and keep your own counsel. And never let Mordred get wind of them. That would be cruelty indeed."

They were sober after that, and I did not think they would talk. If they did, it would mean an end to gentle service in the Queen's household and back to their parents in disgrace, and they knew it. But I was unhappy to know that so many others besides myself could read Mordred's lineage in his face. It would force Arthur's hand, if he was not ready soon.

At last came the summons I awaited. The King was home and begged me to sup with him in his rooms. I went gladly, as eager to hear of his doings as I was to tell of my own. He must have just returned, for as I entered the antechamber and curtsied, his chamberlain Varric was hurrying away with his soaking cloak and boots, and a score of knights were leaving, laughing loudly and slapping each other on the back. Lamorak I saw, back from his travels, and Bellangere the Brave.

"Gwen!" Arthur took me in his arms and kissed me warmly, and the knights smiled at us as they went out.

"You need shaving," I told him, rubbing my cheeks where his bristles had poked me. "But even so, I am glad to have you back. You left in such a hurry! Although we heard what happened, tell me the tale yourself. And where is Merlin now? Is he still here?"

He grinned and called to Varric to bring a bath. "All is well, you will hear soon enough. But first, I must know—how is the boy? What is he like? Will it work?"

I laughed at his impatience, which was so unlike him. "I have no doubt of it, my lord. Yes, he is worthy. He is good and kind and bright. You need have no fear there. But this I must tell you, Arthur. He has your face. It is stamped upon him as clear as on any coin. I am not the only one to notice it."

"Ah. Well, then, matters must be settled soon, I think."

He was sitting on the settle, pulling off his wet leggings, when he stopped and looked at up me quickly. "You do not mind?"

"If you bathe, my lord? No, why should I? I am your wife."

"God bless you, that is not what I meant. But if you thought it was, then you are healed at last."

As always, Arthur knew my wounds and wished to spare me. I went and sat beside him, and placed my hand on his arm. The tunic was icy cold, but his hand was warm. "No, Arthur, I do not mind Mordred's coming. I am glad of it. If you can deal with him, we will have a family. He and I, already, are on the way to it."

He smiled and he kissed me again, with love. "I doubt not you have charmed the poor boy right out of his skin. He comes from a wild land where life is simple. He has never seen anyone like you."

I blushed. "From what I understand, my lord, he appreciates straight dealing, not having had much of it from Morgause."

"Then he and I shall appreciate one another."

Varric and two slaves came in with his bath, and as they bathed him, I sat before the fire and heard all about his wild ride north on All Hallow's Eve. He had ridden all night and had time to reconsider the likelihood of Niniane's story. It seemed to him, in the cold gray light of winter's dawn, that hers had been a vision born of longing, or regret, or even guilt. But by then he was halfway there; it was as quick to continue and verify the tale as to turn back.

When he got to Caerleon Sir Caradoc, the commander, was

amazed to see him, having had no warning of the King's approach. Arthur asked him straight out if Merlin was in the fortress. Caradoc's jaw had dropped, his left hand had made the sign against enchantment behind his back. Swearing under his breath, half ashamed for being so easily duped, Arthur had allowed himself to be escorted to his rooms, and there he ate a good meal and went to bed.

"Then Niniane's tale was false!" I exclaimed. "Yet why would she lie? And she had the nerve to follow you here!"

Arthur smiled, soap suds in his hair. "Stay a moment. You go too fast. Have patience, Guinevere, and let me tell the tale."

In the early morning, Arthur had awakened to the quiet calling of his name. When he opened his eyes, there at the foot of his bed stood Merlin, white bearded, white haired, dressed in his familiar dark robe without so much as a fringe of ornament, and with the same black, unreadable eyes.

"I spoke to him, and he answered me, in his own voice. He came around where I could reach him and gave his hand to me, that I might feel his flesh and know him to be real, and not a phantom."

Behind him, the bath slaves paused in their work and exchanged nervous glances. A sharp word from Varric set them rubbing the King's body with their sponges, but even from where I sat I could see them trembling.

"Were you not frightened, my lord, to see him?"

"No. Not frightened. Not of Merlin. He is a father to me, and I am as dear to him as a son. But I was nearly speechless with amazement." He paused and turned to look at the slaves. "No one who loves me, or Britain, need fear Merlin. Ankat, Menor, do you hear? Whatever he is, man or spirit, he is our protection against the evil men do. Think of him as a lucky talisman and rejoice when he is near."

"Yes, my lord," the slaves mumbled, eyes averted. But I noticed that they stopped shaking and sponged the King with care.

"What on earth did he tell you, Arthur? How did he escape from the burial chamber?"

"Ahhhhh, my dear, that he will not say. I, too, wanted practical answers, but he gave me none. He said only that the walls that can hold him have yet to be built. King or no, I could not keep him where he did not wish to be."

"Then he was not dead? Oh, my dear Arthur! Did you bury him alive?"

Arthur shook his head. "He tells me he was living, but not in

the world of men. He speaks with a tongue I can scarcely understand sometimes. He says he was with his god, who commands
him still."

"Then—then he is not a man?"

"Not as we think of men." Arthur's voice was quiet, and his
gaze slipped off into the distance. "I don't know, Gwen, if I can
find the words to tell it. When Niniane called him 'shapeshifter'
she used the ancient term we use for children's tales—but it will
do as well as any other. He is able to assume the shape we knew
him by—he can take on flesh and bone and blood, at least for a
space of time. But he can also walk among the spirits, pass
through time, he says, and sail across the Light. He can do what
he wills."

"Did he die, then? Or not?"

"Ah, Gwen, your mind runs like mine. I asked him the same.
He told me not to think of death that way. He gave me an answer
that is not an answer: He walks a middle road between the Light
and Darkness. How did Merlin put it? The god permits, for a
while, his flesh to visit where his spirit will always be."

"I don't understand you, my lord. Is he flesh or phantom? Is he
not returned forever, and if not, how long may he stay?"

Arthur shook his head, sending water flying. Ankat knelt hastily to wipe the floor; not stealthily enough—Arthur turned and
begged his pardon.

"I cannot answer you, Guinevere. He is what he wills to be. In
Merlin's words, his body failed him before his work was done;
the god has granted him a gift and has let him return to see it
completed. His magic and his Sight he has bequeathed to Niniane.
He needs them not. Merlin the Enchanter is dead, indeed. But his
power will reach out to us in our time of need: When we need to
see him, he will take shape for us; when we need his counsel, his
voice will speak into our ears. And when at length we need him
no longer, he will vanish." He paused. "Does that help?"

"I hardly know. Where is he, when he has no shape and yet he
speaks?"

Arthur shrugged. "In the gloaming. Between the stars. I am
giving you Merlin's words, my dear, don't be impatient. I cannot
enlighten you more. I don't understand it myself. It is enough for
me that he is here." As he spoke, his voice tightened, and I heard
in it the love and pain he felt for the man who had been by his
side so long.

While Varric shaved him, I asked him if it might not be true,
after all, that Niniane bewitched him and took his strength, so that

he passed for dead but yet was living. Perhaps Merlin's pride might not allow him to admit this, even to the King. He took a long time to reply, but at last, while Varric packed away his razor, he sighed and shook his head.

"No. I put this to him, in a fashion, and he denied it. I know Bedwyr thinks it, and Kay, and others; I have wondered once or twice myself—"

"Do you suspect her, then?"

"I cannot suspect her and keep her as my counselor. The powers he had on earth she now possesses, but he gave them to her freely. I must take Merlin at his word." He frowned. His eyes were far away. "There are dangers ahead. For you and me." He looked at me quickly. "If we doubt him, he cannot help us. And when Niniane arrived at midday, he embraced her with fondness. Had she betrayed him, it could not have been so."

"Can you really not suspect her? She has his Sight, yet she told you he was dead. Either she has not dealt straight with you, my lord, or she is not the enchanter Merlin was, even with his power."

He stood dripping on the heated tiles, while the bath slaves toweled him dry. "You are quick to condemn her, Guinevere."

"Am I? She was quick to condemn me once."

"Ahhh." I did not have to tell him. He knew. Once she had accused me of betraying the King with Lancelot. "Well, it is true she is not the enchanter Merlin was. But had she been guilty of what you accuse her, would she have come to me the instant he appeared to her? And yet she flew straight as an arrow to Camelot, to tell me. You were there. You saw it."

"Yes. I did. Well, I am glad she is innocent of that. But, Arthur, why did Merlin not come to you himself in Camelot if he can go anywhere he wills? Why here?"

Arthur looked away suddenly, and I knew when he spoke he was keeping something back. "There were so many people at court, and he was always shy of crowds. He prefers private meetings."

I did not press him for what he did not say—who was it Merlin did not wish to see?—perhaps it was a secret held close between them, or perhaps the answer would cause me pain.

"Where is he now, Arthur? I must not wait to pay him my respects."

"My dear, you cannot. He is gone. No, not between the stars; rest easy. He's gone south with Niniane to stay with her and

Pelleas awhile. I rode with them the first part of the way and was late getting back, or I'd have been here to greet you."

"But why ever did he leave? Everyone wants to see him and do him homage!"

Again, a shadow darkened Arthur's face. "He would not stay. He did not want to see ... all the people."

"Well," I teased, to lighten his spirit, "if he can come and go as he pleases through the very air, why on earth did he go on horseback, through snow and ice, with Niniane?"

Arthur grinned. "Are you still asking me for explanations? He does as he pleases. In other words, I don't know."

I sighed. "I truly do not understand it."

"Never mind it now."

Varric dressed him in a brown woolen robe, trimmed with rabbit, and a plain belt. Then they hurried away with the bath water and towels, and the King and I were at last alone.

He came forward and took me in his arms. "And now, enough of my tale. I am all ears to hear yours."

"Oh, Arthur, mine is nowhere so exciting."

"Nonsense. Yours is the more important, for the future. Tell me about the boy."

"Which one, my lord?" I countered, smiling, laying a hand against his smooth cheek. "If you mean Gawaine, he is redheaded and hot-tempered, with more arrogance about him than you ever in your life possessed."

He grinned and bent to touch his lips to my neck. "You would torture me with waiting?" Another kiss. "When I have been six weeks away, you would stall me longer?" A third kiss, hot against my flesh. "You wish to deny me, to prove your power?"

"My lord," I breathed, slipping my arms around him, "you need only ask."

The entrance of the chamberlains with trays of steaming food interrupted us. I had not realized until the meal was before me how hungry I was. Arthur, too, after riding most of the day in the snow, was ravenous and fell to eating with gusto. Suddenly I began to laugh.

"What's so funny?"

"Oh, my lord, you have some surprises in store for you! Wait until you see your nephews at table—even by the standards of the soldiers' mess they are uncouth. Kay was shocked."

"No manners?"

"None. Could they see you eat, they would mock you for prissy ways and call you my fancy boy, like as not."

His face darkened. "They would not dare insult you."

"My lord, they are boys and have been raised without restraint. All this is new to them."

"They have done it, then? Is that what you are telling me? And who have they called your 'fancy boy'?"

"Bedwyr and Lancelot both."

"Lancelot! Why, they have not even met him!"

"His reputation runs before him. Remember, they have been living in the barracks."

But this was no solace to him, for they were his soldiers. "Was this insolence punished?"

"Indeed. Bedwyr made them fear for their lives at swordpoint. And they all apologized the next day, on their knees."

But Arthur was distressed. "This is not the beginning I had hoped for. I thought you told me you and Mordred had reached an understanding."

"I was referring to your nephews, my lord, not your son. Mordred is altogether different. He has kept his mouth closed, and observed, and is learning our ways as quickly as he can. He even trains his speech to sound like ours. He says little and hears everything, keeping his own counsel. But when Gawaine attacked me—" I blushed. I had not meant to give out the name. "When those things were said, it was Mordred who defended me to them. And not only me, Arthur, but our whole way of life. I wish you could have heard him. You would have swelled with pride. He told them they ought to appreciate civilization, that they should know when they were being honored and not bite the hand that feeds them. He is so happy to be free of Orkney, Arthur. Camelot is a wonderland to him. It is his dream. He is full of impressions and hope. Now is the time to speak to him."

The servants returned and cleared the trays and left wine warming by the fire. In the next room, they turned down the purple coverlet on the King's bed and, bowing, left us.

Arthur poured spiced wine for both of us and stood beside the fire. He looked pensive. "Were you there when all this was said, Gwen? Did they dare insult you to your face?"

"Ah, not exactly, my lord." And I told him about the scene in the library. He was angry, but when I repeated Mordred's words, he softened. And when I came to Bedwyr's part, he smiled.

"Thank God for Bedwyr's sense! I hope he scared them well."

"Well enough. When will you see them, my lord? They have lived for this meeting."

"It was my intention to receive them formally tomorrow. And

to confirm Gawaine as Prince of Orkney and, if he earns it, heir to Lothian, as well."

"That will please him and perhaps make things easier. My lord, if I may suggest—"

"Yes? Come, Gwen, you know them. What is it?"

"Wear your finery, my lord. And your crown. Nothing impresses them so much as display."

"Is that true of Mordred, also?"

"Perhaps not so much. But they are used to it, you see. Why, they won't stir from their rooms, even for wrestling, without all their copper armbands and silver buckles. And it would not hurt Mordred to see you in your splendor as High King."

He drained his winecup and held out an arm to me. I went to him, and he held me close.

"All right. If you advise it. And you shall be beside me, far more splendid than I. And crowned."

"If the wagons get here," I whispered, smiling. But he was looking ahead, and frowned.

"Now that I am faced with it, I dread it," he said slowly. "I don't know how to tell him. I must know him first, at least a little. Is he so like? Do I not have time?"

"Bedwyr took one look at his face and knew."

"Did he?" He paused. "And where is Bedwyr now? I have not yet taken his report."

"He was worried about the wagons, my lord. I asked him to join us, but he probably went back with the escort to help them through the snow."

Arthur shrugged and, with a smile, began unbraiding my hair.

"More like, he chose to give us privacy." He kissed me again slowly and sighed. "This," he said, "is happiness. After a hard ride, to come home to a beautiful woman. I believe it's a cure for all ills."

There was a large hall in the King's house, and here it was that Arthur held court, met in Council, heard petitions, and gave judgments. It was not as big as any of the halls in Camelot but was a handsome, well-proportioned room with columns holding up a carved ceiling and mosaics of Roman gods upon the floor. Bright tapestries hung against the walls, to keep the wind out, for the house was a hundred years old, and the plaster walls had cracks.

Kay had seen to it, long ago, that a dais was built at one end of the hall, with two gilded chairs upon it. The large one with a Dragon carved upon the back was the King's; mine was smaller, and bore the white stag of Northgallis. Arthur preferred to stand among his knights, or sit at table with them, and not sit perched above them in his high chair, but this formal setting was useful for granting judgments and for impressing newcomers, so he kept the dais.

That morning, all who had come to Caerleon gathered in the hall to see the boys presented to the King. They came for many reasons, but the rumors had been flying, and I am sure most men were there to see what happened when Mordred faced the King. The wagons had arrived past midnight, and poor Ailsa had been half the night unpacking and shaking out the clothes. When I found her in the morning she was cross and grumbling discontentedly; I did not blame her; while she worked, I had been peacefully asleep in the King's arms. I kissed her warmly and obeyed her meekly, and she had me ready in time.

When I saw Arthur, just outside the hall, we grinned at one another. We were dressed in white and gold, with ermine trimmings and jewels everywhere. A great golden torque encircled his neck, etched with dragons and set with gems. And he wore his crown: a simple crested band of beaten gold. Against his dark hair it shone like a diadem. He did not wear it often; for that reason, we all went silent when we saw it, reminded of his authority.

I sank into my curtsy. "My lord Arthur," I breathed.

He raised me and searched my face. "What is it, Guinevere?"

I shook my head, smiling. He did not know he had a majesty about him, a glory of his own that lit him from within, inspiring reverence. But all the others saw it and bent their knees. Arthur stood silent. Then he took my hand, squared his shoulders, and led me into the hall.

The first business, as always, was hearing reports from the knights errant. Gereint stepped forward and gave news from the northern lands and the fort at Olicana where the Tribuit runs. The fort there had been enlarged and the pass widened. Now the road needed renovations. But the country was quiet enough.

Bellangere stepped forward and told of his adventures along the Saxon borderlands, of intermarriages and new towns sprung up, where Briton and Saxon lived in wary peace, of children being born dark-eyed and towheaded. I felt my interest awaken and glanced swiftly at Arthur to see how he took it. He was frowning. Several more were heard from, and then Arthur drew them all together, thanking them well and giving each a gold coin for his service. Then he signaled Bedwyr.

"Bring them in," he said.

There was a scuffle outside the doors, and then all was quiet, and they opened. Gereint led the princes in, Gawaine first, Mordred second, the rest following in order of age. Someone had gone to great lengths to groom them and dress them for the occasion. Their hair was cut, and they wore new clothes of good, soft wool in muted colors—no more necklaces and ornaments of shell, and crude emblems of purple and crimson. Their belts were plain leather, and their boots new. But their copper armbands, crudely etched, they would not part with.

They had been washed well and instructed how to behave. Gereint led them to the foot of the dais and bent his knee. They followed his example, one by one. I looked around for Bedwyr and saw him leaning against the double doors, looking exhausted. So I knew whose work this was. Arthur rose and went down to meet them.

First he raised Gereint, and thanked him for his care of the boys and promoted him on the spot. Gereint flushed with pleasure. The boys, still kneeling, were having a hard time keeping their eyes down. Finally Arthur addressed them.

"You may rise."

They looked small next to the King's height, and I saw that even Gawaine had lost his bluster, awed by the splendor around him. The boys stared in wonder at his garments, at his torque, at his crown, and especially at his wonderful Sword. For once, they were speechless. I looked at them all, but my attention was on Mordred. Half a head taller, slender where they were thick; dark where they were fair; clear-headed where they were bewildered—he looked Pendragon from head to toe in his plain garments. I was amazed that everyone did not see it. Mordred threw me a quick look; his eyes were shining. The others had eyes only for the High King.

Arthur looked them over well before he spoke.

"You are the sons of Morgause, my sister," he said, loud enough for all to hear. "Kings' sons all." The boys glanced quickly at one another, startled. Arthur was making a confession to the hall, and only they did not know it. "Be welcome, nephews. Now, tell me your names."

Gawaine bowed, trying to be correct. "I am Gawaine, my lord. Firstborn of King Lot and Queen Morgause."

Arthur inclined his head gravely. "Gawaine, Prince of Orkney, I confirm you as your father's heir. Orkney will be yours. If you earn it, you shall inherit Lothian, as well. Until then, Tydwyl holds it for me."

Gawaine's mouth dropped open, and he fairly fell to one knee. "Thank you, my lord." A word from Arthur had made him a king and Arthur's servant forever.

Then Arthur stepped in front of Mordred, and the whole room seemed to hold its breath. The King searched his face. I knew what that penetrating gaze was like and wondered that the boy stood it without trembling. He looked up at the King and seemed to lighten and grow taller. At last Arthur spoke.

"And you are Prince Mordred," he said gently.

"Yes, my lord," Mordred whispered. "Only—only I am a bastard, sir, half brother to the princes. I do not know my father's name."

Arthur inclined his head. "That is not a misfortune, Mordred, unless you make it so."

Mordred flushed gratefully and sank to his knee. Arthur passed on to Agravaine and Gaheris. They introduced themselves in turn and made no mistake, to Gereint's evident relief. Even little Gareth the King treated with grave courtesy, asking his name, and how he had fared on the journey, and what he liked best about Camelot so far.

"The horses and the Queen!" was Gareth's excited reply, and Arthur laughed. It was a full-bodied laugh of great joy, and others near us joined in. The hall seemed to exhale in relief.

"I must introduce you to Lancelot," he said. "He is a man of your taste." He winked at me, and I grinned. The boys, even Mordred, were staring at him in shock. They were so young, their world was still simple. But they covered their surprise when the King faced the gathering.

"My lords and ladies, I present to you my nephews, the princes of Orkney, and Mordred, their half brother. For my sake, make them welcome here. From the look of them, they will make Companions one day."

Then he signaled to Gereint to take them off. But to this, it seemed Gawaine and Mordred objected. I heard Gereint say, "There is nothing but business left. You would not enjoy it." He glanced quickly up at Arthur, who was tempted to keep them near him, but shook his head.

"Next time, perhaps," the King said kindly, and the boys were led out.

Arthur sank gratefully into his chair, and I leaned over to whisper in his ear. "Well, my lord? What do you think? He is Pendragon all over."

He passed a hand across his brow. "I am shaking, Guinevere. It was hard to do. And you are right."

"Is he not like you?"

"No," Arthur said slowly, collecting himself. "I confess I cannot see it. He reminds me of Queen Ygraine, my mother. Quiet power. Ambition. Quick pride held in with hard control. He has already learned how to endure."

"Well," I replied, smiling, "then we are both right, for all that is true of you."

Then the first petitioner came forward, and he gave his mind to the business of ruling.

6 ⚙ tbe BOAR buNT

As the great feast day neared, celebrating both Christmas and the King's birthday, the palace was busy with planning and preparations. Arthur saw to it that the boys followed a strict regimen of exercise and study. He provided them all with short swords and spears, except Gareth, and had Perseus, his master-at-arms, begin a rigorous training schedule. Every morning they practiced in the great yard within the fortress walls, and the trained troops who drilled there watched them with smiles. Their idea of a sword fight was to run the blade straight in; they had no idea of strategy. And every afternoon, they would gather in the King's library, where Arthur's hound Cabal lay before the fire, and take instruction from Valerius, Bedwyr, or me. I was usually there.

Several times Arthur himself came in to see how they were getting on. At such times they fell silent and began to concentrate. Gawaine, Agravaine, and Gaheris remained astonished at all they had to learn and that the High King himself thought it important that they learn it. One day while the King was there, Gareth begged Bedwyr to bring out his harp and give them the Lay of Arthur. Bedwyr glanced at the King, who shrugged. While

Bedwyr sang, recounting the events of Arthur's life, the boys surreptitiously watched the King. He had fallen into a study, his gaze
far away. Every now and then a smile would cross his lips. After
the last chord had faded into silence, Mordred spoke.

"My lord King, is it true?"

Arthur turned to him a face so full of feeling, I caught my
breath.

"Yes," he said simply. "It is a true tale."

From the surprise on their faces, I saw the boys had thought it
a myth, like the story of Pegasus, which was also a favorite of
Gareth's.

"The Sword of Maximus," Mordred continued, his eyes fastened on Arthur's face, "is that the very Sword you wore when
you received us, my lord?"

"Yes." Arthur looked at Mordred, and I knew that for him, no
one else was in the room.

"Would you—my lord, would you tell us about the raising of
the Sword yourself?" Mordred scarcely breathed; he looked as if
the words had come out without his willing, and frightened him.

"I will do better than that," the King said, and had a word with
Bedwyr, who went out and returned with the Sword itself, carry-
ing the old scabbard flat across his hands. He knelt before the
King and offered up the Sword with reverence. Arthur drew the
Sword in silence, his right hand grasping the familiar grip without
thought. The boys gathered slowly around, their eyes shining.
They stared at it in wonder, but no one lifted a hand to touch it.

"I will give you its story," the King said quietly, "as Merlin
gave it to me, and as I saw it myself."

As he spoke, his voice low-pitched and commanding, I watched
Mordred's face. The princes were completely absorbed in the
King's tale. Mordred never took his eyes from the Sword. When
the King came to the raising of the Sword from the stone, and the
cold fire that burned in the hilt when he drew it forth in the presence of all the lords and knights, the room went suddenly still.
Something holy was there with us, and we all felt it.

King Lot, Arthur told them, had been the first to kneel, he who
had been Pendragon's enemy but hours before. Thus all the kings
of Britain had united behind him, which enabled him to push the
Saxons back from their lands.

"And the Sword?" Mordred whispered. "Will it protect Britain
always?"

Arthur's brow furrowed.

"I don't know," he answered slowly. "I have always been told it is my Sword." He looked directly at Mordred then, and I saw he was embarrassed, but no one else noticed it.

He sent the Sword back with Bedwyr then, but stayed and answered other questions about the Lay. Agravaine wanted to know how many Saxons he had killed himself, and Gaheris wanted to know whether his mother, too, was a witch.

"No, indeed." The King laughed. "Queen Ygraine was a Cornish princess, and a lovely one, they say. If she bewitched men, it was by her beauty."

"That's how all the trouble came about," Gawaine added, showing off. "She was the Duke of Cornwall's wife when King Uther—" He stopped suddenly, realizing he had gone too far.

Arthur frowned. "I see your mother has taught you well what she wished you to know." But as he could never be less than himself, he admitted the truth. "It is true your grandfather, the High King Uther, lusted after another man's wife. Duke Gorolis attacked the King's troops, which is treason, and died while Uther lay with the young Ygraine."

Agravaine laughed nervously. "It seems that lust runs in the family."

To the surprise of all, color flooded the King's face, and he turned and walked away from them. Of course, the boy was referring to his mother and her train of lovers, but he had hit the King on his open wound, unknowing.

"It seems to me," Bedwyr said easily, stepping into the breach, "that my young lords would do better to keep their own counsel regarding things that do not concern them. Uther Pendragon was a good king, whatever his faults. He held Britain for fifteen years. His son has beaten the Saxons back and holds us in his hand, in peace. For the first time in five generations, Britons may go about their business without the daily fear of war. Be thankful for it. Now go."

They filed out in silence, bewildered and afraid. Not one of them had any idea what they had done to offend the King.

When they were gone, Arthur gripped Bedwyr's arm in the soldiers' embrace. His face was still flushed. "My thanks, Bedwyr."

Bedwyr shrugged. "It was a small service, my lord. He referred to Morgause."

Arthur grimaced. "I know it now." He glanced swiftly at me, still embarrassed. "But there was truth in what he said, and we all know it."

* * *

Since the King had confirmed him the heir of Orkney and Lothian, Gawaine had been friendlier with Mordred. Secure in his superior position to the older boy, he now treated him with an easy condescension. Mordred bore it without change of demeanor; he took it as Gawaine's due and did not resent it. But I resented it on his behalf and wished Arthur could bring himself to talk to his son. He was not without deep pride, but he had no place in the world, and felt it. He had told me so himself.

Sometimes, after lessons were over, he would stay after everyone was gone and talk to me. For some reason, he had come to trust me and knew I would not babble to others the things he said.

"Queen Guinevere," he had said with wide, dark eyes. "What will be my place here? Not that I expect anything—indeed, the High King has been more than generous to me, seeing I am only his sister's bastard. And I do not think he loves me for her sake," he observed acutely, "for he can barely tolerate the mention of her name. But how can I serve him? Has he plans for me?"

I reached out and took his hand. "Yes, Mordred. He has plans for all of you. Why do you think we take such trouble to instruct you? You and your half brothers will be his Companions one day."

"I—I heard him say so, my lady. But I can scarcely credit it. My brothers, yes. They are princes. But I—I have no standing here. Not really. No claim upon him at all."

I knew this must be something the others pointed out to him daily, and I grieved for him. "What do you desire from life, Mordred? What is it you would be?"

He lifted his head and his face came alive. "I want to make a difference," he said eagerly, and I was startled to hear Arthur's very words resounding from the past. "I thought I should die on that godforsaken island, and then there came the summons from the King. And now that I am here, I know that I am where I belong. In the center of things. I feel it. I wish—I wish to do something great, that will be talked about with wonder in a hundred years." He stopped suddenly and withdrew into himself, afraid he had said too much. But the air around us rang with echoes of his words.

"You shall make a difference, Mordred," I said softly. "It will happen as you wish."

He lifted my hand to his lips and kissed it. And ran from the room.

There were hunting parties out every day, and after the boys had gained a little expertise with spears, they were allowed to accompany the men once or twice. On the day before Christmas, Bedwyr organized a boar hunt, for large tracks had been found in the deep woods, and boar would be a great boon to the King's birthday feast. Gareth was kept behind, but the others went. They were gone all day and well into the night. Finally we heard the clatter of hooves in the courtyard and the soldiers' songs ringing in the frosty air. From a window I saw the huge carcass dragged in, saw the cooks' delight as they ran out to greet the hunters, and watched as the men dismounted and dispersed toward the barracks and a well-earned meal. I looked about for Arthur and the boys. At first I did not see them; torches waved and flickered, sending shadows dancing everywhere. Then I caught sight of Gawaine, surrounded by soldiers who slapped him on the back and jested with him. Behind him strode Agravaine, angry, if I read his step aright. Nearby a crowd of men moved forward slowly. Could that be Arthur, walking at such a pace? I gripped Ailsa's arm as she knelt beside me.

"Ailsa! Has aught happened to the King? Can you see?"

"Surely there would have been a courier, my lady—surely Merlin and Niniane would not have left!"

"No, there he is! With Bedwyr. Thank God, he looks all right! But who is that he carries in his arms?"

Two men came running from the house with a litter; the crowd parted for a moment. I gasped. "It is Mordred! Oh, Ailsa! He must be wounded!"

Carefully, and yet with speed, the boy was laid upon the litter. Arthur, with Bedwyr and the rest of his Companions, followed him inside with a solemn step.

I found myself shaking and could barely control my voice. "Ailsa! Send to Bedwyr and bid him come to me at once, if the King can spare him."

I paced my chamber, back and forth and back again, in a fever to know what had passed. How on earth could such a thing happen, with so many people about? How dare Gawaine be so unconcerned? Why was Agravaine so angry? Why had the soldiers treated Gawaine with honor? How could the boys themselves ignore their brother's condition? Surely he could not be mortally wounded—there had been no sense of panic in that yard, but perhaps they had concealed it. I clasped my hands together and spun on my heel. I was not his mother, I could not go to him unbidden. Arthur would send for me as soon as he was able, but how long would that be? What would the physicians allow? They were proud folk, physicians, always sure no one but they could understand their art, always eager to prove their importance by making people wait. When they made kings wait, they were important indeed!

But Bedwyr was a true friend and would bring me news. On the thought, I heard a step in the corridor and heard his voice answer Ailsa's at the door.

"Bedwyr!" I threw open the door, took his hands, and drew him into the chamber. "Bedwyr, what news? Is Mordred wounded? Will he live?"

"Indeed!" He laughed. "Be easy, Gwen, it's a cloud with a silver lining. He was gored, but not badly. He'll be on his feet as soon as they have leeched and bound him."

"Gored?" I cried. "By the boar? Was no one with him? How did such a thing happen?"

Ailsa plucked at my elbow to remind me of my manners. I begged Bedwyr to sit with us by the hearth and sent Hanna for some wine. Ailsa brought him warmed water to wash his hands in, for he had come straight from the hunt, and his tunic bore witness to the slaughter of the great beast.

"Never mind," I told him when he begged pardon for his condition. "I don't mind the smell of boar's blood. But tell me how such a thing could happen, with so many people about to watch over the princes? Was everyone looking the other way?"

"Nay, my lady, pray do not accuse us of negligence. It's not easy to ride keeper on those boys, but because the King was with us, they were well enough behaved. It was just an accident, the kind that may befall anyone, any day."

"Tell me!"

"It was past nightfall when we cornered her, near her lair. I won't name all the knights who killed her—Arthur's was the first spear she felt, and mine the second, but I reckon she didn't begin to lose her fight until she carried fifty. During the chase, the charges, and the battle, be sure the boys were kept away and safe. Indeed, I don't think Gaheris had much stomach for it, but Gawaine was keen enough. At last, when she was on her knees and dying, the King allowed Gawaine to take his shot. It was a good throw, caught her in the throat, and she bellowed mightily. Then Agravaine, impatient for glory, and seeing Arthur signal for the kill, quickly threw his spear—too quickly; his horse shied, unseated him, and dumped him in the snow. The boar turned suddenly and heaved herself up for one last charge. No one expected it—she was all but dead, but boars are unpredictable, that's why protocol must be observed. She whirled and came at him, head down. Agravaine screamed, which only spurred her on. The fool tried to stand and flee, but he'd caught his foot in a buried branch and his horse had run beyond his reach. Mordred, who was nearest, threw himself on top of Agravaine and kept them both down, deep in the snow and as still as he could. Her tusks had been broken in the fight and were sharp as razors. Mordred was lucky she was spent. She gave him a thrust in the side and then died at his very feet."

"Where was Arthur? Did he see it?"

"Indeed, my lady. We all saw it. But it happened too fast to prevent. He was at the boy's side in an instant, with a complexion paler than the snow. But it's a shallow wound, and bled well. That's a good sign. He'll recover."

"Bleeding is a good sign?"

"Indeed. It's always so. A good bleeding prevents festering."

I shuddered, and Bedwyr smiled. "This is something every soldier knows. But you need not know it, my lady."

"On the contrary. I am a soldier's wife." Hanna arrived with the wine, and while she served Bedwyr I rose and walked about. "Bedwyr, you must be leaving something out. I see now why the men congratulated Gawaine. I grew up with five brothers; I know it's good luck to land a spear on your first boar hunt. But why is Agravaine angry? And why, if the wound is a small one, did Arthur carry the boy himself, and why does he tend him still?

"Ahhhh," Bedwyr said, setting down his winecup. I was bewildered by the satisfaction on his face. "I told you it was a cloud with a silver lining. Hear the rest. Once they saw Mordred was not mortally wounded, those ill-bred outlanders turned on him quicker than a whiplash. Gawaine was annoyed that Mordred stole his thunder and had all the King's attention. He felt he deserved praise for his stroke, but because of what followed, he never got it. Agravaine was furious all around. Of course it was his own fault, but he would not admit it. He resented Mordred's protection, he was embarrassed the soldiers were blaming his hotheadedness for the whole adventure, and he took a tongue-lashing from Gawaine, as well, in front of everyone. Gaheris, the coward, stayed well out of it. The minute blood is spilled, he heads for the women's skirts."

"Easy, Bedwyr. He's little more than a child. Give him time."

"Time, my lady, will not change him."

"Was there a fight, then, between the boys?"

"Oh no, with the King there, it never came to blows. When

they turned on Mordred they contented themselves with calling names."

"In front of Arthur?"

"It all took place in front of Arthur." Bedwyr shrugged. "And why not? None of them knew they had any reason to fear the King. They are trueborn princes. Who is Mordred but Morgause's by-blow? No, it never occurred to them to temper their tongues."

"At last!" I cried. "At last he sees what his silence forces Mordred to endure!"

"Normally, those boys stand together, but let anyone do Mordred honor, or even look at him twice, and that is a distinction they are overquick to make. They were all ashamed they had not done what Mordred did."

"And so they should be. They taunted him, then, in front of the King? What did they say?"

"I can't repeat all of it, Gwen, but most of it had to do with his parentage. How dare he try to save Agravaine, a king's son, when Mordred was, as everyone knew, the bastard seed of a witch and her lovesick fancy boy."

"Oh, Bedwyr!"

"That's a mild sample. They let Mordred know in no uncertain terms that he'd taken a liberty he had no right to take. He'd gone above his station, presumed a privilege he had no prayer of ever earning, his pretensions to rank insulted them all, and more of the same."

"I see. And everything they said wounded Arthur to the core. At last he understands Mordred needs the protection only he can give him. But how did Mordred take this?"

"Usually he takes it without the flicker of an eyelash. But tonight he was in pain and frightened and had no defense against such insults. He said nothing to them, but his eyes were wet, and when they had finally stopped and turned away, he swore viciously in the Orkney tongue. And then, in a low voice he thought no one else could hear, he cursed his father, whoever he might be, for begetting him and disappearing, leaving him no word, no legacy, no name, no armor against such insults. He was already, he avowed, a better man than his father would ever be."

I began to smile. "And did Arthur hear this?"

Bedwyr smiled back. "Indeed, my lady. We were both right beside him. The King spoke not a word, but carried the boy in his own arms back to the fortress."

"At last! He will tell him now, to give him back his pride. He wouldn't be Arthur, else."

Bedwyr filled a winecup and handed it to me. "If I am not mistaken, he's telling him right now. I came to you when Arthur cleared the room. Let the last physician depart, and he will speak. I am sure of it. He could not take his eyes off the boy." He raised his winecup to mine. "A toast," he said, "to the successful conclusion of a boar hunt."

It was two long hours before word came. Bedwyr was gone about his duties; around me, the daily routine of the fortress went on undisturbed; the watch changed, the guards patrolled the gates, the barrack lights were snuffed, all together, and Caerleon slept under a light fall of snow.

At first I paced my chamber in a fever and spoke sharply to Hanna when she would have brought me wine. Then I fell on my knees and prayed God might be merciful to both father and son. For Arthur must do what he most dreaded doing: lay open his secret shame to his own son and endure his judgment. And Mordred, who in a moment's rage had cursed his fate, would be faced with another he had not dreamed of, but only at a cost. Too high a cost? Would he be able to forgive his father? Could Mordred, young and pagan as he was, find such mercy in his heart? If he could not, how ever would Arthur bear it?

I was so long on my knees I could hardly rise when Ailsa came to me at last with a hot posset. She wiped my face of tears and redressed my hair, clucking softly and calling me endearments.

"Sir Bedwyr is without," she said, giving my hair a last pat. "There. Now you're fit to see him."

"What?" I cried. "You have made him wait while you dress my hair? Ailsa! How could you?"

"You were not ready to be seen, my lady. Drink that up, there's medicine in it."

It was useless to argue with her in her motherly mood. I downed the posset and hurried out to Bedwyr. "What news, good Bedwyr? Where is Arthur?"

"In the library. Alone."

"And?"

Bedwyr shook his head. "I don't know, my lady. He said nothing. He wants you first."

I fairly ran through the corridors, not caring who saw me. I knocked, but hearing no response, gently opened the door, and slipped inside. Arthur stood alone at the window with his back to me. His hands were clasped behind him, and he looked for all the world like a man admiring the beauty of the midnight snowfall.

I took a breath and gathered my courage. "Arthur?"

He turned and smiled.

"Thank God!" I cried. There was a host of emotions on his face, but the uppermost was joy. I ran into his arms and he held me tightly.

"It is done," he said at last, "and all is well."

"Oh, tell me what happened, Arthur! Bedwyr told me about his wounding and about the things he said."

He led me to a cushioned bench near the fire. We sat together, and he took my hand between his own. The firelight played upon his face and threw shadows along his cheekbones. There was an awe, an excitement, a contained exhilaration behind the gravity of his features. Something long held in had found release.

"First, know that he is not badly hurt. A scratch, really, but it was his first, and frightened him. He is up and about now, and has eaten. He—"

"Up and about? My lord, surely he should rest!"

Arthur smiled. "And will, no doubt, in a little while. At the moment, he is too excited to stay abed."

"How did you tell him, Arthur? I have been on fire to know!"

"His anguish forced me to it, else I might have put it off for the thousandth time. But when he cursed his father, he said nothing that was not true, or well deserved. It was as if he saw into my very soul and aimed his arrows well."

"He did not know it was you he hit."

"No. But I did. And had I told him before, anytime before, these last twelve years, I could have saved him that!" He took a breath and released it slowly. "When the physicians left him and I stayed, he was discomfitted. He felt I must be angry at his outburst—"

"*His* outburst!"

"Just so. Compared to his brothers, it was a whisper. But for Mordred, it was an outburst indeed. He thought, as the princes' uncle, I stayed to chastise him. He assumed I was angry, too, at his presumption. He apologized to me for his rude words."

"Oh, Arthur!"

He passed a hand across his face. "I couldn't bear to have *him* apologize to *me*. The words I've thought so often how to say— they came quickly after that, and of their own accord. I told him I was not angry, but ashamed. His words were not rude, they were no more than truth. He had a right to demand just treatment from the man who begot him. He had a right to be angry for those long years of neglect. I told him that the object of his scorn stood before him and begged his pardon with an abject heart."

"Arthur," I whispered, holding tight to his hands, "may God bless you."

"He was astounded. He stared at me as if I were a demon from the Otherworld. I lost my composure before those eyes and had to look away."

He paused. " '*You* are my father?' he asked me outright. 'You? The High King of all Britain? Who is my mother, then?' " Arthur cleared his throat. "And I told him he had lived with her all his life. My own sister. Morgause." He looked quickly away as he said her name, and I lifted his hands to my lips. "I held my breath, waiting for the first sign of disgust or horror, waiting for those vile Orkney curses to strike again. But he said nothing. He shrugged once. That was all."

"He is pagan, Arthur. It makes a difference."

He raised his eyes. "I know. It was not that he forgave me. It was as if there were nothing to forgive. But it is an ancient sin, and was so before Christ walked the earth." He rose suddenly and paced the chamber with swift, long strides. "Remember Oedipus."

I stood. "That was different. Mother and son. The oldest prohibition. And he was a god-cursed king. You are blessed."

Arthur shuddered. "He sinned in ignorance, and yet his fate came upon him, all the same." He paused in midstride, and his face went white, as if a shadow fell upon him and drowned his spirit. With a visible shrug, he shook it off. "Mordred was not ashamed. He told me it happens everywhere in the islands—there are so few people, they are all inbred." He stopped and faced me. "Gwen, he told me this to ease my distress." He came back to me and took me in his arms. His whole body trembled. "His first thought was not of himself and the future he had just discovered; it was of me. His first act, given the gift of power, was to offer solace to a penitent. Guinevere, he will make a King."

"I know it," I whispered. "I know it is in him. He is Pendragon."

"I—I took a chair at his bedside while he came to terms with it. With all his ambition, he had never dreamed to reach so high. He hardly dared believe it—I had to tell him the story of how it happened, the part that Bedwyr left out of the Lay."

"You never dreamed it, either, at his age. Yet you knew it was your destiny, when you drew the Sword from the stone."

"Tonight I gave him the same future and lived again that revelation, reflected in his face. I wish you had seen it, Gwen. He was reborn."

I drew his face down to mine and kissed him. "It was well done, Arthur."

"He is young for it, but more than willing. We spoke long about the past. I see now what my silence cost him. As you can guess, it has not been easy growing up as Morgause's sideslip. He has seen his father in every handsome face who's crossed her threshold. To his own half brothers he's as much servant as kin. Yet he has always known he was meant for something better than life in Orkney. He's always been quicker, cleverer, and cooler than other boys. He can see three steps ahead, where they see one. He understood it, suddenly, tonight. I have told him I will keep him at court, with his half brothers, until he is grown enough to travel with me."

"Will you acknowledge him, my lord?"

"I have done so to him. But to the people, no. Not yet. It may be a small sin to Mordred, but for an anointed Christian King to announce such a thing, and expect reverence, smacks of hubris. We will give him his due, and let people draw their own conclusions. There is risk here, Guinevere. I intend no deception. But neither do I desire publication of the evil I have done."

"Arthur, if I can forgive you, and Mordred himself does not blame you, why can you not forgive yourself?"

He smiled sadly. "Mordred ought to blame me. It was my doing. But he has not been raised to know sin. As for you, my dearest, you are far too merciful."

He kissed me lovingly, and I held his body close. But tonight there was no urgency behind his tenderness. The boar hunt and the interview with Mordred had taken their toll. I loosed myself from his embrace and made my reverence.

"God has given you a great birthday gift, my lord. You will want some time alone to sort out your thoughts. If you like, I will retire."

"Thank you, Gwen. You know me too well. By the way, Mordred has asked to see you. He is far too excited to sleep and awaits you in the terrace garden. Go to him before you turn in. He will get no rest else."

"It would be my pleasure."

He was watching me with laughter in his eyes. "Do you know the boy is in love with you?"

"What?" I blushed to the roots of my hair. "You are jesting."

"I am not. He is about the right age for first love, and you have captured his heart. So tread softly."

"My lord! I know not what to say! This was not intended."

"Will you attempt to tell me you have never inflamed a man's love without intention? Be easy, Gwen. You cannot help it. Beauty, charm, and sweet temper will sway any man. And as you said, he is Pendragon, and thus your slave."

"Now who is sweet-tempered? You will charm me out of countenance, my lord, and I shall not be able to face him. And you know well, he only wants to tell me all about you."

He kissed me good night then and let me go.

The garden terrace had recently been swept of snow. Mordred paced back and forth across it, his cloak swirling behind him. It was not cold, but hushed and still. I pulled my hood forward and stepped out from the colonnade to greet him.

"My lord Mordred. You wished to see me." I made him a deep reverence, and he hurried to raise me.

"Oh, no, my lady, you mustn't. Not to me. You are Queen, and I am still only a bastard."

His face in the torchlight was light and shadow; it was Arthur's face, as I had seen it by firelight, with shadows beneath the cheekbones, the face of a King.

"You are his son. It is enough for me."

"You knew all along, didn't you, my lady? I—I always had the feeling when I was with you that I was someone special. But until tonight—" He stopped and shivered. I took his arm, and we walked to and fro, to keep warm and to ease his tension. "I cannot believe it yet. It feels so right somehow, but I cannot believe it is me he spoke about. What a King he is!" Even in the dark, his eyes were bright.

I laughed. "He is indeed. Mordred, you have given him great joy."

"Not half so much as he has given me, my lady," he said fervently. "To learn I am Pendragon . . . it is beyond my wildest hope. It is true that I have wanted a place to rule—but Britain!"

"It will not come to you unless you earn it," I said cautiously, not having discussed this with Arthur. "He has publicly declared the Dukes of Cornwall to be his heirs."

He nodded. "I had heard that. I will try to be worthy in every way I can. All I want is a place of my own. I don't mind if it is small."

He had grown up in a queen's house with four legitimate princes already in place. He had never had much that was his own.

"Be patient, Mordred, as the King is. Who knows what is ahead?"

We walked in silence awhile. He moved stiffly, but seemed to suffer little pain. When I looked at him, I saw he was frowning.

"He is ashamed of my begetting," he said in his quiet voice.

"He is Christian, Mordred. For us, it is perhaps a greater sin than for others. All sins of the flesh are so."

"I am afraid, my lady, that every time he looks at me he will be reminded of this shame. I would do anything to ease the pain of that memory for him."

I squeezed his arm. "And so would I. But that is between him and God. Do not worry about it. When he looks at you, he is not thinking of Morgause."

"Are you sure of this, my lady?"

"Oh, yes. Very sure."

He was easier then, but still, something bothered him. "He told me that you think I resemble him, my lady, and that others have noted it. Is this so? I do not see it."

"You have his face, Mordred, but for the eyes. Brow, cheek, and jaw. And his mouth." He looked uncomfortable, and I remembered Arthur's words to me. "But you are like him in other ways, as well," I went on quickly. "You are cool and reserve judgment."

"I wish that were so, my lady," he said unhappily. "But tonight I swore like a fishwife at my own father."

"You had cause. The King knows this. And you did not know your father heard you."

But this was not what worried him; he shifted a shoulder and looked down. He was coming to it.

"The King told me—he was talking about the day when he first knew he wanted to have a son, to pass things on to. He was standing on a hilltop, surveying the lands about him, with Merlin, the great enchanter . . ."

"Yes? Go on."

"He was speaking casually about it, watching me and smiling, but—but when he spoke Merlin's name aloud—something happened." He went still, and I tried to read his features, but we were facing away from the torches and he was in shadow.

"What was it, Mordred? Tell me."

"It was as if a cloud covered the sun. One moment he was filled with pleasure, and then, when he thought of Merlin, he grew cold, like stone, and looked into the distance. I felt invisible. I felt he was afraid." He paused, and a trickle of fear ran up my spine. I, too, had seen a shadow strike Arthur but a little while before, as he talked of fate. "I know Merlin has power, I know he is long-sighted. Even my mother fears him. His visions, they say, are always true."

"Yes."

"Merlin has made many prophecies," he hurried on, trying to get it out before his courage failed him. "From something my mother let drop once—about my future—and from the King's face when he spoke of Merlin, I wondered, I wondered if Merlin had made some prophecy concerning me."

"If he has, I do not know of it," I said, surprised. "Why did you not ask the King yourself?"

Mordred shuddered. "I could not. He went so still. The light in him went out. It felt like death."

I shuddered myself. "Think no more of it, Mordred. If it means something, you will know in time. Merlin himself still lives. Perhaps you can ask him yourself."

"Truly? Where is he, then? I thought he was here in Caerleon, but the soldiers say he is gone."

"That is so. He, um, he comes and goes as he wills, with little notice to anyone. It is the way of enchanters."

"When he returns, my lady, would you take me to see him?"

I smiled. "Oh, no. You would do better to go alone. Merlin likes me not. We do better away from each other."

"He doesn't like you?" He sounded shocked. "How could anyone dislike you? How could there be anything in you that gives offense? You are—you are—" He gulped, and I laid a hand on his arm to stop him.

"It is not personal, Mordred. But to him, I am only Arthur's wife. And I have failed to bear him children. It may be my fate, and Arthur's, but Merlin grieves for it."

He straightened suddenly, as if I had struck him. "I—I am sorry, my lady."

"For what, Mordred? It is no doing of yours."

"That is why he sought me out at last, is it not? Because he has no other sons?" He whirled away from me and strode to the end of the terrace. I stood amazed at his anger. What was in his heart, to make him feel so? When he returned, he held himself stiffly and spoke with constraint. "I see it now. But I will not stay here on those terms. Even more than being the King's son, I want to be—" He stopped, flustered, and then rushed on, "I won't stay here and be a thorn in your side! How can you be so kind to me? Does it not gall you to look at me? How could he bring me here, if he knows how you feel? I will *not* be the instrument of your pain! I would sooner go back to Orkney!"

He moved me to my soul, with his new pride and his sweet infatuation and his generous heart. That in this greatest moment of his young life, he should think of how I felt! Arthur was right; he would make a King. All the bitter heartache of the past weeks lost its biting edge when Mordred spoke those words to me.

"Mordred," I said softly. "Be easy. You are young and you reckon without love. Because he loves me, the King would not have sent for you unless I wished it. And because I love him, I asked him to bring you here, when I knew I could not bear, that he and I might have a son to raise."

He gaped at me and then flung himself to his knees.

"My lady!" he cried. "You are the soul of goodness!"

"Come, Mordred." I raised him and hugged him like a son. "Calm yourself. You must stay with us in Camelot. It is where you belong."

He slowly nodded and kissed my hand. "I should have known," he breathed in a voice so soft I had to strain to hear it. "I should have known a gift this wonderful could only have come from you!"

And while I stood blushing at his fervor, Mordred bowed low, turned on his heel, and left.

THE QUEENS

**The Return
The Slander
The Honor of Lancelot
The Witch of Orkney
The Accusation
The Prophecy
The Witch of Rheged**

7 ✵ ⊙he RETURN

The court moved back to Camelot at the equinox, while the ground was still hard before the spring rains. Then for weeks we suffered through cold, cloudy weather, downpours, storms, and chills. By the end of April the land was green; trees brought forth new leaves, wildflowers filled the meadows, and the horses bucked for joy to be free in their pastures again.

Arthur had been gone eight weeks to visit Cornwall, to pay homage to his mother's deathplace and lay flowers on her grave. And also to meet with Duke Constantine, Cador's son, his official heir. Everyone with a head could guess what he meant to talk about, but nothing was publicly announced.

Once the weather turned fair, I hardly saw the boys. They were all day with the soldiers learning the skills of war. As they improved, they grew more disciplined and began to take pride in their accomplishments, and to see themselves as King's men. This was a relief to me. Arthur had not left it too late, after all. By treating them with honor and courtesy, he had engendered their affection and respect.

Gawaine, especially, had grown more civilized. Part of this was due, I think, to his feeling at last secure in his status as King Lot's heir. Orkney was his, and Lothian if he earned the right to hold it; this was his pride, and it meant so much to him that he held it in, manlike, and did not boast. Part was due to his recognition of Mordred's status. For the King had told him the truth about Mordred. He believed Gawaine had the right to know. Just what Arthur said to him to make him hold his tongue, I do not know, but he kept silent. He and Mordred had a cautious respect for one another and acted more like brothers than ever they had before.

Once spring came, only Mordred and Gareth came to lessons, and not always Mordred. He was quick and learned everything

fast. The only place I found him lacking was in his reverence for
gods. All the boys took instruction from Bishop Landrum; Gareth
was easily converted, Gawaine and the twins preferred the worship of the Goddess they had grown up with; Mordred remained
his own man. He was respectful and willing to bow his head to
whatever god was sacred in a place, but never gave his heart. Indeed, the only worship he gave, he gave to Arthur. I did not press
him; the King himself paid public homage to whatever deity
served his purpose. He told me once he believed all gods were
one God in the end. Perhaps, I thought, Mordred would come to
this in time. One had to make allowances for the lonely life he
had led and the things that had been done to him.

Of Merlin we saw nothing. Niniane returned to Camelot with
the court, but when Arthur left for Cornwall, she took herself off
to Ynys Witrin and to her role as Lady of the Lake. She had kept
away from me of late. At first I put it down to being newly wed;
her husband Pelleas was a handsome king in Arthur's service,
level-headed and strong-willed, as a man must be to marry an enchantress. Then I wondered if perhaps she knew of my doubts of
her I had expressed to Arthur. But Mordred told me it was because I spent so much time with him, and that Niniane could not
bear the sight of him.

"Whatever do you mean?" I asked him.

"Just that, my lady. She will not meet my eyes, but whenever
she comes across me, looks the other way. A great cold comes
from her; it makes me shiver."

"Well," I said to comfort him, "she never used to like me, either, before we got to know one another. I used to think her hos-
tile. She is a powerful magician and not like other women. It is
just her way."

He accepted this and said no more, but I saw he did not believe
that was all there was to it. When she left Camelot, Mordred
breathed easier.

On the first of May Bedwyr and Ferron came to me, wearing
secret smiles, and bade me come on a birthday outing. The boys,
even Gareth, were all out on a two-day deer hunt with the soldiers, and Ferron was enjoying a respite from their care. The High
King, they told me, had left three gifts for me. If I would dress
for riding, they would show me the first. When we arrived at our
destination, they would show me the second. And later that night,
they would show me the third.

Delighted, I did as they bade me, and went with them to the

stables. The grooms had their war stallions ready, bridled in gold, and next to them held Rajid, his blood-bay coat shining in the sun, his mane and tail braided with ribbons threaded with silver.

"What's this?" I said, turning to Bedwyr. "Does Lyonel want Rajid galloped over the downs?"

Bedwyr grinned. "He is not Lyonel's charge anymore, my lady. He is yours."

I gasped, staring. A war stallion! For me?

"Does Arthur know of this?" I cried. Both of them laughed.

"It is his gift," Bedwyr said. How far he had come since that first day we went hawking, when he was loath even to let me ride without a saddle!

The stallion whinnied as I approached him and nuzzled me with affection, blowing his warm breath onto my cheek. It was unheard of, for a woman to ride a war stallion. I had never taken him beyond the ring; now we were riding down the streets of Camelot, in public view. It was Arthur's declaration, as clear as any trumpet, that his Queen was due a warrior's respect. Neither Bedwyr nor Ferron was offended; they seemed pleased, and I was grateful to them.

We rode out King's Gate and along the causeway that crossed the rolling downs toward Ynys Witrin. The stallion was fresh, and his spirits high. I had my hands full for the first hour. The pace was easy; the two knights seemed to have no purpose in mind other than exercise in the soft, clear air. We passed the road that led to Melwas' castle and continued on toward the estuary. The sun was high overhead when they called to me to turn off toward the northern hills.

"We will be met there for a picnic," Bedwyr explained. "That is the second part of your gift."

Indeed, as we neared the wooded hills, I saw the tracks of many horses in the dust. The trail wound up the hill, and we slowed, riding single file. Rajid was winded now, having spent the winter in the stable, and easy as a lamb to handle. Near the summit we came upon a group of horsemen in a clearing, dismounted, and gathered around a fire. Cloths were spread and baskets of food set out; clearly they had been waiting for us. But they were not King's men. They wore no badges. I did not know a single face. But they, apparently, knew me. All of them went down on one knee and made me reverence.

Their leader came forward as we dismounted. He was a young man, about my age, and he moved with grace. I caught my breath as I looked into his face; a handsomer man I had never seen. He was tall, and lithe, and black-haired, with downy brows and clear, long-lashed gray eyes. I felt my chest tighten so I could barely breathe. He was the image of Lancelot, except his nose was straight.

He knelt and kissed my hand. "My honored lady, Queen Guinevere of Britain, I am your servant. We come from Less Britain to take service with your lord, the High King Arthur."

I raised him, trembling, and gripped his hand, so he could not withdraw it.

"Your name, sir?" It came out in a whisper. I thought he almost smiled.

"Galahantyn of Lanascol, my lady."

I held myself still somehow, remembering the eyes upon us.

"Where is he?" I breathed, not daring to take my eyes from his face.

Then he did smile. "On the hilltop. Take the trail to the left. He is waiting."

Bedwyr was grinning, and Lancelot's men were smiling. They had planned this all, I saw, for my pleasure. I tried to school my pace, but five steps up the path I was running, and when I reached the knoll at the top I fell breathless into Lancelot's waiting arms. He swung me around, laughing.

"Oh, Lancelot! Lancelot! You are back!"

"Happy birthday, my sweet," he said, and kissed me eagerly. I held him close and returned his caresses with passion. We stood thus awhile, rejoicing. When I drew away, I thought I caught movement out of the corner of my eye and, turning, saw Galahantyn coming up the path. He had stopped, startled, and looked embarrassed. Lancelot, an arm around my waist, laughed and beckoned him closer.

"You have met my brother, Gwen? Is he not everything I told you?"

"He is beautiful, Lancelot. But we have put him out of countenance."

He put an arm across his brother's shoulders and kissed me again.

"All the world knows I love you," he said simply. Then turning to his brother, who stood with eyes downcast, he said, "Is she not everything I told you, Galyn? Have you ever seen such a woman?"

"Lancelot, that is not fair," I protested earnestly. "What do you expect him to answer, without insult to me?"

At this Galahantyn raised his head and met my eyes. "Indeed,

my lady, an honest answer is an easy one. I do not wonder at my
brother's adoration. When I saw you on your warhorse, you reminded me of the tales the Saxons tell of goddess-warriors, and
you could have been such a one, with white fire for hair."

The color rose to my face, and I made him a deep reverence.

"My lord speaks with a poet's tongue," I replied. "I thank you
for the compliments. I must introduce you to Sir Bedwyr, who
shares your gift."

"Has Bedwyr been paying you compliments, then, all winter, in
my stead?" Lancelot asked with mock jealousy. His face was
near; I could not help it; I kissed him again.

"He is the Queen's Protector now."

"And what is this I hear about a warhorse? You are not riding
Pallas?"

"Rajid, my lord. Arthur's birthday gift."

"Rajid!" he exclaimed, distressed. "What did they geld him
for? He was the best of that year!"

"He is whole, never fear, yet he is mine."

Lancelot whistled softly. "It is because you drew the Sword!"
he said reverently. Galahantyn crossed himself.

"What do you mean? There is no mystery here. The King gave
me the stallion I have been working with six months. Don't look
at me like that!"

I reached an arm to him, and he embraced me. We both forgot
that Galahantyn was there. With his arms around me, he whispered, "Don't you see it is the King's message to his troops? To
put superstitious fear at rest, he must make you worthy in a soldier's eyes. He gives you a stallion not two of his best knights can
sit and proclaims you royal. Pendragon. It is a sign."

"You and your signs." I sighed, kissing his lips softly. "Oh,
Lancelot, I have missed you so!" For minutes then we two were
alone beneath the pale sky, alone in the world, heedless of everything but our great love and our joy at his return. When he broke
away from me at last, Galahantyn was gone.

"Ah," sighed Lancelot, "I see I will have some explaining to
do. Come, let us go down to the others and ease my poor brother's fear for my soul. Let me have the news. What have I
missed?"

"More than I can tell you in a day. And some of it is for your
ears only. But we cannot be private here. Tonight in the library,
with Bedwyr, you shall hear it all."

"I have heard rumors about the Orkney boys," he said, following me down the path. "Has he brought them here?"

"Yes."

"And Morgause?"

"Still in exile."

"Ahh. I'll bet she wears that like a nettle shirt. And Mordred?"

"You have come to the heart of what I want to tell you. He knows."

Lancelot stopped dead, and I turned. There was fear on his face. "He has been acknowledged?"

"Privately, yes. Publicly, no." It seemed to me he felt relief.

"Ah. Well, then. The King is now in Cornwall, I understand?"

"Yes—have you been in touch with Camelot, then? And I did not know it?"

He grinned. "I sent a courier when we landed. Bedwyr thought it would please you to have a birthday surprise, so he sent a message to me secretly, and thus it was arranged. What is the King doing in Cornwall?"

I watched his face closely. "The reason given was to visit Ygraine's grave and pay his respects to Duke Constantine."

"And the real reason?"

"He did not tell me otherwise, Lancelot. But I imagine, as Constantine is his declared heir, he has gone to talk to him about his son."

Again I saw the flicker of fear on Lancelot's face, but I did not understand it.

"When does he return?"

"I know not. We have had no courier. He is expected any time . . . Lancelot." He would have moved on, but I stopped him. "You had better know that Mordred—that Mordred is dear to me. And to the King."

He smiled gently. "I am glad, Gwen. Glad for your sake, and for Arthur's."

I saw he was sincere and it confused me. "Then why are you afraid?"

He paused. "I am afraid Arthur may love him too dearly. He cannot be King, Gwen. You must see that he cannot rule Britain."

All of my defenses went up at once, and Lancelot saw it.

"Why not, if he proves worthy? There is no other child of the King's body who is fit. Mordred is twice Pendragon."

I stopped. Lancelot nodded. "Yes," he said, very softly, "that is the reason. He is a child of incest. You know this. No bishop will anoint him."

Stricken, I turned away from him. "In Wales, when you came on Arthur's behalf to take me from my home, you said yourself—

you asked me to forgive the King this sin. I thought you had forgiven him, as well."

"Indeed, I have," Lancelot said gravely. "He sinned in innocence. I hold nothing against Arthur."

"Then how on earth can you hold it against Mordred?" I cried. "He is the one who was wronged! He is the most innocent of all!" I was near tears. I already knew what he would say. But at least he said it sadly.

"Mordred, by virtue of incest, was not born innocent. He will carry the stigma of his birth all his life. He cannot be anointed. Arthur knows this."

I wept then for Mordred, and he took me in his arms and held me. He tried to bring me comfort. "If the King has taken him into his household and acknowledged him as his son, it is an act of great kindness and mercy. Especially as the boy is dangerous." He gasped then, and swore under his breath.

"What do you mean, dangerous?"

"I—I should not have spoken. Guinevere, forgive me."

I dried my eyes and pulled away, to better see his face. "What do you mean?"

"Please, Gwen, do not ask me. I cannot tell you."

Unreasonably, I grew angry. "I command you to tell me!"

He took no offense, but looked unhappy. "My dearest Queen, if it were my secret, I would obey you. But it is by the King's order I am silent."

"Did Arthur tell you this? Directly? Or did you guess it?"

"It slipped out once, accidentally, when he was thinking aloud. There was no one else present. He bound me with an oath."

"Well, you have not broken it. I have heard something, a whisper only, that led me to wonder if Merlin had ever prophesied to the King about the boy."

I saw by the way he schooled his face to stillness that I had guessed aright. It filled me with foreboding; how dare the old enchanter cast such shadows across our lives! And where had he gone, that I could not reach him?

"There is nothing to be done," I said at last. "He is our son now and is accepted as such by almost all the court. Arthur may be an anointed Christian King, but Mordred is pagan to the core. If kingship is his destiny, he will not need anointing." I smiled at Lancelot's horror. "Never mind. What will be, will be, to steal from Merlin. Let us go down."

He followed me in silence. But when we reached the bottom of the path, before the last turn that would reveal us to the soldiers, I summoned up my courage and turned back to him.

"Lancelot. I have not asked for your news. Your—queen must have been delivered of the child. Is all well? Are you a father now?"

His smile was one of joy and pride. "She bore me a son at the equinox. His name is Galahad."

I curtsied low. "Congratulations, my lord. May he thrive and grow strong."

He raised me and held my hand, searching my face. "You are not bitter? I did not speak before, not wanting to bring you grief."

"Thank you, my dear. But you know I always wished you well. I pray he will grow to be a joy to you."

"Why, Gwen," he said softly, coming closer, "what has happened, to heal your heart?"

I met his eyes defiantly. "Mordred," I said, and turning, led him into camp.

In hall that night we celebrated Lancelot's return. His brother and all his train were made welcome. Now they wore openly the badge of Lanascol they had hid from me before, the screaming hawk with outstretched wings. All the company were glad to see them, and Lancelot was warmly greeted. It was like old times with him sitting beside me, but better, because Elaine was not there. When the wine went round, Bedwyr rose and presented me with the King's third and formal birthday gift. Everyone waited expectantly while I opened the linen wrappings and the inner wrap of soft black cloth. Within was a necklace of brilliant gems, as clear as crystal but so bright they hurt the eyes to look at, strung on a thread of gold. I lifted them for all to see, and the others were as amazed as I was.

"What are they, Bedwyr?" I whispered, awed at the splendor of their reflected light.

"Diamonds, my lady. They come from a distant land, far to the south. Beyond the Inland Sea."

"How beautiful!" I exclaimed, turning them this way and that so they glittered in the torchlight and even the knights at the far table could admire their sparkle.

"Allow me, my lady," Lancelot said, and taking them from my hand, he laid them around my throat and fastened them behind my neck. The touch of his hands made my breath come faster, and I kept my eyes in my lap. It had always been so; it was beyond my power to control. Then he raised me and walked me about the room so that everyone might admire the High King's gift.

After hall, Bedwyr, Lancelot and I gathered in the library for talk. The men stood near the hearth, and I sat on the settle, between them. Bedwyr told Lancelot of all that had passed, of Merlin's return to life, of the boys' arrival, and what they were like. They were due to come back the next day, and Lancelot was to be in put in charge of their sword training, so Bedwyr gave him a full report. He told him everything, even of their poor horsemanship and did not dwell on Mordred more than on the rest.

"Well," Lancelot said, "if they are Lot's sons, they will make warriors eventually. As for Mordred—" He met Bedwyr's eyes and read respect there. "He could come of no finer stuff. It will be my pleasure to teach him his trade."

"You will do him honor, Lancelot, in time. You will see. Whatever you teach him, he will learn it."

A smile touched Lancelot's lips. "Ahhhh. Pendragon ambition. It's in the blood."

"And how have you kept yourself, my lord?" I said quickly. "Who keeps your lands for you and your infant heir?"

This was the first Bedwyr had heard of Galahad, and he slapped Lancelot warmly on the back and congratulated him. Lancelot glanced sidelong at me and grimaced.

"It is good to be back. The winter was a long one. Truth to tell, I am not fond of women in pregnancy."

I smiled, to show I did not mind it. "That is a problem easily solved, my lord."

Both Bedwyr and Lancelot laughed heartily and sat down one on either side of me.

"How refreshing it is to speak straight with a woman!" Lancelot said with fervor, holding my hand. "You deal honestly and set no traps for my tongue."

I did not tell him I had warned him; I did not tell him he had chosen it; all this he knew. "Deal honestly with us, then, King of Lanascol. Who guards your coasts? What is happening in Less Britain?"

He stretched, and sighed. "My cousin Bors is regent. I hope to bring him over next spring. But here is something of importance: I paid a visit to my neighbor King Hoel, Arthur's cousin, King of Brittany. Things are happening beyond our borders that may demand Arthur's attention. I have come to call him to a conference in Less Britain at summer's end. Clodomir, King of the East

Franks, is getting restless. He covets the Burgundian territories that lie on his border."

"He is the eldest son of the great Clovis, is he not?" I looked up at Bedwyr for confirmation.

Lancelot looked surprised. "He is indeed. I did not know you knew Frankish history, Gwen."

"I only learned it lately. Valerius has been teaching the boys. He was dismayed at their ignorance—they did not know Cornwall was a part of Britain, or that Less Britain lay across the sea—you should have seen his face when he realized they had never heard of Rome! He has taught me much that I did not know myself. Before he came to us, he traveled through Frankish lands and spent a month with Clodomir, and afterward with Childebert, his brother."

"King Childebert's all right," Lancelot affirmed. "He is King of the West Franks, and his lands border mine. So far he has been content with what he has. Perhaps it is because we have Arthur behind us. That is one reason I'd like Arthur to visit us in state. If formal ties of friendship are renewed, Childebert will think twice before attacking."

"Is he himself in danger from his brother, Clodomir?" Bedwyr asked, frowning.

"No, but Clodomir underestimates Burgundian power. If it should come to war, I fear he may lose it. If Clodomir falls, Childebert will move eastward, I am sure of it. And the Burgundians will most certainly move north. Then either we shall have the Burgundians at our border, or if Childebert defeats them, a very powerful Childebert with an empire at his back. I like neither. I want Arthur's advice on it."

I was staring into the fire, thinking about the Franks. Where the words came from that I spoke, I know not. "The Saxons lie between us for most of the length of Britain—between Arthur's Kingdom and the Franks. They might turn like a sword in the hand, if trouble arose. Or we could deal with them and become an empire ourselves."

"Deal with Saxons!" Lancelot gasped. "Are you out of your mind?"

I turned to him, startled by my own words. "Am I? How so?"

"I beg your pardon, my dear lady," he whispered, coloring deeply and lifting my hand to his lips. "I apologize abjectly. It is a shock to me to hear—from Arthur's wife—we have only just driven them from the land—"

I glanced at Bedwyr, who was silent and frowning.

"Do I speak so out of turn, my lord?" He shrugged. I turned back to Lancelot. "But we have not driven them from the land. The King has drawn a boundary, yes, which they respect. But twenty thousand of them live on Britain's shores. They cannot be discounted. Would they not be better allies than foes?"

Lancelot shot to his feet, distressed, and paced the room. "You cannot know what you are saying! Saxons as allies! It is a contradiction. They are uncivilized Northmen. They love nothing more than killing, not even honor. Show me a Saxon, I'll show you a murderous dog, by God—"

"Lancelot!" I slid off the settle to kneel before him. "I beg your pardon if I have offended you. I spoke out of turn—I forgot how you have risked your life in battle against them, many times, for all our sakes."

The anger went out of him then, and he raised me quickly.

"I have no right to be angry with you," he said gently. "It is my fault. I am an old dog who likes to lick his wounds and prefers not to learn new ways."

His face was near mine; he held it so, and then stepped away. I sank onto the bench and looked up at Bedwyr, who was watching the fire with no expression at all on his face.

"Now he wishes I were more womanly, and spent more time in the kitchens and the weaving room!" I laughed.

Bedwyr smiled and shook his head. "I think, my lady, he prefers you as you are. As who would not?"

"Thank you, Bedwyr. What a knack you have for saying the right thing!"

And to save us further trouble, he pulled out his harp and gave us some songs about the Saxon wars and the valorous doings of Arthur's knights. What with the wine and warm fire and the fresh air and excitement of the day, I am afraid that I fell asleep as Bedwyr sang, with my head on Lancelot's shoulder and his arm about my waist.

I awoke to the warm clasp of hands and the gentle touch of lips upon my own. I knew without opening my eyes who it was, by the touch of his hand, by the feel of his mouth, by the very scent of the man.

"Arthur!" I cried, throwing my arms around his neck as he lifted me from Lancelot's arms. "Oh, my lord! Thank you for such a wonderful day! Thank you for coming home!" He hugged me tightly, lifting my feet from the ground without effort, and then kissed me.

"I wouldn't miss your birthday if I could help it," he said softly into my hair. "We had a full moon, so we pushed on. How are you, Gwen?"

I pulled away to see his face. "I have never been so happy, my lord."

He smiled. "Then you are easy to please—a good horse, a pretty necklace—"

I laughed up at him. "And Lancelot is back and you are home. We are complete."

Behind me, Lancelot rose, and Arthur turned to greet him. They gripped each other hard and then embraced.

"Welcome back, Lancelot. We have sorely missed you."

Lancelot laughed to cover his emotion. "I have missed events of great moment, I hear from the Queen. Merlin lives? And you have thwarted Morgause and called your nephews into your service."

Arthur glanced swiftly about him. The only people in the room with us were Bedwyr, Kay, and Galahantyn, who had come in with the King.

"My nephews," he said firmly, "and my son."

Lancelot grasped him by the arm and held him. "I congratulate you, my lord, on your mercy. You confer great honor upon him. I look forward to meeting him."

Arthur's eyes were dark, unreadable. "And I congratulate you on the birth of your son. Your lady queen fares well? And you have brought me this fine knight, your brother, for which I am already grateful. See how we increase in fellowship."

I made a low reverence, standing between them. "With your permission, my lords, I will retire. You have much to discuss. Arthur"—I met his eyes—"I will await you."

He nodded, and I left them. Bedwyr ushered the rest out, and I waited down the hall for Galahantyn.

He saluted me, and I fell in step beside him. He had been right at the King's side when he awakened me and took me from Lancelot's embrace; he heard the words we spoke; he had seen my face and could judge, if he had sense, the truth and depth of my reactions. But his face was carefully void of all expression, and I could not tell what he thought.

"Good Galahantyn," I said slowly, "your brother is the finest man I know, next to the King. Have no fear for his honor. I would never shame him. All is well in Camelot."

He looked up swiftly, surprised. "My lady Queen! Forgive me, if I gave you cause to doubt me! It is true that earlier today, I was—disconcerted. But I have seen with my own eyes the worship the King pays you, and you him. Britain's honor is not tarnished, even round the edges, but shines as a bright beacon for others to follow."

I smiled. "You are a poet indeed, sir. Thank you for your forbearance."

"Not at all. It was very good of you and Arthur to receive us this evening, especially as I understand you have visitors of state."

I turned to him, bewildered. "Visitors, my lord? Only you and Lancelot."

He frowned. "But surely—I understood—I know I heard them say the queen had at last arrived."

I stopped and he stopped with me. "What queen? My lord, what did you hear? Who said this?"

He shrugged. "Some soldiers. Young men. Outside the barracks as the High King's troop dismounted. I was flattered the King greeted me so warmly, since the voice I overheard had said the queen would not presume to make her entrance tonight."

"Entrance! Whatever did they mean, I wonder?"

"I beg your pardon if I distress you, my lady. I did ask Sir Bedwyr, but he did not know. He said perhaps you would."

"Indeed, my lord, I do not. Do you remember the exact words you heard?"

"Let me see. One voice said, 'Listen, brother, the queen has returned. She is here in the city, even as we speak.' The second voice replied that she would do well to stay away. The first voice then said, 'Do not worry. She will not make her entrance tonight.' That was all. It made me wonder if my brother and I had come at an inopportune time."

I smiled. "You and your brother are always welcome here, my lord. Any time at all you choose to come. I speak for Arthur as well as for myself."

He bowed. "You do us both great honor, my lady Queen."

"I don't know who it is who has come among us and is staying away, but I'm sure it will come to light in time."

Then I left him to await Arthur in my chamber and did not give another thought to the words I had so casually spoken.

8 ✿ THE SLANDER

The summer sped by. Lancelot proved to be by far the hardest taskmaster the boys had yet known. Until he came, they had been growing proud of their prowess with their new swords and often fought mock battles in the practice yard with the soldiers watching. As they were the High King's nephews, the soldiers gave them respect on this account; but Gawaine and his brothers took it for respect for their skill with swords. Not for long. Lancelot was aghast at their clumsiness, and only his great love for Arthur saved them from disgrace.

As I expected, Mordred and Gareth alone paid him the respect he was due. He gave Gareth his first sword and thereby earned the boy's undying love. This was a special devotion, one that took Lancelot by surprise. The youngster worshipped him. Mordred was Gareth's friend, but Lancelot was his idol. By summer's end, Lancelot loved him as a son.

Once Gawaine challenged Lancelot's harsh tutelage, demanding to know by what right he could treat the High King's nephews with such contempt.

Lancelot laughed aloud. "By what right? Why, the right to save your skin! I would do my lord small service if I allowed you out in the real world with such skill as you have now! Would you like to see real swordplay?" He had seen the King crossing a nearby courtyard, and sent a page to beg his attention for a moment. When Arthur came, Lancelot tossed him a practice sword.

"I am a Saxon prince, my lord," he called out, grinning, touching the sword to his forehead, "and you are a Celtic dog, bred of the Spaniard's seed, Uther's bastard whelp, Dragon's spawn." The boys gasped in horror. These epithets were well-known Saxon curses, all names for Arthur. Everyone knew them, but no one dared speak them aloud. The King caught the sword in the air, delighted, returned the salute, and advanced, calling "Come, then, prince of godless savages, king of the dung hill, emperor of breeding maggots! Come to me!"

The swordfight that followed left all the boys amazed; for a tall man, the King moved like a boy, quick, eager, and graceful, but Lancelot was swifter, if not as strong, and parried him stroke for stroke. After the first twenty minutes, when all the strokes the boys had learned were displayed, from every angle, with every dodge and feint, and with every defense, the two men began in earnest to best each other. By this time, soldiers had begun to gather, and then courtiers, and then townspeople. The sun rose high, and they grew damp with sweat, but fought on without stopping, inventing as they went. Lancelot turned and leaped like a dancer. His sword moved faster than the eye could follow, a bright blur in the noonday sun. But Arthur was Pendragon, and driven to be the best; he persisted, cool and furious, giving way when he had to, but always pushing on. They fought beyond fatigue, each determined to outlast the other. At last, close to exhaustion, Lancelot flung his sword to the earth and bent his knee.

"I yield, my lord." He gasped, smiling up at Arthur, who stood staggering above him, the sweat dripping from his chin. "No Saxon power can withstand you. You have improved—that quick thrust up from below on my shield side, that's a new trick. I'm in your debt. You're the better man today."

Arthur grunted and took his hand to raise him. "Today and always. Fatherhood has made you lazy, Lancelot. We have been at it but two hours!" And they fell into an embrace, slapping each other's backs and throwing punches at each other's shoulders. The boys, who had cheered at Lancelot's submission, took it all in and learned a lesson in manners as well as swordplay.

The King traveled that summer, north to Rheged for counsel with King Urien, then to Galava to see his old friend Count Ector, Kay's father, thence east to York, and on to Dunpelder to visit Tydwyl. He came home along the eastern borders, skirting the Anglish and Saxon lands. He took Bellangere with him, who knew this area and could speak some Saxon, and he saw for himself what the six years of Arthur's Peace had accomplished. Arthur's justice ran the length and breadth of Britain; hill bandits and marauders had been systematically pursued and wiped out. The people of Britain could go in peace about their daily business, could till the land without keeping a sword at their side, and could count on redress for their wrongs. All this pleased him.

But when he came to the Saxon borderlands and saw the easy

communication across the boundaries, the intermarriages, the blood ties that had developed, yes, and alliances, too, he liked it not. A new language was growing there, a broken British-Saxon, that in several valleys threatened to replace pure British speech altogether. He came home thoughtful. I knew from Bedwyr that Lancelot had told him of the words I had spoken in the library, seditious words to Lancelot's mind, but the King never faced me with this.

All he talked to me about that summer was Mordred. The boy was ever foremost in his thoughts. He had grown a head in height and now was taller than I was. If he kept it up, in a year or two he would reach the King's height. His voice had settled in its lower range, and his beard was starting. He soaked up knowledge like a sponge, could ride well, could throw a spear with accuracy if not force, and had grown as skilled with his sword as the least skilled of Arthur's soldiers. He had grown comely, as well, and I noted my maidens' eyes followed him everywhere. But in this it seemed he was less Pendragon than his brothers, who lusted openly after every woman they saw. Mordred kept himself to himself, in mind and body, and devoted himself to learning the craft of kingship.

I had hoped that Lancelot and Mordred would come to friendship and respect. All the princes respected Lancelot for his skill; but except for Gareth, none of them grew to love him. Mordred was always courteous to him, indeed at times he was overly so. I got the impression he respected Lancelot more for his being beloved by King and Queen than for the sake of the man himself. And Lancelot himself would say very little about Mordred. It made me wonder sometimes if he even liked the boy.

Lancelot was with me all summer, as Queen's Protector. Bedwyr went north with the King and spent two months in Brydwell with his wife, whom he liked well and seldom got to see. We were busy enough in Camelot; Arthur had called a convocation of all his nobles for the second week in September, to discuss events in Less Britain and plan the journey; we were all summer getting in supplies. Carpenters built pavilions to house those of the guests who could not be accommodated within the palace; the stables were extended; the smithies were busy at their forges, anticipating new demands for horseshoes and weapons. And in the Severn estuary, the King's ships were gathered and refitted for the hundreds of soldiers and horses and servants they would have to carry across the Narrow Sea.

One day near midsummer, when the King had been gone a

month, Lancelot came to me in the small park Arthur had built between the western tower and the fortress wall. There was an orchard here, which in autumn gave us apples and sweet pears, and a lovely walk between rose beds, with benches set in the shade of the trees. Hanna was attending me, but as Lancelot came up, she withdrew to a far corner to give us privacy.

He had just received a courier from Less Britain, who brought news from King Hoel and from his cousin Bors. The news from Hoel was all about the preparations for receiving the High King, and Lancelot reported all he had said. Then he fell silent.

"And the news from Bors?" I prodded gently, seeing reluctance in his face. "Is all well at home? Surely nothing has happened to your son."

"No, Gwen, all is well. Except—I dislike to tell you this, but you will hear it from others if I do not tell you myself."

I smiled, although I was uneasy, and held his hand. "Courage, Lancelot. Surely you are not short of that, who called the High King 'Dragon's spawn' to his face!"

He smiled. "That was jesting. This is not. Well, you must know it. I have had word that Elaine is with child again."

I stared. "She would not dare!"

Lancelot shook his head, looking a little embarrassed. "You misunderstand me. It is mine."

I gasped. I had no right to feel so, and I knew it, but I shook with helpless rage.

"So!" I cried, tears springing to my eyes. "What a master of control you are, King of Lanascol! So eager were you to come to see me, you could not keep from her bed—she whom you claim you cannot love, and who was just delivered of your child!" I tried to rise, but he held tightly to my hands and kept me there. He looked ashamed. "Oh, Lancelot!" I whispered. "Forgive me! I have no right, and she is your wife." I pressed his hands to my lips. "Do not be ashamed, my love."

His head went up suddenly, and he pulled away from me. Mordred stood at the end of the walk, observing us. He came forward with a steady stride and bowed stiffly. Lancelot rose. Mordred's eyes were on the tear tracks on my face.

"What right have you to treat the Queen so?" he demanded, in his man's voice. "Your place here, sir, depends upon her husband's love. You should save her from distress, not cause it." He bowed to me, and his voice was suddenly soft. "Are you all right, my lady? Is there aught that I can do?"

Lancelot stood straight as a sword, his face a mask. No one, not even Arthur, had ever rebuked him so. From anyone else, he would not have taken it. But for Arthur's sake, he kept still.

"Prince Mordred!" I said sharply, and then paused, lowering my voice. "I do not need protection from my Protector. I thank you kindly for your concern, but I assure you Sir Lancelot has treated me with honor and dealt gently with me in bringing me bad news. There is nothing more to it."

"There are tears upon your face, my lady Queen." He was adamant.

"Women do weep, my lord, for foolish things," I replied, trying to smile.

Mordred stood his ground. He had poise, had Arthur's son. "You, my lady, are not foolish."

"Well, Mordred," I said gently, reaching out to place my hand on his arm, "I am a woman and can grieve for things a man thinks nothing of. Sir Lancelot would never willingly distress me. I do assure you of it."

I could read nothing in his eyes, and he had learned to school his face like any courtier. But his body twitched, as if I had slapped him.

"You would do well to believe the Queen," Lancelot said evenly.

Mordred looked from one of us to the other and bowed deeply. "My lady, my lord, I apologize for my words. I will honor and obey you, for my father's sake." With that, he turned coolly on his heel and withdrew.

"How dare he!" Lancelot muttered, furious. "The nerve to throw Arthur in my face! I tell you, Gwen, he is ambitious—" He stopped, seeing my distress. "I'm sorry," he said quickly, sitting down beside me again. "I know he is young, but—what is it?"

I shook my head. To my own surprise, I was shaking from head to foot.

"He knows now that you love me," I whispered.

"All the world knows that."

"In a general way, perhaps. But Mordred saw it here, between us. And he saw that I love you."

"Will he misunderstand it? Galyn did not."

I spread my hands helplessly. "I do not know what he will think. It is not a secret, God knows. I don't know why he did not believe it before."

"Ahhh," said Lancelot, "I know that."

"You do?"

"Gwen." He took my hands again and held me firmly until I

was still. "The boy is head over heels in love with you. You must know that."

I cleared my throat. "So Arthur told me. I—I had hoped he would outgrow it. He is my son."

"He has grown into it, more like. He would protect you from me, if he could. Now he will add jealousy to his dislike of me. It matters not."

"But it may matter, Lancelot. He does take things to heart. As for jealousy, it is ridiculous!"

But Lancelot was sober. "He is jealous for the King's honor, and for your own. And he does not look at you with a boy's eyes for his mother, but with the eyes of a man for a woman. Let him go to the King with it. Arthur will set him straight."

"He will not take it to Arthur." I spoke with certainty. "I know him. He will hold it inside his soul, closely guarded, and someday it will out. That is my fear. I think I must speak with him."

Lancelot shrugged. "You know him best. But go carefully, Gwen."

When Lancelot left me, I sent for Mordred. He came, all stiff and proper and formal. Little Hanna began blushing and batting her eyelids. I sent her from the garden; Mordred hardly noticed her. He began again to apologize to me, but I stopped him, taking his hands in mine, as he had seen me holding Lancelot's.

"Mordred. Do you know I love you?"

Color flooded his face, and his composure broke. "What?" he whispered. "My lady, what is this?"

"This is a thing I want you to know, to be sure of, to seal in your heart. You are my son, as well as Arthur's."

He looked down, away. "Thank you, my lady."

"I do not say this lightly, Mordred. For love is bound to honor. I could not love a man, and not honor him, as well."

His head came up then, and his black eyes met mine. He began to understand what I was saying.

"The King your father I honor above all men living. He is my husband and my lord. More than that, he is Pendragon, Savior of Britain. There is no more worshipful man in all the world."

He nodded reverently but said nothing.

"Sir Lancelot is his closest friend and most trusted knight. He and the King owe their lives to each other, many times over. This man I also love and honor. As you will learn to do, as well, and as your father does."

He swallowed. There was something he would say but could not.

"You have been hearing kitchen gossip; Camelot abounds with courtiers whose purpose would be served by weakening the King's bond with Lancelot. If you are going to listen to them, use your head, and judge them carefully. Remember this: I am your Queen, and Arthur's wife and servant. Do you understand me?"

"Yes, my lady," he whispered. But in his eyes I saw pain, and adoration, and the agony of unrequited love.

"You are young yet," I said gently, to ease his suffering, "and life is complicated. You will understand in time how it is. Be assured, Mordred, that we have no secrets from the King. His honor is sacred to us both."

Mordred slipped gracefully from the bench to the hard ground and bowed his head.

"You are the soul of kindness and goodness and mercy, my lady," he said quietly. "And I honor you above all." Then he rose and walked quickly away. I was left, bewildered, wondering how it was so clear a message could have so unintended an effect.

Nearly every day I rode out on the downs, in fair weather or poor, with an escort of picked men. Ever since my abduction, Arthur had been loath even to let me out King's Gate, but I would go mad if forced to stay within the fortress walls, so he contented himself with sending a small army of soldiers with me. One hot day that summer I rode out when the heat of the day was past, to spare the horses, and came back toward evening, while light still filled the sky. Ferron was the leader of my escort, and rode beside me. We pulled up near the foot of Caer Camel, where a stream ran through the woods on its way to join the river. We dismounted to let the horses drink, and I knelt on the mossy bank to splash my face with cool, clear water. From the corner of my eye I caught movement and looked up. Some ways away an old woman stooped to gather herbs and cresses. Women from the town often came down to the stream for the purpose, and sometimes brought their children here to bathe, but they seldom came alone. I did not think I had seen this woman before; something about her carriage, or the rags she wore, or the way she moved, struck me as odd. I bade Ferron wait for me, and I approached her to ask her if she wanted escort home.

"Mother," I began. She turned quickly, and I stopped in midsentence, startled. Her face was not old, after all, despite her posture, but in the middle of her cheek was a large, black mole, and from it grew a single long, dark hair, so long it bent under its own weight, and curved down her face. It moved and trembled as she spoke, so ugly, so fascinating, I could hardly take my eyes from it, although I tried to, for courtesy's sake. Her hair was wrapped tightly in a shawl; earrings of bone, crudely etched, dangled from her ears. Her skin was clear and unwrinkled, with fine lines at the edges of her lovely eyes, green and slanted like a cat's. While I stood there tongue-tied, she curtsied awkwardly, her bent, clawlike fingers pulling at her coarsely woven skirt.

"My lady Queen."

"You know me, mother? I don't remember seeing you before."

"I'm new in the district. But everyone knows Queen Guinevere—by her child's hair." She spoke with a heavy lisp, in a hoarse voice that did not suit her age. Although her words were rude, she inclined her head politely. She seemed to be comprised of contradictions; confused, I struggled to keep my thoughts straight.

"Would you like an escort home? The day is going, and I would be happy to lend you the protection of the High King's soldiers."

She smiled, showing blackened teeth. I shivered. "What need have I of men's protection?" she lisped, and pointed with a crooked finger to the basket beside her, full of lichens, herbs, and moss. "I've powers of my own, my dear. It's men who would do well to fear *me*." The noise that issued from her throat was nearer cackling than laughter. The mole hair danced against her cheek.

"I'm sure, mother, you could frighten anyone you wish."

"I'll do more than frighten, indeed I will." She glanced swiftly at the soldiers behind me, and her voice fell to a hiss. "I'm out to geld the randy stallion who's been making rough sport with the girls in town." She nudged me with her elbow and leered. "You understand."

"I have no interest in such matters," I returned quickly. "Take your salacious tales to someone else."

"Stay, lady," she whispered, as I turned to go. "This is a serious matter. He is a King's man."

"All men suffer that distemper," I said sharply. "Keep your daughters indoors, and you've nothing to fear."

"Oh, aye, wise words from a Queen abducted against her will!" I gasped. "Or was it by your leave, after all?" She leered.

"How dare you!"

"It's known all over Britain, lady. What did you do, when the lecher accosted you?"

"I refused him, of course. What do you think?"

"And how much use was that?"

I found myself trembling beyond control. "What are you saying, mother?"

Her lips twisted in an ugly smile; the mole hair twitched against her cheek. "It does my girls no good, either. The ones the lecher cannot seduce, he forces. Three are with child of him now, against their wills. Four babies born last winter, with his stamp upon them. He is a villain if there ever was one."

I shuddered. "A King's man, you say? Mother, bring this matter to the High King himself. Arthur honors women. He will see the man makes reparation."

She held up a fist of greenstuff, with moist, dark roots. "I have a better way, and one more certain of results. See this? This will castrate the rutting stag. A powder of these roots slipped into his wine, and he will never lift his spear again to any woman, even his wife!" She chuckled heartily, the mole hair shivered, and the hackles rose on the back of my neck.

"Surely you would do better to bring this to the King. He will take care of it."

She looked up with narrowed eyes. "In this case, even if he were here, he would do nothing."

"You do not know Arthur."

She shook the herbs in my face. "This is what the girls have asked of Sybil. And this is what Sybil will do."

She glared at me fiercely, and I stepped back a pace. "Sybil, you cannot poison a man so. I tell you, Arthur will see justice done, even to one of his own men."

"Ahhh, but he is more than a King's man. He is the King's dearest friend. So we cannot expect justice from the King." She leaned closer and hissed in my ear. "Not against Lancelot!"

"You lie!" I cried. "It is not Lancelot! It cannot be!"

Her sly smile again. "Indeed? You do not believe me, lady, you of all people? Then do not wonder longer why we cannot tell the King."

"But it's a lie! And you do ill, Sybil, to spread such slanders! Lancelot's honor is stainless! Debauchery is beneath him!"

"As well as you know him, Queen Guinevere, you know him not at all. He has a past that dogs him, like a black shadow, every step he takes. He may spend hours on his knees praying to the Christian God, denying his carnal nature, but when he rises, there is his shadow, back again."

"You lie. He does not yield to such temptation. I know this."

Her green eyes slid sideways, and she lowered her voice. "He does not yield to *you*, my lady. 'Twould mean his life if he did.

No, indeed. But when his fire burns, he comes to town and takes out on our young innocents the pent passion of his dark desires."

"No!" I gasped. "I do not believe you! How dare you suggest it! It discredits you even to think the thought! More like, these girls have been following him about, looking for the chance to lie with him!" Furious, I wiped away a tear. "I bid you stay out of this business, Sybil. If you poison him with your evil herbs, you will face more than the High King's justice! You will face my vengeance, sure and swift!"

She began to laugh, a low, ugly sound. I turned my back on her when she reached out and touched my arm—a light touch and oddly compelling. "Think, my lady, not of the man, but of the children. Think of the precious innocents he has fathered and the miserable lives they lead. They live in hovels; their mothers are barely out of childhood and cannot feed them. Does he send a coin? Or a loaf of bread? He sends nothing to sustain them, and they are starving." She dropped the horrid plants in her basket and faced me directly. "To you he is a friend, kind and loyal. But he shows you only what he wishes you to see."

I drew myself up to my full height, fighting the ache in my throat. "I do not believe you. There aren't any children."

"No? Would you believe Lancelot, if he told you so himself? Ask him, then, ask him about Black Lake in Benoic. Ask him about Vivienne, the Lady of the Lake, and how he used to spend his time with her. Ask him if his Christian father did not beat him for his stolen visits."

I covered my ears with my hands, but still I heard her.

"Ask Lancelot if Vivienne did not prophesy for him:

> 'You will seek love;
> You will find honor,
> Glory shall be your reward,
> And the sins of the flesh your undoing.'

"Ask him if he did not love her more than life and seduce her from the Goddess. Go on. Ask him, if you dare." She moved closer, and I shrank back. "And I have proof, if you are shy of asking or the coward will not admit it."

"He is not a coward! You have no proof!"

"I will send you one of the maidens he debauched. I will have her bring the child she bore him. Poor girl, she will never get a husband now. Is it any wonder she begs my help against him?

And yet she does not ask for death, which I could give him as easily; she begs only for castration. And I will do it."

"No! No, I mean, let me see the girl first. I must hear it from her own lips before I will believe it!"

"Very well. I will send her to the kitchens with a gift of cabbages for the King. Be there tomorrow, at noon, and you may have speech with her. Her name is Grethe." She paused and looked at me thoughtfully. "Her hair is near the color of yours. Perhaps that's what inflamed him."

She turned away, without waiting for my leave, and vanished among the dappled shadows. I watched, rooted to the ground, held powerless by fear.

In hall that night I sat beside Lancelot, but could not bring myself to speak. I had no stomach for small talk. He asked me if I was ill, and did not believe me when I told him nothing was the matter.

I could not get Sybil's words out of my mind; witch, wise woman, sorceress, whatever she was, she haunted my dreams that night and stole my sleep. I was up before Ailsa, well before the dawn, and paced half the morning in my garden. This had once been part of the large, spacious, sunlit garden that ran the length of the women's quarters. Some years ago I had a small portion walled off for privacy. It could be reached only from the terrace outside my bedchamber or from the locked door in the wall.

I paced up and down the garden paths, around the little fountain where the water played in the morning sun, trying without success to convince myself my worries were for nothing. Yes, Lancelot was a passionate man, and as a good Christian he fought against his passions. It was true he loved women and had a weakness for beauty, but what man did not? His seduction by Elaine was an aberration; she had drugged his wine; he was not himself when she led him to her bed. More, she had disguised herself to look like me. Even drugged, he had not gone looking for her.

But what was all this talk about a shadow in his past? A sorceress? A lake near his home in Benoic? A prophecy? Surely that ugly woman was telling lies to frighten me. But to what purpose? For the thousandth time I strove to put these thoughts behind me. I could do nothing until I had met with his accuser. If she came.

At noon I was standing by the back door of the kitchens, looking out on the kitchen gardens. The cooks glanced nervously at one another, and the servants hurried about with lowered eyes. I had no wish to disrupt their business, but I dared not leave. I

waited until the sundial marked well past noon. Just as I drew
breath in relief, I saw a young girl come in by the outer gate.
Dressed in sacking, barefoot, she held a toddler by the hand and
carried a basket under her arm. She looked carefully about. Her
dark kerchief covered a head of bright, golden hair.

With sinking heart I stepped out of the shadow and beckoned
her forward. "Pray, what is your name?"

She dropped me a deep curtsy and made her little boy bend his
knee. "Grethe, my lady. I bring cabbages for the King." The boy
unsettled me. With black hair and gray eyes, he bore no resem-
blance to his mother. Indeed, as Sybil warned me, she was barely
out of girlhood herself; her face had not yet lost the round con-
tours of her early years, yet the child with her could not be less
than two. As I looked at those two innocents, hand in hand, eyes
lowered, my throat closed and I could hardly breathe.

"Keep the cabbages," I whispered. "Grethe, come with me." I
led her to a shaded place in the corner of the building, where steps
that led down to the cellars had been built into the earth. I bade
her sit, but she would not, while I stood.

"Sybil told me, Grethe, how you got your son. But I should
like—I mean, I need to hear the tale from your own lips."

But she only shook her head and would not meet my eyes. I
strove to keep my voice calm and kind. "My dear, I would help
you, if you will let me. If I ask you questions you may answer
with a word or a nod, will you do it?"

She nodded.

"Very well. Sybil told me that you are not wed. Is that right?"

Another nod.

"And that the man who begot your son on you took you by
force? Against your will?"

Two quick nods and a turn of the head away.

"Also, that you know the man's name."

After a long pause, another nod.

"Grethe, I must ask you for his name. I will not supply this for
you. If you wish justice done you and reparation made, you must
accuse him yourself."

The girl trembled but did not speak.

"Grethe, who is his father?"

The toddler looked anxiously up into his mother's face and began to whimper. She leaned down and picked him up and wiped
dust off his leggings. Then she looked up at me. There were tears
in her eyes.

"Lancelot," she whispered, biting her lip and crossing herself quickly.

My knees were jelly. I put out a hand against the wall to steady myself. She watched me anxiously, as the tears made muddy tracks on her dusty face. "I'm sorry, my lady. Truly sorry. But I had to say it."

I nodded, groping for courage. "When did this happen, Grethe?"

"Three springtimes ago, my lady."

"How old were you then?"

She thought hard, counting back. "Thirteen." I shut my eyes. It was not possible he could have done it. Not the man I knew. And yet she named him.

"Has he—have there been—any others?"

She nodded, adjusting the weight of the child on her hip. "Vorn was the first. But there are others."

"You must—it is only fair that he face his accuser. Can you bide here a bit with the child?"

She looked bewildered. "What for, my lady?"

"I will go and get Lancelot—"

"Oh, no!" she cried, gripping the child and swiftly backing away. "No, never!" I reached out and caught her just as she turned to run.

"Grethe! Here—I will not make you face him—take this coin as my thanks for your courage in even coming." She threw the coin down, not pausing to see if it was gold or copper, and gathering the child in her arms, she fled from me as fast as she could.

I collapsed against the cool stonework, shaking, my ears throbbing with the violence of unvoiced sobs. The terror on her face could not have been contrived. I had felt the same when Melwas—when Melwas—Arthur! I cried silently, shutting my eyes against the welling tears. Don't come home, my Arthur! Gone is your fellowship forever! There is nothing here but dust and ashes! Don't come home!

9 ✹ The Honor of Lancelot

For three days I kept to my quarters. Every day, every hour, Lancelot sent to ask if I was ill, if I was better, did I wish to see a physician? He came himself and spoke to Ailsa, but she would not let him up the stairs to my chamber. And while I lay abed and fretted, or paced my garden and fretted, all I could think of was the black-haired child, and the others like him, scrubbing for bread in the village, while coins clinked in Lancelot's purse and silver armbands gleamed upon his wrists. He could not know! I cried over and over. He could not possibly know those children existed! And yet it was his duty to find out.

In the end, it was those fatherless children who drove me from my bed. I arose, donned a fine gown, and bade Ailsa dress my hair. "Light the torch in my garden," I told her, "and await me here. I shall be back within the hour."

Hall was just ending. I waited until the Companions were gathered in the library, and I went straight in. They had not yet lit the candles; the long summer twilight lingered still. Lancelot stood in the corner by Arthur's table, half turned from me, a frown upon his face. Nearby, Lamorak rose from his seat upon the bench.

"My lady Guinevere! How glad we are to see you!"

Lancelot whirled, his face lighting. "Gwen!"

"Thank you, Lamorak. I am over the worst of it, I think."

He withdrew as Lancelot came up. "My sweet, how are you feeling? I've been worried sick about you. You are pale yet, I see, but you've got your spirit back."

"Indeed, I have." It was all I could do to look up into his eager face. "Lancelot, a matter has arisen that concerns us both. I must see you privately."

The smile died. "Shall I bid the men leave? Shall we go into the garden?"

"More privately than in this public setting. We must not, on any account, be interrupted."

He frowned, searching my face. "Name the place, Gwen. I shall be there."

"My own garden. In an hour. Tell no one."

He stifled a gasp. "My dear, do you really think it wise?"

"Of course it is not wise. But we must do it. Ailsa will attend us. No one else. You—you still have the key to my garden gate?"

He nodded, a trifle furtively. "But, Guinevere—"

"Make certain no one sees you." The light in his eyes aroused my temper. "This is not a tryst, Lancelot. Nor a game."

He stiffened and squared his shoulders. "My lady Queen, I will obey you." He bowed formally. I turned on my heel and left.

He came on time. I sat on the stone bench that hugged the garden wall, with the torch behind me, so my face would be in shadow and his in light. He bowed and sat beside me, more puzzled than worried.

"All right, Gwen, what's this about? It must be desperately important, to risk all this."

"What would you say, Lancelot, if I told you Arthur had seduced—no, I mean debauched, a girl barely past childhood, a girl of thirteen. Against her will."

Lancelot gaped. "I would not believe you. He would not do it. What are you doing, Gwen? Is this a test of loyalty you have devised?"

"And that he had got her with child and knew it not."

"Nonsense. You know Arthur better than that. Who has been telling you lies?"

"More, that he never sent her so much as a loaf of bread, though the child was starving."

"Stop this. It isn't funny."

"More, that she lives here in Camelot, not half a league from his home."

Lancelot rose quickly. "Enough! *No one* has ever said that about Arthur!"

I rose slowly and faced him. "No. You are right. But they have said it about you."

He stared at me, uncomprehending, in perfect silence. "What?" It was a whisper, aghast.

"A wise woman told me. It is known throughout the town. And this girl is not the only one. There are others."

The disbelief, the hurt on Lancelot's face was a knife in my heart, but I steeled myself against it.

"And you believed her?" he croaked.

"I have seen the girl. And the child. She named you as his father. To my face."

His jaw dropped. "What?" I stood and watched him as he paled, sank to the bench, and buried his face in his hands. "Oh, God," he choked, "what have I done to you, Guinevere? You cannot forgive me for Elaine, is that it? You will believe any calumny against me, just because I lay with her?"

"No," I retorted. "Of course I did not believe it. Not at first. God knows—God knows I do not want to believe it now. But I saw the girl, Lancelot."

"Christ!" He looked up. "She was lying!"

"Why?"

"How can I know that? No doubt for money."

"Not for money. Poor as she is, she threw away the gold coin I pressed into her hand."

He stared in exasperation. "Then for love, or hate, or jealousy, or fear—how can I tell? I've never seen her—for pity's sake, Gwen, how can I prove I did not do it?" He rose and gripped my shoulders. "Listen. Put aside your anger for just a moment. Remember who I am, what I have done, what we have been to one another." His fingers dug into my flesh; I welcomed the pain; it kept my tears at bay. "I have never forced a woman—I would not do it—it is an evil; it is sin. You know—who better—how circumspect I've been. The only woman I got with child I married, though I cared nothing for her, so the child might have a name. I have always put honor first, *always*"—his voice shook—"even when it killed me to do it, even when I thought I could not survive it, even when it meant giving you up to Arthur. Ahhhhh, God, Guinevere!" He shook me gently, his hands sliding down my arms and across my back in a long caress. "How could you think I would behave so? I would do nothing to hurt you, or shame you, or cause you a moment's grief. How could you think it? What has happened to you?"

Through tears I looked up into his face. "Lancelot," I whispered, "I know you did not do it! My dearest love, can you forgive me? I—I—I am acting just like a jealous woman!"

He bent and kissed me and held me in his arms. "Guinevere, when you lose faith in me, then am I lost forever."

"I am a fool, nothing less." I hugged him tightly. "But you

have an enemy, Lancelot, who has taken pains to construct a slander. It can't be that poor girl. Who can it be?"

I pulled away; he dropped his arms, and we stood watching one another. Together we sat carefully on the bench, well apart, not even our fingers touching.

"That is the question I must answer. Tell me from the beginning how you heard this."

I told him the whole story, leaving nothing out. When I came to the shadow in his past Sybil had recounted, he rose, frowning, and began to walk about. When I described Grethe and her son, he stopped and passed a hand across his face.

"Poor girl. Grethe is her name? I will find her and—"

"No, Lancelot! She is terrified of you! That's why she ran away, she thought I would make her face you. That is when—when I saw her face—I believed—I recognized that terror, you see."

His face hardened. He, who had rescued me from Melwas, had seen the terror firsthand. "It is not me she's frightened of, Gwen," he said very gently. "But whatever it is, she must be freed of that fear. No doubt someone has threatened her. Someone powerful." He straightened. "This Sybil seems to know a good bit about me. You say she's new here? I wonder who she is, who she's working for."

I watched him standing in the torchlight, thinking hard, a tall, slender knight with a supple body, a man in his prime of life. I looked quickly away and fought to slow my breathing; perhaps it had been a mistake to bring only Ailsa. He, too, moved back a pace.

"Well, Guinevere." He drew a long breath. "I suppose you will want to know about Vivienne."

I nodded. "If you will tell me."

"It's not all that important. Really."

"Mmmmm. Is that why no mention, no hint of her has ever passed your lips?"

He smiled bleakly. "If I do not tell you, you will imagine her the focus of my life."

I did not reply to that, but watched him twist his fingers nervously in a nearby vine.

"In Lanascol, deep in the Wild Forest about a league from Benoic, there is a lake. Black Lake. In the middle stands an island. On the island, when I was a boy, lived the priestess Vivienne, Lady of the Lake."

"A pagan priestess?"

He nodded. "A servant of the Goddess, like Niniane."

"An old hag, perhaps?"

He shook his head. "Not quite."

"Loosen your tongue, Lancelot. Tell me, and have it over."

He sighed and sat on the arm of the bench, a good three feet away. "We were forbidden to go there, Galyn and I. My father was a Christian, and a hard one. He feared the Lady. But the villagers loved her dearly; she blessed their births and deaths, treated their sick, danced with them at Beltane, and led their dark rites before the Samhain fires. We were always curious about her. But we obeyed." He stopped.

"Go on. Is this so hard to tell? It's clear you loved her, Lancelot. But everyone has a first love. What is it you dread to say?"

If I was not mistaken, he blushed. "It was more than love," he said quietly. "It was obsession. A thirst I could not slake. I put it down to sorcery, until I met you. Then I knew, as Sybil does, the fault lies in myself."

I twisted my hands together in my lap and kept silent. Suddenly I did not want him to go on.

"I was twelve when I met her. After a fight with my father I rode straight out to Black Lake and swam across to the island. To prove I could do it, to defy him. She was waiting for me and called me by my name. 'Lancelot, Prince of Lanascol, you have come to me at last. Don't be afraid, my lord. You are a better man than your father and will outshine him in glory, could he live a thousand years.' I smiled at that. She always knew how to bring me happiness." He cleared his throat and did not go on.

"What was she like?" I prompted. "Dark or fair? Short or tall? How was she featured?"

He waited a long time, and when he spoke his voice was soft and far away. "Dark. Dark hair, as dark as night. Dark eyes, dark skin, as smooth and soft as silk. A voice like honey. A touch like fire."

"So that is why the men call you Lancelot of the Lake. I have often wondered. Does everyone but me know this story?"

The color rushed to his face. "No. It is not much of a story. But those soldiers from Less Britain have heard the name and—well, you know how soldiers like to jest. It is little more than barracks teasing."

"I see. Go on . . . You had just washed up on shore."

"I visited her often. Whenever I could. I had to sneak out, of course. When I was fourteen, she made me a prophecy, the night

before my father took me to Britain to fight for Uther at Caer
Eden."

"Where he died, and where Arthur was made King."

"My father was wounded there and came home. But when I
met Arthur, I found the service I had dreamed of all my boyhood;
I found the cause, the glory, and the King. I gave no thought to
returning." He smiled briefly. "I was young. But Arthur knew better. For a month each summer, he sent me home to see my father.
Of course, I went straight to Vivienne."

"Of course."

"She was proud of me. She called me a man. And she taught
me many things my father's priest knew nothing of. About
women. About the art of love."

In the flickering light, his eyes met mine and held them. My
heart began to pound, and I pressed my palms into the cool stone
of the bench, to anchor me there. I could not look away.

"I burned for her," he whispered, clenching his fist. "With pain
so fierce I wept, even before my father. And she always, always
quenched the fire and gave me peace and brought me back to
laughter." Beads of sweat stood out on his brow, reflecting the
torchlight. "It was a sickness of the flesh, a desire so deep I had
no respite from it. I thought it was a spell she put upon me. I did
not know, then, it was my nature. When I was here with Arthur,
it was better; she was far away, and we had the Saxon wars to
fight. But let me set foot on a ship for home—I was half mad until I was back in her arms again." He drew a long, trembling
breath and slowly rose. "When I was eighteen my father died. I
went home to see him buried. Something in me changed, when I
wore the crown of Lanascol. I knew it was time to say farewell,
but when I went to see her, she was not there. Had not been there
for months. The village people said she had left them in the
spring, when my father first took ill." He held his hands out helplessly. "I never saw her again."

"That's all there was to it? Where is the harm in that? This cannot be the shadow that dogs you, Lancelot. She loved you, and
you her."

"She is not the shadow." He thumped his fist against his chest.
"The shadow is in *me*. It is the fire in my blood. The fever that
burns my soul. It is not the curse of a sorceress, but a flaw in my
very being. I will never be free of it."

"Lancelot." I reached out a hand to him, and he held my fingers tightly. "This is a plague all men suffer from. Even Arthur."

"Oh, God! That I could have Arthur's strength! Against my will I love you, Guinevere. I cannot help it."

"I cannot help it, either."

"Vivienne was nothing to me, beside you." He trembled violently; I saw he truly suffered, and I saw, too, how cruel I was to bring him here alone. "There are times when I am not master of myself. Believe the truth of that. Else Elaine would not be pregnant."

"Lancelot, you judge yourself too harshly. This is a common foible, not a curse upon your soul."

"The sins of the flesh," he whispered, *"will be my undoing."*

"Perhaps. But with love, and honor and glory, it is hubris to ask for more."

He managed a smile. "Bless you."

We stood and looked at each other. Our joined hands were one hand, indivisible, a sweet secret of the dark. Behind my back I signaled Ailsa, and saw Lancelot's relief when he heard her steps approach.

I raised my chin. "It's time we parted. Everyone will wonder where you are."

He went down on one knee and kissed my fingers. I saw him smile. "There is no one in Camelot," he said, "who does not know where I am."

"You are playing with fire, my lady," Ailsa said primly as she pulled the pins from my hair.

"I know, I know!" I cried, slumping on my stool. "But I had to see him alone!" Through the open terrace doorway we heard the soft thud of the garden door closing and the clink of the key as it turned in the lock.

"Why do you treat him so? What has he done, after all, that other men have not?"

"Nothing," I whispered miserably. "Nothing. But he is Lancelot."

"And what do you want of him? That because he cannot have you, he should forsake all women and deny himself the pleasures of manhood? You are selfish to ask that."

I shook my head angrily, scattering pins all over the floor. "Pleasures of manhood, indeed! What right have men to demand such self-indulgence, when women are denied it, from cook to queen! I tell you, Ailsa, in spite of what I said to Lancelot about a foible, sometimes I think it is merely a convenient lie they tell us, to keep us chaste while they make what sport they please!" I turned on the stool and grabbed her hands, holding hard. "I *hate* it when I know Arthur has lain with some other woman! Even if he confesses it to me himself and begs my pardon—it is a weakness in him and he knows it. *I* do not permit myself such freedoms! And yet, and yet," I breathed, meeting her eyes, "I burn, I ache, just as he does, Ailsa, all the while he is away—and—and for Lancelot, always, always! Since first I saw him—it is a passion I can scarce control! Yet I must bear it without complaint. Oh, God, it isn't fair!"

Ailsa flushed to the roots of her graying hair. "My dear child," she said quickly, "calm yourself!" She hurried to the terrace and drew the curtain, as if by so doing she could protect me. "You will drive each other mad, if you make this known to him. Do not see him alone again, Guinevere, I beg you."

Half laughing, I wiped away the tears that ran down my cheeks. "Dear Ailsa! How can you think he does not know? He has known for years. And Arthur—Arthur has known since before he wed me."

Ailsa stared at me in horror; I slipped to the floor, covered my face, and wept.

A week went by with no word from Lancelot. From Lamorak I learned he attended Council meetings and did not neglect his routine duties in Arthur's absence, but I saw nothing of him. Sir Villers he left in charge of drilling the troops, and Lyonel in charge of the stables. He did not come to dinner and never joined us in the library after hall.

But Lancelot was not the only one I missed. More than once I sent to the barracks for Mordred, only to learn that he and his brothers had all but disappeared. They attended drills every morning and showed up for the soldiers' mess every evening, but between those times no one could find them. I asked around quietly; people shrugged; no one had seen them, and no one missed them much. Mordred's absence bothered me more than Lancelot's. At least I could guess what Lancelot was about.

One morning a page came to me as I sat in the High King's workroom reading from a scroll.

"My lady Guinevere, Prince Mordred begs your attention for a moment."

I rose quickly. "Prince Mordred? Where is he?" Behind the page I saw Mordred in the shadow of the doorway. "Mordred! At last! Come in, come in."

Mordred came and made his reverence. He was very pale.

"Mordred!" I raised him and hugged him. "Wherever have you been? I've sent everywhere to find you!"

He flushed and replied quickly, "I've had matters to attend to in the town, my lady."

"In the town!" I scanned his face and noted his uneasiness. "And your brothers, who have been as hard to find? Were they also in the town?"

He nodded shortly and kept his eyes on the floor. "My lady, I bring you a message from Sir Lancelot."

I stared, astonished. Lancelot send Mordred with a message? "Why, where is he that he could not come himself?"

Mordred flushed again and lowered his eyes. "Please, my lady, do not ask me. I mean no disrespect, but I cannot answer."

His discomfort confused me. I watched his face, half man, half boy, and covered a sigh. If he did not honor me with his confidence, I could not force it from him. "All right, Mordred. I yield. What is the message?"

"My lady, it is more like a riddle. He said that if you were to retrace your steps to the kitchen gardens, you should find there the answer that you seek. But I do not know what the question is." He watched me with curiosity.

I gripped his arm. "When, Mordred? When am I to go?"

"Why, at once, my lady."

My mouth went dry, and I held hard to his arm. "Will you escort me?"

"Of course. With pleasure." But as we walked, his curiosity got the better of his courtier's manners. "What's in kitchen gardens, my lady? Sir Lancelot insisted I come to you at once with the message. He seemed to think it would not wait another hour."

"Indeed, Mordred, perhaps it will not wait." We went through the corridors as fast as I dared without giving the impression of haste. "I only hope it is not too late! Unless I am mistaken, I have waited a week for this."

"Waited a week? What is it, my lady? It can't be something amiss with the cooks; there would be no mystery in that."

Suddenly I stopped and turned to him. "Mordred, I will make you a fair exchange. You wish to know what awaits in the kitchen gardens, which is a secret I share only with Lancelot, and I wish to know what you have been doing in the town, and how Lancelot came to choose you as the bearer of his message. I will tell you the one, if you will tell me the other. What say you to that?"

He considered this indelicate proposal with a thoughtful face, chewing his lip, and at last he nodded. "It is more than fair, my lady, as I have no right to know your business. But where it concerns Lancelot, for my father's sake I wish to know it."

"Mordred." I spoke gently, but in my heart I cursed the palace gossips. "There is nothing about Lancelot that your father does not already know."

He lifted his chin. "I do not trust him, my lady."

"You do me insult, Mordred, to think so little of him."

"Oh, no, my lady! That is not what I meant! I—"

"And that is why I am willing to share this secret with you. To show you the kind of man he really is."

"Very well, my lady. If I am wrong, I will admit it."

At last I could smile. "Thank you, Mordred. Now tell me"—as we started down the corridor again—"where is Lancelot now?"

"In the town, my lady."

"Pray, where in the town, and doing what?"

"He is—he is—dealing with a witch, my lady."

"A witch? You mean the woman Sybil?"

He looked up quickly but took time to frame a reply. "Yes. That is the name she goes by. He is turning her out of town. With soldiers."

A tinge of anger crept into his voice, but I could not imagine why.

"Well, Mordred, he would not do it without cause. She must have breeched the law in some respect. Pray God she did not poison anyone!"

"She did *not* poison anyone!" he cried.

"Why, Mordred, do you know aught about her?"

A quick look away and a light frown. "Enough, my lady, to know she is a difficult woman and a proud one. But she has done nothing to warrant being thrown out of Camelot by the High King's troops!"

He ended on a note of vehemence, but his lowered eyes and compressed lips signaled a reluctance to say more. There was more here than he would tell me willingly, and I decided not to press him.

"And how did Lancelot choose you as his messenger?"

"My lady, I went to the house of the witch and—"

"Why did you go there?"

"To—to find Gaheris, my lady. I heard—I knew he was there. I met Lancelot coming out the door. He commanded me bring this message to you, without delay."

We descended the broad steps into the kitchens. "So you did not find your brother?"

"No, my lady, not exactly. But he was there. I heard his voice."

I greeted the cooks and scullery maids, who made us reverences as we crossed to the garden door. In the cool, shadowed passage I pulled Mordred aside.

"You have kept your part of our bargain, Mordred, and now I will keep mine. I am going to meet a girl who a week ago accused Lancelot of fathering her child." His eyes widened, and I hurried on. "She has come this time, I hope, to tell me the truth. But she may be shy of you, so I beg you, stay well away."

"My lady," Mordred breathed, "how do you know she was not telling you the truth before?"

I met his eyes squarely. "Lancelot denies it, and I believe him." He said nothing, but politely lowered his eyes.

Drawing a deep breath, I pushed open the heavy door and stepped out into the brilliant sunlight of the garden. At first I did not see her and feared I had come too late, but she was waiting in the shadows on the cellar steps. I came up to her; Mordred waited in the doorway.

"Hello, Grethe. Thank you for coming."

She curstied low. Her face was very pale, and her hands trembled. This time she had come without her son. "My lady Queen."

"I have had a message from Lancelot saying you wished to see me."

"Yes, my lady."

"Well?" But she was shaking with fear and could not look me in the eye. Struggling to keep myself calm, I sat on the steps and bade her sit beside me.

"Grethe, nothing good can come of holding back the truth. I will not punish you if you have told me lies; I know you did it to protect your son."

She looked up at that. "You *do* understand, my lady? You really do? I thought, since you had no children of your own, you would only think me weak and foolish."

I winced at the blow—as if childlessness affected the working of one's wits! "Indeed, I understand you better than you know. Anything you do to keep your child from harm will be forgiven. There is no excuse for cruelty to children. That is the one sin I could not forgive. And that is the sin you laid at Lancelot's door, last time we met."

She lowered her eyes. "I know."

"Is it true?"

"No," she whispered, a small tear forming in her eye, to be hastily brushed away.

"Tell me, Grethe."

She shrugged. "Madam, until he came to me this week past, I had never seen Sir Lancelot before." I let out a long breath in relief. "When he came to my father's house, I did not even know who he was."

"Ah, thank God, thank God."

"I thought he was supposed to be a handsome man," she said in her child's voice, "but he had a broken nose. I didn't believe him when he told me who he was, not at first. Why, that boy in the doorway is better looking."

"Judge a man by his actions, Grethe, and not his face. To those who know him, he is handsome enough, indeed."

"Yes, madam."

"Why did you lie to me?"

But she turned her head away and began to tremble. I kept my voice as gentle as I could. "Come, Grethe, surely this is a question you expected. If you did not know what Lancelot looked like, you could not have known that your son resembled him. But someone else did. Who told you to name him to me as the boy's father? . . . Was it Sybil?"

She bit off a cry of terror and stared at me in wonder. "Yes, madam," she breathed. "How did you know?"

"And Sybil sent you to me?"

She nodded quickly. She was shaking from head to foot.

"But it cannot have been for gold. You did not take the coin I gave you."

She said nothing, but simply stared at me in dumb fear, like an animal caged and expecting death.

"What did Sybil expect to gain from such a lie? Do you know?"

She shook her head.

"What threat did she use against your son to force your compliance? How did you fall into her power?"

Here was the heart of her terror. She shoved her fist against her teeth and whimpered.

"Be easy, Grethe, the witch is no longer in the town. Lancelot himself has thrown her out King's Gate and seen her on her way. She cannot hurt you."

Her eyes widened. Suddenly she bent her head and began to weep. "Oh, my lady! She is a sorceress! She told me it did not matter where she was, she would haunt me if I betrayed her! She said she would turn herself into an eagle and carry Vorn away if ever I told the truth! She said she would know every word that passed my lips! We are doomed, we are doomed!"

I put an arm about her shoulders and held her close. "Nonsense, Grethe." I hugged her shaking body. "She said that to frighten you into silence. She cannot change herself into an eagle any more than I can. Once she is gone, you will be safe from her."

She sobbed wretchedly. I waited until the force of her weeping diminished. "Where is your son now, Grethe?"

"At home. With Mother."

"Why don't you go get him and bring him here? You can have a room within the castle, and I'm sure Ailsa can find you some employment. You can keep your son by you in the King's own house. Would you feel safe then?"

She looked up at me in astonishment. I wiped the tears from her dirty cheeks and dried her eyes. "There. That's much better. For your son's sake, Grethe, you must be strong. What do you say? Will you bring him to live here?"

She grabbed my hand and kissed it. "Oh, my lady!"

"Good. Go home and pack your belongings and bring them to the south gate. Ask for Ailsa, the Queen's woman. She will be expecting you."

She thanked me again and curtsied and kissed my hand and blessed me a thousand times and promised good service and undying devotion; when she left the garden in the sunlight, she was smiling.

"That was well done, my lady," Mordred said softly. "You are very kind."

"She was very frightened. And I wish to know why. Eventually I will know it."

He walked me back through the kitchens and up the stairs toward my rooms. "How much did you hear, Mordred?"

"Nearly all, I think, my lady."

"Then you see what Lancelot has done. He did not content himself with denying wrongdoing; he sought out the cause of the accusation and seeks to put it right."

"That is one way of looking at it," he said stiffly.

"Why, and what other is there?"

"You will not want to hear it."

"Tell me anyway."

"My lady, the girl is weak. She acts from fear. Someone frightened her into accusing Lancelot, and now he has frightened her into changing her story. It can't have been hard to do."

"You do not know him," I said sharply. "He would not do it. And you heard her say herself that the witch frightened her into making the accusation."

"I heard *you* say it, my lady. You supplied the name, not her. Please, my lady, do not be angry. I do not know the truth of it. And you were generous indeed to offer her a place in the High King's household. But—"

"Go on."

"I do not believe the witch put her up to it."

We had reached the door to the library, and I stopped and bade Mordred follow me inside. I sent a page with the message for Ailsa; I had intended to take it myself, but then I had not dreamed that Mordred, sensible, thoughtful Mordred, could be so blind.

When we were alone, I sat him down on one of the cushioned benches, and I sat opposite him, where I could see his face. He was pale and uncomfortable, but he held himself straight and did not avoid my eyes.

"Now, Mordred, tell me what this witch is to you. You have defended her at every turn, as if you are loath to think ill of her. Does she have you, too, under her spell?"

"No, my lady."

"But you know her. You have spent time with her. You went to her house."

"Yes, my lady."

"Why?"

He did not answer. He was not afraid or ashamed or guilty, but I saw by his face that I trod on private ground. This time I did not let him evade me. "You must see, Mordred, the importance of this matter. The High King's nephews, and the High King's son, have kept company with a witch who has conspired to defile the good name of the High King's chief lieutenant, his second-in-command, his closest friend. Lancelot has exiled her from the city. If you persist in keeping silent about your part in this, what choice do you leave me but to place the matter in the High King's hands? He will be here in another week. Are you and your half brothers ready to answer the questions he will have?"

"No, my lady." Mordred trembled, but did not give ground. "If I could tell you, my lady Queen, please believe me, I would. I would not have you distrust me for anything in the world! But I have promised the witch I would keep her secrets."

"A foolish promise, Mordred."

"Probably. But she made us all swear by the very things we hold most sacred that we would reveal nothing about her. And I must keep that promise."

"Even before the King, your father?"

Mordred looked up desperately, beseechingly. "Even before the

King. Oh, my lady Guinevere, do you have to tell him? Is it so important? You don't know for certain that she forced the girl to lie, and anyway, Lancelot has got rid of her by now, so couldn't you, couldn't you just let it rest?"

"No," a stern voice said behind me, "she could not."

We both jumped up. Mordred stood at attention; I turned to find Lancelot in the doorway. His appearance astonished me. He looked pale and shaken and very, very angry.

"Lancelot, I am glad to see you. Perhaps, between us, we can come to the truth of this matter."

He bent his knee and kissed my hand, but he did it without thought. His eyes were cold; all his concentration was on Mordred.

"I have come to make my report," he said woodenly. "In private."

"May not Mordred stay? I would like him to hear, firsthand, what you have discovered."

"No need, my lady," Mordred said quickly. "I should be going."

"No." Lancelot spoke with the voice of command, and Mordred froze. "Perhaps you are right, Guinevere. Perhaps he should hear it. But first, I want to know"—he stood before Mordred and frowned down at him—"who is that woman?"

"My lord, to tell you would require me to break an oath I swore."

"Swore to whom? Not to that hag?"

Mordred bristled. "Yes, my lord. To the woman Sybil."

"King's son or no, you are a fool."

"Lancelot!"

He turned to me a face white and drawn with anger and fatigue. "I'm sorry, Gwen. But when you hear—it is no more than truth, though for Arthur's sake, I should forbear to say it. I beg your pardon, Mordred. Your youth, perhaps, forgives you something."

There followed an awkward silence. No one moved. Finally I seated myself on the bench. "I have seen Grethe, Lancelot. Thank you for sending her to me."

"Was she coherent? She's done nothing but weep for three days past. She's been badly frightened."

"She told me you were not the father of her child. She told me she had never seen you before, and when I suggested that Sybil had somehow forced her to the lie, she assented."

Lancelot grunted. "The witch threatened the girl with public exposure and shame. If Grethe hadn't lied, *she'd* be the one tossed out of Camelot instead of Sybil."

Mordred stiffened; Lancelot turned toward him. "It might interest you to know, she confessed it to me. Bold as brass, and as shameless. Your precious witch has kept her ear close to the ground since she's been among us." He turned back to me and passed a hand through his hair. "You see, Gwen, she found out what the girl has tried so hard to keep a secret. She discovered who the boy's father really was. If that were known, why, the girl and her child would have to leave the city. They would have to be discredited. Poor souls, they would be allowed no choice."

"But why?" I whispered. "Who is the father?"

"It does not leave this room." A direct look at Mordred. "After Arthur, the most powerful man in Britain. Bishop Landrum."

"Oh, no!" I crossed myself quickly. But it did not surprise me. "He—he seduced her?"

"A child of thirteen?" Lancelot's voice was bitter. "No. He took her by force. That part of the tale was true. All of it was true, except the name. He *is* the scourge of Camelot. She is not the only one."

"Oh, my God."

"His victims dare not speak. But Grethe told her mother, and the witch found it out."

"But, Lancelot, what did she have to gain by forcing the girl to lie? Why accuse *you*?"

Lancelot's lips twisted into a bitter smile. "In the witch's own words, for her amusement. She wanted to cause us pain. You. And me. And Arthur."

I glanced at Mordred. He stood straight and pale, his face unreadable. Lancelot sat heavily on the bench. He looked suddenly ill. "Ahhhh, Gwen, that's not even the worst of it."

"There's more?" I whispered. "What more could there be?"

"After I sent Grethe here, when I went to the witch's house to face her with it, I found—" He glanced swiftly at Mordred, who kept his eyes fastened on the wall, "I found Gaheris there."

"Yes, Mordred told me—"

"In her arms."

"Wh-What?"

"In her embrace. In her bedchamber. Half dressed."

Mordred gasped. We both turned. The boy was livid, his hand clapped against his mouth, staring at Lancelot.

"He is eleven years old!" I cried.

Lancelot nodded wearily. "Yes."

"No!" The word burst from Mordred, beyond his control. "I do not believe you!" he shouted. "I *will* not believe you! You are only trying to blacken her name because she accused you!" His hands bunched into fists, and he raced from the room.

"Lancelot!" I cried, "Forgive him! He is young himself to know about such things!"

Lancelot shrugged. "He fears more for her reputation than for his brother's safety. I will never understand those Orkney brats. Well, whatever spell she wove is broken now. If he had not believed it, he'd not have run away. And she is gone. The soldiers have orders to escort her as far as Aquae Sulis and send her north. She enters Camelot again on pain of death. Once I charge her in Council with such a crime, her life is forfeit."

"And yet," I breathed, "she has done no more than the bishop himself has done. Arthur must know this."

"You will set the place by the ears, if you tell him. No one will confess it. And in truth, his sin is the more understandable. You yourself believed it possible of me."

"Ahhhh, my dear, can you ever forgive me for that?"

He smiled briefly. "I forgive you anything."

I clasped his hand, and we sat silent for a while.

"I have given the girl a place in my household. She will bring her son to live with us."

He squeezed my hand. "I thought you might. I'm glad you did. She will feel safer here, although she must still see the bishop twice a week. But he will know she has the Queen's protection. For her, at least, that should be the end of it."

"Arthur should know about Bishop Landrum."

He sighed. "Tell him, if you must. He can do little about it, unless the man's victims accuse him."

"He knows I have always loathed the bishop, since I first came to Caer Camel. But he has never understood why."

Lancelot rose and raised me. "And I must tell him about the threat to his nephew. I wish I knew who that woman was. Of a certainty, she is evil."

"Perhaps I should ask Niniane about her."

"Or Merlin."

I shuddered. "I don't know how to summon Merlin. He appears to Arthur now and again, but never when I am there. Have you seen him, Lancelot?"

Lancelot crossed himself. "Once. Away from court. I've no doubt Merlin could put an end to that witch. She thinks he is dead, you know. She boasted to me I could not touch her, for since Merlin's death she was the most powerful sorceress in Britain. I did not enlighten her."

"But Niniane has Merlin's power. She is not afraid of Niniane?"

"No. She is not afraid of any woman. And I fear, Guinevere, she will come back."

"But if she does, you will accuse her!"

"She might wait until I'm gone. She boasted that King's Gate could not keep her from the King."

"She is after Arthur? To do what? If it is Arthur she threatens, then her cause is lost, for Merlin will protect him."

He nodded, thinking hard. "Yes, but she does not know that. And it was not only Arthur that she threatened."

I gripped his arm. "Did she threaten you?"

"Oh, yes. And you."

"Me!"

Lancelot looked away and a flush rose to his cheek. "She said the time would come—despite our vows, despite our wills—she said she had seen it in the crystal—she said you and I will lie together, and so betray the King."

I slid to my knees and held tightly to his hands. "How did she dare! It cannot happen without our will!"

Then he looked at me with hot gray eyes and his strong hands lifted me to his lap. "No," he whispered, his lips against mine, "it will not happen without our will."

I wept upon his shoulder. Arthur! I cried inside my soul, Arthur! Come home now!

10 ✻ The Witch of Orkney

The King came home the first week in September. The kings of Britain followed within a fortnight, all gathering for a great Council to discuss policy toward Childebert and the Franks. With so many preparations, and so many guests to greet, the events of summer faded in importance. Lancelot told Arthur about the attempted seduction of his nephew, but as he had predicted, Arthur could do little about it; the witch was gone, and Gaheris and his brothers were under a stricter regimen now that the King was back. I told him about the girl Grethe and her lie about Lancelot, and how I had believed it, and why, and what the truth was. He saddened when he heard it and ran a gentle finger down my cheek.

"Lancelot would never hurt you by intention," he said gravely. "And if by accident, he would confess it. This you know. Had it not been for Melwas, you'd not have given such a lie a second thought."

"Perhaps not, my lord."

"As for the bishop, he is a man of many sins, but he is still a man of God. I will let him know, in a roundabout way, I will not tolerate such profligate behavior and will give shelter to his victims if they ask it. I will let him know I am considering sending a courier to Rome. I wager he will take the hint."

We had little time for private talk, with so many people arriving and so much public ceremony. Niniane arrived with King Pelleas, her husband, and King Urien of Rheged brought his wife, Morgan, Arthur's full sister. She lodged with her husband in the palace, and I heard from those who saw her rooms that she kept far grander state than I did. Haughty and cold featured, she could scarcely bring herself to speak to anyone lower ranked than Arthur himself. This was fine with me; I did not enjoy her conversation.

The Orkney princes were excited at the gathering of all the men they had learned so much about in Valerius' lessons; most of these had fought beside Arthur in the Saxon wars. But as the boys were too young to be knighted and made Companions, they could not attend the Council meetings and were usually sent out hunting with whatever King's men were going that day. So large a host required a constant resupply of game. Duke Constantine was among the guests; he looked to be a proud man, who would not be easily displaced. Perhaps the King sent the boys hunting to keep Mordred out of his way.

The Council of kings lasted a week. It was resolved that the High King should go to Brittany with Lancelot, to meet with King Hoel and send a message of formal greeting to King Childebert. To represent a united front, many of Britain's lords went with him: Urien of Rheged, Ector of Galava, Hapgar of Strathclyde, Constantine of Cornwall, Drustan of Elmet, and Pelleas, to name a few. My dear uncle King Pellinore of Gwynedd went, also, more to visit his daughter Elaine and see his new grandson than to parley. They were seven hundred men in all, and four hundred horses. The thought of what might happen should storms assail the seas was enough to stop the heart.

Bedwyr stayed as regent and Queen's Protector. As King of Brydwell he deserved a place among this distinguished train, and I asked him if he did not regret having to stay at home and make sure I behaved myself.

He laughed. "The King does me far greater honor by entrusting you to my keeping. Why is Lancelot always appointed the Queen's Protector when he is here? Not for the reason you think, perhaps, although Arthur is an understanding man. It is because Lancelot is most trusted and most able. In all the Kingdom, there is no higher honor." It was a gallant reply, and I thanked him for it; but had I been he, I would have wanted to be traveling.

Parting with Arthur had become easier with so much practice, but parting from Lancelot was difficult indeed. It was mid-October when they set out for the estuary. He would be gone until mid-March, at least. Half the year seemed a lifetime. And since Camelot was full of strangers, we had no privacy for our farewell. Arthur talked long with me the nights of the last week, but Lancelot I bid adieu in the forecourt of the castle, in the public eye.

"Take good care of my lord the King," I told him, doing him deep reverence, "and God speed your way there and back again. We are not the same in Camelot without you, good Lancelot. And as you are a merciful man, give your lady wife a rest from her labors."

His mouth twitched, suppressing a smile. "Gentle Queen," he murmured, "I give her no more labor than she can bear."

"For my sake," I countered, "let her lie idle the long winter, that she may labor and bear no more." Arthur's eyebrow lifted in warning; I gave Lancelot my hand and let him go.

They rode out King's Gate and down the broad causeway to the shore road, and left Camelot behind, ringing with emptiness.

Things were not dull for long. No sooner was Arthur gone than his sister Morgan began to seek out my company. I often went riding with Bedwyr or Ferron, and sometimes Morgan and her courtier Accolon, who dogged her like a shadow, accompanied us. She alone had remained after the host had left; the King had made her welcome, having no other choice, and she had chosen to stay until her husband returned. Arthur was not happy about it, but I told him I did not mind. Until he left, she kept to herself. Accolon never left her side, even at night, said the palace gossip. He was younger than she was, well made and strikingly handsome, with light hair, dark eyes, and a fine complexion. That he was her devoted slave was clear; his adoring eyes followed her everywhere. Her husband King Urien was a graybeard, old enough to be her father.

Morgan was Urien's second wife. His first wife had been dear to him, by all accounts, and had given him four sons, Coel, Uwain, Lyle, and Drian, now grown men who served the King. If he had married Morgan to replace what he had lost, he soon knew of his mistake. She had borne him a daughter, Morgaine, and if rumors could be trusted, had hardly spoken to him since. Her compassion as a mother seemed no greater than her compassion as a wife. Only sixteen months before, at the age of seven, Morgaine had been kidnapped and savagely raped by the villain Heuil, leader of the Strathclyde clan, during a border dispute with Rheged. Arthur had settled the dispute and restored the child to his sister, whose response to her ordeal was to shut her away and treat her like something soiled.

After one of our outings I asked Morgan how her young daughter fared, to see what she would say. She replied, with coldness, that she grew and thrived and had been revenged for her attack. I shuddered at the thought of what she had been through and expressed my deep sympathy to Morgan.

"Well," she said icily, "you should know." And turned away.

I stared after her, astonished. No one had heard her remark but I; I let it pass. I realized then that sharp tongues had been at work, and that at least some in Britain chose to believe Melwas had been successful. If any believed it, it only reflected better on Arthur's mercy, so I said nothing.

When Arthur left, Niniane returned to Avalon. But before she left, she gave the King two words of advice: first, that he should lock King's Gate against all comers, and second, that he should lock up his Sword. Arthur objected to locking the fortress gates. It was his policy, he said, to make Camelot and the justice dispensed in the Round Hall open to anyone in the kingdoms. To lock the gates would be to cut off Britain from her vital center, and he would not do it. But he did lock up his Sword. He was not taking Excalibur to Brittany, for this was a mission of peace and friendship, not of war. So a guard was posted, day and night, outside the door of the Round Hall, where the great Sword hung in its hanger above the High King's chair. No one went in or out without Bedwyr in attendance.

One night when the King had been gone a fortnight, Bedwyr and I were sitting before a good log fire in the library, reading from the scrolls of Xenophon. The wind had risen and promised storm the next day. Drafts whistled through the corridors, around the edges of the tapestries, and made the fire welcome. We had fallen to talking about Lancelot when the door burst open, and Kay ran in.

"Bedwyr! Fire!" he cried. "The stables are afire! Call the sentries—in this wind, it will take every man to save the horses!"

I leaped to my feet, but Bedwyr was already at the door. He turned. "If I cannot be with you, Gwen, get to your rooms. Don't be alone."

I nodded, and he flew away. Now I wished I were a man and not a woman! To have to hide in my quarters with my women, while my precious horses were at risk! Would they have enough men to man the buckets, build a firebrake, and lead the horses out? Would they have time, with this wind? We were so short-handed, with so many troops gone with the King! But I could do little to help. It was man's work, and I had orders to obey.

I went silently along the corridors. It was strange to see no sentries line the walls. As I passed the hallway that led to the Round Hall, I caught movement from the corner of my eye. I turned to look. The torch near the Council chamber had gone out. Why had the guard not relit it? I went to see. When I came to the door, I understood. The guard was not there. Remembering Niniane's warning, I determined to check on the Sword. On tiptoe I grasped the nearest lighted torch and lifted it from the sconce. It was not heavy, but my hand shook, and the door seemed to tremble and sway. I pushed it open slowly, but could hear no sound at all. The chamber was in darkness. Outside the glazed windows I heard dimly the shouts of men, but here was only stillness and peace. I made my way to the great round table and looked up. There it was, still in its hanger, cold and forbidding in the torchlight. I sighed in relief. I did not stop to wonder why the great emerald lay quiet, when usually even the smallest flame set light flashing from its facets; I was so pleased to see the Sword, sheathed in its old scabbard as the King had left it, that I chided myself for my foolish fears and closed the door.

I myself stood guard on it. I disliked to disobey Bedwyr, but the King's orders came first. The Sword must be guarded. Before long, I heard running feet and panting, and a young sentry came racing toward me.

"Who's there, in the King's name!" When he got close enough to recognize me, he gasped and fell on one knee. "My lady Queen Guinevere! What—what's amiss?"

"Nothing. The Sword is there. But when I came by, I found the door unguarded, and so took up the post."

He kissed my hand with fervor. "My lady Queen, you have

saved me from disgrace! Sir Bedwyr was so furious—I was wrong to leave the post, even for fire, but I thought—no matter. You have saved me. I am forever in your debt."

"What is your name, gentle knight?" I asked kindly, for I saw he was young and frightened.

"Hugh, my lady—and I am not yet knighted."

"Arise, Hugh, and take this torch from me, if you will. It grows heavy with holding."

He had it from me in an instant and, relighting the one that had gone out, returned it to its sconce.

"One good turn deserves another," I said, noting the smudges of soot on his face.

"Anything, my lady! Ask it!"

"Tell me about the fire. What is going on?"

Thus far, he said, the fire was contained in the new additions that now stood empty. It had started in the hay, no one knew how. But the King's stables, built of stone, were not yet threatened, and already the horses were being taken to the pastures. People from the town had come to help, seeing the smoke, and it was likely that disaster would be avoided.

"Thank God!" I sighed. "This is good news indeed. Now it will be possible to wait for Bedwyr's report. I thank you, Hugh."

He was profuse in his thanks to me, but I felt sorrow in my heart for him. He would never make one of the King's Companions, for he had no sense. And after this, even though no harm had come of it, Bedwyr would never trust him.

Bedwyr came to me after midnight to make his report. He was tired and out of temper, but pleased with the results. He had washed his face and hands and scrubbed his hair, but his clothes were stained with soot and burned with embers. It had been a near thing, because of the wind.

"If we ever find who set it, I shall take his life with pleasure," he growled.

"Who *set* it? What can you mean?"

"It was no accident, my lady. The hay was newly harvested but well dried. I checked it myself. And we found the ashes of hot coals. That's how it was started. If the Sword had been touched, I would have suspected a diversion, but as it is—" He passed his hand wearily across his brow. "I know not what to think. But someone has done evil, and I will find him."

The next morning, although it had begun to rain, Queen Morgan announced that she and all her train were leaving.

"Perhaps it was unwise to stay and await my lord," she told

Bedwyr in my hearing. "My brother should have left his fortress in more capable hands. After last night, I cannot be sure that we will have mounts left when we wish to go." Bedwyr took it without flinching, but his eyes flashed. I flew to his defense.

"Sir Bedwyr is among the finest men in Britain. Although," I added thoughtfully, "I see where you might find his manner of administration somewhat foreign. He metes out punishment only where it is well deserved, and does not blame children for the sins of their elders. As to horses, my husband's sister is always welcome to animals from his own stables"—I made her a reverence—"that is, if you can ride them."

Morgan stiffened; Bedwyr covered a smile. Even Accolon looked at me with admiration. I began to feel sorry for Urien.

"Thank you, Queen Guinevere," she snapped, "for your gentle offer. As you no doubt rule in Camelot, your advice about governing is clearly worth having. I would beg you remember I am a lady and do not ride stallions. That is for men, and for ill-bred maidens who wish they were."

I heard Bedwyr's indrawn breath and saw the stony faces of the men behind him. When she called me maiden she insulted even Arthur.

"Even were I maiden," I said slowly, letting the words fall singly into the icy silence, "I would have the mother seek healing for a child so abused as little Morgaine and not leave her to suffer nightmares and terrors of the dark all on her own. It has been over a year," I finished softly.

In fury she turned to Accolon. "We will go," she commanded. "I will not stay to be instructed by Arthur's barren wife on child rearing!" With that, she flounced out, Accolon following, and left us in peace. The men in the room were afraid to move. Even Bedwyr glanced at me nervously.

I smiled and took his arm. "Do not fear, Bedwyr. She has not the power to hurt me. If those are her sharpest barbs, I am in no danger. Elaine gave me a tougher hide than that."

Bedwyr exhaled in relief and returned the smile. "She is known for her sharp tongue and the joy she takes in making people cower. But my lady bested her this day."

I shook my head. "To be queen of shrews is no honor. I should not have spoken so to Arthur's sister. I only demeaned myself. Pray, let's hope she keeps her word and leaves."

Morgan was gone by nightfall, and Bedwyr and I looked forward to a calmer stretch of time. There was much to do before we moved to Caerleon at Christmas; the harvest must be brought in, beasts slaughtered and their flesh smoked and dried for soldiers' rations, wool and flax and dyes prepared for winter's weaving, the festivals celebrated and thanks given before the new year at the Samhain fires. Everyone was busy. At this time of year, there was scarcely a village in Britain that could not have used an extra pair of hands. Each morning we rose early, and often by hall we were so exhausted we bid each other good night as we rose from table and went straight to bed.

On one such night a courier arrived just as the wine went round. An Orkneyman by dress, the message he delivered announced the arrival of Queen Morgause.

I looked toward Bedwyr in surprise. He stared, stunned, at the kneeling courier.

"The Queen of Orkney is *here*?"

The man nodded. "She is without, my lord. Awaiting entrance."

My head ached with fatigue, and I grumbled to Bedwyr, "Arthur has too many sisters. What does this one want, I wonder?"

"Not much," came a smooth voice from the doorway, "beyond a courteous greeting from his Queen."

I blushed to the roots of my hair. Queen Morgause stood watching, her escort behind her, as Bedwyr rose and went forward to welcome her to Camelot on the King's behalf.

Never had I seen a woman so lavishly dressed; even her cloak was trimmed with golden beading. Her hair, once red-gold like Uther's, had darkened to dull russet, but she wore it bound in golden mesh; where it framed her face it accented the creamy pallor of her skin. Hands, wrists, neck, and ears were hung with gold and rich enamels, all worked intricately in the way of the northern Celts. Her face had Arthur's bones, but not his features. She had a small mouth and nose and narrow forehead, and lashes too black to be unpainted. Beauty, yes—by anyone's standards she was beautiful, and yet there was something spoiled about it, something slack, stale, beyond its best. But then, she was past thirty.

She acknowledged Bedwyr and made her reverence, a dip of the knee, no more. Cat eyes, long, narrow, slightly slanted, glinted green. I went to Bedwyr's side. She was not as tall as I was, but her shape, even after bearing five sons, would have outdone any maiden half her age.

"Welcome, Queen Morgause." I did not apologize for my rudeness; had she obeyed Arthur's orders and stayed in exile, she would not have heard it. "We have lately had a visit from Queen Morgan. How sorry I am you did not come a month ago, when both your brother and your sister were in Camelot."

She regarded me a moment in silence, and my flesh crept on my bones. The dread I felt seemed so familiar! The eyes narrowed suddenly; sweat broke upon my brow. She turned to Bedwyr. "It is unlikely that either my brother or my sister will regret missing my visit. I came to see my sons, but I do not see them in hall. Are they not here?"

"No, madam, they eat in the soldiers' mess. Let me arrange rooms for you and get you settled, and I will have them sent to you." He did not tell her that the reason they ate with the soldiers was because, even after a year, they had not acquired the manners to eat in hall—except for Mordred, whom the King did not wish to single out.

She looked slowly around the gathering and slowly smiled. "Very well. Show me to my rooms."

Kay bowed low at her side. "My lady, I will escort you."

She turned away, ignoring the arm he proffered. "I will have meat and broth brought to me, and unwatered wine, as well. See to it."

She swept out, followed by her attendants, and Bedwyr and I looked at one another. We had thought Morgan a handful!

"It is no accident she comes when the King's in Brittany," he said with feeling. "She has disobeyed his direct order. But how can I imprison the High King's sister, when he is gone and her sons are here?"

"What do you suppose she wants, Bedwyr?"

He shrugged. "Nothing good, you may wager what you like on that."

"I fear you are right." I did not tell him my deepest fear: that she had come, somehow, to reclaim Mordred.

She swiftly became a general nuisance and as great a thorn in my side as Elaine had been at her worst. She disliked me; not, I discovered, on account of my unthinking rudeness, but merely because I was dear to Arthur. Kay and Bedwyr she treated as her servants and bade them have things brought, replaced when they did not suit her, and taken away when she was weary of them. For Arthur's sake, they held hard to their patience and did her bidding.

Most days, she held court in the High King's library. There she would send for whom she wished to see. Instead of going to the practice field to see her sons' progress, she would send for them and engage them in reminiscences about their Orkney homeland. Gawaine and Agravaine chafed under such treatment; they wanted to show off their prowess with spear and sword. Mordred bore it with grim patience; Gareth frankly fell asleep after a while. Only

Gaheris truly enjoyed every minute in his mother's presence. Indeed, I was amazed at the change in his demeanor. I had thought him a sour, whining child, but now he positively glowed with joy and pride. It was a pleasure, I told myself when I was wont to anger at her presumption, to see the boy so changed. Everyone else was ready for her departure when she had been a week in Camelot, but Gaheris at least had come into some sort of bloom.

She stayed past the harvest, past the fall of the first snow, and the longer she stayed, the more fractious we became. Everything she did rubbed someone the wrong way. And Morgause herself not only enjoyed the disruption of our peace, she went out of her way to make trouble. Once she sent a maid of mine to her chamber, to fetch an amber bracelet from her jewel chest. The girl asked Hadarta, Morgause's chief attendant, to fetch it for her. But Hadarta could not find the chest. She searched everywhere, and flew into a panic, crying out that Camelot was full of thieves, and Morgause would have her life if it could not be found. Little Anis helped her search the queen's rooms; they spent half a day looking for it and weeping. Finally Anis came to me in tears with this silly story and asked me what to do. Neither of them dared tell Morgause the jewel chest was missing; indeed, Hadarta was packing her belongings into a sack, preparing to leave Camelot altogether. Slightly annoyed, I followed Anis to Morgause's chamber and searched the place myself. There were plenty of furs and cushions flung about, and a fine linen tunic too small for a man to wear lying on the floor near the bed—could she be mending it for one of her sons?—but the chest was not there.

"It is a small box," Hadarta wailed, "but very precious! The cover is embroidered with crimson threads and sea pearls! Oh, oh! She will be in one of her horrid wraths, she will have my eyes out!"

"Not in my domain, she won't," I said firmly. "Come, Hadarta. There is nothing to do but face it. Delaying telling her the news will not make it any easier. Come with me, both of you, and we will tell her together."

Morgause lounged in the library before the fire, admiring the rings on her fingers. Anis fell into a curtsy; Hadarta hung shaking at the door.

Morgause listened calmly to my explanation and, with a light little laugh, waved us all away. "Oh! I had quite forgotten! I have the chest with me. And here is the bracelet on my wrist—I found it just after the child went after it."

And that was it: no apology, no regret, no expression of grati-

tude for half a day wasted by two women on her behalf. Anis and
Hadarta were happy enough to escape without punishment, but I
could barely control my anger. Watching me, Morgause's long
green eyes began to narrow and her lips slowly twisted in a smile.
I turned on my heel and walked out.

Not even Arthur's hound was left in peace. Morgause had
brought with her a white-haired cat, which she often kept upon
her lap and stroked. Whenever she brought it into the King's library, she had Cabal kicked out from his place on the warm
hearth, although he cared nothing for cats, so that her darling
might not be affrighted and scratch her with his claws. Cabal was
stiff with age and winter cold; I let him sleep near my grate, but
it was not the same as a good log fire.

Poor Bedwyr had the worst of it. I, at least, could escape on
horseback, for riding was beneath Morgause. She traveled only in
a cushioned litter, lined with velvet. But as regent, Bedwyr could
not escape. The only place he was free from her was in the Council chamber. The guards had orders to physically restrain her if
she tried to enter, but wisely, she did not. Councils grew longer
and longer, and I had wine sent in to the men, which Arthur never
allowed, to help them prolong their session and to signal that I understood.

Dinner became something to be endured. The springs of conversation dried under Morgause's scorching wit; no one cared to ven-
ture an opinion and then be made to look a fool. How I wished we
had a bard, that we might listen to the sweet sounds of music!
Hearing this, Bedwyr offered to fetch his harp and give me a song
or two. I was delighted and begged him to do it. Morgause wondered, with a lift of her lip, how the Kingdom had come to such
a pass, that the Regent of Britain should stoop to harping for himself. Did he garden, too, she wondered, and spin his cloaks himself?
I had opened my mouth to snap back an answer, when I caught
Bedwyr's eye and was silent. He gave us the song that Merlin
wrote for Arthur, about how Britain waited in darkness for a thousand years until the King should be born that would bring her into
light and glory, an everlasting glory that men would forever honor.
As he sang about Arthur, the soldiers in the hall grew solemn and
the women misty-eyed. Only Morgause looked on in half-concealed
contempt. When the last note had faded to a sweet vibration, more
felt than heard, Morgause rose and faced me.

"In my life, I have never heard the truth stretched so. One
might almost believe Arthur had written it himself. As for the
singer, be sure to reward him, my lady Queen, as I hear only you

can do, who are so liberal with your favors, for the honor he has done us all." She made me a low curtsy, and swept out.

Every man in the room was on his feet, crying out in protest. I stared after her, aghast. "Bedwyr, why does she hate me so?"

He gripped my shoulder firmly. "Pay her no mind, my lady. To show anger is to play into her hands. She's a different breed from Arthur."

"Indeed!" I breathed. "Niniane warned me, but I did not believe her. She is a devil."

I fought to keep my temper, but I could not bear the way she treated Arthur's friends as her servants. The final straw came late one afternoon when I had returned from a ride upon the downs and sat in my chamber while Ailsa combed my hair. A page scratched at the door, sent by Morgause.

"The Queen of Orkney is in the library and commands the Queen's attendance," he quavered, knee to the floor.

Ailsa stiffened. " 'Commands' her attendance? Surely not. 'Begs' you mean, Brynn."

"No, madam," the page whispered, trembling. "She said 'command.' "

"Repeat the message," I ordered.

" 'You there, go to the High Queen and command her to attend me. I have heard she has a lovely voice. I wish to hear her sing. Have her come and sing me a song.' "

Ailsa gasped. "How dare she! How dare she send such a message!"

The poor page shook so badly he could hardly speak. "Madam, I told her I could not take the Queen such a message, but, but— she said she'd have me whipped if I did not!"

I went to the child and raised him. "She cannot touch you, Brynn. You serve the King, not Queen Morgause. These are idle threats. Unless you believe them, they have no power. Where is Sir Bedwyr?"

"In Council, my lady."

I hid a smile. "Very well. Take him a message from me. You are to attend him in Council and see the men have wine and mead enough. Do not return to Morgause."

"She bade me return at once with your consent."

"You cannot do that, because you do not have it. Forget her. I myself will give her the reply she deserves."

When he was gone, I returned to the stool and bade Ailsa resume her combing.

"What will you do, my lady?" she asked nervously.

"What I have learned from Bedwyr is best to do," I replied. "Nothing."

I took my time and let Ailsa dress my hair with ribbons and donned Arthur's favorite gown of sapphire blue. It was dark when I went down at last, and the lamps had all been lighted. Anis, Hanna, and Mary attended me. We walked slowly through the corridors, talking and laughing, and as I expected, the library door opened as we neared it, and Morgause came out.

"Ah, there you are at last. I must say, Guinevere, you have kept me waiting long enough."

The sentries near enough to hear her drew breath together; my girls froze. I did not pause, but kept walking.

"What, would you snub the High King's sister?" Morgause hissed.

I turned slowly. "I beg your pardon. Were you addressing me?"

"Is your name not Guinevere?"

"My Lady Queen Guinevere to you, Morgause."

To my surprise, she smiled. "Surely, sister, we may use first names between us. My father was High King of Britain when yours was fighting hillmen for his tiny patch in Wales. Do not imagine you outrank me."

I clutched my gown and stilled myself and answered quietly. "Have you anything else to say?"

"Come sing for me, Gwen. I should like to hear your voice."

I have never done anything so hard, but I turned away without speaking and, reaching out a hand to my shaking maids, continued down the hall. From a distance, we could hear the witch's laughter.

That night, Mordred came to me. I saw him in my antechamber with Ailsa in attendance. He went on his knees, his features solemn, and his voice tight with control. "My lady Queen, you must make her leave. You must find some excuse and make her leave."

I touched his face and bade him look at me. "Mordred, is this your mother you speak of? You wish me to send her away?"

"Yes!" he cried, clasping my hand. "You must! She means nothing but mischief."

"Mischief can be endured. How would your brothers feel about it?"

"Gawaine and Agravaine would not much care. They were pleased at first to see her. As I was. But now, but now she is a nuisance. They want to be soldiering, not waiting on her hand and foot. They are tired of it. We all are."

"Gaheris, too?"

He looked quickly away. "Gaheris—would be better off without her. It is partly for his sake that I have come. Can't you send her back to Orkney? Didn't the High King send her into exile? Hasn't she disobeyed him in coming here?"

"Yes and no. When Lot died, Arthur gave the governing of Lothian to Sir Tydwyl, as regent for Gawaine. That left Orkney for Morgause. Orkney or another husband. She chose Orkney. It wasn't exactly exile, and yet it was. You know better than I how far away Orkney is."

"But when the High King sent for us, he did not send for her. Sir Lukan read the orders aloud. She was commanded to stay in Orkney. So hasn't she disobeyed by coming here?"

"Yes, Mordred. She has disobeyed."

"Then can't you have Bedwyr send her away?"

"As she is the King's sister, we are loath to do it. It is, well, a personal matter between them. Until she gives us good reason to do otherwise, we must treat her with the respect she is due. As Uther's daughter and as Arthur's sister."

His face shuttered. "The matter between them is my begetting." He spoke with no emotion. At thirteen, he already had Arthur's hard control. "He will never forgive her that, and she will use his shame against him, while she feels none. It is clear to me now."

"What is clear, Mordred?"

He looked up at me. "She intends to stay. Here in Camelot. Forever. She intends to take it over, as you have seen. She won't let Arthur stop her; she has a weapon against him. The life you have led this month past, she intends you will lead forever."

I gasped, as much at the pain of hearing him speak so of his parents as at the horror of the future he described. "How do you know this, Mordred?"

He shrugged. "I have heard the way she speaks of my father. I have heard the way she speaks of you. You are—so easy to make angry. Forgive me, my lady, but it gives her such delight."

"When Arthur returns, he will deal with her."

"What will he do? If he sends her back to Orkney, he must have a reason why. That means he himself must publicize his shame. I don't think he will do that."

He was right. Unless Morgause publicly transgressed, or breeched the law, what reason could he give for treating his sister so? He, who was revered as the just King, the wise King, who treated others fairly, no matter what their station—his hands would be tied. I saw why Mordred had come to me. I was not so bound. I could do whatever I willed and answer for it to Arthur, who would be relieved not to have to deal with it himself.

"But even I, Mordred, must have some good excuse. Else it will look like spite and still reflect upon Arthur. She came and made a nuisance of herself and teased the Queen, who could not take a jest and sent the King's sister away. You see?"

"Yes."

"Thus far, she has done nothing but disobey Arthur's wishes."

"I could tell you something she has done," Mordred said slowly, his eyes on the ground. I said nothing but watched his face. Not an eyelash moved. "But—I want there to be another way."

"Perhaps I should speak with Bedwyr."

"Or Merlin." He looked up suddenly. "She would fear Merlin. She has heard rumors of his return, but does not believe them. Can you not ask him what to do?"

"You and Lancelot give me the same advice," I said softly, and watched color flood into his face. "But I do not know how to summon him, even if I were willing. Merlin and I do not, well, see eye to eye."

He drew a long breath. "I see." He paused. "Does the King love Lamorak?" The question came out of nowhere and took me by surprise.

"Of course. He's one of the Companions."

"He's in danger."

"What kind of danger?"

But he rose quickly and bowed. "Perhaps I've said too much."

"All right. I will keep my eyes open. I appreciate your coming, Mordred."

He hesitated, chewing his lip. "Why don't you come to the library one morning, when we are there with Mother? I—I may have something to show you then."

I rose. "If you advise it, I will."

"Perhaps," he breathed, "there will be no need for Merlin."

Several days later I did as Mordred bade me and joined Morgause in the library as she sat with her boys. Gareth was asleep on the hearth in Cabal's place; Gawaine and Agravaine played a covert tug-of-war with their little fingers, and Gaheris curled at her feet, his head resting against her knee. Mordred sat nearby, rolling a chunk of coal between his fingers, working the coal dust into his flesh. He did not look up when I entered, but they all, well trained by Lancelot and Bedwyr, jumped to their feet.

"Good morning, Queen Morgause," I said pleasantly. "You look well rested. I am glad to see it. You may be seated, boys."

Morgause shrugged gracelessly as I sat and took up a piece of needlework.

"We were talking," she snapped, "about private matters."

"The boys are late for sword practice. Perhaps you should let them go and save the private matters until they are at leisure."

Hope lit Gawaine's face, and his mother saw it.

"First I will tell you of the time your father King Lot defeated Caelric, the Saxon king, single-handed."

"Oh, Mother," Agravaine groaned. "We have heard this tale twenty times before. Mayn't we go to the practice field? We'll be in trouble with Sir Berys and Sir Lamorak if we miss more training."

"Don't you worry about Lamorak." Morgause smiled coyly. "He will do as I tell him. As for Berys, he will follow Lamorak's lead. Now, attend me." Mordred shot me a swift glance, and I understood at once the kind of danger Lamorak was in.

She continued with her story, dressing it up with details that reflected on Lot's glory but that could not possibly be true, when suddenly Mordred rose, white-faced and determined.

"Excuse me, Mother."

Morgause looked up, startled. "What is it, Mordred?"

He bent down to her ear and put a hand up to cover his mouth. He whispered something and as he drew away, his dirty fingers touched her cheek. She turned toward me. I gasped. He had left a dark blot on her cheek, and suddenly I knew that face! The long, green eyes, the clear skin, the dark, ugly mole: Sybil!

Shaking, I rose to my feet, staring. She lifted a hand to her face, realization dawning. At her feet Gaheris turned to look up at her. Gaheris! Gaheris and Sybil! I screamed and covered my mouth with my hand. My stomach heaved; on the verge of sickness, I put out a hand to steady myself and found it grasped by Mordred.

"Mordred!" It was more a curse than a cry. He would not look at her, but led me out, calling to the guard.

"Take the Queen to her quarters. She is ill. I will inform Sir Bedwyr."

"Mordred!" I looked back at him through tears. "Oh, Mordred!"

11 ✲ ТНЕ ΛССUSΛТΙΟΝ

When Bedwyr came to see me he found me pacing around my chamber, cloaked and shivering with cold. He stood awkwardly by the door while Ailsa fussed about with possets and hot cloths.

"Mordred sent for me, my lady. He said you were taken ill, and indeed, you look so. What has happened? What's amiss? Was there a courier while we were in Council?"

I shook my head and beckoned him farther into the room. Behind me the thick leather flap hung across the entrance to the High King's bedchamber; I lifted it and checked to make sure no chamberlain was listening.

Bedwyr approached nervously. "What is it, Gwen? It is the King?"

"No." I sat him upon my stool and paced back and forth before him. "Oh, Bedwyr, I do not know how to tell you. I am afraid you will not believe me. We must imprison Morgause. Now. She has committed a grave sin. For the—for the second time. And she is endangering a child."

"Guinevere, be still a moment. If you accuse her, I will imprison her. But first I must know what she has done."

My hands twisted together as I fought for calm. "She has—she is—she has seduced Gaheris."

His dark eyes slowly widened. "Incest?" he whispered, making the sign against evil as I nodded. "Are you sure?"

"I am not the only one who knows it. Let me tell you what happened while you were gone with the King this summer." I told him the whole tale, from meeting the witch in the forest to recognizing her that morning. I told him all about Grethe and her accusation, and about what Lancelot found when he went to Sybil's house to try to clear his name. I left out only my private interview with Lan-

134

celot, as it was nobody's business but mine; no doubt he heard about that already; no doubt it was already stale barracks gossip.

When I finished, he pursed his lips and nodded thoughtfully. "So it was Lancelot who found them together."

"He told Arthur about it, but of course we did not know she was his mother! As Lancelot had expelled her from the city, he thought the problem solved. Had Arthur known—oh, Bedwyr! When Arthur knows this, he will kill her! And then, think of the stain upon his soul! We must prevent it, at all cost!"

Bedwyr took a cup of warmed wine from Ailsa and bade me sit and drink it. I sat on the edge of my bed, with Ailsa's arm about my shoulders, and tried to calm myself. All I could think of was Arthur's face when he learned the truth.

"Guinevere, attend me. I cannot arrest Morgause."

"What?" I cried. "Why not?"

"You cannot accuse her. You have seen nothing. Lancelot is the only one who has seen them together, and he is not here."

"My God, Bedwyr, do you think Lancelot was lying?"

"No, of course not. But I must be fair. She has the right to face her accuser."

"Would you be fair to a demon? To a witch?"

"Yes," Bedwyr replied sensibly, "even to a witch. And so would you. It is Arthur's way. Think, Gwen, if you have seen anything at all."

"I saw—I saw the boy's tunic on the floor by her bed!"

He shook his head. "Even if you *knew* it to be Gaheris' tunic, and I can see by your face that you do not, it proves nothing. There are a hundred other reasons why it might be there."

"But, Bedwyr, this is true! She is corrupting her own son! We must do whatever we can to spare him! If you don't believe me, ask Mordred—Mordred has known it for a long time. Only, only don't ask him to accuse his mother. He was brave enough to betray her to me, but it was stealthily done. If his brothers find out—you know how they are—his very life could be at risk! We must keep Mordred out of it, but send Morgause away, permanently away, from Camelot!"

We argued about it a long time. I wept and pleaded and demanded, but Bedwyr was adamant. He could take no action until she was formally accused, and the only ones who could accuse her were Lancelot and Mordred. Mordred had already risked a great deal in revealing to me what he had kept from Lancelot; I refused to ask him to do more. When Bedwyr had gone, I stood alone in my room and cried Merlin's name aloud.

"If you hear me, King's Enchanter, take shape and come to me! The Kingdom needs you. *I* need you!"

Merlin might not care much about Gaheris' soul, but he would want to keep Arthur's honor clean. And even though I dreaded meeting the enchanter face to face, I would do anything to free Gaheris from the witch's curse.

Days passed; nothing happened. Merlin did not come, and Morgause's behavior did not change. Mordred's brothers, it seemed, had noticed nothing. I avoided Morgause as much as I could. She was cold to Mordred but when she looked at me she seemed always amused. Finally, I could stand it no longer. I rose early one morning after a sleepless night, determined to face the witch myself and demand to know the truth. I had appealed for help and gotten none. I would see what I could do myself, woman against woman.

Wrapping my cloak about me, I hurried through the cold corridors. We'd had a biting frost the night before, and my angry breaths hung in clouds in the freezing air. I climbed the stairs to her apartments and tapped upon the door. No one answered. Annoyed, I pushed it open; Hadarta slept in the antechamber hard by the grate, snoring loudly, an overturned winecup near her pallet. As I stood there, gathering my courage, the inner door opened, and a shirtless boy backed slowly out.

"Before moonrise," he called softly. "I will come again, Mother. I will bring you a present. Wait until you see." In his hand he held the tunic I had seen on the floor. As he slipped it on he turned and saw me. Gaheris froze. And then, as if in imitation of the witch herself, his green eyes narrowed and his lips slid into a sly smile. He said nothing, but passed by me and went silently out the door.

"Come in, Guinevere," Morgause called, stifling a yawn. "I've been expecting you for days."

She sat amid her rumpled sheets, sleepy and unbrushed. The harsh morning light displayed a thousand lines around her eyes, mouth, and neck; her chin sagged, her full breasts flattened in her shapeless shift, the slack flesh on her inner arms shone sickly white, like a frog's belly. And still she smiled at me.

"Does Arthur know you spy upon his guests? That you are a snoop as well as a coward?" The long eyes narrowed and the hairs stood up upon my arms.

"Leave him alone!" It burst out of me before I knew it. "Leave the child alone! You are corrupt and filthy! As you value your life, Morgause, let him be!"

"But, my pretty pet, he enjoys it so." I gasped. She did not bother to deny it! "There is something about a young boy, so new to love, that I find appealing. And there is nothing a boy will not do to please his mother." She was watching me, and as my disgust progressed to horror, so her amusement grew to contemptuous satisfaction. "He's no Arthur, of course."

"Oh, God!" I cried, flinging my hands to my ears. "Stop it! Have you no compassion in you at all?"

"I show you as much as my dear brother has shown me!" She flung aside the covers and sprang out of bed, pulling on a silken robe of dark green. She glanced in her polished bronze at her reflection, then whipped around and faced me. "You bitch. You have no right to outshine me. I will be revenged on you for that. I will tell you what it was like with Arthur."

"You will not! I will call the guard and have you taken to the tower!"

"On what grounds?"

"You—you have lain with your son!"

"And with my brother. But if you accuse me, I will deny it."

"I saw it!"

"No. You saw a boy leaving his mother's room. What harm is there in that?"

"Oh, God! You cannot, you *will* not go free!"

"No?" She smiled again and took a comb to her hair. "I will do just exactly as I please. If you accuse me, I will tell them what a little whore you are. I will name names."

"That is a lie!"

"So? Lies have ruined reputations before now. And they are hard to disprove. There will always be doubts. And be sure I will bring Arthur's shame to light. What a fine, strong youth he was! So eager and so proud. I was his first woman, did he tell you?"

"Of course not! He hates the very—"

"Fresh from his first victory he came to me, all fire and hot breath. He knew nothing."

"My God, have you no shame?"

"None." She picked up a jar of scented balm and began to rub the cream into her skin. Magically, the lines began to disappear. "He was a pleasure to teach, I will say that for him. And he learned well, did he not? Does he please you with those beautiful hands of his?"

"Don't, I pray you! How can you?"

She leaned closer and whispered. "Every time he touches you, my pet, think of me."

"No! Oh, no!" I found myself sobbing into my hands, I, who had come so bravely to her door not half an hour before! Was it witchcraft, or had I just been naive about the depth of cruelty a woman's heart could hold? I wiped away my tears and faced her. "You do not deny, then, Gaheris has shared your bed?"

"Not to you. It amuses me to confess it."

"For this you deserve death."

She shrugged. "In your narrow Christian eyes, perhaps. But none of you can kill me. I do not fear you."

"I will have you imprisoned."

"You can try. Come, Guinevere, I am tiring of this game. You have voiced your outrage. Now go back to bed."

"I will not! Guards! Guards!"

Morgause began to laugh. "You will not even awaken Hadarta, much less rouse a guard."

"What have you done to her? Drugged her wine, I suppose?"

"Clever girl."

"That is enough, Morgause. You are evil, and I will see you put away."

"Will you, indeed? We shall soon see, my sweet, which of us is more powerful. It's been clear for more than a month now, there is room for only one Queen in Camelot."

I gasped at her audacity. "How dare you! And *you* call *me* a bitch! I'll see you flogged!"

"You shallow, empty-headed fool! I'll make mincemeat of you, and *then* see how my brother likes you! I will serve him well for leaving me to rot on that sea-swept rock!"

"Ladies! Ladies!" cried a male voice from the doorway. "What's all this fuss?" Lamorak walked in, looking from one to the other of us in consternation. "My lady Queen, Sir Bedwyr is looking for you. Whatever are you doing here?"

"I have come to lay a charge against Queen Morgause. Take her in hand, Lamorak, and call the guards. I will not stir from this chamber until she is imprisoned."

"What's this? Why, what has she done?"

I hesitated to tell him, until I saw the smirk on Morgause's face.

"The charge is incest. Corrupting a child. One of her own sons."

"What!"

He turned to her, and the face she lifted to him was so totally changed, so full of charm and hurt innocence, I pinched myself to be sure I was not dreaming.

"Good Lamorak, I fear the Queen is ill. Her long barrenness has affected her wits at last." I gasped as I saw the line she meant to take. What a gift she had for finding the sorest spot and plunging the knife straight in! "She burst in upon me this morning, unannounced, and started raving at me. She has got this wild idea about my bedding a boy. No doubt these are her own secret dreams she turns upon me."

"How can you deny it?" I cried. "I saw him here with you!"

"Begging your pardon, my lady, but you did not. There was no one here for her to see, Lamorak. It is absurd and disgusting. What would a grown woman want with an untried boy? Men, experienced men, are much more to my taste."

She sidled up against him and looked up at him with sultry eyes. Lamorak's breathing quickened as he gazed down at her, and his hand slipped stealthily inside her robe. In another moment they would be asking me to leave. I groaned in exasperation. Was there no man in the castle proof against her? On the thought, Bedwyr came through the door.

"Queen Guinevere! There you are!"

"Bedwyr! Arrest her! I charge her now!"

He looked at Morgause and then at Lamorak, who stood beside her, hands at his side. "Well?"

"I deny it," Morgause said proudly. "It is ridiculous. It is beneath me."

Bedwyr grunted. "It was not beneath you once. Lamorak?"

"Uh, my lord, I was passing by and heard words between them, and so came in. I know nothing about it, really. Except I cannot believe—"

"What you believe does not matter. Go downstairs and tell Prince Mordred—"

"Mordred?" Morgause spoke sharply. For the first time I detected a hint of fear. "Where is he? I wish to speak with him."

"Tell Prince Mordred to await me in the Council chamber," Bedwyr finished. Lamorak saluted, bowed to us, and left.

"Where is he?" she repeated.

Bedwyr hesitated a moment before answering and noted the change in her composure. "He was belowstairs as I came by, looking for the Queen, and detained me when I tried to come up."

"If he is still there, bid him come and see me. I have something of importance to tell him."

Bedwyr looked at me.

"He was here when I came to the door, Bedwyr," I whispered. "He was in her chamber. Half dressed. She in a shift, and his smell upon her. At dawn. What more do you need?"

"I deny it!" Morgause spat, seeing Bedwyr's face.

"And sneaked away, no doubt, the coward. You should see him, Guinevere, when blood is spilled, the lily-livered—"

"Silence!" screamed Morgause. "He is not a coward!"

"Indeed?" Bedwyr retorted, his eyes lighting. "Why, he's worse than his twin, who cannot stomach—"

"I'll have you know that Agravaine has killed three men barehanded!" She caught her breath, but too late. Bedwyr was smiling.

"So we are agreed," he said softly, "that we are speaking of Gaheris."

Trapped by her own tongue, Morgause went still. Bedwyr grasped her arm and turned to me. "Mordred did not know you were here, my lady. But he thought Gaheris was. That's why he tried to keep me away."

I exhaled in relief. "So. You believe."

Bedwyr's face went cold. He held Morgause well away from him, as though she were a viper. "Oh, yes," he said. "I believe."

Morgause stiffened. "You will regret the day you crossed me, both of you."

Bedwyr sighed from the depths of his soul. "I regret the day I ever laid eyes on you, Witch of Orkney."

Morgause lay that night in the tower cell and the next day was brought before the Council. I expected her sons to be outraged, but although they frowned and wore long faces, they said nothing. They knew, all of them, the charge was true, and they were torn between anger at their mother's imprisonment and shame for her behavior. Bedwyr had confronted Mordred, who told him the truth of what he knew. But Mordred did not want to speak publicly against his mother. Where he had grown up, the queen did as she pleased, no questions asked, and he did not see why we could not imprison or exile her if we willed. But Bedwyr was worried. It all depended, he said, on whether the Companions could be brought to believe the charges. Most of them thought well of women; none of them would want to believe such evil of Arthur's sister.

Morgause sat in the Chair of Complaint, composed and lovely. Lamorak was not her only admirer at the Round Table. As her chief accuser, I sat at Bedwyr's right hand. The High King's chair, below the Sword Excalibur in its embroidered hanger, remained empty.

Bedwyr got straight to the point. He laid the charge of incest against Morgause and named me as her accuser. The Companions stirred, shocked. Bedwyr then told them what Lancelot had witnessed that summer; had we known then Gaheris' seductress was his mother, she would have been brought before both Lancelot and Arthur and made to answer for it. At this, the Companions frowned and shifted in their seats. If Lancelot had seen it, it was true. There was much discussion between them. Finally, one of them asked who was present when Lancelot revealed what he had seen between the woman and Gaheris. After a quick glance at me, Bedwyr told them: the High Queen and Mordred. There was a small silence. Then Lamorak rose.

"I mean no offense to the High Queen, Sir Bedwyr, but may we not hear from Prince Mordred, as well? Where Lancelot is concerned, we feel, uh, his memory might be more dispassionate, and thus clearer."

I flushed, but held on to my temper. I would have liked to believe Morgause had put him up to that, but it was something any one of them might have said. What was between me and Lancelot had never been a secret. He had said it as delicately as he could, and God knows, there was truth in it.

Sir Bleoberys then stood. "May we not hear from Prince Gaheris, as well? He is accused, as well as his mother."

"He is a child!" I cried. "You cannot ask him to accuse his mother to her face!"

"But my lady Queen," Berys said politely, "are we not asking that of Prince Mordred?"

I shot Bedwyr a desperate glance. "We are only asking Mordred for confirmation of what Lancelot told me in his hearing, are we not?"

Bedwyr nodded and signaled the guard. "Send for Prince Mordred only."

He was not far away and came at once. Plainly dressed and holding himself straight and tall, he looked so much like his father, it was almost like having Arthur in the room. In answer to Bedwyr's question, he confirmed what Lancelot had said. He did not tell them he had refused to believe it. But when Bedwyr dismissed him, Queen Morgause rose.

"Please allow my son to stay." They were the first words she had spoken, and all heads turned toward her. "You have allowed him to hear the accusation against me. I demand he be allowed to hear my reply."

Bedwyr nodded and motioned Mordred to one of the empty chairs. "Very well. What do you say in your defense, Queen Morgause?"

She stood easily and surveyed the gathering with contempt. Richly dressed and hung with ornaments, the silver crown of Orkney with its milk-white stones upon her brow, she was as high-born as every man in that room, and she wanted them to know it.

"My lords. Queen Guinevere. I am wrongly accused of a foul act. I am as innocent as any one of you. Not only do I deny the charges, I am ashamed of you for bringing them against me. I am heartily ashamed. You demean yourselves to even think it. But, my lords, the cause is clear enough. This summer, I gave Sir Lancelot cause to hate me, and we all know, my lords, what that can lead to. No one has a stronger advocate anywhere on earth than Sir Lancelot has in Queen Guinevere." She curtsied prettily in my direction; heads turned; I held hard to the arms of my chair and returned her stony stare. "I pray you, my lords, never say a word against his stainless honor, else you find yourselves in my position."

"What did he do?" whispered one of the Companions.

Bedwyr frowned. "Silence. We are not gathered to accuse Lancelot. Answer the charge, Queen Morgause. The High Queen claims she found Gaheris in your bedroom, half dressed, at dawn. What say you to that?"

"She is lying." She met their eyes, one by one, except for Mordred. "I deny it absolutely. Gaheris is my son. What she suggests is disgusting."

The men nodded, frowned, and murmured.

"Nevertheless," I said firmly, "he was there. Pulling on the tunic he had left on the floor by your bed days before. Setting a tryst for moonrise, promising to bring you a gift. He was closer to me than you are now."

Morgause's lips slid into a smile. "You have been snooping in my chamber, my lady Queen? What is this obsession you have with children? Is it because you are unable to bear any of your own?"

I shut my eyes and drew a deep breath. At least I had seen it coming. She had given me fair warning the day before.

"My lords, have pity on the Queen. Think what she has suffered, unable to bear my brother the King a son. Imagine how it preys upon her mind, day and night, year in, year out, as all about her women conceive and bear. Yet she cannot grow the High King's seed." Against my will, tears crept from my eyes and slowly fell, in long, wet tracks, down my cheeks. Morgause lowered her voice. "Poor woman in a girl's body," she said sweetly, "her barrenness has turned her wits. All she thinks about is children. They must haunt her very dreams. I think, my lords, that this must be how it happened: Still dreamstruck, she came to me and accused me of something she had imagined while she slept. I can find no other explanation. But I forgive her; I would not trade places with her for all the world." She paused. I could not open my eyes. Did they all think me dreamstruck? Did they all think this an answer to the charge? "My lords, is the Queen the only accuser you can find?"

There was silence. Bedwyr cleared his throat. Suddenly a chair scraped against the flooring, and Mordred's voice rang out calm and clear. "No. I accuse you, also, Mother."

I looked up. Arthur's son stood straight, his fists upon the table, and faced the witch. She stared at him, open-mouthed.

"My mother has lain with my brother since before we left Orkney." The men gasped, aghast. "At first I only suspected some intrigue. And even when Gaheris hinted at it—"

"He never did!" she cried, trembling.

"—I thought it was a twisted kind of boasting. He has always needed her affection more than any of the rest of us." He looked around at the men, sad and determined. "But when Lancelot told me what he had seen, I knew it was the truth. All the things I had seen before finally made sense. I knew she would return as soon as the High King left with Lancelot. And when she returned, I kept a watch upon her."

"Dragon's spawn!" she hissed, leaning toward him.

"For Gaheris' sake, I have tried to keep him from discovery. I failed in that. But sooner or later it had to come to light." He looked directly at her. "You knew that, surely. You knew it, and you did not care. You don't much care what becomes of Gaheris."

Her eyes were slits; the look in them made me quail, but Mordred stood fast. "No, you bastard whelp, but I care what happens to *you*! And you will never escape me, Mordred. I have known your fate from the moment of your conception."

"I don't care."

"How like him you are, to turn against me! You will be revenged for that, I do assure you."

"I don't care."

"Brave words, from one who is powerless to prevent disaster! Be certain I will—"

"My lords!" I rose and found my voice. "You have heard the accusation. Will you come to a decision, or must we listen to more of this hateful woman's spite?"

Amid her ranting, the men decided on imprisonment, but away from Camelot, someplace where her sons could not see her except by the High King's leave. They settled on a stronghold in the south, not far from the Winchester garrison. Castle Daure, later known as Castle Dour on account of her temper, was a strong fortress near Saxon lands, held by one Arres, a graybeard king who owed to Arthur the keeping of his kingdom. Until the courier was sent and preparations made, she would be held in the tower.

I took Mordred aside and thanked him for my rescue. Pale and contained, he merely nodded and kissed my hand. Morgause screamed at the sight of it, and as the guards took hold of her, she flew into a rage.

"Bitch!" she snarled. "You two-faced bitch! You barren whore!" Conversation died; men turned; she flung off the grip of her captors. "Cowards! You are all cowards! I curse your children, and all the generations of your descent!"

"Guards!" Bedwyr said sharply. "Hold her. Bind her if you have to." One of them drew forth a length of rope.

Morgause stamped her foot and writhed and swore vengeance upon them all, but they ignored her and bound her fast.

Suddenly she grew calm. "Go ahead, brave men, and bind a woman's flesh. You think that gives you power over me. But you will do my bidding in the end. Guinevere!" She leaned toward me; against my will I shrank back. "Do not think you have beaten me. Do you imagine any fortress in Britain is strong enough to hold me?" She smiled; my innards turned to water. "And those boys of mine whose service Arthur covets, and whose minds you are trying to recast—remember this: They are *my* sons, all of them, and they will never be yours. Not one of them." Her eyes slid to Mordred; I seemed suddenly unable to breathe. "I have sown the seeds of my revenge in them, though they know it not. You cannot remake them. It is already too late." She began to laugh, an ugly sound, full of hate and satisfaction. "Arthur will live to rue the day he sent me into exile!"

"That's quite enough," Bedwyr commanded.

"Silence!" she cried, and froze him with a look. The men went still. The very air began to waver. The spell she wove ensnared the will of soldier, Queen, and prince alike.

"I will destroy my brother. Like Queen Medea, I have brought my enemy a gift that will be his death. He has accepted it; his fate is now out of his hands." I shuddered. I saw it pleased her. "But you, Guinevere, I have already destroyed. Attend and hear your fate. The Great Goddess, who gives life, who takes it and withholds it, listens to my entreaties. You are barren as a mule, and it is *my* doing, it has always been *my* doing! I have sacrificed to the dark moon, in the black pool, every month since you married my brother! It is a powerful enchantment. Because of me, little child queen, the only son you will ever give to Arthur is a son of mine!"

A scream pierced the air. High and wild, it shattered the light and plummeted into nightmare blackness, enveloped by the rotten breath of evil. Pain struck my head; my throat rasped raw—it was my scream, my hate, my terror that lay stretched out on the cold stone floor.

Bedwyr's face swam above me; the witch's high-pitched laughter tore at my wits. "You fools who worship the ground Arthur walks on! He is not the saint you think him! The very crime you accuse me of—" Another scream, was it mine or hers? The door flew open, a great wind rushed in, the cold dark was upon us. Strong hands lifted me and set me in my chair. All the men huddled in the corner, Bedwyr included, hands before their faces, making the sign against enchantment. Across the Round Table, Morgause stood alone, eyes wide with terror, one fist pressed hard against her mouth, one hand held out to ward off a blow. Slowly the faintness passed, and I saw clearly.

Merlin stood before Arthur's chair, black-robed, white-bearded, his flesh seamed with a thousand wrinkles, his eyes as bright as black water. He stared at the witch, and she seemed to shrink even as we watched.

"You!" She gasped, fighting for breath. "You are dead!"

"Yes," he said.

She bit off a cry of terror and collapsed into her seat.

Merlin lifted a long finger and pointed it at her. "I seal your lips upon Arthur. You will say naught against him. Nor against the Queen."

Her eyes widened, but she did not open her mouth.

"The Goddess deserts you. From this moment on, the only power you command will be such as any woman of your age and birth commands." He glanced at the Companions and beckoned them forward. "Take her away and do not fear her any longer. Whatever prison you take her to, there will she stay. I myself will see to it."

Bedwyr bowed. Morgause whimpered. But she was not without courage. "Are you real, Merlin? Or a phantom? Come here and let me touch you."

Something moved behind his eyes. "As real as your shadow, Morgause, which you are never without."

"Except in darkness."

"And where is your shadow in darkness, but lying in wait for the light? It is there, though you cannot see it."

Morgause gasped. "I don't believe you can do it! Wh-What are you? A spirit or a man?"

He lifted his hands, and his black robe spread like wings. "I am Arthur's servant. And you are his enemy. Like Medea, you are cast out, and will not accept your fate. And like Medea, you will be taken away."

"I will tell—" she began, and then her lips froze, though she stamped her foot in anger. At last she spat at him. "Do your worst, then, King's enchanter. Given time, I shall find your weakness and make you pay!"

Merlin signaled to the guards. "Take her away. Go on. It is safe. Though you do not see me with you, I am there, and will protect you from her."

Morgause was led away without a word of complaint. The Companions, tongue-tied and staring, mumbled their thanks to Merlin and filed out. At last only Bedwyr and I remained.

Merlin turned to me and spoke kindly. "You have acted bravely, Guinevere. You have no more need to fear her. Her power is gone."

But for the cold that encased him like a second skin, he seemed the same Merlin I had known, and feared, before.

"Thank you, my lord. I—I am grateful for your coming. I had no defense against her."

He smiled kindly. "You have more than you believe. No one here believed her words but you, my dear, not even Morgause. But for Arthur's sake, as well as yours, I could not let her continue."

"My lord—" I paused, trying to brave the question that had knocked against my lips since first he spoke. "My lord, if—if she has lost her power, does that mean, could that mean, I—I—I could bear to Arthur?"

He took both my hands in his. His grip was warm, real, and brought me comfort, but I knew by the gesture what he was about to say.

"She lied, my dear, when she claimed to have caused your fate. It was an empty, vicious boast. She is no more responsible for your barrenness than you are. Courage, Guinevere. We have spoken of this before."

"Yes, my lord. You told me it would grieve me more than it ever grieves the King. And so it does."

"There is a reason for it."

I looked up. "So Bedwyr told me. But—may I ask you? Is it true?"

Merlin nodded. The great cold that had come in with him seemed to warm as he spoke. "Arthur will live in glory everlasting, as long as men are alive to tell his tale. And that will be in no small part your doing, Guinevere, because he has no son to share it with."

"But, my lord," I said quickly, "he has Mordred."

Merlin froze. The room grew frigid; the air itself turned to ice; a dark cloud took shape around him and from its depths I heard his frosty whisper: "Mordred the Bastard! May his name be cursed forever!" With a sound like a whip-crack, the ice broke, the mist thinned, and he was gone!

I jumped and looked at Bedwyr. His face was white.

"Bedwyr! Am I dreaming?"

He shook his head. "If you are, then I am, too."

"Where did he go? What did I say? Why should the mention of Mordred send him away?"

Bedwyr's hand shook as he reached out to me. "Being merely a mortal man, I cannot say. Ask Mordred what there is between them. He ducked out the moment the enchanter swept into the room. Out that window." He pointed to a window behind the table that gave onto the courtyard.

"He has never seen Merlin before! Why was he afraid?"

Bedwyr shrugged. "I don't know. Why is anyone afraid? Ask Mordred. Come, Gwen, you are tired and in need of rest. And I am, too. In a week we go to Caerleon, and the witch to Castle Daure. There are a thousand preparations, and not much time."

12 ⚙ the prophecy

Three days before we left, Morgause sent to me begging an audience with Mordred. She did not ask to see any of her other sons. I called Mordred to me and asked him if he wished to see her.

He shrugged. "I suppose so, my lady. I know there is something she wants to tell me."

"It is probably something you do not wish to hear. She cannot be pleased with you, Mordred. She must look upon your words in Council as betrayal."

He lifted his eyes to mine and spoke like Arthur's son. "Nevertheless, I will hear her. She can say no word against the King, or against you, either. And as for me, well"—he shrugged again—"she is the one who forced me to choose between her and my father. Attacking Lancelot is one thing: He is a man and can defend himself against her, as he proved. But Gaheris—Gaheris is a child." He shifted uncomfortably. "She enjoys inflicting pain. This is not news. But if she expected loyalty, she should not have let me meet my father. Now I know, as I never knew before, what worship is."

"Ahhhh, Mordred." I reached out a hand to him.

"She cannot hurt me more, my lady. She knows I have cast my lot with Arthur. If she wants to scream at me, let her scream."

"You are a brave man." He smiled at the appellation. "Before I let you go, I will make one request."

"Anything, my lady. Ask it."

"If, in your judgment, what she tells you will affect the King, or the Kingdom, I would like to know of it."

"Of course, my lady. If it concerns the King, it is your right to know. And my lord Bedwyr."

"That depends on what it is. You must use your judgment."

"I will tell you everything, my lady Queen, I promise it."

I smiled at his ardor. "You have been so brave, Mordred, and I owe you so much. If you will take me into your confidence, I would be in your debt." He rose to go. "Mordred." The question came out without my willing. "Why did you run from Merlin?"

His eyes grew wide and he shivered. "My lady, I do not know."

He went to see Morgause and did not come back.

I paced about in a fever of impatience. Something must have happened. A fine, cold rain had soaked the ground and made it muddy. It was not a day for riding or walking out; I sat in my rooms and stitched with my women. It was never a thing that brought me comfort.

I expected Mordred to come to me after dinner, but he did not. When I sent for him, they told me he had gone to bed early. I sent for Berys, who commanded his barracks.

"Have you seen Mordred?" I asked him. "How does he?"

"Well enough, my lady. Only—"

"Yes?"

"He suffers from a heaviness of spirit. He went to bed early and asked not to be disturbed. He told me he would pay you his respects tomorrow."

With that, I had to be content. But on the morrow, he avoided the castle and kept to the barracks. Gareth came in at midday for his lessons, but Mordred was not with him. At last I sent for him, only to be told he had ridden out alone at midmorning for Avalon. Nervously I awaited his return. Niniane was there. So something *had* happened. Whatever it was, it had distressed him to the point of seeking advice from the enchantress he so disliked.

The day was cold and dark clouds hung heavy over Caer Camel. But it did not rain until we were in hall, and then the skies opened. We seemed a melancholy group at dinner. So many were gone from our company; the King's chair was empty. And Mordred kept away.

Finally, when Bedwyr, Kay, and I had gathered in the library, I could stand it no longer.

"My lord Kay," I said, making him a reverence, "the Queen's compliments to Prince Mordred. If he is in Camelot, I would like a word with him."

He look surprised. "Shall I bring him here, my lady?"

"At once."

When he was gone, Bedwyr went to stoke the fire. He set the wineskin near it and then turned. "There's something amiss, isn't there, Gwen? May I know what it is?"

"I don't know myself yet, Bedwyr. But I fear it."

"The boy has been unhappy, Berys tells me. He doesn't eat, and he doesn't sleep. He is afraid of something. Do you know what?"

"No. But I hope to find out."

"He rode out this morning for Avalon."

I shrugged. "He must be back by now. In this rotten weather, where else could he go? Besides, he has made me a promise, and I know Mordred. He will keep it."

On the thought, the door opened, and Mordred came in. His face was pale, but he held himself straight. There were shadows under his eyes. He bowed politely. "My lady Queen Guinevere. I am at your service."

"I expected you before this, Mordred."

His face was stone, but something moved in his dark eyes. "I beg your pardon, my lady. I had matters to attend to. I could not come."

I saw then that he would not speak except in private. I turned to Bedwyr and Kay. "My lords, I would have a word with him alone."

Kay did not like it, but could not say so, as Bedwyr moved at once to go. I motioned Mordred to a seat before the fire and poured him a goblet of warmed wine. As soon as we were alone, he started to shiver.

"Drink this," I said gently. "Say nothing yet." I could see that he was more than frightened; he was moved to his very soul by fear. He sipped the wine and stared moodily into the flames.

"I would rather not tell you, my lady," he said suddenly. "And you, you would rather not know."

"But you have promised, Mordred."

He nodded slowly. "All right. But I warn you, I have seen the lady Niniane. And I have spoken to Merlin. There is nothing to be done."

"You spoke to Merlin?"

I watched his hands grip the goblet, Arthur's hands, strong hands. They were shaking.

"My mother, the queen Morgause," he began, forcing himself to it, "told me she was pleased the King had taken me into his household, and confided in me, and trusted me. She was pleased, she said, to see you so attached to me, and the trust that had grown between us. That surprised me. And then she told me why." He paused and drained the winecup. He turned to face me, then, with that direct look of Arthur's that searched the heart. "It was her plan from the beginning. From before my birth she has raised me to be his undoing. She was pleased because in accepting me, he has donned a garment that will kill him. Those were her words."

I stared. The flames in the grate snapped loudly. Mordred hardly breathed.

"She told me she conceived me because she knew I would be his doom, and she has always hated him. She kept me carefully hidden, and tended, and when Lot died, brought to her, and then sent to Arthur, so that I could be the—the certain instrument of his death."

I gasped. There were tears in his eyes, and in mine. "How?" I whispered. "Oh, Mordred, this cannot be true!"

"She told me she had seen it in the fire, in the stars, in the crystal. But she is nothing if not a liar. She told me also Merlin had seen it. That was why I went to Niniane."

I waited, holding my breath. The future trembled in the silence.

He looked away. "It is true, Guinevere. It is a thing known by those who have the gift of Sight. Arthur's bane, Niniane herself called me. Somehow, someday, whether I will or no, he shall die because of me."

I shot to my feet. "No! You would not kill him! These things cannot happen without men's wills!"

"I would not harm a hair on his head," Mordred whispered. "I demanded to see Merlin. Niniane told me how to find him. She sent me to a wood atop a hill in Avalon as the mists were rising. She gave me the words to say, that would call him forth." He grimaced suddenly. "I felt like a fishwife, spouting charms against the weather!" He ran a hand through his hair, then steadied himself. "You see, like you, I could not accept it. Somehow, I had to make the Seeing false. I was sure that if anyone could break the curse, it would be Merlin. Everyone knows, pagan and Christian alike, there is no one more powerful in all of Britain. So I called him forth out of the mists." He gulped suddenly, and I knew well what courage that had taken.

"He came at once," he said in a shaking voice. "In a spectral shape, shrouded in mist. I—I thought he was a haunting!" He shivered. "It was freezing all around him! And then, as he stepped forth out of the mist into solid flesh, the thunder cracked, and the sky grew dark all around. He was wrapped in a black cloak. All I could see of him were his ancient face and his eyes of ice. How he hates me, Guinevere! I have never met such hate, face to face. I shook so hard I could barely speak."

I took his hand and held his cold fingers tight between my own. And in my heart I cursed Merlin for deliberately frightening the boy. He was Arthur's son!

Mordred stared down at the floor and spoke woodenly, forcing it out. "I told him I loved my father, and on my life I would not harm him. But he said it mattered not what I did or felt. My existence was all that mattered. On the day of my birth, Arthur's fate was sealed. Simply by living I am a danger to him."

I cried aloud, remembering Lancelot's words: The boy was dangerous! And Morgause's threat—here was Medea's gift! Mordred himself! I turned away from him, hugging my arms about me, holding on.

"He said there was a time for everything: good and ill, joy and sorrow, glory and shame, the doing of right and the doing of evil. As Arthur had been begotten in the Light, so I was begotten in the Dark. As Arthur was destined for glory and greatness, so I was destined to bring it to an end. Nothing lasts forever. If I was wise, he said, I would think no more of it than that."

"Oh, Mordred! How cruel! That cannot be all he said!"

"He looked at me as if he would like to watch me burn alive."

Mordred slowly raised his eyes to me, black and full of grief. "I told him to kill me, I offered him my sword."

"No!"

"He refused, saying he would not wound Arthur so. Neither would I, I cried. I was angry, angry at Merlin, and angry at the fates, which could treat a man so unfairly. What had I done? I asked him, to be so condemned before my birth?"

I stood before him, trembling. "What did he say?"

Mordred paused. "The lightning flashed as bright as daylight, and the thunder cracked so near, I jumped. For a moment I could not see him, and I thought he had disappeared. But he was standing looking up into the sky. He was silent a long time. Then he spread his arms, and the wind, which had been gusting, suddenly died. It was not my fault, he said. It had been written in the stars before ever I was born, that Arthur's bane should be the son he begot upon his sister." Mordred turned his head away, and I felt myself begin to burn with anger. He had never been ashamed of it before!

"He is only shifting blame from his own shoulders!" I cried. "It was *his* fault, if it was anyone's! Merlin, the all-powerful magician! He was nearby the night Arthur lay with her. Arthur did not know Morgause was his sister, but Merlin did! Ahhh, Mordred, it is not you he hates, but himself! This explains why he cannot abide you near him, even for Arthur's sake. He feels guilty—as well he should—but will not admit it!"

Mordred looked at me a long moment and then shrugged. "So you, too, my lady," he said softly, "agree I should never have been born." He half smiled as I gasped. "No matter. I think the same. I would rather not have been born at all than be born to kill such a man as Arthur."

"Oh, Mordred, that is not what I meant!" I knelt at his feet and clutched his hands. "You know I am a Christian and it is a grievous sin. But it is Arthur's sin, my dear, not yours."

He smiled sadly. "It is no one's fault. Perhaps Merlin was right. But it isn't fair. Even Merlin must see that it isn't fair. I begged him to release me from my fate. Surely, I said, if he loved Arthur, he would do it." His face grew grim. "If he would not, I threatened to slay myself, to save my father."

"Oh, Mordred, you would not! It would kill Arthur more surely than a swordstroke!"

Mordred shrugged. "He said he could not release me. It was not within his power. Arthur had committed a heinous sin and must pay the price. Nothing he could do, or I could do, would change that. Even my death would not change it now; it would only bring Arthur grief he might be spared."

"Had he—had he no solace to offer you at all?"

"He told me I would be King." I held my breath; Mordred's smile was bitter. "I replied I would sooner die at Arthur's death than succeed him. He smiled, then, and told me to be careful what I wished for." His hand formed a fist, and his jaw tightened. "I told him I hoped Lluden of the Underworld imprisoned him in chains forever! I told him I hoped he roasted long in Hell! Enchanters are nothing but meddlers!" With an effort, he calmed himself and drew a deep breath. "He said one thing more before he went back into the mist and the rains began. Guess what it was."

"I'm sure I cannot," I breathed.

" *'Take what comes and live without complaint. What will be, will be. Life is woman's gift; death is God's.' "*

This timeworn commonplace was known as Merlin's litany, so often had it fallen from his lips. There was not a child in Britain who did not know it. And this was all the comfort Merlin could offer Arthur's son!

"Oh, my God, my God!" I bent my head, weeping. "How can it happen without your will?"

"I don't know. But it will. I will be the cause of it, somehow. I would never raise a hand against him, but just by having been born, I will be his death. Oh, the gods are unjust!" he cried suddenly, and buried his face in his hands.

I rose and sat beside him, and cradled his head in my arms. When we both were calmer, I said, "The King knows."

He nodded. "Yes. I know he knows. I remember now the times he has recalled it, when he was with me. I remember how the light left his face. And guess who told him! Merlin, of course." He clenched his fist. "He was only a little older than I when he learned it—that his own half sister carried his child, who would one day be his death! Can you imagine it? He should have killed her before she bore me! I should never have been born! How has he managed to be the man he is, knowing this?"

He rose suddenly and began to pace the room. I could not watch, he reminded me so of Arthur.

"The King knows, yet he took me in," he said fiercely. "Not only took me in, but searched for me. Educated me. Trained me. Trusted me. He has done me nothing but honor. And for what? That I should reward him by bringing him his death? *I will not do it!*"

He tore at his hair and then stopped, willing himself to stillness.

"I have made a vow." His voice was quiet again, but deadly serious. "I have vowed I will not outlive him. No one, *no one*, will be able to accuse me of that ambition."

I knew he referred to Lancelot. But before I drew breath to defend him, Mordred came and knelt before me. He looked suddenly young and lost.

"Why did he do it, my lady? Why did he take me in, knowing I am his fate? Can any man be that brave? Or is it that he would rather see his death approaching than wait, unknowing, for the blow?"

"I do not think it was bravery so much as love," I said gently, taking his hands. "He would do what is right by you, whatever the outcome."

He nodded, swallowing. "I will do the same by him. I will serve him with my life. If this—cruel injustice cannot be averted, at least I can show him that by my will I love and honor him."

I stroked his hair, and he laid his head in my lap. So Bedwyr found us when he came in later, in a pose of love, with tears on our faces.

Two days later the court moved to Caerleon for Christmas, and Queen Morgause left for Castle Daure. Arthur had wanted to be home by Christmas, but storms had closed the seas, and we had no word. We went about our business, Mordred and I, as if nothing were amiss. He was resolved upon his course of action, of loyal service until death, and in an odd way this had calmed him and matured him. I was the one who could not sleep at night, haunted by bad dreams and ghostly voices. Merlin was wise to stay clear of me, for I was eager to give him a piece of my mind. Rumors drifted in that he had been seen near his precious cave in South Wales. I determined to ride there and face him, but was prevented from going by a snowstorm. The storm became a blizzard and kept us penned within doors. I thought some days I should scream in frustration.

"Oh, Arthur!" I cried alone at night. "Come home and take this burden from me!"

Bedwyr was my only solace. If he knew of the dreadful prophecy, he did not show it. He was calm, and kind, and wise. If he was puzzled by my moodiness and outbursts of anger, he did not reproach me, but put it down to womanly weakness, or loneliness for the King.

Christmas, the King's birthday, the feast of Mithra, passed without word from the King. And then at last the weather broke, and we had two weeks of thaw. I rode out every day, on Pallas if I wanted a long gallop, on Rajid if I needed a challenge to my skill. Bedwyr became worried and spoke to me thrice about not risking my neck while under his protection.

"I am pursued by enchanters!" I retorted. It was the only clue he had to what was wrong.

The day the King returned I was out riding. Berys was the leader of the escort, and although I had led him leagues from Caerleon, he followed meekly and let me have my way. I was well paid for such foolishness, for on the way home his horse threw a shoe, and we went at a walk all the way. It was well after dark when we reached the fortress. The sentries met us with evident relief.

"The King is back and wants to see the Queen!" they cried in greeting.

Berys swore under his breath. "Just my luck, by Mithra! Now I am for it!"

"The fault is mine," I told him. "Don't worry about the King. He knows me."

He grinned, and I realized suddenly it was the first time in a month I had made anyone smile.

I hurried to my quarters and found Ailsa ready with my bath. From her chatter I gathered that the King had returned at midday and had been closeted all afternoon with Bedwyr, Gawaine, and Mordred. Thank goodness he had learned from other lips of Morgause's crime and imprisonment, although with Gawaine there he would learn little enough of the details. How far away that trouble seemed to me now! How swiftly had my worry over the corruption of Gaheris been swallowed up by my fear for Mordred! How much had happened—and all of it dreadful!—since Arthur had left Britain!

The King took his dinner in his rooms, still in conference. Ailsa brought me some bread and soup, but I could eat none of it. I did not want to greet the King in public. I was not sure I could trust my tongue. So in spite of Arthur's orders that I was to be brought to him as soon as I was ready, I waited until the page reported that Mordred and Gawaine had gone.

He was in his sitting room with Bedwyr, standing before the fire. I avoided looking at his face and curtsied at his feet.

"Welcome home, my lord." I tried to hide my agitation, but of course he saw it. When he took my hands to rise me, his grip was firm. As always, I felt calm and warmth and strength flow from him, and I looked up in desperation. "Oh, my lord!" He embraced me then and held me close while I struggled against tears.

"I know what it is, Gwen. Go ahead, let it out," he said softly, and at long last I let go and sobbed like a child in his arms.

"It is not fair!" I cried against his breast. "Oh, Arthur! God could not be so cruel!" He held me until my weeping subsided and pressed a cool cloth gently to my brow. Bedwyr handed him a cup of scented wine, which he put to my lips and bade me drink. I felt dizzy with so many tears and collapsed into the chair. Arthur sat across from me, holding my hands. Bedwyr stood gazing at the flames.

"Oh, my lord! This is a terrible thing! I shall go mad unless you help me! Has—has Mordred spoken with you? Does Bedwyr know?"

He answered me calmly. "Mordred has made his report, and Gawaine his. And Bedwyr has told me what they could not. I know all about Morgause and your bravery on behalf of Gaheris. Thank you, Gwen. No one else I know would willingly face my sister. Including me." He paused. "I have approved the Council's actions."

"My lord, I do not mean the trouble with Gaheris!"

"I know, my dear." He touched his lips to my hand. "About the prophecy that worries you—no, Mordred did not speak of it. And yes, Bedwyr knows. I have just now told him of it." He paused, frowning. "I wish you had shared it with him, Gwen, and saved yourself such suffering. You are naught but skin and bone and sorrow. He tells me you have had no rest for weeks. It is no wonder you are ill."

"It was not my secret to share," I whispered. "Oh, Arthur! Tell me it is not true! Niniane would not come to me, and I would have gone to Merlin, but—"

He smiled, a shadow of his grin. "There was a timely snowstorm. Yes. And now you see why Merlin has avoided Camelot and comes to me only in private. He cannot bear the sight of Mordred, although for my sake, he does not say so."

I shuddered. "If Merlin loved you, Arthur, he would never have told you this!"

He sighed. "I know this is hard, Gwen. It was hard for me once, too. That's why I never told you myself. But what is it, after all? Just an event foreseen. Knowing or not knowing will not change it; all it will do is bring joy or pain to those who know. I can see that my son has accepted this. It has made him a man. And it must have been more difficult for him than ever it was for me. You will have to accept it, too, my dear."

"I cannot!" I cried, and appealed to Bedwyr. "Bedwyr, make him see it must be somehow averted! His own son!"

Bedwyr's smile was sad, and his eyes were full of grief. But he only shrugged and said gently, "Listen to Arthur, Gwen. If he can bear it, then we all must, for his sake."

"Arthur! Speak with Merlin! Let it not fall to Mordred—what has he done to deserve it? He is innocent. Let him be free of this!"

"Yes, he is innocent," Arthur agreed. His warm brown eyes held my own, and I felt the soft, light touch of his will, soothing, calm, serene. "We must both do all we can to help him, to protect and honor him, to ensure that his fate will be undeserved."

I was held, helpless, in the web of his powerful love, and gradually felt my anger drawn from me, until I was left empty of grief. I slipped from the chair, sat at his feet, and kissed his hands.

"Leave us now, Bedwyr," I heard him say.

"My lord," Bedwyr said softly, and went out.

Arthur lifted me in his arms and carried me into his chamber. He undressed me quickly, wrapped me well in warm blankets, and put me in the bed. Then he stoked the fire and brought me watered wine and made me drink it. He called for the page and sent for hot broth. When it came, he took it and fed me himself. When I could take no more of it, he set it aside and, sitting down beside me, looked into my face.

"Why would you not let Bedwyr tend you?" he asked gently. "He is sick with worry about you. You do not eat or sleep. He feels he has failed me."

"I did not know he felt so, my lord. He has been so kind to me, and my thoughts were always elsewhere—I did not notice his distress. It was selfish of me. I will beg his forgiveness."

Then he smiled and gently touched my face. "That is more like the Guinevere I know. Let it be. I kept him here this evening to show him what it was that ailed you, so that he did not feel it was his fault. He knows it now."

"How did *you* know, my lord?"

"I looked at Mordred's face, and I knew the witch had told him."

"I made him tell me. He did not want to."

"He should have been stronger. But he loves you."

I closed my eyes on that, but two small tears slipped out. "Oh, Arthur," I whispered. "I do not want you to die."

"Ahhhhh." He breathed it out slowly and kissed the two tears. "Now we are coming to it. It is death you fear. You are young, and you have not felt its touch before."

How could he know? Did he know my every thought?

"I fear *your* death. I cannot envision life without you. And to die by his hand—"

His finger closed my lips. "Don't, Gwen. We don't know that. Not even Merlin knows how it will happen. Only that it will. And that is not such precious knowledge, for every man must die. I do not think about it. It is what we do in life that matters."

He was so calm, so strong, so sure, he gave me strength. I looked at him in wonder. "Is it because you are a soldier, you do not fear death?"

He smiled lightly. "Every soldier fears death, before every battle. But not during it; there is not time. And yes, it is easier, to have faced it and come away. Now listen, while I tell you another of Merlin's prophecies."

"No! Please, no more!"

"You will like this one," he said, coming closer, pulling the pins from my hair. "He promised me I should have time to accomplish what I most desired. Time and to spare, he said. So, you see? You need have no fear that this wicked day of destiny is near, for I have plenty of plans still to carry out. Many things remain to do. But I will need you beside me to do them."

He took my hair down and let it fall around my shoulders. What with the warmth of the fire and the wine and the hot broth, my shivering had gradually subsided, and I began to relax within my warm cocoon of blankets. When he was with me, death seemed infinitely remote.

"Arthur," I whispered.

"My love."

"You are—you are such a force for life."

He smiled and kissed me gently. "And you, my dearest, are more than life to me. I am nothing without you. Now sleep. I will sit here by the fire."

"But—"

"There will be plenty of time for love." He grinned. "This also Merlin told me."

I laughed. It seemed like the first time in years.

13 ❁ The Witch of Rheged

"What on earth did you say to my sister?" the King asked with a smile, looking up from the papers at his desk.

"Your sister, my lord?" I waved away Hanna, who was fanning me, and turned in the chair to see him better. The library doors were open to the terrace, where Kay, Bors, Galahantyn, Bedwyr, Lancelot, and I sat languidly in the midday heat in the shade of the Camelot oak. Nearby, the new fountain, an alabaster dragon tipped with gold on claws and tail and fangs, spewed spring water in a refreshing tinkle of sound. It made us feel cooler just listening to it. We had barely moved the last hour. Only the King had energy enough to work. I peered into the cool dimness of the chamber. He had just broken the seal on a scroll, which he read with some astonishment.

"Yes," he said, beginning to frown. "My sister Morgan. Witch of Rheged, as she likes to style herself. Listen to this." He paused and, keeping his finger on the close and flowing penmanship of her scribe, began to read carefully in Latin. " 'And whereas your good lady Queen did insult me, in the company of sundry lords and princes, who will bear witness to this on their oaths as King's men, and as this took place in the royal city of Camelot, albeit while you yourself, my good lord King and brother, were abroad with my most reverend lord King of Rheged, I do beseech and require of you justice to the satisfaction of our honor, as we two Pendragon'—I can't make this out, I think she wants a hearing— 'and set aside the enmity between us of past years, by setting aside the very root and cause, which, however lovely, brings forth naught but a rank and barren blossom—well, I guess the gist is clear enough. Oh, yes, she goes on to wish me 'happiness and increase' and refers once again at the end to my youth and Urien's strength. He was fifty when he got Morgaine on her. I suppose she means to tell me it is never too late."

In spite of myself, the color rose to my face. I lowered my eyes. The bruise still gave pain, when tapped sharply.

"Oh, God." Lancelot groaned, watching me. "Not again. You settled all that years ago, Arthur. She can't be serious. She's just being nasty."

"But why?" asked the King, rising and coming out to join us. He sat on the plinth of the fountain pool, facing me. "She says here"—he tapped the letter—"that she's coming to Camelot to settle the matter. What matter? What happened while I was gone last year?"

I looked up from my lap and met his eyes. "I should have told you, my lord. But it seemed so small a thing at the time. The morning after the stable fire, when Queen Morgan left with her train, she said some very rude things to Bedwyr." The King glanced at Bedwyr, who nodded. "I only meant to defend him," I continued, "and return her remarks in kind . . . you know, my lord, the sort of things women will say to each other in a fit of temper, where a man would keep silent. It really was nothing at all."

Lancelot and Kay, who had heard nothing of it, sat up a little straighter.

"Did you insult her, Gwen?" Arthur asked calmly. "If you did, I am sure she deserved it. But I must know what you said."

Good Bedwyr jumped in to my rescue. "Your lady sister insulted you, as well, my lord, which was what upset the Queen."

"Oh?" He raised an eyebrow and turned to Bedwyr. "How so?"

"Ah, she implied your marriage to the Queen was, ah, unconsummated."

To my relief, Arthur laughed. "Oh, I see. A catfight. Say no more. I will disregard it. She also says here that she is bringing Morgaine, her daughter, and to be sure to let Guinevere know. Does this signify anything?"

I lifted my chin. "Yes, my lord. I had no right to do it, but I told her to her face she was an unloving mother, to leave the child untended for so long. That is the insult. But see now, she will bring her, so perhaps it was all for the good."

"Ahhh. Perhaps. But I like not the tone of this letter. She asks for a formal hearing. It sounds almost like a Plea of Complaint."

"Against the Queen?" Lancelot sat forward and would have risen but for the look on the King's face.

"I assure you, my lord, it was a small thing!" I cried. "When she was gone, I thought no more upon it!"

"Nor did I," Bedwyr said quietly.

"I—I suppose I should have remembered it, and told you, but so much else was happening—with Queen Morgause—and I forgot," I finished lamely.

The King's eyes were kind, but his face was grave. "Be easy, Guinevere. I do not blame you for this. As you said, it is a small thing indeed. What you said to her, if impolitic, was true. But it seems she would make something of it. I would like to know what."

He looked around at the company in expectation.

"It is clear," Lancelot said hotly, "that she wants the Queen put away." Bors and Galahantyn looked at him swiftly.

The King shook his head. "No. That is what she wants us to think. She was just indirect enough to hope we would think so. But I have publicly declared I will not do it. This is known throughout Britain."

"It is known in Less Britain, as well, my lord," Galahantyn offered.

"So. What is it she wants?"

But no one answered him. He rose and paced slowly back and forth before us. The very air shimmered as he passed.

"When is the lady Morgan arriving, my lord?" Kay asked. "And with how many?"

"In a week. With twenty men and the child."

"Not with King Urien?" I asked quickly.

The King stopped his pacing and looked sharply at me. "No. That is what makes this so interesting. Urien is in Cornwall to see his youngest son married to Constantine's sister. I will wager he knows nothing about this."

"Her husband's son wed to the sister of the High King's heir?" Lancelot asked. "And she the High King's sister? This smells of ambition."

"Oh, Lancelot," I said in irritation, "you smell ambition everywhere."

He flashed me a look, and Arthur saw it.

"I don't like it," Bedwyr muttered.

"Nor do I." Arthur sighed. "She is up to something. But I fear we will have to wait to see what it is."

A page appeared at the library doors and bowed from the waist. "My lord King! Sir Lamorak is returned from Castle Daure, my lord, and requests a word with you."

"Bring him here."

"Yes, my lord."

"What's this?" Kay asked. "You recalled Lamorak from the Winchester garrison?"

"Not exactly." The King smiled wryly. "I should have done last winter, but now it is too late. He is enamored of Morgause and no doubt comes to beg me for her freedom. For the third time."

Lancelot rose. "Shall we leave you, my lord?"

The King waved him back to his chair. "No, no. He knows what I will say. He will be glad to appeal to you. Watch him well. Do you remember Lamorak?"

"Of course, my lord. A good knight, bold and sensible. A good shot with a bow. A fine swordsman."

"With an eye for women," Bedwyr added.

The King rolled up Queen Morgan's letter and tucked it in his tunic. "You will find him changed," he said shortly.

Lamorak came in behind the page, knelt at Arthur's feet and kissed his ring.

"My lord King! My thanks for this audience. You do me great honor."

"You have given me good service, Lamorak. I will hear you," the King replied politely, raising him.

Lamorak was a well built man of middle height, about Arthur's age. He had never married; rumor had it he loved women too well and never could settle on a single one. His demeanor now was one of boyish eagerness; with shining eyes and flushed face and fluid tongue, he described Queen Morgause as a changed woman, a sorrowful and humble penitent who, under the encouragement of good King Arres, had give up her pagan ways and accepted the True Christ. She had confessed her sins, he said, and received absolution. She had forgiven them all, even Merlin. But now she spent the long winter nights weeping for loneliness and the hopelessness of her condition, doing Arthur worship always, and praying mightily for his soul. She would beg, and he begged for her, to spend her last days in freedom, living quietly in some distant corner of Britain, wherever the King might choose to send her.

At the end Lamorak lay on the paving stones and kissed the hem of the King's robe. Arthur said nothing, but glanced at his Companions with a meaning look. I saw Galahantyn was moved by the knight's desperate pleading, and Bors, too, had a face of sympathy. But those of Arthur's men who knew Morgause looked sickened.

"Good Lamorak," Lancelot said gently. "Beg not so piteously for the freeing of a witch. She is not some innocent, unjustly imprisoned. This abject pleading does you no honor."

Lamorak rose, and some dignity returned to him. "Sir Lancelot, she is witch no longer. All her charms and magic she has renounced for the True Christ. She repents of her past deeds, sir, and lives now a Christian life."

"Then," Bedwyr said dryly, "she should beg permission to remove to a nunnery."

Lamorak flushed. "My lords have sport with me. No matter. This is a lady wronged, and I would see her righted."

"No." Arthur said it flatly, and the word hung heavy in the unmoving air. "Your intentions may be honorable, Lamorak, but you are led astray."

"But, my lord—"

"I have not wronged her," the King said quietly. "It is she who has wronged me. And my wife. And her sons. And more than once. She has no one to forgive. And she has not asked those she has injured for forgiveness. For the crimes she has committed, she deserves death. But I do not kill women. She will stay where she is."

Lamorak drew himself up and met the King bravely. "I am betrothed to her, my lord. With your permission."

Arthur stared at him, shocked beyond speech. Lancelot looked away in pain. Bedwyr put a hand to his brow, unable to watch. Kay scowled.

I rose. "Sir Lamorak." I dipped him a curtsy, and he bowed to me.

"My lady Guinevere."

I put a hand on his arm and felt how it trembled. "You are an honorable man, and lately of the King's fellowship of Companions. We have missed you since you have been stationed at the Winchester garrison."

"Why, thank you, my lady."

"Have you thought well, my lord, about this step you take? Does Gawaine know you would be his stepfather? What think the twins?"

He paled slightly. "I have said nothing yet, my lady. First I seek the King's permission."

"Ah. Let us give this some thought." I took his arm, and we strolled around the fountain. The splashing of cool water kept our words from other ears. "What is it a man seeks in marriage? A warm bed, a loving pair of arms to come home to, a ready smile, a forgiving heart? Yes, if he is lucky. But these any village maiden can provide. What does a man want who marries a queen?"

"It's not that!" Lamorak gasped. "Do not accuse me of hubris, my lady. This is not because she is the High King's sister! I love the lady!"

"You misunderstand me, sir. I meant, any queen. You must know she has held the reins of power in Orkney since her husband's death. She is a woman of strong will. Would you agree?"

He licked his lips nervously and nodded. "What of it?"

"What will you come home to, Lamorak? A woman who can listen to your cares and understand them? Who may speak her mind, but bow to your will in a dispute? Who will temper her judgment with soft words, when it disagrees with yours? Who will put anger aside for your sake? Will Queen Morgause put you, who have never ruled a kingdom, higher in her estimation than herself?" The longer I went on, the more uncertain he became. I spoke very kindly to him, and he had no resistance against kindness. "Happy is the man whose wife loves his honor more than he does. Will Queen Morgause put your honor before her own?"

I could see he knew her well enough, despite infatuation, to know the answers to these questions. He wavered. "I—I know not, my lady."

"We will grant you time to rethink it, dear Lamorak. In the meantime, stay with us awhile and renew your friendships here. If at month's end you still seek the King's permission, ask then. But do not ask today."

He knelt and kissed my hand and, bowing to the King and his Companions, left us hastily.

Arthur rose and came to me, taking my hands between his own. "Thank you, Gwen."

"I spoke the truth, my lord. And he heard it. He has not yet lost all his sense."

"He is besotted," Sir Bors muttered.

"Bewitched, more like." Bedwyr added. "If she is Christian, I am King of Rome."

Kay laughed. "They are lovers, surely. How else did he know she wept all night long?"

"He is her pass to freedom," Galahantyn observed acutely.

But Lancelot said nothing. He sat in quiet agony, his eyes aflame, watching and trying not to watch our hands clasped together. Arthur let go of me and turned. Lancelot looked away.

"Blessed is the man," the King said, "who does not have sisters!"

Queen Morgan came to Camelot in state, riding at the head of her company with Sir Accolon at her side. In a closed litter some way behind rode her daughter the princess Morgaine. It was said that since her terrible ordeal, the child had not uttered a single word; she could hum a melody but she could not speak, and she hated the sight of men. It was my dearest hope that Niniane would take charge of the girl and heal her.

The King stood on the castle steps with his company of knights, gave his sister the ritual kiss of greeting, and saw her installed in her rooms. Then he washed his hands of her and returned to his work. Two steps he took in precaution. He sent to Avalon for Niniane, and he sent a message to Urien in Cornwall, begging his attendance in Camelot as soon as the festivities were over. He gave Urien no specific cause to come, but counted on his loyalty to bring him.

I was kept out of Morgan's way, which suited me well. We had no relief from the heat, and I and my ladies sat all day by the fountain in their garden, or in mine, stitching and listening to birdsong. It was enough to drive one out of one's wits. Everyone's temper was frayed. When I saw the King in the evenings, it was all I could do to be civil to him.

"What has your precious sister come for?" I would accost him. "Make her speak—has she some complaint of me? I will see she regrets it! Oh, Arthur, do *something*! If I have to stitch another cushion I shall scream."

And he would laugh and give me cool fruit drinks, chilled with ice they kept in the cellars, packed in straw. He was almost too sweet-tempered to bear.

Finally, Queen Morgan went to see the King. He came to me shortly after, to tell me what she had said.

"I have called a Council meeting in the Round Hall, at her request, when the heat of the day is past. She wishes to make a formal Complaint, but will not tell me what it is. You must be there, Gwen."

"Whatever pleases you, my lord."

"It does *not* please me," he said, suddenly cross, staring at the dull white sky. "But you must do it. Christ! Why won't it rain?"

When the Council met two hours before dinner, the heat had grown worse instead of better. The sky was darkening, but the air was still and oppressive. It hung so heavy, it took effort to breathe. Arthur and his Companions gathered in the Round Hall, mopping their brows and looking damp and ragged. I sat on the King's left hand. Lancelot took his place on his right. Directly opposite the King was the Chair of Complaint, sometimes known as the Perilous Chair, on account of some judgments given against false accusers. Here sat Queen Morgan, robed in rich velvets and crowned with the crown of Rheged, cool and steady, looking not in the least uncomfortable. That was when I knew for certain she was a witch.

Behind her chair stood Accolon, handsome and proud, dressed lavishly to match her. He held himself still, but he had not her steadiness. His eyes darted here and there, watching the faces of the Companions, and more than once drifted to the High King's Sword and then quickly looked away. I shivered suddenly, though the heat was stifling.

When everyone was gathered, Queen Morgan rose. "My lord King, my brother, and all you gentle knights, I come to bring Complaint against the Queen."

There was muttering among the Companions, and Lancelot shifted in his chair. The King stared at her, waiting.

"When last I was here, as your guest, you, my brother, had no sooner taken ship for Less Britain when your lady Queen turned upon me and insulted me to my face. Sir Accolon will verify it; and if he tells the truth, Sir Bedwyr will, as well. I have no doubt," she continued as Bedwyr, on my left, stiffened with anger, "that it is difficult for a backwoods princess to be brought so high, by your favor and grace, my lord, and all in all, she has done well, and is beloved of your company. But without your strong hand to guide her, she is a ship cast off from moorings. And this time, my lord, she has foundered upon Pendragon rock."

If she thought the way to get at Arthur was through flattery, she was mistaken. He sat perfectly still, but his nostrils flared and his eyes looked right through her. Beside him, Lancelot barely controlled his fury; I could read his thought upon his face: backwoods princess indeed! It made me smile, and Queen Morgan, seeing it, began to lose her temper.

"I am the daughter of the High King Uther and his Queen Ygraine! I will not be insulted, my lord King, by anyone in the kingdoms, without redress. It is my due."

Arthur considered her long and then answered. "I know of what this 'insult' consisted. I know also of the words you spoke to Guinevere. This is not a matter for the Council, Morgan, but for you two women only. It seems to me that apologies are due on both sides. Let us dismiss this matter."

"No!" She was truly angry now, and her haughty features looked hard and cold. "I will have redress! You are famous for your justice, my brother—would you withhold it from your own kin? I will not have anyone speak to me so!"

The King sighed wearily. "What redress do you seek? The High Queen will apologize." I rose.

She paused and gathered everyone's attention. "She has dishonored you, my lord King. Put her away."

The Companions shouted in protest; the noise filled the hall. Arthur was surprised, and showed it. He could not believe she had come all the way from Rheged for this. He did nothing to stop the shouting, but waited until the noise of dissent abated. Gently he took my wrist and sat me in my chair. He felt my trembling and said softly, "Courage, Guinevere." Then he faced his sister. "No."

"Hear me out, my lord. You will see the words I speak are truth. You are enchanted by her beauty, as is every man in this room. How not? And if she had done Britain her duty in bearing sons, I should demand less. But in truth, my lord, she has failed you and betrayed Britain; she has ended the Pendragon line and put a final stop to what you and our father have accomplished. This is not news—this she can see herself. But Pendragon must be her enemy, else she would step down of her own accord, and do you the grace and favor you have done her. But she has not; she is content to do your line dishonor and bring it to a close. She is not Queen enough for you, my lord, however much you love her. Not Queen enough to put your honor before her own; not Queen enough to treat your sister with common kindness; never mind the loving favor she bestows upon your Companions." Here Bedwyr gripped my hand beneath the table and held on tightly. "And her favors, my lord"—her voice went smooth and silky— "are so generously bestowed! Can you not see with your own eyes, brother, how she treats Sir Lancelot, or Sir Bedwyr, or King Melwas?"

I gasped, and the Companions stared at her dumbfounded. The implication was perfectly clear. The deliberate mention of Melwas cast the same shadow over them all; she meant they were my lovers, and every man there knew it.

Arthur shot to his feet, white-faced. His right hand pushed hard on Lancelot's shoulder, keeping him in his seat.

"That is enough." His voice was flat, and when one saw his eyes, the room grew colder. "This is unpardonable."

I held tight to Bedwyr's hand and kept dry-eyed. Later he showed me where my nails had drawn his blood.

"You have had more redress than you deserve," the King said in a low voice. "I have allowed you to publicly insult my wife. I should have known you better."

Amazingly, Queen Morgan looked contented with this response and smiled a smug smile.

"There is no question here of betrayal, madam, except on your own part. All Britain knows I will not put the Queen away. Neither"—and he let his glance fall on the stunned faces of his Companions—"will I allow her to leave me, so long as I am King. That is an end to it."

"I insist that she go." Morgan's eyes were bright and eager; what did she hope from this defiance?

The King leaned forward, furious. "I refuse."

Queen Morgan shrugged and signaled Accolon. The young knight stepped forward and came to the edge of the table.

"King Arthur of Britain," he said formally, with barely a tremor in his voice, "my lady the Queen of Rheged is dishonored by the Council's refusal to give her redress for the wrongs done her." He had got it by rote; this was planned. He drew a glove from his belt and threw it on the table. "On behalf of my lady the Queen Morgan, I do challenge King Arthur to personal combat—with the Sword of Britain against the Sword of Rheged. I contest your right to rule."

Everyone gasped. Arthur looked bewildered behind his shock. Lancelot jumped up, shaking from head to foot.

"Traitor!" he cried. "You foul, murderous traitor! I will kill you myself before you lay a hand on the King! How dare you!"

"Lancelot!" Arthur held his arm but could not still him. The room was in an uproar. Everyone was shouting. Queen Morgan looked quietly pleased; Accolon stood white and determined beside her. My eyes went swiftly to the Sword, behind the King's chair. Something touched my neck like a cold draft, and I felt the hairs rise. When I looked away, I felt Morgan's icy gaze upon me and shivered.

Amid the hubbub, Arthur collected himself and grew thoughtful. He could not fathom her intentions, but his immediate course was clear. "I accept the challenge, Sir Accolon. On the morrow we meet."

Again the knights protested, each one offering to fight for the King, each one protesting that he should not risk his person for such a one as Accolon.

Arthur raised a hand and silenced them. "I thank you, my lords, for the offers. But he has challenged my right to rule. And she has challenged the Queen's honor. I will meet him myself, and with pleasure. Kay, see to the arrangements." He looked at Morgan. "Now get out."

She swept out with stately dignity, Accolon in her wake. The Companions crowded around Arthur.

I turned to Bedwyr. "Let me go! Let me go!" He released me, and I sprang from my chair and flew to my rooms. Suffocated, oppressed with misery, I ran to my garden to find solace in private tears. I wept long and heartily. No matter what I did, I brought grief to Arthur. Morgan was right—I was not Queen enough for him. It had never occurred to me to leave him, to withdraw, but had I been less a backwoods princess and more a queen, I should have thought of it and done it. And now? Would it be too late? He had declared he would not let me leave, but perhaps that was to defend my honor in that public place. Perhaps he would allow it, if I went quietly without his knowing. The old wound was reopened, and I felt I could not bear it any longer. But to part from him now—I would be but half myself without him. Yet how could I stay, and subject him to insults for my sake! He was forever defending my honor with the blood of his body!

I wept until my head felt like splitting, and still the tears flowed freely. Suddenly I felt a cool touch upon my temples and a gentle hand stroke my brow. I lifted my head to see a child, thin and dark and pretty, at my side. Her face was narrow, her expression somber, but her warm brown eyes were luminous and filled with love. She hummed a little tune, and as she touched me, I felt my tears subside.

"Who are you?" I whispered, taking her little hand in mine. "Who are you, who looks at me with Arthur's eyes? What is your name?"

She said nothing but kept humming, and then very gently kissed my cheek. I reached for her and hugged her to my breast, this little angel with the healing hands. She embraced me; her thin arms, delicate as a bird's wings, went round me, and I was comforted. Without warning, she stiffened, then broke away and left me, quick as a wink. I looked round for her, but she had vanished. I did not believe in fairies; I thought I must have dreamed it.

Then I saw Arthur coming down the path to me, more upset than I had ever seen him. He knelt beside me on the flagstones and took me in his arms. "Dear Gwen! How she has hurt you!"

"My dear Arthur," I cried, laying my head on his shoulder. "Why is it I am such a heavy stone around your neck? I cannot bear that I should be the one to put you in jeopardy! Your sister was right in that—until you are free of me, you will forever be defending my honor against slanders that are nothing but truth!"

"I knew it!" he whispered fiercely. "I knew you would take it

so. For this, and not for Accolon, I will be revenged upon her!"
He pressed me close and held me while I wept in his arms. "Listen to me, Guinevere, for I do not say this lightly. You are the joy in my life. Have you ever thought what it is to be a King? Daily am I besieged by other men's problems, pressed upon by a crowd of personalities around me, always easing the friction, finding the smooth path, making the way straight, always giving, giving, giving. I cannot tell you what pleasure it is to come at last to you. There I can be free of obligation. I can say anything to you. This is a rare thing in a woman; so for this I treasure you and would have none other."

I listened to him and was struck with wonder. These were Bedwyr's words from Arthur's lips.

"My—my lord, I thank you. But I wish you would not take up arms for me." Because the day was hot, the breast of his tunic lay open, and I ran my fingers over the scar on his shoulder. "The Saxons never harmed you in all the years you fought them," I whispered. "The only mark you bear, you got for me, by Melwas' blade. I am ashamed of it, Arthur. It should not be thus."

He tried to smile. "What, would you have me covered with scars, like old Caius Lucius?"

"Please, Arthur," I begged, the tears returning, "please let some other fight in your stead. I could not bear it if you suffered injury on my account."

"My dear wife," he breathed. We stayed thus, silent, arms clasped about one another, struggling for command of our emotion.

I felt a light touch and looked up. The sweet child stood behind us, one hand on Arthur's head, one hand on mine. My tears dried, and I breathed more easily. Arthur looked up and saw her. She did not move, but looked straight into his eyes, so like her own, then gently touched his face with her small hand. He dared not even breathe, lest he break the spell. The child stepped closer and gently took his head in her frail arms, cradling him against her slim body. The King closed his eyes. Two small tears welled up and spilled down her rounded cheeks. Lightly she touched his head above his ear, and caressed the spot as if it pained him. From nowhere came a low voice, ghostly, that echoed around us.

"Thus shall it be on the last day, the wicked day, when the King sends his spirit home. He shall lay his head down in her gentle lap, and lay down his burden at last . . ." The voice trailed off into silence. Even the birds were still.

Then Niniane stepped out from the shadows, holding her head in pain; the King opened his eyes and sat up; the child ran to

Niniane and hugged her skirts. I reached for Arthur's hand, shocked to my very soul.

Niniane sank down on the stone bench, head bowed. The child touched her temples and began to hum.

The King gripped my arms, breathing fast. "Stay with me, Guinevere, I pray you. Don't leave me."

"My lord!" I whispered, meeting his eyes. The moment passed. He steadied himself and drew a long breath.

"Is there aught I can get for you, Niniane? I know Merlin used to take a potion after visions, but I know not how it was made."

She looked startled. "Did I prophesy for you, my lord? My head feels like it, but I can remember nothing, except darkness and flame. Yes, I can see by your faces I said something of importance. Let this child finish . . . thank you, Morgaine, that is better." The little girl sat down on the bench beside her and waited quietly, swinging her thin legs back and forth. Niniane smiled lightly; the harsh lines from brow to hairline told of her headache, but her eyes and voice were back to normal. "This is Morgaine, Queen Morgan's daughter. She has the gift of healing and of Sight. She is especially sensitive to pain in others. That must be what drew her here, for I was on my way to the Round Hall to see you when she disappeared from my side. She is now in my care." She raised her chin. "She will be Lady of the Lake after me."

"Thank you, Morgaine, for comforting the Queen," Arthur said gravely to the child. She kept her eyes down and would not look at him.

"She does not speak," Niniane went on. "But she has the gift of thinking in pictures, which can be seen and understood by an adept. In this way, she has told me something of importance, my lord, which you should know."

"Tell me."

"The sword hanging in the Round Hall is not Excalibur."

I gasped, and the King started. "Are you certain of this?"

"She knows where the true Sword is. In a dark place, underground. Safe. Somewhere in Rheged. After I have taken Morgaine to Ynys Witrin and dedicated her to the Lady's service, I shall go to Rheged and find it for you."

Arthur nodded. "Now I understand my sister's plan," he said slowly. "She never expected me to put you away, Gwen. In fact, she chose as her demand the one thing she knew I would not do. All she wanted was a confrontation, so her poor dupe Accolon could issue his challenge."

"So now that you know the sword is a fraud, you will not fight him? This duplicity can be revealed, and all will be well."

But the King shook his head. "No. I will meet him. His honor demands it. Let him have the chance to change his mind."

"But you will not fight with the weapon they have substituted? Surely they have designed it to shatter in your hand."

He was adamant. "There are more ways to kill a man than by running him through with a sword. If Accolon does not yield to me, he will die tomorrow."

"He will die tomorrow," Niniane repeated absently, but the words on her lips sounded final. She rose to go, and we both rose with her.

"I have frightened you, Guinevere," she said with concern. "Your hands are like ice. I beg your pardon for it. What did I prophesy?"

"Only my death," Arthur said with a light smile, and a gentle kiss to my forehead. "But I promise, I shall not fall to Accolon."

In fact, the contest with Accolon was barely a contest at all. Accolon came magnificently dressed; the King wore his plain fighting garb. I watched Queen Morgan's face as the men approached one another. When the King put his hand on the hilt of the sword and accepted it without thought, her face lit and her eyes grew eager. I felt sickened; he was her own brother, yet she wished him dead. If Lancelot looked for Pendragon ambition, he need look no further than Ygraine's daughter Morgan.

Accolon, knowing the weakness of the King's sword and wishing to put a quick end to the contest, lifted his weapon and swung with all his might. The King blocked the blow; his sword shattered in his hand.

"An omen!" Queen Morgan cried. "See how the sword fails him!"

But before the words were out of her mouth, Arthur drove the jagged remnant of the blade into Accolon's face, then reached for his dagger and stabbed him to the heart, all before the poor knight could lift his sword a second time.

The King knelt down at Accolon's side and spoke to him and took his hand. When he died, the King saluted him and turned away. Not a single tear graced Morgan's eye; she was angry and kept declaring that God had sent an omen to Britain, that Arthur was no longer worthy of the Sword.

Lancelot laughed. "The Sword of Britain, Madam? Or that piece of glass? So this is why you came to Camelot!"

At a sign from the King, a guard formed around her, and she

was taken prisoner. That night Urien arrived and learned all that had happened. He was closeted with the King for hours, and when they parted, both men looked at ease with one another.

"He has put her away," Arthur told me later. "He has given her into my keeping and is content to leave Morgaine with Niniane. I will send Morgan to Castle Daure to join her sister. The garrison at Winchester can be fortified to supply the troops. Let the two of them match their wits and magic against one another. As long as they are out of my hair!"

"What did she hope to gain?" I asked him. "Did she think to replace you herself? Surely she knew the men would not follow her or Accolon."

"I think she intended to present Urien with an accomplished fact and persuade him to take over the Kingdom himself. I tell you, Gwen, he is glad to be rid of her and would have put her by long ago, but for fear of offending me."

He stood behind me, brushing my hair. With the coming of dark the heat had given way before a light sea breeze. I had bathed, although the entire castle thought me strange to want hot water in summer. But it refreshed me more than chilled wine, and for the first time that day I felt at ease. The danger to the King was past, and he had suffered no hurt for me.

"Will you be in any danger without your Sword, my lord?" I asked him.

"No, Gwen. It is a symbol now, more than a weapon. It has been years since I lifted it in battle."

"Then all is well," I said with relief. "Niniane told me once that you were destined to be the victor in every field you took—I should have remembered that."

"It was Merlin's prophecy," he said in a tight voice, "before it was hers."

I turned on the stool and clutched his wrist. With great care, he set down the brush. "Like that of today?" I said hoarsely. "Had you heard that before?"

He shook his head. He was not afraid now. He had already accepted it. "No. The vision came to her there in the garden. It was new to me."

"What does it mean, my lord? That—that you will be slain? That cannot be, if Merlin's vision is true, and you are always victorious."

He looked puzzled. "I don't know what it means. But what is this? Do you try to argue with visions?"

I stood and slipped my arms around his body. "I mean only that perhaps Niniane is not the seer Merlin was; perhaps it was not a true vision."

"She has Merlin's power," he said gently. "Don't distress yourself, Gwen. Put it behind you."

"Do you believe these things she sees must happen? Don't you believe that men's wills count? Are we God's puppets, or do we earn His love by making choices for good or evil?"

He stepped back from me and looked into my face. "We are responsible for our actions," said the King.

I swallowed. "Then perhaps these dark fates may be avoided, if we will. I have thought long about this, Arthur. Perhaps these are warnings only, of what will come if we stray from the right path. If we make our own futures, who is to say what they will contain?"

He frowned and took a turn about the room. What love he bore for Merlin, never to question him! I felt suddenly guilty that, like Eve, I offered him uncertainty, where before he had made his peace.

"What are you telling me?" he said. "Today, in Morgaine's embrace, I felt my death blow." He raised his hand and touched the side of his head. "Do you mean that what I felt was only possibility? One among many?"

I began to tremble. "I—I think—oh, Arthur! Remember what else Merlin told you! That it should be Mordred's doing!" The sudden pain on his face brought tears to my eyes. I ran and knelt at his feet. "Forgive me, my lord."

He raised me and said slowly, "I had not forgotten."

"But he will not do it!" I cried, and then everything I wanted to say came rushing out in a tumble of words. "This was my first thought, when Niniane spoke today, that it could not be true, not that vision and the one of Mordred both, because he will not raise a hand against you. This I know, he has sworn it to me! Morgause terrified him—how evil, to tell her own son he would be the death of his father! But he thought, as Niniane told him, it might be something indirect, like, like falling from a horse on your way to see him, or some such thing. This would be beyond his power to prevent. But this horror of today—this he can and will prevent! For Mordred loves you, Arthur. I know Lancelot thinks him ambitious, but he will not know the boy. He would not harm you if his life depended on it. He has suffered so from this foul prophecy! But if you are to die in battle—and how can that be, if you are always victor?—then by his will, Mordred can be free of this thing! He has sworn not to outlive you." I gasped. I had gone too far; I had not meant to tell him that.

He looked at me a long while in silence. "A boy's oath, that the man must break. He will be my heir." His voice was flat. I dared not move.

Rarely was he out of temper and rarely had his wrath touched me. But this time I had offended him deeply. The skin around his nose and mouth looked pinched and white, his eyes cold and black. Slowly he turned his back to me and walked out on the terrace. Only then I felt my knees shake and clutched the bedpost for support.

"Arthur!" I whispered. Would I never learn to guard my tongue? But for me, he would have peace of mind. I was forcibly reminded of my words to Lamorak—how pompous they sounded now! The King came to me for comfort after the day's ordeal, and I wounded his heart.

He stood stiffly by the parapet, staring out at the dark garden below. I knew by the way he held himself that he fought his own fury. I sank to my knees and whispered a quick prayer, for Arthur's sake. He must get past this anger, and understand that what drove both me and Mordred was nothing but fear for him. He could command fear; could he admit, and forgive, that we could not? I trembled again at the thought of what I had done. If he could not get past it, what then? Surely our close fellowship was ended, and he would trust me no longer. I bowed my head as tears slipped out—how was the Witch of Rheged proved right about me, after all!

After a long while, I heard his step and felt him touch my hand. "Arise, Guinevere. I would talk with you a moment."

I looked up quickly; he was calm, the black anger gone. "My dear lord, please forgive me. Lately I am but a thorn in your side."

His features warmed; he almost smiled. "Hardly that." He led me past the leather curtain and into his own chamber. He sat upon the great bed and beckoned me to sit beside him. "I cannot long be angry with you, Gwen. But I must know this about Mordred."

Haltingly I told him about Mordred's distress when Morgause had told him of Merlin's prophecy and about the solemn vow he had made.

"Lancelot," Arthur said evenly.

"Yes, my lord," I said sadly, looking away. "I fear that was the reason. Mordred suffered great anguish, Arthur, and I believe he still means to keep his vow."

"He is young yet." Then a whiplash of anger cut across his

voice. "Between you, you have robbed me of my future!" Stilling himself, he took my hair in his hands and slowly let it fall through his fingers. "'Gwen. You must make an effort, for my sake, to ignore these prophecies. They are nothing, really. They do not affect us. They are simply things seen by those who have Sight to see them. If they are true, they are true, and if false, false. Live as though you had not heard them. My sweet wife, it is the only way. Give up trying to decipher them and reconcile them; you have not that gift, thank God. Forget them."

He leaned slowly forward to kiss my cheek and neck and throat. With a sigh, I let go of my fear and my worry—he took them all upon himself.

"Thank you, Arthur," I whispered, and found his lips on mine.

Gently he pressed me back against the bearskin coverlet and leaned over me, filling my vision. "I am a King, and I do what I must. When he is King, he will do the same. Understand this, Gwen."

"Yes, Arthur," I breathed, "you are right."

He smiled slowly. "And now, is your fear gone?"

"Yes, my lord," I said, reaching for him.

But he resisted, holding himself away, looking down at me. "Are you sure? A moment ago it consumed you, body and soul."

I lifted a hand to his face. "You have the power to dispel it, my lord," I said softly. "You have always had this power. Since the first day I met you, Arthur."

Gently he caressed my cheek with his finger and then ran his hand slowly down my shoulder and over the soft fabric of my gown.

"Do you remember how frightened of me you were then?" he asked with amusement, watching my face. "You put me in mind of a wild filly; you wanted to run."

"I remember it well. You gentled me like a master."

He laughed lightly. "No, hardly that. Does it not seem odd to think we were strangers once?"

I caught his roving hand and pressed it to my lips. "Come, Arthur. I have not your patience."

"And now," he continued, smiling, "you are like dry tinder awaiting the spark. See what comes of overcoming fear?"

I took his face between my hands and drew him down to me. "If you possess the spark, my lord, bear in mind that too much wind may blow it out."

Then he laughed with pleasure and kissed me.

THE DRUIDS

The Homecoming
The Messengers
The Isle of Mona
The Prisoner
The Judgment

14 ❀ The Homecoming

"Well, Gwen," Arthur said, smiling, "who do you think is coming to see us?"

Council had just broken up, and the Companions lounged leisurely near the windows in the Round Hall, passing the wineskin and enjoying the breezes of early summer. Lancelot and Bedwyr stood near Arthur. They had been arguing as I entered the chamber, but broke off, and turned to me with lightened looks. I knew a courier had come that day from Wales, and I knew that several of the knights errant had returned to report on their travels, but I could not guess what it was that so pleased Arthur.

"Who, my lord?" I asked, as he raised me. "An old friend from Wales, perhaps?"

"Close to the mark," he replied. "An old friend, indeed, and one you have not seen since well before you came to Camelot. But not from Wales."

"Not from Wales? But before I came here I did not know anyone who was not from Wales! Unless you count my tutor Iakos?" I glanced up and saw his eyes were dancing.

"Someone you liked better than Iakos, I imagine. Someone tall and fair and handsome, to use your words. A king's son when you knew him. Now a king."

"Not Fion!" I cried. "Oh, Arthur! Is it really Fion? Is he coming to Camelot at last?"

"Not to Camelot. We go to meet him in Gwynedd." He turned to Bedwyr. "Do you remember him? The Prince of Ireland? He came to meet us along the Glevum road when his countrymen had ransomed him from Pellinore. He'd led a raid on Pellinore's coast and been caught. Gwen was the one who found him half dead on the beach and wrapped him in her cloak, though it was midwinter, and saved his life, thereby enslaving his affection."

Lancelot was watching me, and I felt a slow blush rise to my face.

"It was nothing so dramatic. He would have lived in any event. It would take more than a winter's night on a Welsh beach to silence Fion. Where have you heard these fantastic tales?"

Arthur laughed. "Why, he told me so himself. He talked about you a good deal, as I remember." I looked away, but could not keep from smiling in delight. I had not seen Fion in ten years, since I was fourteen and had stumbled upon him, a wounded pirate with golden hair and eyes of unbelievable green. He was the first man who ever spoke poetry to me, or sang to me, or tried to win me. This was at an age when a grown man's admiration means more than life to a lass; had he asked for me, I would gladly have married him.

"It was Fion who proposed her for Queen, was it not?" Bedwyr asked.

"No, no," I said quickly, feeling Lancelot's eyes still on my face. "That was my cousin Gwillim. At least, that was what Pellinore told me."

"True enough," Arthur said easily, "But it was Fion's praise of you that decided me. I knew him to be an honest man."

"Just how well did you know him?" Lancelot blurted. "I thought he was Pellinore's hostage."

I grinned at Arthur, delight getting the better of sense. "He was the handsomest man I've ever seen! Oh, it will be so wonderful to see him again!"

Arthur laughed outright as Lancelot colored. "You see, Lancelot, we are but second best. In her heart there is another who comes first."

To hide my face I made a deep reverence between them. "Not so, my lords." The jest had gone far enough, and Arthur knew it. He slung an arm about Lancelot's shoulders.

"Things are as stormy in Ireland as they ever were, with six cousins after his throne. Even his marriage to a northern girl did not stay the plotting against his life. So he has sent a message seeking counsel."

"But I thought he was not coming to Camelot."

"Indeed," Arthur said, lowering his voice, "he is not. He is setting his enemies a trap. He has given out that he comes to Camelot to consult with me. That is a month's journey by sea and land and back again. Plenty of time for the pretenders to foment a riot. But he will do no more than touch land in Gwynedd, pay us his

best wishes, and return to catch them red-handed. If he is successful, he might be able to unite his realm."

It sounded like Fion. He was a better poet than a leader of men;
quick and clever, he could charm his way out of anything. Except,
perhaps, the ambitions of his relations.

"Oh, Arthur! Won't you take me with you? Please, my Lord,
just this once!" Ever since King Melwas had kidnapped me, Arthur barely let me ride three leagues from home without the entire
army at my back. To go home again, actually to go home and see
the Western Sea and the wooded mountains of my girlhood! My
thoughts must have shown upon my face, for Arthur slipped an
arm about my waist.

"Yes, you are coming. But it will not all be pleasure. I have
need of your diplomatic skills. Besides—" He hesitated, and
smiled again. "I doubt either you or Fion would forgive me if I
went alone."

"You are right about that! When do we leave? And with how
many?"

"In two weeks. With half the army."

"So many? To greet Fion? Ahhhh. I see there is more to it. Do
you expect war, then? What is amiss?"

"No," Arthur said quickly, "or you should not come. Not war.
But the situation is difficult."

"What situation?" Their faces grew grave, and Lancelot and
Bedwyr avoided looking at one another. I felt a sudden foreboding. "What has Maelgon done?"

I knew, of course, that Elaine's brother Maelgon was king now
in Gwynedd, poor Pellinore having broken his neck in a hunt the
previous autumn. My cousin Maelgon was but a younger, stronger
version of the hot-headed Elaine, and was capable of almost anything. He was certainly capable of picking a fight with any one of
his neighbors, but the King had said he did not expect war. On the
other hand, with half the army along he was clearly ready for it.
I thought of the Welsh lords I knew, of my brother Gwarthgydd
the King of Northgallis, and the kings of Powys and Dyfed and
Guent. They had all liked Pellinore well enough and were loyal to
Arthur. I did not think it likely Maelgon could stir them up against
Gwynedd in so short a time. But whom else might Maelgon have
offended?

Arthur glanced at me and shook his head. "I told you both," he
said to Lancelot and Bedwyr, "she knows the man."

"I do indeed. You frighten me by your silence. What has he
done?"

Arthur sighed wearily and began to pace back and forth. The men near the windows stopped their idle chatter and stood quietly, listening. At length the King turned and faced me. "Maelgon has taken it into his head to purify Gwynedd. To wipe out the Druids."

I gasped, and my hand closed automatically over the crucifix at my throat. This was a thing Arthur had feared for years. Christian power was growing in Britain, and he knew there would be those who tried to win a name for themselves by championing the Christian cause and justifying slaughter in the name of righteousness. And this, Arthur abhorred.

In distress, I looked at Lancelot, but his face told me nothing. He stood stiffly, waiting, looking nowhere. With every passing year Lancelot grew more devout, as if by prayer and fasting and strict adherence to his faith he could purge from his soul our long, deep-rooted passion. But Arthur, an anointed Christian King, respected the old ways and was well known to honor the gods sacred to any place. He had worshipped at the Mithraeum in York; he had honored the Great Goddess; he was known to stop at wayside shrines and leave offerings to the Elder Spirits; he had been formally blessed by both the Archdruid Salowen and the Lady of the Lake. His broadmindedness had been marked and appreciated by his people. Only a small group of fanatics dared to criticize his fairness. But the Bishop of Landrum was among them and had preached more than once against such tolerance. And the bishop's power was growing.

Salowen the Druid! I thought suddenly. The Isle of Mona, the Druids' Isle, lay but a league off Gwynedd's shores. Even in Pellinore's day they had caused trouble with the Christian community, always competing with Father Martin for recruits, their schools and music outshining anything the Christian brothers could produce. Mona was an ancient seat of learning, and her sacred grove of Nemet one of the holiest places in all Britain.

"Arthur," I whispered, "do not tell me he has done insult to the Druids on Mona's Isle."

"He has done worse than insult" came the cruel reply. "He has done murder. Not directly, but through another."

"In a good cause," Lancelot murmured, and I stared at him, astounded.

Arthur frowned, but checked his anger. "A man should not be murdered for calling his God by a different name," he said firmly, looking around the room and catching everyone's eye. "I will not have that said of me, nor of any who serve me." He did not look directly at Lancelot, but the point went home.

"Amen," I said quickly, praying Lancelot would take the hint and be still. "How did it happen?"

Arthur resumed his slow pacing, his hands behind his back. There was utter silence in the room. Then it was that I noticed that the gathered Companions stood in two groups, Kay, Gereint, Gryfflet, Sagramor, and the other Christians by the open window, behind Lancelot, and Villers, Dryaunt, Bleoberys, and Bellangere with the other pagans nearer Bedwyr. Already was Arthur's council divided.

At last, Arthur spoke. "Did you know a youth named Balyn in Gwynedd? I believe he was the son of one of Pellinore's nobles."

"Yes, I think so. There are two of them, are there not? Twins? Balyn and Balan. Rambunctious boys, as I remember, the type to find trouble everywhere. And not very clever."

"Your memory serves you well. Not clever enough by half. They were very close as children, as twins are, but when they came of age they fought over a maiden. It grew into a feud, they say, until their father split them up in order to protect them from each other. He himself owed a favor to Salowen, so he offered him Balan's services for a term of years in repayment of the debt. Balyn he sent into Pellinore's service. Pellinore made him a Christian."

"Ah, yes," I said, recalling to mind the rather thick-featured boy with badly cut hair who always said his prayers aloud, at twice of the volume of anyone else. "He was very enthusiastic about whatever he undertook; but he seldom looked ahead toward consequences."

Gryfflet moaned under his breath. "Aye, my lady, you know the lad all right, may God rest his soul and the Good Goddess preserve his spirit from harm." Gryfflet, at least, was making an attempt to straddle the fence.

I turned to him. "He is dead? Do you mean he was Maelgon's agent?"

"He led the raid on Mona's Isle at Maelgon's command," Arthur said shortly. "Nine Druids were slaughtered, including his brother Balan, whom he slew himself, not knowing who he was."

"Dear God!"

"The priestess Viviane was beheaded," Villers growled.

"Three Christian lives were lost." This from Gereint.

"And Balyn himself was slain by Balan, who, at Salowen's

command, had sworn peace with his brother a year hence," Bedwyr finished sadly. "But he knew him not."

My hands twisted together as I looked at all their faces. "This is terrible! Is there now a holy war between Druid and Christian in Gwynedd?"

"Not yet," Arthur said, watching Lancelot from the corner of his eye. "That is what we go to prevent. I will talk sense into Maelgon or remove him from his throne." Now I saw Arthur's need of me; Pellinore's widow Alyse must be kept from interfering in such treatment of her son; she was not a weak-willed woman, and she had been powerful once.

"You had better talk to Salowen, as well," I said nervously, and was gratified to see Lancelot's expression soften. "He will want revenge."

Arthur came to a stop. "I have sent to see him. If I can get him and Maelgon into the same room and talking, there is a chance we can settle this. But if we cannot"— his voice sounded hollow, and his gaze looked far beyond the chamber wall—"then all I have done has been for naught. Once Briton is pitted against Briton, the Saxons need not even lift an ax to conquer us."

At the mention of Saxons, the two groups of knights drew closer together; Lancelot met Bedwyr's eyes.

"Arthur," I said firmly, taking his arm and bringing his thoughts back to the present, "it will not happen. You will see when we get to Wales. I am sure I can make Alyse see sense, and I'll wager any amount you like Maelgon still fears her. And don't forget Fion. The tongue he carries in his head can charm anyone with ears. All will be well. I am sure of it."

We left as soon as the solstice celebrations were ended. Mordred, who had just turned fifteen and been inducted into the army, was coming with us. Being only a new recruit he could not ride with the King, but was stuck at the back of his company where he swallowed dust the whole way. Even so, he was thrilled to be coming, especially as Gawaine, at fourteen, could not.

The journey to Wales was easy and swift; we had glorious weather, the roads were dry and we made excellent time. There was only one incident along the way to mar my joy at setting out for home. I rode the first part of the way with Niniane. She was on her way to the Lady's shrine at Avalon, and we provided her escort as far as the causeway across the marsh. But she was not good company. She was distracted, barely listening to my attempts at conversation, wincing at the bright sun as if it hurt her eyes. As we left the rolling downs and came to a flat plain by the river Camel, she shuddered and moaned aloud.

"Niniane!" I whispered, putting out a hand to her. "What is it? What is amiss?"

She shook her head impatiently and waved away my questions. "I don't know. It is nothing. Let me be, I pray you. This—this place stinks of death."

I looked about, but could see no carcass anywhere, nor any cause for her complaint. "The plain of Camlann?" I wondered aloud. "Why, it is wonderful country for galloping. And the air is sweet."

But her breath was coming fast and labored, and she cried out angrily, "It is a battlefield, I tell you! There are dead men all about! And so near Avalon . . ." I was frightened, then, lest she be having a vision of some horrible misfortune, and I called to Arthur to attend us. He rode over immediately and spoke to her. But as soon as she heard his voice, her irritation left her, and she faced him calmly. "Beware of false messengers!" she cried, and the voice that came from her lips was not her own, but the hollow, ringing voice of the god. I crossed myself quickly, and Arthur took her arm to steady her.

"What messengers, Niniane?" he asked softly. "Welsh messengers? From Gwynedd?" But she only shook her head, unable to speak, and slumped in the saddle. Arthur made her drink from his flask and soon brought her round. But she remembered nothing she had said, either about messengers or battlefields. I was distressed, but Arthur shot me a warning glance, reminding me not to worry about her Seeings. This was not unusual behavior from Niniane, who carried Merlin's power within her, so we let her be. At least she no longer felt a horror of the beautiful country we rode through. And I strove to follow Arthur's advice and put her words behind me, since I could make no sense of them, and I owed him obedience to my promise.

We rode into the forecourt of Pellinore's castle one fine summer afternoon. Everything was much the same as I remembered, only smaller. The stables, I saw, had been well maintained, and the outbuildings looked all in good order. I wondered, with a secret smile, if Maelgon had discovered and repaired the crack in the wall where Elaine and I had eavesdropped on so many of Pellinore's councils. Maelgon himself greeted us at the threshold. He was a well-built young man, strong and able, with Pellinore's stern visage and bushy brown beard, but not, underneath it, his endearing warmth. And though it was a hot day, he was dressed in every piece of finery he owned, from the heavy crown of Gwynedd to embroidered cape, jeweled belt, and gold wristbands encrusted with gems. Arthur, bareheaded and dressed in simple traveling clothes, was much the finer figure as he stood before Maelgon and accepted his homage.

Vainly I looked about for Alyse; by all rights she should have been there, but she was not. Instead, a timid wisp of a girl with thin dark hair and overlarge dark eyes stood trembling at Maelgon's elbow, overdressed as he was, looking like a child in her mother's clothes. I covered my shock as Maelgon introduced us to his bride Anet. She was the youngest child of old Caw of Strathclyde, whose sons had given Arthur such trouble after his death. Her brother King Hapgar had ruled there since Heuil's defeat, and although he himself had sworn allegiance to Arthur, he was powerless to keep his quarrelsome siblings in line. The worst behaved was Gildas, Heuil's pet and now a Christian priest. This arrogant philanderer had studied once in Ireland and now fancied himself a second Plato, a modern Pliny, a poet and a recorder of events, well above the rank of common men. He was more dangerous to cross than a viper; he could, and would, for spite or a piece of gold, ruin a man's reputation with a single stroke of his pen.

I regarded little Anet with sympathy. What an upbringing she must have had! With twelve wild brothers for companions in childhood, perhaps she knew no other response to life than seeking shelter. Arthur greeted her gently, and she almost smiled at him as she knelt to kiss his ring. But me she could only stare at, trembling, as if I were some demon come straight from Hell to fetch her. Though I spoke softly and chose my words to please her, she could not utter a sound, but licked her dry lips and shrank from my touch.

We were given the finest rooms in the castle, outside of Maelgon's own. Ailsa and I found ourselves standing in the very chamber Elaine and I had slept in as girls. The bed was the same, and the pearwood chest at its foot, but there were new pieces, as well, all worked in the old Celtic patterns they still cherished in the north.

"I will wager you, Ailsa, that this is little Anet's room, and Maelgon has turned her out of it on my account. No wonder she hates me!"

"Hates you, my lady? Certainly not."

"You did not see the way she greeted me. She could not bring herself to look me in the face."

Ailsa chuckled as she began her unpacking. "Not from hate, you may be sure. I saw her when your back was turned. She could not take her eyes from you. It is not hate, Guinevere, but envy. A little slip of a lass like that would give anything she possessed to be as strong and as beautiful and as sure of herself as you."

I turned from her, finding the room suddenly oppressive. "No doubt that will end as soon as she finds herself with child," I said bitterly, and left before she could try to offer comfort.

I went up to the tower to see the sea. None of the sentries were men I knew, but they all knew me and let me pass. How wonderful to look again upon the Western Sea, stretching endlessly blue and beckoning beneath the summer sky! For the first time in many years I longed for Elaine's company; I could almost hear her eager, conspiratorial whispers in my ear. Her spirit seemed to hover in the salt breeze. I had noted well how much more warmly Maelgon greeted Lancelot, his brother-in-law, than Arthur, his King. I would have to remember that Lancelot had special standing here, on Elaine's account; he would have to remember it, too. Why, I wondered suddenly, had I come? This was not the homecoming I wanted—Pellinore gone, Alyse in seclusion, every childhood memory of Elaine saddled with the cruel acknowledgment that she was Lancelot's wife. How could I have thought this would be bearable?

I heard a step behind me and turned. "Arthur!"

Beyond him, the sentries had snapped to attention and stood staring at the sky beyond the parapet with concentrated effort.

"Well, I have found you at last. These are not tears of joy at homecoming, I think," he said gently, brushing my cheek with his finger. "It's not quite what you expected, is it?"

I shook my head, and he took me in his arms. At length, when I was calm, he loosed me and leaned upon the parapet, looking out toward the sea.

"This is the view you have always wanted to see from Camelot," he said with a smile. "I can see why." He hesitated. "We can always go to Caer Narfon, Gwen. The soldiers would prefer it; there are better barracks. And the King's house is not bad. It's been rebuilt since you last saw it."

"No," I said firmly. "Not even for you would I give Maelgon such pleasure."

He grinned. "Good. Then we will stay and make him behave

himself." His gaze traveled slowly over the castle grounds, the paddocks, the meadows, the wooded hills within his view. "So this is where you lived. I wish the Saxons had not landed in the north that spring. I should have liked to come and take you out of Wales myself." I looked away. And if he had come? Then Lancelot would not have come in his stead. Arthur shifted. "Lancelot suffers more than you do. As kin to Maelgon, he must listen to his bragging and laugh at his jests." I felt a blush creep into my cheeks, but I had ceased to be amazed that Arthur read my thoughts. "Tell me more about Maelgon. What do you suppose made him choose such a child for a wife? She cannot be much of a helpmate."

"Maelgon would sneer at the very idea of a helpmate. He is a bully, Arthur, pure and simple. And she, poor girl, must have been bullied her entire life. They are probably well suited . . . But what her life must be like!"

"She is in awe of you, you know," he said quietly. "Like Mordred. Like me."

"Flatterer. You are only trying to cheer me up. But how is Mordred?"

He straightened and laughed. "Last I saw him he was covered with dust and sore from the the saddle and trying in spite of it all to be dignified." He paused and lowered his voice. "I have asked him to be my eyes and ears among the men, and in the village. As he is pagan himself, he can go where the Christians will not. And in the tavern, men take little notice of a youth his age and in their cups may let something slip."

I moved closer to him and watched his face. "And what is it you seek to know, my lord?"

His lips thinned. "I want to know where Salowen is. He has sent no message."

"And what do you want of me?"

As he turned toward me his features softened. "I leave the women to you. I want Maelgon weakened, even a little. There is no check to his power, I find. No one will oppose him."

"No doubt he has banished all those who ever offered him advice he did not like."

"Awe is a powerful weapon, Gwen," Arthur said slowly. "Use it." He smiled suddenly, took my hand, and slid it through his arm. "Give Maelgon a wife like mine, and I can leave him with an easy heart . . . Come, come, don't blush so. This is not flattery, but truth. And now you must come with me, for I am bidden to bring you to Alyse. She has been asking for you, and I offered to act as page."

That, at last, made me smile. "Well, you haven't the least idea how to go about it. You must bow your head and lower your eyes. You cannot look me in the face; you cannot touch me."

With a bark of laughter, he bent and kissed me, then lifted me in his arms and carried me past the sentries and down the tower stairs.

I hardly recognized Alyse. She sat in her rocker wrapped in shawls, small and thin and faded. She who had been a powerful queen and Pellinore's right hand, the leading force in my childhood, she was an old woman. Leonora and Cissa, who still attended her, did not look half so changed.

She was pathetically happy to see me and rose to kiss my hand, embracing me with tears of joy. "Ah, Gwen, how good of you to come with the King! You grow more beautiful with every passing year! How I wish dear Elen could see you now!"

Startled at the reference to my mother, whom she never mentioned in my hearing, I mumbled some reply, and Leonora hastened to make tea at the grate.

"I looked for you in the forecourt when we rode in, Aunt Alyse."

"I could not be there," she said with a spark of her well-remembered anger. "I am not on speaking terms with Maelgon."

"No?" I was amazed. Of her three sons, he had always been her pride. I waited, but she was not ready to talk about Maelgon.

"Let me look at you, my dear. How you delight me! You bring the sweet air of summer in with you—I could almost feel young again." Her grip on my arm was strong and steady. I sat across from her and observed her closely. She wandered on, remembering the old days, but remembering them quite differently than I had known them. "I always knew you were destined for greatness, Guinevere. Everyone could see it." This, though she had schemed and fought to get me married early and out of the way so Elaine could pursue Arthur! I glanced quickly at Leonora and caught her hiding a smile.

I handed Alyse her tea. "I am sorry to learn of Pellinore's death. He was almost as dear to me as Father."

"Thank you, Gwen. They say he never felt the blow that killed him. That's a mercy. He never bore pain well. Always demanding to be cosseted and nursed for the smallest scratch." I nearly smiled, unable to envision the brawny Pellinore acting like a child. But I was gratified to see Alyse treat her beloved husband as she always had and not enshrine his memory in soft words just because he was dead.

"And how do you get along with your new daughter-in-law, Anet?"

Alyse snorted unkindly, and the years seemed to drop from her. "Just the type to suit Maelgon. A convent flower, not hardy enough to last a year on this rocky soil, I warrant. Do you know, Guinevere, that since that old devil Caw put her in the convent at the age of five, she had never seen the outside of it until Hapgar gave her to Maelgon?"

"Not even to go home? Do you mean she spent her whole life there?"

"I do, indeed. And by all accounts, it's no more than a jumble of rubble with thatch for a roof, hidden in some godforsaken valley in the wild mountains of Strathclyde. Her Latin is atrocious, and her speech is thick with old Celtic expressions our grandfathers had forgotten!"

I laughed at her indignation. She was faded and wrinkled, yes, but not old; it was her will that commanded her flesh, and if that could be revived, Alyse could yet become a forceful ally.

"Why did Maelgon choose her, then?"

She looked at me slyly. "Why do you think? Not for her beauty, poor thing. Maelgon's ambition extends beyond Gwynedd, even beyond Wales. No daughter of Powys or Dyfed was good enough for him. Alliance with Rheged would have suited him best, but of course Urien has no daughters to speak of." Thus did she dismiss little Morgaine. Alyse was returning to form, and Cissa and Leonora were smiling. "So he looked to Strathclyde. Hapgar's daughters are eight and ten, but Maelgon had not the patience for a long betrothal. So he took Anet. She is twenty, if you can believe it."

"Twenty! I did not think her above fifteen!"

Alyse laughed unkindly. "And even after he saw her the young fool would not be dissuaded." She closed her eyes and sank back into her chair. "Such willfulness. It reminded me of my sister Elen. Everyone advised her against Leodegrance. Northgallis was too small; he was nearly old enough to be her father, with grown sons already from a former marriage; she was so beautiful she could do so much better! But she would hear none of it. She loved Leo and would have him or none other." She sighed deeply as my face flamed. How did she dare speak so about my father to my face? But I held my tongue and reminded myself sternly what I was about.

"It is possible, you know, Alyse, that the little convent flower is only waiting for the gardener's hand to bloom into something lovely. Who has her trust?"

Alyse shrugged. "God knows. I do not. And I care not, Guinevere. That is behind me now."

I took her hand and held it in my own. "And if Pellinore were to walk in that door right now, what would he say to hear you say such things? He would scold you for faintheartedness and bid you train the girl to her task. She will never be a queen without you."

She opened her eyes and smiled slowly. "Pellinore never scolded me in his life, and you know it well. He did not dare." The smile faded. "And I do not wish to hear it from you. It matters not to me if Maelgon has a queen or a doormat for a wife. He chose her. Like Elaine, he has made his bed and now must lie in it."

I left her soon after for she was tiring, and I had no wish to discuss Elaine's marriage. She begged me to come see her daily, and I agreed. Already she looked better than she had when I arrived, and her interest in affairs was reviving. Before I left I drew from her a promise that she would attend dinner with us every night of our visit. Whatever there was between her and Maelgon, I felt sure neither of them would voice it in Arthur's presence.

In this I was right. They never so much as looked at one another. But this only served to make conversation at dinner more difficult. Maelgon our host did not want us there; we were interfering in his affairs, but he was obliged to make us welcome. Arthur did not want Maelgon to know his real purpose in coming to Gwynedd, which Maelgon was trying hard to learn, but he wanted to know what the current situation was, which Maelgon was trying hard to hide. Anet kept her eyes in her lap and spoke to no one. Alyse plied Lancelot with questions about Elaine, her daughter, which he strove to answer in a low voice so that I would not hear. What with that, and the necessity to chuckle at Maelgon's jests and nod at his asides, poor Lancelot looked as comfortable as a cat on hot bricks. The awkwardness of the situation grew amusing, and when Arthur, catching my eye, winked at me, I nearly laughed aloud and disgraced myself. I looked forward to less formal talk after dinner, when the mead was passed around and the men talked more freely about affairs of state.

I should have remembered we were not in Camelot. Too soon for me, little Anet rose and led the women out. Alyse retired immediately to her chamber, but I was obliged to follow Anet to the meeting room and engage in pointless chatter while we waited for the men. After a time, it became clear that the men were not coming. Perhaps I should have expected it, knowing how different Maelgon was from Arthur, but it was a blow. I sat on the long bench by the unglazed windows, looking out on the paved forecourt, the grassy embankment, and beyond to the woods, longing for the freedom to escape to the stables. If this was to be nightly repeated, I should go mad. The men were discussing events of importance, while we idled talking about the weather. My gaze alighted upon a woven hanging that was new to me, and I sat up a little straighter. It was skillfully worked and designed by someone with a sense of color and style. It depicted an ancient Celtic king being feasted by his companions after a successful cattle raid. The firelight threw half his face in shadow, and his eyes seemed to burn through the very fabric. I rose, shocking the women into silence, and went over to get a closer look. The source of these wondrous effects then lay revealed; here were threads of many colors I had never seen before, shades and gradations of common colors, and hues completely unknown in nature.

"Whose doing is this?" I asked, turning back to the women.

To my amazement, little Anet rose, trembling, and made me a reverence. "It is mine, my lady."

"This is wonderful work, Anet. Did you design it? Where did you get the dyes to make such colors?"

Her face flushed crimson with my praise, but some of her shyness left her as she approached. "Thank you, my lady. Yes, I designed it. It is taken from a woodcut of King Cunedda I had in childhood. But I added the firelight. It was done at the convent, for there all the women are skilled in weaving. And Sister Boudice showed me how to make many of the dyes, but some of them I discovered for myself."

Her eyes glowed as she spoke, and all hesitation disappeared from her speech. In my heart I thanked God for revealing to me her gift.

"Do you mean you invented these dyes? Why, they are wonderful. I wish you would show me your workroom, that I may see how it is done."

She curtsied, flushing with pleasure. "Nothing would please me more, my lady. Would—would you care to see it now?" She looked so hopeful that I assented at once. Not all the women followed us; probably they saw enough of the weaving room during the day. There were three looms, one of ancient make, twice the size of the others. The room itself had been extended, at the expense of Alyse's garden, and contained great vats for dyeing, benches and tools for the preparation of the dyes, twenty or so spindles, quantities of raw wool and tubs for washing and bleaching. Once started on her topic, nothing would stop Anet's tongue, and during the next hour I learned more than I had ever wanted to know about the preparation of plants, lichens, roots, barks, and earth to get the dyes she used. She was an accomplished spinster and could spin the finest thread I ever saw. She showed me sketches she had made on parchment for a large hanging for the dining hall. Maelgon stood at the center, surrounded by his ancestors, with his precious hunting dogs at his feet. I thought this in questionable taste, seeing how Pellinore had met his death, but of course the pose was Maelgon's idea. I praised her work, and she blossomed under the praise. Anet was a skilled craftsman whose lot it was to be a queen. And while her nature might be unsuited to her role, she had pride. She could do this one thing very well, and she knew it. It was a beginning.

I bade her sit with me upon the bench while I fingered a skein of woolen thread. She had lost some of her awe and spoke readily about the quality of thread, which wool suited her best, how the blue-fleeced sheep of Rheged grew the finest wool for cloth.

Slowly I turned the skein in my hand. "Ask Maelgon to procure you some," I suggested. "He is on good terms with Urien. You could keep your own flock."

She gasped. "Oh, I do not dare! Ask him for something for myself?"

"Why not? It would be to his benefit, as well. It costs him little, and gives you great pleasure. Surely he would like to add to his livestock. Why not try it?" She trembled and grew shy again.

"I lack the courage," she whispered. "He does not listen when I speak to him."

I took her hand and leaned close to her, lowering my voice. "Ask him in bed. There even a king is defenseless against a woman." Her little face grew red, and she giggled, covering her mouth. I laughed with her, but in truth I pitied her heartily. I could not imagine that Maelgon had much tenderness in him.

"Do you—with the High King?" She gasped, her eyes wide.

"If it is important enough. He is a man, after all."

"Everyone knows you share the High King's counsels."

"If I have his ear, it is because he has learned to trust me. But that takes time, Anet. It did not start out so. And you have been

married, what? Less than a year? It is time to make a small beginning. You are not asking for a sword. This is a woman's concern,
and Maelgon should not object. You have your sphere of influence here in the castle. Make it your realm, as Alyse did."

She looked lost and frightened. "But—I am only—what if no
one does my bidding?"

"You are queen," I said firmly. "They will do it. They expect
to. Have you never given anyone an order?"

She gulped and looked nervously about the room. "Only my
women. Only in here. Here—it is safe."

"Who enlarged this room? Who dared to sacrifice Alyse's garden?"

"Maelgon," she whispered, looking hastily away. "He asked if
I needed more room for the looms. He was glad to do it."

So he had deliberately provoked Alyse. He had made it clear to
her he was king, and she had no power over him. This steadied
my resolve.

"Did it please you to lose the garden?"

"It pleased me to enlarge the room. But I was sorry to lose the
garden, and Queen Alyse was so angry."

"Well, then, why not enlarge the garden? At this time of year
the gardeners will have time to do it. I know which blooms Alyse
likes best. What say you? We will go together in the morning, and
you will give the order for it."

She had been ready to object until I offered to come with her.
But she finally agreed and thanked me profusely for the trouble I
took.

"No thanks are due me, Anet. It behooves us all to please
Alyse. Gwynedd, Wales, even Britain will be the stronger for it.
I only wish I knew why she has quarreled with Maelgon."

"Oh, I can tell you that!" Anet exclaimed, as I stared, astonished. She blushed faintly, but her joy in our newfound sisterhood
had loosened her tongue and she told me the truth without
prompting. It seemed that when Pellinore died he had been buried
without proper Christian ritual. Father Martin had succumbed to
illness the previous summer, and although the bishop in Caerleon
had promised to send a new priest to Gwynedd, none had arrived
when Pellinore had his accident. Alyse had wished to wait, even
months, to see him properly buried, but Maelgon had refused and
finally had performed the rites himself. It was his right, as king,
but Alyse was furious, resenting his kingship as much as his use
of power. Afterward, when the promised priest finally arrived,
Maelgon publicly rejected Alyse's demand to have Pellinore dis-

interred so his body could be properly blessed. Instead, he bade the priest say the blessings above the gravesite. For, he said, what difference could a few feet of earth make to the Almighty Creator?

"Queen Alyse was very angry," Anet whispered, shifting uncomfortably. "Maelgon was not very polite."

"That I can well believe," I agreed dryly. "Politeness does not run in this family."

"She said in front of everyone that she would never speak to Maelgon again until he had apologized for his rudeness."

"Then she played into his hands."

"Yes, my lady. It seems so. I know that he laughed."

I turned to look at her. She had fine, dark eyes and a straight nose. If her hair were better dressed and her gowns more carefully chosen, she might yet make a presentable queen. "Anet," I said suddenly, "would you rather be Queen of Gwynedd or a princess of Strathclyde?"

Her jaw dropped. "What do you mean?"

"Listen carefully. Your future is in your hands. If you care for Maelgon, or for your place here in Gwynedd, attend me well. Maelgon must change his ways or yield his throne."

"Yield his throne?" she whispered, shaking.

"Why do you think Arthur is here?"

Her hand flew to her mouth, and she covered a shriek. Clearly, she had no desire to return to Hapgar's court and be pawned off to one of his petty lords.

I slipped an arm about her waist and hugged her gently. "Do not be afraid. That is the last resort. And you can do much to prevent it."

"I?" There were tears in her eyes.

"Yes. You. You share Maelgon's bed. You have the opportunity to sway him. He must learn that the greatest Christian virtue is that of love."

"You—you mean the—the Druids?"

"Yes."

"Oh, my lady Guinevere! I told him—everyone told him—it was wrong! It was cruel! But he has a hate within his soul he cannot control! I knew he would bring suffering upon us all! I knew it!"

I cradled her against me, rocking her as she wept. "He is a man now, and a king. He *must* control it. Without control, how can he rule? Discipline can be taught, Anet. He can learn it."

"But—but how?"

"Little by little. We will start with small steps. First we will give the order to enlarge the garden."

Late that night when Arthur came to me, I told him all that had passed. He was pleased. It had been harder going with Maelgon. Most of the men were still drinking and looked to be at it till dawn. Maelgon would not let Lancelot go, no doubt hoping that in time the drink would loosen his tongue.

"All I have been able to learn," Arthur said wearily, "is that he has scouts posted throughout the forests, watching all the approaches to Gwynedd. If he does not expect an attack from Salowen, he is giving a good imitation of it."

I shivered. I would not want to be in Maelgon's boots, with a Druid's curse upon my head, never knowing from which direction violent death would come.

"Surely Salowen must know you are here."

Arthur shrugged. "Even the Saxons know I am here. Let us hope he can get a messenger safely past the scouts."

"And Fion? When does he arrive? Will Maelgon make him welcome? How long will he visit?"

At last Arthur smiled. "I should have known who was foremost in your thoughts all this while. Thanks to you, he is on excellent terms with Gwynedd. We have had no message from him, either, but we should see him soon."

"You know very well, my lord, that he is not foremost in my thoughts."

"Do I?" he whispered, coming closer and putting his hands into my hair. "Then you must prove it to me. This may be a homecoming for you, my lovely wife, but to me it is like stepping into a strange sea. I cannot get my bearings."

15 ⚙ THE MESSENGERS

By the end of our first week in Gwynedd Alyse was walking with me about the castle, gaining strength daily, and beginning to look forward to seeing Fion again. In her eyes he would always be Pellinore's ransomed hostage, but I did not think that would bother Fion. To get her out in the sun again, I asked her to take me to Pellinore's grave, that I might pay him my respects and place flowers upon his resting place. This she did with great dignity, saying little, and keeping her eyes dry. On the way back I took her past the garden. In a week the gardeners had almost doubled its size and had built a little bower where she could sit and doze out of the bright sun. When she saw it, she stopped as if struck, and I felt her hand tremble on my arm.

"Did Maelgon do this?" she whispered.

"No, madam. Anet gave the order for it."

"Anet?" She turned slowly toward me, and I saw tears in her eyes. "This is your doing, Guinevere, may God bless you. Anet never gave an order in her life."

"I do assure you, she did. She told me herself she felt responsible, since it was on account of her looms that you lost it."

She shook her head. "Maelgon was responsible. Yet he permits this? Has he seen it?"

"Oh, yes. He has seen it. But he is too busy worrying about Arthur to worry about gardens."

A small smile twitched at the corners of her mouth. "And well he should worry," she said under her breath.

Just then Anet looked out from the weaving room and waved to me. "My lady Guinevere! I want your advice!" She lifted her skirts and came hurrying breathlessly up the path. "The cooks are angry because we have taken the carrot bed and the vines—I have an idea for expanding the kitchen garden, as well! Oh!" She stared in disbelief at Alyse, who stared in wonder at her.

"My lady Queen Alyse!" She gasped, falling into a curtsy. "Please forgive me—I did not know it was you!"

Slowly Alyse put out a thin hand and raised her. "Anet. My daughter." They looked at one another in silence for a moment. Then Alyse released her hand and slowly smiled. "Guinevere tells me I have you to thank for replacing what my son had taken away."

I shot Anet a warning glance, and she read my thought. Gulping, she nodded shyly. "Does it—I hope it pleases you, my lady? If there is aught you do not like, or would rather rearrange, you have only to say so."

"And you will see that it is done? Thank you, Anet. That is a generous offer."

"Oh, Queen Alyse, I would do anything to please you!" The truth of this heartfelt avowal was so clearly written on the girl's plain face that even Alyse was moved.

She patted Anet's hand as we walked together through the garden. "Perhaps you would care to take some refreshment with me this afternoon, when the heat of the day is past? Guinevere has been coming daily to see me, but we are tired of reliving old times and could do with some new conversation."

Anet was nearly struck speechless by the honor being done her, but commanded her fear enough to accept politely. When she had excused herself and returned to her weaving, I bent and kissed Alyse's soft cheek.

"That was graciously done, my lady queen. You will not regret it."

Alyse chuckled. "Well, it was what you wanted, was it not? I am not blind, Guinevere. I see what you are after. And I owe it to you. For the garden."

It was never easy to fool Alyse.

One night at dinner, when the heat of the hall was oppressive, the air unmoving, the torches smoking and everyone's temper was frayed, a sentry came to Maelgon's elbow and announced the arrival of a messenger for the High King.

"Who sent him?" Maelgon asked gruffly.

"He will not say who sent him, my lord, but he says to tell you he bears a message from Salowen to the High King Arthur."

Maelgon's eyes blazed. "Throw him in the dungeons and let him cool his heels! I will not have the filthy vermin in my hall!"

Arthur's body went taut, and his eyes grew cold. But he waited.

The sentry licked his lips and shuffled his feet, but made no move to obey. "My lord—"

"Well?" Maelgon cried, slamming his tankard on the table.

"My lord, I cannot. He is a King's man." The sentry looked nervously at Arthur, and Maelgon glared at him, but at length, having no choice, waved his hand in assent.

Into the room walked a slim youth in a plain tunic, bearing himself like a soldier, and showing neither fear nor awe. When he approached Arthur I gasped aloud. It was Mordred! Arthur rose, and Mordred bent his knee.

"My lord King."

"Arise, Mordred. You have a message for me?"

"Yes, my lord."

"Is it a private message?"

"No, my lord. It may be publicly given."

"Who sent you?"

"I don't know the man's name, my lord. But I know that he is a Druid from Mona's Isle, and the message is from the Archdruid Salowen."

"And how did you come to be the bearer of this message?"

"I was in the town with some soldiers when a boy approached me and took me to this man who had the message." Then he lifted his face to Arthur and flashed him a quick look full of pride and love, before dropping his gaze to the floor once more. "I put myself in the way of it," he murmured.

Arthur did not move, but I sensed his pleasure and approval as surely as if I had seen him embrace the boy. "Give me the message."

Mordred stood very straight and closed his eyes to get it word for word. "Salowen, leader of the Sacred Order, who serves the Goddess in Nemet and walks between the standing stones, sends greetings to Arthur, High King of Britain. Hear this, King of men. The Great Goddess has been raped by heathen murderers and cries aloud for vengeance. Before the new moon falls from the sky, death will fall upon Gwynedd." Here the men stirred, and Maelgon would have spoken, but Arthur lifted a hand, keeping his eyes on Mordred's face, and they were still. "Because the High King has shown himself to be a just man, Salowen will speak with him, if he wills. But not so long as he lives beneath the roof of Maelgon the Murderer, or eats his food or drinks his wine. Let the High King remove to Caer Narfon with no protection but his own troops, and Salowen shall meet him at his pleasure."

Mordred opened his eyes and looked up at Arthur. "That is the message, my lord. But the man told me that every night and every day until the new moon, Mona shall be invisible to men, that none may find it." All around the table men crossed themselves, but Arthur looked with pride upon Mordred. It took courage to recite that message before Maelgon himself, and I could see the boy's legs were shaking. Arthur thanked him gravely and sent him back to the barracks with an escort.

As soon as the door shut behind Mordred, Maelgon spoke. "If the Druid approached him, my lord, the boy must be a pagan himself."

Arthur, still standing, turned. "Yes."

"Did you know this? Why did you bring him here? Only Christians are welcome in Gwynedd."

A hush fell over the company. More than one of Arthur's men knew that Mordred was his son. For a long moment Arthur said nothing. When he spoke at last, the very gentleness of his voice revealed the depth of his anger. "I choose my soldiers, Maelgon, for the strength of their sword arms, not for the names they call their gods. If you wish to contest this, say so. We can settle this tonight. Sword against sword."

Maelgon blanched. He knew now that the High King was willing to wage war over the Druids. He glanced hopefully at Lancelot, but Lancelot's eyes were on Arthur, awaiting a signal.

"Of—of course my lord is welcome to choose his soldiers by any standard he deems fitting," Maelgon stammered hastily. "But in Gwynedd we are all Christian."

"I am glad to know it," Arthur replied evenly. "Let every Christian keep the commandment to love his neighbor as himself, and we need worry no longer about who is pagan and who is not."

Maelgon opened his mouth to object, but found everyone staring at him and thought better of it. Swiftly Arthur leaned across the table until he breathed into Maelgon's face.

"If aught happens to that boy while we are in Gwynedd, you shall answer to me with your life. I promise it."

Maelgon drew away and Arthur straightened. The moment passed before anyone knew what had happened, yet fear swept the room. Alyse and Anet huddled together. The sweat stood out on Lancelot's brow.

Someone broke the silence with a nervous cough, and Maelgon bowed his head. "As you wish, my lord King."

Appeased, Arthur took his seat and signaled the wine bearer.

Relief loosened everyone's tongue and soon the hall was noisy with conversation.

"What did he mean about the isle becoming invisible?"

"It is an old Druid trick. But half their power is in the minds of their believers."

"What do you mean? What trick?"

"The calling of the mists. Old Salowen's a master at it. He doesn't mean the isle will disappear, just that he will shroud it in mist so you can't see it from shore. That's all."

"It's true! I was fishing out past the point in the coracle at dusk and saw a great mist creep off the sea in the west!"

"Well, don't excite yourself. The isle is still there. You have only to go through the mist to find it."

"Go through a Druid's mist? Who would dare?"

"My lord Arthur," Maelgon said loudly, stilling the other voices. "Do you intend to leave for Caer Narfon to meet with Salowen? I assure you, I will not stand in your way."

Lancelot lifted his goblet to hide a smile. Arthur, straight-faced, answered politely. "Thank you, King Maelgon, but I will see Salowen at my leisure. And it would be a shame to leave so soon, after the hospitality you and your good queen have provided us. We will stay until we have feasted our honored guest. We await Fion."

Maelgon shrugged rudely and left it there, but it was obvious to anyone with eyes that he was furious. It was a relief to me when Anet rose to lead us out. I only hoped that she had sense enough to know better than to ask Maelgon for her blue-fleeced sheep tonight.

Three days later we had another messenger. Arthur, Maelgon, and most of the men were out hunting when Maelgon's scouts brought in a young man in ragged clothing, bound at the wrists and beaten to senselessness. They threw him in the dungeon to await Maelgon's return. I learned of this through Ailsa, who had been dozing near a window when he was brought in. I went at once to Anet and let her know if it. She stared at me blankly.

"Surely, my lady, we can wait to know who he is until Maelgon returns."

I sent her women from the room and sat her down. "This is an opportunity for you to do great good, Anet. And to increase your power. At Camelot, I visit the dungeons almost daily to speak with the men there. Not to console them, but simply to be kind. I do not need to see that they are not mistreated. Arthur is a fair

man. But he wishes those he must imprison to learn from their
mistakes and not to leave with a grudge against his judgment. I
simply go to see them, and be seen by them, and listen to their
complaints. We do not have many who return, once they are
freed."

"You want me to go see this man?" She began to tremble, and
I held her hand firmly.

"I will go with you. If he is a messenger, which is what Ailsa
thinks, it is wrong to imprison him."

"You want me to free him?" Anet whimpered. "Oh, no!"

"No, you cannot free him. But at least you can see that he is
not cruelly treated. You have the right. This is your domain." I sat
beside her and spoke more gently. "They have taken his weapons,
if he had any, Anet. You cannot come to harm. Maelgon's sentries
will obey you. Why not? It will be like the gardeners, you will
see. Come, let us go now."

Anet went unwillingly, only because she could not deny me.
The sentries looked astonished to see her, but to a man they bent
their knees and let us pass. We found the prisoner senseless on the
dirt floor, his hands still bound, a filthy gag in his mouth. He was
a mere youth with his beard just beginning. In the corner of his
tiny cell two rats sat boldly watching him. To my surprise, Anet
hardly noticed the vermin. It told me something about the convent.

At her order, given in a shaking voice, the guards unbound the
boy, removed the gag, and washed his face. It was all we could
do for him, and it was little enough. But the change it wrought in
Anet was wonderful. She grew excited at her power to ministrate
to the needy, and boldly asked the guard to send to her the scouts
who had brought him in. Astonished, the guard demurred, until I
murmured sweetly that King Arthur was expecting a messenger,
and we hoped with all our hearts that this was not the man. The
guard broke into a sweat and said at once he would send for the
scouts.

When we were back in the fresh air of the garden, I hugged
Anet and kissed her for joy. "Well done! Well done, Queen Anet!
I could not have done it better myself!"

She colored and then said eagerly, "It was so easy! That poor
youth! He is hardly more than a boy, and they beat him so!"

"They probably think he is pagan. Perhaps he is. Here in
Gwynedd, that seems to be enough."

"Do you think Maelgon will be offended, when he hears?"

"That you had his face washed? Can he be that petty?" Then,

because I knew the answer to that, I hurried on. "You know, Anet, that every queen has the power to give protection to those who ask it of her. In old Celtic law, not even your husband could violate that protection. Because it is a powerful weapon, you must use it wisely and sparingly. But if you do not use it, you give up the right."

"But this man has not asked it of me."

"No, I am not thinking of this man. But in the future, there may come a time . . . In order to grant protection, you must have the power to enforce it. Give Maelgon's sentries time to get used to obeying your commands. Then one day they will do it without thought."

"I shall go into the dungeons every day!"

When Maelgon returned, he had the scouts brought before him, and learned, as we had already done, that they had stopped the youth upon the road into Gwynedd. That he was pagan was clear enough; he wore the symbol of the Mother on a thong about his neck. They did not even have to put him to the test of the Lord's Prayer. He had confessed quite openly he was not Christian, and they had not waited to hear more, but had taken him prisoner.

Arthur was furious. He openly demanded to know why his laws were not obeyed in Gwynedd, and when Maelgon stood up to him and claimed the right to govern his own kingdom as he saw fit, Arthur, with his hand on Excalibur's hilt, and every eye in the room upon his hand, asked if that meant he could do insult to anyone he pleased without redress. There was silence. Were those laws? Arthur demanded. Was that justice? Had not the High King sworn to protect the rights of his people, down the the lowliest peasant? Did not Maelgon agree that this man had been unjustly treated? They did not even know yet what his crime was.

Grudgingly Maelgon backed down, and everyone exhaled. The prisoner, now awake, was brought before them. He fell on both knees in front of Arthur and kissed his boots. His name, he said, was Nuathe. His mother served the Lady's shrine at Avalon. He bore a message for Arthur from Niniane, the Lady of the Lake.

"Give me the message," Arthur said.

"Do not go to Rheged, my lord!" Arthur looked startled and waited for the rest, but nothing more came.

"That is the message, Nuathe? Nothing else?"

"That is the message, my lord. The lady Niniane gave it me herself. She bade me hurry. I was chosen as the messenger because I ride fast."

Arthur frowned, and Maelgon, seeing his chance, began to

grumble. "What sort of a message is that? Are you telling us the truth, boy?"

"It is the sort of message Niniane might send," the King cut in. "And in any event," he added lightly, "he was speaking to me."

Arthur thanked the youth for bringing him the message, and for enduring such hardships along the way—this with a pointed look—and begged him to rest well before his return journey. Maelgon took the hint, and housed the boy with honor until he left, escorted by Maelgon's troops, two days later. After all, it was known throughout Britain that to harm a King's messenger was to insult the King and was asking for bloodshed. Before he left, Nuathe publicly thanked Anet for her treatment of him while he lay in the dungeons and praised her for her Christian charity. All of Arthur's train did Anet honor, and Maelgon could do no less than join them.

Three days later we had a third messenger. This one, although a pagan, came dressed as a soldier and carried a messenger's pouch; Maelgon's scouts let him pass. He arrived at sunset, as we all gathered before going into dinner. He bowed politely to Maelgon, to me, Alyse, and Anet, then went on one knee before Arthur. He came, he said, from Rheged.

Arthur took the scroll from his hand, examined the seal, broke it, and beckoning the torchbearer nearer, slowly read the message. His face grew grave, and he read a second time. Then he tucked the scroll in his tunic and faced the messenger. "Your name?"

"Cathbad, my lord."

"Whom do you serve?"

"Sir Uwain, my lord. King Urien's son."

"Are you a Christian, Cathbad?"

The man's eyes flashed, and he hesitated just a moment. "No, my lord. I am not. I serve the Mother."

"Do you know what this message says?"

"No, my lord. It was sealed before it was given to me."

"Tell me what you know of events in Rheged."

I watched Arthur anxiously, wondering why he was treading so carefully, wondering what the scroll said. Lancelot watched him, too, frowning. Maelgon looked at Cathbad in disgust.

"King Urien has been summoned to the defense of Strathclyde. King Hapgar sent a message begging his help a week hence. The Picts have broken their borders and attacked in great numbers." Anet gasped and sought my hand. "King Urien thought that many lives might be saved if you could but show your face in Strathclyde, my lord. Since you are by chance halfway there already, and the Picts know it not." He paused. "They would not stand against you."

Arthur's frown deepened. "Is Urien going?"

"Indeed, my lord. We are bound by treaty to do so. Preparations were well under way when I left."

"Does Uwain go with him? Who stays as regent?"

"Coel stays, my lord. The eldest son. All the rest go with him. This is a major attack."

Arthur drew a deep breath and bade the man rise. "Thank you, Cathbad, for bringing the message. Get you a night's sleep. In the morning we will take up our arms and accompany you back to Rheged."

This set the castle buzzing. Maelgon was of course delighted to be rid of Arthur and was consequently ebullient and condescending throughout dinner. Arthur himself was silent, and though the conversation among the men centered on the savage Picts and the glory of war, he would not speak about it.

I excused myself early from the women and went up to the tower to think. It was a fine, warm night and the stars were out. In the northwest the mist still lay upon the sea. Salowen's mist, they were calling it already. We had been in Gwynedd a fortnight and nothing had been done about the Druids. In five days the new moon would rise, and Arthur would be in Rheged. Without him behind me, would I have the courage to defy Maelgon should the need arise? Why was Fion not here? I felt now as Arthur felt. I could not get my bearings.

Arthur came to me before midnight. I heard his voice bidding the sentries keep watch upon the stairs and leave the parapet to us. When I turned to greet him, he took me in his arms and kissed me hungrily, unbraiding my hair and letting his lips slide down my throat.

"Arthur! What is the matter?"

He laughed hoarsely and pulled me closer, kissing my lips. "I do not want to go, Gwen. This is the false messenger. I am sure of it."

"Then do not go, my lord! Niniane has warned you twice about it!"

Abruptly he loosed me and began to pace back and forth along the parapet. "I must go. Urien is a major king and ally. If he calls me, I cannot delay."

"But if the messenger is false, then he does not call you."

"Yes, but I cannot really know that until I get there, Gwen.

Suppose Nuathe was the false messenger? Have you ever seen him before, among any of Niniane's attendants?"

"No, my lord. But it is his mother who attends her. Not Nuathe."

"Still. It is just possible his message was a lie."

"Sent by whom?" He shrugged. I thought carefully back. "He came in on a red roan, lop-eared. I've never seen that horse before."

"Probably borrowed from the garrison at Caerleon, or hired from some inn. Surely he didn't ride it all the way from Ynys Witrin. Not if he was in a hurry."

"Then perhaps it was Mordred's message that was the lie."

His head came up, and he stopped his pacing. "I've thought of that. Mordred cannot identify the man who gave it to him. He was robed and his face hooded. If it was indeed Salowen who sent it, it could easily be a lie. Truth and untruth are much the same to the Sacred Order. But in that case, I must still go to Rheged. And the moon is waning fast."

"But you suspect Cathbad. I saw it in your face."

He smiled bleakly. "Let us hope no one else is so observant. Yes, I suspect him. For one thing, he told me exactly what was in the scroll. No more, no less. As if it were rehearsed. He admitted he could read. Does he imagine all couriers are so educated? And the scroll itself. It is Urien's seal, right enough, but the Latin is not quite right. It has an odd flavor, like those old scrolls found at York years ago, which Valerius swears are verbatim translations from the Celtic tongue. And I know Urien's scribe. His name is Junius. He was trained by his father, who was a Roman." He turned away and began to pace once more. "Cathbad was dressed like a soldier, but he did not carry himself like one. Did you see his eyes when I asked him if he served Christ? It was as if I had offered him poison. If he is not a Druid himself, I am a Saxon." He paused. "And the timing is so perfect. Something is about to happen here in Gwynedd. But the King's presence is a problem. How to remove the King? Send him a plea for help he cannot refuse. It is just too obvious."

"Then don't go."

He whirled and faced me. "I must. Even though I know it to be false. I must go. Men are not given perfect knowledge. I cannot be sure. I cannot risk offending Urien if I am wrong. It would cost too many lives."

"What would you like me to do? How can I help you?"

He sighed and stared up at the night sky. "Wait here for Fion and watch Maelgon every second. I am leaving Lancelot in command of half my troops. He is the obvious choice; he has Maelgon's ear, much joy it brings him. Talk to him about Maelgon. Learn as much as you can. And take him out riding now and again. He will lose his wits if he has no release."

I went up to Arthur and took him in my arms. I could feel the tension in his body. He was strung as taut as a bowstring before the arrow flies.

"Arthur," I whispered. "All will be well. God has not brought you here to stab you in the back. Go, do what you must do, and come back quickly. We will be here, awaiting your return. Have faith in us."

"Ah, Gwen," he breathed, bending down to me. "How I rely on you!"

16 ☙ The Isle of Mona

With Arthur gone, Maelgon grew light-hearted and everyone around him breathed more easily. Anet received his promise for her sheep. Maelgon publicly complimented her upon the new garden, and even went so far as to apologize to Alyse for his high-handed treatment of her. Happiness, it seemed, had been restored.

But Lancelot was uneasy. Maelgon could not be trusted out of sight, he grumbled. He did not fear Arthur enough. Following Arthur's instructions, I took Lancelot away for a while each day. Sometimes we rode, sometimes we walked, and we kept our talk to political events: Maelgon, Arthur, the Druids, and the future of Gwynedd. Lancelot firmly believed that the Druids, with their mists and magics, were dying in Britain and that our future belonged in Christian hands. But while he approved of Maelgon's wish to have a Christian kingdom, he did not believe that Maelgon had a right to persecute men simply for being pagan. Maelgon's treatment of Nuathe had shocked him, as it had many of Arthur's men. Maelgon, he admitted solemnly to me, as if it were news, had not the temperament for kingship.

Spending less time with Maelgon, Lancelot began to relax a little and smile more. He was kind to Anet, whom he called my pupil, and complimented her upon the new way she wore her hair. And he found time to spend with Alyse. I tried to anticipate their meetings and leave them alone, but I was not always successful. Alyse could not imagine why it distressed me to hear Lancelot speak of Elaine and Galahad.

We had no more messengers. It was too soon to hear from Arthur, he had barely reached Rheged. He had taken Mordred with him, since the boy was safer fighting the Picts than staying with us in Gwynedd.

On the night of no moon a deathly hush descended upon Gwynedd. The sea mist seemed to hover just yards offshore. Few soldiers slept that night, and in the morning everyone was grumpy. Whatever was coming was coming soon; the new moon rose at midnight.

About midday, tired of the edginess that enveloped the castle, I coaxed Lancelot out for a ride. Maelgon had bragged he would go hunting and then called it off at the last minute. His scouts had formed a tight ring around the castle, and he had archers posted at every window. In disgust at such cowardice, Lancelot rode out openly with me and a small escort. We rode up into the hills I had known so well as a girl. The air was sweet with pinescent and the woods alive with birdsong. It reminded me of that day, long ago, when we had met.

"Lancelot! Do you know where we are?"

He grinned. "I was thinking the same. The clearing is up ahead on this path, is it not?"

I nodded. He gave the signal to dismount and handed the reins to the captain of the escort. "Take the horses down to the stream to drink, then post a guard and rest awhile. There is a small clearing around the bend in the path. I will be there with the Queen."

"Yes, my lord."

The clearing was smaller than I remembered, crowded with scree around the edges, the grass grown long. Near the center, where Lancelot had stood when I first saw him, grew a young laurel. I plucked a leaf from it and crushed it between my fingers, releasing its sweet scent.

"This is the place," I said softly, half to myself. "I could never forget it."

Lancelot took my hand. "Yonder is where I first saw you. Sitting on your white mare with your mantle thrown back and your hair loose around your face. Never in my life had I seen such a beautiful woman." Gently he pushed a few stray strands from my brow. "Never in my life will I see such another." He stepped closer, and trembling, I turned away from him. A great oak stood at the edge of the clearing, must have stood there for generations, and I leaned against it, grateful for support. Slowly Lancelot walked toward me. I was no more capable of telling him no than of growing wings for flight. When he put his hand upon my waist I leaned into him. When he touched his lips to my face and whispered to me, all I could say was "Lancelot. Lancelot." And when he began to kiss me, first softly and then with sweet demand, I held his body close and clung to him, wishing with all my heart this would never end.

Suddenly he was gone. Rough hands grabbed me and something foul was thrust into my mouth. My hands were bound behind me. Gasping for breath, I saw Lancelot on the ground, kicking and writhing while seven men in ill-dressed skins gagged and bound him and took his sword. One he kicked in the groin, another in the knee. The leader lifted a club and smashed his head. I drew breath to scream, but choked on the gag. With a grunt, Lancelot lay still. It had all happened in a moment, and in absolute silence. The birds still sang undisturbed in the treetops.

There were twelve men altogether. They bound Lancelot and tied his senseless body to the oak. A thin stream of blood seeped from his ear. Then two of them lifted me as easily as they might carry a brace of quail and headed down an animal track toward the shore. Since I could do nothing against them, I lay still, but I could not keep the tears from my eyes. Had they killed him? Would he live? Would his own soldiers find him there at length? If he lived, he would wish himself dead before he faced Arthur's men bound and gagged, the Queen taken and his sword gone. Oh, my Lancelot! How cruelly the fates were wont to treat us!

The men carried me a long way, without speaking so much as a whisper. I knew we were getting near the sea; I smelled it. Near the water's edge, they dumped me rudely on the sand, stripped off their skins, and buried them under a rock. From the same hiding place they drew forth robes, roughly sewn of coarse gray cloth, and donned them. For belts they had only simple twine. Two by two they ran into the brush and pulled out little lightweight coracles made of bone and wood and tanned skins, well waxed.

"Gorn, you and Llyd take her. Yours is the biggest."

"She will sink it. Let Bilin have her. His is strongest."

"If she comes with me there will be no room for Nidd. I cannot paddle her alone."

"Do as I say, Gorn. The soldiers will find him soon. So what if she is taller than we thought? Try it. If she struggles, strike her."

Hands grabbed me and hauled me into the tiny craft. I could not believe they were going to trust these primitive constructions to the sea. They rocked and swayed and spun about, dangerously deep in the water. I shut my eyes and in my heart said every prayer of penitence I knew.

Time crawled by in silence. The only sounds were sea sounds, the chuckle of water as the waves lifted and dropped us, the soft kiss of the paddles, the muffled cry of seabirds. I felt unaccountably sleepy and struggled to open my eyes. We were enveloped in gray mist so thick the robed men seemed to disappear before my eyes, although they were certainly there, pressed hard against me, swaying with the effort of keeping the horrible little craft afloat. I felt a sob well up within me and gulped to keep it down. I knew now who these creatures were. They were Druids, and we were going to Mona's Isle.

To me it seemed like years before we reached the shore. Even then the men were quiet, talking to each other in low voices, two of them carrying me as they had before, the others carrying the little boats and hiding them in the bushes. Then they marched single file through the pine woods that grew close to the water's edge, and up a small rise and out of the cold mist, into brilliant sunshine. I looked about as best I could. We were in a sheep meadow, where sheep and goats grazed with a shepherd boy and his dog in close attendance. It looked for all the world like any peaceful meadow in Britain.

Suddenly I heard chanting. It began as a low hum, steady and throbbing, but as we approached its source I could distinguish the words, ritual and meaningless, chanted to a pounding rhythm that beat heavily, insistently like a hammer at the smith's forge. The men's gait changed; now they marched to the chant, swinging left and right. I felt the steady pounding in my belly, and thought I would be sick. Above us on both sides rose dark standing stones, breathing cold upon my neck, pricking my flesh like eyes on one's back. At the end of the avenue the men stopped. I tilted my head back and saw a tall man in a white robe standing before a wide door carved into the hillside behind him. His hood hid his face. He raised his hands in a solemn blessing and then said curtly, "Take her below. The cell is prepared. Well done."

As the men began to move, he came around to get a better look at me, and I saw, tucked in his embroidered belt, the long crescent knife of sacrifice. The white hood bent lower, and within its shadow gleamed a row of sharp, even teeth. He was smiling. I fainted.

When I awoke I lay upon a narrow pallet in a small cell. The floor was dirt, beaten hard and swept clean. Walls of undressed rock sweated moisture. Through a crevice crept a draft of sweet air. There were no windows, and only one door, low and curved and ill-fitting. Beside the pallet was a stool of carved wood, and on it, a horn cup and a candle. I sat up as memory flooded back and groaned. They had wrenched my shoulder when they dropped me on the beach. I moved my arm tentatively; stiffness, no more. Where the cruel rope had torn my wrists, and the gag cut my mouth, someone had applied a soothing balm. The smell was familiar—oil of spikenard? I shook my head to clear it and, bracing my hands against the rock, I managed to stand, although my head was spinning. I gasped, looking down at myself. I was dressed in a white Druid's robe and nothing else! I was naked beneath it. They had taken my tunic, my leggings, even my undergarments and my boots. My bare feet were clean, my hair was clean—they had stripped me and bathed me and even scented my hair! Surely they must have drugged me to do so much without my waking! I began to shake, and sat down quickly upon the pallet. That I was being carefully readied for something was certain, but for what?

Someone scratched upon the door and then slowly pushed it open. A young man's face looked in, and he smiled when he saw me awake. Nodding politely he came in holding a wooden pitcher.

"Good evening, my lady. You must be thirsty. Would you like some more water? Why, you haven't touched your water yet."

"I don't know what's in it."

He grinned. "You think it might be poisoned? Poison is a dirty tool. Servants of Christ may stoop to poison. We do not. See? I will drink some myself." This he did, with no ill effects. When he refilled the cup and passed it to me, I drank gratefully.

"Thank you. What is your name? May I know it?"

"Kevin, my lady."

"Thank you, Kevin. I am in your debt."

He set the pitcher upon the little stool and bowed to me.

"Who are you, Kevin? Why are you kind to me, when the others were not? What are you doing here? May I ask these things?"

"Well, you may ask them," Kevin said easily. I judged him to be about nineteen, but it was hard to tell. "The ones who brought you here are servants, really. I am a graduate of the School. I am an acolyte. Soon I will be an initiate."

I attempted a smile, but my mouth was stiff from the gag. "Congratulations."

"Can you stand, my lady? Would you like a hand?" He extended his hand, strong and warm, and I took it. I was taller than he was by a head. He took a step back and surveyed me slowly from head to toe.

"You are a beautiful woman," he said bluntly. "It was a pleasure to prepare you."

I blushed, affronted at such directness. "What did you do to me? Prepare me for what?"

Kevin smiled. His teeth looked very white in his short black beard. "Do not be afraid. We who served the Goddess take vows of chastity from full moon to new. But tomorrow, when you are made one of us, if you are willing . . ."

"Made one of you? Is that what I am prepared for?"

"It is a lesson to Maelgon. You will be offered to the Goddess. If She claims you, one of Maelgon's own family shall be numbered among us. A just retribution, don't you think?"

"How am I to be offered? How will She claim me?"

"Ahhh." Kevin sighed. "Now you are asking questions I may not answer. You must wait for dawn, when the new moon stands above Nemet."

I shivered and clutched the robe about me.

Kevin smiled and backed toward the door. "Do not be afraid, beautiful one. Salowen himself has consecrated you to the Goddess. You have been done great honor."

"Salowen! Was he here?"

"Indeed. He oversaw the preparations."

My hand went to the crucifix at my throat, but of course it was not there. Kevin observed the gesture and smiled again.

"We are not savages," he said gently, "no matter what they teach you about us. You will live to see your husband and children again. Good evening." And he closed the door behind him.

"Children!" I gasped. "I have no children! Kevin! Kevin! Come back! Who do you think I am?"

But the door was locked, and no one answered my pounding. I threw myself on the pallet and wept until I was beyond feeling. Hours passed. I tossed fitfully, unable to sleep. I did not know what awaited me. The Goddess I had worshipped as a child, the Goddess Niniane served, was the Good Goddess, the Mother of men, whose gifts were life and health and fertility. To Her belonged the spring blooming, the full, rich living of high summer, the planting and harvesting of all good things, the yearly renewal of life. But here on Mona Salowen worshipped the Dark Goddess, the Great Goddess, who lived in Nemet and exacted retribution for one's sins. Her gifts were justice, victory, vengeance, and death. And yet they were one Mother. Like the gold coin of Britain, with Arthur's image stamped on one side and his deadly Sword Excalibur on the other, so did the Goddess have different faces She turned to men.

"O Holy Mother," I whispered, kneeling on the dirt floor and clasping my hands tight. "Blessed Mary, Bearer of Light, Giver of Death, whatever name it pleases You to take, Mother, hear my plea. Spare Lancelot's life and deliver me from the trial that awaits me. Send me Arthur! Send me Merlin! If escape be possible, oh please, please rescue me. If not—if not, give me strength to endure what is ahead. Let me not shame Arthur, whatever happens, more than I have done already. O Mother, Mother, give me strength!"

After this, I was able to sleep. But I woke as soon as the door opened. It was Kevin, bearing a new candle.

"Kevin!" I leaped up and went to his side. "Oh, Kevin, what hour is it now?"

"The new moon has risen. I have just come from the ceremony." Indeed, there was a milky calm about him, and his voice was thick with sleep. I wondered if it were true, that the Druids drugged themselves for worship, and if so, why?

"Kevin, tarry a moment, I pray you." I placed a hand upon his arm, and he turned swiftly to me, a light in his eyes. Only then did I remember that his vows of chastity no longer bound him, and I stepped back a pace, holding hard to my courage. "You told me before, I should live to see my children again. Kevin, I have no children. Do you not know me? I am Guinevere, Queen of Britain. King Arthur's wife."

He went pale and stared at me unmoving.

"I must see Salowen the Archdruid. If he is able, after the ceremony—send him to me at once. I must see him before the dawn. His very life, the future of the isle itself, is at stake."

Slowly, with great care, Kevin turned away from me and lit the candle with a steady hand. Then he went to the door and stopped. "If he will see me, I will tell him what you have said."

"Make him see you!" I cried. "Surely there must be one among your number who knows me by sight! Bring him here." But the door was closed, and Kevin was already gone.

I waited a long time. I sat on the pallet and dozed, hearing the Druids' chanting in my dreams, but waking afterward to deathly stillness. Suddenly, when I had nearly given up hope, a robed figure slipped silently into my cell. I blinked to make sure he was not a vision. His hood was thrown back, revealing a thin face with narrow eyes, a long, hooked nose, and thin, cruel mouth. His white hair was cropped close to his head; I could see the bones of his skull. Around his neck he wore a thick collar, beautifully patterned. His hands, long and thin and sensual, made a quick sign over my head, and then disappeared into the folds of his robe.

"I am Salowen," he said. His voice, deep and rich and vibrant, was that of a man half his age and twice his size.

I struggled to my feet and made him a reverence. "You do me honor, Salowen, to see me. I asked you to come because I fear you have made a mistake."

"I do not make mistakes."

"If you think taking me will anger Maelgon, you are in error."

"You are his sister."

I gasped. To be taken for Elaine! What cruel irony was this?

"I am not his sister! Elaine is in Less Britain with her sons. She has never left since she went there as a bride. Surely you must know this!"

He nodded calmly. "As I know that you have befriended your brother's wife, the new queen, and have reconciled her to your mother."

He had spies in Maelgon's very household! "My mother is dead. I grew up in Gwynedd as Pellinore's ward. Queen Alyse is my aunt, although she has been as a mother to me."

"And Maelgon a brother."

"No. I never liked Maelgon, and he never liked me. He always was a bully. That is why Arthur came to Wales, to bring peace between you or remove him from his throne."

"Ha!" He laughed harshly, and the patterned collar around his neck began to move. My hand flew to my mouth to cover a scream. The collar slowly unwound itself into a great snake, sliding down his arm toward me, its eager tongue flicking in and out.

"Do not move," Salowen commanded. His long hands stroked the slithering flesh as the snake descended, sliding gracefully across the floor, brushing my feet. Gracefully the snake lifted its head, wrapped itself around my legs, and began to climb. I shut my eyes and held myself still. I was terrified that I might faint. I

heard a low-pitched whistle, and at once the snake retreated, un-
coiling gracefully from about my ankles and returning to
Salowen's outstretched hand. When he had settled it again about
his neck, and I had begun to breath, he smiled, showing his little
cat's teeth.

"That is a point in your favor. It is well known that the lady
Elaine cannot abide serpents."

"It is well known that Elaine has never left Lanascol!" I retorted angrily.

Something flashed in his eyes, and I shivered. "It is well
known," he hissed softly, "that Guinevere has never left Camelot."

"How can I prove who I am? Is there no one here who knows
me?"

"There is Cathbad. If he returns in time."

"Cathbad! Then—then it was you who tricked Arthur into leaving Gwynedd?"

Again he smiled, and again a frisson of horror slipped up my
spine.

"Tell me this," he said softly, leaning closer, "if you are not
Maelgon's sister, what were you doing in the forest, alone with
her husband?"

I flushed scarlet, avoiding his eyes. There was no reply to that.
Pleased, Salowen stroked the snake and regarded me dispassion-
ately. "If you are Guinevere, then are you Maelgon's cousin. And
if you are dear to Maelgon's sister's husband, so much the better.
You are a woman like any other. The Goddess herself shall judge
you."

"I will not become one of your cult!"

His smile grew broader, and his voice grew softer. "Indeed, you
will not. Is that what Kevin told you? Kevin is an acolyte. He
knows little. But he will know the truth before dawn."

He turned away from me.

"What will you do? Be sure you will answer to Arthur for it!
Have you not the courage to tell me?"

He whipped around. His eyes were burning slits in his face.
"You wish to talk about courage? You will need it. At dawn you
will be offered to the Goddess. If She accepts you, She will spare
your life and you will owe it to Her always. If not, you will die."

"It is three hundred years since the kind of sacrifice you speak
of was banned in Britain!" I cried, fighting back a sob.

"And it is a thousand years since a priestess of the Goddess
was beheaded at her prayers," he spat.

"I am not responsible for that."

"And I am not responsible for the Goddess' judgment."

"How—how will I be judged?" I whispered helplessly.

"By fire."

In the still predawn Kevin returned. He carried a tray of food, which he placed carefully on the floor by my pallet. I sat watching him. His hand shook, and he did not want to meet my eyes.

On the tray was a slice of new bread, a comb of honey, and a cup of goat's milk, warm and fragrant. It was the ritual meal of sacrifice, as I had heard it told in stories when I was small. In the old days, before the Romans came to Britain, the Druids sacrificed once a month to their bloodthirsty Goddess. In the old days.

"I'm sorry, my lady," Kevin said in a low voice. "I did not know."

"You are forgiven."

"I wish there were something I could do."

"Get word to Arthur. Afterward—somehow, get word to him, and see he learns the truth."

Kevin bowed his head. Surely what I was asking was forbidden by his vows. "I will do it."

"Thank you. God bless you."

"I will pray the Goddess to spare you." He gestured toward the tray. "Please, my lady, drink the milk."

"I cannot touch it. I will be sick."

He looked up briefly, pleadingly. "I have put something in it to help you. That is all. To help you." Then he rose and left.

God had answered my prayer. I was not to be rescued, but here was something to enable me to endure. Even so, I had not the courage to take it until I heard them coming for me. Then I downed it all in one swallow.

The procession moved slowly. They formed two lines, gray-robed and softly chanting, with me between them and Salowen at the head. The chanting was tuneless, more a gentle rhythm than a song, and they shuffled to its beat, left, right, left, right, through tunnels lit with smoking torches, left, right, up shallow steps, left, right, and out into the damp dark thick gray mist. I hardly felt my feet touch the ground. The beat was in my blood, bearing me onward. My gray-robed companions vanished in the mist; I followed Salowen, the white-robed, who led me into the dark grove where a mystery awaited. The path narrowed, the chanting quickened, trees leaned down to caress my face with their light fingers as I passed. Ahead stood a great circle of standing stones in a wide clearing. The mist gathered strength and swirled around the clearing, bearing me up and up onto a platform in the center. A thick rope was placed around my waist and tied to a pole behind me, pinning my arms to my sides. Before me stood Salowen at an altar. On the altar lay a black stone, hollowed out, and beside it the gleaming knife of sacrifice. So this was Nemet, I thought calmly. In the old days, this is where the victims met their end. I gazed about the clearing. Gray-robed figures huddled at the feet of the standing stones, swaying to their chanting, filing in to take their places. All of them were hooded.

Suddenly Salowen raised a great staff above his head and the chanting stopped. In the guttural language of Druids, he cried out some ritual words, looking to the heavens, and the Druids replied. This he did thrice; then the staff descended and the chanting began again; this time the cadence changed. It was deep, vibrant, dolorous, and slow. Salowen began to speak above the chanting, reciting the wrongs done the Druids over the centuries and justifying the vengeance he was about to take. I did not attend him. I leaned against the pole and watched the thin, bright crescent of the new moon creep above the treetops. How lovely she was, how pure and innocent—how far from earth! Everyone who had ever been dear to me I then remembered, my father Leodegrance, Gwillim, Gwarth, everyone who had been so kind to me in Gwynedd when I was an orphaned stranger; everyone who had welcomed me to Camelot, all Arthur's Companions, his commanders, and his soldiers. Good Bedwyr, my friend, who now held Camelot in the King's absence, and Kay, Gereint, Ferron, and a hundred others. But to Lancelot and Arthur, I could not bring myself to say farewell. Heaven held no joy for me without them.

Salowen raised the staff again, and the chanting grew quick and restless. Men began to shuffle about in small knots, circling slowly around me. Three of them held torches. Faster, faster, eagerly the chant beat against my ears, closer, closer came the fire, stinking of resin, stinging my eyes with smoke. The brushwood under my platform must have been damp with Druid's mist; it took them a long time to light it, but at last, it caught. Through a wall of shimmering heat I watched them slowly back away, hoods falling askew, mouths slung open in excitement, devouring me with feral eyes. They had all gone mad.

A wild yell rent the morning; a black horse broke through the trees bearing a knight with a slashing sword, singing a victory paean. Other voices took up the cry—from the woods came a phalanx of foot soldiers with shields and swords, scattering the

Druids, cutting them down. The stallion screamed as he neared the flames, but for Lancelot, he bore them. Down came the deadly sword, the rope fell from me, and I swooned in his arms as he lifted me and carried me away.

I dreamed that I was home at last, or in Heaven; I was somewhere I had always longed to be.

Slowly I opened my eyes, but could see nothing. As my senses returned to me, I heard sound—no more than a whisper, near my ear. Someone was praying. I lay protected, enveloped by strong arms, wrapped in a cloak, gently held, gently kissed.

I slid an arm around his waist and pulled him closer, until the length of his body pressed against mine.

"Oh, Lancelot," I whispered.

"Guinevere. Thank God."

"Is this a dream? Do I live?"

In the dark he found my lips and kissed them. It was the only answer I wanted. Tears welled up and spilled freely forth. He held me while I wept and whispered sweet endearments to me, words that I remember to this day. At length, when I was quiet, he arose. I saw then that we were in a large cave with smoothly rounded walls—man's work. Lancelot went to the cave mouth and spoke to a soldier there. It was dark beyond. I lay on a mat of leaves and bracken covered by a soldier's cloak. Lancelot's own cloak was wrapped about me, and underneath, I still wore the white robe of sacrifice. Where were we? And what had happened to the day? The men spoke softly and dared no light. We could not yet be in Gwynedd.

Lancelot returned with a skin of weak wine, and bade me drink.

"We are still on Mona's Isle?"

He nodded but said nothing.

"This wine is bitter. Have you any water?"

He shook his head. "We could not find a spring, although there must be one about. This place is clearly used regularly. It was perfectly clean."

"What day is it? Have I slept long?"

He smiled, and I lifted a hand to his face, that face which I had thought I should never see again!

He caught my hand and held it against his breast. "You have slept since you fainted. You were probably drugged."

"Yes. Kevin did that for me. I took it willingly."

"The murdering bastards. There are not so many of them left now."

"Did you find Salowen? The leader in the white robe?"

"I saw no one in a white robe. Was he there himself?"

"Yes. Lancelot, I told him who I was. He was going to sacrifice me anyway. Arthur must know this."

"He will know it," he said shortly.

"He took me because he thought I was Elaine."

He bit off a cry and bowed his head. "It is my fault he took you for Elaine."

I kissed his hand and stroked his hair. "You did nothing without my consent. I am to blame, as well. Tell me what happened, from the beginning. Have we time? The last I saw you, they clubbed you and left you for dead."

"We cannot leave before daylight. There is plenty of time." He made light of the beating they had given him, but in fact he still suffered from dizzy spells and sometimes saw things double. The troopers had found him and brought him round. They had tracked the Druids as far as the beach, where they found Lancelot's sword buried with their skins under the rock. Lancelot was all for dashing across the channel at once, but could barely sit on his horse. The troopers sensibly made him return to the castle, where Alyse took charge of his care and would not allow him to rise or speak.

"She probably saved your life."

"Perhaps. But, Guinevere, I did not want to live. To hand you to Maelgon's enemies through my weakness—"

"Stop." I placed my hand over his mouth and leaned into his embrace. "Do not dwell on it. We were both at fault. But God is moving. Can you not feel it? We are part of a pattern. And we are not yet come to the end of the skein. Go on with your tale."

Gereint had been his lieutenant. Through Gereint, he commandeered what fishing craft could be found in the village; Maelgon's ships lay at anchor in Caer Narfon, half a day's ride away. Gereint had canvassed Arthur's men for volunteers. And even though it meant going through the Druid's mist on the night of the new moon, every man of them had volunteered. There was only room for thirty in the boats, and Gereint picked men who could swim or row. While everyone was at dinner, Lancelot escaped Alyse's vigilance and made his way to the stables. He wanted cavalry, but it was a long swim. Five men brought their horses; only his own stallion Nestor survived. While the men took turns at the oars and fought the current, Lancelot spoke to the horse, cajoling and encouraging him across by the sheer strength of his will. Every time they tired and feared they could not go on, they seemed to hear

Merlin's voice in their ears, ringing from the sea, the air, the sky, compelling them to greater effort.

"Merlin?" I whispered, awed. "Did you see him?"

Lancelot shook his head. "No, but he was there, more a shadow than a shape. A voice. A presence. But he gave us the strength to get across."

An hour before moonrise they struck rocks on the eastern shore. They managed to get everyone safely landed, but lost the boats and nearly lost Nestor on the beach. If they had not stumbled across a stream within a hundred yards of shore, two men might have died, and the horse certainly would. Fresh water and rest revived them; they posted a guard and slept as best they could. Lancelot, who could not sleep, roused them well before dawn, and they scouted the shore for, as he put it, the Druids' lair. Nestor, stiff and exhausted, hobbled along behind him.

They found the Druids by their chanting. They formed a phalanx, but when Lancelot smelled the smoke, he did not wait to make a battle plan, but spurred Nestor to action and burst in among them. When he had me, he had not dared to return to the clearing to his men for fear of putting me at risk. For although they do not carry swords, Druids are deadly fighters. Their knives fly silently through air, wood, or stone, men claim, and never miss their mark. Indeed, when he met Gereint at the appointed meeting place and gathered the men, he was astonished at their losses. The Druids had scattered immediately upon the attack, offering no resistance, but melting into the misty woods. In vain did Gereint's men search for them, daring them to step forth. And one by one, as the soldiers hunted them in the brush, they were cut down by swift-flying knives without ever seeing the hands that threw them.

When they regrouped, Lancelot had but twelve men left of the thirty who had come. And although many Druids had died that morning, we were still outnumbered many times. They had taken to the hills to look for a defensible spot where they could tend me. The cave gave onto a ledge of rock that overlooked a small valley. It was easy to defend, if your enemy had swords. Gereint stood guard at the cave mouth; the men and horse rested in a grove below the ledge. They had no fresh water. At dawn, they must scout for a spring or a stream and try to snare a rabbit. The rations they brought with them were all but gone; they had to plan an attack on the Druid's storehouses if we were to survive until Maelgon or Arthur could mount a rescue. He spoke with confidence, but I knew it was for my sake. Our chances did not look good. Although he did not say it, I knew he was afraid for Nestor, as well. After the swim and the day's trek into the hills, it would be a miracle if the horse survived.

I told him then about the coracles that lay beached somewhere along the shore and about the sheep meadow and the goats. He dismissed the coracles—he would not trust me to one, he said, and would not ask Nestor to make that effort twice. But the sheep and goats were a boon, indeed, and I heard the relief in his voice. I told him about my conversation with Salowen, and about who Cathbad was, and everything that had happened to me. It all came tumbling out, as I sat in his arms and we waited for dawn.

"Did you arrange with Maelgon to come rescue us if we did not return?"

"The coward says he cannot come himself; he must wait upon Fion. But he sent two couriers after Arthur."

The shadow at the cave mouth moved, and Gereint approached softly. He bowed to me, smiling kindly. "My lady Queen Guinevere. I am glad to see you awake."

"Thank you, Gereint. I am glad to be awake."

"My lord, we think we hear the sound of chanting, far off down the slope. Gryfflet has volunteered to scout them and see what they are up to."

Lancelot did not move, but his arms about me tightened, pulling me closer. "Is he strong enough?"

"He is the fittest among us."

"Let him stay out of knife range, then. I cannot spare him."

"Very good, my lord. I will tell him."

"Gereint!" Gereint turned back and I felt Lancelot tremble, and still it. "Is Nestor standing?"

"Yes, my lord."

"Send young Sagramor into the hills above this cave to seek a spring. There must be one about. Guinevere tells me she has seen a meadow where they tend sheep and goats."

"That is good news."

"Indeed. It is our best hope."

Gereint returned to his post, and Lancelot and I sat silent, holding each other in peace, waiting. Before long we, too, could hear the chanting. No more than a murmur at first, it stirred the air and grew into a low hum that snaked around the cavern walls and set my heart racing. Lancelot rose and went out to Gereint. They left the ledge, and when he returned, Lancelot was alone.

"Tell me," I said, sensing he was braced to give me bad news.

"Gwen." He sat down beside me and took both my hands. "We

are surrounded. They are coming up the valley, shoulder to shoulder through the trees, in a tight ring. They know we are here."

"Can we defend against them?" When he did not answer, I brought his hand to my lips and kissed it. "Come. Tell me. I can face death if I am with you."

"Ahhhh, my beautiful Gwen, you are braver than I," he whispered, pulling me to his breast. "The men are hidden among the rocks. Nestor is set free in the forest. It is all I can do. If only I had brought an archer!"

I took his face in my hands and kissed his lips. "Lancelot. It is not your fault."

"We have an hour, perhaps. No more."

He drew me down onto the makeshift pallet and held me, whispering to me between kisses. "We have always known—since first we met—that this was a love sent to us from Heaven—Guinevere—I cannot bear to part this life—without having held you in my arms thus, at least once—at least once—permit me, my dearest love, to lie with you."

His seeking hands slid under the Druid's robe and found my flesh.

"Lancelot," I breathed, joy and terror battling in my soul, "I cannot deny you." And I gave myself up to his ardor.

He was so unlike Arthur, whose delight in touching and native gift of patience gave him the power to shape a woman's desire as skillfully as ever a potter shaped his clay. He could start with nothing and build to pleasure by slow degrees, with joy and care and laughter, until the heart cried out for its sweet release; or, himself ablaze, could fire the body in a flash to meet his need. Lancelot's passion was a conflagration, burning and unmanageable. I gave myself to his flame, feeling nothing but heat and wild excitement, fed by his eager fury. I had no will but his will, no future beyond this moment; without a look back I surrendered to his engulfing holocaust. His body crushed me; I could not breathe; cold terror gripped my soul; suddenly I saw clearly into the heart of this consuming blaze: It was ash. Cold. Dead. Forgotten. Crying out, I hammered at his shoulders in panic.

"NO! Lancelot! I cannot! I cannot do it!"

He backed away at once, gasping for breath, with glazed eyes that knew me not.

"Oh, Lancelot, Lancelot, forgive me if you ever can. But I cannot do it. It is death."

"Gwen!" he whispered, shocked. "My God!"

We stared at one another, and I fumbled to sit up and straighten my robe.

He sat beside me and passed a hand across his brow. "Dear Christ, am I possessed? This is madness. It will be the end of us, forever."

"Yes."

I saw he was shaking as badly as I. I could not voice the terror in my soul. Twice in one day I had stared into the abyss, black and beckoning, from which there was no return. The approaching Druids frightened me no longer. The steady thrum of their chanting anchored me firmly to the dark, cool earth, and I welcomed it.

"I love you, Lancelot," I whispered sadly, touching his hand, "but there is no hope for it."

"Guinevere, forgive me."

"My dear, you are forgiven without asking." I drew a ring from my finger and placed it in his hand. It was the love knot cast in gold that my father had given my mother during their courting. "Take this, Lancelot, and keep it by you. I love it dearly. Take it in exchange, if you will, for what I cannot give you."

He pulled the leather lacing from his tunic and, threading it through the ring, tied it about his neck. "If it is the last thing I ever do, Guinevere, I will protect your honor."

A strange calm came over him. He rose and handed me up. With great dignity, he walked me halfway to the entrance to the cave. Beyond, the sky was lightening. Treetops swayed gray-green in the early breeze and the valley erupted in birdsong; it would be a beautiful day.

"Guinevere, if it should come to death, we will not wait here like trapped rats. We will climb up the hillside and find a cliff that reaches out over the sea below. If there is no help for it, we will choose death together, you and I. Are you with me?"

I smiled at him and took him in my arms once more. "I am always with you, Lancelot."

With great tenderness, he bent his head and kissed me farewell.

"For shame!" a voice cried out in anger. "Unhand the Queen, you blackguard! For shame! My God—it's Lancelot!"

There in the cave mouth stood two men with drawn swords. Foremost was Maelgon, staring open-mouthed at Lancelot. Behind him, with eyes only for me, stood Fion.

17 ✤ The Prisoner

Lancelot's sword leaped to his hand, but Maelgon did not advance. Confused, he wavered and lowered the weapon. I could see his thought upon his face. His exalted standing among the kings of Britain lay in his being my cousin and Lancelot's brother-in-law. As outraged as he felt he ought to be, it availed him nothing to be outraged at us.

But as Maelgon lowered his sword, Fion stepped forward and crossed Lancelot's blade.

"In the name of Arthur of Britain, yield or die." There was iron in that lilting Gaelic voice, and I saw Lancelot go stiff with anger.

"Lancelot!" I flung myself to my knees between them as they each moved forward. "Do not harm him, I pray you! This is Fion!"

But even as I spoke, Lancelot lowered his sword. He knew he had no right to defend me against anyone who spoke in Arthur's name. Fion's swordpoint touched his breast. With his sword at his side, Lancelot took one step forward into the blade, drawing blood as Fion hastened to withdraw. Acknowledging the gesture, Fion inclined his head, sheathed his weapon, then extended his hand.

"Yield your sword, sir, in the King's name."

Lancelot hesitated, then bent his knee to the ground and offered up the sword in the ritual gesture of surrender, with the blade held flat across his palms. Fion took it. Lancelot was now his prisoner.

"Fion." I rose shakily and looked at my old friend. The morning sun behind him threw his face half into shadow but lit the bright gold of his hair and glittered off the great jewels at shoulder, wrist, and waist. His face had grown rugged with the cares of kingship, and he now carried himself like a warrior, but his eyes, brilliant green and smiling, were unchanged. He was still the handsomest man I had ever seen.

"My lord King Fion," I said with firmness, making him a deep reverence. He let his eyes travel slowly from my hair, loose and unbraided, to my bare feet.

"My lady Queen Guinevere." He bowed gracefully from the waist and, with laughing eyes, said gravely, "How the fashions have changed in Britain since I left!"

It broke the tension, and everyone relaxed a little.

"I do assure you, my lord, I would I were better gowned to greet you. But the Druids dressed me." I became suddenly aware that the chanting had stopped. In the valley now we heard only the voices of soldiers, calling out to one another and singing victory paeans. "Have you subdued them? Have you found Salowen?"

"Subdued them?" Maelgon broke in. "Aye, you could say so! We have sent them all to meet their precious Goddess face to face!"

"Do not kill them all, for my sake!" I cried, ignoring Maelgon and speaking only to Fion. "There is at least one among them I would save. Not everyone took part—spare the innocent, I pray you!"

Maelgon snorted, and Fion glanced at him swiftly.

"We have disarmed every man we could find. Those who offered fight are dead. When we find their headquarters, we shall gather them for your inspection, and you may decide who lives and dies, if you wish."

I shuddered, and Fion reached out to take my arm. Lancelot moved instinctively to protest, then stopped himself in time.

"You, Lancelot. I remember you now. When I knew you last, you were Arthur's closest friend and ally." His voice was cold. Lancelot flushed, but held himself still and said nothing. My heart sank. I could see he was prepared to accept all the blame for everything that had happened; he had already convinced himself he deserved it. "You will come with me, sir. I will take you to Arthur."

"Now, now," Maelgon grumbled uneasily, clearing his throat. "I will take charge of him, my lord Fion, if you like. He is my sister's husband."

At this Fion turned to him and stared. "Elaine's husband? Then I had better keep him close for his own protection. Between you and Arthur, he can be judged."

Maelgon, who never could see beyond the end of his nose, was at a loss for a reply.

I gripped Fion's arm and looked up into his face. "I pray you, my lord Fion, before you judge what your eyes have seen, listen to me. I will tell you truth."

He drew closer, and the smile returned to his eyes. "Fair enough, fair Queen. Let me hear your speech."

"Above all men on this earth, Arthur loves and honors Lancelot. And I do promise you that Lancelot loves and honors Arthur. He would die for Arthur gladly, no questions asked. You do him an injustice to think him traitor. He saved my life this day past, and not for the first time. Why do you think the Druids came after us? Yesterday at dawning the Archdruid Salowen tied me to a stake and offered me to the Goddess." Fion's eyes widened, and he glanced quickly at Lancelot. But Lancelot was stone. "He did not merely threaten, he bade them light the fire."

"Fire?" Fion whispered, incredulous. "They gave you to the fire? That is the fate reserved for—"

"Traitors and whores. Yes. I know it. And they lit the fire. If it were not for Lancelot, I would not now be with you. Lancelot and his companions rowed across in the night, braving the Druid's mist on the night of the new moon, losing boats and horses, and rescued me at the very moment I succumbed to the smoke. They have tended me all night, going without water or food. When we found ourselves discovered and surrounded by the Druids before dawn, we prepared to die." I looked up into his brilliant eyes, so near my face, and hoped he remembered the day he bid me farewell in Gwynedd. "What you saw, Fion, was our farewell."

He did remember it. I saw his features soften, and he straightened. "Well, Lancelot. If I have misjudged you, I beg forgiveness. You have saved the Queen from a cruel fate, and all Britain is in your debt. I, too, thank you from my heart." He held out Lancelot's sword for him to take.

But he did not take it. Bowing stiffly, Lancelot said in a tight voice, "You are merciful, my lord. But my gracious Queen does tell but half the truth."

"Lancelot!"

"It is my fault she was abducted by the Druids. If I am the villain who put her at such risk, surely it is no more than my duty to save her from it. This justice demands. You do well, my lord, to doubt me. I have wronged Queen Guinevere, and I have wronged King Arthur. I cannot take the sword back. Give it to Arthur. I am in his hands."

"Lancelot, I forbid you to do this! Are you mad? But an hour ago you swore me protection!"

He looked at me then. I could not bear to see such pain in his eyes. "I swore," he said gently, "to protect your honor."

"This is not the way! Think, Lancelot, how you would hurt him!"

"He will know it, Gwen. There is no help for that. All it takes is one look at your face."

"Or yours!" I retorted angrily. I hated the martyr in him. Why could he not forgive himself? "Do not sacrifice Arthur on the altar of your guilt!" He turned away, but there were tears in his eyes. Fion looked slowly from one of us to the other.

"This sounds," he said coolly, "like a lovers' quarrel."

"No, no," Maelgon cut in hastily, "I'm sure it is not. The Queen my cousin spoke truth. They said farewell. Nothing more. She would not dare. It would be her death."

Fion cast him a look of mild contempt. "You do not know Arthur." He looked sadly at Lancelot and at me. "You must both return to Gwynedd with me. Whether you go to Arthur as prisoner or free man, as Queen or penitent, I leave to you. But to Arthur you must go. There is more here than I have time to unravel. Or"—with a long look at me—"than I desire to know."

He moved back and gestured for us both to walk before him. But as we stepped onto the ledge and into the bright morning sun, we heard scuffling above us, and a shower of pebbles and dust fell over the lip of the cave at our feet.

"Who's there!" Maelgon cried, drawing his sword. Down the rockface slithered a young knight in a torn tunic, with a wineskin slung around his shoulders and a rope in his hand. At the other end of the rope staggered a tall thin man in a filthy white robe. The young man gave the rope a forceful tug, and Salowen fell in an ungainly huddle at his feet.

"Sagramor!" Lancelot cried. "Well done! Is that the archdruid?"

"So he claims," Sagramor replied with a grin. "He's cursed me and all my descendants about a hundred times. What a tongue he has!"

Salowen struggled to stand. His wrists were bound and bleeding, and his face cut and bruised where Sagramor must have struck him. But he pulled himself up to his full height, looking upon us all with grand contempt. He still had his dignity, and he said nothing.

"He tried to kill me at the spring," Sagramor continued lightly, coiling the rope. "But his aim wasn't very good. I didn't think those knives ever missed. But he was out of sorts because I killed his snake." Salowen's eyes slid to him for a moment, full of hate.

"*This* is the man who put you to the fire?" Maelgon cried excitedly. "Cousin, speak! Is it he?"

"Yes."

"King Maelgon—" Fion reached out to stay his arm, but too late. With a mighty thrust, Maelgon's blade split the Druid's body from throat to groin. Without a sound, he staggered and collapsed into a pool of his blood and innards. Gagging, I hid my face on Lancelot's shoulder, and his arm came around me.

"Sagramor!" he called. "Is that water you carry? Bring me some for the Queen!"

The water revived me; sweet and cool, it eased my sickness. I made Lancelot drink of it, also. Fion stood between us and the slaughtered Druid, to screen me from the sight. Maelgon delighted in hurling the bloody remains off the ledge and stomping upon the dark-stained earth.

"Food for kites," I whispered. "That is all he is become. And by his own lights, he was a religious man."

"I will build him a cairn, to mark his deathplace," Fion promised. And he did. Before we left the Isle of Mona two days later, he built the cairn with his own hands.

Fion's ship lay at anchor in a sheltered bay, and it was there they took me. At first I was dizzy and light-headed, but when Fion brought me broth and bread, I felt better. I had not eaten, I realized, since before I took Lancelot riding in the woods. Was it only two days hence? It seemed to me I had been on Mona for half a lifetime. I saw to it that my brave rescuers were fed, as well. For two days Maelgon's men scoured the island for stragglers, buried the dead, tended the wounded, and questioned the Druids they found. I refused, to Maelgon's disgust, to identify my tormenters. How could I be sure? They had been robed and hooded; I had been drugged. And I did not want any more to die because I named them. Salowen was enough. Their power was broken. Nestor they found grazing placidly in the sheep meadow, fully recovered from his ordeal. But however hard the soldiers searched for the sacred grove itself, or for the avenue of standing stones that led to it, they could not find it. Nemet had disappeared.

They did not find Kevin. I grieved to think him dead on my account. Maelgon and Fion, and even Lancelot, could not understand my tears. They put it down to the terror I had undergone. But Arthur would have understood it.

Maelgon at length decided to sever his ties with Lancelot and treat him as a traitor. In a tight place, he probably reckoned, blood ties to the Queen outranked ties by marriage to the King's dearest Companion. He insisted Lancelot be confined to the ship and allowed no contact with anyone, save the servants who brought him food. Fion objected, on the grounds that what Lancelot had done to save the Queen was known and attested to, but what he had done to disgrace me or the High King was unknown. Nevertheless, Lancelot assented to imprisonment with a willingness that surprised everyone, except me. If he had shouted from the hilltop, he could not have proclaimed his guilt more clearly.

Leaderless, the Druids who wished to remain on Mona's Isle to tend their sheep and live quietly were permitted to stay. Their knives were taken from them.

We were a solemn procession, coming home to Gwynedd. I was given immediately into the care of Alyse and Anet, who seemed to have come to friendship in my absence. They were wild to know what had happened, and how and why, but I feigned exhaustion, kept to my rooms, and held my tongue. Maelgon had not the nerve to throw Lancelot into the dungeons, much as I knew Lancelot himself wished to go. Instead, he confined him to his quarters to await the arrival of the King. On the third day a royal courier arrived. The hoax about the Picts had been discovered as soon as they reached Rheged, and Arthur was on his way back as fast as he could ride.

When I heard this from Anet, I rose from bed and bade Ailsa bathe and dress me. I chose a deep-blue gown to wear with the sapphire earrings Fion had given me as a wedding gift. My hair Ailsa dressed with sapphire netting and strings of river pearls, scenting the long coils with rosewater imported from Gaul. She shook her head, mumbling under her breath about duplicity and wickedness and the snare of beauty.

"Ailsa," I said firmly, "when a woman wages battle, she is entitled to any weapon she can lay her hand to. Hush your chatter, and send to beg an audience of King Fion."

Most of Fion's train were still housed in his ship, Maelgon having few rooms to spare. But Fion was given a chamber of his own, and this is where he saw me. He sat near the window with two of his companions; when I entered, they leaped to their feet, eyes wide and mouths agape. Fion, too, I noted with satisfaction, was struck dumb by the change the gown had wrought. I made him a deep reverence. "My lord King Fion."

He cleared his throat. "Queen Guinevere. Be welcome."

"Thank you, my lord. I have come to beg a favor of you. But I would prefer to speak privately."

With a wave of his hand he dismissed his companions. Fion came forward and took both my hands. "I have been hoping for this, Guinevere. Are you quite recovered? I heard you lay abed, ill from your long ordeal."

"Oh, yes, my lord, I am recovered. But my ordeal is far from over."

"Ah." He leaned down and softly kissed my cheek. "Don't be so formal with me, lass. I'm still the man you knew as Pellinore's hostage."

I smiled up at him and saw his eyes grow luminous. "Indeed? Then I am still the orphaned princess, standing in the shadow of Pellinore's daughter."

At this he laughed and handed me into a chair by the window. "By all the saints in Christendom, you never stood in anyone's shadow! Did I not tell you, when last I saw you, that a great future lay before you?"

"You did indeed. But how could you have known?"

"By my eyes!" he exclaimed. "God does not bestow such uncommon beauty on a maid to have it hidden in a corner of the kingdom. It is a gift with a purpose. Only from the heart of Britain could your light blaze forth to bathe this embattled land in its resplendent glow—"

"What a tongue you have, Fion!"

"There was only one man for you, Guinevere."

"He is the finest man, the strongest, truest, bravest, and most beloved in all the world."

"Ahhhhh." He exhaled with what seemed to be relief and kissed my fingers. "I am glad to hear you say that."

"I know you doubted me. And after what has happened, who will not?" I looked unhappily out the window, where the wooded hills lay still and shimmering in the heat of high summer. "And because it is Lancelot," I said slowly, "I fear that Arthur, too, might doubt."

Fion hesitated. "Surely, if anyone can relieve him of that doubt, you are the one."

"I pray so. But—but because it is Lancelot—"

I fell silent and felt Fion's eyes on my face. At length he spoke. "As the Greek poets tell us, the gods do not give lightly of their gifts. If they shower a man with virtues, they will see he suffers for it, or endures a cruel fate, or is born with some fatal flaw, to insure against hubris."

I turned to him, my eyes filled with tears. "Yes," I whispered. He took my hands, and held them. "And yours is Lancelot." I nodded.

He leaned very close and lowered his voice. "Tell me truth. Are you lovers?"

"No." I returned the pressure of his grip and faced him directly. "No. Never. But who will believe it now?"

Joy returned to his features, and he sat back, relieved. "Who needs to believe it, besides the King?"

"How can you ask that, and you a king yourself? You would be thought a fool by all your people."

He laughed lightly. "I am already. But I take your point. . . How did he ever become husband to Elaine? It is easy to see where his heart lies."

"She seduced him," I said shortly. "By a cruel trick designed to hurt me. But she has hurt everyone by it, not least of all herself. Now she is in Less Britain. It is Lancelot's home. She will never see Wales again."

"Ahhhh." He smiled lightly. "It seems she and Maelgon have that in common; they act before thinking and take one step farther than their eyes can see."

"Indeed."

"Well, my lass, if you wish to convince me of your innocence, you have only to declare it. I do believe you. But with Maelgon's men and Arthur's, it is another matter."

"I know."

"Lancelot is not helping matters."

I rose in agitation and paced the room, twisting my hands. Fion rose and stood, watching.

"He believes he is protecting my honor by taking all the blame upon himself. He does not see that all he is doing is proclaiming his guilt—and mine—far and wide. Sometimes I wish—sometimes I wish he had but the smallest splinter of Arthur's sense!"

"Or yours."

"He cannot be allowed to speak with Arthur. Not alone, and certainly not in public." I turned toward him and knelt upon the floor. "This is the favor I come to beg of you, Fion. He is your prisoner. You have his sword. Do not allow him speech with the King. For all our sakes."

Gravely he came and raised me and held me gently in his arms. "My sweet lass, I do not see how I can prevent it. Maelgon has imprisoned him, not I. To my way of thinking, saving you from the flames forgives him all his other sins. I'd honor him myself, but he refuses to be honored."

"But you have his sword. By formal right, he is yours. Speak to Arthur yourself. He knows Lancelot well. He will know what to do. Just don't let Lancelot open his mouth."

"And what," he said slowly, "would he say? What's at the bottom of this, Gwen? How did you come to be abducted in the first place?"

I held him firmly in my arms and looked into his handsome face. "We visited the clearing in yonder woods where we first met. We were alone, but the escort was within call. He held me in his arms, as you are holding me now, and kissed me. That is all. We were attacked by twelve men and subdued before he could draw his sword."

"He must," whispered Fion, "have been besotted." He bent and kissed me himself, a warm kiss with passion behind it. I pushed him away lightly and saw him smile. "Ahhh, gone are the days when a Celtic king had to share his queen with his allies! Now I am as guilty as Lancelot."

"More so," I returned, "for we were in the open woods, not unattended in his chamber."

He loosed me and grinned. "Cleverly managed, my lass. If Arthur can get the better of you, I salute him."

I smiled back. "He is not easily deceived. Indeed, few have had the courage to try. He must know the truth, Fion, but not the whole truth. For his own sake, and for Lancelot's, and for mine. It will hurt him so!"

"Certainly it will. But are you going to tell me that after all these years with you and Lancelot living daily at his side, he could not bear that hurt? Come, Guinevere. You have sense. He will know it all. Lancelot was right, you know. All it takes is one look at your face." I covered my face with my hands. "What would you have me do?" he went on gently. "I cannot prevent the High King from talking with his lieutenant when and where he wills. This business of the sword is formality only. The only power I have over Lancelot is what power he grants me. You know this. We are in Maelgon's house, on Maelgon's lands. I am Maelgon's guest. If Maelgon wants to call a formal council and lodge a formal charge and demand the King's Judgment, I cannot prevent him."

"Council!" I cried. "Charge! What charge? He would not dare! Oh, the scoundrel! He thinks he sees a chance to climb to power over Lancelot's body! The braggart! The bully! The swine!"

"Surely," Fion said calmly, "he is not the first."

"Oh, Fion, Fion! You must prevent this! Do not let him take charge of the proceedings. He is a coward at heart, I know him. Face him, and he will back down."

Fion sat me down and gave me water from the carafe. When I was calmer, he spoke in a friendly, sensible tone. "I've enough on my hands at home, lass. I'll not risk war with Gwynedd, even for you. And for what? To spare Arthur pain he cannot be spared? You say he knows Lancelot well. Then he will know what drives the man and what to do to save him. He is not High King for nothing. I should imagine he could handle Maelgon with one arm tied behind his back. It seems to me the only tough problem Arthur has is you." I stared at him. Fion looked at me with great kindness. "There is something you are keeping from me. You, who were put to the fire and escaped death by minutes, you have not once mentioned the Druids. All your thoughts are upon something else. I do not ask to know it. But what is a kiss in the woods? You would not be so afraid, for so small a transgression. Will you fear Arthur might discover I kissed you here? No, I thought not. If I can see this, do you really believe Arthur will not?"

He offered me his kerchief, and I wiped the tears from my cheeks.

"You are right," I whispered at length. "I can keep nothing from Arthur. And it is from me he must know it. Oh, Fion, this will be the hardest thing I have ever done."

"Harder than facing the fire?"

"A thousand times harder."

He smiled and clasped my hand. "I am glad to hear it. You do love him."

I shrugged, unable to see past my tears. "I love them both."

Late that night Ailsa scratched at my bedchamber door, to say that Queen Anet was without and wished to see me. I was not yet abed, being too restless for sleep.

"Let her come in to me, Ailsa. At this time of night, it must be some secret thing, or something urgent. Stay within call."

To my surprise, Anet was dressed and cloaked, and so alive with excitement that I hardly knew her.

"Why, Anet! What means this?"

"Oh, my lady Queen Guinevere!" She sank to her knees and clasped her thin hands together. "Oh, my lady, I must tell you what I've done—what has happened—I pray you will forgive me—but I was following your advice, and Queen Alyse agreed—she has helped me, indeed—I wouldn't have known what to do but for her, and for you. Oh, say you will not be angry with me!"

I suppressed a grin. "I will try not to be angry, Anet, but first you must tell me what it is. How alive you look! You are quite changed."

She nodded eagerly. "Indeed, I am! Maelgon says he hardly knows me! Oh, but he does not know what I have done! And he will be so furious with me when he discovers it! Tell me what to do!"

I drew her up onto the bed beside me and calmed her as best I could. "First tell me what you have done."

"I have given sanctuary—protection—to a Druid!" she whispered.

"Oh, Anet! Under Maelgon's very roof?" She nodded, her eyes huge. "Where is he, then? He is not in the chapel!"

"No, no, he stays in Alyse's rooms during the day, and at night he sleeps in the garden bower. It is not patrolled. I take him out every evening through the weaving room when Maelgon has retired."

"How did this happen? How came he here? What does he want?"

"He wants to speak to the High King. He came ashore the morning Maelgon and King Fion left for Mona's Isle. King Fion's ship had landed at nightfall, and Maelgon met him on the beach with the news of your abduction and Lancelot's attempt at rescue. They made ready to sail again as soon as they could, but the wind died. Just before dawn they departed, and before the sun was at half height, this Druid came ashore in the smallest boat I've ever seen. He came to *me*, Guinevere, to me!"

"Well, you are queen, Anet. It is right that he should."

"He—he threw himself at my mercy, with tears in his eyes, and said he had dolorous news for King Arthur and must speak with him in person. He had vowed he would do it. So I had no choice, had I? Did I do the right thing in taking him in?"

I gripped her arm suddenly. "Vowed to whom? Anet, what does he look like! Describe him!"

"W-Well," she stammered, taken aback at my eagerness, "he is about Maelgon's height, and young, with a black beard and white teeth."

"His name! Do you know his name?

"Why, yes. It is Kevin."

"Oh!" I cried, "Thank God! He lives! Yes, my dear Anet, you

did the right thing! Oh, I bless you for it!" And I kissed her and hugged her and wept upon her shoulder.

Startled and delighted, she embraced me. "He wanted to see you, my lady, as soon as you were better. He was so happy when you were rescued. And he has been so worried about your illness. But we heard today that you were up and about, so he begged me to ask if you would see him."

"News travels fast. I only went to see Fion."

She looked at me sideways and dropped her gaze. "If you are not yet well enough, of course, the visit can be postponed." She had not been spending time with Alyse for nothing, I noted with amusement.

"I daresay I could manage it, this once," I replied, and she laughed gaily.

With Ailsa clucking in distress behind me, I threw on a cloak and followed Anet silently down the back stairs, through the weaving room and out into the moonlit garden. We were not in much danger of observation; the garden stood at the back of the castle and only the women's rooms looked out upon it. Nevertheless, we strolled slowly arm in arm, feigning leisure, until we reached the bower. It was dark within, but I saw Kevin by the whiteness of his smile.

"My lady Guinevere! The Goddess spared you! How glad I am to see you safe in Gwynedd!"

I smiled and clasped his hands. "She sent me Lancelot. And not a moment too soon. Without your help, good Kevin, I should not have withstood the trial that awaited me in Nemet."

Anet crossed herself quickly, and Kevin made the sign of peace between us. He begged me to relate what had happened, so I told the story. Anet grew still as I told it, and Kevin bowed his head.

"So," he said slowly, when I finished. "Salowen is dead. It is a sad ending for a great man. Of course he was wrong to abduct you, even if you had been Maelgon's sister, but he was possessed by hate after Maelgon's attack. The priestess Viviane—you heard what Balyn did to her?"

"Indeed we did, may God rest her soul."

"She was a great and powerful woman. And beautiful, they say, in her youth. They were lovers, when Salowen was young, and she was the Guardian of Nemet. You would find it hard to believe now, but he used to be a man of peace, with great charity toward others, even Christians. That is why I did not believe—even when they told me—what he meant to do to you."

"It's all right, Kevin."

"No, my lady, it is not. By his act, Salowen has put our very future in jeopardy. What will the High King do, when he learns of it? We shall be lucky if he does not burn the island from end to end."

"That is not Arthur's way."

"No? It is Maelgon's. And he is our neighbor. Are there any left living on Mona?"

"Some. But many died, Kevin. I feared you were among them."

"I could not take part in the ceremony. But neither could I prevent it. I did what I could. I spent the hours before dawn seeing to it that the brushwood was well watered. It was odd." He hesitated. "There was a spirit there, black-robed, with an ancient staff and an icy breath. He was new to me, but he was powerful. While he was by me, I worked with the strength of ten and did not tire. At dawn, when we heard them coming, he bade me take a coracle and come across to find King Arthur."

"Oh, Kevin! I owe you my life, indeed! You and Merlin! It was your doing the fire would not take! Bless you both! A matter of minutes was all that lay between me and next world, I assure you."

"Ah, my lady Queen," he breathed, and held me in strong hands and kissed me firmly on the lips, while Anet gasped. He released me and fell to one knee. "I beg you will let the High King know I am here and that I wish to plead with him for mercy toward the Druids. We are in his power now, all of us. And Maelgon would destroy us. I place myself under your protection, if you will."

"No," I said slowly, "I think the protection of Queen Anet will suffice. This is her house, not mine. But I will undertake to speak with Arthur, if—if he will hear me."

"Thank you. I could not ask for more."

When we were back in the weaving room, Anet finally found her tongue.

"Did they really tie you to a stake and set it afire?" she quavered. "Oh, I did not believe it when Maelgon told us! Queen Alyse said they would never dare!"

"They did dare."

"But Kevin tried to foil their plans? Then he has betrayed them. What will happen to him now? Can we make him a Christian, do you think?"

"On the contrary. I was thinking he might make a good leader for those who remain. In his heart he worships the Light. With

Kevin in charge, perhaps Nemet would not be such a fearful place."

"He was bold to kiss you, my lady! Why did you allow it?"

I sighed and drew her arm through mine. "Druids have not changed in a thousand years, Anet. In the old days, before the Romans came to Britain, customs differed. A Celtic king, like the King Cunedda in your tapestry, took a beautiful woman to wife for a purpose. Her sovereignty was something shared by all his people. If a lord, a priest, or an ally, or even someone lowborn performed a great service to the king, the king was honor bound to grant the man a favor. Nine times out of ten, it was the queen."

"No! I never heard such a thing!"

I smiled down at her. "You were raised in a convent, my dear. I grew up on these tales. Let us thank God we are living in more civilized times."

"Is that—is that why you and Lancelot—" She stopped as I froze. "I mean—I didn't mean to—oh, Guinevere! Forgive me!"

"Finish your question."

"No! I dare not!"

"Finish."

"I have made you angry now, and I never intended to! It's just that I did not believe it when they said that you—you and Lancelot were—were—lovers in the woods when you were taken." She gulped and covered her mouth with her hand, shaking.

"Who told you this?"

"No one. Everyone." It was a whisper.

I turned away, surprised to find myself trembling as violently as Anet. "Arthur is not Cunedda. Arthur is as Roman as he is Celt. You presume too much!"

"Oh!" She gasped, sinking to the floor. "Please, please forgive me! I am ashamed I spoke!"

I sighed wearily. I had no cause for anger at poor Anet. And if I could find no answer for her, how on earth would I ever answer Arthur? I raised her from the floor and made her face me.

"There is both truth and untruth to what you have heard. To understand, you must be willing to set aside your judgment."

"You—you would not betray the King!" Anet breathed in terror.

I held her firmly by the shoulders. "I would not, and I have not." She nearly swooned in relief, but I shook her and bade her attend me. "Think of Arthur as a great tree, the tree of Britain. I am the flower, the froth, the transient bloom upon the bough. Lancelot is the strong branch that supports me; yet he is nothing without the tree itself, and neither am I. Without Arthur, we die; and without us, he is made less than he is." I looked into her face, and saw by her sadness that she began to understand. "We try, all of us, to walk the straight path. But we are none of us without flaw." She began to cry, and I let her go.

In the dark, still room I sat in the shadow of the ancient loom and gazed out at the midnight garden. We were all held powerless in a sticky web of intrigue, secrets, fears and desires, plotting at cross purposes, caught up in our own petty plans, accomplishing nothing. We awaited Arthur's coming like the onset of the winter gale: destroying summer's leavings, sweeping the past away. Only Arthur could do it.

18 ✿ The Judgment

"Guinevere," Alyse said firmly, "I must speak with you." Coming down the length of the garden in the midday sun, she seemed once again the queen of my childhood, a powerful tyrant who brooked no opposition. I was annoyed to find myself trembling and made an effort to stand straight and still as she approached. Behind me in the weaving room Anet watched from the window. I had spent the morning there, trying without success to occupy my mind with threads and patterns. But the constant clacking of the looms gave me a headache, and in irritation I quitted her company to seek peace in the garden. There was no peace to be found. Alyse took my arm and guided me toward the bower. If she could not say what she had to say in public, I did not want to hear it. But lacking the courage to tell her this, I was bound to listen. She came straight to the point.

"We must do something about Maelgon. He is on the verge of doing Gwynedd irreparable harm."

"How so?"

She shifted uncomfortably. "Have you not heard, then? I

thought Anet must have told you. He has concocted some wild story about you and Lancelot together in the woods—I am ashamed of it, Gwen, and pray you will forgive him for it. He does not care that he disgraces his poor sister, and thereby his mother, with the tale. He gives out the man attacked you—forgive me, my dear, but it is best that you know this beforehand. He wants to call a Council and bring a formal charge against Lancelot—Lancelot, of all people!—thinking, the half-wit, that this will somehow please the High King and gain him a place at his side! I told him he had been out in the sun too long, to think so. There is no one closer to Arthur than Lancelot, and if he thinks to please the King by telling him this sordid tale, then he deserves what Arthur will do to him! But *I* do not deserve it, Guinevere, *I* do not! The King is expected at sundown. Somehow we must keep Maelgon silent. Clearly, you owe him nothing. In your place, I would probably let Arthur destroy him. But he is my son, and Pellinore's, and Elaine's brother—if you ever loved us, Guinevere, will you not help us now? Speak to Maelgon! Warn him of his danger."

I believe I stared at her. I know that I was speechless.

"What a fool he will look when Lancelot denies it! There is no point to it! He is embarked upon a course that can only bring him ruin! He thinks, because he has destroyed the Druids, he is a great power in Britain that Arthur must reckon with! The pig-headed child!" She paused, plucking at her skirts in anger, and I cleared my throat and found my voice.

"What if Lancelot does not deny it?"

"What do you mean? Why shouldn't he?"

"He was responsible for me, when the Druids took me."

"You were set upon by twelve men! What kind of odds are those?"

"But it was his doing that the odds were twelve to one. Besides, he has done something—else that Arthur would not like and is feeling guilty about it now. You know his sense of honor, Alyse. If he feels he deserves chastisement, he will take it in any form it is offered."

She looked at me sharply. "What do you mean by that? That he would accept punishment for an offense he had not committed?"

"That is exactly what I mean. He has done it before."

She snorted in disgust. "Well, Elaine told me he could be insufferable. Don't misunderstand me"—this as I flushed scarlet and moved to protest—"I am not unhappy with the match. He is a good husband to her; he has given her a kingdom and sons every

year. Two healthy boys she has now, and another on the way. She
has no cause for complaint. If there is no love between them,
well, God knows that is common enough. And she only has to
tolerate him in the winters. That is little enough to bear, it seems
to me ... Guinevere, you are shaking. Have a seat, my child.
What is amiss? Are you ill?" She drew me down onto the bench
beside her and pressed a hand to my brow. "Surely, this is nonsense about desiring punishment for anything because one is
guilty of something. It is foolishness, pure and simple. You are an
old friend of Lancelot's. Can you not make him see sense?"

I wanted to laugh, but my throat was so tight I could make no
sound at all.

"I bade Anet speak to you about it, because we agree that
Maelgon is cutting his own throat, but she told me today to let
sleeping dogs lie. So I came myself."

"It was good advice, Aunt Alyse."

"Maelgon is my son. I cannot sit idle and watch him destroy
his future—" She broke off and rose unsteadily. A great silence
filled the garden. The looms had stopped. Alyse bent her stiff
knees in a curtsy, and I looked up. A tall man stood at the end of
the path in the shadow of the gate. Around us the world held its
breath.

"Arthur," I whispered, rising slowly as Alyse sank to the
ground and bowed her head. In a dozen long strides he was with
me, had his arms around me, held me so tightly I could barely
breathe, and hid his face in my hair. And I did not know until he
embraced me how I had longed for his embrace! His strength and
his joy gave me the peace I had been seeking; he was my rock,
my rest, my certainty.

"Arthur!" My tears flowed freely down my cheeks and soaked
his tunic. I hardly knew if they were tears of joy or pain. "Oh, Arthur, Arthur, at last!"

"You are alive!" he breathed. "Alive! Nothing matters beside
that!"

He kissed my tears and kissed my lips with a desperate joy that
stirred me to my soul. Nothing mattered, nothing mattered beside
this.

He held me a long time. Alyse had gone, the weaving room
was empty—the day stood still and time silent, all for us.

"When I heard—what Cathbad told me—Guinevere, the light
went dark."

"Yes," I whispered, remembering the approach of the abyss.
"The light went dark."

"What a fool I was to go! When Niniane twice warned me—"

"Don't," I begged, putting a finger to his lips to stop him. "Don't, Arthur. You, of all people, are not to blame."

"I left you."

"But for foolishness, I would have been safe enough. When did you hear of it?"

"Cathbad told me of the sacrifice. Not willingly, you may be sure. We caught him trying to escape one night in Rheged; I suspected him and had him watched. In fear of his life, he told me their plans." He stopped. "I nearly killed him. Had Ferron and Bellangere not dragged me off him, I would have. I lost my wits, I think." He pulled my head to his breast and kissed my hair. "I put all my faith in Lancelot."

"He saved me, Arthur, at the last moment. But he was not alone. Merlin was there. And one of the Druids helped me. They—they thought I was Elaine."

"Salowen may have thought so. But Cathbad knew the truth. And he let the plans go forward." I shivered at the cold in his voice.

"Salowen is dead."

"Yes."

"You knew?"

"Fion met me on the road two hours hence with a small party. He said they had been out hunting and seen our dust."

"Did he? Bless the man! He is a true friend."

He pulled away and looked down into my face. "Did he come to me at your request?"

"Yes, Arthur."

"Ahhhh. To blunt the force of Maelgon's accusation, no doubt."

"You have spoken to Maelgon?"

"He met us at the outer gate. He would not stand aside until he had voiced his grievance. I had to command him to move out of the way, so I could come to you." He kissed me again, slowly and with love. In his arms, I found the courage to face my fears.

"Arthur, have you spoken to Lancelot?"

"Not yet."

"He has taken it all upon himself."

"Well," he said slowly, "he is responsible."

"Not alone. I—I share the blame, Arthur."

He took the blow with barely a tremor; still, his eyes were kind. "He saved you from the flame. For that, I will forgive him anything."

"Don't let Maelgon bring a formal charge. Please."

"I cannot prevent that, Gwen. He has done so already. We meet tonight."

"Tonight?"

"It is his right. I must hear him. But I will make short work of it, I promise you. It is easy to see what he is after. I want the women there—will you be ready? Are you recovered enough?"

With a lie I could postpone it, but I could not lie to Arthur. "Yes."

"Don't distress yourself so. You can't believe I would bring judgment against Lancelot."

I held him tight and fought back tears. "You have not seen him yet."

With a firm hand he lifted my chin and looked long and searchingly into my eyes. What he saw there brought him pain and bitter joy. At length he dropped his hand and said sadly, "What you have done has scarred your soul. That is punishment enough, I think."

"Lancelot will die if you forgive him."

He shrugged. "I can deal with Lancelot. It is you, Guinevere, whom I must heal."

I stared, stunned to hear Fion's words so soon repeated. Arthur turned. Maelgon and Anet, Fion and his companions, Ferron, Gereint, and Bellangere awaited us at the gate.

"Duty beckons," Arthur said gently, offering me his arm. "You who faced the Druids with such courage, you must be brave yet awhile longer."

Maelgon called the Council an hour past dinner. Ailsa laid my gown out on the bed while I paced the room in distraction. How had things come to such a pass? Why could not this embarrassment be avoided? Why, oh why, should everything I did reflect shame upon Arthur? That I was the root of all this sorrow was plain enough. The King had spent all afternoon with Lancelot and afterward had paced the garden alone, his hands clasped behind his back, looking solemn. I had seen him from my window, when I could bear to look.

"Come, my lady, it is time to prepare."

She had laid out my finest gown, my best jewels, and had the sapphire netting ready for my hair.

"Oh, Ailsa. Put them away. I cannot wear them."

She stared blankly, uncomprehending. "But—my lady—"

"I will not go dressed for a celebration, when I am the source of such distress! Dear Lord, save me from hubris! Find me something plain. Dull. Ugly."

"But where—"

"Send to Cissa. There is an old trunk in Alyse's room, I think. I remember a gray gown. If they have not given it away, I will wear it."

"But, Gwen! You cannot—"

"Very well, I will go myself!" I cried impatiently.

Scowling, Ailsa dipped me a curtsy and hurried to the door. But there she turned. "If I were you, I should worry about pleasing the King."

"Oh, God!" I wailed. "If only that were all that mattered!"

She returned some time later with a dove-gray gown. I bade her remove the lace trimming from bodice and sleeves and declined the jeweled belt Cissa had sent.

"One would almost think," Ailsa said sourly as she bent over her task, "that you wish to be a prisoner yourself."

I stopped pacing to face her. "That is precisely what I wish! Maelgon may treat me as a victim, but I am one with the accused. And I want Maelgon to know it. It is the only thing I can do to help save Lancelot."

Her eyebrows lifted. "Lancelot! You cannot think he is in real danger, my lady. The High King would never condemn his closest friend."

"Oh, Ailsa, it is not that simple. In council friendship cannot be considered. Arthur must pass a Judgment the council will accept. Maelgon counts on Alyse and Anet to side with him. And they might, to protect the honor of Gwynedd. I have done my best with Anet, but he is her husband, after all. That leaves me, Fion, Lancelot, and Arthur. Fion will be diplomatic of necessity, and I know already what Lancelot will say. What can Arthur do? If he gives a Judgment that contradicts the council, Maelgon will contest it, and we shall have war. That is what Arthur came here to prevent. His very fairness will tie his hands. I must do whatever I can to make Maelgon think twice." I lifted the soft, dull fabric in my hand. "Arthur will not like this, but I think he will forgive me the gesture."

The gown fit snugly and without its laces was plain and self-effacing. I wore no jewels, no earrings, no adornments of any kind. At my command and against her will, Ailsa pulled my hair back from my face and bound it with a thong. If I did not look like a prisoner myself, at least I looked like a penitent. Not even Maelgon could mistake the signal.

The page arrived to fetch me, and I turned to Ailsa. "Well? What think you? Am I plain enough?"

She smiled in her motherly way and made me a reverence. "You have done your best, my lady, and a valiant effort it is. But the effect would surprise you."

"Whatever do you mean?"

"The color of the gown sets off the perfect beauty of your skin. You have a matchless neck and shoulders. I do not worry any longer about the King."

"Ailsa!" I cried in panic. "What are you saying? It cannot be! You think to humor me, that is all!"

She smiled again. "Of course, of course. The page is waiting, my lady. You must go." And she pushed me out the door.

When I entered the council chamber everyone but Arthur was already there. Thank God it was a small council, with only the six of us and no advisors, no lieutenants, no servants. Only four men guarded the door, two of Arthur's and two of Maelgon's. I recognized Gereint and Bellangere, trusted friends both and men who could keep their mouths closed. Predictably, Maelgon wore all his finery, even his crown. Anet was in her new gown, and her hair was dressed in the way Ailsa had taught her servant. She looked almost pretty, but the change in her went deeper. She was calm and self-possessed, even though she was excited. She was a woman who had found a joy in power. I did not think she could go back now to what she had been before.

Alyse, stiff and formal, sat beside her. She looked at me with dismay and disapproval, but said nothing. By her words that afternoon she had placed herself in my debt, and she dared not speak against me now. Fion, on the other hand, was astonished. When he rose to hand me to my seat I saw the question in his eyes.

"What can I do to serve you?" he whispered as he bent over my hand.

"Defend Lancelot," I murmured.

"Aye, that I could guess myself. But how far?"

I looked up into his brilliant eyes. "Keep this foremost in your thoughts: Where would I be now without him?" He squeezed my hand in answer.

Lancelot himself I could barely look at. He was dressed as plainly as I and sat straight in the chair opposite Arthur's empty seat. Around his neck he wore a leather thong, half hidden by the tunic. I knew with certainty that it held my ring, and wondered what on earth had possessed him to wear it here. He was furious with me, as well. His black brows came down over his eyes when he saw me, and he scowled at me across the table. At least, I thought in grim amusement, we did not look like lovers.

The night was warm and damp, with sea fog cloaking the shore and valleys. A thick mist crept in through the narrow windows and haloed the torches with light. There we sat, we six, watching one another in silence and waiting for Arthur. Time passed. Maelgon began to frown, and sent a page to discover if aught was amiss with the High King. It was unlike Arthur to keep anyone waiting. The page reported that the King was coming. But still we waited. Lancelot began to worry; Alyse looked pointedly at me; I shrugged. Anet cast a nervous glance at Maelgon, who was slowly growing angry. And Fion, his eyes dancing, looked amused.

At last we heard his steps. The soldiers snapped to attention. The High King paused in the doorway, gathering everyone's eye, and entered. It was worth the wait. He was plainly dressed in white, cool and majestic, the crown of Britain shining in the torchlight against his dark hair. Around his waist he wore his jeweled swordbelt, and at his side hung wonderful Excalibur, the great emerald blazing from the hilt. He shed light all about him, and as he moved the mist seemed visibly to part and let him through. We all rose. Maelgon, already sweating in his heavy, colored velvets, bowed as he passed. I made my reverence to the floor. After a long hesitation, Arthur raised me. His eyes ran over the gown and met mine. I could not read his face. There was a gravity about him that I feared.

He signaled the guards to close the door, then stood and looked slowly around the council table, searching every face. The air was so still I could hear voices far off in the outer courtyard, but in that chamber I did not hear so much as a breath. At last the King spoke.

"Let God be my witness, I will have the truth spoken. King Maelgon of Gwynedd, bring your complaint."

Maelgon rose, looking hot and uncomfortable, knowing he had not Arthur's air of command, and resenting it.

"My lord King Arthur," he began. "We of Gwynedd beg your Judgment upon Lancelot. As king, I am responsible for all that happens on our soil, but a tragedy has occurred, my lord, for which I will not accept the blame. A grave injustice has been done to your lady wife, my cousin Queen Guinevere, while you were in Rheged. As my lord knows, she was kidnapped by Druids and taken against her will to Mona's Isle. This travesty took place on my lands, and I will not bear that shame without redress. My lord, it was not through my doing she was taken. She was in the company of Lancelot, and of no other." He licked his lips. "He may be a loyal and faithful knight, he may be first among the King's Companions, but he has failed you, my lord, in his protection of the Queen." He stopped and looked nervously about. No doubt the humility he saw on Lancelot's face gave him courage, for he straightened and drew breath. "I formally charge Lancelot with negligence in his care of the Queen." Maelgon's eyes flitted to each face around the table. No one moved. "Indeed, my lord, I charge him with more than that. When my lord Fion and I came to his rescue, we found him alone with the Queen. We found them—" He hesitated and dropped his gaze, unable to withstand Arthur's steady glare. "We found them in an embrace. My lord, I believe he was alone with her all night."

Silence fell on the small company. My eyes were in my lap. I could not look up. When Arthur spoke, his voice was ice. "Which of them do you accuse? What is the charge?"

"Oh, no," Maelgon sputtered, hastily retreating, "my lord mistakes me. I lay no charge against the Queen, my cousin. After her ordeal, no one could blame her for clinging to any one of my lord's soldiers for support. It is Lancelot who is guilty of taking advantage of her state, of seeking that from the Queen which he had no right to ask. I accuse him of—of—of," Maelgon stammered, seeing Arthur's face, seeing his future go up in smoke before him, "of conspiring to betray the King," he finished, sweating.

"I have heard you. Sit down," Arthur commanded, his face pinched with anger. Maelgon sat.

Arthur looked toward Lancelot and bade him rise. "Lancelot, I have heard your account of these events today from your own lips. I do not ask to hear it repeated now. But I charge you to answer three questions, upon your oath and before God. Have you ever conspired to dishonor me or my wife, Guinevere?"

Lancelot faced his friend and met his eyes. "No, my lord."

"Have you been negligent in your care of my Queen?"

"Yes, my lord."

"Last," Arthur said, a trace of warmth creeping back into his voice, "did you risk your life, and those of your companions, to save Guinevere from the Druids' fire?"

"Yes, my lord," Lancelot replied woodenly, staring hard at Arthur. Clearly, they had come to some agreement—how Arthur had managed it I could not guess—but Lancelot said nothing beyond the barest truth; in exchange for what? What was Arthur's part in the bargain, that would restore Lancelot's honor in his own eyes?

"Sit down," Arthur commanded. Lancelot obeyed. "My lord Fion, you accompanied King Maelgon to Mona's Isle. Tell me how you found my lady Queen. Of the charge of negligence you can tell us nothing, but address, if you will, the charge of betrayal."

Fion rose, standing at ease, and spoke in a conversational manner. His beautiful voice, melodic as a bard's, captured every ear. "Well, my lord, we found your Companions trapped at the head of a tiny valley. The Druids were approaching with drawn knives, knowing they had no escape. The Queen had been taken to a cave to give her rest and revive her. She had been drugged, as I understand it, to enable her to undergo the burning without shame." At this Anet clapped a hand to her mouth, and Alyse began to mumble under her breath about reaping what one sows, looking straight at Maelgon. Arthur's face was stone. Fion went on as easily as if he had been talking about the weather. "She spent the night in a drugged sleep, guarded by both Lancelot and Gereint, and awoke to hear the Druids chanting. There was no need for silence, my lord. They chanted to let Lancelot know his fate approached him."

I looked up and met Lancelot's eyes. In that moment we both relived the terror of that dark morning. I began to tremble. Beneath the table, Arthur took my hand.

"When my lord King Maelgon and I fought our way through them and reached the cave, we found Lancelot and the Queen together, as Maelgon says, in an embrace. But they were at the cave mouth, my lord, not hidden in the dark recesses. The Queen tells me they were saying farewell, knowing death to be but a knife throw away. I believed her then, and I can see no reason to doubt her now. Lancelot, when challenged, surrendered his sword to me as a token of his faith." Fion reached behind him and brought forth the sword, placing it on the table in front of the King. It lay sheathed in its old, plain leather scabbard, the cross of rubies on the hilt winking balefully in the mist. "Indeed," Fion continued, "he stepped unarmed into my swordpoint, drawing blood, to signal his innocence."

Maelgon snorted rudely but Arthur's eyes were warm as he thanked Fion and bade him take his seat.

But Fion hesitated. "My lord King, as we speak I am fighting for my kingdom's life at home. I have left my wife in the care of trusted lieutenants. It is easy enough for me to imagine myself in your place, and I would tell you this: If ever my wife were made to face the trial your Queen has faced, I would bestow my everlasting blessings upon the man who saved her from it. It would not matter to me what else he had done."

A smile touched the corners of Arthur's mouth. "Thank you, Fion." Lancelot looked away in despair. Gently Arthur loosed my hand and bade me rise. "Guinevere, you have heard the charges made against Lancelot. What answer do you make?"

I faced him. "My dear lord, the charge of betrayal is false. No man loves you more than Lancelot. And as for negligence—" I lowered my eyes and took a deep breath. "My lord, there is no one at this table who does not love you, or who would knowingly do you a disservice. I am sure"—and I raised my head to look at Maelgon—"that if we had it to do again, each one of us would act differently. I, for one, would not ask Lancelot to ride out with me when vengeance of some kind was expected from the Druids. And Lancelot would not dismiss the escort, that we might have private conversation. And I feel certain, my lord, that Maelgon would not call in all his scouts from the forest to ring the castle so tightly, thus leaving the beaches unpatrolled. And even you, my lord," I said quickly, as Maelgon drew breath in anger, "you would not go to Rheged. You probably would not allow me beyond King's Gate."

Arthur listened unmoving, watching Maelgon.

"What happened was an accident of fate. We were all at fault. We were none of us at fault." I turned directly toward Lancelot. "But since my friend Lancelot stands accused, let me remind everyone of this. It was Lancelot and no other who cut me from the Druid's stake when they had already lit the fire. I owe him my life. Should you find him deserving of punishment, I beg you will allow me to share it with him, in repayment of the debt." Lancelot leaned forward and buried his head in his arms to hide his face. As he moved, the ring fell free from his tunic and swung forward on its thong into the light. Arthur stared at it, speechless. "And— and if it were not for the quick action and bravery of King Maelgon and King Fion— Oh, my lord," I pleaded, laying a hand on Arthur's arm, seeing the grief on his face, "do not be deceived by appearances. All is not as it seems. These are Lancelot's kin, his wife's family. He honors Gwynedd, he would not bring shame upon it."

"I quite agree." Alyse spoke firmly, rising. "My son is new to kingship, my lord Arthur, and has not yet attained Pellinore's wisdom. There is truly no cause for discord between him and Lancelot. They are brothers. Listen to your lady Queen, my lord. I know her words to be truth."

Maelgon sat open-mouthed in anger, then leaped to his feet. "What nonsense is this? My lord, my mother has retired from life these nine months past. Disregard this unseemly advice—"

"Unseemly advice?" Arthur cut in coldly. "She told me to listen to my wife, your cousin."

"I will not bear any part of this shame!" Maelgon cried, his face red. "Your lady wife was abducted, and it is Lancelot's fault! I demand your Judgment upon him!"

Arthur rose and drew himself to his full height, facing Maelgon.

"My Judgment he shall have," the King said slowly. Maelgon exhaled, appeased, and sat down. "But I have not yet heard from Queen Anet. I would like to know her counsel."

Maelgon stared, and Anet flushed.

"My lord," she quavered, rising to face him. "I am the last person to wish shame upon Gwynedd, or blame upon one of your Companions. My lord Maelgon may be new to kingship, but he is wise and able, and cares as deeply about the honor of Gwynedd and the glory of Britain as my lady Queen Alyse or his father the great King Pellinore." She stopped uncertainly; both Maelgon and Alyse were staring at her in amazement.

"I am sure you are right," Arthur said kindly. "Have you any counsel to give me about the charges?"

She clasped her hands together tightly and did not take her eyes from his face, drawing strength from his very presence. "I know nothing about them, my lord. But I cannot imagine that any insult was intended, to you, to Gwynedd or to Britain. As to what the Queen has endured, I did not know a woman could possess such courage. To my mind, honor is due not only to the Queen, but to Lancelot and Maelgon and Fion for saving her life, which was twice in jeopardy. I wish—my lord, I wish we could celebrate her safe return and disregard how she came to be taken from us!"

Arthur smiled. "That is my wish, as well, Lady Anet. Maelgon is lucky to have such an intelligent woman at his side." Maelgon, who had jumped up to protest, stood sputtering aimlessly at this compliment, proud that his wife should receive such commendation from the High King, at the same time angry that she dared to voice an opinion different from his own.

While these three were standing the doors flew open and a group of soldiers pushed into the room, shouting and cursing, calling for Maelgon's attention. Lancelot shot to his feet, and Fion be-

side him. Between them the soldiers hauled forward a man in a
Druid's robe, with blood streaming from his nose and one eye
swollen shut in a bruised and battered face, and a slim youth with
black hair, bound by the wrists. The mist seemed to thicken with
their entrance, and I leaned forward to see them better.

"Arthur!" I whispered, clutching at his sleeve. "Oh, stop them!
It's Mordred!" He drew breath in slowly and went still, watching
Maelgon.

"My lord Maelgon!" the soldiers cried. "We found them in the
Queen's garden, my lord! This is a Druid from Mona's Isle, he
confesses it!"

Maelgon stepped forward, and Anet behind him.

"Arthur!" I whispered. "Do something! They have bound him!"

"Be still a moment," he said softly. "He is not hurt. Let me see
what Maelgon does."

"You again!" Maelgon sneered at Mordred. "You cannot stay
away from the vermin, can you? Want to be one yourself someday, is that it? You filthy pagan, stand aside." He turned his back
on Mordred, leaving him bound, and turned to Kevin. "What are
you doing in my precincts? How dare you set foot in Gwynedd
without my leave! I will have you horsewhipped, you pagan
snake!" And he raised his fist to strike that beaten face yet once
again.

"No." The word fell into the pause like a rock into a still pool.
Anet, trembling visibly, stepped forward. "No," she repeated. "Do
not strike him. He is here with my permission, Maelgon. He has
my protection."

Every eye in the room turned full upon her. Maelgon's fist was
still raised, arrested, above his head. The color drained from his
face. *"What?"* he whispered, incredulous. *"What* did you say?"

"He is here with my permission," Anet repeated, her small
voice gaining strength. "He came ashore the morning of the sacrifice, having done what he could to save the Queen on Mona, and
begged for my protection. He wants to speak to the High
King."

As she spoke, Maelgon regained his color and, with it, his temper. "Protection be damned!" he shouted. "You have no right to
disobey me! I am king!" He shook his fist wildly in the air, grind-
ing his teeth, his spittle frothing upon his lips. Anet, shaking,
stood her ground.

"Nonsense," Alyse said coolly, rising. "Every queen has the
right to grant protection. It does not depend upon the king's desire. To deny her this right is to dishonor Gwynedd, and

Strathclyde, as well. You have given no order, Maelgon. She has not disobeyed you. She has shown sense and calm and tolerance. She is to be commended."

Maelgon slammed his fist down on the table. "Tolerance!" he shouted. "Not to Druids! This is a Christian land!"

"I hope," Alyse retorted, "you are not going to question her devotion to her faith."

Maelgon looked at his convent wife and scowled. "No, no, of course not. That is not what I meant. But—"

"This man performed a service to the High Queen, and thereby to the High King. He has been granted protection in order that he might speak with Arthur. I suggest you let him do that, if your men have not already beaten him beyond the power of speech."

"I will hear him myself first!" Maelgon snarled, trapped between his women. "I wish to know what he was doing with this, this unholy miscreant in the garden."

I gasped at his reference to Mordred, but Arthur stilled me with a touch upon my hand.

"You. Druid. Attend me."

"His name," ventured Anet, "is Kevin."

Maelgon ignored her. "Druid. What were you doing in my garden?"

Kevin, stiff with pain, looked him squarely in the face and said nothing. He had about him something of the milky calm I had seen in him before, when he had just come from a ceremony in Nemet. Slowly he turned toward Anet and, raising his bound hands, made a sign before her face.

"What is he doing?" Maelgon cried. "Stop him! Guard!"

The soldiers grabbed his shoulders, but Kevin offered no resistance and stood quietly.

"My lady Queen," he said thickly, through swollen lips, "the Great Goddess has blessed you with child. You have done me a service and in return I give you this knowledge. At the spring equinox you will be safely delivered of twin children, one male and one female. The son you bear will add his light to the greater glory of Britain, and your daughter shall be beloved of the finest warrior in the realm." He stopped suddenly and shook himself awake to find the entire company staring at him.

"My lord Maelgon," he said in surprise. "I was coming to see you. I must speak in private with the High King Arthur."

Maelgon was caught completely off guard. His anger was swallowed up in his confusion. Anet, trembling and blushing, was led away by Alyse to take her seat. Maelgon had been honored, and he knew it. But he could not bring himself to thank the Druid. "What were you doing in my garden?" he repeated dumbly. "Why were you there?"

Kevin frowned, as if trying to remember. "I was waiting to see the King, my lord, and then he came himself into the garden to speak with me."

"You lie," Maelgon returned. "He has been in this chamber all this while."

Kevin looked about, bewildered, and then saw Mordred.

"Here he is. Ask him yourself." Then to Mordred: "Tell them, my lord, that you came to me while I waited for you, and that I asked for your mercy toward my people."

"What impudence is this?" Maelgon cried. "*This* is the lad you took for the King?"

Kevin looked blankly at Maelgon. "Yes, my lord. The High King of Britain."

Mordred, his dark eyes wide with terror, looked helplessly toward Arthur. And at last, Arthur stepped forward.

"Maelgon. Stand back." Through the misty lamplight they made a path for him, and he stood before Kevin, tall and glowing, making the Druid look small and dark. "Untie his hands. And the boy's."

"But—"

"Untie them!" Arthur snapped, and the guards obeyed. "They are not armed," Arthur said evenly to Maelgon. "Your men have seen to that." Maelgon grunted and Arthur addressed Kevin. "I am Arthur, High King of Britain. It is I you seek. Kevin, leader of Druids, do you know me?"

Slowly Kevin's eyes traveled upward from his glittering sword to his face and rested there. A look of puzzlement swept his features.

"King Arthur. Yes, my lord. I know you. Then who is—" He turned swiftly to Mordred and passed a hand across his eyes. "But I saw the crown. I saw it. The very one you wear, my lord, I saw it upon his head."

There was a deathly silence in the hall.

"Treason!" Maelgon croaked, but he trembled, afraid. Mordred froze, his eyes on Arthur's face.

"Kevin," Arthur said slowly, "have you never had the Sight before?"

Kevin stared in surprise. "The Sight, my lord? Why, no, only Salowen has—had—" He faltered. Arthur took his arm to steady him.

"It has passed to you," he said gently. "And his power, as well, if I judge aright. You came to ask my mercy for your people, and your Goddess herself has given your people into your hands. You lead them now, Kevin. From this moment forward."

"But I am unready!" Kevin whispered, astounded. "The initiation! The ceremony!"

"Come south with us when we leave Gwynedd. Niniane, Lady of the Lake, can perform the initiation. You would do well to learn from her. When you return to Mona you will be Archdruid in Salowen's place."

Kevin knelt at his feet and kissed his ring. "You are more than merciful, my lord King. And I am undeserving."

"No," Arthur replied, "for your aid to Guinevere you deserve whatever is in my power to give."

Kevin's glance slid swiftly to Mordred, still standing rooted at his side. "And this youth, my lord? What does this Seeing mean? Will he be of service to you?"

"Indeed, that is my hope," the King replied with a quick smile. "He is my nephew, my sister's son. He serves me now, and may come to kingship in time, if God is willing."

Maelgon stared at Mordred in wonder and at Arthur with growing consternation.

"Mordred," Arthur said gently, "what were you doing in the king's house tonight? Did you come to see this Druid?"

"Oh, no, my lord," Mordred replied, licking his dry lips. "I did not know he was there. I came—my lord, I came to see the Queen." Arthur lifted an eyebrow but did not interrupt him. "All the men were talking about her abduction, my lord, and her terrible ordeal. They wondered if she could withstand it. They thought she might lie gravely ill and the news be kept close. No one had seen her, my lord, and everyone knew you had been all afternoon pacing in a brown study." A wry smile touched the King's lips; Lancelot saw it, Mordred did not. "So the captain of my company bade me see what I could discover about the Queen. I came to the garden, my lord, because the Queen is known to walk it of an evening. I did not know she was in Council. The only one there was Kevin, and he addressed me strangely." Mordred gulped. "He talked about a crown and such. I was about to leave when the soldiers grabbed us."

"You see the Queen before you now," Arthur said. "Does she look ill?"

Mordred glanced at me shyly and lowered his eyes. "No, my lord. Sad, perhaps, but not ill. And very beautiful."

I felt heat slowly rise to my face as Arthur smiled. "She is indeed. Thank you, Mordred. You may take this report back to your captain."

Mordred knelt and kissed his ring. Maelgon's soldiers stood aside to let him leave, but closed again around Kevin. Clearly Maelgon, who was losing his case against Lancelot, was not about to let Kevin escape his grasp. But before he could open his mouth to speak, Arthur turned and faced him.

"Maelgon, I am ready to give my Judgment, upon Kevin and upon Lancelot."

As this was what Maelgon had called him there to do, he dared not object, but he grumbled as he nodded, and signaled his men to keep hold of the Druid. We returned to our places around the council table. Everyone sat but Arthur. In the misty light everything around him looked dim and dark, but Arthur himself shone forth like a beacon, in his white raiment and his bright jewe' .

"When I came to Gwynedd, I found this land at war, Christian against Druid." He slowly looked at the faces turned to him around the table. "This is the cause of all our distress. This is why the Queen was taken. If harmony is not restored there will be worse to come. I will root out the source of discord," Arthur said firmly, looking at Maelgon, "wherever it lies. Anyone who serves me serves my cause." He turned to Kevin. "Loose him," the King commanded and the soldiers obeyed. "Kevin, step forward. For the wrongs done your people, for the murder of the priestess and the massacre of worshippers, I grant you Mona's Isle in perpetuity. And I forgive you the abduction of my Queen." Kevin sank to his knees as everyone gasped. "Your people shall have my protection for as long as I hold Britain. But because none but you lifted a finger to prevent the sacrifice of what is dearest to me, I will require that your worship be restricted to Mona. Your people are free to come and go in Britain, but not to worship here, not to recruit, proselytize, pray, teach, practice magic, heal, curse, or even sing. Do not thank me. This is a death sentence I pass upon you. But you will have peace." His hand moved to Excalibur's hilt. "If you are threatened again, send for me. I will destroy your enemies."

Maelgon was livid, but held his tongue. Anet's hand touched his sleeve, begging restraint. The Druid had changed her life with his words, and she sought to remind her husband of it. Arthur must have read my thoughts; he leaned his hands on the table and said quietly to Maelgon, "This man has given you a great gift, if you but knew it. If you have sense, you will thank him for it."

Maelgon scowled but seeing Anet's face, relented, and signaled his guards to leave the room.

Kevin bowed to Arthur. "I am unworthy of the honor you do me, my lord. I have not Salowen's power, but I will serve you any way I can. You have but to command me."

"Druid! Disperse this mist!" Arthur commanded.

Startled, Kevin raised a hand, and a breeze sprang up from nowhere, thinning the mist and blowing the clouds from the stars. Kevin himself gasped in surprise, but Arthur smiled.

"You will serve me well," he said.

Speechless, Kevin withdrew, and the soldiers at the door, all Christians, crossed themselves as he passed by. Then, as silence settled upon us, all eyes turned to Lancelot.

"Rise, Lancelot, and hear my Judgment."

Lancelot stood stiffly, and I found my hands twisting together in my lap. If Arthur forgave him, Lancelot would labor all his life under the burden of that obligation, and Maelgon would not be able to bear the slight. Yet everyone had voiced a plea for mercy, and Arthur had moments before publicly forgiven the Druids. How could he now hold Lancelot to blame?

The two men faced each other in the clear light.

"Of the charge of betrayal which Maelgon brings against you," Arthur said slowly, "you deny it, and there is no other witness but the Queen. I free you of this charge." I whispered a small prayer of thanksgiving. Lancelot stared steadily at Arthur.

"But I find you negligent in your care of my Queen," Arthur said heavily. "In all the years I have known you, this is the only time you have failed me. Because it was you alone who saved her from a fate not even a dog should undergo, I do forgive you as her husband. But as King I cannot forgive it; through your action was her life put in jeopardy; I require of you penance before I see your face again." He stopped, and Lancelot began to breathe. Life returned to his features, and he knelt gracefully before Arthur.

"My gracious lord, name what penance you desire. I shall faithfully perform it."

"Of that," Arthur said, warmth returning to his voice, "I have no doubt. You will accompany King Fion back to Ireland with a troop of men of your choosing. Place yourself under his command. You may not return to Britain until his country is at peace and his rule no longer threatened. However long that takes, so long shall you be parted from us."

Lancelot looked at Arthur with worship on his face. "My lord," he said fervently, "it shall be done."

"This is your doing, Guinevere," Maelgon growled. "I will not forget it!"

"And when you return," Arthur continued, "you will stop a month in Gwynedd and rebuild on Mona's Isle all that has been so recently destroyed by Christian troops. And I make you, Lancelot, a Christian king, responsible for keeping the peace between Mona and Gwynedd. You will come yearly to Gwynedd to visit with Kevin and with Maelgon. I am sure that, as you are his sister's husband and kin to him, King Maelgon will not object."

Maelgon, who had half risen in protest, sat down again and fidgeted uncomfortably.

Arthur straightened and looked about him. "What say you to this, Fion?"

Fion flashed him a smile. "I bless the day I came to Britain," he replied. "Everyone honors me here."

"Queen Alyse?"

"Very satisfactory, my lord. Honor is conferred all around."

"Queen Anet?"

"Thank you, my lord, for your mercy."

"Guinevere?"

"My lord has pulled a swan's egg from a wasp's nest. It is well done."

"King Maelgon? You have heard my Judgment. Do you accept it?"

Maelgon hesitated, frowning as he worked it out. He had wished to be rid of the Druids. And Arthur had banned them from Britain. But Kevin had been honored, and he dare not attack Mona again. He wished to lay blame upon Lancelot, and Lancelot was being blamed. But Lancelot was being honored, also, and was no less powerful than before. On the other hand, Lancelot's ties of kinship would be renewed perforce, and Maelgon's ties to power could only be strengthened thereby. He did not like it; this was not how he would have done it; but he could find no flaw in Arthur's Judgment.

"Very well, my lord," he assented at last. "I will accept it."

Gravely Arthur turned to Lancelot and took up his sword from the table.

"Arise, Lancelot. Take back your sword and commend yourself into Fion's service. Go now and return to us swiftly. The Queen and I will pray for your safety every day you are gone from us."

Lancelot took the sword from his hands and flashed me a look of joy.

"For the glory of Britain will I go." And he kissed the King's ring.

Arthur walked with me back to my chamber. He dismissed Ailsa and closed the door behind us. He took off his swordbelt and carefully laid the Sword upon the chest in the corner. His crown he removed with his own hands and placed upon the Sword. Then he stood and looked at me. "You are the bravest woman I know."

"How did you do it, Arthur? How did you find the right path? You have given him back his dignity, and your friendship is undamaged. I did not think it possible."

He came toward me and took my hands. Lightly he rubbed his thumb against my finger where my mother's ring had always been. "Well," he said very gently, "there has been damage, but not beyond repair."

"Arthur," I whispered, meeting his eyes and feeling again the tremendous power of his affection, "do not misunderstand it."

"I hope I do not."

"It was in exchange for what I could not give him. He had done so much for me."

"I know."

"And—it was a lesson to us both, not to be forgotten."

"And what did you learn?"

I raised both his hands and kissed them, then looked up into his face. "You are the end and the beginning. I love you, Arthur, more than life."

He drew a long breath and let it out slowly. "Then I am glad it happened. And I forgive you for it. Now, Guinevere, can you forgive yourself?"

I stared at him, and suddenly, amazed, I understood. What I had so clearly seen in Lancelot—the guilt, the remorse, the self-recrimination—both Fion and Arthur had seen in me.

"I—I don't know. Sometimes it seems that everything I do does you harm."

"I am unharmed." Again he touched the place the ring had been. "Even so, I am unharmed."

"Oh, Arthur, I never meant to hurt you!" I looked quickly away and stilled my trembling. "I thought I should never see you again, and I owed him my life."

His hands slid slowly up my arms and cupped my shoulders. His touch was comforting; he steadied me.

"Gwen, I understand it. Let it go." I looked up. His warm brown eyes held me, offering solace. "He is my friend, too."

I saw he meant it; he *was* unharmed; in some incomprehensible way we three were closer now than before, and would always be so, bound forever by our love, whose boundaries we had so recently discerned. To me, it was the lifting of a great burden, and for the first time since we came to Gwynedd, I felt lighthearted.

"Thank you, Arthur. Then I am not afraid any longer."

He smiled in relief. "How many times must I tell you, you need never be afraid of me?" He stepped closer. "Indeed, you are the one men would do well to fear. Who brought Alyse back to life? Who put spine into Anet? It is your doing Maelgon was soft clay in my hands, as it will be largely your doing if there is peace in Gwynedd. He is a new man with those two women at his side. I could not have done it, Gwen, without you."

I flushed with pleasure at his praise and ruffled his hair. "What a tongue you have in your head, my lord King! I suppose you did nothing at all!"

He laughed, freeing my hair from the thong and running caressing hands along my shoulders to my neck. "The next time you try to look plain," he said lightly, "do not choose a simple gown. It only proclaims to all the world that your beauty lies in your bones and your skin, and not in your ornaments. I have wanted nothing the last hour but this." He bent his lips to my neck and kissed me.

THE MEN OF ORKNEY

Seeds of Discord
The Murder
The Beating
The Heir
The Slaughter

19 ❀ seeds of discord

The summer Mordred turned seventeen, Arthur knighted him. Both he and Gawaine had become members of the King's army on their fifteenth birthdays and had enjoyed the honor of entering into official manhood. They had traveled with the King on his journeys around the Kingdom, had sat at the back of many meeting halls, and at the farthest table in even more dining halls. The glamour had rapidly worn off. Mordred was content to watch, and wait, and listen to the councils of his elders, but Gawaine chafed at inactivity. He was forever longing for a good fight.

Seventeen was young for knighthood, but all the Companions knew Mordred deserved it, rumors about his parentage aside. He was an able fighter and a good swordsman; only Lancelot, Galahantyn, Bedwyr, and the King could best him. But more than that, he had a cool head in a crisis and could always look three steps ahead and judge consequences. He had the makings of a statesman. The only thing he lacked, it seemed, was Arthur's ability to lead men by inspiring their love. Lancelot said he had no endearing warmth, no inner light, no central reservoir of strength and serenity for men to draw on. He was young for that, I retorted. Arthur had had it in abundance at fourteen was his reply.

The second reason Arthur knighted Mordred was to elevate his status, while not yet acknowledging him openly. He no longer had to sleep in the barracks, but was given rooms in the castle. He was one of the High King's Companions and sat in the Round Hall with the other knights at Council.

The uneasy tension between Mordred and Gawaine was strained by this elevation, but not to breaking point. Gawaine knew Mordred was the King's son. But he also knew he would soon be a king in his own right, well before Mordred could ever

261

hope to rule. And he knew the King was not ready to declare Mordred openly his heir.

It seemed that Lancelot's judgment had been acute. Christian power had grown in Britain during Arthur's long reign. Most of the kingdoms were Christian, as were most of the knights who now served him. The only man Bishop Landrum would bend a knee to was the High King himself. On Ynys Witrin, the monastery of Christian monks grew as powerful as the Lady's shrine. Only the hill folk, and men from the outland kingdoms of Orkney, Lothian, and parts of western Wales, still worshipped old gods. And Mithra, the soldiers' god, even Mithra was remembered only on his great feast days.

This was a problem for Arthur, for as Lancelot had predicted, there seemed to be no question of Mordred ever becoming an anointed King. Duke Constantine of Cornwall, who had grown more manifestly devout as Mordred grew in favor, was fond of reminding all who would listen that Britain must have a Christian King. But until Arthur acknowledged to the people of Britain that Mordred was his son, such talk as Constantine's could be scoffed at, and forgotten. So Arthur kept quiet, and kept the peace, and gave Mordred honor and status in other ways.

That same summer Agravaine and Gaheris turned fifteen and joined the company of men. They celebrated by getting drunk and tearing up the town in their revels, picking fights with soldiers and accosting every woman they saw. The King made good their damage with gold to all who asked for it and chastised the twins for this behavior. But his words were remembered only until the next chance for rowdiness came along. Gawaine was of their temperament, but his future as heir to Orkney meant much to him. Neither Agravaine nor Gaheris had aught to look forward to but what honor they could gain by killing the King's enemies—and the country was at peace.

I stood in the library garden three weeks after the solstice, directing my women as they pruned the roses. Fion had sent me some lovely glass bowls for my anniversary, which he never forgot. These were of many shapes, some deep and some shallow, all etched in the pretty way the Irish have. The bowls turned the light and set it shimmering in the very air. I poured clean water into them and, filling them with roses, set them in the King's room, in his library, and in Mordred's room and my own, to please the eye and scent the air. I was teaching the art of pruning to my two newest girls, Claire and Linet, when Claire clumsily dropped her knife and, blushing, tucked a stray wisp of hair into her net. As I opened my mouth to chide her, I saw Mordred coming down the walk toward us, and I smiled.

He was as tall as Arthur now, although he would never have his father's shoulders. But he had his face and was a handsome youth, admired by all the girls in Camelot.

"Queen Guinevere." He bowed politely.

"Why, Sir Mordred, how glad I am to see you. I miss the days when we were daily together."

"As I do," he said fervently. "I thank you, my lady."

I saw he would talk with me, so I gave some last instructions to the girls, which I doubt they even heard, and led him off deeper into the bower.

He adjusted his pace to suit mine and kept his voice too low for overhearing. As a courtier, he was skilled. "My lady, I have just come from the King. I was with him when a courier came, and I asked if I might bring you the message. As I see you so seldom nowadays," he finished, smiling shyly.

"I am glad of it. Tell me."

"The message came from Castle Daure. From King Arres."

I glanced at him quickly, but his face was carefully neutral and his eyes were on the ground. "From King Arres?"

"He begs the King to allow the Queen of Orkney a last visit with her sons."

I stopped, and Mordred stopped with me but did not look up. "A *last* visit? Is she ill?"

"No" came the quiet answer, "but she is on the verge of taking orders and will remove to a nunnery next autumn where men are not admitted."

I stared at Mordred. Was it possible Lamorak had told us all the truth? "I was not aware the King had given her leave to go."

Mordred looked up at last, his dark eyes unreadable. "Indeed, my lady, he has not. She has not asked him. This is the first he has heard of her plans."

"So she has got King Arres to do her bidding? If she is truly Christian, no doubt Arthur will let her go."

"I advised him against it." Mordred drew a deep breath. "Every word from her lips is a lie," he whispered. "This is some trick she has devised to regain her freedom or renew her hold over Gaheris—I don't know what she is planning, but I know, I *know* she lies. She is no more Christian than I am. Arthur should disregard Arres' request."

"He cannot. On the chance it might be true. He must at least make an effort to find out."

He nodded. "I know. But I like it not. He tells me that some years ago she enslaved Sir Lamorak, who even bid for her hand in marriage. And that you talked him out of it."

I smiled. "He is flattering me, Mordred. I did nothing of the kind. Arthur sent him to Brittany to serve King Hoel, to cool his ardor and hope that he would wed a Breton lass. I have not heard what became of him."

Mordred looked grim. "I will tell you. He is back now in the King's service. Sir Gereint passed through Winchester last spring and says that Lamorak is stationed there at the garrison, second-in-command. He still sees her."

"Well, he has not renewed his request for her hand in marriage," I said with a frown.

Mordred looked uneasy, then shrugged. "He claims he is still betrothed to her and, from what Gereint told me, enjoys all the privileges thereof."

I glanced up to see his face and caught a quick blush on his cheek. If Mordred, her cool-headed bastard, felt shame for her behavior, what would her hot-blooded sons think if they knew?

"This is rumor, surely. If she is preparing to live a life where men are not admitted—"

"Exactly, my lady! It is all a lie! Not about Lamorak—I've no doubt he is her lover. She has never denied herself the indulgence of even her smallest desires. When I was a child"—his voice shook—"I remember a constant stream of men going in and out of her apartments. I used to see my father's face in every one of them." He looked away and squared his shoulders. "In any event, Arthur has decided to grant Arres' request and send us. But he is uneasy about it. He will send Sir Sagramor to the nunnery to find out if she really plans to retire there. And he has decided to ride south and inspect some fortifications not far from Giants' Dance; it is an excuse to accompany us the first part of the way."

I smiled. "That sounds like Arthur."

"Where is Merlin?" Mordred asked softly. "Why can't he do this, instead of Arthur? The King risks himself to come within a hundred leagues of her!"

These were his parents he spoke about, and it grieved my heart to hear it. "For years Merlin has been no more than a shadow and a voice. Now Arthur believes Merlin is gone. He says he has gone to his gods in that cold Welsh cave of his. The King even pays a servant to tend the place, that it may retain its holiness, and so honor Merlin." To my surprise, Mordred looked stricken. "Don't be distressed. Arthur told me it was a sign we needed to worry about Morgause no longer."

Mordred grunted. "He is worried enough about her now."

"When do you leave, and who attends him?"

"Within the fortnight. Gawaine is at Caerleon and must be sent for. Bedwyr, Gereint, Villers, Galahantyn, and Bellangere attend him." He paused and lowered his eyes. "Lancelot stays as Protector."

I grieved to see he still could not accept it. "And Gaheris? Does he know?"

"Yes. He and Agravaine followed the courier in, to hear his news."

"How did he take it? Is he eager, or afraid?"

He hesitated. "He is beside himself with joy."

"He must be guarded! Oh, Mordred, do not let her see him alone!"

He shivered. "Believe me, my lady, the troops who escort us have orders to attend us every minute. Orders given in the presence of Gaheris. The King takes no chances."

We walked on in silence. I was as worried for Mordred as for Gaheris. His brothers never knew the part he had played in the accusation of Morgause. They blamed Lancelot, who was not then even in Britain, and they blamed me. I feared Morgause might take joy in telling them the truth and setting brother against brother for her amusement.

"He will take me with him when he goes to talk treaty with the Saxons," Mordred said suddenly, brightening.

"Will he? I am so glad, Mordred. You are ready for it."

"Readier than most, my lady," he said, warming to it, "for I have learned some Saxon on the sly."

"Really? From whom? Have we Saxons in Camelot?"

"Indeed we do. Two of them are grooms in the stable—Saxons are magicians with horses—Lancelot employs them all unknowing! They told him they were Irish, and he put down their straw-colored hair and strange accents to that. I have taken the trouble to make their acquaintance and learn what I can of their tongue. If they speak slowly enough, I can understand them."

I watched him thoughtfully as he spoke. Lancelot was right about him; he saw opportunity everywhere. As he would need to, to be a King.

"Are you sure they are not spies?"

"Oh, no, my lady. They are not. Each carries a blood price on his head and left the territories to save his skin. All they want is to work with good horses and be left in peace. They curse their former king and have sworn allegiance to Arthur. And anyway," he finished, "I tell them nothing of what passes. I go to them only to learn."

"This is excellent, Mordred. You may perhaps do the King your father a special service, if you understand their speech, and they know it not. You can attest to the truth of the translations. More than that, you can listen to what the soldiers mutter to one another and see how the land truly lies."

He nodded eagerly. "That has been my thought, my lady. Their nobles, their 'thegns,' I must have speech with, to find out whether it is only King Cerdic who desires to deal with us, or if his men are behind him."

"And our men?" I asked with hesitation. "Are they behind the King? Or is there grumbling and superstition? Do they think it reasonable we talk with Saxons, or do they think the King is growing soft?"

I saw by his disconcerted look that I had hit a bruise. He wished desperately that I had not asked him. Arthur had evaded the question with assurances, but Mordred answered me.

"Opinion is divided, my lady. Among the young men—" He gulped hastily, seeing my face, and changed his wording. "I mean, among the youths of my age, some would follow the King even into the gates of Hell, but some prefer to hate the Saxons, mostly because they want war. These would fight their own kin for a rag of glory, if they thought these could get away with it."

"You might be describing your own brothers," I teased him, to lighten the tone.

He smiled. "Indeed, I am. All but Gareth, who, like me, takes no joy in killing. My brothers are among this group, and some black Celts from Wales. Most of the Christians are behind Arthur. As for the older—er, the proven warriors, who fought with the King in the Saxon wars, they are divided, also. Some cannot let go of their hatred and look beyond it. The others will do whatever the King commands, because he is who he is and has done what he has done."

"Amen," I whispered.

"The foremost of those opposed," he said slowly, "is Lancelot."

I touched his hand and smiled at him. "Do not worry about Lancelot. He is opposed with his lips and his head, but his heart and his sword are with the King. He would follow him anywhere, even beyond the gates of Hell. Do not for a minute doubt him."

"If you say so, my lady." But he did doubt; I could see it in his face.

I shook my head. "Ah, Mordred. It is my fondest dream that you and Lancelot should grow in trust and friendship. You both are men of honor, and you love the King. But neither of you will know the other. There is some great reluctance between you."

Mordred took my hand and bent his knee to the ground. "You are so full of gentleness, my lady, you would have everyone you love, love each other. And when I am with you, it seems almost possible. But, dear Guinevere, beyond the sphere of your influence, beyond these castle walls, lies a world of slanders, lies, fierce competition, and mean acts. To be in your company, yours and the King's, it is like coming up from the depths to breathe pure air."

I took his head in my hands. "Is life so difficult for you, Mordred? Are you still badgered about your birth? If the King's silence makes it troublesome, tell him."

He shook his head quickly. "No, no. Let that be. I understand the silence. It must be so. Only—" He paused and swallowed audibly. "Only I sometimes wonder what the future holds for me. He has never told me what he intends."

I touched his cheek. "If he has not told you, I cannot," I whispered. "But you know him, Mordred. He is your father, and he loves you. What would you do if you were he?"

He looked at me with his black eyes, wise and deep and tragic. "But I am not enough like him," he said so softly, the words hovered on the edge of sound. I felt a thrill go through me like an arrow of truth.

"No two are the same. But there is much of him in you. If you cannot see it, I can. And knowing Arthur, what do you think he will do?"

He kissed my hand with fervor, and I raised him. His face was flushed with excitement.

"Go with God," I told him, and sent him back to Arthur.

Lancelot and I strolled in the garden after hall. The night was warm and scented and dark with a new moon. Some light spilled from the open library doors, where a single cresset burned, but the depths of the garden were deep in shadow. Claire and young Linet attended me, but they sat discreetly by the fountain in the light, comparing the valor of the young knights they worshipped and, out of custom, paying us little attention.

In darkness, Lancelot clasped my hand and held it close against his breast. We walked thus, silent, taking pleasure in the still beauty of the night and in the touch of our flesh.

"I wish, Gwen, I could bring Galahad to meet you. I worry sometimes that he is kept too close at home."

"I would be honored, Lancelot," I replied, "to meet your son. What do you mean, 'kept too close'?"

"Oh," he said lightly, lifting my hand to his lips, "he is too fond of his mother."

"That is normal for a boy his age, I think. Soon his heroes will be men."

He shrugged. "I am not there enough. And she sets his mind against me, young as he is. He would be better off living here. Like Mordred. Like Gareth." It was the nearest he had ever come to telling me about his life with Elaine. I could see well it was death to him.

"Then leave the other two with her and bring him. You are his father."

He shuddered and then looked quickly away. My heart filled with rage against Elaine—that he should dread that confrontation so! Lancelot, bravest of men!

"I would like him to grow up like Gareth," he said quickly. "He left his mother early enough, it seems. He is full of gentleness and honor and the love of doing right. Galahad strives for high ideals, but knows only those his mother feeds him. He should be at Arthur's court."

"Then bring him," I said warmly, slipping my arm through his and entwining my fingers in his own. "Shall Arthur send for him?"

He looked down at me, and a stray wisp of light caught his smile. "No, my lady Queen. This I can do myself."

"Brave Lancelot!"

He laughed and drew me close. "This is a great myth you women raise us to believe: that you are powerless and we must risk life to protect you. I have yet to know a woman who does not rule her husband in anything she wills." He kissed me softly, letting his lips linger on mine.

"You know *me*."

"You pretend you do not rule Arthur? Why, three years ago he felt about Saxons as I do. You would no more have caught him treating with their leader than—than bathing in boiling oil. And now he proposes to parley with Cerdic himself, and talk new treaties, as if the thieving dog were his equal!" With an effort, he calmed himself and lowered his voice. "I know who has his ear, Gwen. Don't think I cannot guess whose idea this is."

We walked on a little farther, and I gave him time to settle his emotions. Like Gawaine, he was quick to anger, but unlike him, he was just as quick to cool.

"Is Cerdic a thieving dog," I asked gently, "or a ruler beset by greedy lords at his back and a growing population on his shores? In all these years he has kept his word to Arthur and not strayed across the border anywhere. And yet, you know, his chieftains must be hollering for more land every year and spreading rumors about his growing age and unfitness for his crown. In his boots, my dear Lancelot, what would you do?"

"I would keep my word," he said with some defiance.

"And so he has. The King asked for this parley, only to set the stage for the future. If they meet in friendship now, perhaps his chieftains will wait to see what comes of it; and in the meantime, they will be our buffer against the Franks."

"Yes, yes, I know the reasons," he said impatiently. "But even now that Clodomir is dead, we are not threatened. Childebert has treaties with me and with Hoel. So why do we need a buffer? And what makes him think the Saxons will listen, or abide by what is agreed?"

"They will listen, because he is Arthur of Britain. And Cerdic has shown that he can keep his word. We have nothing to lose, Lancelot, and much to gain, perhaps, in the future."

He sighed. "I know your dream of a united Britain. But there might be a lot to lose. Many are against it."

We had reached the stone bench that hugged the wall at the end of the garden. I could see nothing here, it was so black. I put out my hands and laid them against his chest. His own came up and covered them.

"And you, Lancelot? I know you disagree with Arthur, but will you follow him?"

"Unto death," he whispered, and kissed me. For a moment, I allowed myself to respond to him, giving in to the demanding fires that burned in me whenever he was near. But at last, trembling, we broke apart and sat together on the bench, remembering who we were.

"You are right, Lancelot. He does this because of me, and because of Mordred, who has caught fire with this idea. But although Arthur sees the sense in it, he is not eager to pursue it far. He says it is not his destiny."

"That's Merlin talking."

"I know. But he believes Merlin. He has always believed everything the old enchanter said."

"He wasn't always old, you know, Gwen." I heard the smile in his voice. "Bedwyr knew him when he was not much older than Arthur is now. In his prime. And when I met him, at Caer Eden, where he stood beside Arthur in front of all those gathered lords, he was magnificent! With Uther dead, and the Saxons camped across the river, there wasn't a man on the battlefield who'd have risen for the boy Arthur if Merlin hadn't been there. His very presence was more powerful than the entire host of war leaders. You should have heard my Christian father mumbling all the ancient protections! He sounded like a Druid!" He laughed lightly. "He was a strong enough man then. Tall and dark and silent. Terrifying, at times."

"Don't I know it! Lancelot, did you know that Merlin is dead?"

"What, again?"

"No, I mean it. Last spring, before we left Caerleon, he came to Arthur in his sleep and said good-bye. 'I am gone to my fathers; I will be with your children; you shall live forever in glory, the once and future King.' It is odd, is it not? But Arthur understood it, it seems. He awoke in tears, and yet he did not grieve. But he said that Merlin was truly gone, taken into the hill by the god who dwells there. Now the place is holy and tended as a shrine."

Lancelot grunted but said nothing.

"I wonder if it is because Arthur believes Merlin dead that he holds himself to this destiny of his—to hold Britain safe from the Saxons. I keep thinking, how much safer would we be, if they were part of it!"

"They tried to be part of it once," Lancelot protested, "in Vortigern's day, and nearly destroyed us. Perhaps in time they might become civilized, but really, Gwen, they are primitive savages."

"Well," I said, "let be. You know them, and I do not. Niniane does not see any harm in the trip for Arthur, so I hope I shall not have cause to regret his going."

Just then we heard voices, and a light came bobbing uncertainly down the path. Lancelot dropped my hand and rose. It was a page, and behind him, a courier.

"My lord Lancelot, Queen Guinevere," he said hastily, "an urgent message for you, my lord. Will you receive it here?"

Lancelot drew the man ten paces away and heard him. By the lantern light I saw him take bad news and grow solemn. He thanked the man and gave him a coin and sent him off to his meal and bath. Then he came back to me.

"What is it, my dear? Nothing's amiss with the King?"

In the new darkness I could not see him, but heard his voice, full of contrition. "There is no word from Arthur, or from Arres. This was from my home, Guinevere. Alas, my wife is dead."

I gasped. "What? Elaine dead? Oh, Lancelot, how came this? She is younger than I am!"

He felt for my hands and held them tightly. "She was delivered early of a stillborn daughter. They could not stop the bleeding."

"Oh, Lancelot, how terrible!" It was how Arthur lost his first wife, and I knew the horror it brought a man, to be the cause of a woman's death. "May God give rest to her unhappy soul," I whispered. I felt him come closer in the darkness.

"Pray with me, Gwen. I should feel more grief than I do. I did not love her, and she hated me, but she bore me three sons, and she was my wife. Help me mourn her."

So we sank to the ground and knelt side by side, hands clasped in prayer upon the bench, and together we prayed for the salvation of Elaine's departed soul. Lancelot was deeply moved, not by grief, but by self-recriminations. All that he had ever said or done, or not said or not done, on account of Elaine, he now remembered. He took her death upon him, and felt he owed God for it. It was his way—I could not change him.

And I, I remembered our childhood days together in Gwynedd. Bright, happy, full of life, she had welcomed me into her home with open arms, never once pitying her orphaned cousin; she had made me feel at home from my first day. How I had loved her for it! She led everywhere, and I followed. I remembered our gallops along the stony beach upon our fat ponies, and the time she tried to teach me Irish braiding—it took Ailsa three hours to get the knots out of my hair! And how we eavesdropped on her father's councils, and stole cream from the kitchens, and plied our tutor with mead to escape our lessons ... and how, when I had stumbled upon a half-dead Irish pirate early one frozen winter morning, Elaine, her cheeks flushed with excitement, had brought me the news that he was a real Irish prince and worth ransom! Thus Fion had entered our lives, and so began, in all innocence, a competition between us for the notice of men. Poor Elaine! How sad that only at her death should my anger toward her finally slacken! Now that she had suffered a heavier punishment than any I would have laid upon her, I pitied her from the bottom of my heart. From childhood she had worshipped Arthur, as prince, as King, as man, only to see her rival wed him. And although she had hated the man she married, she had done her duty and had borne him sons. What had I wanted from her, but love for Lancelot? She was no more capable of that than I was of love for Melwas—dear Elaine!—if only she could forgive me! If only it were not too late!

Eventually, when the night was well spent, we heard whispers behind us in the dark. I finished my prayer, crossed myself, and turned. Linet and Claire stood there with a candle, their eyes wide in wonder. They dipped quick curtsies, and the light trembled, casting shadows.

"What is the matter?" I asked softly. "Why have you come?"

"My—my lady," Claire whispered, shaking, "it grows late and we were worried. We did not hear your voices. And—and we felt we neglected our duty. As your chaperones . . ." Her voice trailed off. Lancelot knelt, head bowed, his back to them.

I rose, wiped the tears from my cheeks and guided them slowly away. "We have come to no harm, as you see. Sir Lancelot has had bad news. Now wait for us by the fountain. I will be with you in a moment." They went obediently, and I watched them thoughtfully. I wondered if they had been sent.

When I returned to Lancelot, I found his thoughts running the same way.

"Spying on us, were they?" he asked, rising. "Who sent them?"

"I don't know. Let's not jump to that conclusion."

He sighed with a great weariness. "There is a faction of young men who have taken against me. You had better know this, Gwen, especially as Arthur will not hear it spoken of. They are young yet, but their power is growing. All the Orkney boys are in it, except Gareth."

My heart beat suddenly fast, and I felt my anger rising. "Do you include Mordred in this group?"

His voice was very gentle. "Oh, yes. By some he is thought the leader. He and Agravaine. They would catch us in some amour, if they could. They think I lie with you and so betray the King."

"They do not dare! Tell me this is not true!"

He slipped my arm through his and started back down the walk. "But it is true and cannot be discounted. And in my heart," he breathed, so low I could barely hear, "in my heart I am guilty. Whenever I lay with Elaine, in my heart it was you I held. This is a sin."

"Dreams are phantoms!" I protested. "We are all fools in our dreams! You cannot be guilty, Lancelot, of sins your flesh has not committed. I will hear no more of this. This is folly."

He squeezed my arm. "That is just what Arthur says."

"Well, Arthur knows the truth. You are the last man on this earth who would betray him."

At last I heard the smile back in his voice. "Thank you for that. I only spoke to warn you. Sometimes the appearance of a thing is all that is required to produce conviction. You know the saying: Where there is smoke, there is fire."

"Only fools think so." We approached the light, and he gently dropped my arm, so that we walked without touching.

"There are plenty of fools about," he said lightly. "We should, perhaps, be more careful of the smoke."

20 ✸ ᴛʜᴇ ᴍᴜʀᴅᴇʀ

Arthur returned a day or two later, having seen the boys halfway to Castle Daure. He had waited near the Great Plain to hear if there were trouble, but all had apparently gone well. Morgause received her sons without incident, and they would stay a fortnight in her company before Mordred and Arthur left to meet the Saxons. Relieved, Arthur threw himself into the daily routine of ruling, joining me and Lancelot on occasion for a day hawking or a good gallop over the downs.

One evening, after a hard ride, a hot bath, and a good meal, we sat late in the library, playing chess. The doors stood open to the garden and the sweet scents of summer, of roses, honeysuckle, and new-cut grasses, drifted in on the soft night breeze. With us, stretched on the benches asleep or recounting the day's events over a cup of neat wine, were the best loved of the Companions, Lancelot, Bedwyr, Gereint, Ferron, Lyonel, Bleoberys, and a few others. In the corner, a trio of my maids sat and stitched.

With a deep sigh of contentment, I gave my mind to the game.

Arthur and I were usually well matched, but that night he was not at his best. His beloved hound Cabal had died that morning while we were out hunting. The news had met us upon our return, and he had grieved to hear it. Within the hour the houndsman had brought some young dogs to the King, and he had chosen a new Cabal, white-coated and dark-eyed, with paws and ears too big to suit his size, and a mischievous eagerness that made the High King laugh. As he sat before the chessboard, Arthur held young Cabal in his lap, and twice put his bishop in jeopardy while he played with the pup's floppy ears. At length the dog, eager to regain Arthur's attention, shoved his nose under the King's arm and pushed hard. Pieces flew off the table and Arthur bit off a cry of disappointment.

"Just when I was about to trap your knight!"

"My lord is dreaming!" I laughed, leaning down to pick up an errant pawn. "You were four moves from checkmate, maybe less."

He grinned. "Nonsense! I had you right where I wanted you."

"Indeed? What kind of strategy is that, to lose two pawns to every one of mine?"

"Why, a ploy to disarm you through overconfidence."

"What a clever strategy! Is this how you won Britain, my lord King? No wonder the Saxons could never get your measure!"

Two or three of the men looked our way, smiling.

Arthur shook his head. "When you are too sure of yourself, my dear, you make mistakes."

"Do I, indeed? Would you care to name them?"

He laughed outright and set the dog upon the floor. "No, I would not. I am not such a fool as all that. I grant you the game, Guinevere. Does that content you?"

"To be given as a gift something I had earned already?" I retorted, smiling up at him as he rose to stretch. "Nothing will content me but to hear your admission that I bested you tonight."

He took my hand and raised it to his lips. His eyes met mine, and heat rose to my face. "Ask it of me again when the night is over." I heard chuckles from the men and felt Lancelot's eyes upon me clear across the room. The dog, impatient of attention, leaped up on Arthur's chair and thence to the table, scattering the pieces wildly all over the room. With loud cries of laughter, the men chased the dog and scrambled for the pieces on all fours, while the pup ran circles all about them, yapping in glee.

In the middle of this mayhem, a knock came at the door. Arthur was beside me, on his knees, whistling for the dog, and I saw his face as he glanced up. He went suddenly pale, and slowly rose, the black queen falling unnoticed from his fingers.

Kay stepped in, grim-faced, and bowed. "My lord. A courier. From Castle Daure." Behind him, white as a nether spirit and still dusty from the road, stood Gareth. Alone.

"Bring him in."

In the corner, little Linet, a pretty dark-haired child with eyes bright as a bird's, looked up and smiled shyly at Gareth. She was only thirteen, but already had lost her heart. Gareth fell to his knees at Arthur's feet, so consumed by some strong emotion he neither saw nor heard anyone else in the room.

"Uncle," he whispered. "Uncle."

At Arthur's signal, the maids gathered up their work and departed, the Companions rose, bowed, and filed out in silence. Someone grabbed the dog. Lancelot awaited me at the door; I made Arthur a reverence.

"No, Gwen. Stay. You, too, Lancelot. The boy will need your aid."

I looked down at Gareth's bowed head. I knew my thoughts were one with Arthur's: Something had happened to Mordred.

"Arise, Gareth," the King said quietly. "Gwen, a winecup. Drink this, son, and sit down. Collect yourself. Whatever it is you have ridden so far so fast to tell us will still be true five minutes hence."

Gareth obeyed. At fourteen, he was a well-grown youth, as strong and thickly built as his brothers, but of a kinder nature. His gentleness and good humor lent his plain face an honesty that the others' lacked. He trained daily with Lancelot and had grown to love honor. The wild streak so apparent in his brothers was tamed in him, and civilized.

Arthur stood before him. "All right, Gareth. What has happened?"

The boy looked up with eyes dulled from suffering. "My mother—Queen Morgause—is dead."

I gasped. "Dead! How?"

"She was murdered." He spoke lifelessly. Arthur reached out a hand to his chin and raised his face. Through the dust on his cheeks were trails of former tears; he met Arthur's eyes directly; he was telling the truth.

"How?" Arthur asked sharply. "Who?"

Gareth turned his face away and dropped his eyes. "My lord, Gaheris killed her."

"Gaheris!" I cried, sitting hard on the bench beside him. "Oh, no!"

"I think," Arthur said slowly, "you had better take your time and tell us the whole story. Lancelot, set a guard upon the door and see we are not disturbed."

With an effort, Gareth stilled his trembling and, drawing a deep breath, began to speak. "At first, everything went smoothly. Mother greeted us all with the show of loving warmth she always puts on for strangers." I bowed my head to hear him speak so; even Gareth! "Sir Lamorak took charge of our escort and saw that we were well attended. We got to see her in the evenings, in the common room, either in the company of Sir Bellok, the garrison commander, or of Sir Lamorak, or of King Arres himself, who did us the honor to come and greet us. We were never alone with her. Gaheris—Gaheris began to chafe under such surveillance. And Mordred took to staying awake nights, just to be sure he slept. My lord, I think he kept watch over Gaheris, covertly, all the while."

"Bless him," I breathed.

"But then—" He shivered suddenly. Lancelot's hand came down upon his shoulder, and his voice steadied. "If only Mordred had enlisted my aid, we could have watched in shifts! One night he dozed off and woke well past midnight to find Gaheris gone. Although it was so late, he made his way to her rooms without difficulty. No one even asked his business. No one, he told me later, appeared to think twice about a youth making his way to her apartments after dark."

"Oh, Gareth!" I clasped his cold hand.

"They were only surprised that he did not know the way. When he came to her chamber, he found Gaheris weeping at the door. They heard voices within, and laughter, and sounds enough for Mordred to know—and, and Gaheris, too, may God forgive him—how she was engaged. Mordred sought to draw him away, but Gaheris refused to leave. Finally, Mordred took him by the shoulder and shook him, pointing out that such obsession was a sickness, and when Mother was alone they could come back. At this Gaheris apparently went wild, drew his sword, and kicked open the door."

He stopped and drained the winecup. "I will give it to you, my lord, as I heard it from Mordred's lips that very night. I cannot ever, ever forget his words. His voice was so cold." He wiped sweat from his brow and Lancelot tightened his grip on the boy's shoulder. "They found her in bed with Lamorak, coupled, and so absorbed in each other they were slow to react. Mordred grabbed his arm, as Gaheris began shouting obscenities—this probably saved Lamorak's life. He leaped out of bed and made for the chair where he had left his sword. Mordred of course assumed Gaheris would try to slay Lamorak, so he was completely unprepared for what actually happened." His voice grew tight, but he kept on. "Gaheris turned to Mother, lying naked on the covers and, with a cry of such anguish that it froze them to where they stood, brought down his sword across her neck."

"Dear God!" I stared up in horror at Arthur's face. "Oh, Arthur!"

He passed a hand across his brow and crossed himself.

Gareth plowed on in a lifeless voice. "Gaheris fell to weeping and flung his sword away and began embracing her body amid the bloody sheets. Then Mordred urged Lamorak to dress and get going, to put as much distance as he could between himself and Gawaine before the news was out. He got Lamorak away and bid him hie back to Brittainy until the storm blew over. Then he locked the doors behind him, gave Gaheris into Agravaine's care, and came and told me about it. He bade me take horse at once and come to you. He said I was the one courier you would believe. But I think, my lord, I think he wanted to get me out of that awful place!" His voice finally broke, and he covered his face with his hands. Lancelot sat beside him and with an arm about his shoulder, hugged him to his breast.

After a moment, Arthur spoke. "How did Gawaine react? Do you know?"

Gareth struggled for composure. "Yes, my lord. I—I was there when Mordred told him." His smile was bitter. "You know Gawaine. Nothing will serve but he must kill Lamorak. Not even Mordred could make him see reason. Mordred told him Lamorak was her betrothed—that this was known by five or six of your Companions—and that it gave him a right to her bed. But Gawaine will have it that Mother was dishonored."

"Is he mad?" I cried. "His mother is dead by his brother's hand!"

"He has no love for Gaheris. And he knows it was no rape. But her death is a small thing, beside her honor."

"Her honor!" But I said no more; Gareth was her son, as well.

"And Agravaine, too, is breathing revenge." The boy faltered. "He considers it all Lamorak's doing and wants an eye for an eye. I know he always protects Gaheris, but—and now Gawaine is the leader of our clan. We are headed for disaster! It is too soon, too soon. I can't believe she is gone."

"Come, Gareth." Lancelot spoke in a low voice full of tenderness. "Come with me to the chapel. Together we will pray for the salvation of her soul. There is great comfort, I have found, in heartfelt prayer."

Gareth's eyes widened. "Oh, my lord! I had forgotten! Kay told me about your wife and daughter! To lose two of your kin in one stroke—and here I am grieving for a mother I did not love in life."

Lancelot glanced at me swiftly, then raised the boy. "Whatever turmoil lies within your heart, prayer will ease it and give you the peace to sleep."

Gareth nodded. I could see he was close to exhaustion. "Very good, my lord, I thank you. I would like to go."

I glanced at Arthur but he shook his head, and Lancelot and Gareth went out together. When the door had closed, Arthur turned to me. "Let them be. He is better alone with Lancelot, and Lancelot alone with him." He took my hand and held it between his own. "Gwen, the hour is late, our fellowship is broken. Would you take it amiss if I asked you to retire? I have to fetch the scribe, have orders written out, and there are couriers to send. I will be late, I fear."

There were new lines in his face and a drawn, weary look around his eyes. I thought suddenly, and for the first time, *He is no longer young.*

"My lord, may I await you?"

He half smiled and brushed his lips against my hand. "I would like that very much."

He was very late, but at last he came. I had wine ready, and cool fruit drinks, and cold water, and had filled the bowl on his nightstand with fresh roses. I waited in my own room until Varric left him, and then I went in.

"My lord Arthur." I walked into his embrace, and he kissed me fondly.

He was not too tired to smile. "Ah, Gwen. Bless you for waiting. I am so weary of it all. Let us have peace a moment."

We went out onto the terrace to enjoy the coolness of the night. He sat in the chair, and I stood behind and rubbed his shoulders. At first it was like pressing fingers into bronze, but with time, his flesh grew more human to the touch. At length he sighed and thanked me, and I came around and sat at his feet, my head resting on his knees.

"By her death, Morgause has sown the seed of blood feud into my company of knights," the King said flatly. "Even now, I am not free of her curse! Gawaine has sworn to avenge himself on Lamorak. Should he succeed, Lamorak's cousin, Drustan, King of Elmet, will be avenged upon Gawaine. We shall have the kingdoms at war with one another at a time we can least afford it."

I took his hand and held it hard. "What steps have you taken?"

He sighed again. "I'm going to have a devil of a time convincing Arres that I will not hold my sister's death against him. But I have sent him a message explaining things as best I can. I have banished Gaheris. If, as I believe, he has lost his wits, he will come somewhere to the fate he deserves. I cannot kill him; that would divide the Kingdom right down the middle. Thanks to Mordred's quick thinking, Lamorak has vanished. If he has sense, he will not go to Drustan, which is where Gawaine will look for him. He has a distant relation in Cornwall and friends in Brittany. Either place would serve him well. When and if this blows over, I will welcome him back into the Companions. He has done nothing amiss. I am the last man on earth who could condemn him."

"Stop it, Arthur. That is behind you."

He shrugged. "For the present, I will keep Gawaine and Agravaine close by me. I have ordered them home at once. Time may temper their hatred. I have no doubt that Gaheris will get word to Agravaine, and I hope that Mordred, through him, will be able to keep me informed as to what happens. I can do no more than this, but wait."

I kissed his hand, and he gently stroked my hair.

"Lancelot feels more sadness at the passing of a wife he did not love than those wild boys do for their own mother," he said softly, in sorrow. "Even Gareth is more shocked than sorry."

"That is the difference in the man."

A smile touched his lips. "Yes. It will be good to have him back with us again the year round." He stopped there, but looked down into my upturned face. I reached up and put my arms about his neck, drew his face down and kissed him. It awoke the flame in him, and he responded, drawing me up onto his lap.

"My lord," I breathed, "in time, all will be well. And see, Merlin was right. There was no more need to fear Morgause."

He sighed. "When I am with you, Gwen, I can believe it. I can believe almost anything, even that Gawaine will grow into sense in time."

"He may, with age. He is but sixteen." I paused. "My lord, is it true that some of the young men have taken against Lancelot?"

He went still a moment, then nodded. "Yes. From envy. They

see he has the trust and favor of both King and Queen. This is a natural thing. They are a small group, boys without power and small hope of gaining it. Pay it no mind."

"But, my lord, is Mordred one of them?"

He looked at me sharply. "No. Who has said so?"

"Lancelot himself thinks so. I did not believe it."

He sighed. "Agravaine is the leader. A fifteen-year-old hothead whom Lancelot could slay with one arm tied behind him! It is ridiculous to pay them heed. Mordred bears Agravaine little love, but recognizes the blood tie and would keep him from harm if he could. That is why he goes to their meetings, and drinks and dices with them, to protect me and Agravaine. If Lancelot has seen them together, he has drawn the wrong conclusion."

I exhaled in relief. "I am so glad, my lord. I was afraid—I wish them to be friends, and not enemies."

"As do I. Sometimes," he said heavily, "I wish we could escape court and all its intrigues, and take up arms in the open field against a worthy foe—good, clean fighting is preferable to this!"

I ruffled his hair. "To a man, perhaps. But most certainly not to me, who must wait here until the battle's end for news. It is like sitting upon hot coals."

But he did not smile. His gaze was distant and pensive.

"A coin for your thoughts, my lord."

With an effort, he smiled. "Oh, I am feeling my age, is all. My days of leading armies into battle are behind me."

"I pray to God they are," I said with fervor, "but that has nothing to do with age, but with the success of your leadership as King. Why, you are but one and thirty! Ambrosius was your age when he took Britain!"

He grinned and suddenly looked twenty again. "What a honey-eyed tongue you have, my child queen."

"Child, my lord?" I put a hand to his cheek. "You do not treat me so."

He kissed my neck, my throat, my shoulder, and his fingers sought the fastenings of my gown. "I know your body better than my own," he whispered. "You have not changed a whit, in all the years I've known you, except to grow more precious to me."

My breath caught as I felt his hands against my flesh, and I began to tremble. "We will stay young together, then," I breathed. His hands moved; his warm eyes grew fierce.

"We are as we do," he growled, and lifted me and carried me indoors.

That night was unlike any in my memory; the heartache and

emotion of the past hours found vent in a wild, desperate loving that gripped us both and then, talons in, would not release us. We slept, and woke, and slept again, exhausted. At dawn the King awakened me with kisses and made sweet love while the birds sang to us beyond our window. When he finally arose from bed, his step was that of a young man and not another word dropped from his lips about the complaints of age.

On a beautiful day a week later, Arthur and his host left for the Saxon territories. Lancelot and I bid them farewell on the castle steps. It was a formal leave-taking; the men who went had to know this was an embassy of state. They were not a large army, for Arthur did not wish to threaten Cerdic, but they were all mounted, for the Saxons feared the power of Arthur's cavalry. The King invested Lancelot as regent and Protector of the Queen. I scanned the faces of the troops and could detect no raised eyebrows or sidelong glances. Bedwyr was going, and Galahantyn, Bors, Ferron, Villers, Bellangere, and Gawaine. Mordred, too, of course. In the three days they had been home, he and Gawaine had hardly spoken, but in the army they would be required to be civil to one another. Agravaine was left behind; his outspoken hatred of all things Saxon made him a dangerous companion behind Saxon lines. And gentle Gareth, who would have been welcomed by the King, was only fourteen and still in training.

I kissed Mordred on both cheeks and handed him a packet wrapped in soft linen.

'This," I told him, "is for Cerdic's lady or, if he has none, for the leading woman of his house. Tell her it is from me."

Mordred looked surprised. "What is in it, my lady?"

"A small necklace of silver, of Celtic design. And a net of little sapphires and river pearls for her hair."

He looked disconcerted and glanced swiftly at Arthur. "But, my lady, their—I hear their women wear their hair as maids do, in plaits, always down."

I smiled. "Give it to her anyway. You don't know women, Mordred. If she likes it, she will find a way to wear it."

Arthur grinned and took my hands. "He has time to learn it. Well, good-bye, Gwen. Keep the Kingdom for me, and take good care of Lancelot."

I kissed him on both cheeks, and then, remembering Lancelot's words about smoke and fire, I kissed him full on the lips. "I keep everything of yours near my heart, my lord," I said, just loud enough for the closest men to hear.

His eyes were laughing at me, but he gravely inclined his head. "I rely upon you."

Turning, he gave the order to mount and go. We watched them out King's Gate.

"Lancelot," I said softly, as the last horse trotted out of view, "did you know you are employing Saxons in your stables?"

His eyebrows lifted, and he offered me his arm. "I did. They are born horsemen. But I didn't know you knew. Who told you?"

"Mordred. He has been learning their language from them. He thinks you believe them to be Irish."

He laughed. "There is a lot about me Mordred doesn't know." We passed through the door as he spoke, and I saw Agravaine just entering the hall. At Lancelot's laughter he stopped dead and glared at us both, before turning on his heel and going back swiftly the way he had come. "They give out that they are Irish to avoid the ire of the people. They are common men, not warriors. Do they worry you?"

"Oh, no. I just found it hard to believe you couldn't tell a Saxon from a Gael. Mordred should have known better."

"Indeed." He said no more, but walked on with a set face.

"Lancelot."

"My lady?"

"When do you take the troops out for drill?"

"Arthur said to give him a couple of days. First we will drill in the downs, then farther east. By the time he meets with Cerdic, we should be within shouting distance of the border."

"Take Agravaine with you."

He stopped, startled. "Why Agravaine? He makes nothing but trouble. No commander wants him in the company. Giving him an order is like swimming upstream, much effort is expended for little result."

I met his eyes. "Nevertheless, take him. He is trouble looking for a place to alight. Give him work, the hope of a fight, anything but the inertia of castle guard duty. He will be a danger if he stays here."

He thought on it and finally nodded. "There is sense in that. And his horsemanship could do with work. I will give him to Gereint; he will stand no nonsense." He smiled. "But Gereint will make me pay for it, someday. Still, perhaps it will take the boy's mind off his brother. Have you heard what they are calling him?"

I nodded. "Yes. Gaheris Yellowbelly, killer of women. For his own sake, I pray he stays away from court forever."

We had reached the parting of our ways, and he bent over my

hand. "Britain is too small a place to hide such a one forever. We will see him again."

21 ❁ The Beating

"My lady! My lady! Oh, please wake up! Please come!"

I opened my eyes. A candle wavered inches from my face, and a small white hand plucked urgently at the bedcovers.

"Who is that? What's amiss?" The candle fell back, and slowly Linet's frightened face came into view. Her robe was hastily tied about her bedgown, and her dark hair, braided for the night, was disarranged.

"Linet! What has happened?" I slipped out of bed and made her sit down upon it. She was shaking. I took the candle from her and set it on my nightstand.

"It's Claire," she whispered. "I came for Ailsa first. When she saw her, she sent me to awaken you."

"Don't worry about that," I said, chafing her hands. Her fingers were ice cold, although the night was warm. "Tell me quickly, child. What has happened to Claire?"

Her teeth chattered, but she struggled valiantly to speak. "He has beaten her!" she cried, gulping. "There is blood, and—and her face is askew—and I don't know why she ever allowed him—I am afraid she will die!"

"Die?" I gasped, throwing my robe about my shoulders. "Beaten? Who has done this? What are you talking about it? Who has been with her?"

I clutched her shoulders and held her still, holding her eyes. "Tell me, Linet."

"It was—it was Agravaine," she whispered, the tears spilling from her eyes. I said nothing, but took the candle and bade her follow me.

The girl lay on a pallet in her room. Ailsa bent over her, pressing cool cloths to her head, a bowl of bloodied water on the floor beside her.

"My lady!" she cried in distress. "Oh, see poor little Claire. She cannot speak, poor child. I think the beast has broken her jaw." I came up beside her and looked down at the beaten girl. Her face was bruised and already swollen to twice its normal size. Her lips were thick and broken; her nose awry and crusted with drying blood, her eyes swollen half shut. A thin stream of blood had trickled from her ear and now lay drying on the pillow. And her jaw was crooked. I knelt at her head.

"Claire. Can you hear me? This is Guinevere." But she could not speak, and I could see it would pain her to nod. I took her hand in mine. "Two fingers for yes," I said quickly, "and one for no. Can you hear my voice and understand me?"

Yes.

"Can you speak?"

No.

I turned to Ailsa. "Send the page for the King's physician. Quickly!" She rose and left. Then to Claire: "Did Agravaine do this?"

Yes.

"Do you know why?"

Yes.

"Does Linet know why?"

Yes.

"You are a brave girl, Claire. I will see justice done. Be patient awhile longer, and we will ease your pain. May I ask Linet to tell me why?"

A long hesitation, and then, slowly, yes.

I looked up at Linet, who stood trembling by the bed. "Tell me, Linet."

Her eyes widened in fear. "Oh, no, my lady. I cannot! Indeed, I cannot!"

I pulled her down to kneel with me at Claire's side, where she had a very clear view of the poor girl's face. Anyone could see that she would be deformed forever.

"Do you wish this crime to go unpunished?"

"Oh, no, my lady!"

"But it will, unless you speak. Claire herself would tell me, but as you see, she cannot." I rose and paced the room, suddenly reluctant to probe further. But there was no choice. "Answer my questions, then, Linet, if you cannot speak out. Take her hand. She will signal to you when you go wrong. Am I right in surmising that this was not the first time Agravaine was in these chambers?" As Linet's room was next door, this was something she would know on her own.

"Yes, my lady."

"He is her lover?"

"She is—sort of promised to him, my lady. I mean, they are betrothed, only it is unofficial."

"Of course," I said bitterly. "It is always unofficial. He would have to have the King's permission. And mine." I stopped and looked at Claire. "Do you still have affection for him, Claire? Do you wish to be his wife?" Despite the pain, she shook her head. I was relieved to see it. If I knew the type of man at all, Agravaine cared nothing for her and would never take her now. He had used her and for what? For the satisfaction of his lusts? Any girl would do for that. But only a Queen's maid could give information about the Queen. I drew a deep breath. "What did he want of her, Linet? Did he ever ask questions about me? Or the King? Or Lancelot?"

Linet shrank back, unwilling. Claire looked pleadingly at her and moved her fingers. Linet was clearly terrified. Her very fear told me what I wished to know.

"Linet. I will not be angry with you, no matter what you have to tell me. Take courage and speak. Agravaine is the High King's nephew, and what he does has implications for many futures. The truth here is important. Do you wish Gareth to be dishonored?"

Her eyes flew up to mine then, and she stared. "Oh, no!"

"Then tell me, for God's sake, before the physician comes! What did he want of her?"

"He—he set us to spy on you and—and Sir Lancelot, my lady," she blurted, looking away.

"Ahhhhh. I thought as much." I knelt down at Linet's feet and gently took her hands. "My dear Linet, do not fear to tell me. I know well what is in Agravaine's mind. He wishes to have proof that Lancelot and I are lovers." She gasped. "Is that not so?"

She nodded, staring at me in horror.

"He cannot come by such proof, for we are not. I do not fear him. So why, I wish to know, do you?"

She looked wildly at Claire, whose eyes were on my face. She looked surprised.

"Answer me."

"I—we—the—we—oh, my lady, please forgive us! But we thought it might be true! Agravaine said we must unite to save the King's honor!"

I held tightly to her hands, for she shrank from me. "Why did you think it might be true?"

She shook from head to foot and would not meet my eyes.

"We saw you together often. Sometimes—in the garden, holding hands. And—and once Claire saw him kiss you. In the way of love, not of friendship."

I smiled at her and lifted her chin so she could see I was not embarrassed.

"Yes," I said gently, "these things are true. I do confess them. They are evidence of love. And I love Sir Lancelot. All the world knows this. The King himself knows it. But you must be careful what conclusions you draw from this."

They were both staring at me now, but their fear was leaving them. I rose and stood before them. "The King knows my heart. He would not leave me in Lancelot's care if there were not trust between us. Do you understand this? That there can be love without surrender or betrayal? I would not expect Agravaine to understand it, but you are my women. You know me better."

"Oh, my lady!" Linet cried, in tears. "I told him it was impossible! For Ailsa guards your door. And I have seen the tenderness between you and the King. I told him it could not be so! But—but—" she gulped, and stopped.

"He probably told you," I said slowly, "that where there is smoke, there is fire."

She nodded eagerly. "His very words! And when he came tonight, we told him we would not spy upon you longer, for we were convinced he was wrong. We told him of the dark night of no moon, when we crept up upon you in the garden when we had not heard your voices, for thus he had instructed us, and—and we found you praying."

"Is this what inspired his rage?"

"Yes, my lady. He called us fools and cowards. He would not believe it, but would have that we were lying on your behalf. He said he knew that Sir Lancelot had the—the key to your garden gate upon a thread around his neck. He had seen it. He lost his temper, and—and struck Claire. Again and again and again!" She covered her face with her hands and wept.

A slow anger began to burn within my breast. Ailsa arrived with the physician, and I went out to find the page.

"Send Lancelot to me. Here, in the girl's room." I pulled a ring off my little finger. "Give this token to him and say I request his presence urgently. A matter has arisen that must be settled now. Be sure and tell him," I added bitterly, "that I am well attended."

He was longer than I expected. The physician had completed his ministrations and was shaking his head sadly over the beaten girl. He had given her a sleeping potion, so she was beyond her pain. When Lancelot entered, I understood his delay. He was carefully and completely dressed, down to his sword and his boots. His own chamberlain accompanied him, and stood outside the door. Ailsa and Linet clutched at their bedgowns and lowered their eyes. I myself had been careful to fasten my robe up to my throat and down to my ankles, although the night was warm. When he knelt before me and placed the token in my hand, he did not meet my eyes.

"My lady Queen Guinevere. I am at your service."

"See, Sir Lancelot, what has been done to my poor maid!"

He went to Claire and spoke with the physician. She would heal, the man said, except for the jaw. She would live, if she could eat soft foods, but she would probably never speak again. Poor Claire. If she was ashamed to go home, then her future lay in God's service, in some convent where vows of silence were respected.

When Lancelot turned from her bedside I could see he was angry.

"Is it known who did this thing?" he asked me.

"Yes, my lord. It was the High King's nephew, Agravaine."

He drew breath slowly and met my eyes. The message passed. He understood it all. "I see."

"I will have justice done, my lord. He shall not go free of this."

"Indeed he shall not. But justice might be better served by awaiting the High King's return," Lancelot said carefully.

"But he might be weeks! This must be dealt with now. I will not have the women under my protection made sport of by King's men."

He nodded slowly. He saw I understood the gravity of the situation. It fell to Lancelot to punish Agravaine and make his hotheaded opponent his deadly enemy for life. But it was a matter of honor, and Lancelot understood it well.

"Do you wish to be present when I confront him?"

"I most certainly do."

"Think carefully on this, my lady. He has little control of his tongue."

"There is no other choice. He violated my protection. I must be there."

Lancelot glanced sadly toward the sleeping girl. "What is the maid's wish? Does she wish to wed him?"

"No. Yesterday, perhaps it was her ambition. But now she would not take him as a gift."

His eyebrows lifted. He inclined his head. "I shall send for him first thing in the morning."

"Lock him up tonight. Now. Put him in the tower under guard. He does not deserve a moment's freedom while she endures this pain."

Everyone was staring. Lancelot met my eyes and waited. He commanded Camelot. This was in his purview, not in mine. But I was his Queen, and he had sworn to obey me. Yet I knew, even as I glared at him, that I could no more try to command him than I could try to command Arthur. With as much grace as I could summon, I made him a low reverence.

"Forgive me, my lord. I am in an intolerable position."

He moved instinctively toward me, but stopped himself at once. Before others, he would not even touch me. "I understand your anger, Guinevere. The man who did this will be punished. But I cannot imprison Agravaine until I have confronted him and heard his defense. You know this well. It is not Arthur's way."

"But in the meantime, she suffers. It is not fair."

"No," he agreed in a gentle voice, "it is not fair. But I will not make two injustices where before there was only one."

"As you will, my lord."

"Thank you, my lady." Then he guarded his face and said carefully, "I think you might investigate the manner of the man's entry into these apartments."

I was startled. Since Agravaine had been her lover, I had assumed Claire had let him in. "What does my lord mean? Linet, did she not give him entrance herself?" The frightened girl shook her head and cowered in Ailsa's arms. "Then how did he come to be here?" But she could not speak, before all these people, and merely shook with fright. Somewhat impatiently, I turned to Lancelot. "If you know aught of this, sir, please tell me."

He cleared his throat, frowning. "There is a way in, through the postern gate, into the ladies' garden. It is known in the barracks as the Gate of Heaven."

"Who dares to call it so!" I cried indignantly. Of course I knew of the gate; Lancelot himself had come that way once. On the thought, I felt my face flush with color, then grew angry at my own reaction. I was innocent; he had come to me for private talk, not for love. I lifted my chin and faced him. "I take responsibility for that. Henceforward the gate shall be sealed. And while we are speaking of garden gates, does my lord still have the key to the gate of my private garden, which Sir Kay gave you many years ago? If so, I should be glad to have it returned." I held out my up-turned palm.

Linet and Ailsa gasped aloud; but Lancelot's composure never wavered. I saw from the flicker in his eyes that he guessed at Agravaine's accusation.

"It is in my possession, my lady, but not upon my person. I will have my chamberlain bring it to you, immediately I return to my apartments. I beg your pardon for keeping it so long; it had slipped my mind I had it."

I nodded. He had said before witnesses what I had given him the opportunity to say.

"I accept your apology. Until this matter arose, I had forgotten, also. Clearly, I must guard my women more closely than before. I am beholden to you for your advice."

He bowed, and after promising to call me in the morning before Agravaine was brought before the Council, he left. The physician left close on his heels, and we women were alone.

I turned to Linet. "Is this true, what Sir Lancelot tells me? Have many men gained entrance by the postern gate? Speak, Linet, and do not fear me. But I must know the truth."

"Since I have been here, my lady, Agravaine and Gaheris are the only ones I know of. But it is rumored that over the years—" She stopped, seeing my face. I had been a fool not to suspect it, as several of the maids who served me had got pregnant first and husbands later.

"Has Gareth been here? Or Mordred?"

"No, no!" Linet cried, weeping. "Oh, no! Don't think it! Gareth would not, my lady! And Sir Mordred—what would he want with your waiting women?" She clapped her hand over her mouth and turned away, sobbing. I gave it up. There was nothing to be done now but deal with Agravaine. But my heart was heavy that night, for I felt myself partly to blame, through negligence, of what had happened to poor little Claire.

Had the full Court been assembled, Agravaine would have been called to the Round Hall to be accused before his fellow knights. But most of the Companions had gone with the King; others were traveling the Kingdom as knights errant. Only a few remained in Camelot. These, Lancelot assembled in the King's library, before he had Agravaine brought in. I sat on his right hand, as Agravaine's accuser in Claire's place.

Gareth came with him. It was clear from his bewilderment that he had not spoken to Linet and knew not why his brother was summoned before the Council. But I saw that Agravaine knew. He stood somewhat defiantly before the assembled knights, and his smile, when he bowed to me, was nothing short of insolent.

"Agravaine of Orkney, son of Lot," Lancelot began, "there is a formal charge laid against you which I call you to defend."

"Who brings this charge?" he asked boldly, looking about him at the gathered warriors.

"I bring it," I said slowly. He froze. "I bring it on behalf of a maiden in my service, whom you have beaten and maimed."

I saw Gareth pale and look swiftly at his brother. It was a mean offense and beneath him, but he saw the truth of it in his brother's face, and it sickened him.

"Last night," Lancelot continued, "you secretly entered the apartments of the Queen's ladies and beat a girl named Claire of Swiftwater, whose father serves King Pelleas. There is a witness to the beating; one Linet, daughter of Lucius of York." Here Gareth flushed and then began to anger. At least, I thought irrelevantly, her affection for him was returned. But Agravaine seemed unaffected. He just stood there and looked at Lancelot with hate.

"I witnessed the harm you did the girl, as did the King's physician and the Queen. She will never speak again, nor chew. Her jaw is broken." The knights looked astonished and murmured among themselves. They were gentlemen all, and such behavior had been beneath them, even as boys. "What have you to say in your defense?" Lancelot asked.

Agravaine sneered. "Since when is it a crime to strike a woman? The wench contradicted me. She deserved it."

I shot to my feet, trembling in fury, so angry I could find no words to speak. He did not even bother to deny it! Lancelot took me gently by the wrist and held tight. Gareth pulled futilely at Agravaine's elbow. Lancelot rose and forced me slowly back into my chair.

"It has been a crime in Britain," he said to Agravaine in cold rage, "since the day that Arthur met Guinevere. This is not Orkney; this is a civilized land. The King respects women, and so do all those who enjoy his favor. You are a coward, boy, to raise your hand to one who has no defense against you. I am ashamed of you; so is your own brother. Where is your honor?"

"You dare to call me coward! If you think," Agravaine sputtered furiously, "that I am going to stand here and listen to *you* speak of honor! You, of all men! You, you snake in the grass! We all know what goes on whenever the King's back is turned! Your lust is infamous! We know you lie with the—"

"Agravaine!" Gareth cried in horror. "Be still, I pray you! If you force his hand, and he calls you out, you are a dead man. Think twice, I beg you! For our dead mother's sake; for the sake of our exiled brother; Gaheris needs you living. Curb your tongue!"

The anguished words got through to him, and Agravaine stood silent, flushed with anger. Lancelot himself was barely in control of his temper. But he did not want to have to kill Arthur's nephew and begin a blood feud. If he killed one of them, he would have to kill them all.

Into the strained silence, I spoke. "The girl has been permanently maimed. She will never be able to speak; she will never marry. You have robbed her of her future. Unless you make her restoration, her father will be after your head."

But Agravaine was not ready to admit defeat. "I demand a hearing of the full court. I will not be judged by this—this conspiracy of intimates. I will go to my uncle the High King—"

"Yes," I cut in softly, "why don't you do that? Go tell Arthur how you violated my protection, how you insulted the Queen's privacy and tarnished her name." Agravaine went white. He knew well that Arthur had, more than once, risked personal combat against better men then Agravaine, to save my name. "You dare not do it. It is as much as your life is worth." He swallowed, and Gareth took him aside, speaking to him softly and furiously. They argued for several minutes, while Lancelot canvassed the other knights and found, as he expected, that they were unanimous in their condemnation of his act.

At last Agravaine shrugged Gareth off and turned back to Lancelot, looking sullen.

"If I am in the wrong, I beg your pardon," he said gruffly. "I lost my temper with the girl. I did not mean to harm her."

"That's as it may be," Lancelot said flatly, "but harm you have done. And restoration you shall make, as much as is in your power. Her future is in her own hands. If she chooses to retire to a religious house, you will pay her upkeep, you and your heirs, for her lifetime. If she chooses to return to her father, you will pay what ransom he deems fit."

Agravaine was aghast. "And if I cannot pay it?"

"What you cannot pay in coin, you must pay with service, by the sweat of your brow. The Earl of Swiftwater will have work that needs doing. Every religious house has the need of strong man's labor. One way or the other, you are responsible for her."

Agravaine shifted from one foot to the other, while Gareth continued to urge him to accept this judgment. I could see that he was debating whether he might not do better if he brought the case to Arthur, but he did not wish to risk the power of my pleading with the King. At last he gave way and shrugged gracelessly. "As my lord wills."

Lancelot inclined his head. "So is this judgment given and accepted. Take care, Agravaine, that you do it. I myself shall hold you to it."

Unbelievably, Agravaine smiled slowly. "As long as you have power, you can try." Gareth grabbed his arm and, bowing quickly to me and to Lancelot, dragged him away, still whispering furiously.

The nearest of the Companions turned to Lancelot. "My lord, you have made an enemy this day."

Lancelot sighed wearily. "I have indeed. But I saw no way around it."

"There was no other way," I assured him. "You have done the right thing; if he despises you, it is to your credit. Think no more upon him."

"On the contrary," Lancelot said. "When we go on maneuvers, I shall keep him in my own company, where I can keep an eye on him. I want no foment at home while the King is on such a delicate mission."

"Can you not take Gareth, as a page? He seems able to influence him for the good."

Lancelot's expression softened, and he looked at me gratefully. "An excellent idea. Gareth will be a comfort to us both. I thank you, my gracious Queen, for the suggestion."

"Anything," I replied lightly, meeting his eyes, "to bring you ease."

Lancelot took the army out the next morning, and they stayed on maneuvers within half a day's ride of Cerdic's stronghold until Arthur and his cavalry left the Saxon Shore and rode into their camp to join them. They all returned to Camelot together on a hot, dusty day in August. I stood on the castle steps with Kay and Ailsa and several other of my women who had husbands among the returning knights. They were a weary group when they arrived, hot and covered with grime. By my order, Varric had prepared the King a hot bath, and I sent him to it as soon as the greetings were over. He looked tired, but not unhappy, so although he said nothing of what had passed, I knew the meetings had gone well.

Mordred and Lancelot came up the steps together behind the King, followed by Bedwyr and Gawaine. Their faces were set, and except when they greeted me, none of them smiled. This, I thought, was Morgause's legacy: The seed of discord was sown in Arthur's Court and had taken root. Agravaine himself I did not see. He must have kept well out of sight among the soldiers.

I went in to wait in the library garden. When he had washed the dust of travel off and changed his clothes, Mordred came to me there. We sat by the fountain, where the splash of water cooled the air and hid the sound of our words from other ears. He was eager to tell me all about the journey and about the strange sights he had seen. They had been well treated, he assured me, royally so. Cerdic himself was an old man now, and attended by his son Cynewulf, who was just short of Arthur's age. This man had the look of a warrior, fierce and stern, but Cerdic was still the leader. He was a legend among his own people. It seemed, Mordred said, that each village had its own king, and until Cerdic had united the West Saxons, one village had had little in common with its neighbor. Even now, the West Saxons felt themselves a people apart from the East Saxons and South Saxons. They spoke of these tribes as if they were separate peoples, and not all from the same homeland.

"It sounds like Britain, before Arthur," I said.

Mordred nodded. "Cerdic is no Arthur, though. He has united the West Saxons, but so far as I could tell, looks no further. But as reverently as Cerdic was treated, it was nothing to how they treated Arthur. They never stopped staring at him. He was a legend come to life. The servants shook as they served him, afraid to touch even his cloak. He was served first, even before Cerdic, and given the best of everything. Nothing was too good for him."

I smiled. "And rightly so. They can never defeat him."

"Well," Mordred said, "Cerdic at least knows that. I don't know about Cynewulf. And truly, my lady, I doubt it would be possible to push them into the sea. They are too many, and have been there too long. Cerdic himself was born there, and his father before him."

"Yes. Which is why we must deal with them. Tell me how it was and what agreement you came to."

Mordred hesitated, then chose his words with care. "I think perhaps it will take more time than I had envisioned, my lady. You see, they are not, well, not really civilized, at least by our standards." I could see he was disappointed, but did not want to disappoint me. "They govern by council. All the thegns have a voice; Cerdic is war leader, that is the role of the king."

"And when there is not war?" I asked him.

"Then his role is diminished. In Cerdic's case, his reputation as leader is well established, and no one questions his authority, but this is unusual. When Cynewulf becomes leader, he will have to prove himself. This much I gathered from Cynewulf himself, for we had some time for private speech. He of course talked about wars with the South Saxons, but that was probably no more than a diplomatic choice. They very clearly want more land and are looking westward."

"So you think we will have peace only until Cerdic dies?"

Mordred shrugged, looking down. "That is what the King thinks."

"And you, Mordred? What is your assessment?"

He looked up, and the eagerness was back in his face. "I think we have no time to waste. If there is war ahead, we will be ready to fight it. But if we can establish trade links with the West Saxons, then they might have something to lose by attacking us; at the same time, if we send them goods from a civilized culture, dressed stone, bricks, iron plows, wool garments, imported silks and tapestries, jewelry—why, everything that we can do that they cannot, then perhaps we may raise the level of their living and make them more like us."

"What, have they not these things now?"

"Well, they have jewelry. It is of beaten gold or copper, all in the shapes of animals. The workmanship is skilled, but the design is primitive. Why, when the queen saw what you had sent her, the whole tribe was amazed. They could not believe that human hands had made that sapphire net or worked that necklace. They thought it was from our gods." He grinned. "And you were right, my lady. When Cerdic's queen was told the net was for her hair, she had it redressed on the spot and wore it."

I laughed. "All women are alike in their vanity."

"You have her thanks." His black eyes twinkled. "They have heard of you there, of your great beauty, your white-gold hair and your dark-blue eyes and your ageless skin. They have a song about you, which they sang for us on our first night there." I blushed to hear this and lowered my eyes, but Mordred continued. "They picture you as a warrior queen, riding a war stallion and holding aloft a jeweled sword." I gasped in dismay, and Mordred laughed. "Don't worry, I think the image is patterned after one of their warrior goddesses. It is a great mark of respect."

I rose and paced before the fountain, wringing my hands. "You don't know how much I regret ever having touched the Sword! I wish I had not done it!"

Mordred rose and stood awkwardly. "Be easy, my lady. The King does not regret it, this I know. So why should you? He says you saved the Kingdom that day. He recalls it with fondness."

I stilled myself and smiled at him. "He is a good man, and generous with his praise. But I was wrong to do it, and this every one of his soldiers knows. But about the Saxons, Mordred, I am amazed at what you have told me. What do you mean they have no bricks or stone? Can this be true?"

"Oh, yes. They build entirely with wood. None of the buildings is very big, and the roofs are all of thatch. The walls of most are only sticks and branches, bound together and cemented with wattle. They dig pits, and have their floors below the level of the earth, to keep out drafts. In the larger dwellings, these are boarded over and serve as storage places beneath the floor. The only dwelling we saw that looked like it took more than a day to construct was Cerdic's own meeting hall. A single room only, but very long, with a hole in the middle of the roof, above the hearth, for the firesmoke. This is where all of Arthur's party slept, and where we met and dined, for it was the only place big enough to hold us all. I tell you, my lady, such a place as this"—and he spread his arms wide to indicate the whole of the castle—"this would surpass Cerdic's power of imagination. They would not believe it unless they saw it." He smiled again. "I know, because I tried to describe it, but Cynewulf thought I was boasting."

I stood amazed. How could such primitive peoples wield such power? How could they ever have threatened to destroy us?

"What are their horses like?" I asked, knowing they had them, although they did not use them for war.

Mordred grinned again and shook his head. "You would laugh to see them. They are more like ponies than horses, thick-bodied and short-legged, dun-colored, with stripes down their backs. And small eyes."

I thought of the animals in Lancelot's care, those tall, fleet, graceful steeds with large, dark eyes that spoke of their foreign blood. No wonder neither Lancelot nor Mordred doubted the Saxon grooms!

"Do they use iron at all?" I wondered.

"Yes," Mordred replied. "In their weapons. I make no disparaging comparisons there. They don't use swords much—I saw some, but I did wonder if they were taken from our dead in battle. But their spears are full seven feet long and tipped with cold iron. And their two-headed axes." He shuddered. "They tie feathers to them for each man the ax eats—they think of them as live things, needing sacrifice. I saw many of them. Cerdic's own was so covered with feathers it could be taken for a bird. And each one stood for the life of a Briton." His voice went cold and low and deadly; I stared openly at him. I had never seen this hard anger in him until now. But he was Pendragon, and speaking of Saxons. Perhaps it ran in the blood.

"And did you, Mordred, have a sense of whether the thegns are more interested in war than peace?"

He shrugged. "They want more land. They live by farming. The soil thereabout is rich and fertile but their numbers press upon them. They are excellent boatmen; their craft are shallow and they prefer to navigate waterways and settle by them. They don't build roads. They want territory inland from Rutupiae, on the river Thames. They would prefer not to fight for it, if they can bargain for it instead. This is what Arthur holds out to them, to bind them as a buffer state between the Alemans, the Burgundians, the Franks, and us. At the moment, they are pleased at the prospect of more talk. I do not think they will try war. At least"—and here he gulped—"not while Arthur lives."

He said no more. I wondered if he was thinking of his oath not to outlive the King, the oath that had made Arthur so angry.

"Well, then, it sounds like a successful journey, taken all in all," I said. "Be not disheartened. It is a small step, but a step nevertheless. And if you had not been here to champion this cause, dear Mordred, I know well the High King would never have gone." I paused, but he said nothing. Clearly, there was something on his mind. "And now, to more immediate matters. I assume Lancelot has told the King what passed with Agravaine." His eyes flew to my face, but their expression was carefully guarded. "How does this place you, Mordred? You may not love him, but he is your half brother."

He shifted uncomfortably and struggled with himself awhile. "Why do you always ask me such pointed questions?" he said at last, in distress. "Most women would skirt such unpleasant issues, but you always face them head-on. It's as hard as answering the King."

I put a hand on his arm and felt him tremble. "It is my way," I replied gently. "I am unwomanly, perhaps, but then, I am Queen. How can I aid and advise my lord if know nothing of these things? I am chained to his castle, Mordred. I cannot go where you go; the King does not take me on his travels. When once he did—well, you know what happened. I am a danger to him outside these walls. So I have no way of knowing what passes within Britain, if the men I love will not speak to me."

He slid to the flagstones at my feet and kissed my hand. "Oh, dearest Guinevere! I meant no disrespect, you must believe me! Unwomanly! How could you think it? I meant only—"

"Hush, Mordred," I said, smiling and ruffling his hair. "I know what you meant. Do not be afraid to speak your mind. You are my son. I will keep your counsel."

He collected himself then and met my eyes. "Well," he said at last, "I condemn Agravaine, of course, for his base action. And I cannot deny that Sir Lancelot's judgment was fair. But—"

"But?"

"But it would have been more politic to wait for the King's return," he said carefully. "There are those who object to the judgment because it was Lancelot who gave it. Had he waited for Arthur—"

"Ahhhh. He wished to. But I would not let him, for the maid's sake. He knew well it would make him an enemy, but for my sake he went ahead. You cannot deny his courage, Mordred."

"No, madam, I do not. But he has made more enemies than only Agravaine. There is a faction of young men growing ... Agravaine has sway with them. Most of them think it no great crime to strike a woman. They think Lancelot a proud man who reaches too high. They also think—" He stopped and lowered his eyes.

"Yes," I said sadly, "I know what they think." Mordred still looked away, and I turned to face him. "And you, Mordred? What do you think?" He looked up then, and again I could not read his thoughts.

"I believe what you tell me, my lady," he said quietly. "You have told me the rumors are not true. But that does not mean Lancelot has nothing to fear."

"So he told me himself."

Mordred's eyes widened. "I am glad he knows it. There are those who would dislodge him from his place near the King. Please, my lady, guard yourself when you are with him, for the very walls have eyes." He stood abruptly and bowed. "Forgive me if I have said too much."

"No, Mordred, you have told me nothing I did not already know. Are there any—any men of Arthur's age who feel the same?"

"Not to my knowledge," he replied. "These are all young hot-heads eager for action. This long peace does not suit them. And since they dare not speak against the King, they plot against his second-in-command."

"And you?" I said softly. "You play a double role here, do you not? They think you are one of them. Is this hard for you?"

A bitter smile touched his lips. "Oh, I am used to that, my lady. I have played a double role for most of my life, it seems. They trust me because they know I have no love for Lancelot."

He straightened suddenly and squared his shoulders. I turned to follow his gaze and saw the King coming out from the library.

"Say nothing to the King about Lancelot!" Mordred warned. "He will not hear it talked of!"

Mordred bowed to his father. I went to greet him, and as always, he took me in his arms and kissed me warmly.

I smiled up into his face. "Welcome home, my lord."

"Thank you, Gwen. I am sorry you and Lancelot had trouble while I was gone."

I glanced swiftly at Mordred, but his eyes were politely on the ground. "I am sorry, too, my lord. The timing was poor; but we did not choose it."

He sighed and handed me back to my seat. He sat beside me, where Mordred had been, and Mordred moved back far enough to give us private speech.

"I have spoken with Agravaine," he said, coming directly to the point. "I have told him that had I been here, his punishment would have been harsher, for the King cannot ever give the appearance of favoring his relations and still be considered just. I would have had him dismissed from my service, as well. There is no honor in hating women."

"How did he take this?"

"Oh," Arthur said, his mouth twisting in a grim smile, "he did not like it. But there was nothing he could say. I wanted to make him feel he had got off lightly, but he is determined to carry a grievance against Lancelot." He paused. "Is the maid still here? I would have a word with her."

I took his hand and kissed it fervently. "Oh, my lord, I bless you for this. Yes, she is here. As soon as the swelling has subsided, she will send for her father and go home. The physicians say she may not travel yet."

"The poor girl," he said sadly. "I will send her with a royal escort when the time comes. I will do her all the honor I can, seeing he is my nephew, and my responsibility."

"Thank you, my gracious lord. It will mean much to her. It means much to me."

He slid an arm about my waist, pulling me closer. "I know not what it is in their blood, that makes them treat women so. Perhaps they always hated Morgause and did not know it. I am thankful that Lancelot dealt with Agravaine so fairly. Even so . . ." He let it drift.

"Mordred and I have been talking about the Saxons," I said, to change the direction of his thoughts. "Are you pleased with the mission, or do you think it was a mistake to go?"

"Oh, I am well satisfied. They fear us still; they know our power. My demands are reasonable. They will not break the peace." He turned and beckoned Mordred forward to join us. "It will take time, but we will get their cooperation in a defense treaty."

He talked for some while about the journey, including Mordred in the conversation, but it became slowly clear to me that he was keeping something back; that he was speaking optimistically for his son's sake, or for mine, but hiding something dark behind his words. When at last Mordred begged to be excused, Arthur embraced him and let him go. I watched him out of earshot and turned immediately to the King.

"And now, my lord," I said, laying a hand on him arm to prevent his going, "what is amiss? Tell me your true thoughts. These were words only, and not what you believe. Is there war ahead?"

He looked startled and then chagrined. "You would make life easier for me, Gwen, if you did not know me so well."

But I would not be diverted. "Tell me, Arthur. I can see in your face, you do not believe we can ever deal with Saxons."

He frowned and began his steady pacing, hands clasped behind his back. "All right, then. You are right. I do not trust them. As long as I live, they will be our buffer. They have no choice in that. But what you and Mordred dream of, that they should become part of us one day, whether through trade or any other means—no, this I do not believe will happen."

"Why not?"

"They are savages," he said shortly. "Cerdic is a gentleman by their standards, yet you would certainly call him a savage. The differences between us are too great. What you dream of will take more time than we have." He spoke fiercely and with conviction. "Cerdic talked of tribes in the far eastern lands, more primitive and savage than even the Saxons. They are on the move. They are leaving their grasslands and crossing the mountains in the hope of plunder. They destroy everything in their path. These are the people who are pushing the Saxons out of their homeland, who are pushing the Burgundians westward and northward, who are pushing the Franks. Eventually, we, too, will be pushed. While I live, if Merlin is to be believed, we can hold them." He stopped suddenly and turned to me. His eyes were dark. "But after I am gone, will we be strong enough to stop them? They will come across the border like the storm tide over a sea wall."

I was shaking from head to foot. "Then you must live, my lord! Live until we have civilized the Saxons!"

He laughed, but there was no mirth in it. "Then must I live five hundred years!" He shook his head. "No, Guinevere. They will never be like us. We are so far beyond them, you would find it difficult to imagine. When they come across the border, they will kill everyone in their path. They know not mercy, nor honor, as we see it. They will kill for the sheer joy of taking life. Their axes thirst for blood. It will not be like the Romans. The Saxons will destroy us, or drive us into the hills and starve us. Either way, we will be gone. They are our fate."

"My lord Arthur!" I cried, falling to the ground in tears, wringing my hands. "Oh, no! God would not allow such things to happen! All this that you have built cannot go for naught! You have made Britain! We were tribes ourselves, and now we are a nation! Please do not think we ever could go back! What has happened to you to drive you to such black thoughts?"

He came to me, raised me gently, and held me close. "I'm so sorry, Guinevere. Do forgive me. It was thoughtless of me to distress you so."

"No, my lord, I asked for your true thoughts. If these are they—I brought them upon myself, and I thank you for your honesty. But do you really think these things?"

He shrugged and kissed the tears from my face. "Sometimes. I had bad dreams there. Perhaps it was the unaccustomed food."

"Can we speak with Niniane? Could she not dispel these fears?"

"I have asked her this before. She sees no further than my death." I shuddered, and he pressed me closer. "Let it be, Gwen. If it comes, it comes. In the meantime, we will do what we can to avert it. That is why I went, after all. In case there is some possibility of preventing annihilation."

"Is that why you went, my lord? I cannot believe that such a primitive people could destroy a civilized land. If we are so far advanced, how can they conquer us?"

"The example lies everywhere before us," he replied. "Even Rome herself is not immune, if some of the strange tales that have reached this shore are true. When men rise above the level of killing for joy, like Bedwyr, Lancelot, myself—we leave ourselves vulnerable to those who still have savage instincts, like Agravaine, Gaheris, Gawaine."

"You must be stronger than they."

"Yes. As long as we are stronger, we shall hold them." He said no more, and my thoughts cowered before the vision of Britain without Arthur. But he was in his prime—surely, we could look ahead to thirty or more years of peace! And who knew what the Saxons would be like in thirty years?

"Tell me of Gawaine," I said, to change the subject. "Does he back a treaty with the Saxons? Does he feel his brother unjustly punished?"

Arthur sighed and, taking my arm, began walking. "For once, Gawaine is holding his own counsel. I have told him clearly what I expect from him. I fear he thinks Agravaine's punishment too severe—if he is willing to forgive Gaheris the killing of their mother, he is not likely to see a mere beating as much of a crime, although it was base. But I have told him I abhor it and, as his King and uncle, will hold Agravaine to Lancelot's judgment. If Gawaine wants to rule in Orkney, he will see things my way or keep quiet. It is as much as his future is worth to oppose Lancelot. In anything." His voice was cold.

"It seems," I said slowly, "that Gawaine is learning some hard lessons rather fast."

"Let us hope it makes a man of him." He came to a halt and, drawing a deep breath, took both my hands and faced me. "Oh, yes, and Gwen"—he hesitated for a fraction—"I am to let you know that Lancelot leaves for Lanascol tomorrow."

This was news to me, and I am afraid my face gave that away. "But why, my lord? He is not in danger?"

Arthur smiled. "When did he ever turn his face from danger? No, he asked permission to go home to see his wife's grave. He will be back before winter and will bring his eldest son with him." The laughter lines deepened at the corners of his eyes. "And you will have another boy to raise."

"Oh, Arthur, that would be wonderful, if Lancelot is willing." But I was thinking, Why had he not told me this himself? Why send Arthur? Then Arthur lifted my hand to his lips and kissed it, and held it against his smooth, shaved cheek. His eyes were deep with some great grief.

"What is it, Arthur?" I whispered. "Does he not have your blessing?"

He started three times to speak, but could not bring himself to it. I began to fear he had some dreadful news to tell me.

"Arthur, what is it? Will aught happen to him while he is away? Has Niniane seen anything?"

"No," he said gently, "not that. Be easy, Gwen."

"What then?"

He drew a deep breath and spoke. "You both have heard the rumors. I want you to know that it is my wish that he bring his son to Camelot, and that you and Lancelot raise him together. It would give you both great joy to be as parents to the boy. I would like to see it. He has had so little joy in his life."

I gasped and dared not breathe. He had himself broached the forbidden subject! While he struggled to find the words, I held hard to his hand.

"What joy he has found, Gwen, he has found with you. I bless you for that."

"Arthur!"

"I know it cannot be helped. But it grieves me that I should be the cause of his suffering. His is such a noble heart!"

"My dearest lord!" I cried, blinking back tears and taking him in my arms. "It is not your fault! He loves you better than his own self, and his joy is to serve you!" I felt how he trembled, and I laid my head against his chest.

"There is nothing to be done. I will not give you up," he said.

"And I would not go."

"It is God's will, I suppose. But it is cruel. I would ease his pain by any means in my power. But you are the means, Gwen."

I raised my face to his. "My sweet lord, I will with pleasure raise his son, if he wills. But it is because of you that he brings him here. You are the lodestone that draws us all to your side. Arthur, do not pretend it is me! We are none of us anything without you."

He kissed me with sudden feeling, right there in the garden, and I heard the quick, soft steps and gentle rustling of courtiers, knights, and servants fading swiftly into the castle depths, leaving the King alone.

22 ✺ The Heir

From the first, Galahad foiled the King's plans. Although the boy was an eager student of Bedwyr and Valerius, he would learn nothing from me. He was always polite, at times overly so, but his heart was closed to me. He was only five years old when he first came to Camelot, yet already Elaine had trained his thoughts against me. And against Lancelot. I was shocked to find that so young a lad disliked his father. His boyhood hero had been his uncle Galahantyn, whom he worshipped. As time went by, and Galahantyn spent more time in Lanascol, holding Lancelot's lands and caring for his younger sons, this worship Galahad transferred to Arthur. Bedwyr encouraged this, hoping that as he grew older, and saw how Arthur loved Lancelot, he might in time be softened toward him. But this did not happen.

Galahad was a strange boy. Like Mordred, he was quiet and held his tongue. One never caught him in a hasty speech or careless act. Even at five, he was serious and thoughtful. But while Mordred loved life and could laugh at himself, Galahad rarely smiled and had no sense of humor. When he was not at lessons, or learning riding or swordplay, he was in the chapel praying. He thirsted for a glory unattainable even in Arthur's Kingdom.

He had a great disdain for beauty, whether in man or woman; he thought it a temptation to do evil. This was odd, for he himself promised to outdo both his father and uncle in physical beauty. He preferred plain clothing, wore no decoration, and shunned all forms of ceremonial trappings. Had he been ugly, it would have pleased him better. He sought holiness in squalor, Lancelot said. It was the only unkind thing I ever heard him say of his son. But it was true. I sometimes wondered if his young life was a burden to him, the way he bore it so solemnly.

As time went by, I saw clearly that his dislike of me and his

303

disapproval of his father were grounded in our love for one another. This was perfectly understandable. If the boy had loved his
mother dearly, he must have seen that his father did not. And
when he came to Camelot, he must have discovered, as everyone
else had, it was I who had Lancelot's heart. Naturally, then, he de-
spised me. I tried every way I could think of to reach him and
make him think better of me, but to no avail. Lancelot and I both
grieved for him. Had he been blessed with a more loving, open
nature, he might have given us such joy. But he was not that kind
of child.

His censure of us hurt his father deeply and put a strain upon
the affection between us. Lancelot was careful never to be with
me alone, and when we were with others he forebore to touch me.
Even the ceremonial kiss of greeting he denied himself, when his
son was watching. Since we were no longer easy with one another, we began to long for each other more and miss the companionship we had shared for so many years. Some nights I could not
sleep, wishing only for the touch of his hand in mine. Thus, on
the rare occasions when circumstance threw us together unobserved, and this long smoldering passion found vent, we were
driven close to the edges of control and left quaking with fear at
the strength of our feelings. I began to see how wise Arthur had
been to let us be; with freedom, this other long love had not endangered that I felt for the King. But now, this maddening pattern
of long restraint and brief, fierce release looked to drive us both
toward some disastrous conclusion.

Lancelot could not ignore his son's censure. "He is my con-
science speaking," he would say to me. "He knows that in my
heart, I sin against God, for I covet what is Arthur's. I am not able
to ignore him." Pleading with him did no good. He felt he deserved the torture the boy put him through. But I did not feel I deserved it, and there was no one I could confide in. I certainly
could not talk to Arthur about it. He would let no one bring the
subject up in his presence; and even when we were alone together,
he would steer around it. Since the day he had opened his heart
to me about Lancelot, he had grown so sensitive, it was as if he
protected a tender wound. My love for Lancelot he had accepted
long ago, but he did not want to be reminded. On occasion I
would find him looking at us both with helpless compassion, but
truly, there was nothing he could do.

Galahad's closest friend at court was young Gareth. Although
the Orkney prince was nine years his senior, Galahad was always
ahead of his age in everything. Gareth treated him as a beloved

younger brother and took him on outings and taught him tricks with bow, sword, and spear. He had the boy's confidence, if anyone had. And yet, although Gareth loved and honored Lancelot above all men, he was never able to sway Galahad toward a more lenient regard for his father.

When Gareth entered Arthur's service at fifteen, he and Linet became formally betrothed. Being a gentleman, he promised her he would not come to her bed until they were married. Before that, he wished to have the approval of her father, who lived in York. So one fine spring day in Gareth's sixteenth year, Arthur sent Gareth and Gawaine on a mission to Festus, governor of York. He had appealed to Arthur for settlement of a minor dispute among the bishops there, which touched not on religion but on their property. Gawaine was now a man of eighteen, newly knighted, and one of the King's Companions. This was the first time he had been the leader of a diplomatic mission, and he carried himself with great pride. He did not know that Arthur was relying on Gareth's presence to ensure that proper judgment was rendered.

Linet's father Lucius was a prominent man in York, a landowner and a knight in good standing with Festus and with Drustan, King of Elmet, whose stronghold at Caer Mord lay but a day's ride beyond. Linet's grandfather was old Caius Lucius, who had served with both Ambrosius and Uther in Britain's wars and had gained for himself the honorable reputation of being the most battle-scarred man in the Kingdom. He was himself descended from a Roman governor in the time of Maximus. Linet could hardly come of higher lineage, and the match pleased both Arthur and Lucius.

Festus held a great feast upon their arrival, and unbeknownst to them, he had invited Drustan himself to the celebration. Drustan was a big man, a graybeard by this time, but hard as iron and with a reputation of a tough and deadly fighter. He was a proud man and had only been slowly won to Arthur's service. But the Angles lived close along his southern borders, and he saw the sense in uniting against the barbarian foe. He was an honest soldier and a just man, and since he gave thought to what he did, he had small patience for quick tempers or hotheadedness. Thus he was not well pleased to find Gawaine sitting near his elbow at dinner, for Lamorak, whom Gawaine had sworn to kill, was his nephew by marriage. Being Drustan, he took this bull by the horns and asked Gawaine outright how the matter now stood with him.

"Are you my sworn enemy, Sir Gawaine?" was how he put it.

"Or, have you grown into sense since you swore vengeance upon my nephew Lamorak?"

He had a booming voice, and everyone near him heard this: Gareth, Festus, Lucius, and a score of other men. Gawaine had to think quickly, which was never his strength. He and Gareth were surrounded by Elmet's friends, and many of Drustan's own soldiers sat in the hall. And even Gareth might not defend him, for he abhorred blood feuds. To declare himself Drustan's enemy would be the height of folly. So he denied it.

"My lord," Gawaine said stiffly, "I bear no one in your house ill will. Once I was Lamorak's enemy, for I felt he shamed our mother. But it is true that our mother was herself as guilty as he."

"Then you forgive Lamorak," Drustan pressed, "and withdraw your challenge to him?"

Gawaine swallowed hard. "Yes, my lord. As far as I am concerned, he is one of the High King's Companions, as I am, and I would greet him as such."

Drustan slapped him hard upon the back. "I am glad you have come to your senses, lad!" he cried. "For I have called Lamorak out of his Breton fastness and bid him stay the summer with me. I intend to apply to King Arthur to have him accepted as one of your number in Camelot. It is appropriate he should have your backing. Thank you, boy. You may tell the King, when you return, that Lamorak should be here by the solstice."

Gawaine was silent and continued so for the rest of his visit in York. This was unlike him, as everyone knew, but no one could fathom the cause. The judgment he gave in the bishops' case was a fair one, being a compromise, and everyone praised his sense. When he left, he left with everyone's thanks and best wishes. Gareth stayed on at Caer Mord at Drustan's invitation; Gawaine returned to us alone.

He never gave Arthur Drustan's message. Instead, he gave it to Agravaine, who was in secret communication with Gaheris. In doing so, he considered he had kept his bargain; for he did not come against Lamorak himself, and he had not promised Drustan, or so he thought, that he would send no other. In this and in other things, his mind worked like a child's. Although even children knew that truth must be told from the heart, and not from the lips only.

One day not long after, Agravaine disappeared. Mordred came to Arthur as he walked with me, to tell him this, and to discover whether the High King had perhaps sent him on a mission. On learning Arthur had done no such thing, Mordred told us he was sure Agravaine was on his way to meet Gaheris.

Arthur frowned. "Where is the boy hiding, Mordred? Do you know?"

"My lord, I know nothing with certainty, but I believe he is somewhere in the hill country west of York."

"And what do you think this disappearance signifies?"

"My lord, I know not, but they rarely dare a meeting. Something important must be going on. And it cannot bode well."

Arthur looked at his son a moment and then nodded. "Well, then, I will send you to York with greetings to Festus and a message to Lucius. Keep your eyes open, Mordred, and see if you can find them or discover what they may be up to. It is time I spoke with those boys. If you can get word to them, say that I have charged you with a message for Gaheris; that if he publicly repents his crime and swears to accept such penance as I shall give him, he may be received again at court."

Mordred bowed. "You are merciful, my lord, to treat the ruffian so. Truly, it is more than he deserves."

Arthur sighed. "Men like Gaheris have a way of getting what they deserve. Yet he is my nephew; I must do what I can for him. Gareth is staying the summer with Drustan; perhaps he can help make Gaheris see sense."

So Mordred departed and Lancelot breathed easier at court. Mordred traveled north into wild and hilly lands. There were still outlaws in the deep forests there, and travel could be chancey, but he was a King's man, well trained and young, and he reached York without trouble. Festus received him with delight.

"You're just in time, my lord," he cried, "to celebrate Lamorak's return from Brittany! He's here now, a guest in my house, and tonight we will feast him long and well!"

Mordred knew at once why Agravaine had come. He asked quietly after the twins; no one knew anything about them. But York was a big place, nearly a city, with a thousand places to hide.

Lamorak was guest of honor at the feast. He looked fit and healthy, and younger, Mordred thought, now that he was free of the witch's curse. The feast lasted late into the night, with an excellent bard and excellent wine, Lamorak's gift from the vineyards of Gaul. Before they broke for bed, Mordred pulled Lamorak aside and bade him take an escort on his journey to Elmet, and told him why. But Lamorak, full of wine and confidence, scoffed at the idea that two such ruffians could harm him.

"Then let me ride with you, Lamorak. If we are together, they will not chance a meeting, and I have messages to give you from the King."

Lamorak grinned drunkenly. "*You* carry messages from the King? A fine thing—I'd rather go alone than with a bastard of that witch. Oh, all right, Mordred. I owe you my life, after all. If it's so important . . . Be ready at noon, I'll meet you at the town gates."

But when Mordred arrived at the gates near midmorning, he found Lamorak already gone. He had left after breakfast, the sentries told Mordred, he had ridden out alone, chuckling to himself.

Grimly Mordred set his spurs to his horse. After a half-day's hard gallop on the dusty road, he had given up all hope of preventing disaster when he heard shouting beyond the next bend. Summoning one last burst of energy from his exhausted horse, he galloped forward.

He was almost in time. Even as he watched, Lamorak, whose sword was engaged with Agravaine's, was felled from behind by Gaheris in a coward's killing. He toppled from his horse, pulling Gaheris' sword from his hand. Gaheris leaped down and, whipping out his dagger, cut Lamorak's throat. At this Mordred shouted, and his shout was echoed by another farther up the road. Drustan himself had come to greet his nephew and rode forward at the head of a small party of knights. Foremost among them was Gareth, who galloped forward, screaming.

"Agravaine! Gaheris! Touch him not! Oh, oh, what have you done?" He went white when he saw Lamorak was beyond help.

Gaheris retrieved his sword and wiped it on Lamorak's clothing. "Fear not, little brother. I have revenged our mother's honor."

"Honor!" Gareth cried in horror. Then, seeing Mordred: "Dred, are you in this?"

"Certainly not," replied Mordred coolly. "I came to stop them, but I was too slow."

As the High King's deputy, it was his duty to arrest the twins, but already Drustan's troops surrounded the four Orkney boys with drawn swords.

"So," Drustan said, hard and furious, "this is how Sir Gawaine repays my trust! I will see you both hanged."

"You dare not!" Agravaine shouted. "Our uncle the High King will destroy you!"

Gaheris, looking spent now that his goal had been accomplished, remounted sluggishly and swung his horse to Agravaine's side. "We have no quarrel with you, sir. You would be wise to let us go."

"My lord," Gareth quavered, seeing Drustan losing control of his rage, "let me speak with them a moment." Drustan glared at him, then finally nodded and drew his knights away.

Gareth faced the twins, with Mordred behind him. "Please my brothers, be reasonable. You cannot expect him to let you go, when you have killed his nephew in cold blood. You have broken the High King's laws."

"It was a fair fight," Agravaine insisted. "We challenged him outright with his crime."

"Two against one is not fair," protested Gareth.

"I saw the killing," Mordred said quietly, and Gaheris stiffened. "Gaheris took him from behind. That's not in any of the rules of combat I know."

Gareth looked sickened. "You dishonor me, Gaheris. Drustan is a fair man, and his anger is righteous. Let yourselves be taken captive; behave and beg his pardon. I can probably get you off with your lives."

"The High King—" Agravaine began, but Mordred cut him short.

"I would not wave the High King's name about, as if it were a banner of protection. You know well whose side he will take in this affair. You have shamed Gareth, you have shamed me, and you have shamed Arthur by this deed."

"Then," Gaheris said boldly, "do not tell him of it! You always were a snake in the grass, you bastard brat!"

Mordred stared him down and then turned away, disgusted, to fall back with Drustan's men. But Gaheris, suddenly enraged, raised his sword and attacked. Gareth blocked his way and parried his sword thrust, crying a warning to Mordred. Many things then happened at once: Mordred whirled, Drustan's knights spurred forward, Gaheris attacked Gareth, screaming in fury and foaming at the mouth. Gareth, Lancelot's star pupil, fought his brother off and pierced his sword arm to make him drop the weapon. But one of Drustan's knights, eager for vengeance, threw a spear. It struck Gaheris' chest and came out his back. He screamed and fell from the saddle. Agravaine lifted his sword, to find it taken from his hand by Mordred.

"Don't be a fool," Mordred growled. "That way lies death."

Gareth, in tears, knelt in the dust by his brother, and with Drustan's help cut the spear shaft so he could lie easily on the ground. He was senseless, but did not die. They fashioned a body sling, and several of the knights carried him on foot back to Caer Mord. Lamorak's body was slung over an empty saddle. Gareth rode back beside Agravaine and argued with him all the way. Mordred, feeling both helpless and responsible, rode at Drustan's side. At last Drustan turned to him and spoke.

"I have heard about you, Sir Mordred. You are Arthur's son, are you not? By the witch-queen, mother of these boys?"

Mordred froze. In all his life, he had never been asked this question outright, had never even discussed it except with Arthur and with me. He had grown used to the fact it was a subject everyone avoided. And as the King had not publicly acknowledged him, he was at a loss for a reply. But he felt, after what had just passed, that he owed this man the truth.

"My lord king," he said at last, "I am."

"And why are you here, then? In the cause of your brothers? Or in your father's cause, if the two are different?"

"My lord Drustan, the causes are indeed different. I came north at King Arthur's request to find out how things stood with Gaheris. We suspected Agravaine would get in touch with him, I had instructions from the King to find them both and discover what they were up to. But I was too late. As for Lamorak, my lord, he was well loved by my father and would have been welcomed back at court. I believe the High King was trying to clear the way to bring him back, when he sent me to seek Gaheris."

"Ah, then Agravaine's boast is a vain one."

"Indeed it is!" Mordred cried. "I have made it clear to him, as well. You need not fear Arthur's vengeance, my lord. His anger will be all on your side. He will never hold Gaheris' death against you."

"And you yourself, Sir Mordred?"

Mordred looked away. "Like Gareth, I am ashamed to be their kin. Gareth is an honorable man. But I have had a bellyful of the others."

Drustan laughed shortly. "It was Gawaine who set this up, for besides Gareth, he alone knew Lamorak was coming. Let King Arthur know this, Mordred, when you return. I have no wish to pit kingdom against kingdom in a blood feud, when we have enemies enough beyond our borders. But let him know that when I next come to Camelot, I would speak with Sir Gawaine. Alone."

Mordred nodded, heartsick and weary. What Arthur had most wished to avoid had come to pass. Morgause's curse lay upon his Kingdom still. With Gaheris dead, and Gawaine's future so threatened, what would Arthur do?

But as it turned out, he did not need to do anything, for Gaheris did not die. He was a year recuperating in Drustan's castle, under guard, but he lived. Mordred and Gareth stayed at Caer Mord a full month, doing Drustan service, and they kept Agravaine with them. Finally, after Agravaine had begged Drustan's pardon most abjectly, Drustan formally forgave him and allowed him to go. For Agravaine had at least engaged Lamorak face to face.

These three returned to Camelot one hot day in July, and that was the first any of us heard about this terrible affair. They came to the King in the library, where he sat working with his scribe, while Bedwyr, Lancelot, and I waited upon his pleasure in the garden. Thus we all heard this tale together. Bedwyr was stricken with sadness; Lancelot alternated between fury at the insult done the King and pride in Gareth's noble behavior. I watched Mordred's face throughout, and saw his grief and his anger at his inability to prevent this tragedy. How he longs for power! I thought to myself. Arthur alone was still.

When they had told everything, all eyes turned to the King. He rose and walked out into the garden, staring at the sky. When he returned, his expression was grim.

"Agravaine." The youth paled and went down on one knee. "My lord."

"When you took service with me, you took an oath not to lift a sword against any man, save only the King's enemies. Lamorak was not my enemy. He was a trusted knight and still served me. Your oath is broken. You are dismissed from my service." Agravaine gasped, and Gareth closed his eyes in sorrow.

"But, my lord—" Agravaine whispered, unable to believe it.

"Go," Arthur said flatly. "Get your belongings from the barracks. You can find a room in town, if you want to stay. Gawaine will give you protection, no doubt, since I judge you did his bidding." Dumbfounded, Agravaine opened his mouth to protest yet again, but Arthur cut him off, showing temper.

"Be gone before I call the guard!" Agravaine fled.

Arthur paced back and forth, scowling. Lancelot and Bedwyr stood at attention. Mordred and Gareth were on their knees. At last the King sighed deeply and put his anger behind him. He stood before Mordred and Gareth and addressed them solemnly.

"I thank you both for your noble efforts on my behalf. If Drustan remains my ally, you have done me a great service. Gareth, I will honor you publicly in Council; you have shown calm and sense and honor in a matter that must have touched your heart nearly. For this, I am grateful."

"Thank you, my gracious King," Gareth murmured. Arthur raised him, clasped him, and kissed him. "Go to your brother Gawaine and tell him I will see him here in an hour. Try, if you can, to make him see the gravity of this affair."

Gareth promised and withdrew. The King turned back to Mordred, whose dark head was bowed in anguish.

"My lord," he cried, "please forgive my failure! I should have prevented this and could have, if I'd had my wits about me!"

A smile touched Arthur's lips, but Mordred did not see it. "Rise, Mordred, my son. You are not to blame for this."

Mordred's eyes flew to the King's face. Arthur grasped his arms and embraced him. "Even had you ridden at their side, even had you cried a warning to Lamorak, you could not have prevented his slaughter. They would have killed you first, to get to him. And I need you living."

Mordred drew a trembling breath, and color flooded his face. For a moment they stood thus, father and son, holding each other. Bedwyr and Lancelot stood flattened against the walls, staring straight ahead, unseeing—the sentry's stance. Arthur was the first to turn away, deeply moved. "I thank God you and Gareth were there," he said slowly. "As it is, we shall have peace awhile longer, if I can deal with Gawaine. Tell me how Drustan stands in this."

Mordred swallowed, stilled himself, and gave the King his report. Arthur seemed satisfied and nodded.

"There is hope," he said.

"But, sir, there is one thing more. You should know," Mordred said slowly, with a tremor in his voice, "you should know that Drustan asked me straight out if I were your son. It was just after the killing, we were bearing Gaheris and Lamorak back to Caer Mord and he needed to know where I stood. But he asked me, instead, who I was." He hesitated, and the King met his eyes.

"I hope," Arthur said carefully, "that you told him the truth."

"Yes, my lord," Mordred said, relieved. "I could do naught else. So—so now he knows."

From where I stood I could see him shaking, and my heart went out to him. Tell him, Arthur! I cried in my thoughts, it is time to let him know your intentions! But Bedwyr and Lancelot were there, and I did not think he would. Arthur stood looking gravely at his son.

"It is well he knows," he said slowly, "so he will accept you one day as his King, should he outlive me."

Mordred went white; his eyes widened in amazement; my own

filled with tears. Lancelot and Bedwyr were staring at the King, Bedwyr with warm approval, Lancelot with worry and dismay.

"My lord," Mordred whispered.

Arthur smiled. "You did not think I would leave Britain in Constantine's hands, while my son is living and able? You are my heir, Mordred, none other. Give me another year, and I shall publicly declare it."

"My lord," Mordred breathed again, at a loss for words.

"You have things to learn yet," Arthur said gently. "But you are worthy." Then he grinned. "If you don't believe me, ask the Queen."

When Mordred looked to me, my kerchief was over my face, and I began to weep. This broke the tension, and all the men laughed. I drew Lancelot and Bedwyr out into the garden and left Arthur some time to be alone with his son. At length, he bade us all leave him, Mordred, too, for Gawaine was due, and he wished to speak with him alone.

While the King met with Gawaine, Mordred sought me out. I had gone to the stables to visit Rajid, and he found me leading the stallion out to graze. When I saw by his face he wanted private speech, I beckoned him to walk with me, and we went down the path to the meadows beyond King's Gate. As we passed the outer ramparts, Mordred lifted a hand, and four sentries fell in smartly behind us. I smiled to myself. Clearly Arthur's soldiers recognized Mordred's authority.

When the stallion had settled down to peaceful grazing, and the sentries stood some fifty paces off, Mordred seemed unable to begin. He fidgeted and looked away, clearly moved by strong emotion but unable to speak his mind.

"Well, Mordred," I said gently. "He has told you now what all Camelot has known for years. And Duke Constantine, as well, unless I miss my guess. You are his heir."

Mordred straightened and met my eyes. "I can hardly believe it. I have both wanted this and feared it."

"Feared it, Mordred? You? Fear power?"

He looked away quickly. "Guinevere, do not forget my oath."

This was the rub. I had half expected it. I reached for his hand and held it tightly in my own. "When you made the oath, Mordred, what was in your mind? Remember back to that day."

"I did not want Lancelot to accuse me of ambition," he said slowly.

"Yes. But you are Pendragon. Ambition, the drive to be the best—it is in your blood. Lancelot knows this. And now he knows, as he did not know then, that you love and honor the King."

"And," he continued, as if I had not spoken, "I wanted to thwart the prophecy. I still want this. If I die with him, how can I be his death? I want to deny this curse more than I want anything else, even"—he swallowed—"even being High King." He shook his head slowly. "He has done me such great honor. I will give up anything, even the future he offers, to be free of this prophecy. But Niniane says this is beyond my power. Oh, Guinevere," he cried, "what am I to do?"

Arthur's words had lit a fire in him; he glowed with pride, with confidence, with the knowledge that he had at last received the call to his destiny. He had been born to kingship—looking at him now, no one could doubt it. And yet he was ready to renounce it, to accept death instead of glory, and all for Arthur's sake.

My eyes were on the ground. Near my foot Rajid's lips gripped the meadow grasses, his strong teeth softly tore the shafts, which sprang back into place at half their height. As time passed they would grow tall again, as if the horse had never been there, for although the shaft was gone, the root still lived.

"Take your mind off Arthur and Merlin's prophecy," I said suddenly, looking up into his black eyes. "Think of Britain. Think of the people all over Britain who live in peace. All Merlin ever said or did, he did for Britain, and Arthur after him. We are bound into a nation now. Keep our welfare always before your eyes, and God will guide your steps."

He slowly sank to one knee, pressing to his lips the hand that still held his. Where the words had come from, I did not know, but I felt suddenly edgy and fearful, as I used to feel in Merlin's presence. I actually turned my head to look behind me, but of course no one was there.

"My dearest Guinevere," Mordred whispered. "You are a Queen, indeed!"

I raised him quickly. "Come, Mordred. I have said nothing you do not know already, in your heart. Had you asked the King, he would have told you the same."

He looked solemnly at the ground and moved the toe of his boot over the short blades of grass cropped by the horse's teeth. "Let me tell you my dream," he said in a low voice. "It is a dream that consumes me. . . . All men may be warlike, but everyone in his heart values peace. I dream that someday—beyond our lifetimes, surely—but someday, all the civilized world may be one nation! Britons and Saxons, Franks and Bretons, Romans, Egypttians, and men of other nations we know nothing of—they will all sit down together and talk of peace. Yes, I know it sounds impossible. But look at Arthur. Not so long ago men would have said it was impossible for Britain. But he has shown us how it may be done. Men serve gladly if they are well led."

This was a speech for Mordred; his eyes were shining and his face was alight. Then did I see his father's spirit in him, and I made him a low reverence.

"My lord," I whispered, "what a King you will make!"

He smiled shyly. "I have said too much. But I wanted you to know what is in my heart . . . However, these are dreams, and there are practical matters to be faced. How will he get the Christian lords to accept me? Even to Lancelot I am an unholy abomination."

"It is not as bad as all that. I am Christian, and I accept and love you. Do not worry about Arthur. If wisdom and patience can accomplish it, it will be done."

"Wisdom and patience," he said slowly, "and the love of the people."

I took his hand and held it hard. "When they know you, Mordred, as I do, they will love you."

He met my eyes and lifted my fingers to his lips; together, hand in hand, we turned back toward Camelot.

What Arthur said to Gawaine, I do not know, except that it was harsh. I am sure that he forbade him to seek revenge against Drustan, even if Gaheris died. Whatever chastisement he administered, Gawaine took it and kept silent. He took charge of Agravaine, paid for his lodgings in the town, and saw that he went to his yearly service for the Earl of Swiftwater. But he was no longer as friendly with Gareth, and Mordred he avoided altogether. To ease matters, Arthur kept him moving. When he traveled, he took Gawaine with him, leaving Mordred co-regent with Lancelot. When he was home, he sent him to Caerleon, or Cornwall, or Rheged, or Lothian. Thus was Gawaine's deadly energy put to use and friction prevented.

In this way, Gawaine became known as the High King's right hand, a forceful knight who shared the King's counsels and knew his mind. His quick temper was put down to his youth. Men respected him.

Meanwhile, Mordred and Lancelot came to an understanding. Thrown together as they were by Arthur's orders, each knowing the other bore a special place in the King's heart, they learned to work together. Gradually, Lancelot passed more and more of the daily work to Mordred, allowed him more freedom to make decisions, and finding him a sober, careful, hardworking man, let him take the reins of power into his own hands. Lancelot was still the Queen's Protector, but as time went by he allowed Mordred to assume most of the work as regent. In return, Mordred treated Lancelot with new respect and seemed to like him better.

"I may have been wrong about him, Gwen," Lancelot said to me once. "He is a good man and will make a good King. He understands men. His judgment is never colored by his feelings. This used to make me think him cold, but he is not. I used to think the army would not follow him. But now most of the soldiers are his age or younger, and have known since their first day here who he is. Perhaps, after all, Arthur is doing the right thing."

"That you should doubt him!" I cried, delighting in his words. "And when has Arthur ever done a wrong thing?"

"Not," Lancelot said very gently, "since he begat him."

One day late in summer I went riding on Rajid. The King was in Rheged, and Gawaine with him. Mordred sat in the workroom, reading petitions. Lancelot was out on the downs, drilling new recruits. I came in from my ride, dismissed my escort, and told Lyonel I would tend the horse myself, for I enjoyed it. I rubbed him down and brushed him, and put him in his big box, which looked out on the paddocks. He was tired, and stood quietly dozing. Grateful for a moment of solitude, I sat cross-legged in the clean straw in a corner and pulled an apple from my pouch. I was suddenly reminded of my girlhood in Gwynedd, when I used to hide in my horse's stall and overhear the grooms spreading palace gossip. Twenty years dropped from me as I sat there, for once again I heard voices coming down the aisle.

"I just don't understand it," a boy's voice said. "A good knight slain, your brother mortally wounded, and all for a woman? Why do men do it?"

"You will understand the attraction of women someday!" the other voice laughed. "Even when they are not witches, they weave a powerful spell."

"There are no witches," the young voice said firmly. "That is superstition."

"You may think so," the other replied indulgently, "but I know better. My mother was one. She had power."

"Then it was God's power, or Satan's. There is no other." This dogmatic assertion I recognized as Galahad's. The other voice, the gentle one, was Gareth's. They had pulled a horse out of his stall and, by the sound of it, were grooming him.

"Well, have it your way, then," Gareth said. "She had the devil in her, I will not argue that. But women can be angels, too. Linet is such a one. And the Queen is another."

"You know," Galahad said stiffly, "how I feel about the Queen."

"Yes, but you are awfully quick to judge her, for one so young. Can she help it if she is beautiful? It is a gift from God."

"But my father loves her!" the boy cried in anguish.

"And if he does?" Gareth's voice was gentle. "What of it? So does my lord Bedwyr. So does Galahantyn, Bors, Lyonel, Mordred, Ferron, and a hundred others I could name. So do I. Would you condemn us all?"

"Yes."

Gareth laughed. "What a young wolf you are! Time will teach you tolerance, I wager. The Queen has always treated me with kindness and forbearance. She is good, and gentle and charming, as well as lovely. It would be base of me indeed not to return her affection and respect."

"That is not what I mean," Galahad objected. "You know my father loves her in a different way."

But Gareth skirted the question. "What has she done, little prince, to hurt you so? Why do you hate her?"

"She was cruel to my mother!" He was near tears and struggling to control them. How my arms longed to reach out to him in comfort! "She hated my mother and banished her from court!"

"Now, now," Gareth said soothingly, "who has been telling these tales? All the world knows your mother was the Queen's best friend in childhood. They grew up together. Why, the Queen brought your mother to court when she married the King, and kept her near. Are these the marks of hatred, or of love?"

"My mother told me it herself," Galahad declared. "They were friends until she married my father. Then the Queen turned against her and sent her away. The Queen loves my father, Gareth. And he loves her, as he never loved my mother. He loves her not in the way that you do, or Sir Bedwyr. He loves her in the same way that the King does. As a wife. I know this to be true."

"Hssst! Hush, young tyrant! This is treason you accuse your father of! Now tell me truly, Galahad, were you there when the Queen broke with your mother? Do you know both sides of this quarrel? Then you do not know the truth of it, but only your mother's version. Let it be. It does not concern you. Why, if I had believed every tale my mother told me, where should I be now? As for Lancelot, he is a man of honor. If he were not, neither King nor Queen would love him. He has not betrayed the King, nor the King's bed, and he never will."

"He has broken God's commandment in his heart," came the implacable reply. "In God's eyes, he has lain with her a hundred times!"

My face was wet with tears, and I pinched myself hard, to keep from sobbing. My poor, dear Lancelot!

Gareth sighed heavily. "Oh, let it be. You cannot know that. If God so condemns every man who ever lusted after Guinevere, then in God's eyes Arthur is a thousand times cuckolded! Such things are fancies only. Forgive him, Galahad. We cannot help whom we love."

"I will not forgive him."

Gareth grunted. "Well, well, perhaps in time you will come to see the honor in him. No one is without sin, Galahad. Not even the High King. You must learn to forgive it."

"Mordred is an abomination." I gasped aloud, but they did not hear me, for the horse moved at that moment and scraped his hoof against the stone flooring.

"Watch your tongue!" Gareth cried. "He is my brother!"

"Yes," Galahad replied calmly. "He is your brother and your cousin both. He is abomination."

There was a long silence. At last, Gareth spoke gravely. "If you wish to live, little prince, you will learn to keep your thoughts to yourself. Mordred may well be your King someday."

"If he attempts it," Galahad said slowly and clearly, "I shall slay him."

"Oh, God!" I whispered, covering my face with my hands. "Oh, God! Oh, God help us all!"

Gareth hushed him and took him outside with the horse. I sat in Rajid's stall for over an hour, weeping. Galahad was then seven and a half years old.

23 ❀ The Slaughter

It was a black night. Thick clouds raced across the moon's face, and the trees in my garden bent double in the wind. I knelt at my bedside and prayed for the King's safety. What must the sea be like on such a night? The heavy leather flap between our chambers lifted in the gust, then fell to with a loud slap. Varric had not shuttered the unglazed windows in the King's room, for the night was not cold. But I had a good log fire in my own grate.

Even after prayers I felt restless and could not sleep. The castle was quiet, but I could not shake the feeling that something was amiss. The pretty songbird in his willow cage was fast asleep, head tucked under his yellow wing. From the antechamber I heard Ailsa's snores. I wondered if the noise kept Linet awake. We had had six new girls come to us that summer, and good Linet had given up her room and moved in with Ailsa, as her wedding was nigh anyway. I should miss her company terribly! Four years she had been with me, and a sweeter, kinder maiden I had never known. Now at seventeen she was a real beauty and hopelessly in love with Gareth. How lucky they were to marry for love! They waited only for the King's return to accomplish it. Gareth was now eighteen and knighted, a treasured Companion of the King. Lancelot loved him more dearly than his own son; he was incapable of meanness or dishonesty and could always be counted on to defend a just cause. I smiled to myself. It seemed like only yesterday Gareth had come to Camelot, a little boy holding tight to Mordred's hand. Now here he was grown and about to be married. Well, I told myself, at least Camelot was his home, and although Linet would exchange my service for his, she would live here and I should see her.

A stray draft set the flames dancing in the grate, and I shivered. What was this strange foreboding? Surely it could not concern the

King, for Niniane had sent no warning. The country was still at peace. Mordred's dream of a trading treaty with the West Saxons looked possible now that the Council had ratified Arthur and Cerdic's defense treaty. Only the situation with the Franks was unstable—but Arthur himself had gone to lend strength to Hoel. This was not a real threat to our peace, not yet. To honor Lancelot, Arthur had taken Galahad as his personal page, and also Gawaine, who now led a troop of cavalry under the King's command. Mordred was regent, and Lancelot Protector, as had been so twenty times before. Nothing was amiss or out of place. Then why could I not sleep?

I went to the glazed doors that gave onto my terrace and watched the angry wind beat down my garden plants. I knew what I should find in the morning—apples and pears all over the paving stones, split and bruised, a feast for the late bees. And leaves everywhere, and broken branches—oh, God! What was this heartache? I clasped my hands together at my breast and felt the pounding of my heart within. Something was amiss. I thought suddenly of Agravaine. He was just back from his yearly duty at Swiftwater, and Mordred had informed me that there was a meeting tonight in the room Agravaine and Gaheris shared in the town. I thought the King had been lenient with Agravaine; after dismissing him from service, he had commuted the sentence and agreed to let him return after three years, if he behaved. Such mercy angered me, but Arthur told me the boy had to have a future he valued, or nothing could temper his rashness. He had only one year to wait now, and although he had not killed anyone, which was all Arthur expected by good behavior, he remained an active thorn in Lancelot's side and a lodestone for every dissatisfied young hothead in the army. Because we had peace, kings and dukes lived to be old men, and their ambitious sons grew restive and eager to snatch power. These were the kind of men Agravaine gathered around him. Gaheris, healed of his dreadful wounds and bearing horrible scars, lived with him, forever banned from the King's presence and having nothing in his heart but hate. Mordred they no longer trusted, since he had begun to assume power in the King's absence and had come to better terms with Lancelot. But Mordred was clever and kept a close watch on their movements and their meetings. Gareth was never of their party, for he loved Lancelot more than any man but Arthur, finding in him the father he had never had. Thus far, Mordred assured me, their meetings did no more than give vent to their feelings; they drank and diced and whored and slept it off. But I did not like having such ruffians so close. Was it this that made me nervous? Mordred knew of the meeting; surely his spies would watch the house. All the castle guards were loyal to the King. Lancelot, Mordred, and Gareth were the three best swordsmen in Britain, after the King, so what was to fear?

I shrugged and drew the soft curtain across the terrace doors. The truth was, I thought with a grim smile, I missed Arthur. I missed his company and the peace of mind his presence brought. And I missed him for another reason. When he was gone, Lancelot and I could not so much as look at one another. But when Arthur was there, when he was with us, we could touch and gaze and find some little relief. How cruel, I often thought, that it should be so. No one, not even Galahad, dared speak about us to the King. Thus did he grant us his protection.

Suddenly I heard footsteps and whispered voices below my stairs. Trembling, I stood by the fire and tried to compose myself. In a moment, Linet came up and peeked hesitantly into the room.

"My lady Queen! You are up! A courier has just ridden in, with a message from the King."

"Let him come up then." She beckoned behind her, and a young man, still breathing hard from his exertions, stepped into the room and knelt at my feet. In his hand was a scroll with the High King's seal.

"I come from the coast my lady," he recited quickly. "The King put ashore today at Potter's Bay. He pushes on with the cavalry without delay; he may be no more than an hour or two behind me. He gave this to me himself and bade me deliver it into no hands but your own." He ducked his head, his message complete, and withdrew hastily.

"Stay, Linet," I bade her, "until I have read this, to see if there is some reply."

I broke the seal and saw the neat Latin hand of Arthur's scribe. It was a short note only, to inform me of his early return and imminent arrival. But the language was urgent and hidden in it was a warning. 'Send for Lancelot and Mordred,' it said, 'and tell them this news, but do it secretly, that no others may know of my coming, or even guess at it.' After that, it was signed with his love. I looked up at Linet.

"Three things, Linet. First, see that the courier is housed apart and is allowed to speak with no man until morning. Impress upon him that his mission is secret. No one is to know he comes from the King."

"Yes, my lady. He is very full of this knowledge already, my lady. He would not tell us from whom he came, but I would not let him see you without knowing the source of the message."

"Who among my women knows his errand?"

"Only myself and Ailsa."

"Good. Next, send a page to Sir Mordred to beg him come to me at once. Do not tell him why, only that it is an emergency. Tell him the Queen commands his presence."

"Commands?" Linet asked, startled.

"Third. Send to Sir Lancelot with the same message. Command him to attend me here. At once."

Her eyes widened, and she curtsied low. "Yes, my lady."

"Oh, and one thing more. Perhaps most important of all. See that I am well attended. I want six or seven maids below, fully dressed, and you and Ailsa in this chamber. You have ten minutes."

She flew downstairs, and I went back to the fire to scan the letter. What was it Arthur feared, that he could not say straight out? Some treachery at home? From whom did he wish to keep his coming secret? I tucked the letter in my pocket and pulled my little stool to the hearth. There was another chair in the corner, which I dragged over, and then I got a third one from the King's chamber. When all was ready, I inspected myself in the polished bronze. My robe was of cream-colored velvet, with long, close-fitting sleeves and a high throat. Only the toes of my slippers showed beneath it. It was the chastest garment in the entire castle. My hair was braided for the night and held in a net. Satisfied that no one could take me for a siren, I sat on my stool, closed my eyes, and waited.

Within minutes I heard Lancelot's voice belowstairs, urging Ailsa to hurry and refusing to ascend before her. Linet came in first, then Ailsa, gray-haired and bent with the pains of age. They took their places at the doorway and curtsied as Lancelot entered. He was fully dressed, but shod in slippers and had come, this time, without his sword.

"Guinevere! What is it?" he cried, taking my hand and pressing it to his lips. Our eyes met and locked; then carefully, he lowered his and bowed.

"I have had a message from the King," I told him. "Let us wait for Mordred."

He looked up in surprise. "Did you send for Mordred? He's not in the castle. I know this, because a half hour since I tried to find him myself and bade his chamberlain send to me when he returned. I have heard nothing yet."

I gasped and felt my breath come faster. "My lord, you came to me alone?" I whispered.

Anger and bitterness flashed across his face, instantly suppressed. "No. I am not a fool. Three men attend me beyond the outer door. One of them is Gareth. He was up, unable to sleep. So I brought him."

At that moment, one of my maids appeared at the doorway, breathless, to say that Sir Mordred could not be found.

I nodded. "Very well, Lise, tell them to keep looking. See that he comes to me the instant he is found." She scurried back down the stairs to her post below, and I bade Lancelot take a chair.

As he read the King's letter, I held my hands to the fire to warm them. They trembled uncontrollably. At last, after scanning it a third time, he put the scroll down.

"Well?" I asked. "What does it mean, my lord?"

He shook his head. "I do not know. He has had some information is my guess." He glanced swiftly at Ailsa and Linet. Ailsa had been with me since Northgallis, and Linet was Gareth's betrothed. He could trust them. "It seems he fears some treachery, but in truth, Gwen, I know not what it is."

"Well," I whispered, "so long as you and Mordred are free of suspicion, I can bear the waiting. The courier said he might be here within two hours."

"Good." He shut his lips tight on the word, then looked into my eyes with longing. I had to look away to keep from blushing.

All of a sudden we heard raised voices and the heavy tread of boots. Then a hoarse shout, from the King's room! Lancelot leaped to his feet and faced the curtain. I screamed as a sword thrust through—suddenly the room was full of men, armed and stinking of stale mead—one Liander was foremost, a Welshman. He was drunk. His sword waved before Lancelot's face. Mellyot from Gwynedd was behind him, and then Agravaine, Gaheris, Collgren, Mador, Lovell, and last, behind them in Arthur's chamber, I saw Mordred running up. Everything that happened, happened at once, and yet I saw it—I see it still—as if it happened in a different time, slowly unfolding like the petals of a flower.

"Put up your swords!" Lancelot shouted. "I am naked!" It went against all the rules of knighthood to attack an unarmed man, but their intent was clear from their faces. All their swords were drawn.

"You are ever naked when you lie with the Queen!" Gaheris screamed, pushing Liander forward. Lancelot ducked the raised sword, grabbed my little stool, and brought it up against Liander's sword arm, at the same time landing a hard blow across his wrist. The man bellowed in pain as the bone snapped, but in the next instant he lay dead at Mellyot's feet, run through by his own weapon, which Lancelot now held before him.

"Cowards!" he cried, enraged. "Swine! Get out!"

"Traitor!" Gaheris and Agravaine howled together, surging forward. Then the room was alive with clashing swords, and blood sprayed everywhere.

"Gare-e-e-th!" Linet screamed, backing toward the landing, clutching Ailsa. "Gare-e-eth!"

I pressed flat against the wall, unable to breathe, watching Lancelot defend himself against them all. His rage was an unholy thing, wild and possessive. He was blind to all else but the pressing blades. He did not see Gareth come bounding up the steps to his aid; he did not hear Mordred shouting to them to stop, in the King's name. He slew Agravaine with no more thought than he'd waste on a Saxon, he slew Mellyot, and Lovell behind him. Gareth came forward, sword raised in his defense; Lancelot saw the weapon only and ran his blade through Gareth's breast. He turned to the next foe, while Linet fell screaming over Gareth's body. When Agravaine fell, Gaheris had turned to me, blood lust in his eyes.

"Bitch!" he shrieked. "Whore! This is your death day!" I gasped as he leveled his sword and came at me. But Mordred got between us and engaged him. Lancelot whirled and took him in the throat. Gaheris, killer of women, died at my very feet, and his blood soaked my slippers. Mordred looked up to find Lancelot's sword pointed at his breast. Contempt swept Lancelot's features; he lunged, and Mordred blocked the blow. I cried out, but he never heard me. Linet was wailing, the women were all screaming, and the King's guards were thundering up the King's stairs. Everyone else was dead.

Mordred was skilled, but no one could match Lancelot man to man; yet Lancelot did not kill him. He had opportunity, more than once, and I saw that even in his fury, for Arthur's sake, he would preserve his son's life. Finally, with the guards at the curtain, Lancelot locked his blade and tripped him, wrenching the sword from his hand. Mordred staggered.

"Coward!" Mordred gasped, reaching for his dagger. In exasperation more than anger, Lancelot ran his sword through Mordred's shoulder. The dagger dropped; Mordred lunged, slipped, knocked his head against my bedpost, and fell senseless to the floor. Lancelot stood alone in the slaughter, covered in the blood of his attackers, breathing heavily. Slowly his vision cleared, and he saw me.

"Gwen!" he gasped. "Is that blood yours? Are you hurt?"

Dazed, I looked down at my spattered robe and stepped out of the pool of Gaheris' blood. I could not speak, but shook my head. He came to me and took me in his arms, pressing me close. His whole body shuddered violently, and I felt him sob. I was numbed. I felt nothing. I saw, without interest, that even the bed hangings were spattered with blood; my mother's little stool was broken, the fine needlework slashed beyond repair, the birdcage lay trampled on the bloody carpet, the bird gone. Eight men lay dead, and the King's son wounded, and all by his hand.

The guards at the curtain didn't know what to do. They looked anxiously at me for some sign. Linet wept uncontrollably over Gareth, and Ailsa with her. Finally, Lancelot seemed to notice them. He looked up and shook his head, as if to clear it.

"What is that? Who has fallen?"

Then, slowly, feeling flooded back, and with it, terror. I gripped his arms, to keep him by me.

"It is Gareth."

"GARETH?" he cried. In anguish, he tried to free himself from my grip. "Dear God! Gareth! Let me go, Gwen, I must see to him!"

"No, my lord. Don't add to her pain. I saw the stroke. He is dead."

"I will be revenged for it!" he cried, on a sob. "Who slew him?"

I did not answer, and Linet looked up then. He saw his answer written on her face. He went still, grew pale and began to tremble.

"No! No!" he whispered frantically, turning to me in desperation. "No, tell me it was not I! Please, Gwen, if you love me!"

I wished I could weep, but the tears would not come. My throat ached so that I could hardly speak.

"You were not yourself, Lancelot," I whispered hoarsely, "when you killed him."

"Ahhhhh!" he cried, and covering his face, sank against the wall.

Then I beckoned to the captain of the guard. "Take Sir Lancelot to his chambers and guard them well. Let no one in or out save the King's physician." To everyone there, it sounded as if I was putting him under house arrest, and they were all amazed. But I was thinking of Arthur, who was due in soon, with Gawaine at his side. The guards were for Lancelot's protection.

"Take Sir Mordred to the physicians first and have them see to
his wound. He is not mortally hurt, I think, but we must be sure.
And after that, clear the bodies from my room." I shuddered.
"Alone of them all, take Sir Gareth to the chapel. His will be a
burial with honor. The others—I will instruct you later what to do
with them."

The captain bowed low, relieved to have definite orders. "It
will be done, my lady."

"After that, have this room cleaned. Take everything out. I—I
cannot bear it!"

"Yes, my lady," he said swiftly, afraid of tears. I turned and
helped Ailsa pull Linet from Gareth's body. She was faint with
weeping and as limp as a rag. We got her downstairs and put her
to bed with hot bricks in her blankets and a cold cloth on her
brow. Poor Ailsa was not much better. I made her take some
brandy and put her to bed, as well. The six maids who had been
below during the slaughter stood huddled by the door. They were
frightened out of their wits but could not leave until dismissed.
When Ailsa was settled, I dismissed them, all except one, whom
I bade stay and keep watch upon the others. Then I went out and
stood in my sitting room, alone and dazed. I did not know what
to do. Bedwyr! I thought. I must find dear Bedwyr! I rummaged
through Ailsa's trunks until I found a cloak. It hid most of the
bloodstains. With this wrapped around me, I hurried through the
corridors to the King's library. The sentries stared at me as I went
by, against regulations. As I reached the library door, Kay came
around the corner and saw me. His jaw dropped.

"Queen Guinevere!"

He ran up and took my arm. I had not realized I was shaking
so, until I felt his firm support. "Come, my lady, come in here. I
will light the fire."

"Bedwyr!" I whispered.

"Yes, I'll send for Bedwyr." He snapped an order over his
shoulder to the nearest sentry and gently led me into the room. It
was cold and dark, and the fire had long gone out. I was astounded at this; in my mind's eye I had seen it as I always saw
it, warm and bright and comforting. I could not be thinking
clearly. Perhaps Kay was right when he put me in the King's big
chair and covered me with blankets.

He lit the fire himself, good man, and tended me like a servant
until the page brought Bedwyr. He was quickly dressed, and still
tousled from sleep. I had not thought how late it was.

"What's up, Kay?" he said, covering a yawn. "The sentries look as if they've seen a ghost."

"They've seen the Queen, which is near enough. Here, boy!" he called out to the page. "We'll need some warm spiced wine and some hot bricks. Be quick about it, there's a lad."

"What's amiss with the Queen?" Bedwyr asked sharply, and then coming to where Kay stood, he saw me in the chair and gasped.

"Gwen!" He took my hand. "She's cold as ice! What in the name of Mithra has happened? There's blood in her hair!"

"Aye." Kay kept his voice low, although no one else was in the room. "There have been doings aplenty this night. I've just come from Sir Mordred and the physicians—he's been in a swordfight."

"Does he live?" Bedwyr cried, paling.

"Aye, he's very lucky. Got his shoulder sliced is all. It's clean. He was awake. He would not say how he got it. He bade me go and rescue the Queen."

"Rescue?" Bedwyr whispered, staring at me. "From what?"

"Krinian made only a brief report. I will tell you what I know. There are eight men dead in the Queen's bedchamber, and she has locked Lancelot in his room and put guards at his door."

Bedwyr whistled slowly and dropped to his knees, holding my hands and looking worriedly into my face. "Is this true?" he asked softly. "Gwen, can you tell us?"

My teeth began to chatter, and I clenched my jaw to keep them still. Bedwyr rubbed my hands between his own. Arthur's hound Cabal came up and pushed his head in between us, sniffing, nosing under the blankets. Bedwyr shoved him aside.

"When the physicians are free, send them here," Bedwyr said. Kay rose as the door opened, and the wine and warming bricks came in. He arranged silver goblets on a tray nearby and set the wineskin to warm above a flame. Then he went to a shelf behind the King's work table and took down a silver brandy flask. He poured a little in a cup and held it to my lips.

"Drink this, my lady. Just a sip will do." But it smelled foul, and I turned my face away. Bedwyr's grip on my hands tightened, and he pleaded gently with me.

"Please, Gwen. Please take some, for my sake. Arthur trusts us to take care of you, and we would not betray that trust." And because once before I had ignored his ministrations and suffered by it, I obeyed him and swallowed the fiery liquid. It left me gasping, and my eyes grew wet, but still tears would not come. I shivered as the fire burned in my belly, then slowly spread its gentle warmth throughout my body. I felt better, and Bedwyr saw it.

"By all the gods that are," he breathed, "I bless your courage! Say nothing yet—I see you cannot do it. Let me slip these bricks under your feet." He lifted the blankets and cried out in horror.

"Kay! See this! Her shoes are soaked in blood! And the hem of her robe—no wonder the dog was interested. By the Bull, there has been a battle!"

Kay came over, frowning, and sent for a bath slave, for towels and hot water. "Bring her women here!" he commanded, and I struggled to arise.

"No!" I cried, my voice a shadow of itself. "No, they cannot come! They cannot—they saw it—they are abed—they cannot—do not ask it of them!" Bedwyr gently pushed me down into the chair. I could not believe how little strength I had.

Kay turned toward me and spoke kindly. "They saw this blood-letting? Then we will leave them and tend to you ourselves. Dear God, I wish the King were here!"

I gasped, suddenly remembering his letter. He was almost here! He was coming! But it was a secret, and I could not tell them! I looked wildly from Kay to Bedwyr.

"Gawaine!" I cried, and my voice flew free, echoing off the walls. They jumped. "Oh, find him, Kay! Take Gawaine and lock him in a safe place and let him speak to no one—*to no one*—until the King has heard it. As you value your life, do this!"

Kay looked bewildered. "But Sir Gawaine is in Brittany, my lady, with the King."

I groaned, hugging myself, and rocked slowly forward and back. "Gawaine will be here. He will be here within the hour. Do not let him speak to anyone. Not anyone. It is as much as his life is worth. If he dies, I shall die with him."

Kay stared, astonished, but Bedwyr's eyes narrowed. He caught the change of reference; he knew I spoke of Lancelot at the last. In an instant, he saw a glimmer of what had happened, and rose, taking command.

"Do as she says, Kay. Set extra guards at the entrance, in case he rides in. Stop him at King's Gate and have him escorted. Be sure to treat him with honor, but seal him off from rumor. There is more here than we yet know. Trust the Queen."

Kay obeyed and left us. Bedwyr knelt at my feet.

"What is it, Gwen? Here, take this wine and sip it slowly. It will calm you. Trust me. It is Lancelot you fear for, is it not?"

I took the wine and nodded, shivering and rocking, my eyes upon the fire.

"After this night's work, Gawaine will want to kill him?"

I nodded again and drank thirstily, emptying the cup.

He took it from me. "Then Lancelot has slain one of his brothers?" I met his eyes and groaned.

He gripped me hard, to stop my rocking. "Which one? Agravaine? Gaheris?"

From deep within me I felt the pain beginning, and my breath came in quick gasps, as it fought its way up and out.

Bedwyr began to shake me and call my name. "Guinevere! Stop! Oh, Gwen! Please don't!"

But it could not be stopped. I heard wild laughing and then an unearthly shriek; it was my voice; it came from me, my body ripped by searing pain, and I bent double, falling into Bedwyr's arms.

"Ahhhhhhhh! All! All! He has killed them all! Oh, Bedwyr, what will Arthur do!" I was sick, I think; I lost my senses for a while, but I remember the sweet, sickly smell of it through the fog of feeling, as he held me tightly across both his arms and sat with me close to the fire to warm me. He wept himself; I remember his tears falling on my cheek. He wept for Gareth; he wept for Lancelot; he wept for Arthur and the good fellowship of his Companions, now forever broken. I pressed my face into his shoulder and gave myself to weeping. I lay racked with sobs, I don't know how long, until I was exhausted and could no longer cry, but only twitched helplessly with grief. I believed myself close to death; I even wished for it.

Bedwyr groaned and kissed my face.

"We must believe, my dear Gwen," he whispered. "It is the will of the gods. We must believe."

At last the door flew open, and I heard Arthur's voice.

"Bedwyr! Where is the Queen?"

Bedwyr straightened quickly. "Here, my lord!"

In four strides he was with me, and I looked up into his face. He paled, and his eyes grew dark.

"Guinevere!"

"My lord," I whispered, but no sound came out. He pulled aside the cloak and looked at my bloodstained robe.

Gently he took me from Bedwyr and placed me in the chair. Behind him stood Kay, and the bath slave, and a host of dusty soldiers.

"Get out! Close the door!" he barked. "Kay, do I not still employ physicians?"

"Yes, my lord," replied Kay, who was not used to rebukes from the King. "But at present they are with Mordred."

Arthur hesitated a fraction, then said shortly, "Is he mortally wounded?"

"No, my lord."

"Then surely he can spare one of them to tend the Queen. Get him!"

Kay withdrew. Arthur glared at the bath slave, who deposited his burdens at the King's feet and dashed out. Gently Arthur removed the sodden slippers and washed my cold, stained feet himself. He would not let Bedwyr assist him, and Bedwyr, remembering a time long past when I had bathed the King, did not insist. He dried my feet and wrapped them in the warm towels the bricks had come in, then placed them on the bricks.

"Why is she not attended?" he snapped at Bedwyr.

"She would not let us send for her women—she said they saw what happened—I gathered they were in the same state."

Arthur's face looked pinched. "But she is the Queen," he said evenly, "and they her servants. Go yourself and bring one of them here with a robe. This thing reeks—I will have it off her. Go."

It was odd, how I could see him and hear him so clearly, and feel the touch of his hands, but I could not speak, or move, or do anything of my own will. I felt empty and drained of strength. I was content to give myself into his care. Slowly, awkwardly, he got the filthy robe off me and rubbed my poor body with the blankets, and wrapped me tightly in them. Bedwyr was back soon after, dragging poor Lise in her nightdress, carrying a blue robe. The child had been weeping, for her face was swollen, and she was frightened to death to find herself face to face with the King. But he had no time for courtesies.

"Stand at the door, let no one enter," he commanded Bedwyr. Then he directed the poor child to help him dress me. She blushed a thousand shades of pink at my nakedness, but Arthur was gruff with her and bore no hesitations. Try as I might to help them, my limbs would not obey me. Between them, they got me dressed at last. Arthur tucked the blankets in around me, thanked the girl, and dismissed her, and then called Bedwyr in. Kay and the physician were close behind. God bless Arthur, he would not let the man leech me; he knew I had a horror of it. So the physician contented himself with mixing me a posset and advising more heat to my feet.

"She's had a shock," he told the King. Arthur kicked him out. He stood Kay and Bedwyr before him.

"Tell me what you know."

While they spoke, I began to feel a lazy warmth seep into my limbs, and gradually, as I relaxed, I drifted into sleep. When I awoke, Cabal had his head in my lap, and the King stood before the fire, alone, watching me. I tried my limbs gingerly and found they obeyed me. I pushed myself up straighter. I felt lightheaded, but myself again. Cabal's tail beat eagerly against the floor. Arthur came and knelt at my feet, taking my hands. His face was grave, the lines of care carved deep from nose to mouth. His warm, loving eyes were desperately worried. I tried a smile, and found that my lips moved at least a little.

"Oh, Arthur!" It came out in a whisper. "I am glad you are home!"

He kissed my hand and laid his head in my lap, whispering a prayer of thanksgiving. He did not care that I heard it. I stroked his hair gently. The dog's big tongue licked my hand in joy.

"You will want to know what happened."

He lifted his head. "There is no need. I have seen Mordred."

I shook my head. "He did not see it all. I saw it all, Arthur. I saw it all."

He closed his eyes and bowed his head. "So you did. All right. Tell me."

I told him all of it, without a tremor; it was like taking a great burden, which I could hardly bear, and placing it on his strong shoulders. He bore it for me, and I could breathe again.

When I finished, he sighed deeply, and a smile touched his lips. "And after that, you had sense to give clear orders to the guards and to tend Linet and Ailsa. I tell you, Gwen, you have more courage than many of my soldiers. If you could learn to wield a sword, I would make you a captain of my horse." Then he rose and paced once about the room.

"Where is Gawaine?" I asked him suddenly.

"With Ferron. In the Round Hall. We were met by your orders at King's Gate. I saw them obeyed. I knew there was a reason."

"Have you—have you spoken with him yet?" And he knew by my voice that I did not mean Gawaine.

"No," he said wearily. "Not yet. You came first."

"He was naked, and they attacked him."

"I know, Gwen."

"He did not even know Gareth was in the room, until after."

"I know."

"And Mordred—he thought he was one of them—it was an easy mistake to make, he followed them in. And he had three chances to run him through and let them pass. He only wounded him to disarm him."

"So Mordred told me."

I stopped, my lips dry. Arthur handed me a winecup, and I took it. My hand was trembling. "What will you do?"

He looked at me with compassion and then sighed. "I don't know. But after this, Britain will be too small to hold them both."

I met his eyes. "Yes. I see that."

He shrugged. "Then they have taken it out of my hands."

I said nothing. He was right.

He could not keep Gawaine waiting much longer, so at last he sent for Lancelot. He bade me keep my chair and himself stood near me, so that we received him together. Lancelot came, scrubbed clean and ready for the road. Grief for Gareth had already etched new lines in his face. He saluted Arthur and kissed his ring. When he rose, he stood with a soldier's straightness and waited for his commander's judgment. But Arthur, who loved him, embraced him.

"Lancelot!" he cried in a low voice. "Was there no other way?"

Lancelot shrugged, but his eyes were wet. "I am your servant, Arthur. Do with me what you must."

Arthur spread his hands out helplessly. "What can I do? I must send you home. You cannot stay in Britain. And keep a guard around you, all the days of your life."

Lancelot nodded. "You are merciful, my lord. It is more than I deserve."

Arthur swung an arm around him and gripped him by the shoulders. "You are my right hand. My shield. My other, better self. A warrior with stainless honor. A man without compromise. You deserve better of me than banishment. I only do it to save your life."

Lancelot cleared his throat. "And Galahad. Will you keep him with you? He is better here than in Lanascol. With me."

"Whatever you will."

"That's all I ask. Except—" He paused, and with an effort kept his voice steady. "Except to beg your pardon for wounding your son. I saw his raised sword in front of the Queen—I wanted only to disarm him, but he is too good a swordsman."

"Thanks to your teaching," Arthur said, his voice gone suddenly rough. "Lancelot, I know well all you did was in defense of the Queen. You saved her life tonight. You know what that means to me. It is not a gift I can repay. Were it not for Gareth, I could square things with Gawaine and keep you here. Everyone else deserved to die."

Lancelot nodded but could not speak. He would never forgive himself.

Arthur embraced him again and kissed him on both cheeks. "I will have Ferron arrange an escort. You'd best be gone tonight. The ship we took still lies at Potter's Bay. I'll send a courier to the captain." He looked at us both with sadness. "I give you an hour to take your leave of the Queen. Be gone when I return." Tears crept from Lancelot's eyes as Arthur left, setting a guard upon the door.

Lancelot sank to the floor at my feet, and I cradled his head in my lap. There was nothing to say. Arthur might sail to Lanascol, but unless Gawaine should die, I would never see Lancelot again.

"Guinevere," he said at last. "Do you remember when I came to take you out of Wales, long ago, and you did not believe me when I told you the kind of man King Arthur was?"

"Yes, my dear, I remember it well."

"Now you see the truth. There is not another like him in the world."

I smiled. "Sweet Lancelot, this is not news."

He looked up and held my gaze. "When I am gone, do not grieve for me and pine for what might have been. Give him the love you would have spent on me. He is worthier by far."

"Lancelot," I slid down and sat beside him, and embraced him. "Dearest Lancelot. I would do it if I could. But you know well what is between us is beyond my power. From the moment of our meeting, I have loved you. I will love you always, past parting, past death."

He kissed me and held me close. "If I had life to live again," he said, "I would change nothing."

He held me thus and kissed me, and we talked of times long past, of Wales and of Camelot when the Kingdom was young. We even came to laughter once or twice. We had not shared such closeness since I tended him on Ynys Witrin, ten years before. And we kept coming back to Arthur.

"He has done it," Lancelot marveled. "He has fulfilled our dreams. Where he has fallen short, it is because other men failed him."

So in Arthur we found solace for our souls; and when at last he took his leave of me, our eyes were dry. We shared a pride that Arthur's honor was untarnished. When he had gone, I wept most bitterly awhile, but these were tears of self-pity, and I soon stopped them.

I sat by the fire and stroked Cabal, afraid to look into the future, afraid to recall the past. When Arthur returned, he found me thus, and joined me on the hearth.

"Well, I have done what I could, Gwen."

"Was Gawaine wild when you told him?"

"Indeed. But there is only one door to the Round Hall, and I stood before it. Had I not been High King, I think he might have run me through, to get to Lancelot."

"He is safely away?"

"Yes. With Ferron and an escort. I made it quite clear to Gawaine I want no more killing here. He understands the twins behaved as traitors and, had they lived, must have suffered hanging. Their lives were forfeit the moment they entered your chamber. But Gareth—" He paused and shrugged. "Gareth's death is cause for vengeance. Not even Lancelot denies it. I had to allow the justice of his complaint."

"Of course, my lord. Where is he now?"

"I sent him to see Mordred. He wanted a firsthand account; he wants to vent his anger and say his piece. Mordred will listen. I am tired of it."

His face, turned to the fire, looked carved in stone; a noble face, but lined with care and weary of the burdens a King carries. Mordred is twenty-one, I thought suddenly. I am glad of it. But will he ever be as strong as this King?

"I have given Gawaine Orkney. After we bury Gareth with full honor, I will invest Gawaine with kingship. Then he will travel north to take up his rule."

I let out a long breath in relief. "How wise you are, my lord! Sending Gawaine north and Lancelot south."

He shrugged. "Temporarily expedient. Orkney is a small place for a man of Gawaine's energy. He will be back."

"He cannot go to Brittany without your leave?"

"He is a king now. He can do what he wants. He can risk my displeasure and the consequences it brings."

"But he will swear allegiance to you when you invest him?"

"Oh, yes. But then, he made an oath to Drustan once."

I clasped his hand tightly and, once again, drew strength from him. "Oh, Arthur, how I grieve for your good fellowship of knights, now torn asunder! It is not right that you should have to give your time to these feuds and rivalries, when there is so much else to do."

He smiled briefly and lifted his shoulders. "If Kingship were only battles, it would be easy," he said. "This may turn out well, Gwen. Who knows? They may both live to serve me; the group of rebels is disbanded; our treaties are not affected. And Lancelot in Lanascol makes Less Britain stronger, and that is where trouble will next arise."

With a gasp I recalled his letter. "Arthur! Why did you send the letter? What treachery did you fear? Was it this?"

He laughed bitterly and shook his head. "No, indeed! I wish now I had never sent it! If Lancelot had not been followed to your chamber—"

"Never mind that," I broke in hastily. "Why did you send it?"

"I had word through a traveling merchant that Constantine was on the move, and with troops. To me, that meant only one thing: an attempt on Camelot, and Mordred. But I did not like to say so, in case he had an informer here."

"Do you suspect that, my lord?"

He sighed and passed a hand across his brow. "With Gawaine beside me, I suspect everyone. He sees phantoms everywhere. No one is safe from his suspicion. Not even Mordred."

"Why Mordred? He knows your plans for Mordred."

"Yes, but he does not like them. Remember, as a child, he was used to thinking Mordred a fatherless bastard, and beneath him."

"But now he knows he is your son!"

"Yes," Arthur said wearily, "but he suspects him of the same ambition all Agravaine's friends suffer from—of wishing to supplant their fathers upon the throne."

"You know this is not true of Mordred."

"Yes." Arthur spoke gently. "I know it. I did not say Gawaine was wise or knew men. Just that he is eager to see slights everywhere. It is my blessed sister's legacy to me, this bloodbath, this disruption of my peace."

I grieved to hear him speak so gloomily and longed to bring the light back to his face.

"Tell me about Mordred, my lord. I meant to ask after him before. How fares he? Is he in pain?"

Arthur grimaced. "Pain enough. Lancelot knew well what he was about and missed the bone. The physicians have stitched it, as Merlin taught them, and with luck he will keep the use of his arm. But it is his first real battle wound," Arthur said, sounding a little amazed, "and he is a grown man."

"That is a testament to your Kingship. Tell me what he said

about the attack on Lancelot. And where was he when we could not find him?"

"Ah, yes," Arthur said, brightening. "He was in the town, spying on Agravaine and his friends. They were drunk and tending to violence, and he wished to keep them from causing trouble. Someone came running from the castle to say Lancelot had gone secretly to the Queen's room, alone."

"This, though he brought three attendants and came at my summons!" I cried, aghast.

"I know, Gwen. This news roused them. They thought they saw their chance and took up their swords and broke into my apartments. Mordred followed them, and when he saw what they meant to do, he tried to stop them. But they were too many and pushed him aside. He sent for the house guard and ran after them to my room."

"Just in time to stop Gaheris and save my life!" I shuddered. "Did he really threaten you?"

"Indeed, my lord. He called me names and leveled his sword at my heart."

"Mordred told me what he said," he said shortly. Then his voice softened. "Yet he was loath to name Lancelot as his attacker. He kept silent before Kay and Bedwyr. He only told me because I commanded him, straight out. He assured me that Lancelot mistook him for one of the conspiracy."

"Yes," I said sadly. "Lancelot always mistook him."

Arthur rose and helped me up. "Well, it is over. I pray God for a space of peace, to bury the dead and regroup. Can you sleep, Gwen? Or would you like a potion?"

"Oh, Arthur!" I cried, shivering. "Do not send me back to my quarters! It will take a week to clean away the blood!"

He gently put his arms about me. "That is not what I meant. Of course you shall not go back. Stay with me until you are ready to brave your chamber again. But can you rest, or should I send for a sleeping draught?"

Relieved and comforted, I slipped my arms around him. "Such rest as I can find in your arms, my dear Arthur, is all the rest I desire."

At last, at long last, his face lit with joy, and he smiled.

ThE hIGh KING

The Threat
The Queen's Dilemma
The Rescue
The King
The Wicked Day of Destiny

24 ✹ the threat

I was out riding when the courier came from Brittany. It was a cold March day with a fitful wind and small, fierce showers of rain. Not a day for sailing, but ships could always get across if the message was dire enough. I rode with Bedwyr and Ferron and three others, far across the downs to the eastern woodlands, just for the pleasure of exercise and riding free in the wind. Ferron teased me that I enjoyed riding in bad weather, but Bedwyr seemed to understand my restlessness. I believe he felt it, too.

Truth was, the King was aging. He was but forty, with a third of life ahead, and yet he laughed less often, brooded more, and seemed sometimes to long for times gone by. Ever since Lancelot's banishment five years before, grief had grown upon him and slowly encircled him, until even his closest friends longed for the daring warrior they had once known. Bedwyr was near his age and was not so changed. I did not understand this deep sorrow. Sometimes the King was more my father than my husband, though only five years older; when he called me his child queen, it made me want to scream. He knew he was changing, and he knew I was not.

When he sent Lancelot away, it took something out of him that could not be replaced. Only a few of us could make him smile: Bedwyr, Mordred, and especially Gawaine. Gawaine was the high-spirited Companion whose jests and boasts and antics could bring light into the King's face. And for this I honored him. He loved Arthur deeply and would have done anything he asked, excepting only forgive Gareth's murder.

So we galloped over the downs that day and missed the courier. We little thought the future was so close upon us. I raced Ferron, and won; raced Bedwyr, and lost by a nose; for my new stallion was only four and, although faster than Bedwyr's gray, could not go ten strides without bucking. At last, tired and laughing, we turned for home. Halfway back, we were met by horsemen bearing the High King's banner. The messenger's face was grave. Sir Bedwyr and Sir Ferron were summoned at once to Council in the Round Hall. They saluted me and left. The remaining guard formed close around me, and we followed hard upon their heels.

In the stable Lyonel and two grooms were gathered around a tired black gelding whose head hung low. They had covered him with blankets; his coat was drenched, his neck steaming. The grooms sponged his legs with cold water. That was when I knew there had been a courier.

I beckoned Lyonel closer. "When did the courier ride in, Lyonel?"

"About an hour hence, my lady."

"And where from?"

He cleared his throat. "From Less Britain, my lady."

I met his eyes. "From whom?" But he shook his head. He would have loved to tell me the man came from Lancelot, but he did not know. I thanked him and went back to tend the stallion myself. While I worked, my thoughts drifted to my old friend, so long gone from me. Arthur had been twice to see him and had told me he looked well. He and Galahantyn had formed a strong alliance with old Hoel, their neighbor, and had treaties with King Childebert of the Franks. Galahantyn had married a Breton girl, who adored him, and she was raising Lancélot's younger sons along with her own. He seemed, said Arthur, to have found a sort of peace in this close family and to have grown into a king.

I looked up as a groom led another horse in. This one I recognized: a chestnut mare with a white star and a white stocking on her near hind. She belonged to Niniane, and she was sweating. I went immediately to find Lyonel.

"Did a messenger leave Camelot for Avalon after the courier arrived?"

"Why, no, my lady. What's amiss?" he replied, seeing my distress.

I shrugged. "I don't know that anything is amiss. But Niniane is here. Send a groom to see to my stallion. I must find her."

All I could think of, as I hurried to my quarters to bathe and change, was that Niniane had come unbidden. That meant she had known through her Sight that she was needed. Something of great importance had happened, or was about to happen, and it concerned Arthur.

My girls dressed me quickly, and before the hour was out I was waiting nervously in the King's library for the Council to be over. If only I were allowed in Council! As the High King's advisor, Niniane, alone of all women, could attend. To exclude me was mere foolishness; the King shared all his thoughts with me, and took my advice and valued my opinion enough to argue with me when we differed—what more did his Companions do? Some of them, like Gawaine, did not even do that, but simply shouted out their feelings and gave no thought at all to what they said. Simply because I could not lift a sword—I laughed to myself and quit this foolish thinking. I had no desire to be numbered among the men; rarely did I wish for the honor of sitting through the drudgery of Council meetings. I was merely impatient for news!

I strode across the room and back again, Cabal following at my heels. I tried to imagine what the news could be. Had Hoel died? He had been ailing for years. But he had grown sons who had sworn allegiance to Arthur and who were friends of Lancelot. Hoel's dying could not be a disaster, however unexpected. And if Niniane were here, the news must be dire. Could aught have befallen Lancelot? But Galahantyn was there, and loyal. All Less Britain was bound with treaties. Perhaps Childebert had died, or been supplanted. That might require Arthur's presence across the Narrow Sea. But would it bring Niniane out of her fastness? I shivered. Niniane's presence frightened me. I feared that whatever news had come cast some shadow across Arthur's destiny. But that meant Saxons. Arthur and Mordred had only last autumn sealed the trading treaty that was so dear to Mordred's heart. It was the first step toward friendship between the mainland kingdoms; it acknowledged the West Saxons' right to the territory they already had occupied for sixty years, from Seal's Bay to Rutupiae. Even if Cerdic should die, his son would be a fool not to honor a treaty that acknowledged their place on British soil. Where, I thought desperately, where could the threat be?

The country was quiet. Gawaine, King of Lothian and Orkney, held the north. Hapgar held Strathclyde, and Coel, Urien's eldest, ruled in Rheged. Drustan and his sons held the northeast solidly for the High King, and between my brother Gwarthgyd in Northgallis and Maelgon, who had sway over the lords of Powys and Dyfed, Wales was secure. Cornwall, I thought suddenly, only Cornwall might betray him. On Mordred's twenty-fifth birthday not quite a year ago, Arthur had at last declared his son to be his heir. To his own surprise, the country did not rise up in protest, or bring up the ancient scandal, or deny Mordred's right to kingship. The sin that ate at Arthur through his life and made him sensitive to every touch upon it was forgotten by most other men. It was old news; everyone knew Mordred was the High King's son. Only Duke Constantine nursed a grievance. He proclaimed it loudly to any who would listen, but since even a fool could see his motives, men smiled and shrugged and drank to Mordred's health.

I did not think Constantine could command much of a following, certainly not against Arthur. Nor could he foment trouble in Less Britain, not with Lancelot there. Arthur's wise rule, Arthur's treaties, Arthur's friendships—these things held Britain strong and safe. Where lay the threat? I could not see it.

"Well, Cabal," I said, patting him kindly, "we will just have to wait."

They were in Council four hours. When they broke, I heard shouts of joy and laughter in the halls, and someone sounded a horn, a call to arms. The door flew open; I jumped up; the King entered, smiling, his arm around Mordred's shoulder. The years had fallen from him in a single day! He was alight and happy. I knew what it meant. He was going to war.

Behind him came in Bedwyr, Gereint, Bellangere, Agglaval, Dryaunt, Villers, and Bors, all jesting with each other. I had seen to it that the wineskins were full of warm, spiced wine, and pitchers of mead stood on a low table. Men found counseling thirsty work.

"My lord Arthur," I greeted him, dipping him a curtsy.

He swung his free arm around me and, lifting me off the floor, kissed my lips. "I have stirring news, Gwen. We are raising an army."

"I guessed that much, my lord. Who is our enemy?"

He grinned and turned to Mordred. "I told you, she is the only one who does not like to hear it."

He had walked us to his writing table. Now he stopped and looked back at the gathering of knights around the fire across the room. They filled their cups and raised a toast to him.

"Arthur of Britain!" Bors cried. "Victory and long life to the King!"

"Long live Arthur!" the knights chorused. Arthur inclined his head. When he turned to me, he spoke gently.

"We are not yet directly threatened, Gwen, but if we do not go now, with a show of strength, war will be inevitable."

"But who, my lord? Who is our enemy?"

The smile left Arthur's eyes. He told me straight out. "Rome."

I gasped. *Rome.* Was it possible? Arthur grasped my elbow and sat me down in his own chair.

"Arthur!" Bors called. "Do you believe Gawaine can raise a thousand? When Tydwyl never mustered above five hundred men?"

Arthur glanced swiftly at Mordred. "Stay with her and answer her questions, if you will. She will have many. I will join you when I can."

Mordred sat on the edge of the table. His eyes were shining.

"Rome?" I whispered. "This is folly, Mordred. Would Rome threaten us again?" But before he could answer, a shout of joy went up from the knights. I saw them gathered around Arthur, pounding him on the back, prophesying slaughter and boasting already about great feats of bravery. I stood.

"I must get out in the air," I said quickly. "Have you a cloak?" He brought me Arthur's, heavy and warm and lined with fox pelts. I wrapped it around my arms to keep it off the floor, and Mordred followed me out to the garden. It was misting, but the air was sharp and clean. I breathed in deeply and walked along the damp paths among the sleeping plants. Mordred followed patiently.

"All right," I said at last. "Tell me about it."

It appeared there was a new Emperor in Rome, one Justinian, who hoped to return the Empire to her former glory. He had sent one of his generals, Lucius Quintilianus, also called Hiberius the Spaniard, to demand tribute of King Childebert and King Hoel in return for "protection."

I stared aghast at Mordred. "Protection! From whom? Do they think to invade us again, as in the days of the Emperor Claudius?"

"The King thinks they look for an excuse for it," Mordred admitted. "The tribute demanded is more than Hoel could ever pay, and Hiberius knows it. The Romans claim that they will keep the Burgundians from our borders, if we pay the tribute."

"The Burgundians!" I cried. "But the Franks have held them off for years! What nonsense is this?"

"Yes, my lady. But Rome has stirred them up."

I stared at him. "I see the game. Did you say, Mordred, that *we* are being blackmailed? Has the demand for tribute come to *us*?"

"No, my lady. Not yet. But the King knows that if Hoel and Childebert have been approached, sooner or later it will be asked of him. The threat will not be reduced by waiting. The time to act is now."

I nodded. "Clearly. What will he do?"

"Hoel and Lancelot and Childebert have gathered at Kerrec for council. They believe their only hope is in a joint defense, and a strong one. No one knows the strength of Hiberius' army, or even of the Burgundians. But a strong front now, with Arthur of Britain behind them, might give the Romans pause. They know well he has never been beaten."

I managed a smile. "The Unconquered King. I hope they know it. How many men will he take?"

"Ten thousand, if he can raise them."

"Ten thousand!" I gasped. "Is it possible?"

Mordred flashed one of his rare smiles. "There is not a man in Britain, youth or graybeard, who would not drop everything to fight for Arthur. He is a legend. And he will win."

I faced him nervously. "Then why is Niniane here?"

He looked surprised. "I did not know she was."

"What! Was she not in Council?"

"No, my lady. I don't even know if the King knows. He said nothing to me about it."

Puzzled, I fell silent. Around us the March winds rose and sent the folds of Arthur's cloak flapping. I welcomed the cold rain on my face; it cleared my head and kept my fears at bay.

"How odd," I said suddenly, "that we should stand here speaking of these Romans with such horror. Nearly every man in the Council chamber is descended from a Roman; the King, you, and I are all descended from a Roman general, a Spaniard even, one of the conquerors themselves. Had Maximus left when Rome withdrew her troops, we would not be here."

"But Rome did leave," Mordred said quietly. "She cannot now think to take us back under her mantle, after having left us to fend for ourselves against barbarians! This is what so angers Arthur. The arrogance of the demand! That Rome thinks she can claim us at her will! She abandoned us when we were little more than a scattering of hill tribes; now we are one people, and now we are our own masters."

"Indeed. Now we are worth something. Tell me, will the King take Excalibur?"

"Since there may be fighting, I should think so," Mordred replied, watching me closely. "Why?"

I shrugged and, feeling uneasy, adjusted my hood about my face to hide it. "No reason. I just had a thought. The last time the Sword left Britain . . . you know the story. When Maximus himself raised it against the King of Rome, it availed him nothing, and he died."

Mordred gripped my arms and forced me to look into his eyes.

"Rome was not then Britain's enemy," he said firmly. "Rome had left. It was Maximus' folly to pursue her. This time she comes to us. She *is* our enemy. And the Sword was made to protect Britain from her enemies. The end will not be the same."

Tears sprang unbidden to my eyes. "Oh, Mordred, I pray not!"

"Fear not, Guinevere," he said gently. "We will protect him with our lives. Lancelot and I, and Bedwyr and Gereint, and every knight in that room, and in the Council. He is worth more than life to us. Trust that old fox Merlin. If it comes to battle, he will be victorious."

I nodded, drying my eyes on the King's cloak, and, taking his arm, headed back. "You are going with him, did you say? Tell me who else goes. And how many men?"

This diverted his thoughts from Merlin and his dreadful prophecies, and he named three-quarters of the kings of Britain and nearly every lord I knew.

"Why, Mordred, there is no one left," I said when he had finished. "Who will be regent?"

"You will, Guinevere," said Arthur's voice. I looked up, startled, to see him at the doorway, smiling.

"Whatever do you mean, my lord?" He held out his hand, and I took it. He led me back inside, where all the knights were gathered behind him, smiling at me.

"The Council has decided to leave you in charge," he announced, regarding me with pride. "Not a single voice dissented."

I stared at him.

"Long live the Queen!" Bedwyr cried, and they all shouted, raised their goblets, and drank. For a swift moment, I thought this the jest of drunken men, but the King's face told me otherwise. He, at least, was sober and was brimming with pride.

"My lord King," I said shakily, doing him a low reverence, "I know not what to say. I thank you for the honor you do me, but do you think it wise? I cannot command troops, my lord."

He raised me and held both my hands. "I believe you could, you know," he said gently, and then smiled. "But you will not have to. I leave Ferron here as commander. The lords in your Council are all men you know: Kay, Lyonel, Gryfflet, Villers, Clegis, Dynas, and Bleoberys. With Ferron that makes eight. And Mordred will return before the battle to relieve you of the regent's duties, by your leave. I take him with me that he may meet Hoel and Childebert, and join our council of ally lords. It's more than time they got to know each other. But then he will return—I can't risk both of us—so you need not rule longer than you must, unless you choose to. I leave that decision to you."

There was no doubt any longer that he was serious. The weight of such responsibility set me trembling, and I gripped his hands hard, to stop it.

"If you have such faith in me, my lord, I dare not doubt myself. Tell me—tell me what dispositions you have made around Britain—who is left for defense?"

Arthur glanced swiftly, triumphantly, at the knights. By my question, it seemed I had confirmed his faith. He sat me in his great chair behind the work desk and began to pace.

"Drustan sends his sons with me, but stays to hold the east. Old Tydwyl will hold the north for Gawaine. Kay's son holds Galava, Hapgar's brother Pertolys holds Strathclyde, Maelgon's brother Peredur Gwynedd, Coel's brother Uwain is regent in Rheged." He ticked off the other kingdoms one by one, all of them held by old men or untried youths. Except for Cornwall. Constantine himself stayed in Cornwall.

"He has lately had a quarrel with Childebert," the King said carefully, "and I judged it best to leave him behind. A thousand of his men come with me, the best part of his army. But I have given him the guardianship of the West. It is an honor that I hope will heal his pride." Then his face softened. "It is thanks to you, Gwen, we can leave Britain so lightly defended. To the east sit the Saxons. Thanks to you, we have treaties with them and must consider them allies, at least at present. And thanks to you, the Irish have kept to their own coasts these twenty years."

"No thanks to me, my lord," I protested, "but to your own wise statesmanship!"

Arthur laughed. "Nonsense. Fion's been in love with you since he first set eyes on you. That's why he keeps peace with us." I blushed at this, and the men grinned. "Never mind," the King said in a kind voice. "Whether it is due to you or me or destiny, we have no threats from our neighbors. You will be safe here, Gwen. If I doubted it, I could not leave you."

"Thank you, my lord. How long until Mordred's return? And yours?"

"Hiberius requires his answer by the first of June. Mordred should be back shortly after. I hope I can be back by the solstice, having sent the Roman on his way. If not, by midsummer, surely. The more men we can muster, the less time it should take. Give me a month to gather the army; three weeks to make the crossings; by June we should be ready for battle."

I took a deep breath. "Very good, my lord. I can manage that, I think." Then I grinned. "But if I am gray when you return, it is your doing!"

Arthur laughed and raised a toast to me, and the men joined him. I caught Mordred looking at me unawares; he blushed when he caught my eye and turned away.

Niniane came to dinner, but sat where I could not get speech with her. Afterward, she sought an audience with the King, while Bedwyr, Kay, Mordred, Ferron, and I sat by the library fire and discussed plans. When Arthur joined us, he looked solemn but content, so I judged she had not brought him evil tidings.

Late that night when I had the King to myself, I asked him what she had said; it was none of my business, but I thought he would tell me. He demurred at first but, when he saw my fear, gave in to comfort me.

"It is nothing she has seen through her Power," he assured me. "Just what she calls a feeling in her bones. But, as with Merlin, her bones never lie. These are important matters we are facing; they matter to Britain's future. She came to see how seriously we took this summons."

"Did she predict nothing, then? Victory? Defeat? Stalemate?"

By starlight I saw his smile. "You should know by now, Gwen, it is ill luck to speak to a commander about defeat or victory on the eve of battle."

"This is not the eve of battle, Arthur. You are evading me. What did she say?"

He reached for me under the bearskins and pulled me close against his body. "Will you not be diverted, even for a moment?"

"How can I, when I fear for your life?"

"Do not fear it. What she told me was perhaps the best thing she could have said. She said my fate was in my own hands. It is something every king likes to hear ... Why do you tremble, Gwen? This is not bad news."

"I do not like it when Niniane speaks of fate."

He shrugged and touched my hair. "It's the way enchanters talk. Think nothing of it."

"With your permission, Arthur, I will speak to her myself."

He laughed. "She warned me you would try to. You worry too much, Gwen. Remember Merlin's words: *Take what comes and—*"

I clapped a hand over his mouth and whispered furiously, "If you say that to me again I will scream aloud and wake the castle! Dear God, how tired I am of that stale advice!"

He began to laugh in earnest, with true delight, and it was impossible not to laugh with him. He was once again the warrior King of Britain, and the spirit of his youth had returned to him. I gave up my questions and joined him in his joy.

The truth is, Niniane avoided me. During the month it took to gather Britain's army at Caer Camel, she flitted between the Lady's shrine on Ynys Witrin, her husband's fortress in the River Isles, and Camelot. She saw to it no one ever knew exactly where she was, or when she was expected. In spite of all the preparations, I kept a constant eye out for her. And in spite of the constant planning and changing of plans, she was always there when her advice was needed and always gone by the time I got wind of it.

There was an immense amount to do. Couriers flew daily in and out of King's Gate; kings and dukes and earls and lords from every corner of Britain began arriving with their troops, on horses, on ponies, and on foot. Everyone rallied to the High King's call. He had given them twenty years of peace; now they were eager to fight under his Dragon standard. We did not bother to enlarge the stables; there were too many horses to accommodate them all. They were tethered to horse lines behind the soldiers' tents. The open meadows inside the the fortress walls were soon filled; troops and tents spilled out down the hill itself, and onto the downs below. They gathered around their commanders and were grouped more or less by location; the wary Cornishmen together on this side, the boisterous Lothians on the other; the cheerful warriors from Rheged on the south slopes, the taciturn Northumbrians on the east. The Welsh contingents disgraced themselves in my eyes, for the North Welsh condescended to the South Welsh, and fights broke out. They had to be separated from one another at the end, the men from Guent in one place, from Dyfed in another, the men from Powys yonder, and those from Gwynedd under my own watchful eye.

I saw my brother Gwarthgydd, older now than my father had been when he died. He was very glad to see me and said I had not changed a hair since my girlhood—this was his favorite refrain, but if he expected me to believe it, he was disappointed. He had left his son Gwillim, my dearest childhood companion, to hold Northgallis, and had brought his brothers with him to fight for Arthur.

This huge army needed food, and water, and boots, and horseshoes and weapons. The street of smiths was busiest of all; they never slept; they worked in shifts; their forges were alight for a solid month. My women spun and wove and sewed: war cloaks, tunics, leggings, robes, and mantles; slippers, stockings, caps, belts, and gloves; and most important, banners with the High King's emblem, the Red Dragon on a field on gold, for every company wanted one to carry. I made the King a sash to wear across his tunic, a token from his lady of the finest, crimson-dyed silks in the storerooms. In tiny golden stitches I made a dragon, and a castle and a cross, and stitched the initials of his name over the breast—AR, "Arturus Rex." If Hiberus should meet him face to face, I thought, he would know with whom he had to deal. I worked long and intently on this project—I told myself it was for Arthur, but I knew it was to keep my mind from other things.

Nearly every evening after hall I went to the chapel and prayed. Some years before, Arthur had built a small chapel on the castle grounds, to save me the walk to the church. Bishop Landrum always waited for me at the church, eager to help me in my devotions. He was disgusting. He leered at me and stared lewdly down my gown and sometimes even smacked his lips when he came near to speak. He never bathed and smelled worse than the compost heap. He had aged unpleasantly, his lust growing with his years, until all my maids were terrified of him. He called himself a servant of God, yet had fathered over twenty bastards by girls in the town. I could tell he believed all the rumors about Lancelot and thought that if he could bring himself to approach me, he might have me. So I had begged Arthur for the chapel, and he built it for me.

Usually, I was alone there and stayed long to enjoy the peace. But one night when I came in, a young soldier was there, head bent, back bowed in prayer. I took my accustomed place, some distance away, and began my prayers for Arthur's safety and the preservation of all he had built in Britain. At length, when I had finished, I rose from my knees to find the young man beside me, although I had not heard a whisper of his approach. I looked up into the breathtakingly handsome face of Lancelot's son Galahad. At fourteen, with black hair shadowing his striking features, he was the image of how Lancelot must once have looked. But his sky-blue eyes, bold and merciless, were Elaine's. There was a light about him; in that setting it seemed like a holy aura, the touch of God.

"My lady Queen," he said solemnly, "there is no use praying to God unless your heart is pure."

"Good sir, God knows my heart. I hide nothing from Him."

He shook his head. "The bishop knows your sins, madam. Renounce my father, Guinevere, and be cleansed."

Alone of all the men in Camelot, including Arthur, he dared say this to me! But for Lancelot's sake, I treated him gently. "The bishop casts stones, my lord, yet he is not without sin."

His eyes flashed. "Your prayers will not be answered."

"Judge me not, Galahad. Look well into your own heart, before you seek to know mine. Good evening."

I left him and walked out with as much dignity as I could summon. He had been the bishop's favorite since he first came to Camelot. I was always astounded that he revered the man, that he was so very easily fooled about some things and so difficult to fool about others. I hoped fervently that Arthur was planning to take him to Less Britain and was much relieved when Ferron confirmed that this was so. Lancelot would be glad to see him again, at least for a little while, and I did not think I could bear him about much longer. Whenever I went to chapel, after that, he was there.

Finally, in the last week, Niniane came to Camelot to stay. Pelleas, her lord, was leaving, and she came with him. I sent for her; she sent back to say she was engaged and would speak with me on the morrow. I sent again; the page could not find her. I rode myself to Avalon, to find she had just left. Angrily I went to Arthur, who did not need to be bothered at such a time, and demanded that she grant me an audience. He heard me out with patience and told me she had just left him, saying she would meet me after hall in the orchard. She did not come to dinner, and I suspected another ruse. But when I came to the orchard, she was there. The apple blossoms were just out, dancing like white froth in the April breezes. Niniane sat on a stone bench in a pose of meditation, eyes closed. I signaled my two maids to wait and went forward to see her alone. She did not change her attitude when I came up; I stood before her and waited. At last she sighed and opened her eyes.

"Greetings, Queen Guinevere. You wish to see me."

"I do indeed, Lady Niniane. Why have you been avoiding me?"

She smiled, ever so slightly. "Perhaps because I do not wish to answer your question."

She was straight with me; I gave her that. She had always been so.

"And why would you not wish to answer it?"

She sighed again and faced me. There was no expression on her face at all. "I do not see into the future as you look into your bronze, my lady Queen. Great events, those that move history, throw portents ahead, for those who can read them. But most of life is as dark to me as it is to you."

I sat, suddenly weak in my knees. "And yet you came here. Unbidden, and on time. You must have seen some such portent. Did you not?"

The night was soft, and all around us the earth smelled sweet with new growth. But when I looked into Niniane's eyes, the air grew cold and rank. She looked away and showed me her profile. She drew a deep breath slowly and let it out. "Yes. The world is about to change. There are great events ahead. The wheel of time is turning. Things will not be as they were before." She stopped and closed her lips tightly.

"Niniane!" I cried, trying desperately to control my rising panic. "Niniane, tell me what you foresee!"

"No." Her voice was flat and empty. "I cannot. It is forbidden. But because you are dear to him, and fear for him, I will answer you one question. Choose it well."

I gasped and kissed her hand. There was only one question to ask!

"Will he return?" I cried, as the tears slid down my face. "Will Arthur return to Britain?"

She turned to me slowly, and I thought for a fleeting moment she felt relief. "Yes," she said very softly, "he will return." Then she rose, made me a graceful reverence, and departed.

I sat alone for a long while in the spring twilight and let my tears flow unchecked. He would return; that mattered most. But a fear yet nagged at me. She had sat here, dreading something; yet she had not dreaded the answer she had to give. I began to fear that I had asked her the wrong question.

The night before they left, all the lords gathered for a great feast. The army numbered over twelve thousand men; not even Arthur had expected so many to answer his call. Hoel and Lancelot and even Childebert had sent ships across the Narrow Sea; ten ships lay in the Severn estuary, and a score more in the small harbors along the southern coasts. Even so, they would all make several trips; the crossing would take weeks to accomplish.

I could not partake of the meal; the wine was rich and unwatered, and the men grew rowdy, as they do on the eve of battle, to cheer themselves and banish fear. I led the women out early and went straight to my quarters. Usually the King stayed late, for the men needed his presence; but there was no battle on the morrow, only leave-taking. They let him go early, for they knew he had his good-byes to make.

I waited for him in his chamber. I had dismissed Bran and Varric for the evening, saying I would tend the King myself. They had understood. I dressed in his favorite gown of mine, a blue one, and brushed my hair and let it fall unbraided. I was determined not to weep. Niniane had promised he would return.

I heard him coming; in the antechamber he stopped and spoke to Bran in a low voice, then came up the stairs with a firm step and paused in the doorway. Meeting his eyes was like taking a blow to the chest; my heart began to pound, and tears sprang to my eyes.

"This is not good-bye, Gwen," he said gently.

"I know, my lord. But it is farewell." He came across to me, and I gripped his arms. "In spite of everything, Arthur, in spite of the great honor you have paid me, in spite of your obvious joy at leading the army again, in spite of the righteousness of the cause, my heart is heavy. I do not want you to go."

He wrapped his arms around me and hugged me tightly. "Come, come. We will not be parted for very long. Before you know it, it will be midsummer, and we will be idling around the fountain complaining of the heat."

I managed a smile and blinked away the tears. "And when did you ever complain of anything, my lord? You describe the rest of us, perhaps, but not yourself. Sometimes, Arthur, you are too sweet-tempered to bear."

"Your praises go to my head," he said lightly, "but I can be as angry as the next man. You have seen me so."

"Sloth and incompetence annoy you," I replied, "but little else. What a King you are, Arthur! Remember that Britain will not be Britain without you here, but a mere shell of herself, her innards gone. Every minute you are away will seem like days to me!"

He stood back and looked down into my face. "Why, Gwen, those are sweet words to carry with me. I will remember them."

He led me to the bed and sat down beside me. "Listen, now. This is how I regard it. What is the very worst that can happen? What do you fear most?"

I swallowed hard and tried to copy his calm speech. "That you will be slain on the battlefield and not return to me."

He smiled. "That is your woman's heart speaking. I can think of worse fates than death. So be it. Now, what is the best thing that can happen? What do you most desire?"

"That Hiberius should beg your pardon and withdraw before a single sword is drawn!" I whispered fervently.

He laughed. "Well, we are agreed on that. And now, what is likely? Surely it falls somewhere between the two. I believe Hiberius will test us and give us battle to see our strength. But, united, we will defeat him and come home the victors. How many men return with me depends upon his numbers and his determination. But I will be back, Gwen."

I nodded. "So Niniane has told me."

"She has?" He looked so startled, I knew he had been speaking more from his heart, to comfort me, than from belief. "Then she has told you more than she told me. Well, then, where is the cause for fear?"

I sighed and lifted my hand to his face. "I don't know, my lord, but I do fear for you." He took my hand and kissed my palm.

"Put fear away," he whispered. "Let there be nothing but joy between us tonight."

I yielded to him willingly and for a while forgot the darkening future. But later, as we lay spent from pleasure and waiting for sleep, my thoughts turned again to Niniane, and to Arthur, and to Mordred. The world would change, she had said—what could that mean? I thought Arthur was dozing, but then he spoke, in a voice so low I pressed closer to him to hear it.

"Guinevere, if the fates are cruel and part us forever, I would have you know this: In all my life I have loved no one more than you. Were we permitted to live our lives over, I would take you again to wife, and none other. I have been given many blessings, but the dearest one to me is you."

"Oh, Arthur," I whispered through tears, "this sounds like good-bye." He would not let me speak, but kissed me and held me close in his arms until the dawn.

They left at midmorning. The King rode out resplendent in a cloak of purple, with a circlet of gold on the brow of his helmet and the crimson sash across his chest. Above him flew the Red Dragon of Britain. On his belt hung his great Sword. His gray stallion was excited by the press of horses and soldiers and danced all the way to King's Gate, where a great shout was raised by the gathered armies beyond the walls. The stallion reared; laughing, Arthur brought him down and gave the command to march. Within an hour, all we could see of him was the dust he raised on the plains below.

25 ✹ The Queen's Dilemma

God bless Arthur, he sent me a courier every day, and when he got to Less Britain, sent me one every week, to let me know how he fared. His crossing was easy; he made Kerrec in good time and was heartily welcomed there by Lancelot and Hoel. They met with King Childebert to plan their strategy and wait for the rest of the British forces to land.

Meanwhile, our little household at Camelot ran smoothly. We had only a hundred men left in the barracks, but Ferron drilled them daily. Niniane returned to Avalon and kept watch over King Melwas' young cousin, who held his fortress for him. We posted scouts along the Saxon borders, but Cerdic kept his word and gave us no cause for fear. It truly seemed that Britain lay quiet in peaceful slumber, hardly knowing her lord was away.

And then one night a courier arrived. Kay, white-faced, brought him to me as we sat in hall. He had not come from Arthur, which I guessed from the freshness of his clothing; he had come from Niniane. The message was short and to the point. Duke Constantine was lately come north from Cornwall with an army of four hundred men. She bade me take care, for he meant to take Caer Camel. I blanched as I heard this, then asked the messenger tell it again to all the knights who sat at table. To a man, they were furious and shouted out their protests. What did he think he was about, defying Arthur's orders the moment he was gone?

I thanked the courier for his speed and bade him sup with us. He gave me what little news there was: The last of the King's ships had left the estuary, and the Summer Country was quiet. But they kept good lookouts, I observed, to get news of Constantine so soon. The courier dropped his eyes. Melwas' cousin had not thought to post lookouts; the lady Niniane had seen it in the fire.

At that I rose and excused myself from the company, bidding the eight knights who formed the Council to meet me in the King's library after the meal. I went there immediately, to have a moment to think. Clearly, Constantine meant mutiny. As guardian of the west, he could move his troops through Cornwall, through Dumnonia and, skirting the Summer Country, even through Wales. But to approach Caer Camel defied Arthur's orders. And why patrol with four hundred men? No, he meant to take Arthur's fortress, whether to wrest it from him or to hold it for him made no difference. He was dealing with a woman now and saw his path to power clear.

Could we prevent him? That was the question. Could we hold Caer Camel, outnumbered four to one? And if we could, for how long? Six months? Three months? One? We were now halfway through May; this was not the time to send for Arthur, nor for Mordred, who was meeting for the first time the ally kings with whom he would one day have to deal. Could we hold out against the duke, or must we give him battle? Four to one were not odds I liked.

The knights hurried in a short time later, led by Ferron, all muttering their outrage and voicing threats. I got them settled and asked for their advice. They assured me, and Kay confirmed this, that the fortress could be held by a handful of trained men against an army of thousands. The walls could not be breached, King's Gate could not be forced; the battlements could be held by the archers forever. But the thought of a siege filled me with horror. Worse than the loss of freedom was the fear of leaving the rest of Britain on its own, with Camelot, its heart and soul, cut off by Cornish troops. I voiced my fear, and to a man, they were willing to fly out King's Gate and do battle, four to one. I shook my head.

"My lords," I said, "I will not be responsible for such slaughter. We cannot allow ourselves to be drawn into a battle. If he means us ill, that is to play into his hands. But we must be sure of his intentions. Until he declares himself our enemy, Constantine is Arthur's ally. If he knocks upon King's Gate and begs entrance of me, I must let him in."

I could see by their faces they thought me naive, or witless. Two of the younger men, Dynas and Clegis, scowled darkly.

"But, my lady!" Dynas objected. "You cannot let them in, not in such numbers! Once inside King's Gate, they will take us!"

"The man's a fox," Villers growled. "He's been waiting for the chance to get Mordred out of the country. He will give out that he comes to offer you support. He will say anything to get inside."

They all voiced their agreement; no one doubted that Constantine was our enemy, and a devious one at that.

"Then, my lords, we must devise a strategy. We cannot fight him; nor can we wait, cut off from Britain, for the High King to return. Once Constantine surrounds us, he will be High King in all but name."

They all looked at one another, nervous and unhappy, but no one spoke.

I glanced toward Ferron, who was frowning. "My lord, can you not think of some way to stall them?"

He cleared his throat. "Not with so few men, my lady. One hundred against four hundred are poor odds."

"Not fight them, Sir Ferron. Stall them. Slow them down."

Silence blanketed the room. Clegis and Dynas stared sullenly at the floor. I guessed that this was not the kind of talk the men were used to. Fighting was something they understood: good, clean fighting out in the open air. Not one of them, I was willing to wager, had ever tried to outwit his opponent. To a man, they lacked Arthur's patience for planning, talking, and waiting for the slow unfolding of events. I began to appreciate the skill it took to rule such men.

"Would my lords feel easier if I sent to Wales for troops to come up behind him?"

In relief they voiced their assent. But Sir Gryfflet shook his head. "Don't send to Gwynedd for troops, my lady. Maelgon's brother Peredur is lord there now, and Maelgon holds a grudge against you for banishing his sister to Less Britain. Where she died."

I stared open-mouthed at this nonsense. Before I could speak, Sir Clegis confirmed it. "Maelgon is loyal to the High King, my lady, but I would not count upon his loyalty to you."

"Banish his sister!" I cried. "This is fools' chatter! Her husband took her to Less Britain—the husband she alone chose out of all men—to bear his son, which she conceived of her own will. God knows—God *knows* I would have kept them both in Britain and unwed! I should have liked to send her back to Wales and her precious brother!" The men looked quickly at one another and shifted in their seats. I gripped the edge of Arthur's table and fought for calm. What these men had heard were only rumors. If Maelgon had indeed turned against me, it was because I had publicly opposed him in Gwynedd, when he accused Lancelot and I defended him. He was too much a coward to admit it openly. And these men, I wondered, could the same be said of them? Did their loyalty to Arthur extend to his person only, and not to me?

Just then the door behind them opened; they all looked round. Anna, a plain maiden of seventeen and the only one of my attendants with any sense, poked her head in.

"Not now, woman!" someone grumbled. "We're in Council!"

She looked straight at me, her brow puckered with worry. "My lady, I beg pardon for the interruption, but—"

"Unless it's a courier it can wait," Dynas cried. "Be gone, maiden!"

I raised my hand for silence. Since Linet had gone home to York, Anna was the only woman besides Ailsa I could talk to, and I relied upon her. "What is it, Anna?"

"It's Ailsa, my lady. She has fallen down and can't rise. Or speak, or move. I have sent for a physician but I judged you would want to know."

I gasped. "Ailsa!"

"For pity's sake," Clegis murmured, "the King's Council interrupted for an old woman's fall!"

"You judged rightly, Anna." My voice shook, but whether with rage or sorrow I hardly knew. "I will come at once."

The men turned. "But, my lady!" It was Dynas and Clegis together. "What about Constantine?"

I paused at the door. "Fortify yourselves with wine and mead, send for the scribe, and await me. I will return directly."

I reached for Anna's arm, and we went out together.

"How they resent your power!" she whispered. "What fools men are!"

Kay's calm voice floated clearly down the corridor. "My lords, do as Arthur does and put your faith in the Queen. She will not disappoint you."

I squeezed Anna's arm as we hurried away. "Not all men, Anna. Thank God, not all men."

They had put Ailsa to bed. When I went in, the physician was bending over her, prying open her eyes, and shaking his head. He bowed to me and backed away. A sob welled in my throat as I looked down upon her face, so thin and old and gray, and so suddenly! I sat upon her coverlet and took her hand in mine. How soft and slack the wrinkled skin, how light the bones! I bent and kissed her pallid cheek. She slept, breathing noiselessly, but it was a deeper sleep than she was used to; neither sound nor touch awakened her.

"Ailsa," I whispered. "Dear Ailsa!" I pushed a lock of thin hair from her brow. "When did this happen? Where did she fall?"

"In your chamber, my lady." Anna said with a hand upon my shoulder. "She was folding a gown just come from the fuller's. I heard a noise—she did not call out—and ran up to find her lying on the floor. Her eyes were open then. She knew me, I'm sure of it, but she could not move or speak."

I turned to the physician, who bowed again. "What do you make of it, sir? Come, tell me the truth. I can see by your face how grave it is."

"I fear, my lady Queen, there is little that can be done. It's the sleeping sickness. If she awakens from it, she may live awhile longer. But she will not regain the use of her right arm. See the way her face is slackened. That is a sure sign of the sickness. And if she does not awaken, then death will follow."

I fought down the sob. "How long?"

He shrugged. "Two days. A week. It is hard to tell."

"And until then?"

"We will keep her warm with hot bricks at her feet and rub her chest with salve. If her breath stays quiet, she may recover. It is not unknown."

That slim hope was all that he could give me. I sat with her, holding her hand, until the bricks and hot water arrived. Then, as I was in the way of the physician's ministrations, I went out with Anna.

"Oh, Anna, I do not like the look of her. All the life is gone from her so suddenly! Only this morning she was chiding me about the state of my hair . . . she always took such pains with it . . . she always took such care . . ."

I faltered; Anna held me tightly and, unable to bear it any longer, I wept in her arms. Ailsa was the only mother I had ever known, and no mother could ever, anywhere, love a child more than my dearest Ailsa had loved me. When I said I wished to arrange a pallet by Ailsa's bed and sleep by her through the night, Anna assured me she would see that it was done.

There was nothing else I could do. I wiped my eyes and returned to the library with Anna, hand in hand. We entered abruptly and found the men in heated argument. Kay, Ferron, Berys, and Lyonel were defending me to Dynas, Clegis, and Villers. Gryfflet stood between them, listening. They broke off of a sudden when they saw me, and some of their faces went red. Dynas and Clegis were young men, too young to have fought with Arthur in the Saxon wars, but Villers was an old friend—I looked at him in surprise, and he had the grace to color and look away. He had lately become a Christian; it crossed my mind that Bishop Landrum might have been busy with his tongue.

"Gentlemen." They were staring at the tear tracks on my cheeks. "My lords all, hear what I have decided. I will send first to Northgallis. Gwillim my kinsman will come to my aid. His wife is the King of Dyfed's daughter; between the two kingdoms, he can command a hundred men or so. And I will send to Drustan of Elmet. Since Arthur's generous recompense for Lamorak's murder, he has been a staunch supporter of the King. He might even come himself. Will that do?"

Relieved, they assured me that a hundred men on either side of Constantine's army could give him a battle he might not wish to chance.

"But," Gryfflet ventured, still sitting on the fence, "can they come in time? Even with swift couriers, and allowing time to muster what men are left"—he counted upon his fingers—"it will be a fortnight, at least, my lady. Constantine will be here long before that."

"Not," I said quietly, "if we can slow him down." They looked at one another and again went silent. "If you will, my lords, leave that part of it to me."

They agreed to this without much argument; no one asked me what I proposed to do. Kay got them settled drinking mead before the fire. I sat at Arthur's desk and beckoned to the scribe. He drew out his parchments and quills and mixed his ink, while from the pouch at my waist I took the regent's seal. With Ferron standing by, I dictated the letter to Gwillim, and below the scribe's neat Latin hand, I wrote it myself in Welsh, for I did not know if Gwillim kept a Latin scribe. My father certainly had not, but even Wales had grown more civilized since then. I sent the same message to Drustan. When the ink dried the scribe sealed the scrolls with wax. Carefully I impressed the wax with the regent's seal. Ferron summoned couriers, and they went off at once, taking the northern road through Aquae Sulis to stay out of Constantine's way.

The scribe began to collect his things, but I bade him stay. "I have another message, good Julius. Bide a moment while I consider what to say."

Ferron looked at me hopefully, but said nothing. Any move of Constantine's was important. But this was treachery—Niniane had seen it through her Sight, so it was true—and clearly Arthur needed to be told. I did not wish to alarm him, for it might come to naught. I dared not ask for Mordred, or one of his top commanders, and yet he had to know the threat was real.

"Address this to Arthur, High King of Britain," I said slowly, and Ferron sighed in audible relief. I smiled up at him. "What did you fear, my lord? Did you think I would keep this from him and try to be King myself?"

"By the Light!" he swore softly. "It is not unknown!"

"Well, by the grace of God, I am not Pendragon and have not that ambition. I am his servant. How shall I tell him of this threat, without calling half his army back?"

In the end, we simply stated the facts as we knew them. I asked for a company of men on good horses to come as swiftly as they might, to help take Constantine from the rear in case he sat down in front of Caer Camel to besiege us. The message was sealed, and the courier sent.

I rose and turned to Ferron. "Thank you, Ferron, for your aid and for your defense of me. I know some of the younger men, especially the Christians, think it unseemly for a woman to govern men."

Ferron smiled. "Fools come in many colors, my lady. Pay them no mind. They have yet to learn that leadership wears different cloaks."

"Why, Ferron, I thank you for those words."

He bowed. "You raised the Sword of Britain, my lady. You are not like any other woman these men have known. Give them time to get better acquainted. They probably think"—and his eyes narrowed in laughter—"that you've done little else but weave Arthur his war cloaks. They will learn, my lady Queen, the lesson we all have learned. Give them time."

I said nothing, but made him a reverence to the floor. Once my foolish arrogance had endangered Ferron's future; now his forgiveness, so generous, so undeserved, touched my heart.

When we reached the women's quarters, I pulled Anna aside. "Anna, I must ask a service of you. It will require courage."

She straightened and dipped a quick curtsy. "Queen Guinevere, I am your servant. Command me."

"You must take a message to Niniane. To Avalon. Tonight."

I heard her indrawn breath, and her eyes widened, but she did not shrink from me. She was a brave girl. To every Christian woman, except perhaps to me, Avalon was a forbidden and frightening haunt of dark rites and pagan spirits. Girls her age could not remember, as I did, the days when the Good Goddess was worshipped throughout the land. Anna feared what dwelt behind the whitewashed pavilions of the Lady's shrine; but I recalled with fondness the clean, sweet-scented cells, the cool calm of the House of Healing, and the still beauty of the tended orchards encircled by the Lake. The only thing to fear at Avalon was Niniane herself, aloof and powerful as she was. She had served Arthur well these many years—would she now serve me?

"My lady, I will do it," Anna said firmly.

"Bless you, Anna. You will come to no harm, I promise you. I will give you a token to show the guards at the gates. You must ride alone—not secretly, but silently—I do not want the Council to know."

At once her interest quickened, and she nodded eagerly. She was seventeen and still unmarried; no one had yet offered for her, though she was a better woman than all of my pretty girls put together. Naturally enough, this had engendered in her a contempt for men's opinions; she was always eager to prove that she could do without a warrior's help.

"Say to Niniane—herself, mind you, no other—say to Niniane the High Queen begs her assistance—yes, begs—for the Kingdom's sake. Tell her we have sent for reinforcements, thanks to her warning, but we need a fortnight. For Arthur's sake, if not for mine, I beg she will call upon her powers and bring wind, storm, flood, or mists, or whatever catastrophe she can devise to bar Cornwall's way. Once he crosses the Camel, once he comes to the plain of Camlann, we are besieged and the heart is cut out of Britain! Then are we held captive, trapped and powerless, at the Duke of Cornwall's whim."

"Oh, my lady." I saw she trembled.

"Take heart, Anna. Niniane will heed my call. I am sure of it, else I would not ask her."

She swallowed. "It's not that, exactly."

"What is it, then?"

"Can she—my lady, can she really do such things?"

I smiled. "Oh, yes. Do not doubt her power. If she willed, she could raise mountains from the sea. But she has a fierce pride and must be cautiously approached. Take care to speak politely and hide your crucifix under your tunic. Plead for the Kingdom, Anna! I would go myself, in an instant—but Arthur would breathe flames if he knew I went without the Council's knowing."

"And they would never let you go. Never mind, my lady, I will do it. I will slip out now to the stables and be back before moonset."

I gave her the token. She curtsied, then paused on the verge of going. "My lady—"

"Yes, Anna?"

"Did you—did you really lift the High King's Sword?"

She stood perfectly still, but I could feel her fear across the space between us. She was barely seventeen, about to undertake a mission—alone and in secret—she had never dreamed of doing. I reached out and clasped her hand.

"It is one of the tales they tell," I said slowly, lowering my voice to a whisper, "and in truth, nothing is beyond a woman's strength if the need is great enough."

"My lady Queen," she breathed, "I believe it." She smiled shyly. "I will be back before moonset, and no one will know I've gone."

Four days passed. Ailsa slept and did not awaken. Every hour, it seemed to me, she grew smaller and thinner than the hour before. I saw that she had warmed bricks put to her throughout the day and night. By her bedside I kept a carafe of sweet water, for when she should awaken. Every few minutes I moistened a cloth and pressed it to her mouth. All it did was chap her lips. Without water, I knew, she could not live long. I did not sleep much. My heart was too heavy and would not allow me peace.

Ferron came by twice daily to report on Constantine's progress. We had sent scouts out at once and so learned of his quick march from the coast, his turning eastward well south of Ynys Witrin, and his steady approach from the southwest. But when Ferron came to summon me to Council, I waved him away.

"But, my lady"—he frowned—"the men are growing restless. Berys and I daily drill the troops, to keep them occupied and give Clegis and Dynas something to do, but time is running out. Something must be done. In three days Constantine will be at the banks of the Camel. We must devise a plan."

"Oh, Ferron! I cannot come now—I cannot even think—my thoughts are like dry leaves in a wind—"

"But the men are all gathered in the Round Hall."

I looked down at Ailsa's gray face. Anna sat in the corner, eyes averted, wrapping an herb-soaked cloth around a steaming brick. Slowly I shook my head. "I cannot leave her, Ferron. She is near death. I must be here."

"Guinevere, I pray you to attend us. The Council is divided, you must know that. Half of them want to take him on, face to face, if only because they are tired of waiting."

I looked up briefly. "Teach them patience, then. Set them an example. Do what you can, Ferron. You must see that I cannot leave her. She is a mother to me. I would never forgive myself if I were not here . . ."

He hesitated, bowed low, and left.

"My lady!"

I jerked awake. It was very dark; the candle had gone out. A shadow darker than the rest, Anna leaned over the bed. "My lady!"

Too frightened to breathe, I jumped up from the pallet.

"Dear God, Anna—" I stopped. Ailsa's eyes were open and looking up at me. "Ailsa! Oh, Ailsa! My dear nurse! Bide a moment, pray, and take some water. Help me, Anna!" I lifted her head and shoulders—how light she was!—and put the cup to her lips. She could barely manage to swallow; most of it dribbled from her lips, but some of it went down. Anna placed a warm brick at her feet, then went for broth. I held Ailsa in my arms, and whispered to her and thanked God that she still lived. Her lips moved. I bent my ear close to her mouth and heard her breath, just on the edge of sound.

"Guinevere."

"Oh, Ailsa! I am here! Do not struggle yet with speech. You will be stronger soon. I am here, my dear love, I am here." I lit the candle and held her in my arms and told her what had happened and begged her take more water and assured her that everything would be all right in time; all the while she watched me with eyes full of fear.

She took a little broth when it came, a very little, then fell asleep as I sang to her and stroked her hair.

When she slept, her sleep was light and quiet, with little sighing breaths, the way she always used to sleep. Gratefully I kissed her brow and rose.

"Shall I send for the physician, my lady?"

"Later, Anna. Let her rest a little longer undisturbed."

"Will you be going back to your chamber, then?"

"No. No, I will stay here with her until she is quite recovered. And in the morning, I suppose I ought to show my face in Council."

"Would you like me to attend you?"

"Thank you, Anna, but not this time. Not in the Round Hall. To men, that is a sacred precinct. Stay by Ailsa and give her more broth if she awakens."

"Yes, my lady."

In the Round Hall the men sat with gloomy faces. They were a small gathering, eight sitting around a table built for thirty. Above the High King's chair Excalibur's hanger hung empty, and the great chamber, so often full of voices and the robust companionship of men, rang hollow like a gourd with its innards missing.

Kay looked glad to see me, and Ferron, relieved, asked kindly after Ailsa. But the others stirred in their seats and glared at one another. They had reached an impasse—some wanted war, some preferred to wait out the siege until our reinforcements came, and some wavered, undecided. Without Arthur, they were like nervous horses, pulling against one another with more passion than sense, and with little result. How they missed his steady, guiding hand!

In the middle of their arguments a scout arrived, still dusty from his ride, and fell to one knee at Ferron's feet.

"My lord! It is amazing—a miracle—they were bewitched, I think!"

"Speak sense, Aranor. Remember you are a soldier."

The youth gulped and twisted his hands together. "My lord! Duke Constantine has disappeared!"

"What!"

"Regis and I were watching from Berin's Hill, south of the Camelford—"

"I know your posting," Ferron said sharply. "Go on."

"We watched them camp, my lord, but—but in the morning, yesterday morning, they—they disappeared!"

Ferron scowled. "They got past you unseen, you mean, you young scamp. Sneaked past while you were sleeping."

"No!" the youth cried. "We checked the ground! They did not get by us! My lord, please believe me. I could follow the tracks of an army without getting down from the horse. We slept in shifts—they did not pass us!"

"Then where did they go?"

"My lord, we could not tell. A great mist crept in that night, all up and down the valley, encircling their campsite. It came down from the Lake. We saw it come. It did not lift in the morning, but seemed to draw strength from the sun and grow thicker. Toward midday it drifted back to the Lake, and—and the army was gone! We—we covered all the ground between where they had been and the river. My lord, they did not come this way, and they are not there. The tracks led toward the Lake." The boy gulped. "I don't know why they would change course, my lord. And I—I don't know where they went."

A couple of the men made the sign against enchantment, and the Christians crossed themselves. Ferron still scowled skeptically.

"Believe him, my lord," I said. "He is telling you the truth."

At that, they all turned to stare at me.

Kay cleared his throat. "My lady, do you know aught about this?"

"My lords, you agreed to leave that part of it to me." I looked around at all their startled faces. "Constantine has not disappeared, he has only been misled. Eventually he will find his way again. Thank you, Aranor, for your news. It could hardly please us more."

As soon as the scout was gone, Clegis spoke. "And when he comes, my lords, what will he find? An army of King's men too frightened to step outside the gates!"

"Too wise to step outside," Berys countered. "Don't be a fool, Clegis."

I raised my hand for silence. "I am the one who must answer to Arthur for the Council's action," I reminded them. "And I will not risk your slaughter. If we can even the odds, that's a different matter. But until help comes, I forbid the gates to open."

Several of them shifted in their seats; Dynas and Clegis scowled. These were strong words, and they resented hearing them from me. But my thoughts were with Ailsa, and I was almost out of patience.

"But, my lady," Clegis cried at last, "we cannot sit here and do nothing while the traitor approaches!"

"Certainly we will not," I said calmly. "We will do what we can. Sir Clegis, you are the finest archer in the High King's army. Pick thirty men—we can spare no more—and train them to hit their mark at a hundred paces. See that we have five times the arrows you would expect to need, to kill four hundred men. I give you five days." His jaw dropped. "Can this not be done?" I asked innocently.

He colored. "It will be done, my lady Queen."

"Thank you, my lord. I am sure I may rely upon you. Dynas, I charge you with readying our defense against an attack of fire arrows. If it comes to confrontation, I don't expect Constantine has the stomach for a siege. Bid the coopers get busy. We'll need water vats and men to carry buckets. I can spare you five soldiers only, but you may organize a brigade from the pages and grooms and chamberlains. They will need drilling, of course. Take all the time you require. With so many gone from Camelot, they have little enough to do."

"I will do it!" Dynas cried eagerly. "I had not thought of fire arrows!"

Ferron of course was in charge of the fortress defense, and Kay of the castle's, but with these two young hotheads busy at other tasks, their own plans would run a smoother course, I thought. And I saw by the half-concealed amusement on their faces that they thought so, too.

They were all talking about siege defenses when I left. I smiled to myself. They had formed a plan, and hardly a man there knew how they had done it. Ahhhh, my dear Arthur, I thought as I walked quickly back to Ailsa, how they all must be as putty in your hands!

Three days later Constantine was discovered mired in the bogs at the southern reaches of the Lake of Avalon. How he had come there, no one knew. But everyone knows how easy it is to lose one's way in a fog.

For those three days, Ailsa was much the same, more sleeping than awake, unmoving, and saying nothing. I had hoped that, once she came out of her deep sleep and opened her eyes, she would come to herself again, but the physician told me not to expect it. When she was awake, she knew me. But although she listened to my voice and smiled a trifle when I sang to her, she could not respond, even with the lift of a finger. And when she slept, her breath rattled lightly in her chest. The physician frowned when he heard it, but said nothing beyond advising more salve.

Day and night I sat at her side; Anna and I took our meals in her little chamber. I found solace recalling events long past when Ailsa had helped me through one scrape or another, and I knew by her eyes that Ailsa enjoyed it, too. Anna, bless her, listened to my reminiscing without a word of complaint, laughed when I laughed, and once or twice was moved to tears.

"Oh, Anna!" I cried. "There never was such a guardian in all the world as Ailsa! She knows me better, even now, than I know myself. But for Ailsa, I should have betrayed—I should have yielded—always she held up before my eyes the honor of Gwynedd, the honor of Arthur, the honor of Britain, and bade me do what I knew was right! Ah, Ailsa, my mother in life, without you I should not now be Queen!"

I chanced to look down and found her awake and looking at me, thin tracks of tears sliding sideways down her cheeks. I fell to my knees and kissed her hands. "You know it's true, my darling Ailsa, don't you? You and Arthur, between you, have kept me on the straight path. Without you, I should long ago have yielded to temptation and betrayed the very things I hold most dear."

Half her mouth moved in a smile; her lips began to work. But as I bent down to listen, a knock came at the door, and Ferron burst in to tell me that Constantine was on his way again and fast approaching the Camel river.

"Come out of your fastness, my lady, I beg of you! The Council needs you!"

"Ferron, Ferron, I cannot come—"

Behind him came Kay's voice, stern and sad. "You must choose, Guinevere, between Ailsa and Britain. Remember Arthur once made such a choice."

"Oh, God!" I cried, pressing my hands against my face. "I am only a woman! Surely that choice will not be asked of me!"

"But it is," Ferron pressed. "Clegis has roused Villers and Dynas and even Gryfflet almost to frenzy. They will not listen to a word we say—against orders, Sir Villers is rousing the army, even as we stand here!"

"Then give him an order he can obey!" I cried, my eyes on Ailsa's withered face. "Bid him take twenty men and cross the river. Set fire to the land on the other side, six leagues either way. We've had no rain for weeks and the land is mostly brush and meadow grasses. Let it burn toward Constantine; let him see a wall of flame. It will take him a day to get around it. A whole day of precious time."

For a long moment the men stood silent. Then Ferron grinned and bowed. "My lady Queen."

A hot afternoon, stuffy and still. Anna wiped my brow with a cool cloth, as I wiped Ailsa's. The sun beat down upon the castle walls and warmed the stones that encased us. Somewhere, I hoped, the flames were still burning around Constantine; in that little chamber we were roasting alive.

Ailsa was whispering, but it was mostly nonsense. She roamed a world where past and present mingled, and I could not follow half she said. Her breath came harder, no matter what we did to ease her, but she did not seem to know it. Arthur, Uther, my father Leodegrance, Alyse and Pellinore and a hundred others marched through her thoughts in a confused parade; she did not hear me when I spoke to her or listen when I sang.

Through the window we could see dark clouds building in the distance, slowly swelling and creeping toward us. Rain might

bring us sweet relief, but it also signaled danger. It would put out
the fires that had, for two days, kept Constantine at bay.

"Those men are fools!" Anna grumbled in my ear. "Sir Dynas
is speaking treason! I overheard him with Sir Clegis when I went
to fetch the water. He does not intend to obey you, my lady, even
if you command him to his face. He says since women are not
warriors, they cannot lead men!"

"Hush, Anna. I know what they are saying. It's even possible
that it is true."

"But, my lady!"

"I should be with them. I know that; but I cannot go. I am not
Arthur. Listen to her, my dear, sweet Ailsa. She is not in her right
mind. I am so afraid, Anna—once, Arthur put his grief behind
him, for Britain's sake. But I—I cannot seem to let go of mine."

When I closed my eyes I still saw Arthur, hands clasped in
prayer, a shadow of himself, consumed with grief for Merlin's
passing, consumed with the fear he had buried him alive in the
stony ground. It was the Sword that had roused him and brought
him to his senses; the great Sword, a gift of the god, which protected Britain from her enemies. But the Sword was not here now.
He had taken it with him.

That night the skies opened. I lay on the pallet at the side of
Ailsa's bed, listening to the wheeze and shudder of her breath. A
silent seed of fear took root inside my heart and set me shaking.
This could not happen, not now, not after so much. It was nearly
summer; the sweet warmth of the afternoons and the sun on her
face would bring her back to health, if I could move her outdoors!
But moving her the physician flatly forbade. He said she would
not survive it, and that was easy enough to believe, seeing what
little nourishment she took. We were doing all that we could—
what more could we do?

All that dark day her breath rattled loudly. We lit a coal fire in
the grate and sprinkled herb water on it to steam the air and give
her an easier breath. Anna brought me news that the Camel was
in full flood, raging and impossible to ford. She crossed herself
quickly and smiled.

Ailsa woke at dusk and looked at me beseechingly; her lips
moved, but no sound came out; she was in need, and I did not
know what she wanted! Anna and I brought her everything we
could think of: blankets, bricks, tea, broth, water, wine, salve,
soap, furs, and even ribbons. Then my glance happened to fall on
the kerchief on the floor where we had collected all the charms
and jewels the physician had taken off her.

"Her amulet!" I cried, lifting the soft, leather pouch full of lucky talismans. Something moved behind her eyes. I placed the amulet in her hand, and her spirit charms, too, and her prayer beads; her fingers, so long immobile, closed around them; her eyes fluttered shut, and she slept. I did not know whether to weep with joy that she could command her fingers or weep with sorrow at what her request betokened, but I wept.

Toward dawn I was awakened by a harsh, grating sound. I sat up; in the dimness I saw the glint of Ailsa's eyes. Her mouth was open; the horrible sound came from her throat!

"Lady Elen!" Her hard, rasping voice rang loud in the room. A thrill of fear raced up my spine. Elen was my mother, dead these five and thirty years. "It is done . . . You are delivered . . . of a daughter . . . A queen . . . like no other . . . One day she will make you proud." She gasped horribly, fighting for breath. I bent over her. Her eyes looked into mine. "So proud." The eyes rolled back, the racking noise faded to a sigh, Anna's hand came down upon my shoulder.

"No! Ailsa! Ailsa! Don't leave me! I need you still!"

Gently Anna's hand pulled me away. "Come, my lady. Let me cover her face."

"My lady, they have crossed the Camel! The floodwaters abated enough to let them through!"

"My lord Ferron, she takes no heed. Can you not let her grieve for the old woman? She loved her as a mother."

"But, Anna, she is regent. We cannot act without her."

"Have they sent a messenger?"

"Not yet."

"Are they shaping for attack?"

"Not yet."

"Then, I pray you, leave her awhile longer. She cannot attend you now. As you see."

"But how soon?"

"Ah, sir, that I do not know."

"My lady, Sir Ferron has come thrice to see you. Duke Constantine is camped upon the plain of Camlann and has sent a messenger begging entrance."

I stared at the shrouded figure on the pallet. "How dare he, when she is not even in the ground? Beg him say a prayer for her, my dearest Ailsa."

"I'm sorry, Sir Ferron, it must wait awhile longer."

* * *

On a gray morning in a warm rain we buried her. Bishop Landrum spoke the words that sealed her body in the earth and her soul in heaven. I blessed him in my heart, when he allowed my dear Ailsa Christian burial. In life, she had worshipped not only Christ but every god she knew.

26 ❁ ТНЕ ᚱᴇSCUE

I opened the curtain to see Arthur standing by the window in a loincloth, his flesh shrunk to no more than a shroud upon his bones.

"Britain needs you, my lord! Take up your Sword and lead her."

"I am powerless to do it. Britain will have to wait."

"No!" I wept aloud. "I will lead the men myself, if you will not! Though a woman, I can die as easily as you!"

"Put down the Sword, Guinevere."

"I cannot! Oh, come and take it from me, my lord! It is so heavy!"

His hand gripped the hilt; light flashed from the living blade and burned my eyes.

I looked up. Sunlight streamed into my chamber, dazzlingly bright. I was in my own bed; I could not remember how I got there. But I remembered my dream.

"Anna, how long have I been here?"

She knelt nearby, head bowed against the coverlet, but when I spoke, she raised her head. "Oh, my lady! A day and a night!"

In irritation, I pushed the covers aside, sat up, and then stopped, dizzy. "What has passed? Where is Ferron?"

"Outside, my lady. Council has just ended." There was fear in her eyes, but also hope.

I paused. "How do we stand? Tell me, if you know."

"Elisane is below with a tray of food. I will tell you while you eat. I beg you not to argue with me, my lady, I can see you are dizzy. It's been over a week since you've had a proper meal."

While I ate she told me what she knew. Constantine had finally arrived and sat down at the foot of Caer Camel, blocking the Roman road and commanding the approaches to King's Gate. There he had sat for three days, every morning sending his second son, a youth named Markion, with a message begging an audience of the Queen.

"And what answer did the Council give him?"

Anna, as always, spoke straight. "None, at first. But as so long a silence demanded explanation, they finally told him you were ill and could not receive him."

"They should have told him it was grief. Constantine would delight to know they were all held helpless by a woman's weakness. It would have fed his pride and made him overconfident. I do not mind their scorn."

"My lady, their pride would not allow it. They would never admit to helplessness, not King's men."

I sighed. "Well, and what did Constantine say?"

"He laughed at them." Anna smiled. "He called them cowards and accused them of hiding behind a woman's skirts."

"How like him."

"But angry as they were, they took it and did nothing. Sir Kay made them obey, at swordpoint."

"Did it come to that? Bless Kay. It must have been hard for them."

I pushed aside the tray of food. Already I felt less lightheaded.

"He cannot be serious about war. He dare not make Arthur his enemy. His eldest son, his heir, Sir Meliodas, worships Arthur—he is with him in Brittany, leading the Cornish troops. I can't believe the duke truly wants a battle, unless he is using his sons to hedge his bets. Have we seen any sign of Wales or Elmet?"

"Not yet, my lady. They are daily expected."

"And where are the men now?"

Her smile faded. "On the practice grounds, my lady. Falling in, for battle. The horn sounded but half an hour ago."

"What! Are they mad? Who led them?"

"Sir Villers, my lady. And—"

"Dynas and Clegis, yes, I know."

"And Sir Gryfflet and Sir Bleoberys."

"Ahh, dear God, Berys gave in to them, did he? He swung the

balance for war—well, what can you expect from rule by Council? The fools will kill themselves, and Arthur will hold me to account." I rose, and found my legs were steady.

"But—does not the Council always make decisions?"

I nearly laughed. "Don't you believe it, Anna. Arthur rules Britain. No one else. The Council is for consensus. And no one ever disagrees with Arthur. Long experience has taught them he knows well what he's about." I reached for my comb. "Quickly now, there is little time! Bring me my best gown, the blue one, while I put up my hair. And bring me my crown."

I stepped out into the bright June sun of the forecourt. The Council, on horseback, were mustering the troops, each commander giving his men instructions. Ferron and Kay had not yet mounted but stood with their backs to me, their very postures bespeaking their anger.

Someone called out and pointed. Several of the soldiers fell to one knee.

Kay and Ferron whirled. "My lady Queen!"

I strode down to where they stood, and they each bent a knee to the ground. "What goes on here, my lords? What is meant by this defiance?"

"My lady," Ferron began, glaring sideways at Villers, "in your absence, the Council has decided to give the blackguard fight."

Silence fell across the courtyard. Even the horses stood still.

"How dare they? Who gave the order?" No one moved. I turned to Villers. "Sir, you will follow me to King's Gate and bring the soldiers up behind me. Sir Clegis, I see your men are ready on the battlements. Bid them fit their arrows to their bows and when I go out the gate, aim them, every one, at Constantine."

Ferron gasped. "You are not going out!"

"My lady!" Kay cried in a strangled voice.

Villers slid from his horse and fell to both knees. "My lady Queen, do not take this risk on account of me!"

"You leave me no choice, sir. But it is not much of a risk, with Clegis' archers at the ready—if he so much as draws his sword, he will die."

I turned to face the troops, who stood gaping at me. "I know you men are loyal to King Arthur. Be patient yet awhile longer, I pray you. Together, we will protect Arthur's fortress and keep Britain whole. And I will spare your lives, if it is in my power. Now." I took a deep breath. "I will speak with Constantine."

They shouted protests, and Kay and Ferron begged me strenuously not to go, but I did not slow my pace, and no one laid a hand upon my arm to stop me. At King's Gate, Kay, near panic, forbade the guards to open the gates.

"I'm sorry, Kay, my old friend, to give you such trouble, but I must countermand the order. Guards. Open the gate." The poor guards shook, shrugged apologetically at Kay, and swung open the double gates. "Villers, stay here. If the archers let fly, you must needs attack. But until then, stay well out of sight."

"Guinevere!" Ferron cried. "You cannot go out alone! I am coming with you."

He shook from head to foot and had turned pale. I yielded; he would never be able to face Arthur, else.

"Very well, but leave your sword and dagger here. If you come, come naked."

He obeyed me without protest and followed me outside.

We took Constantine by surprise. We were well out into the sunlit meadow before his sentries saw us and sounded the alarm. I stopped within thirty paces of the gate. Above us, atop the length of the outer walls, Clegis' archers had their arrows ready. Clegis himself I saw, above the gates; he saluted smartly and bent his knee.

"Stay behind me, Ferron, and keep your eyes open. Don't shake so. It is too beautiful a day for death."

Ferron shook his head. "I have never faced a warrior without my weapons," he admitted. "Never mind an army."

I managed a smile for him. "Without fear, bravery is impossible."

He gave me a half smile back. "So Arthur has told his troops a hundred times."

The thunder of galloping horses turned our heads. Constantine and his commanders rode toward us at speed, with his army running up behind him. When they neared us, they slowed and formed a broad semicircle around us.

"They're in fighting position, my lady," Ferron murmured behind me.

I nodded. Duke Constantine himself was a man just past the prime of life, with gray flecks in his beard and lines around his dark, angry eyes. But he was as fit and lean as any warrior ten years his junior. He glared at me a long moment, then slid off his horse, signaling his commanders to stay on theirs. He walked toward me. Some whisper of sound made him look up, and he saw the long ridge of arrows aimed at his heart. He stopped.

"What sort of welcome is this?"

"Do you come as friend or foe, my lord duke?"

"As friend, of course."

"Then where is your greeting?"

Scowling, he bent his knee to the earth and bowed his head. His commanders glanced quickly at one another. I looked hard at them; one by one they saluted.

"Rise, Constantine, and be welcome to Camelot." Immediately he relaxed, and his hand no longer hovered near his swordhilt. "Forgive, if you will, the Council's stalling. It is my fault; I was abed."

"I am sorry to know my lady Queen was ill," he said gruffly. "And pleased to see you are now recovered."

"Tell me how you found the state of the country on your ride north from Cornwall."

He shrugged impatiently. This was talk that usually waited for a good seat at table, a pitcher of mead, and a leg of fowl. "Quiet. Not a whisper of discontent."

"And how was your journey?"

He looked at me sharply, but I kept my face straight. "Smooth, my lady, and swift. In spite of nasty weather."

"Ahhh. I am glad to hear it. But why swift, my lord? I thought perhaps you had had some news of unrest that we had missed, but you tell me it is not so."

I nearly laughed at his chagrin. How he wished he had thought of that before!

Instead, he came out with the excuse he had prepared. "I have brought you an army, Queen Guinevere, for your defense, since the High King left Camelot so lightly garrisoned. And as a warning to the Saxons," he added, as an afterthought.

I made him a deep curtsy, pleased to find him slow. "What a very generous gift. I thank you, my lord, on the High King's behalf."

His commanders relaxed, grinning at one another. The army, watching them, stood at ease. Constantine jerked his head toward the archers. "Why do they still threaten me, my lady? Call them off."

I smiled sweetly and spread out my hands. "They are my only weapon, my lord duke. You wear your sword, your men are armed. As you see, Sir Ferron and I are not. I will call them off when your men are well inside."

This suited him perfectly, and he smiled. "Very well. Let us go in."

"Of course," I added lightly, "you will come without your

swords." He froze. "You are not our enemy, my lord; we are not yours. There is no need for weapons."

He took a long moment to control his rage enough to answer. "I have brought you an army, Queen Guinevere. But they cannot serve you without weapons!"

"Of a certainty," I replied pleasantly. "We shall return them. And I do not refer to your commanders, Duke Constantine. Only to your men. Have them stack their weapons outside King's Gate as they come in. Sir Ferron will collect them and give them back, when he has trained them and they have sworn allegiance to the High King Arthur. I thank you from my heart for this generous gift, my lord duke. How you will keep Cornwall without them is beyond my ability to imagine."

"They are not Arthur's men!" Constantine cried, reddening. "They are mine! And they do not move without their weapons!"

I feigned surprise. "Then they are not a gift, after all? My lord, what did you bring them for?"

"To keep you safe from Saxons! But they do not swear allegiance to Arthur. They are Cornishmen, and follow me!"

"Well, my lord, if they are yours and not Arthur's, you had better take them back to Cornwall. We are safe enough from Saxons now."

"This is tyranny!" Constantine shouted hoarsely. No woman had ever spoken to him thus, and it was more than his pride could bear. He took three sudden strides toward me; Ferron pulled me back as something whistled through the air and thudded into the turf a stride from Constantine's boots. A single arrow stood half buried in the ground, the shaft still quivering. Constantine stepped back, the color gone from his face.

"Another step," Ferron warned, "and you're a dead man."

On the rampart, Clegis saluted me and notched another arrow. I shrugged off Ferron's arm. "I beg you, Sir Ferron, give the duke a chance to save his skin. My lord, I beg your pardon. In Arthur's absence, his men are anxious to protect me. Make no sudden move, I pray you. I cannot answer for their actions. You see how it is. I am sorry, but I'm no Arthur."

The duke glared, fighting for composure. "You don't fool me, you Welsh witch! You planned this insult! In all my life I've never been treated so! You will let me in the gates, and be polite about it, or—or—"

I waited calmly for him to speak the treason that would seal his fate forever, but suddenly the lookout sounded his horn and the archers on the wall pointed, shouting, to the plains beyond. From where we stood, we could see nothing, but the alarm could mean only one thing.

"My lord duke!" I called out, loud enough for all his commanders to hear. "Make your decision now! If you want war, you shall have it, but the contest will be more closely matched than you had planned. My reinforcements have arrived."

Constantine swore viciously under his breath, cursed me for a barren bitch, and swung on his heel. As he reached for his stallion's reins, we saw his scout ride up at a fast gallop.

"My lord duke! We are surrounded! They come from the west and from the east and from the south! Five hundred men or more! And a host of cavalry!"

"Damn all women!" Constantine shouted, leaping into the saddle and flinging his horse's head around. "I've been wronged, and I'll take what's due me! I'll be back!"

The last we saw of him, he was leading his troops down onto the plain as fast as they could go.

All we had to do the rest of that brilliant day was watch from the towers. Drustan from the east and Gwillim from the west met an army of horsemen riding fast from the south. The Dragon banner flew bright in the summer breeze, red on gold, unmistakable. The men from Elmet and from Wales gathered under the Dragon and took their battle stations. Villers led Camelot's forces out King's Gate to take the ground Constantine had yielded. Surrounded, Cornwall dug in his heels and waited. Arthur's commander, whoever he was, showed calm and sense, and sent to beg a parley. We watched from the towers as they met and spoke. Not until the shadows began to lengthen did Constantine turn and give the signal to retreat. The King's forces let them pass, then closed behind them and followed them on their way.

I drew a deep breath and sighed. "All is well. Thank God for Arthur's friends and allies! I wanted to avoid bloodshed at any cost." Beside me, Kay and Ferron smiled indulgently. "Whoever Arthur sent must be honored and commended. Will they be back by nightfall? Let us feast them well."

"Don't expect them until tomorrow," Ferron advised. "No doubt they'll see Constantine at least halfway back to Cornwall, just to be certain he goes."

Sure enough, four hundred men rode in King's Gate in the bright sun of midmorning. Drustan was there, and Gwillim my cousin; and leading them was Mordred.

"Oh, Mordred!" I cried with joy, hugging him in greeting.

"How glad I am to see you! I am more thankful than you can know that he sent you! I asked only for one of his commanders."

"I know. I saw the letter," he said, smiling. "But he was angry he had misjudged Constantine and thought I should be here. You must tell me what happened."

I hugged Gwillim and thanked him most sincerely for coming to my aid. And Drustan, who was well past sixty but had come himself, I sat at my right hand at dinner. We celebrated a long time, and gave them food and wine and song and, finally, rest.

It was late in the evening before Mordred and I had time for talk. We strolled in the garden with Kay and Ferron, still discussing Constantine's bold move and Mordred's thwarting of his plans. Now that Arthur's declared heir was back in Camelot, Constantine had no excuse for leaving Cornwall.

"You will stay, won't you, now that you are here?" I asked, clasping his hand.

"Yes, my lady. I am to stay until the King returns, as regent, if you are willing to give up the post to me."

"Willing! Oh, yes, indeed I am willing! God knows I have had my fill of such responsibility; how he has borne it all these years, I cannot guess. I have aged a decade since his going!"

"Well," Mordred said, grinning, "you do not look it. You look but twenty, if you look a day."

I squeezed his hand, glad to feel laughter again. "Thank you, my lord. I will believe every word you tell me from now on!"

"I must send a report to Arthur tonight, for he is beside himself with worry. Only half his mind will be on Rome until he knows that you are safe."

"And how does my lord?" I asked him anxiously. "How do they treat him? Is he honored? Is his health good? Are they ready?"

"He is well and he is honored," Mordred said with pride. "He is a King among kings. He has become the arbiter of all their disputes; their battle leader; their judge. The Franks have a name for him: Riothamus. Beloved judge. It began among their soldiers, when he settled some impossible dispute to all their liking. They know his fairness now. His own troops have the hardest chores; it is seen he favors no one."

Kay and Ferron asked about the Romans and their dispositions. Mordred told them what he knew, although clearly he had left them before their final plans were set. Hiberius demanded the tribute by the first of June. The Franks and Britons proposed to send a party to treat with him and negotiate the demand; also, to get a look at his numbers and their equipment. Mordred was to have been the leader of this party, until my letter changed Arthur's plans.

"Who went in your stead?" Kay asked. "Bedwyr?"

"No," Mordred said slowly, frowning, "he was the obvious choice, of course. But Arthur wanted someone of royal blood. He sent Gawaine."

"Gawaine?" I gasped. "Send a hothead to negotiate with Romans? Is he mad?"

Mordred shifted and schooled his face. "He believes Gawaine has steadied and matured. He gave, as evidence for this, his treatment of Lancelot."

"What of Lancelot?" I whispered in panic. "Arthur said Gawaine had promised not to harm him!"

"So he has, my lady. That is what I mean—"

"He has forgiven him for Gareth?"

"No," Mordred said patiently, "but he has stood before Lancelot and promised not to kill him while they are both in the High King's service."

"What does that mean?" I asked blankly.

"It means Lancelot is safe while Arthur lives. To do him honor for that promise, the King sent him with the party to the Romans."

"But surely," I protested, "Gawaine could see that if he did not promise, Arthur could not keep him in Brittany! What foolishness is this? What has happened to my lord?"

Mordred shrugged. "If he errs," he said quietly, "it is on the side of mercy."

I rose, clasping my hands in distress. "He knows himself he has always been blind to Morgause's wiles and has never seen her sons for what they are!" I gasped as I realized what I had said. "I beg your pardon, Mordred!"

He shook his head. "I do not," Mordred said solemnly, "think of myself as Morgause's son. No offense is taken."

I reached out a hand to him. "Thank you, Mordred. You are Arthur's son, indeed." He touched his lips to my fingers and let me go.

"How long have you been gone, Sir Mordred?" Ferron asked. "When was this mission to the Romans? Who else was in the party?"

"I have been traveling six days. They left soon after I did. They should have come to some conclusion by now." He named the knights who had accompanied Gawaine: Bedwyr and Gereint from Britain, Hoel's two sons, Galahantyn and Bors from Lanascol, and three of Childebert's best men. But to Gawaine of Orkney had gone the honor of leading them all.

I fell silent and worried over this while he talked awhile with Ferron and with Kay. They sent a message of reassurance to Arthur and made plans for the disposition of the troops he had brought home. But I fretted over Arthur. What was he about, trusting Gawaine? We should have war, for certain, if anything happened to spark Gawaine's quick temper.

At length Kay and Ferron left us, and Mordred and I sat alone in the dark garden, with a single cresset burning by the door.

"And how is Lancelot?" I asked quietly. When he did not reply, I placed my hand upon his arm and searched his face. "Do not begrudge me this, dear Mordred. Your father does not."

He opened his mouth to speak and then changed his mind. "He is well," he said at last. "He looks about the same. He had not been with the King five minutes before he asked 'How does the Queen?' "

I smiled. "And I will wager any amount that Arthur answered him without hesitation. Come, Mordred, you are a man now. Have you never loved a woman?" I knew he had two bastard sons; I had heard him speak of them to Arthur. But I did not know who their mother was, or if he loved her.

He lowered his eyes. "Oh, yes, madam. I have, indeed."

"Then you know its power; such a passion cannot be trifled with."

"I know it."

"A wise man recognizes this and accepts it."

He lifted his chin. "Are you asking me to condone it?"

"No. Just to accept it and forgive me for it."

Mordred remained very still. After a long while, he nodded. "Very well. But someday, Guinevere, I will remind you of these words."

I took his hand between my own; in shape and size and feel, his hand was so like Arthur's, even down to the calluses made by his stallion's reins. "So be it. Now tell me what I want to know—did he seem happy? Was he downcast? Do his sons delight him? Does Galahantyn's wife care for him well enough? Does he still miss Camelot? How did he greet Galahad?"

Mordred withdrew his hand and rose. He walked away some distance, staring up at the sky, then returned and stood before me. "Guinevere, I do not see him with your eyes. I cannot tell you everything you want to know. I am sure he would rather be back here in his old place than rule in Lanascol. But he seems content enough. I have not seen his younger sons. He greeted Arthur like a brother. There is nothing changed between them."

"Ahhhh. I am glad of that. And Galahad?"

Mordred began to pace back and forth. He had his father's stride.

"I would rather you did not ask me," he said finally.

"Why?" I cried. "What has happened?"

"They have had a falling out. It is not serious—I mean, not to Britain. For Arthur's sake, they have put their words behind them and are united in his service. But it was a close thing."

"Oh, Mordred, you distress me! How did this come about?"

"Must you ask me? Really, you would rather not know."

I rose, and he stopped his pacing to face me. "Mordred. You have gone too far not to go on. If you will not tell me, I must ask Arthur. Which of you can tell me with less distress?"

"I can," he said at once, and handed me back into my seat. "Very well, then. You know that Galahad has commissioned himself the High King's personal guard, ever since he first accompanied the King as a page, years ago? Well, he sleeps outside his tent at night—yes, right outside on the very ground, whatever the weather. He rejoices in personal discomfort. He follows the King everywhere; Arthur can go nowhere without him. How he bears it, I don't know. I could not."

"Does he not fight for the King? I thought he was skilled as a swordsman."

"Oh, yes, very skilled. He has Lancelot's quickness. But—I know this is hard to remember, because he is so tall and solemn—he is only fourteen and not old enough for the army. Even if he were"—and I heard a smile in his voice—"I don't know a single commander who would want him in his company. No one is good enough for Galahad, and he lets everyone know it."

"Mordred," I said suddenly, "do not take him lightly. I believe he is dangerous, and he bears you no love."

"I know that," he said. "And I know why. Don't worry. I watch him."

"He is feared by many, because he speaks with God."

"Or he says he does," Mordred replied with a smile. "That's a claim that cannot be disproved, and so has no value. Don't distress yourself with fear about Galahad; his vision is so single, he is blind to everything outside it. I have a plan for him. Arthur is going to send him on a quest."

"A quest for what?"

"For the grail and spear that lie hidden somewhere in Wales. The rest of Maximus' treasure, that his captain brought home to his wife. Excalibur she could not bear to keep, believing it the cause of her husband's death, and so sent it north to Caer Eden with the captain, but the grail and spear she kept. No doubt she buried them somewhere. We will tell Galahad it is holy and send him after the grail."

"Mordred," I whispered, shaken, "you are blaspheming!"

"No, my lady," he said gently. "I would not mock your Christian God. Merlin himself thought them sacred, saying they lay protected by the god, away from the eyes of men. And he should know." But then he smiled. "Galahad will dedicate his life to this if he thinks that only he is pure enough in heart to find it. It is a fit punishment for hubris, is it not?"

But I shivered with foreboding. "Only God punishes hubris."

"And so it will be. If his God loves him, he may find this treasure. I will not stand in his way. Only the lady Niniane knows where it is." He grinned. "And because she is a pagan, he will never ask her."

"Has Arthur agreed to this plan? It does not sound like him."

Mordred sobered instantly. "He was against it at first, but after what happened with Lancelot, he has changed his mind."

"Well, now you *must* tell me! Clearly, this is of importance. Tell me now."

He came reluctantly and sat beside me. "Remember that you asked twice for this."

"Go on, Mordred."

"When we first came across to Kerrec, we found old King Hoel in a terrible fury. His niece had been kidnapped by outlaws in the Perilous Forest. She was sixteen and was on her way home with her nurse and an escort of Hoel's men after a visit to Kerrec. She never arrived. Her father sent a message to Hoel asking what had become of his daughter, and Hoel was beside himself with rage. Arthur suggested that he and Lancelot gather a small force and find the girl, while they waited for the rest of the army to come across the Narrow Sea. You can imagine how readily Hoel assented to this offer!"

"With such powerful men for adversaries, I am almost sorry for the outlaws."

"Ahhh," Mordred said sadly, "you will not be. Only a handful of us went—Arthur, Lancelot, Bedwyr, Galahantyn, Gereint, Bors, and myself. And Galahad."

"Why did he go, if so many others did not?"

"You may find this difficult to credit, but it is like him. No one asked him to go. He just came. He showed up, mounted and ready, at the King's side as we set off, and because he was not in the army, Arthur felt sorry for him and let him come. We traveled the route the girl had taken and found clear signs of an ambush. These outlaws were not clever men, they left a trail a child could follow. We came to a lake, and in the center was an island. From the island came the sound of weeping."

I looked down in sorrow, remembering Melwas, a cold knot in my stomach. I had thought that terror was behind me, after all these years.

There was but one boat beached on the shore. As Mordred, the Orkney man, was the only seaman, he rowed them all across. When they came ashore they found the old nurse, dressed in torn scraps of clothing, covered with bleeding scratches and dirt and sand.

The tale the woman told horrified them all. Five outlaws had ambushed them and slaughtered their escort. The women were dragged to this place and raped by all five outlaws. The princess Elen had not lasted past the second day; they had stripped her and thrown her into a shallow pit and burned her bloodstained clothes. The old nurse was nearly out of her wits with terror; her age had been no protection. When the monsters had finally gone, the day before, she had used what remained of her strength to drag rocks and dirt over the pit to bury the poor girl. In Arthur's arms, the poor old woman died. They had buried them both well and placed crosses over the graves and said prayers over them.

Then they had gone in search of the murderers. The outlaws had divided, fearing pursuit, so the party divided as well, following the various trails. Arthur and Mordred had gone together, Bedwyr with Gereint, Galahantyn with Bors, and Lancelot had collared Galahad and led him away from the King. They each found their man and killed him. But Lancelot and Galahad had found the last two together.

"When we gathered at the appointed meeting place," Mordred said slowly, staring hard at the garden walk, "Galahad's face was bruised and swollen, his lips were cut and crusted with blood, and he had lost two teeth. Everyone assumed he had been injured in the fight and so said nothing. But I noted that Lancelot was stiff with fury and that Galahad glowed with the joy of righteous suffering. He held his head high and was too proud to reply to anyone's solicitous remarks. When we got to Kerrec, neither father nor son could speak a word to each other; after ten days of this, Arthur finally summoned them to a meeting, and so discovered what had happened."

He stopped suddenly and passed his hand across his brow in a gesture so familiar I felt a stab of acute loneliness.

"Were you in the room?" I asked softly.

In the dark I saw his eyes flash. "At Arthur's request." He sighed. "Well, delaying the tale makes it no easier to tell. Here is what happened. They met the two outlaws; one of them, an old soldier gone to seed, drew his sword; the other, half his age and better armed, ran. Lancelot went in pursuit of the second and left Galahad to dispatch the first. When Lancelot had killed his man, he heard screams of terror coming from the spot where he had left Galahad. Racing back to rescue his son, he found—he found Galahad standing above the ruffian, unharmed, and with a bloody sword." Mordred stopped again. My hands twisted in my lap and I swallowed. My dear Lancelot!

"What had he done?" I whispered.

Mordred shrugged. "He had stripped the man and cut off his genitals and thrown them to the kites."

I gasped and pressed my fist against my mouth. Mordred went on in a flat voice devoid of feeling. "Galahad was raving. He would not kill the man, but shouted verses from the Scriptures about an eye for an eye, or some such thing. The outlaw, who had been a soldier once, begged Lancelot for death. Lancelot dispatched him with a stroke and gave him peace. But then— Galahad began shouting about the whore of Babylon, and the defilement of women—the rape had turned his wits, Guinevere, you must believe this. He had been unable to take his eyes from the naked body of the princess when we found her. It is time he lay with a woman." He paused and then said slowly, "The filth that came from his mouth made Lancelot ill. It was some minutes before he realized that when Galahad spoke of a whore who castrated men and stripped them of virtue, he was referring to you."

"To *me*?"

Mordred went on as if he had not heard me. "Lancelot strode up to him and struck him across the face with all the strength he had. And told him if your name ever passed his lips again, he would kill him and delight in doing so."

"Dear God!" I cried. "Oh, Lancelot! My poor Lancelot!" Weeping, I looked up at Mordred and found him watching me. "He said these things to Arthur? To his face?"

Mordred nodded. "What was worse, Galahad showed no regret.

He admitted all this freely. He did not beg the King for forgiveness, although he knew Arthur has called men out to combat for smaller insults than that."

"Indeed!"

"Clearly the boy is mad. There is no question now of his ever serving Arthur with his sword. He can't be trusted. Arthur demanded that father and son swear their peace in his presence, and he will bring Galahad home when he returns, but something must be done with him to keep him out of the way. Hence the quest. That very night, Arthur assented to it."

"Oh, Mordred!" I whispered, covering my face with my hands. "How they are both wounded on account of me! In that, Galahad is right—I am a curse to both of them!"

He put his arm around me and comforted me while I wept upon his shoulder. "If it is indeed a curse, it is one neither of them would live without. You are not to blame for this, Guinevere. The boy has lost his wits."

"I am not thinking of Galahad," I cried. "But of Lancelot, who will never forgive himself for the fact that his own son spoke those words and wounded Arthur. And of Arthur, who will forgive it but will be unable to forget it. They cannot be as brothers now!"

"Their friendship is deep, and of long standing," Mordred said quietly. "They have weathered storms as bad as this. And they have a war to fight together. As time passes, these wounds will heal."

I fought to collect myself and be calm. What he said was true of Arthur, but I knew well that the wound Galahad had given Lancelot would never heal.

"Will there be war, then, do you think?"

"Of a certainty," he replied.

I searched his face in the scented darkness. "Are you sorry to have had to come home, and miss it?"

He faced me, but I could not read his expression.

"No, indeed," he said calmly. "I am well content to let Arthur, duke of battles, lead Britain's troops to war. I would rather be here at home, ruling as regent."

A pain struck my chest and I shivered, but I did not know why. I drew the regent's seal from my pouch and placed it in his hand. "Take this, then, and relieve me of my duties. I am glad it was you he sent, Mordred. Will you keep me informed of all that passes?"

He stood and raised me, and then bowed low. "I will treat you, dear Guinevere, with all the respect and honor my father pays you. Indeed, I will endeavor to make the difference between us, King and regent, as small as it may be."

27 ❁ The KING

Mordred was an excellent administrator. Under his hand, the Kingdom ran smoothly. He carried all the details of daily routine in his head and knew how to get his plans accomplished. He knew which men had power and how they stood with others and who was jealous or nursed a grievance, and who was loyal. He dealt deftly with the Council; never had their meetings been over so quickly and with so much decided. He seemed to know everything that was happening in every corner of Britain; he daily received and sent messengers, and I believe he had spies, as well. He knew how to treat men and he had their respect, if not their love.

Recognizing the threat that Constantine posed, he at once set about raising an army to replace in some measure the one that had gone with Arthur. He sent messages to every reigning ruler in the Kingdom and frankly explained his position. While Arthur was away, the stability of Britain was threatened by an ambitious lord. He requested men for the common defense. Where lords demurred, saying their numbers were depleted past bearing, Mordred paid them a visit, a courtesy call, he said. But afterward, he always got his men. Soon we were five hundred strong in Camelot. And I confess that I breathed easier with such strength at hand.

He kept his word to me and talked to me of all his plans and all his dispositions. He worked hard every morning and after Council at the King's desk in the library; he got quickly through the written work that Arthur so disliked. He kept two scribes busy at these times and could have used a third. The men drilled daily; when he had time, he liked to drill them himself, but usually it

fell to Ferron. But almost every day, he made time to take his exercise with me and Ferron and Anna when we rode out. He was
kind, attentive, and always courteous. Even so, without the daily
running of the Kingdom to keep me occupied, and without Arthur,
or Lancelot, or Bedwyr, I grew lonely.

I often found myself standing alone in Arthur's chamber. It was
kept clean and swept and aired, just as when he was at home. I
stood on the polished wood floor and let my gaze travel over the
few pieces of simple furniture, the bare walls, and the old silk
banner above the great bed. It impressed me now as it had on my
first day in Camelot: a soldier's room, simple and direct, a place
of stillness and of peace. I would stand there and feel my loneliness drain from me; he was still there, in that room. I felt his presence. And I came away with an easier heart.

Sometimes I went to the top of the northwest tower, for privacy
and a chance to think. Arthur and I had often gone together, remembering our first time there, on our wedding night, and smiling
at it. But sometimes I would go alone, and sometimes in the past
had found him there, studying out some problem or simply surveying his dominion. Now that he was gone, I found it restful just
to stand where he had stood and look at the fertile lands all about
me, giving thanks for the peaceful beauty of the country. From
this tower I could see the old Roman road that ran up from the
river Camel and would watch the troops drill, or the men go forth
to hunt, or a messenger ride in.

On the day of the solstice I went to the tower, feeling lonely
and ill at ease. On this day of all days I wished Arthur were there.
Twenty years ago we had been married. Sometimes it seemed like
yesterday to me—except that at fifteen I had known nothing of
men, had feared Arthur, and had thought I could not live without
Lancelot. I smiled to myself, as I watched a dusty courier galloping along the causeway, heading for King's Gate. How I wished
he was bringing the message that the High King's ships were in
the estuary and that before nightfall he would be here! When I recalled his last night home and his great tenderness toward me, I
was filled with the ache of longing. What I would not give to hold
him in my arms again!

I put these thoughts aside, as they led only to weeping, and I
wished to feel the joy that this day always brought me. I thought
instead of Britain, and how she prospered, and how lucky I was
to be alive in Arthur's time. He had been crowned at fourteen and
had led Britain for twenty-six years! And for twenty years we had
not had so much as a skirmish! Imagine, an entire generation

growing up in a land at peace! It was almost beyond comprehension that such a miracle could happen in such a wartorn land as Britain. God must indeed love Arthur beyond all others.

I heard a soft tap at the tower door and turned to find Mordred behind me. I knew instantly it was not good news—not from his face, which was always well schooled and unreadable, but from the mere fact that he had come himself and not sent a page.

"My lady Guinevere," he said quietly, "please forgive the intrusion. But it is important."

My hand crept to my throat, then I straightened, stilling myself. "What is it, Mordred? You have had news from Less Britain?"

"Yes, my lady. Would you not prefer to come down to the library to hear it?"

"Certainly not. Tell me now. Is my lord well?"

He cleared his throat. I thought he looked uneasy. "Yes, my lady. This letter is from him." He handed me a scroll, and I recognized the flowing penmanship of Arthur's favorite scribe. "It is short, as you see, and dictated in haste. It is as we feared, Guinevere. Gawaine's embassy ended in disaster, and they are marching to war." I scanned the note, but it gave just bare details. Mordred would have the complete message from the courier's lips. I drew a deep breath and bade him tell me all he knew.

"It seems they had no sooner ridden into the Roman camp when trouble broke out. While the diplomats in the party were meeting, Gawaine accosted some Roman youth he thought showed him arrogance; an argument arose over a trifle; Gawaine ran him through on the spot."

I gasped. "He *killed* him? How did he dare? He was sent to talk, not to fight!"

Mordred's shrug was eloquent. "The youth turned out to be a nephew of Hiberius himself, so the insult is not likely to be forgiven."

"I should think not. Is Gawaine in disgrace?"

"Well," Mordred said slowly, "he has forced Arthur's hand. I should tell you, perhaps, of the conversation we had before I left." He paced back and forth a bit, then came to the parapet beside me and gazed across the rolling fields toward the Tor. "When you asked why Arthur sent Gawaine instead of someone more level-headed, I did not tell you all of Arthur's reasoning. He knew it would come to war. The embassy was only a stalling tactic, to get a look at their strength. But in his heart he felt that the sooner they met in battle, the better. The Burgundians were mustered, but Hiberius is lately come from Rome and probably does not have all the reinforcements he would like. Thus he agreed quickly to the proposal of an embassy. When Arthur chose Gawaine, he knew there was a chance there might be trouble. But if they fought the sooner for it, so much the better. Now it has come to pass. He says in the note they have gathered their forces and are marching to meet the Burgundians at Autun."

I shut my eyes and said a quick prayer to God for his safety.

"I knew it," I whispered. "I knew he would take the field himself. Oh, Mordred!"

He took my hands. "Do not fear, Gwen. He will not lose. You know Arthur."

"Yes," I cried, "and so do they! They will not come against him unless they outnumber him three to one—and even if he lives, what of those who fight with him? Mordred, if they meet in battle, so many will die!"

He nodded. "Perhaps. But fewer than if they waited until the Romans were ready. In a way, perhaps, Gawaine's hotheadedness has worked to advantage. It is unlikely they could outnumber him three to one."

I leaned upon his arm and tried to smile. "You would give me courage. Thank you, Mordred. But I think I will go to my chamber. When—when does this dreaded event take place?"

He looked at me with compassion; I remembered Arthur's words to me once when I had expressed horror at war: "How can war be evil? Fighting is as natural as breathing to men; and if your cause is just, where is the dishonor?" Mordred was Arthur's son, I saw. To him it was a matter of honor and glory, and certainly not a dreaded event.

"My dear Guinevere, it may be taking place even as we speak. The courier has been on the road a week."

"Dear God!" I whispered, feeling faint. Mordred bent toward me in concern, and I fought to collect my wits. "Then we may hear—within a week—all the world may change!"

He felt how I trembled and slipped an arm about me to support me. "Please, Guinevere, take courage. The King will be victorious. All that will change is that the Romans must leave Gaul, this time forever."

I straightened and stepped out of his embrace. "You will keep me informed, Mordred? Do not let this show of weakness make you fearful of sharing news with me. I will be braver next time."

His features softened. "You are brave enough now. I will indeed keep you informed of any messages I receive. Now, shall we go down together?" He offered me his arm.

"No. No, thank you. I have changed my mind. I would like to stay here awhile, and pray."

He bowed and left me.

Life went on unchanged. Daily Mordred sent for me and went over what news there was from around the Kingdom. Daily he rode out at my side. I had every chance to see him at work and see how Arthur's men took to his leadership. He was respected and admired. He was an able man, known to be clever and far-seeing. These weeks of being sole regent were the first chance he had ever had to rule. It had so long been his heart's desire, and he had had so many years of apprenticeship, it was as if a sleeping plant had at last turned its face to the sun and started to grow. It seemed to me he grew in stature daily.

At first I was elated—when he came to be High King, he would be a good one, as I had always known he would, and Britain would not suffer under his leadership. But then I grew uneasy, for an oak can never be put back into its acorn, or a falcon, once flown, go back into its egg. During these weeks, Mordred tasted power, and it agreed with him. When Arthur returned, he would find his son a king in all but name; he would have to find him some territory of his own to hold, for I doubted now that Mordred could go back to being merely his advisor and his heir. But what lands could Mordred, bastard prince of Orkney, call his own?

I pushed aside these thoughts, for no one could settle it but Arthur. I kept Anna by my side all the day long, and read to her, or sang to her, if I could bring myself to it, or rode with her and talked. She had more thoughts in her head than weddings and beddings and the catching of husbands. She was a great comfort to me.

It was Anna who told me that the young men of Britain, the sons and nephews of Arthur's friends and Companions, and even their grandsons, were growing restless under Arthur's rule. They thought the High King grew old and set in his ways, she said, and they were eager for a younger man to lead them. She knew this hurt me, and she told it to me gently, but I could hear the truth of it in her voice.

"All young men feel so, I believe," she said. "In your youth, my lady, young men had the Saxon wars to fight and a young King to lead them. But these young men thirst for power and are tired of peace and civilization."

"Tired of civilization? Anna, what can you mean?"

"I mean only that they want to be kings in their own lands and set their own laws and run their affairs as they see fit. They care nothing for Arthur's way of governing. They laugh at the notion of justice for common folk."

Was it possible? That young men raised in Arthur's Peace should wish to push us back into the violent dark? Why, we should be no better than the Saxons, with each kingdom at the other's throat!

"Oh, no, Anna, I cannot believe this! Simply because they are impatient for glory, they would tear down all the High King has built? It is wild oats, surely, and nothing more. And do they think that Mordred will be different from his father? He is a civilized man—none more so."

Anna was fond of Mordred; as fond as she had ever been of any man, although he had never so much as cast his glance her way. She could speak of him without blushing or growing shy, but she admired him and often followed him with her eyes and let affection warm her voice when she said his name.

"Sir Mordred is from Orkney, where ways are different," she replied. "These young men I speak of are all from the wild lands in the north and some from Wales. However Roman he behaves with Arthur, they think it only one of many cloaks he wears, and that in his heart Sir Mordred is of their blood. After all," she added softly, "he is a pagan."

"Do they accuse Arthur of being Roman? Why, at this very moment he risks his life to drive the Romans out! Can they not see this? Are they blind?"

Here she patted my hand and smiled. "Yes, indeed they are, my lady. Blind to anything they prefer not to see. Perhaps your assessment is the right one, and these are wild oats. In time they will settle down, as their fathers did, and be glad to be part of Britain."

I shuddered. What future was left for Britain without a strong King at her center, giving her laws and granting justice, protecting her from enemies without and within? Why, without Roman civilization, we should be back in the time my father used to speak of, when there were twelve kings in Wales alone, each fighting with the other while the Saxons rowed their longboats up our rivers!

"Dear Anna, keep your ears open, and tell me what you hear. It seems the times are changing fast. Arthur will need to know this, when he returns."

* * *

We had six days of rain; then the sun broke forth in splendor and the heat of summer was upon us. A week went by, then two weeks, and still we heard nothing from Less Britain. I began to sleep better. No news is good news was a saying older than Merlin.

Between the stables and my gardens, I kept myself busy. And after hall, when I went with Mordred and Anna and Ferron and some others to the King's library, I would sit quietly in the scented cool of the summer night. I'd let my thoughts wander and see the King's face in Mordred's features and hear his voice in my ear.

One brilliant morning I walked in the library garden with Anna. Some of the younger maids were learning the art of caring for roses, and they laughed gaily together and chatted with the gardeners as they had their lessons. Anna and I stood some way from the fountain and spoke quietly together. The door into the library was open, and we could see Mordred in the dimness, at the High King's desk. Even as we watched, he rose and stood at attention. A page backed away; a courier approached, filthy with the dirt of travel, and went on one knee. I gripped Anna's hand—I dared not breathe.

"Victory is ours!" I heard him hoarsely cry. "My lord, the Romans are defeated!"

I began to weep in silence. Anna gently led me away to the back of the garden. I knelt where once I had knelt with Lancelot, and gave my thanks to God for answering my prayers. So great was my relief, I could not rise, but stayed leaning on the bench, hands clasped, for a long time. I never heard Anna leave me. But when I heard Mordred's steps approaching, and I turned, Anna was gone, and the maids and the gardeners, as well. We were alone.

I looked up smiling and had opened my mouth to speak, when I saw his face and was struck dumb. There were tear tracks on his cheeks! Mordred, who never showed but a fraction of what he felt, Mordred had wept.

My throat went dry; I could not find breath. Mordred sat slowly on the bench and took my hands between his own. He himself was barely in control, and he trembled.

"Guinevere—"

"Victory," I whispered, "I heard him say it. We won the day. I came to give thanks."

Mordred nodded slowly, but his eyes were full of grief. "Yes," he managed. "The day was ours. Hiberius himself was killed, and his forces recalled to Rome. The Burgundians are defeated. The threat is—is past."

"Then why—no! Do not tell me!" I cried, as he opened his mouth to speak.

He held my hands hard. "The King is—Arthur is dead."

I simply stared at him. I felt nothing. Wrapped in numbness, I could neither weep nor speak. I shook my head.

Mordred sighed wearily. "I will tell you what the courier said. I have a—a dispatch from Lancelot, written in haste from a field dressing station, before he—while he could still speak. He is badly wounded," he went on quickly, "and not expected to live." I closed my eyes in pain and bowed my head. "They took the field ten days ago, with the High King leading the troops from the west; it took all day. It was a long and bloody fight. You were right, it seems, about their numbers. They dared not face Arthur of Britain without a force superior to his. But still he beat them. He broke them, Gwen, by midafternoon, and they retreated. The rest of the fighting was desperate skirmish only, with ragged bands of men putting up resistance here and there. Lancelot and Bedwyr were near him; Bedwyr was wounded, but is able to stand. At the end of the day, they could not find the High King. Lancelot lay gravely wounded on the field, and in the field hospital, after he had dispatched this message, he told the courier what he had seen. The High King was fighting with Gawaine near the banks of a small stream to Lancelot's left, when a small force of savage Burgundians burst out of ambush; one minute the King was there, and the next not. The Dragon was seen to fall. From the litter, Lancelot directed troops to the spot, and they searched but could not find him."

I found my voice. "Then he is alive. Somewhere."

Mordred looked pained. He swallowed. "It is possible, my lady, but not likely. You see—I don't think you know what happens after a battle. Men crawl out from nowhere, it seems, like ravens, to strip and rob the dead. Sometimes the troops, too, if they are not well led. Within an hour of falling, a man is cleaned of all his belongings, his weapons, his jewelry, his clothing. Sometimes they take his life, if his own men have not yet found him. When—when Lancelot sent men to search the place, scavengers had already been there." He reached inside his tunic and slowly drew forth a torn strip of crimson silk. It was the sash, hacked to ribbons and stiff with mud and dried blood. I took it in my hands. There at the ragged edge were the golden, interlocking letters, *AR*. "They found this by the stream," Mordred whispered, choking.

I seemed to feel a great cold grow inside me; my limbs were lifeless, my lips so stiff I could barely move them.

"Even naked, the King's body would be known," I whispered. "He lives, Mordred. He lives. The lady Niniane told me he would return."

His eyes flashed, then grew dull once more. "Did she? Did she say how?"

"What do you mean?"

"Did she say how he would return? Living? Or on a bier?"

I believe I screamed. Every day, every hour, I had comforted myself with this prophecy, and I had not thought of this! No wonder Niniane had shown relief!

"When Lancelot got to the field station," Mordred continued, "he sent this message. Rumors of Arthur's death are sure to flood Britain fast—he advises us to act as if the King were dead, to hold together. Soon—within a week—we will know for certain. There are search parties out every day. But as Lancelot points out, at the battle's ending, if he lived, he would have sent someone with a message. They waited hours, Gwen. They heard nothing."

I sat still, hearing his words, but unable to feel them. It could not be true; and yet, how could it be false? Of course Arthur would get word to his commanders, if he lived. The bitter irony of it ate at my heart: Lancelot on his deathbed telling Mordred he must be King! My dearest Lancelot! Lancelot and Arthur—both felled in one wicked day! It was too heavy a grief to bear; I could not bear it; I pushed it aside.

"You had better be King now, Mordred. When they find him—if he is—when they send you his ring and his Sword, we will crown you. But—but you had better take the title, for Britain's sake."

Mordred raised me from the ground and kissed my cheek. "What a noble Queen you are," he whispered, "to think of this amid your great grief. As you say, it must be done. But I want you to know that I would give anything not to have to do it."

He meant it; for once, his heart was in his eyes, and I read his love for Arthur there. "I will come," I said without a tremor. "I must. There may be some who would not accept you, else. We must be united."

So I went before the Council, grave men all, and after Mordred read aloud Lancelot's brief message and advice, I told them as clearly as I could that this was what King Arthur had desired, that his son Mordred be confirmed as High King after his death, and that all the kings of Britain swear allegiance and fealty to him as they had to Arthur. So it was done.

And after, I left them to their somber celebrations and let Anna guide me to my chamber. But there I bade her leave me. Alone, I stood before the leather curtain and gathered my courage. Slowly I lifted it and passed into his room. It was still and calm and clean, and I drew a deep breath. But my spirit did not lift; the place was empty; he was not there. From below his stairs I heard the sound of weeping. Gentle Bran, no doubt, had just heard the news.

"Oh, Arthur," I whispered to the air, "do not desert me! Who is left to bring me comfort and help me bear this grief? There must be something of you left here." I knelt by the trunk and threw up the lid, growing frantic to find something, anything, that bore his smell, his feel, any mark of his spirit. I lifted out his favorite winter robe of plain brown wool, trimmed with rabbit. I pressed it to my face; but of course Varric had sent it to the fuller's before packing it away, and it was clean, devoid of any trace of Arthur. I shook it out, and a moth flew free. Alarmed, I looked more closely. Over the left breast I found a hole made by the moth's tooth—and I burst into tears.

Bran flew up the stairs; Anna came running in. Between them, they got me into my own bed. I remember little of it. For days I lay unthinking, unseeing, unresponsive to entreaties, beyond grief and beyond hope.

When at last I arose, I began to accept the fact that Niniane was right: The world had changed. I forgave her for not forewarning me—had I known the truth, we could not have shared that last, sweet night together. As it was, Britain was still whole, and Arthur's son was King. Now it was time to give thought to where I should spend my future, for I had no doubt that, as soon as he could get the army home and see things settled, Mordred would get himself a wife. I must leave Camelot.

But when at length I went to talk with Mordred, I found he was not there. He had gone, with a troop of men, eastward to meet with Cerdic. The news of Arthur's death had indeed raced across the Narrow Sea and had reached the Saxons almost as soon as it reached us. They had sent an embassy, asking for a parley. I questioned Ferron, who had stayed as my Protector, and he said simply, "Cerdic has declared the treaties with Arthur void." Well, I thought, it was not surprising. Cerdic's treaties had been with Arthur, and now Arthur was gone. Mordred had gone to ratify the treaties in his own name, and it was right that he should. So I said nothing. I spent my days on the turret of the southwest tower, which overlooked the entrance to King's Gate, and all the lands between Caer Camel and the far woodlands, toward Brittany. Daily I watched couriers ride in, but none from Less Britain. We had no more news.

At last Mordred returned and sent for me. I went to him in the library and curtsied at the doorway.

"My lord King," I said quietly. He extended a hand, brown from the sun, and raised me. I looked up into his eyes and hardly knew him. He was tanned and relaxed, and happy and vibrantly alive.

"My dear Guinevere," he said softly, "you need do me no reverence—not you. Are you well enough to sit with me awhile? I would talk with you."

"Yes, my lord. And I would talk with you."

He dismissed the other courtiers and led me into the garden. He spoke very gently and watched me closely to see if I attended. When he saw I did, he gradually grew more natural and told me quietly all about his visit with Cerdic. He had been very successful. Cerdic had not only ratified the terms of the treaties he had had with Arthur, but he and Mordred had come to a new agreement. Cerdic's son Cynewulf was then in his Saxon homeland, organizing yet another "rescue" of his people to Britain's shores. Cerdic needed more land. Mordred, on the other hand, wanted landing rights in the harbors of the Saxon shores, for trade with the Saxons, with Bretons, Franks, and even the Alemans of northern Gaul. They had struck a deal. Cynewulf would be allowed to land his longboats unchallenged; British ships would have rights of passage along their shores. It was a giant step forward in friendship between the two peoples, a giant step along the road to making them one nation. I congratulated Mordred and wished that, for his sake, I could feel joy. But that part of me that looked forward had died when Arthur died.

Exultant though he was, Mordred was sensitive to my sorrow. "You are pale, Guinevere. How many days has it been since you have ridden out in the fresh air?"

I shook my head. "I do not feel like riding, Mordred."

"Not feel like riding? It is not the Guinevere I know who speaks! Is there aught that I can do to ease your sorrow?"

I managed a smile. "Indeed, I hope there is. I have come to ask for your advice."

He looked pleased and bowed low. "Any way that I can be of service—just name it, it shall be done."

I looked away. "You may think this foolish, Mordred. But then you are not a woman." I paused. "We women must depend upon men for our keeping. And now my protector has gone from me, I—I am adrift. It is a consequence of childlessness I had not considered, until now. I have thought of returning to Wales, but it is a long time since it has been my home. I cannot go to Gwynedd. Pellinore is dead; Alyse blames me for Elaine's early death; Maelgon despises me for other reasons. And even in Northgallis—Gwarth has four brothers, all with wives and children. Gwillim is still my friend, but he is married now, and—and I cannot live with him. I know what would happen. He loves me still, and his wife would hate me. I would go to Ynys Witrin and live with the ladies there, if Niniane would take a Christian, but it lies hard by Melwas' castle. And *nothing* will persuade me, loyal to Arthur as he has been, to set foot on his lands again." I shuddered, and Mordred touched my arm to interrupt me.

"Dear Guinevere," he whispered, "there is no need for you to go! Stay here in Camelot—it is your home. I will protect you. It will be my pleasure, for as long as you live."

I blushed under his gaze and looked down. "You are kind, Mordred. Very kind. I thank you for the offer. But you know well that someday soon, perhaps within the year, you will wed, and bring your own Queen to Camelot. I cannot stay here, like some worn-out gown still hung in the corner, because no one knows what to do with it."

"Guinevere!" Mordred looked aghast, and he went down on one knee before me. "Guinevere, do not speak so."

"Rise, Mordred! You are King now, you ought not to kneel before me."

"I will do as I please, my lady Queen. I will not have you think such thoughts! I beg you not to consider leaving! I have no plans to wed, nor will I make any—"

"What of the mother of your sons?" I asked gently, touching his face.

He trembled and shook his head. "They are by different mothers," he said quickly. "Those women matter not. They are content as they are. I have seen to that. My heart is—they have not my affection. Please, Guinevere, believe me. You matter much more than they."

He rose suddenly and paced back and forth before me. "The night before I left Brittany, the King spoke with me well into the night. About what should happen if—if he did not come back. The last thing he said, the last but most important, was about you.

He bade me promise to protect you and care for you all the days of your life. I promised him, Guinevere, I promised willingly. So let me do it. It is Arthur's wish, as well as my own."

I bowed my head. "All right, Mordred. I thank you from my heart. In a year or so, you may feel differently, but—"

"Never!"

"—but for now, I will worry no longer about it. For this I thank you."

He raised me from my seat and kissed my hand. "Guinevere," he said fervently, "you are still Queen here. You need not ever bend a knee to me."

But I dipped him a curtsy as I left him. He was, after all, High King.

Time passed, and still no news came from Brittany. Mordred told me the reason.

"A summer storm assails the Narrow Sea," he said. "They say the wind blows out of the north, cold and strong, all day and night. Messengers going south may get across in record time, but no ship in Brittany can sail beyond the harbor. One good thing has come of it, though. Cynewulf is also held ashore. Some on the Council do not like this treaty, and I would win them over before he is here in fact."

"Then is our army stranded?"

"They are on Hoel's lands, and safe. The threat to them is past. This gives them time to reorganize and heal their wounds. We should know the truth of things as soon as the wind changes."

I looked at his face, Arthur's face, profiled against the sunlit garden. It was a strong, young face, full of authority and promise and the joy of wielding power, and doing it well.

"Mordred," I said softly. "What if—what if the courier brings the news that the King lives and has landed? What then?"

He turned to me, helplessly, beseechingly. "I—I will yield to him, of course. He is my father."

I drew a long breath of relief. "Will you, Mordred? Can you? Do you swear it?"

He nodded and swallowed hard. "I have thought of it every night since the news of his death. It would not be easy to give up kingship, even for a time. But he is Arthur. Even were he not my father, I could do no less."

I went to him and hugged him tightly, my eyes wet with tears. "You are a good man, Mordred. And I love you dearly. You grow daily more like him, do you know that?" I thought to please him by my words, but the joy had gone out of his face.

Eventually, the wind changed, then we had news. Not at first—I later learned that the army's ships had been caught in a squall and gone astray. The first ships that landed were trading vessels, and everyone on board had heard a different story. So the first things we heard were rumors—the King lived, the King was dead, the King lived but was mad. Lancelot had died of his wounds; Lancelot had recovered but could not yet walk. Gawaine lived and led the army, usurping Arthur's place. Gawaine lived and had vowed to kill Lancelot before he left Less Britain. Gawaine lived and supported the raving King, loyal to the end, while Bedwyr led the troops. Mordred and I looked at one another and knew not what to think. As we had heard no rumors of their deaths, we took Gawaine and Bedwyr to be living, and so knew that eventually we should have the truth.

But the first messenger to come was not from the British ships, but from the Saxons. The messenger, afraid for his life in Camelot, nevertheless braved the troops to give Mordred his report. Cerdic was furious and called Mordred to account. British ships had landed on his coasts, blown eastward by the fickle winds. This was allowed by the new treaty and so the local people had not panicked, but simply retreated inland to allow them passage. But the same ill wind had blown Cynewulf and his company ashore nearby. Most of those new immigrants were farmers, but some were thegns and fighters. They knew nothing of the treaty, of course, but saw in the presence of the British ships opposition to their landing. However, they had held back their attack, in case the Britons should prove peaceful. But no sooner had the Britons put ashore than they attacked, led by a wild young warrior who cried aloud for Saxon blood. And so battle had ensued, Cynewulf's men were defeated, and the land about laid waste as the Britons, ragged and weary but still a fighting force, moved north.

Nervously the counselors heard this news.

"What was landed first," Mordred asked, "horses or men?"

"Men," the Saxon replied, "and they had lifted the Dragon banner above a tall man with a great sword that shone like light. Everyone there had thought it was Arthur."

Mordred went white. "Are you certain it was Arthur? Were there any there who knew him?"

The Saxon shrugged. It was not certain; nothing was certain, but that the Britons had landed on the Saxon shore and attacked, unprovoked.

Mordred shook his head. "Had it been Arthur, the cavalry would have landed first. If he meant war. Of course, it is possible that they were merely shipwrecked and felt themselves threatened by Cynewulf's armed force."

The Saxon nodded. "That is why King Cerdic sends to you, King Mordred. The fault may be on both sides. But the fact is, the Saxons and the Britons are once again at war. The treaty has been broken."

The knights around the Round Table looked at Mordred nervously. But Mordred had his father's calm. "Return to Cerdic with the message that I will come to his aid immediately with the army. I beg him to be patient. If this is Arthur, there should be no danger. Was it not Arthur himself who made the first treaty with your people? He would never break a promise he had made. If it is not Arthur but some remnants of the army, they are confused and afraid. I will show myself and bring them back home and make reparations to Cerdic for what damage they have in error caused."

With this the Saxon had to be content and took himself back to his territories. Mordred gave out orders to gather the troops and prepared himself to set out the next day. But first he came to find me.

I knew from his face he was beset. He looked both pleased and dismayed, relieved and frightened, angry and full of hope. He went on his knee at once and grasped my hand.

"Gwen, there is a chance he is alive!"

I gasped and sank into a chair. After all this! After the hard work of acceptance, to have hope given back! I did not trust myself to speak, but squeezed his hand.

"I've had a message from Cerdic." He gave me the report, and finished, "some among them think it was the High King who led the Britons. I leave tomorrow to find out if this is true."

But here my courage left me. What I had been through, after hearing of Arthur's death, I could not go through twice. The scar upon my soul was deep and still bled. I dared not bare myself for another blow. I dared not hope. I turned away from Mordred and withdrew my hand.

"No," I whispered. "It is not he. It cannot be. He has stood face to face with Cynewulf; he knows the man. He would never have attacked."

"But Gawaine might have," Mordred persisted, surprised at my reaction. "From what the courier told us, it sounds just like him. And who else could it be, under the Dragon banner?"

"Bedwyr, perhaps." I sighed wearily. "Gereint? Who knows? But if it had been the King, they'd have known it. There would be no doubt."

Mordred chewed his lip, watching me. "Tomorrow I leave for Cerdic's side, and we move south together. The defense treaty binds me to this action. But I am not sure it is the best course—it will look as if we march against our own troops."

He was asking for my advice! With an effort, I met his eyes and gently touched his face, Arthur's face. "You are High King, Mordred. Of course you must go. Stay Cerdic's hand and bring our poor troops home."

He squared his shoulders. The gesture brought fresh tears to my eyes. "When we meet them," he said firmly, "we will parley. I will show them how misunderstanding has arisen. At all costs, I must avoid bloodshed. For all our sakes."

That night, after Anna had dressed me for sleep and brushed my hair, I knelt by the open terrace doorway and said my prayers. As I rose and turned toward the bed, I saw light creep under the leather curtain and heard soft voices in the King's room. Without stopping to think, I pulled aside the curtain and went in. Mordred stood there, just come from hall, and Bran stood trembling behind him, holding a night robe.

I gasped and met Mordred's eyes.

"No!" I whispered. "Not his chamber, Mordred. Not yet. Please."

"My lady," Mordred began, and then stopped. He waved his hand, and Bran fled down the stairs. Mordred came around the bed and stood before me.

"Guinevere, I would not alarm you. Have I misunderstood you?" His voice went very low. "Did you not this very day confirm me in my Kingship, while there is yet hope that—"

"Not his bed. No. Not yet." I twisted my hands together, my eyes on the familiar bearskins. "I still—I can't—I still remember—" I looked up at him and shook my head. "Then I must go, for I am not your Queen."

He took my hands and pressed them to his lips. Instinctively I drew back, but he pulled me closer and, before I knew it, held me in his arms and kissed my lips and my face with eager passion. Before I could even comprehend it, he was on his knees, his arms about my waist, his face buried in my skirt.

"I would make you my Queen, Guinevere," he cried, "if you would have me! I have loved you these fifteen years, since my first day in Camelot—do not shrink from me, I pray you! I am not Arthur, I know it well, but I am his son. Can you not find some corner of your heart for me, or does he have it all?"

He looked up at me beseechingly, but I was speechless. There was nothing I could say. "Do you hate me?" he whispered. "Am I evil? You are so good, Guinevere, and I have loved you for so long! Tell me, please, that there is hope for me. You said yourself I was your King. You said it today, in spite of the news I brought you. Please—please, while I am away, consider my plea, and when I return let me know if there is hope for me. I see by your face you are affronted. Remember how you once spoke to me! Of the power of passion and how it overrules us! You begged me to accept it, in your case. Can you not accept it now in mine? You asked me once if I had ever loved a woman—you are that woman, Guinevere! By all that's holy, I do love you, as much as life. I intend no insult, my dearest love. I would only honor you as Arthur has always honored you, and I would love you as he always has."

As he spoke, his face revealed his soul. I recognized the blaze of passion in his eyes; I had seen it often enough in Arthur to know its meaning. In this, too, it seemed, he was Pendragon. Trembling, I freed myself from his embrace and stepped back.

"My lord," I breathed, "these words were better not spoken between us. How can I answer you, Mordred? I have always regarded you as my son."

Pain and anger flashed across his face, instantly suppressed. He rose, rather stiffly. "Regard me thus no longer. You are not my mother."

"Oh, Mordred, I would not hurt you for the world. I bear you naught but love. But—"

"But not that kind of love?" he asked gently, recovering his composure and guarding his face. "I tell you now, I will wed no other."

"Then Britain has no future!" I cried, clasping my hands to my throat. "Mordred, there is no sense in this! This is folly. You must marry, to keep his line alive. Let me go, my lord, and seek shelter where I may. While you are King, I cannot stay here!"

"You *must* stay." He reached out and held my shoulders firmly. "You *must* stay. I command you. If you are gone when I return, I shall seek you out and find you. You cannot hide from me. Be sure of that. We will settle this another time." He dropped his hands and looked about the room. "I will not sleep here tonight. Do not fear it. But when I come back—" He left it at that, bowed low, and left me.

I was still standing there, shaking, when Bran crept up the stairs.

"My lady?" he called anxiously. "Are you all right? Oh, please, my lady, do not look at me so! I would never betray the King! But the King is—and Sir Mordred bade me serve him, and he is—King."

"Be easy, Bran. I do not fault you. But I—I would ask a favor of you this night."

"Anything, my lady!"

"Will you sleep here, on this side of the curtain? Bring your own bedding, if you like, no one will mind. But I would have warning of—anyone's approach."

He understood and did not bat an eyelid. "Yes, my lady. With pleasure I will do it."

So I slept that night with Anna in my bed and Bran at the entrance to my chamber. I dared not look ahead. I prayed that wherever Arthur's spirit was, he had looked the other way. And not for the first time, I cursed my beauty, which had caused me so much more pain than pleasure in my life. Truly, it was a burden.

In the morning, Mordred left for the Saxon territories at the head of a great army. Not until he had been gone three hours did I draw an easy breath. Ferron, who was left in charge, was jubilant and, seeing me downcast, came to cheer me.

"Be easy, Queen Guinevere, the King will be home soon."

I looked at him in puzzlement, then shrugged. "How can he, when he has but left, and no one knows the end of his journey? But it matters not to me."

Ferron stood rooted to the ground, shocked. "I mean King Arthur, lady!" he cried.

I turned away. "No more of this, I pray you. I cannot bear it."

He grabbed my arm in anger and spun me around. Then his face softened. "Has no one told you? Arthur lives. The messenger minced his words in Council, seeing he was speaking to Mordred, but the Saxon grooms have told me what they overheard him saying to his servant." I met his eyes slowly. The world around me began to spin. "Cynewulf saw him and knew him and sent word to Cerdic. It is Arthur. He has returned."

I fainted.

28 ⊛ The Wicked Day of
Destiny

Two days later we received a courier from Mordred. He bore
two messages, one for me and one for Ferron. Together we received him and heard his news. Mordred had met with Cerdic,
and their forces rode south together to meet the men come from
Brittany. Cerdic was angry. British troops had landed armed in his
kingdom, a kingdom whose sovereignty Arthur himself had guar-
anteed, and had killed his people. As their king, he had no choice
but to gather his thegns and foot soldiers and give them battle.
But this Mordred, his ally, was determined to prevent. He wished
to reassure Cerdic, but he also wished to protect his men. If it was
true that Arthur led them, then this should be easily accomplished,
he told Cerdic. If Gawaine or some other led them, as was likely
from their warlike behavior, all would be well once Mordred met
them.

"And did Mordred and Cerdic seem easy with one another?" I
asked the courier.

He licked his lips nervously. "Passably easy, my lady. But the
Saxons are very angry. The treaty has been broken, and someone
must pay. They ride together as allies, but not in close friendship.
It looks like a ticklish business to me."

"What did Cerdic have to say about Arthur?" Ferron asked,
glancing at me sidelong. "He has had time to gather information.
Were there any who could say with certainty whether the King is
among these men, or no?"

The courier swallowed and met his eyes. "Yes, my lord. One of
the thegns who had gone to greet Cynewulf's landing party was
a veteran of the Battle of Agned. He saw the King and recognized
him. He says it was Arthur."

I trembled and turned away to seek a chair. My eyes watered, and my knees would not support me.

Ferron spoke with him a moment, then dismissed him, turning his back to read his letter. I retired to a corner, afraid to open mine. I would have left Camelot within an hour of Mordred's going, if Ferron had not given me hope that the King was still alive. Trembling, I broke the seal and unrolled the scroll. It was not written in the scribe's hand, but in Mordred's own. The lettering was labored and took me a long time to read.

My lady Queen Guinevere, he wrote, *how can I ever beg your pardon? I have spoken the unspeakable and will regret it all my life. I apologize most abjectly for my rude and hasty words, and for the doubt and suffering I have caused you. I swear, on my life, that I will never again approach you in such a manner; you are safe from me, my lady, all the days of your life. I beg you will not flee your home on account of me; I do not wish to break my promise to Arthur, to keep you well and care for you, but I will not prevent your leaving, if you wish it. Should you stay, you will do me honor. I shall keep to the quarters I now occupy, for they are grand enough for such as me. You need never fear me. I am now, and will always be, if you will forgive me and show me the mercy for which you are well known, your loving son, Mordred.*

I stared blankly at this missive. Was this the same man who had embraced me in Arthur's chamber? I had never known Mordred humble before. I wished to believe him, but I could not discount the fact that he knew, when he wrote it, that Arthur was alive.

I looked up and saw Ferron watching me.

"What will Mordred do, my lady? Can you hazard a guess? He says here, it seems likely that the King lives, but he cannot understand why he comes home through the Saxon lands, swords drawn, instead of putting back out to sea, or crossing westward toward Potter's Bay and Britain. He says it has the appearance of deliberate provocation, and Cerdic is outraged. Thus far he has held his hand, but unless Mordred can get speech with the King beforehand, he fears there might be fighting. He assures me and asks me to assure you that he will not raise his hand against Arthur. But neither does he offer to abdicate his crown. What will he do, when faced with it?"

I shook my head. "I don't know, Ferron. Three days ago I would have said that he would yield to Arthur. He has promised me that. But now—I don't know. Indeed, I wonder if he knows himself."

Ferron cleared his throat. "You should know, my lady, that there are rumors everywhere. About you and Mordred."

I looked up swiftly. "Rumors of what?"

Ferron hesitated a moment only. "Bluntly, of marriage. That Sir Mordred has long loved you is well known. Lately, the gossip goes, you have shared his bed and agreed to be his Queen."

I gasped. "Do you believe this?"

"No," he said at once. "I know better. But while you stay here, it is a difficult rumor to disprove."

Tears sprang to my eyes. "What would you have me do? Fly from Camelot as my lord is nearing home at last? Oh, Ferron, he must be sick to death of fighting! I know why he presses onward, although Mordred does not! He is weary and looks forward to find the shortest way to his desire. A Saxon beach is not the place to take counsel and discuss the merits of various routes! Picture him! Stranded on a beach, shipwrecked perhaps, with a Saxon force approaching and the cruel sea at his back! Every instinct in him, every fiber of his being, would urge him onward, and through them, in a straight line to home. He knows, yes, he knows that the Saxons cannot stand against him. Once his men are back, and tended to, and given rest, there will be time to mend the fences he has broken. If only Mordred would let him be!" I stopped, fought back a sob, and continued in a whisper. "How will he feel, when at last he gets here, weary and grieving for all those he has lost in battle, and looks for comfort in my arms, to find that I am flown because of foolish, disgusting, ridiculous rumors about his own son!"

Ferron came to where I sat and knelt beside me. He was moved, I saw. "You are quite right," he said softly. "I understand it now. Forgive me, my lady, for the suggestion. You think only of the King. I should have, also."

"In my heart, I don't believe Mordred will stand against him. But you will know better how the soldiers feel. Are they Arthur's men, or Mordred's?"

Ferron frowned, considering the question. "Those that went to Brittany, all twelve thousand—every man was Arthur's. But those that Mordred raised here this summer, they are mostly young men, the sons and younger brothers of those who left with Arthur. They have sworn themselves to Mordred."

"Then there are two Briton armies?"

"I really do not know, my lady. Are there two Kings?"

Through tears I looked out to the garden, shimmering in the dry, late summer heat. "If they cannot speak, or reach terms—

Mordred will not face him. He must fall back. But Cerdic cannot. I fear the Saxons will attack him, and Mordred will not be able to come to his aid, because he is Cerdic's ally."

"But, my lady, you said yourself the Saxons cannot stand against him. This is a prophecy of Merlin's, is it not?"

I nodded. "Yes. But he is weary, Ferron. I feel this in my soul. And Merlin—" As I spoke the name, I gasped aloud, and my hands flew to my throat. I felt the blood drain from my face.

"Guinevere!" Ferron cried, catching me by the arms, and shaking me gently. "Guinevere, what's amiss? What is it?"

"Merlin!" I whispered in terror. "Dear God, I had forgotten! That deadly, fearful prophecy he made! Never in all these years could I envision how it could come to pass—and now I see! Oh, Ferron, all is lost! May God forgive them both!"

He did not understand me and begged me to tell him, but I could not. I could not lay that fearful burden on another. He took me to my quarters and gave me into Anna's care. I begged her to pack my trunk and make ready for departure.

"Are we leaving, my lady?" she asked in great surprise. "What has happened?"

"I am leaving, Anna. You need not come with me, unless you wish. I cannot stay and watch this. I cannot stay!"

She sat me in a chair and brought me water. "Where you go, my lady, there will I go, also. I will not leave you in these troubled times. Where are we off to?"

"I don't know, I don't know, Anna!" I cried in distress. "To Caerleon, perhaps? No, held by Mordred's men. Too near Maelgon. And not south—Duke Constantine will be upon them like ravens after a wolf fight. And not north—Drustan's sons lie dead in Gaul and Drustan himself is old enough to be my father. He cannot live much longer. And who will rule Elmet when he is gone? Hapgar was killed along with Coel of Rheged—their sons may be those lovers of the cold, north wind you spoke of. East then—but who will take me?"

"The Saxons lie east," Anna said sensibly.

I began to weep once more. "I am not afraid of Saxons." Anna tended me and comforted me, and at length I shared my fears with her. As always, she was calm and sensible and gave me good advice.

"You can know nothing until the Saxons meet the British. Then must King—Sir Mordred choose his fate. Wait and see what happens. And in the meanwhile, we can stealthily make arrangements for a sudden departure, should the necessity arise."

I yielded to her sound advice, and we talked long that evening, taking supper in our quarters and seeing no one. In the morning I went to the stables. Good Lyonel was overjoyed to see me and gladly consented to the favor I asked. He set two swift geldings aside for us and gave us saddle packs, the kind the soldiers used, and made a solemn oath never to reveal, except to Arthur, what he had done. I did not tell him when or where we were going; only that we were. His eyes misted, and he kissed me farewell in kindness, but he did not ask me why I left.

Anna and I packed well for the journey and hid the saddlebags in the straw and waited. Long days went by, dry and hot; nothing moved on the downs but dust devils, playing in the parched grasses. Ferron was worried about me and begged for my company.

"Call me when the courier comes," I said. "Until then, I would be alone."

He came on the day the weather broke and rode in drenched from rain. The skies lay low and black on the hills. Thunder rolled up the valleys and pounded on King's Gate. It sounded like a thousand evil spirits clamoring for entrance. I shivered and reminded myself I was a Christian.

Ferron summoned me to hear the courier's message. He had no letter, but had got his tale by heart. The High King—for it was he, indeed—had gathered his forces on a rise and saw below him the Saxon army and the Briton, marching together to meet him. He had not waited to greet them or send a messenger to beg a parley—veteran that he was, he had attacked.

In my mind's eye, I saw him, weary to death and sore of heart over his losses, confused by the Saxon hostilities after he had treated with them for peace, bewildered, perhaps, by the rumors of King Mordred coming in arms against his father. I saw him as he must have stood, looking down upon them, Mordred and Cerdic talking together even as they came in sight of him. I could imagine his grief, and his fatigue, and then his anger, as the old, cold hatred gripped his soul; and the Sword trembled in his hand, crying out for Saxon blood. No, to Arthur it must have seemed that the Saxons had turned against him, and he must have thought, if his son loved him, he would join his cause.

King Mordred, continued the courier, had recognized the High King and had withdrawn the Britons from the field. Ferron glanced at me swiftly and looked relieved. He would have parleyed, repeated the courier, but was given no chance. His host fell back and were returning to Camelot, for he refused to lead his troops against King Arthur. He would return home and wait for him here.

And Arthur, I thought, always cool and far-seeing in battle, had seen his son turn, not to come to his aid against the Saxons, but to desert the field altogether, leaving him alone to fight Cerdic with the ragged remnants of his strife-torn army.

By nightfall, the courier continued, Mordred's troops received word that Cerdic's forces were broken and had fled in disarray before the High King Arthur, who stopped only to regroup and bury his dead before pressing onward. Within three days Mordred's army would be here; within seven Arthur himself would come. Then, said the man, staring straight ahead, trancelike and unseeing, the Kings would parley and fences would be mended, misunderstandings cleared, and peace restored.

No, I thought sadly, none who knew them well could think so. Father and son they were, both proud men, each feeling betrayed by the other, whom he loved dearly, both Kings of the same land. Which one would bend the knee and say: I was wrong, my lord?

I shook myself out of my dark thoughts and found the courier had gone. Ferron tried to look cheerful, but I soon spared him the effort.

"I will retire, my lord. I am not well. I thank you for your care of me; we have had good times together; let us remember those days and not what is to come."

He let me go; perhaps he understood me better than I gave him credit for. I found my maids peacefully sewing, as unaware of the doom that threatened as they were of thunder on a dry day. But Anna was not there. I passed into my sitting room and thence to the stair to my chamber. I stopped, holding my breath. I heard voices above. One of them was Anna's, and the other was male. I went up silently and paused in the doorway. The room was dim, for the day was black, and Anna had lit no candles. The curtain across the terrace doors was partly drawn. Anna stood there, fastening the latch. Beside her in the dimness stood a tall, cloaked figure, dripping wet, and whispering his thanks.

"Anna!" I whispered, seeing by their quiet movements this was a secret thing. "What goes on here?"

She whirled to face me. "My lady!" The cloaked figure went down on one knee.

"Queen Guinevere."

I walked quickly to him. "I know your voice. Who are you?" His hood slipped back; he looked up, smiling. It was Galahad! I stepped back and caught my breath.

"Galahad! What means this? How did you come here?"

His smile was sly. "By the garden gate, my lady, and up the stairs. A family trick." Then he bit his lip and crossed himself. "My lord, forgive me," he said to no one. "I will not err again."

I glanced at Anna. I had shared with her some of Mordred's story, enough for her to know this boy was not in his right mind. She backed quietly against the nightstand, where, since the night of Gareth's murder I kept a jeweled dagger, and surreptitiously opened the drawer. But Galahad bore no weapons, no scabbard, not even a knife tucked in his belt. What did he want?

I had not raised him. He still knelt before me. In the dimness, he looked beautiful, calm and serene; so must his father have looked, once, when his whole future lay before him. Lancelot had been his age at Caer Eden, when he first met Arthur.

"Have you news of my lord?" I asked him swiftly. "Fares he well?"

Galahad turned to me a guileless face. "Who is your lord, Queen Guinevere?"

"You know well who!" I retorted. "I ask after Arthur, and none other!"

He paused. "May I rise?"

"Will you behave?"

He smiled again, a smile that made me shiver. "I am tamed, lady. Your lord and husband has bound me round with oaths. I will not harm you. See? I come naked."

I raised him, and he thanked me. He was taller than I was by a head, and so handsome a youth, it took one's breath away. He had eyes that entrapped the gaze and mesmerized the mind, if one looked at him too long.

"Why are you here?" I asked him bluntly.

"I come from Arthur," he replied. "I have a message."

"You?" I gasped. "You travel with him? Were you aboard his ship?"

"Oh, yes," he said easily, brushing the water off his cloak. "I have been at his side this long while. I am his beloved, now that Gawaine is dead."

I swallowed hard. "Gawaine dead? How came this? Where did he die?"

"On a Saxon beach. He led the charge, and I was right behind him. I saw it happen. Cynewulf's ax got him. He died in Arthur's arms, when it was over."

"So—you have fought for the King, after all?"

"I have rid the earth of a hundred godless savages!" he cried, and then faltered suddenly. "I owe the King my life, twice over. Would I could be so cool in battle!"

I trembled and walked about the room to still my fear. "And how fares Arthur? Does he sleep? Eat? Is he weary?"

"He is angry. Fury drives him. His allies attacked him and bar his way." He shrugged. "That's what comes of making treaties with heathen bastards. Their oaths are soon forgotten."

I shook my head. "You don't understand it, Galahad. There is much more to this than you can see. But no matter. Has he his health?"

But again, he did not seem to understand me. "He is sick at heart, and weary. There is a knife in his back. The traitor kills him."

"Traitor! What traitor?" I gasped, fearing his answer.

"Mordred, of course," he replied calmly. "We saw him, plain as day, come take the field against us—against *us*—and beside Saxons!"

"Dear God!" I whispered, sinking to a chair. "It has come." I grasped at the last straw. "But Mordred never raised a sword against him!"

"No, the coward! The King attacked, and the coward turned and ran! It broke his heart."

I bowed my head. All was lost. It was time to be going. "One more thing. Does—does your father live?"

His eyes flamed, but he kept still. "I knew you would ask it— but I have promised the King politeness. Bedwyr lives and fights with us. Of my father, I say nothing."

"Please, Galahad."

"No."

I gave up. "Give me your message, then. Are you going back to Arthur? Will you take him a word from me?"

He reached in his tunic for a scroll as he shook his head. "I have a mission. I'm going on to Ynys Witrin to seek audience with a witch. The King would see her. Then I must purify myself at the monastery there. I have a Quest, you see."

He handed me the scroll, bowed low, fastened his cloak, and put his hand to the latch.

"Go with God, Galahad," I said softly.

He turned back and raised his hand in benediction, making the sign of the Cross in the air between us. Then, with a strange smile upon his lips, Lancelot's poor tortured son let himself out into the storm and crept out of Camelot by whatever way he had come.

"Anna, a light," I said softly, shivering from the encounter.

With trembling fingers I broke the seal and slowly puzzled out the words. He had written it himself.

My dearest Gwen, I pray this finds you well and whole and free. I do not believe the rumors. I am beset on all sides and fear for your safety. Get you gone from the traitor Mordred and fly to Amesbury. I will take back what is mine and, when I am free, will come to you there. The abbot will take you without questions. He is beholden to me. Be quick and silent. The fox is sly. I hold you in my heart and trust you. Your once and future King, Arthur.

And at the bottom, hastily scrawled: *Forgive my sending Galahad. He has promised to treat you as his mother—there is no one else—I cannot spare Bedwyr. Lancelot lives. He will join me as soon as God gives him strength to walk. Pray for us both.—A*

My heart leaped with joy in the same moment it sank in despair.

"We are lost, Anna!" I whispered, rereading it with speed. *The traitor Mordred.* "Oh, Anna! We are lost!" *I will take back what is mine.* Oh, my dear Arthur, how take it back? Only by killing your son—and when we meet, what will you say to me then? "Come!" I said, thrusting the letter in my pouch. "My riding clothes. Quickly! It is time to go!"

"Now, my lady? But the storm!"

I laughed at her and saw her eyes widen in amazement. "Do you not know this about me, Anna? Why, I love riding in bad weather! Come."

It took us four days to make the journey, and for four days the skies were dark and leaden, cloaking our passage. Each night we spent in a peasant's cottage. The poor people of Britain gave us shelter, never asking who we were, but understanding the desire of women to seek shelter in the house of God. It was an omen of change.

The abbot took us in, good man, with tears at Arthur's letter. I did not want his finest rooms, but begged for a small cell. I needed no ornaments or furnishings beyond what the other women had; I needed only Anna nearby. He gave me what I asked for. My window looked out past willow trees to the river that wound slowly southward toward the great plain, and the Giants' Dance, where Ambrosius and Uther lay buried.

Ambrosius had been born here—hence the name of the place—and now it lay but a day's ride from Cerdic's lands. But this did not concern me. The Saxons might be entwined in Arthur's destiny, but I knew in my soul that they played no part in mine.

I could not think of Camelot without an ache in my throat. It had been my home for twenty years, and I knew every foot of it—chambers, towers, gardens, stables, and grounds. I thought of it as I had seen it for the first time, on that bright summer day: shining and golden upon its green hill, with flags flying gaily from its towers; a citadel of greatness and glory! The Kingdom was new then, and we had all been so young! I knew I should never see it again. Whatever the future held, I could not go back. I had but one room now; but it was more than enough for my needs.

I kept to my cell, apart from the others, joining them only for prayers in the little chapel. I knew from their sidelong looks and hushed whispers that they knew me, and I did not want their worship. Anna stayed by my side, and together we knelt and prayed for Arthur and Mordred, together we took our meals, together we took the air in the walled garden or in the grounds.

We often walked to the water's edge, arm in arm, saying nothing. It was a time of waiting. The weather cleared, and we had those calm, bright days that make September welcome, with cool breezes in the morning and the warmth of summer at noon. Leaves edged themselves with yellow, then gently fell and rustled underfoot. My heart was held by some unnatural calm; I did not weep or sigh, but found joy in the careful perusal of small things: a bird's feather, dropped upon the lawn, held soft and tickling between the fingers; the gleam of morning sun on the dewy grasses; the pleasant chuckle of the brook as it danced and frothed around the boulders in its way; the beauty of sunsets, the soft glow of chapel candles, the gentle, soothing strokes of Anna's brushes in my hair. I kept my thoughts to these, and so survived.

One lovely afternoon as we sat beneath the willows Anna told me stories of her childhood. I attended now and then, but my thoughts were on the tiny creatures that ran up and down along the rough willow bark. What heights they scaled, these mighty runners! What cliffs they overshot and valleys fell into, all unharmed! It amused me to watch their frantic efforts—did they have goals? I wondered, or did they scramble about undirected, for the sheer joy of running? And what end would they come to? A spider's web, most likely, or food for birds.

On the thought, I heard screaming in the sky above me and felt a cold horror grip my soul. I looked up—ravens in flight, no more, heading westward—but I felt the day grow dark behind the shadow of their passing.

"My lady Guinevere!" Anna cried. "Why do you shake so? Why do you weep?"

I rose unsteadily, and she took my arm. "Let us go in and pray."

"What is it? Oh, please tell me, what have you seen?"

"Nothing," I whispered, "nothing at all. Only ravens flying westward. Men believe—they can scent a battlefield fifty leagues away."

"Oh, no, my lady, these are old wives' tales. I am surprised that you believe them. It is the season for their movement, that is all."

But I knew, as we knelt in the chapel, that Arthur walked the earth no longer. He was gone from me forever. I knew it by the heaviness of my spirit and by the grief that shadowed me, a brooding thing, waiting upon a courier's word, waiting to engulf me. I would not recognize its presence and give it entry, but put on my white veil of mourning and prayed, day and night, for the salvation of Arthur's soul.

On the seventh day, the abbess came to me.

"My lady Queen," she said with a curtsy, "Father Albin wants you to know we have a soldier with us, convalescing, who would speak with you."

"A message?" I asked quickly. "From whom?"

"Not a message, my lady. The man is from the village and left with the King to fight in Brittany. He returned only yesterday, to recover from his wounds."

I clasped my hands together and held them hard. "Is he coherent? Does he wish to talk?"

She raised her eyes to me, and I saw compassion there. "Yes, my lady. When he learned the Queen was here, sent hither to await the King, he asked to see you. Will you come?"

"Indeed I will."

I dropped my veil and followed her. We passed Anna in the garden, and she left her task at my signal and came to me. Behind the convent cells was the house of healing. Avoiding the main chamber, which smelled, we were taken to a small, rude hut of wattle. On a dirt floor, strewn with straw, lay a pallet with the sick man, wrapped in bloody rags. It was a far cry from Niniane's House of Healing, and I doubted anyone could recover here. A servant tended him and placed stools for us, then ducked out.

"Kerwas." The Mother addressed him gently. His face was gray, and his eyes dull. I did not know much about healing, but to me he looked beyond their help. "Kerwas, this is the Queen."

She glanced at me. "A servant will be within call, if you need him."

I thanked her and turned to the dying soldier. He was about my age, at a guess, but ravaged by hard use and pain. He looked me over carefully.

"Are you truly the Queen?"

I was dressed in a plain gown of dull gray and wore no ornament of any sort. He had no way of knowing who I was.

"Yes, good sir. I am Guinevere of Britain, Arthur's wife."

"Let me see your face." Obediently I lifted my veil and drew it back. Anna loosed a pin and brought my hair forward. He sighed and closed his eyes.

"Good Kerwas, I would not tire you, but if you bear a message from my lord, or even news of him, good or ill, I would hear it."

"I have news."

"Does he live?" I blurted, not intending the question, and pressed my fingers against my lips, fearful of his answer.

He opened his eyes and looked into my face. "I do not know, my lady. But it is unlikely."

I nodded. "Go on," I whispered. "Tell me what you know." Anna gave me a clean cloth for my eyes.

"I was with him," he said slowly, "in the battle of Autun. I fought there in the company he led. We broke them. We broke the Burgundians and the Romans, and they outnumbering us five to one."

I smiled and slid off the stool to sit at his side. I took his rough hand in mine. It was cold, and I chafed it gently.

"My lord is the victor," I said softly, "in every field he takes."

He closed his eyes. "Aye," he said, "and the enemy knew it well. But near the end of the day, when we were mopping up and driving out the stragglers, we were ambushed."

"So we heard from Lancelot. He got a message home."

Kerwas grunted. "No doubt he meant well, but 'twould have been better for us all if he hadn't sent it!" He shifted in discomfort.

"Tell me about the ambush."

"Well, they came at us from behind, and we fought them across the stream. Savages they were—I will not tell you what they did. We were a handful only, thirty foot soldiers and only the King and Sir Gawaine on horseback. They must have been a hundred, easy. Maybe more. But the King has a cool head; he kept us in formation, and we repulsed them. Nay, we followed them into the wooded hills and killed every last man of them by nightfall."

"How many did you lose?"

"Half, my lady. But they lost all."

"You are a brave man, Kerwas. Were you injured?"

"No, my lady, not there. We had magic that day, God be praised."

"Why did not the King send a messenger back to the field headquarters, to report his whereabouts?"

The pale eyes opened, then, and met mine. "My lady, he did."

"He did? They—they never received it."

"We know this now. He sent young Dunstan, a fast runner, to Sir Lancelot. We were two days in the hills, scouting for stragglers and burying our dead. On the way back—"

"Two days! Why so long?"

He looked away and stared pensively at the thatched roof above his head. "Ahhh. The King was weary, my lady. And we thought, since we had sent Dunstan, there was no hurry. We would be at Autun a week, easy, just burying the dead. But on the way back, we came across Dunstan's body, locked in a death grip with a Roman youth, beside the stream. Then we hurried and found the troops in a panic because the King was lost. There was rejoicing when they saw his face, I can tell you!"

A glimmer of a smile crossed his lips. I called for the servant, but no one came, so I lifted his head myself and gave him a drink of the broth the servant had left.

"Everyone is always glad to see Arthur," I said gently, and pillowed his head on my lap.

"Aye, my lady. That's true enough." He looked better, and spoke stronger and kept his eyes on me. "But we held no celebrations, for Sir Lancelot was wounded and lay near death. For three days the High King sat at his bedside while he raged in fever. Sir Gawaine was always at the King's elbow and came out to give us news from time to time. The physicians were sure that Lancelot's suffering would end in death, but the King would not leave him. No one knew, until Lancelot passed the fever and opened his eyes and spoke, of the message he had sent home to Britain. Then was the King distressed and sent another courier off that instant, but in his joy at Lancelot's recovery, he did not think to double-check. We learned later, the man was thrown from his horse in the Perilous Forest and died of a broken neck."

"It seems, indeed," I said slowly, "as if God wished Britain to think him dead."

"Aye, lass. I mean, my lady. We stayed until Lancelot could be moved and our dead had been buried and their belongings gathered. The King made a list of all those killed and sent another messenger home."

"Another?" I cried. "But he never got here!"

"He left as the winds were rising on the Narrow Sea. Chances are he was drowned. We escorted Lancelot to his home in Benoic. We carried him on a litter. He vowed to follow us to Britain as soon as he was able, to fight the traitor Mordred."

"Mordred!" I gasped. "Dear Kerwas, you have left something out. Why did the High King think his son a traitor *in Brittany*?"

"Aye," Kerwas said slowly, with some reluctance. "I have indeed left something out. Constantine sent a letter."

I froze, staring at him. "Constantine? Duke Constantine of Cornwall?"

"Aye. The winds favored his courier, although they stymied ours."

"He sent a letter? To the King?"

Kerwas watched me carefully, and it seemed to me that he guarded his face, as much as was in his power.

"Why are you afraid, my lady?" His head lay in my lap, and he could feel my trembling.

"Duke Constantine is no friend of mine, nor of the King's. He bears me a grudge. I am surprised that he would send to Arthur, and surprised that my lord would read it."

"But he did read it," Kerwas said firmly. "And it brought him sorrow."

"And how," I asked, "do you know all this? Were you in his councils?"

"My lady, I stood guard upon the entrance to the tent. I was there when the courier brought the letter. Lancelot lay calling out in his fever. The King asked for quiet on his behalf, so he could hear his moaning and know that he still lived." I shut my eyes, and he went on. "The camp was quiet. The night was hot; the tent flap lay open. The King read the letter in silence, but Sir Gawaine, who was always with him, was not so skilled, and worked out the words aloud."

"And what did he say?" I asked, trembling, afraid that I knew already.

"I am no courier, my lady. I have not got it by heart. But the gist of it was this, if you will forgive me."

"I will forgive anything but falsehood, Kerwas. Tell me."

"He wrote to say that Sir Mordred had declared himself High King of Britain, without waiting for confirmation of Arthur's death, and was gathering a new army, loyal to himself alone. The duke predicted that when and if the King returned, he would stand against us. As he did."

"No," I said swiftly, "you judge too quickly. He did not. Not for that reason."

"He did," Kerwas said harshly. "I was there, and saw it."

"All right," I said to soothe him, for his color was not good. "But think back to Brittany, and how you felt then. Would you have opposed him, Kerwas, if Arthur were not with you?"

"If King Arthur were dead, my lady, then Sir Mordred would be King. Of course we would not oppose him."

I sighed. I had known the men were loyal Britons, all. I had known it. "Thank you, Kerwas. Go on with your tale. What did the King say?"

"Well, he understood it. He knew the message Lancelot had sent. It was to be expected, he told Gawaine. Mordred was only following his instructions. But Gawaine did not like to hear it. The duke wrote that Sir Mordred was meeting with the Saxons, all on his own authority, without even taking counsel."

"But of course. He had to. If the King was dead, the treaties were void. Cerdic sent for him."

"So Arthur said, my lady. But Gawaine accused Sir Mordred of rank ambition. I heard him cry that Mordred had not waited even a day to see if the rumors were true."

"He could not wait, for the Kingdom's sake," I protested. "And it wasn't a rumor. It was a written message from Lancelot. And in any event, waiting a day, even a week, would have gained us nothing."

Kerwas watched me with interest and with some fear, and I strove to calm myself.

"So the King said," he agreed. "But Gawaine said otherwise."

I looked away. My dear Arthur, with Lancelot fighting for life and Gawaine shouting in his ear that his son wished to betray him! Had no one loved him enough to stand by him in his need?

"Always, always the same story," I whispered. "The cold Orkney blast that destroys whatever he has labored to build! . . . Well, go on, Kerwas. I know Duke Constantine said more. I know his hatred for Mordred. I can even guess his next lie. He no doubt mentioned me."

That took Kerwas by surprise, and he looked at me intently. "It came last," he said, "but touched the King nearest, by his voice. The duke claimed that Mordred courted you, consorted with you, and planned to make you his Queen."

"And? Surely he did not content himself with such vague accusations?"

"All right, my lady, if you will have the truth, I will tell it. He claimed you had consented, and the wedding day was fixed."

I pressed the cloth to my face. "Oh, Arthur!" I whispered. "My dear husband and my friend! You were alone!"

At last Kerwas closed his eyes and sighed.

"I knew you kept faith," he said in some relief.

"But did the King know it, Kerwas?"

With an effort, he gripped my hand. "Indeed so, my lady," he said in a low voice. "It's my belief he never doubted you. I'm a married man myself, my lady. I'd have known, by his voice."

We sat silent a little while. Anna had left to fetch the servant. Now he came, bringing water and a blanket. Anna begged me to arise from the soiled and matted straw, offering to take my place herself. But I would not let her. His sickness did not offend me, nor his smell, I know not why. I wanted only to sit with his head in my lap and hear him talk of Arthur.

"Well, then," I said, when he was comfortably settled and refreshed, and breathing easy. "Well, then, what happened next? If my lord did not believe the letter, how did he ever come to suspect his son of treachery?"

"You have Gawaine to thank for that—him and Lancelot."

"Lancelot! Why, they are sworn enemies! Are you going to tell me that they were one in this?"

"Gawaine was like a gadfly, always buzzing about the King, never leaving him in peace. Every word out of his mouth spoke ill for Mordred."

"I can easily believe it," I said sadly.

"It was Gawaine who told Lancelot about the letter, as we carried him back home. Most of it he took in silence." He stopped, and I touched his hand.

"You needn't tell me. I know well what part of it upset him. He believed it, then?"

"No. He never believed you had consented, my lady. He believed you trapped by circumstance. But he believed that Mordred was ambitious and looked to secure his title by taking you to wife."

"He always distrusted Mordred."

"Each of them pressed the King to hurry. When we left Sir Lancelot, he swore he would not be far behind us. But when we came to take ship for home, the winds were against us."

"So I have heard."

"And when we at last made land, we were blown off course."

"Were you shipwrecked, Kerwas? Were the vessels destroyed?"

"Ours was, my lady. Most were heavily damaged and could not put back out to sea. But ours and Sir Bedwyr's were destroyed."

"Ah, Bedwyr," I said, my eyes misting. "I am glad Bedwyr was with him." Kerwas cleared his throat, and I felt my heart sink within my breast. Was Bedwyr gone, too? "Go on, Kerwas. Finish your tale."

"It is easily finished. It is all killing. No sooner had we landed than we saw Saxon troops approaching. We were less than two hundred ashore and only twenty horses. Gawaine would not heed the King's call for patience. He saw we were outnumbered and rallied the forces under the banner. He had a young black-haired devil with him, who cried out for heathen blood."

I paled. "Galahad?"

"Aye, that's the name." He made to spit and then recollected my presence, and cleared his throat instead. "We attacked them and broke them. The King would have asked for parley, for he suspected some mischance. But Gawaine raised the war cry and led the young men forward. We veterans would have waited with the King, but our hand was forced. We broke them, but there Gawaine received his deathblow, and died later on the beach. With his last breath, he begged the King to send for Lancelot, to revenge his death."

I let out a long breath. "Then at the end, he forgave him. God be thanked for that."

Kerwas grunted, and I helped him to a more comfortable position.

"Kerwas," I said suddenly, "did you know you were on the Saxon Shore?"

He tried smiling, but could not bring himself to it. "No, indeed. We thought we were in Britain. Only the High King wondered, but even he was not sure."

"Ahhhh. That explains why you thought Cynewulf came to fight."

"Well, didn't he?"

"No, indeed. Never mind it now. What did Arthur do next? Organize the army and push for home?"

"You know him well, fair lady. That's exactly what we did. We knew soon enough we were in Saxon lands; we passed many villages, and the people there were sore afraid. But we let them be; King Arthur said they were our allies. He wished to move with speed, before news of the beachfront battle got to Cerdic and was misunderstood."

Too late, I thought sadly. How the fates had worked against him!

"But we fought several skirmishes along the way, my lady. It seems the news had spread, and though we left them in peace when they did not oppose us, when they gave us fight, we fought them."

I nodded. "How not? I see how this disaster came about. And I have heard from Galahad's own lips about the battle against Cerdic."

Kerwas trembled, and a tear fell from his eye. "Aye, that was a sad day. Until that day, the King had hope his son was not a traitor. But when he saw him, riding abreast of Cerdic, their forces coming upon him together"—he gulped—"he lost his patience. I have been a soldier these twenty years, my lady. I have never seen a man so angry. He rallied us for attack. 'Now,' he said, 'we will see which side he chooses!' But when we broke from the woods and came at them—Mordred turned and ran. That was what wounded the King so. He would rather have fought him, man to man, than see him run away."

"Did he see it thus?" I cried. "Or did you hear this from Galahad? He wanted peace! He had sworn in my presence he would never raise his hand against his father! And he kept that oath, that day. If my lord Arthur would not wait to speak with him, what choice had he?"

"We did not see it that way, my lady. The men didn't. I don't know what Arthur thought. He said little. But after we had buried our dead and set fire to the battlefield, we pressed on toward Camelot at double march. The King was heard to say he would be revenged."

I closed my eyes. Anna came forward and pressed her kerchief to my brow. "Take some water, my lady. Have some refreshment."

But I shook my head. "Thank you, Anna, but no. We are coming to it now. This brave man was with my lord to the end, it seems. Go on, dear Kerwas. Do not fear to tell me the worst. I have known already these seven days."

"Is that how long it's been?" He sighed and paused for breath. "We came to the Camel valley late one evening. We were only a league from home. But between us and Camelot lay Mordred's army. A lady rode into camp in the early morning, a fine lady upon a fine horse."

"A chestnut mare? A slender woman with dark hair? An air of authority and power?"

"I see you know her."

"It was the lady Niniane, Queen of the River Isles and Lady of the Lake. She is the King's enchantress."

"Ahhhh. So. She stayed till dawning. When she left, she was fighting tears, and the King looked bitter. But he sent a knight as messenger to Sir Mordred, to request a parley."

"Thank God!" I breathed. "They spoke then? Face to face?"

"Yes, my lady. Around noon. With the armies all around them. They met in a tent near the river's edge. They talked for about an hour."

Even knowing the ending, I felt a great rush of relief. They were cool men, both, and possessed of patience. So they had sat and spoken together, father and son. I would be forever glad of that.

"You don't happen to know what was said?"

A bitter smile touched his lips. "No, my lady. I was close enough to see, but not to hear. We raised a cheer when they came from the tent, for they came out arm in arm, the King wearing his war helm, with the crown upon the brow. Mordred's head was bare. We thought—we all thought it was over, and all was well."

"And why wasn't it?" I asked softly, stroking the hair from his face. He closed his eyes, weary of talking.

"I don't know, my lady. Suddenly there was shouting; we looked up and saw soldiers fighting—how it came about, I will never know. But when have two armies faced each other, ready for battle, and not fought? Suddenly we were at war. Someone raised a paean—King Arthur saluted his son and turned back to his troops. Sir Mordred stood there, rooted to the ground, and watched him go. Then my captain called me, and we formed the phalanx. It had begun."

"He knew," I whispered, as the tears began flowing, "he knew, and chose the time. What a King he was!"

Kerwas lay still a long time and then at last drew breath. "Near midafternoon I was wounded, run through by a sword. I lay on the turf as the battle was waged around me. I lay unknowing for some of the time, and when I awoke, the sun threw shadows long. I heard someone calling 'The King has fallen! Look! The Dragon is down!' When I looked up, I saw Sir Lancelot, with tears on his muddy face. In his arms, he bore the High King Arthur." Kerwas coughed and spit out bloody froth; I hugged him close and wiped his lips with my sleeve. "He was awake, but groaning. There was blood in his hair, and a great wound—" He stopped. Gently I stroked his head, above his ear.

"It was here," I whispered.

He struggled to open his eyes but failed. "Yes," he breathed. "How could you know? It was—dreadful. They took him, I think, to Ynys Witrin, to the shores of Avalon. Lancelot carried him, although he was barely healed. I—I have come to the end, my lady. I know no more. They came with the litter and carried me back. No one speaks of it, except to say he is gone."

I kissed his forehead; his flesh was cold. "Yes," I managed, "I know he is gone. Thank you, Kerwas. There is only one thing more. What happened to Mordred?"

His breath came fast and shallow, and I bent low over his lips to hear his speech. "I know not," he whispered. "I heard nothing of him." He paused, and his body shuddered. "Now I have told it," he breathed. "Bless you." He went limp in my lap, and I hugged him tightly as my tears splashed down on his lifeless face.

"Stay, Kerwas," I whimpered, "oh, dear God, stay with me!"

It was Anna who drew me away, I think, and put me to bed. Black grief fell upon me when Kerwas died, the grief I had fought off so long, and for days I was senseless to all but pain. I wished for death; I prayed for it fervently—anything to be with my dear Arthur!

Nevermore would he hold me in his arms, or whisper sweetly in my ear in the still of night. I would never hear his voice again, or his laughter, or feel his lips against my hair. Gone forever were those loving eyes and the calm strength that supported me through every woe. He had become part of my own flesh, it seemed, part of my very soul, this man whose outstretched hand I had once feared to take.

Britain would miss him, certainly. But Britain would have other kings. It was I, Guinevere, who would not survive his passing, who would miss him a thousand times an hour in unmeasurable ways. He was more than a king to me, he was my world: my sweet spring, my rich summer, my brilliant winter dawning; he was my sleep, my rest, my peace, my joy, my very life—how could I go on without him? I closed my eyes and prayed to God to join my soul with his. I was unable to look back, dared not look forward, and could not bear the present. What was left for me, but death?

But death did not come.

Cruelly, the black grief passed and left me numbed and exhausted, without even the will for thought. When at last I rose from bed at Anna's begging, I sat alone in a chair, listening to the wind. The unbearable emptiness that was my future stretched out before me like a dead gray sea, flat, dull, and comfortless, without direction, without end.

"Oh, God," I whispered. " 'How I have wept, day and night, before you . . . How my soul is filled with trouble . . . Lover and friend you have taken from me, and all my acquaintance into darkness!' "

Anna, always at my side, took my hand and held it gently. "My lady, hold hard to faith. This is not the end."

"Without Arthur, it is the end."

"Ah, but 'A man's days are as grass, he flourishes as a flower in the field; the wind passes over and he is gone. But the mercy of the Lord is from everlasting to everlasting.' "

Everlasting! It had been Merlin's promise! I nodded suddenly as my heart lifted. "Yes."

Anna squeezed my hand, misunderstanding.

Everlasting! He would live forever, beyond this grief, beyond this life, beyond even my imagining. He was not gone; he would never leave me. He was everlasting, the once and future King.

✹ EPILOGUE

I was alone in my cell when the abbess came for me. For hours I had been trying to pray, but I could not stay on my knees. The darkening sky and freshening breeze among the willows by my window made me restless; something was about to happen. And then I thought I caught the thud of a horse's canter from the road beyond the monastery walls. When the abbess finally knocked, I was half expecting her, and stood serene before her hasty curtsy. Kind woman, she had never learned the art of dissembling, and her weathered face betrayed her disapproval and her fear.

"My lady Queen."

"Please, Mother," I murmured as a small thrill of terror shook me. If the rumors that had flown about the land the past weeks were true, I was no longer Queen, and whoever had come for me might well have come to take me to my fate. Indeed, it was hard to imagine another reason for a visitor, or for the Mother's fear. But I had heard only one horse.

"My lady," she began again. "You have a visitor in the garden."

She did not continue, and I waited. With lowered eyes, she seemed to seek guidance from the polished stones of the floor. "I told him you do not receive visitors, my lady. He bade me give you this, and ask you to come."

I gasped. In her hand she held his ring, the great ruby with the Dragon of Britain carved small. I took it from her, trembling. It was warm, as if it had just come from his finger. My knees shook and for a moment I feared I might fall.

"Mother!" I cried. "Is it the King?"

Then her sad eyes met mine, her compassion overcoming her fear. "No, my lady. It is not the King, but a King's messenger. He has ridden hard but will not tarry long. Time presses upon him."

"I will go at once," I replied, and with her help adjusted the white veil of mourning over my face. She walked with me as far as the garden entrance and then, with a quick obeisance, left me.

I did not see him at first. The garden was small and private, surrounded by high walls. Pear trees stood silent, slowly turning color in the autumn light; the herbs of summer were gone; the roses recently pruned; only golden chrysanthemums blazed at the corners of the walks. A last ray of sun escaped the approaching storm clouds and lit the smooth alabaster of the Virgin's statue.

Then I saw him. He was kneeling before the statue, head bent in prayer, a weary knight, the dust of travel still upon his clothes. But I would know that back anywhere, among thousands, and in spite of myself, my heart leaped within me.

The Mother's disapproval was now clear to me, and her fear, as well. She would never fear for my death: What was that, but going home to God? But she feared mightily for my soul.

I walked slowly toward him. He rose and turned, and I lifted my veil. He had washed his face, and his hair and his hands. We looked at one another a long time. Then he went on one knee, took my hand, and pressed it to his lips. I caressed his black head, wondering desperately why I should feel so pained by the silver threads I found there. He led me to a bench and we sat silent, looking at one another in a kind of quiet desperation, because we had said good-bye forever, long ago.

"Gwen," he said at last. There were new lines in his face, and a weariness in his soul, an admission of defeat that was new to me. I did not need to ask what it was. I opened my hand and looked at the King's ring.

"It is true, then," I whispered, daring the words for the first time. "Arthur is dead."

"I helped to bury him," he said in a low voice. "Niniane took him to Ynys Witrin. The priestesses prepared him. The monks dug his grave. It was—it was dreadful."

"And you were hurt?"

Light leaped to his face, and he quelled it. "Yes. But it's better. I accompanied him; there was no one left."

"What? Did none survive?"

"None. Gwen, they are all gone." His voice shook, and he bowed his head. I sat stunned.

"Kay? Ferron? Gereint? Galahantyn?" I whispered. "Even Bedwyr?"

He nodded, head down.

"And—and Mordred?" That steadied him. He looked up, the old dislike in his eyes.

"Mordred killed him. It was Mordred's hand that struck the blow, cursed be his name forever! Mordred opened his head. He fulfilled his fate, as Merlin predicted. You backed the wrong horse, Gwen."

I took both his hands. The pain between us was unbearable.

"God called Arthur home; God guided Mordred's hand. It had to happen. If we don't believe that, we shall go mad." I felt the bitter tears on my face, and I felt his eyes on them. "You have been away a long time. You have heard rumors. I know what they are. But, my dear, this you must believe. There was never any King for me but Arthur."

He kissed my fingers. "I never doubted *you*, Gwen. But I have always doubted Mordred. He was ambitious."

"Was?" My voice broke. "Oh, dear God, no! Is he dead then? By whose hand?"

"By Arthur's" came the cruel reply. "Arthur slew him in the same instant he received his death blow."

The truth was so plainly written on his face that I burst into tears and had to hide my face in my hands. Angrily he paced the garden walk.

" 'Strewth! I never thought to see more tears shed for a traitor and a King-slayer than for the King!"

I prayed God for the strength to recover myself—this was a grievous blow indeed. I had believed, in spite of the rumors, in my heart of hearts, that Mordred must be ruling as High King, biding his time until the remnants of Arthur's army would rally to him, and he could ratify his precious treaty with Cerdic the Saxon and secure Britain's borders forever. My dear Arthur! My poor Mordred, who fought so hard against his fate! Whatever was the future to hold for us Britons now? Were we, in fact, still a nation at all? Or was I a Welsh princess once more, and Lancelot a Breton, as we had been in the dark days before Pendragon?

"Are we in the hands of the Saxons, then?" I cried, and he turned to me in surprise.

"The Saxons? No, not yet. Constantine is King. Who else?" He sounded bitter. He came back to me and sat down. "I thought you grieved for Mordred. I know you loved him, though I will never fathom why."

"Dear God, I loved him too much. But not as you and others think, you who should know better."

"I never—"

"Yes, you did. In your heart you have doubted even me."

He bowed his head. He would never understand what had been between me and Arthur's son, who had fought so hard and cared so much. To Lancelot he would always be a traitor. To Lancelot, and to all of Britain.

"I have grieved for Arthur this fortnight past," I said slowly. "In my heart I am with him, as he is with God. But Mordred is gone from me forever. That devil's spawn Merlin was right. His name will be dragged through mud for centuries to come. No one but I will ever know his goodness."

There was silence between us, but thunder rumbled far off, and Lancelot stirred.

"I have not yet told you why I came. Three things I have to tell you. Then I must be off." He glanced sideways at the door, and suddenly I was afraid.

"Are you pursued?"

"Of course. By both Constantine and Cerdic. For different reasons. The last of the Companions. Never mind. Before Arthur died, as Morgaine held his head in her lap, he spoke of you."

I bowed my head, not knowing what was coming. The dying words of a King were powerful by every magic known to man. But I knew that since it was Arthur, they would be merciful.

"He blessed you, Gwen. And he expressed the wish that when your time comes, you be buried with him, in the same grave."

The tears ran freely down my face as I felt the love of that strong heart reach out to me, even from death.

"I have left instructions for this with the abbess, or her successor. She has promised upon the Book of God that it shall be done." He paused, and by the strength of his control, I knew what was coming next. "I am on my way home to Less Britain. My lands are divided, my troops scattered. If my sons are to have any birthright, I must go back and put things straight. If Constantine wants me badly enough, he can come find me. But he will not. Cerdic will be watching his back." I smiled inwardly. Here we were, finally alone and unobserved at this singular time in our lives, and we talked of affairs of state. It was fitting, I thought. See how far we had come. But I smiled too soon. "If you would do me the honor, my dearest Queen, my only love, I would take you with me, and you should spend the rest of your days with me. Come out of your fastness, Gwen. Come with me. This is our chance at last. There will never be another. Come with me now."

His heart was in his eyes, and I knew well that nothing had changed between us since the first moment we had met; we had waited all our lives for this. He desired this, and yet he feared it. He was reluctant, and yet his eagerness was like the flame of youth. For so many years I had loved him but had been held by stronger vows. And now, at last, we were free.

I looked up at the swirling sky, the dark thunderclouds piling against one another in oncoming fury, and felt again the bitter agony of deep desire. I saw Ygraine and Uther, bound in a powerful passion that held a kingdom together but lost them their son; I saw Merlin, with his damning eyes, all his powers focused on Britain and her preservation, who let no one, man or woman, stand in his way; and I saw Arthur, sober and patient and kind, waiting for my decision, waiting to see if at the last, and for such a reason, I would betray his memory, his work, his Kingdom. I thought of Elaine, who had struggled once with such a passion, and I forgave her, after all these years. Last, I am afraid, I thought of my promise to God.

"Thank you, sweet Lancelot, for the invitation. God knows I have waited many years to hear it. But I cannot, my love. It is too late."

He kissed me then, and in his touch I felt both joy and sorrow. In a perverse way, he was glad I had chosen to stay. He knew it was impossible and wrong, but it had been impossible not to ask. He still depended, as he always had, on my judgment. Only I knew how close I had come to giving in.

"My precious Gwen," he whispered, going down on one knee. "You are steadfast and unchanging, the only virtue in a wicked world." He drew my hand to his cheek and kissed my palm. "There is one thing more. I had a vision on Ynys Witrin, after we buried Arthur."

I stared at him. "*You* had a vision?"

He nodded fervently. "I do not know if it was God who sent it, or Mithra, or Niniane, or even Merlin. They all spoke to me. I was to come to you when it was safe, bearing a message."

For half a second I both hoped and feared he would command me to go with him, quoting divine direction, but he had never been a subtle man.

"You are to write it down, Gwen. The story of your life. Of Arthur's deeds. Of the times."

If he meant to shock me, he succeeded.

"*Me?* Write it down? A woman's words? Whatever for?"

"Merlin spoke with his voice of power. He commanded you to do it, and not to question—"

"That sounds like Merlin."

"—and to be faithfully honest, as you are. Those were his words, Gwen. 'Faithfully honest.' And you used to think he disliked you. Do it, and tell the world the truth about us, and the truth about Mordred, if you like. There's no harm in it, is there?"

I thought about this awhile, holding his hand and letting his head rest in my lap, knowing that this time it would truly be the last time.

"No one will listen to a woman. And there is no one alive now who would believe a word I said. It wouldn't suit their purposes."

"Then perhaps it shan't be read by those alive now. Perhaps it will come to light when times have changed and the people of Britain wish to know the truth about their King and Queen."

Like Arthur, Lancelot knew how to win me over "The people of Britain" never failed. And suppose he really had seen a vision?

"All right," I said. "I suppose I might try. It will give a purpose to the years I have left."

He rose and took my arm as the first few raindrops splashed on the warm, gray stone of the garden walls. I walked him to the gate, but there we lingered, the postern guard eyeing us, reluctant to come to our final parting. Suddenly I remembered the ring, which I had held in my hand all this while.

"Am I to keep this ring, or are you to take it to Lanascol?"

"It is yours. I took it from his finger."

"Did he bid you bring it me?"

"He was beyond speech."

My throat ached suddenly, but I persisted. "And his Sword? Where is that?"

He cleared his throat uncomfortably. "When I heard his death sigh, I became enraged with grief," he said in a low voice I had to strain to catch. "I took the Sword out of his very hand and threw it into the Lake of Avalon. You could say it has disappeared."

I looked at him in frank astonishment. "Why did you do that?"

He braved himself for his reply, standing somewhat stiffly. "I heard Merlin's voice, telling me to do it. 'From the deeps of the Underworld has it come, and so shall it go home.' "

Merlin's words sounded strange on Lancelot's lips, but I believed them nonetheless. Arthur had believed that Merlin died, but Merlin's spirit was alive in the world after his passing. This was fact.

"If Excalibur has gone, then Britain is forsaken," I whispered. "We are dead, Lancelot. Our time is past."

He nodded heavily, and that weariness of spirit which I had

first noted in him returned once more. "Yes. It is over. I shall disappear into Less Britain, and you shall vanish within this fastness. Forever. Unless you leave our tale behind you."

I clutched suddenly at his sleeve; he could not go, not yet. I would never see him again.

"Lancelot! I have forgotten to ask about your son! Does Galahad live?"

He looked up, unfooled. "Yes."

"Oh, I am so glad!"

"I found him at the monastery. He helped me—with Arthur."

"Ah, the poor boy. Where is he now? Will he return with you?"

A bitter smile. "No. He will go wherever I am not. He stays in Britain to fight for Constantine."

I held hard to his hand. It was easy to see the wound Galahad had given him would never heal.

"There is hope, then, after all," I urged softly. "Niniane once prophesied 'A son of Lancelot will raise the sword of righteousness; he will keep the Light in Britain.' You will see, Lancelot, Britain will be preserved."

"Well," grumbled Lancelot, "he's a good enough swordsman."

I touched my lips to his hand. "He is more than that. My dear, if our time is past, his is just beginning. With warriors like Galahad to fight our battles, surely our dreams will not die with us."

At last he smiled. "Ahhh, Gwen, what faith you have! You were not Arthur's wife for nothing."

"Arthur's Kingdom will not die. Britain will endure. Arthur's efforts have not been in vain."

Lancelot crossed himself solemnly. "Amen. If Galahad can be a part of the Britain you envision, I will die content."

"He is destined for greatness," I whispered, watching his eyes. "There is something in him—I don't know what—that drives him always onward. Perhaps he will be a great king. Perhaps we shall live to see it."

He shook his head. "There is only one Arthur."

The breeze blew up suddenly, cold on the back of my neck. I gripped his hand as he withdrew it.

"Sweet love, I must go."

"Now?"

He kissed me formally, courtier to Queen, for eyes were watching.

"Go with God," I managed.

"Good-bye, Guinevere."

The storm broke.

THE CURSED

BY

DAVE DUNCAN

In the beginning were the fates, dispensing unto mankind in equal measure their light and their darkness, their sorrow and their joy, their blessing and their curse . . .

SHOOL is Time, the Slow One, stealer of youth, guardian of what has been and what is to be, maker of ends and beginnings

IVIEL is Health, Star of Evening, bringer of wounds and sickness, Star of Morning, the healer, the comforter

MUOL is Passion, the Red One, bringer of love and hatred, maker and destroyer

AWAIL is Change, the Inconstant One, the fickle one, ruler of the night

OGOAL is Chance, the Swift One, the joker, spinner of fortune

JAUL is Thought, who is Reason, the Bright One, dispenser of truth and falsehood, maker and breaker of law and justice

POUL is Destiny, the Great One, giver of life and death, the mover, queen of days

1 ✹

In Tolamin, it began with a runaway wagon. Two horses came careering down the narrow street in panic, trying to escape from the terrible racketing monster pursuing them. Its load of pottery ewers clattered and rolled; every few seconds another would bounce right out to explode on the stones and splatter contents everywhere. Bystanders leaped for the safety of doorways or pressed back against walls. There was no sign of the driver.

A child stood directly in the wagon's path, thumb in mouth, an infant clad only in a wisp of cloth, staring blankly at the doom hurtling down upon him.

The boy's mother rushed out to snatch him away to safety, but her foot slipped and the two of them sprawled headlong together, directly under the plunging hooves. Horses and wagon flashed over them and continued their headlong progress to certain destruction at the river. The woman scrambled to her feet, clutching her child. Apparently neither had suffered as much as a bruise.

"There!" Jasbur screeched. "You see that?"

"Lucky," Ordur muttered.

"Lucky? You call that lucky? I say it's impossible. I say somebody is *influencing*!"

Ordur scratched his head and thought about it. He wasn't thinking too clearly these days. "Suppose it could be."

"Suppose? Hah! You're even stupider than you look, you know that?"

"You, too!"

"You look like a moron, but you're not that smart. You don't have the brains of a lettuce."

"You, too!"

That was the best Ordur could manage in repartee these days. He knew he was slow. It wasn't fair of Jasbur to call him ugly, though. Jasbur was just as bad: short and bent, almost a hunchback. His face was a grayish, swarthy shade, as if it had not been washed for years, and gruesomely wrinkled. The whites of his eyes were yellow; he slavered all the time. Although the fringe of hair around his head was silver, its roots were dark. There were patches of shadowy dark stubble on his cheeks and more on his bald pate. His teeth were nastily prominent, his clothes tattered and filthy.

The wagon had reached the dock. The horses veered to right and left; trappings broke miraculously to free them. The wagon sailed on by itself, passing narrowly between two moored barges and vanishing into the water. Jasbur crowed witlessly at this further evidence of fatalist influence upsetting the normal probabilities of the world.

But talk of lettuce had reminded Ordur that his belly ached. He peered up the long street, then down it. There were a lot of people standing around, mostly staring after the wagon. An excited group had gathered around the woman and her child, babbling about their miraculous escape.

"I'm hungry. Haven't eaten all day!"

Jasbur shrieked in derision. "All day? It's barely dawn! You mean you didn't eat all day yesterday!"

"And I'm still hungry."

"Whose fault is that? You're supposed to be a beggar, but you look so bad you give children hysterics. Women set their dogs on us because of your ugly face."

"You, too."

"Half the people in this town don't eat. It was your idea to come to Tolamin, and it was a stupid idea."

Ordur didn't think it had been his idea, but he wasn't going to argue with Jasbur today. Maybe tomorrow would be better. "You eaten today?"

"No, nor yesterday neither!"

"Don't like this town," Ordur announced. "It smells."

"Curd brain! It's all the burned buildings. It was sacked, you numbskull."

As if to emphasize the point, a ruined shell of a house farther up the hill collapsed out into the street in a cascade of bricks and charred timbers. Dust flew up in black clouds. People screamed.

"There!" Jasbur cackled. "Months it's been standing, now it falls down. I tell you, there's somebody influencing!"

"Who?"

"How should I know?"

Lightning flashed, and thunder cracked almost overhead. Ordur jumped. "Oughta get out of here!"

"Naw. Thunder at this time of day? How often d'you see that?"

"Don't *see* thunder, Jasbur. See lightning. Hear thunder."

"Bah! There's an Ogoalscath around here somewhere. Let's find him." Jasbur hobbled off down the hill on bandy legs.

Ordur strode after him. "Why? How'd you know he's this way?"

"I don't, but he will be, you'll see."

Surely wise people would go away from an Ogoalscath, not toward him? But if Jasbur said to go this way, then Ordur would have to. Jasbur wasn't being very nice to him just now, but he did seem to be the smart one. He said he was, so it must be true.

Lightning flashed again, thunder rumbled, rain began to fall in grape-size drops.

2

In Tharn Valley, it began with a bad tooth. Bulion Tharn was no stranger to having teeth pulled. Any man who lived long enough to outlast his teeth had been blessed by the fates—that was how he liked to look on the matter. He had been fortunate in having Glothion around. Glothion was the blacksmith, the largest of his sons, with limbs like an oak. Old teeth tended to shatter when gripped with pliers, but Glothion could pull them with his bare fingers. It felt as if he were about to snap the jawbone, and the way he steadied his victim's head under his arm would surely crush some unfortunate's skull one day, but nine times out of ten he could yank a tooth cleanly out.

This time had been one of the other times. Bulion should have stood the pain a week or two longer, perhaps, to let the rotting molar rot some more. He hadn't. He'd been in too much of a hurry, and Glothion had pulled the crown off.

That meant real bloodshed. Wosion had insisted they wait three days, until the fates were propitious, and by then Bulion had been almost out of his mind with the pain. It had taken Glothion and Brankion and Zanion to hold their father down while Wosion himself tried to cut out the roots with a dagger.

He hadn't found all of them, obviously. Now, two days later, Bulion's face was swollen like a pumpkin and nigh hot enough to set his beard on fire. He was running a fever. The pain was a constant throb of lightning all through his head.

He was very likely going to die of this.

There were surgeons in Daling. The odds that he could survive the two-day ride there were slim. The odds that any leech or sawbones could help him now were even slimmer.

It seemed the fates were ready to close the book on Bulion Tharn.

3

In Daling, it began when Tibal Frainith came to Phoenix Street.

Gwin was helping Tob the stable boy replace the wheat sheaf over the door. She was needed only when a cart came along and threatened to sweep ladder and Tob and wheat sheaf all away together, but her presence discouraged passing urchins from attempting the same feat. Meanwhile, she could clean off the road with a broom—not just because it made the entrance more appealing, but because it meant less dirt to be tracked inside. She could have sent a servant to do all that, but then it would have taken twice as long. She welcomed an excuse just to go outside. It seemed she did not leave the hostel for weeks at a time nowadays.

Meanwhile, the staff indoors were probably sitting around eating and talking when they should be working. Morning was busy time. The last guests had just left. There was a stable to be shoveled out, water to carry, beds to make, bread to bake, bedding to air, and all the interminable cleaning. The Flamingo Room needed fumigating again, having still not recovered from the sailors who had infested it with bedbugs the previous week.

Morning sunlight brightened the narrow streets of Daling as gladly as a baby's smile. Stonework shone in the color of beech wood. The cobbles were polished little islands, each one set off by dark mire in the crevices between them, giving the roadway a texture of coarse cloth, a cobble carpet, dipping here and there into noxious puddles, although even they reflected the sun. Exterior windows were rare, but a few bronze grilles gleamed joyously; and all the doors were limed to a brilliant white.

Phoenix Street was occupied by pedestrians and horsemen and much idle gossip. Every few minutes, an oxcart would come clattering and rattling along, usually being chased by small children trying to cadge a ride and being shouted away by the carter. Strolling hawkers called their wares, stopping to talk with the women at the doorways.

The old wheat sheaf hit the cobbles, disintegrating into a cloud of dust and a mess of rotted straw where Gwin had just swept. She clucked annoyance and hastened to pass up the replacement bundle to Tob. He took it without a word. Not even his own mother could call him swift. The only good thing about Tob was that he was too stupid to be dishonest.

She laid into the straw with her broom, spreading it out for hooves and wheels to crumble. She tried not to remember that self-same sheaf being hung—thirty-six weeks ago, a day as hot as this one promised to be. She had been helper then, too, but it had not been a half-wit stable boy up the ladder. It had been Carp himself. Now Carp was rotting in an unmarked grave somewhere near Tolamin. Karn and Naln had followed their father. She was the only one left now—widow, bereaved mother, innkeeper, Gwin Nien Solith.

"Gwin!"

She spun around, blinking into the sun.

The speaker was tall, lean, clean-shaven. He bore a bulky pack sack on his shoulders. His smock and breeches had never been dyed and now were a nondescript gray. They were ordinary Kuolian garb, yet of an unfamiliar cut, as if they had traveled far from the loom that birthed them. He had steady gray eyes and brown tangled hair, worn shorter than was normal for men in Daling. Bone and sinew lay close under his skin. Yes, tall. He was smiling at her as if the two of them were old friends, close friends. She had never seen him before in her life.

"I don't . . ."

He started. "Sorry! I am Tibal Ambor Frainith." He bowed.

"Most honored, Tibal *Saj*. I am Gwin Nien Solith."

"Yes. I mean I am honored, Gwin *Saj*." He was blushing.

Blushing?

Pause.

The expectant look remained in his eyes. She could not recall being thrown off-balance like this for years. She did not forget faces. He was at least as old as she was, so why were his cheeks flaming red like that?

A stranger in town would seek out a hostelry. Carp Solith had won a good reputation for the Phoenix Street Hostel; his widow had sustained it so far. Most of her business came from repeats, established customers—merchants, farmers, ship captains—but first-timers were not rare.

So why was she gazing tongue-tied at this man? Why was he staring down at her with that blush on his cheeks and that wistful, disbelieving expression in his gray eyes? There was something strange about his gaze that she could not place.

"The Phoenix Street Hostel," he said in his unfamiliar accent. "Everyone will . . . Everyone told me that it's the best hostelry in the city, Gwin *Saj*." He spoke too softly, stood a little too close.

A lead pair of oxen emerged from Sailors' Alley, with another following.

"They spoke no less than the truth, Tibal *Saj*."

"I need a room, Gwin." He still seemed mildly amused that she had not recognized him. He was a little too quick dropping the honorific.

"Rooms are my business, Tibal *Saj*." Why else display a wheat sheaf above the door?

Tob was still up the ladder, tying the sheaf to the bracket. The oxcart was advancing along the road. Tibal backed into its path, holding up a hand to stop it, all without ever taking his eyes off Gwin.

"You came by way of Tolamin?" she said. He must have, to be arriving in the city so early in the day.

He hesitated and then nodded. The wagoner howled curses at him.

"How is it?" she asked.

Tibal blinked and frowned. "Much the same," he said vaguely.

Whatever did that mean? The Wesnarians had sacked it in the fall.

The teamster hauled on the traces and brought his rig to a clattering halt with the lead pair's steaming muzzles not an ell from the lanky stranger—who still ignored it all, still stared at Gwin.

Tob came slithering down the ladder, leering with pride at having completed an unfamiliar task. "All done, Gwin *Saj*."

"Take the ladder down, Tob."

"Oh. Yes." The lout moved the ladder. Tibal stepped out of the way, so the team could proceed.

"You almost got yourself jellied there," she said.

"What?" He glanced at the cart and its furious driver as if he had been unaware of their existence until she spoke. He shrugged. "No."

There was something definitely odd about Tibal Frainith, but he raised no sense of alarm in her. Almost the reverse—he seemed to be signaling friendship. Not asking for it, just assuming it. Curiously reassuring, somehow . . . clothes neither rich nor poor . . . carried his own pack. Not a rich man, therefore. Soft-spoken. Not a soldier. Not a merchant. A wandering scholar, perhaps? At least he wasn't proposing marriage yet. Lately she spent half her days fighting off suitors who wanted to marry a hostel, and she was going to lose the battle.

She opened the door, setting the bell jangling. "I'll show you the rooms we have available." They were all available, but she would not admit to that.

He stepped past her. As she was about to follow him inside, a voice said, *It has begun.*

Startled, she jumped and looked around. There was no one there. Tob was just disappearing into the alley with the ladder, heading around to the back. The wagon had gone. The voice had not come from Tibal Frainith.

So who had spoken? Her nerves must be snapping if she was starting to hear voices. With a shiver of fear, she followed her guest inside, shutting the door harder than necessary.

DEL REY ONLINE!

The Del Rey Internet Newsletter...

A monthly electronic publication, posted on the Internet, GEnie, CompuServe, BIX, various BBSs, and the Panix gopher (gopher.panix.com). It features hype-free descriptions of books that are new in the stores, a list of our upcoming books, special announcements, a signing/reading/convention-attendance schedule for Del Rey authors, "In Depth" essays in which professionals in the field (authors, artists, designers, sales people, etc.) talk about their jobs in science fiction, a question-and-answer section, behind-the-scenes looks at sf publishing, and more!

Online editorial presence:

Many of the Del Rey editors are online, on the Internet, GEnie, CompuServe, America Online, and Delphi. There is a Del Rey topic on GEnie and a Del Rey folder on America Online.

Our official e-mail address

for Del Rey Books is delrey@randomhouse.com

Internet information source!

A lot of Del Rey material is available to the Internet on a gopher server: all back issues and the current issue of the Del Rey Internet Newsletter, a description of the DRIN and summaries of all the issues' contents, sample chapters of upcoming or current books (readable or downloadable for free), submission requirements, mail-order information, and much more. We will be adding more items of all sorts (mostly new DRINs and sample chapters) regularly. The address of the gopher is gopher.panix.com

Why?

We at Del Rey realize that the networks are the medium of the future. That's where you'll find us promoting our books, socializing with others in the sf field, and—most importantly—making contact and sharing information with sf readers.

For more information, e-mail ekh@panix.com